VERITAS

Monaldi & Sorti

Translated from the Italian by Gregory Dowling

First published in Great Britain in 2013 by Polygon,
an imprint of Birlinn ltd

West Newington House
10 Newington Road
Edinburgh
EH9 1QS

www.polygonbooks.co.uk

9 8 7 6 5 4 3 2 1

ISBN: 978 1 84697 257 7

The publishers acknowledge investment from Creative Scotland
towards the publication of this volume.

British Library Cataloguing-in-Publication Data
A catalogue record for this book is available on request from the
British Library.

Typeset by IDSUK (DataConnection) Ltd

Printed and bound by Grafica Veneta, Italy

Authors' Note

Any reference to places, people and events – however bizarre they may seem – is *not* the fruit of our imagination but taken from sources of the period. We ask readers, whenever they have any doubt as to the truthfulness of what they are reading, to consult the endnotes and the bibliography, where they will find fully documented proof. What we especially enjoy is digging out of the archives those oddities of history which, were they not true, would be considered implausible.

"The horrendous battle is no longer between Trojans and Achaeans, but now the Danaans are fighting even with the immortals."

"Jove the Father created a third lineage of talking men, a brazen one, in no way similar to the silver one: sprung from ash-trees, violent and terrible.
They were keen on the works of Mars, bearers of grief,
and all sorts of violence; they ate no wheaten food,
but were hard of heart like adamant, fearful men."

(HOMER, *Iliad*, and HESIOD, *Works and Days*, in:
B.A. BORGESE, *Rubè*)

Contents

An Appointment

✠

The great room is all a-glitter, with the bronze of its furnishings and spiral decorations, and its glowing candles.

Abbot Melani keeps me waiting. It's the first time, in over thirty years.

Until today, whenever I arrived at our appointments I had always found him already waiting, tapping his foot impatiently. But now it is my turn to gaze continually towards the severe monumental doorway by which I entered over half an hour ago. Defying the freezing, snow-laden wind that sweeps in and sets the doors creaking on their hinges, I vainly strain my ears and eyes for the first signs of the Abbot's arrival: the drumming hooves of the four-horse carriage; the first glimpse, in the torchlight, of the horses' plumed heads as they draw the ceremonial black carriage to the foot of the entrance staircase, where four old footmen, huddled in their snow-dusted greatcoats, are waiting for their even older master, ready to open the carriage door and help him, one last time, to descend.

As I wait, I let my eyes wander. The room is richly ornamented. From the arches hang great drapes with words embroidered in gold; the walls are swathed in brocaded mantles, and veils adorned with beads of silver form a gallery of honour. Columns, arches and pilasters of sham marble lead towards the central baldachin, which is a sort of truncated pyramid resting on a platform six or seven steps above floor level and surrounded by a triple row of candelabras.

At the top, two winged silver creatures, kneeling on one leg, their arms outstretched and the palms of their hands raised heavenwards, perch in expectation.

Twisting branches of myrtle and ivy adorn the four sides of the baldachin, each of which proudly bears the coat of arms – picked out in fresh flowers, apparently plucked straight from the hothouses of Versailles – of the Veneto nobility: a piglet on a green field. At each corner stands a flaring torch on a tall silver tripod, adorned with the same coat of arms.

Despite the grandeur of the *Castrum* and the splendid accoutrements, there are very few people around me; apart from the musicians (who have already taken their places and uncased their instruments) and the valets in their black, red and golden livery (who, with their freshly shaven faces, stand motionless as statues holding ceremonial torches), I can only see down-at-heel noblemen looking on enviously and a crowd of workmen, servants and gossiping women, who, despite the late hour and the icy cold of the winter night, gaze around themselves in ecstasy, waiting for the procession.

Taking its impulse from my eyes, my memory starts to wander as well. It abandons the snow and the leaden Parisian winter of the deserted Place des Victoires which lies over the threshold, where biting northern wind swirls around the equestrian statue of the old King, and it swoops back, far back, to the gentle slopes of the Eternal City on its seven hills, to the top of the Janiculum Hill, and the dazzling heat of a Roman summer many years ago. It was on that occasion, surrounded by different nobility, amid more ethereal architecture of papier-mâché, with a different orchestra trying out music for a different event and valets holding torches that would illuminate another story, that I caught sight of a carriage trundling along the driveway of Villa Spada.

How strange are the workings of destiny: at that time I had no idea that it was about to reunite me with Abbot Melani after seventeen years of silence; this time I know for sure that Atto is going to arrive, but the carriage that is bearing him towards me refuses to appear on the horizon.

My train of thought is briefly broken by one of the players, who bumps into me accidentally as he climbs down from the platform. I raise my eyes:

Obsequio erga Regem

is embroidered in gold characters on the black, silver-fringed velvet drape that adorns the tall column of false porphyry in plain style opposite me. Another column, identical to this one, stands on the other side, but the writing is too far away for me to read.

In my whole life, I have only attended one such event. Then too it was a cold night and it was snowing, or raining, I think. There was certainly cold and rain and darkness within my heart.

⊰⊱

On that occasion too I was in Atto's company. We were part of a great bustling crowd: people were streaming into the room from all sides. Every corner was so packed that Abbot Melani and I could only elbow forward two paces every quarter of an hour; it was impossible either to advance or to retreat and we could see nothing but the ceiling decorations and the inscriptions hanging from the arches or placed at the tops of the capitals.

Ob Hispaniam assertam	*Ob Galliam triumphatam*
Ob Italiam liberatam	*Ob Belgium restitutum*

There were four columns bearing mottoes. They were of the Doric order, the symbol of heroes, and very tall: about fifty feet, in imitation of the historic columns of Rome, the Antonine and the Trajan. Between them, on the *Castrum*, an imitation night sky made of veils was adorned with golden flames and gathered upwards in the centre, in the shape of a crown, by gold cords and sashes tied by four gigantic buckles in the form of majestic eagles, with their heads resting on their chests.

Alongside them, Glory, with rays radiating from her head (in imitation of *Claritas* on the coins of Emperor Constance), held a laurel crown in her left hand and a crown of stars in her right.

Behind us, just beyond the great doorway, twenty-four valets were awaiting their lord. Suddenly the hubbub died down. Everyone fell silent and a glimmering light assailed the darkness: it came from the flaring white torches borne by the scions of the nobility.

He had arrived.

છ∽ન્જી

The sound of drumming hooves coming to a halt on the pavement outside jolts me from my memories. The four footmen, palely gleaming with snow in the winter night, are finally moving. Atto is here.

The candle flames flicker and blur before my eyes, while the doors of the church where I am awaiting him are thrown open, the church of Notre Dame des Victoires, the basilica of the Barefoot Augustinians. From the black carriage emerges the red velvet of the bier, glistening in the torchlight: Atto Melani, Abbot of Beaubec, King's Gentleman, *Cittadino Originario* of the Most Serene Republic, many-time Conclavist, is preparing to make his solemn entrance.

The old servants bear the coffin on their shoulders; it is engraved with the piglet on a green field, Atto's coat of arms. From beneath the gallery of honour formed by the black veils with silver beads, some mourners make their way through the two wings of bystanders: they are the few people to whom the formerly illustrious name of Atto Melani, the last witness of an age now swept away by war, still – perhaps – means something. The four footmen proceed right to the heart of the *Castrum doloris*, the funereal catafalque, and, having mounted the steps of the truncated pyramid, they consign the corpse of their old master to the open arms of the two silver genu-flecting angels, the palms of whose upturned hands finally receive what they have been waiting for.

On the catafalque hangs a funeral drape of black velvet with silver fringes, on which is embroidered in golden characters:

> *Hic iacet*
> *Abbas Atto Melani Pistoriensis in Etruria,*
> *Pietate erga Deum*
> *Obsequio erga Regem*
> *Illustris*
> Ω. *Die 4. Ianuarii 1714. Ætatis suæ octuagesimo octavo*
> *Patruo Dilectissimo*
> *Dominicus Melani nepos mestissimus posuit*

The same words will be engraved on the sepulchral monument that Atto's nephew has already commissioned from the Florentine sculptor Rastrelli. The Augustinian Fathers have granted the site in a side chapel close to the high altar, opposite the sacristy door. Atto will therefore be buried here, as he wished, in the same church where lie the mortal remains of another Tuscan musician: the great Giovan Battista Lulli.

"*Pietate erga Deum / Obsequio erga Regem / Illustris*": the words are repeated on the two side columns, only the nearer of which I had been able to read before. "Illustrious for his devotion to God and his obedience to the King": in reality, the former virtue is in conflict with the latter, and no one knows this better than I.

The orchestra begins the funeral mass. We hear a castrato singing:

> *Crucifixus et sepultus est*

"Crucified and buried," intones his reedy voice. I can make out nothing else, everything flickers and wavers around me: the faces, colours and lights blur like a painting that has fallen into water.

Atto Melani is dead. He died here, in Paris, in rue Plastrière, in the parish of Saint Eustache, the day before yesterday, 4th January 1714, at two in the morning. I was with him.

❧

"Stay with me," he said, and breathed his last.

I will stay with you, Signor Atto: we made a pact, I made you a promise, and I intend to abide by it.

It matters not how many times you broke our pacts, how many times you lied to the twenty-year-old boy servant and then to the father and family man. This time there will be no surprises for me: you have already fulfilled your obligation towards me.

Now that I am almost the same age that you were when we first met, now that your memories are mine, that your old passions are flaring up in my breast, your life is *my* life.

It was thanks to a journey that I found you again, three years ago, and now another one, the supreme journey of death, is bearing you away to other shores.

Safe journey, Signor Atto. You will get what you asked of me.

Rome

JANUARY 1711

✠

"Vienna? And why on earth should we go to Vienna?" My wife Cloridia stared at me wide-eyed with surprise.

"My dear, you grew up in Holland, you had a Turkish mother, you came here to Rome all by yourself when you weren't even twenty, and now you're scared of a little trip to the Empire? What am *I* supposed to say, seeing that I've never been beyond Perugia?"

"You're not telling me we're going to make a trip to Vienna; you're telling me we should go and live there! Do you happen to know any German?"

"Well, no . . . not yet."

"Give it to me," she said, and she irritably snatched the document from my hand.

She read it through again for the umpteenth time.

"And just what is this donation? A piece of land? A shop? A job as a court servant? It doesn't explain anything!"

"You heard the notary, just as I did: we'll find out when we get there, but it's certainly something of great value."

"Right. We'll go all the way there, clambering over the Alps, and then perhaps we'll find it's just another trick played by that scoundrel your Abbot, who'll exploit you for some other crazy adventure and then throw you away like an old rag, leaving you penniless into the bargain!"

"Cloridia, think for a moment: Atto is eighty-five years old. What crazy adventures do you think he's likely to embark on now? For a long time I thought he was dead. It's quite something that he's actually hired a notary to pay off his old debt to me. He must feel the end approaching and now he wants to set his conscience at rest. In fact, we should be thanking God for granting us such an opportunity when things are so hard for us."

My wife lowered her eyes.

6

৵৽৹

For two years things had been bad, extremely bad, for us. The winter of 1709 had been very severe, with endless snow and ice. This had led to a bitter famine, which, together with the ruinous war that had been dragging on for seven years over the Spanish throne, had thrown the Roman people into dire poverty. My family and I, with the new addition of a six-year-old son, had not been spared this fate: a year of bad weather and frosts, something never seen before in Rome, had made our smallholding unproductive and wiped out my prospects on the land. The decline of the Spada family and the consequent abandonment of the villa at Porta San Pancrazio, where I had undertaken many profitable little jobs over the years, had made our situation even worse. My wife's efforts to halt our financial ruin through the art of midwifery had, alas, proved insufficient, even though she had been practising it for decades to great acclaim, and now had the help of our two daughters, aged twenty-three and nineteen. The famine had also increased the number of new mothers who were penniless, and my wife assisted these with the same self-denying spirit with which she attended to the noblewomen.

And so the list of our debts increased and in the end, in order to survive, we were forced to take the most painful step: the sale, in favour of the moneylenders of the ghetto, of our small house and holding, bought twenty-six years earlier with the little nest egg left us by my father-in-law of blessed memory. We found shelter in the city, taking lodgings in a basement that we had to share with a family from Istria; at least it had the advantage of not being too damp and maintaining a fairly constant temperature in winter, even in the hardest frost, thanks to the fact that it had been dug into the *tufo*.

In the evening we ate black bread and broth with nettles and grass. And in the day we got by on acorns and other berries that we scraped together and ground up to make a kind of loaf, garnishing it with little turnips. Shoes soon became a luxury and gave way, even in winter, to wooden clogs and slippers stitched together at home from old rags and hemp-twine.

I could find no work, none at least worthy of the name. My slight build often counted against me, for example in any job that involved lifting or carrying. And so in the end I had been reduced to taking on the vilest and most sordid of jobs, one that no Roman would ever dream of accepting, but the only one in which I had an advantage over family breadwinners of greater stature: a chimney-sweep.

I was an exception: chimney-sweeps and roof tilers usually came from the Alpine valleys, from Lake Como, Lake Maggiore, from the Valcamonica, the Val Brembana and also from Piedmont. In these poor areas the great hunger forced families to give up children as young as six or seven seasonally to the chimney-sweeps, who made use of them to clean – at the risk of their lives – the narrower flues.

Having the build of a child but the strength of an adult, I could offer the best guarantee that the job would be done properly: I would screw myself into the narrow openings and clamber up agilely through the soot, but I would also scrape the black walls of the hood and flue with greater skill than any child could apply to the job. Furthermore, the fact that I was so light saved the tiles from damage when I climbed onto the roof to clean or adjust the chimney pot, and at the same time there was no risk of my dashing my brains out on the ground, as happened all too often to the very young chimney-sweeps.

Finally, as a local chimney sweep, I was available all year round, while my Alpine colleagues only came down at the beginning of November.

I myself, to tell the truth, was often obliged to take my lively little son along with me, but I would never have made him clamber up a flue; I merely used him as a small apprentice and assistant, this being a job that requires at least two people.

To reassure the customers of my skills, I would boast a long apprenticeship in the Aprutine Mountains (where, as in the Alps, there is a long tradition of chimney sweeping). Actually I had no real experience. I had learned the rudiments of the art only at Villa Spada, on those occasions when I had been asked to climb up the flues to solve some unexpected problem, or to repair the roof.

And so, every night, I would load my barrow with tools – rasp, palette knife, wire brush, butcher's broom, a rope, a ladder and counterweights – and set off, never without first seeing my consort give her sleep-befuddled child a loving hug. Cloridia detested this risky trade, which kept her awake at nights, praying that nothing would happen.

Wrapped in my short black cloak, by the first light of dawn I would have reached the outlying areas of the city or the nearby villages. And here, uttering the cry "Chimney-sweeeep, chimney-sweeeeeeeeep!", I would offer my services.

All too often I would be greeted with hostile words and gestures; the chimney-sweep arrives in the winter, bringing bad weather with him, and so is considered a figure of ill-omen. When people did open their doors to us, if we were lucky my son would receive a bowl of warm broth and a scrap of bread from some kindly housewife.

A black jacket buttoned on the left, below my arm, to prevent the buttons from snagging on the walls of the chimney, and closed all the way to the top, the sleeves tied tightly at the wrists with string, to stop the soot entering; knee-length trousers of rough moleskin, which did not hold the dirt, with protective patches on the knees, elbows and bottom, the points of greatest wear when clambering up the narrow flues: this was my uniform. Narrow and black, it made me look only a little less tiny and scrawny than my son, so that I was often taken for his slightly elder brother.

As I wormed my way up the flue, my head would be swathed in a canvas sack, hermetically sealed at the neck, to save me, at least in part, from inhaling the soot. Hooded like this, I looked like a prisoner condemned to the gallows. I was completely blind, but in the flue there was no need to see: you worked by touch, scraping with the rasp.

My son would wait down below, trembling with fear lest something should happen and he should be left all alone, far from his dear mother and sisters.

In the fireplace and on the roof, however, I would climb up barefooted, so as to be unimpeded and thus able to brace myself and push more efficiently. The problem was that it reduced my feet to a mass of bruises and sores, and so throughout the winter, the period when I had most work, I would walk with a limping, unsteady gait.

Working on the roofs was often extremely dangerous: however, it was a mere nothing to someone like me, who had once climbed the dome of St Peter's.

❧

The most painful aspect of our poverty, however, was not my wretched job, but our two girls. My daughters, unfortunately, were still unmarried, and everything indicated that they would remain so for a long time. The Lord God, praise be given, had endowed them with an iron constitution: despite their privations, they were still beautiful, rosy and florid ("Thanks to their three years of breast-feeding!" their mother would say proudly). Their hair was so gorgeous and glossy that every Saturday morning they would go to the market to sell the hair that got caught in their combs during their morning toilet for two *baiocchi*. Their health was a real miracle, as all around us the cold and famine had taken a heavy toll.

My two girls – sweet, healthy, beautiful and virtuous – had just one flaw: they had not a penny of dowry. More than once the nuns had come from the convent of Santa Caterina Sopra Minerva, which annually distributed large sums to the families of poor girls who would agree to take the vows, to try to persuade me to send them to the cloisters in exchange for a neat little nest egg. The girls' robust constitution and perfect health attracted the nuns, who needed strong, humble sisters to do all those chores in the convent that the nuns from noble families could not be expected to do. But even at our worst moments I had politely declined these offers (Cloridia was rather less polite; shaking her breasts angrily, she would berate the nuns to their faces: "You think I breastfed each of them for three years to see them end up like that?"), and in any case my girls themselves showed no inclination for the veil.

Already fully acquainted with the joys of maternity thanks to their experience as assistant midwives, they yearned to find husbands as soon as possible.

Then the cold ceased and the famine too. But the poverty did not vanish so quickly. After two years, my daughters were still waiting.

A futile anger would gnaw at me whenever I saw my elder daughter's face grow asbstracted and sad without a word being said (she was already twenty-five years old!). My rage was not directed against a blind and cruel fate, far from it. I knew perfectly well whom to blame: not the cold, nor the famine that had laid all Europe low. No. I had a name in mind: Abbot Melani.

A ruthless schemer, an interloper, a man of a hundred deceits and a thousand tricks; master of the lie, prophet of intrigue, oracle of dissimulation and falsehood; all this, and more, was Abbot Atto Melani, a famous castrato singer of former days, but most especially a spy.

Eleven years earlier he had grimly exploited me, even putting my life at risk, with the promise of a dowry for my daughters.

"Not just money, houses. Property. Lands. Farms. I shall make over your daughters' dowry. A rich dowry. And, when I say rich, I am not exaggerating." Thus he had duped me. Those words were still engraved in my memory as in my bare flesh.

He had explained that he had various properties in the Grand Duchy of Tuscany: all valuable, with excellent incomes, he had specified, and he had even set down a promise in writing, in which he engaged to establish in my daughters' names a marital dowry, each with incomes or properties that were "substantial", all to be defined before a notary of the Capitol. But he was never to take me to that notary.

Having made use of my services, he had gone off to Paris on the sly, and all my wandering from lawyer to lawyer, from notary to notary, in search of someone who might give me some hope, had proved useless. I would have had to file a very expensive lawsuit against him in Paris. In short, that document containing his promise was mere waste paper.

And so he enjoyed his riches, while I endeavoured to drag myself and my family from the desperate swamp of indigence.

But now I was summoned to appear before a Roman notary. He had been charged, by a colleague in Vienna, with the task of tracking me down and delivering to me a deed of donation signed by Abbot Melani.

What exactly it consisted of was a mystery. The asset, which the notary considered must be something of great value ("a piece of land, or a house"), was described by abbreviations and numbers, probably referring to Viennese registries, all of which were totally abstruse. Abbot Melani had moreover opened an unlimited credit in my favour at an exchange bank, so that I could provide for the journey without any financial hindrances.

As for me, I just had to present myself at a certain address at the imperial capital, and there all would be revealed and I would receive what was due to me.

It was not, unfortunately, a donation in the Grand Duchy of Tuscany, as the Abbot had led me to believe back then, but much further off, on the other side of the Alps even.

However, in our current dire straits, it was manna from heaven. How could we refuse?

Vienna

FEBRUARY 1711

✠

The drum roll resounded over the bare snowy plain that lay before the city walls. Its powerful thunder interwove with the silvery serpentine sounds of the parade trumpets, the military pipes and horns. This martial commotion was redoubled by the echo that bounced off the massive walls, amidst fortifications, ravelins and earthworks, so that it sounded as if there were not just one line of players, but three or four, or perhaps even ten.

While a military regiment drilled outside the city walls, from within the ramparts we felt upon us the severe gaze of church spires and palace pinnacles, belfries crowned with crosses and castellated towers, serene domes and airy terraces – a host of sacred and profane rooftops that warn the traveller: what you have reached is not an anonymous cluster of men and things, but a benign cradle of souls, a powerful fortress, a protector of trade, blessed by God.

As our carriage drew close to the Carinthian Gate, the entrance to Vienna for travellers from the south, I saw those proud and noble pinnacles rise up one by one against the leaden sky.

Supreme among them, as the coachman pointed out, was the lofty and sublime spire of the Cathedral of St Stephen, a dazzling fretwork of intricate decorations, with the added embellishment of a gleaming mantle of snow. Not far off was the sturdy octagonal campanile of the church of the Dominicans. Then came the noble bell tower of St Peter of the Holy Trinity, as well as those of St Michael of the Barnabite Fathers and St Jerome of the Coenobite Franciscan Fathers, and then the pinnacle of the Convent of the Virgins at the Gate of Heaven, and many others besides, crowned by onion spirals, typical of those lands, each culminating, at the very top, in golden globes surmounted by the holy cross.

Finally, there was the symbol of the supreme imperial authority: I espied the great tower of the Caesarian Palace, in which Joseph the

First of the Habsburg House of Austria, glorious Sovereign of the Holy Roman Empire, had reigned happily for six years.

With the music of the military regiment calling us to discipline, the grandiose fortified walls of the city obliging us to modesty and the innumerable bell towers of the city disposing us to the fear of God, I began to picture to myself the sinuous curves of the Danube, which, as I knew from the books I had perused before our departure, flowed on the far side of Vienna. But above all I silently invoked the name of the leafy dark mass, which now, between one cloud and another, began to take shape on the horizon, gentle with its hilly rotundities, and yet mighty, as it loomed steeply over the waters of the river and gazed silently eastwards: the city's silent and heroic sentinel. It was the Kahlenberg, the glorious mountain that had saved the West: it was from this woody promontory, overlooking Vienna and the river, that the Christian armies, twenty-eight years earlier, had freed the city from the great siege of the Turks, and delivered Europe from the threat of Mahomet.

It was no surprise that I remembered those events so clearly. All those years ago, in September 1683, while everyone in Rome and Europe was tremulously awaiting the outcome of the Battle of Vienna, I was working as a servant boy in an inn, where I served lunches and dinners. There I had met my wife, Cloridia, and, among the many guests in the hotel, a certain Abbot Melani.

Screwing up my eyes, with the carriage wheels creaking as they forced their way out of yet another ditch, I saw a ray of sunlight strike the little building on the summit of the Bald Mountain, perhaps a church – yes, a little chapel, the very one where (so memory – or rather history, as it was by now – told me) a Capuchin father, at dawn on 12th September 1683, the day of the decisive assault, had said mass and harangued the Christian commanders before leading them to the bloody but blessed final victory over the Infidels. Now I was going to touch with my own hand, or rather my own feet, the shining relics of the past; I myself would tread the gentle hills of neighbouring Nussdorf, where the infantrymen of the Christian armies, battling from house to house, from barn to barn, from vineyard to vineyard, had driven back the wretched curs of Mahomet.

I turned with emotion to Cloridia. With our little child sleeping in her lap, my wife said not a word. But I knew that she shared in my reflections. And they were not light thoughts.

We had endured a grim journey of nearly a month, setting off from Rome at the end of January, not without first anxiously prostrating ourselves before the sacred relics of Saint Filippo Neri, patron of our city. Abbot Melani had seen to it that we always obtained seats well inside the carriages and not the far less comfortable ones by the doors. After changing horses at Civita Castellana and spending the night at Otricoli, we had passed through the Umbrian town of Narni, then Terni and finally, at midnight, ancient Foligno. And in the days that followed, I, who had never travelled beyond Perugia, had spent each night in a different city: from Tolentino, Loreto and Sinigaglia, a city situated in a charming plain looking onto the Adriatic Sea, up to the Romagnolo cities of Rimini and Cesena, and then Bologna and Ferrara, and even further north, up to Chioggia on the delta of the river Po, and Mestre at the gates of Venice, and then Sacile and Udine, capital of Friuli Veneto, a notable and splendid city of the State of the Most Serene Republic. And I had then seen the nights of Gorizia and Adelsberg, arriving happily in Ljubljana, despite the fact that snow had been falling incessantly from the moment of our departure until our arrival. And then I had slept at Celje, Maribor on the Drava, Graz, capital of Styria, Pruch and finally Stuppach. Equally numerous were the cities that I had passed through, from Fano to Pesaro and Cattolica, a small town in Romagna, and from there through Forlì and Faenza. We had travelled along the river Po, passing through Corsola and Cavanella on the Adige, and along the Brenta. We had passed through the delightful town of Mira and reached Fusina, where one enters the waters of the great lagoon of Venice. And, finally, we had sailed along the river Lintz in one of those small boats that are rightly called wooden homes, since they possess all the comforts of a house. Twelve men rowed it and went so fast that in just a few hours the view before our eyes had changed from rocks to forests, from vineyards to cornfields, from great cities to ruined castles.

The cold and the snow that had accompanied us throughout our journey seemed to have no intention of leaving us. Now we were finally at the gates of Vienna, anxious as to what awaited us. The city about to welcome us to her bosom, which we had so long dreamed of, was justly known as the "New Rome": it was the capital of the immense Holy Roman Empire. Under its dominion lay, in the first place, Higher and Lower Austria, Carinthia, the Tyrol, Styria, the Vorarlberg and the Burgenland: the hereditary lands of the Habsburgs, the so-called Archduchy of Austria above and below the Enns, over which they had reigned as archdukes long before being crowned emperors. But the Holy Roman Empire also embraced countless other lands and regions, on the coast or in the mountains, such as Krajina, Istria, Dalmatia, the Banat, Bukovina, Croatia, Bosnia and Herzegovina, Slavonia, Hungary, Bohemia and Moravia, Galicia and Lodomeria, Silesia and the Siebenbürgen; and it watched over the German Electorates, including Saxony and therefore also Poland; and since the Middle Ages it had been (or it used to be, or would soon be) also Switzerland, Swabia, Alsace, Burgundy, Flanders, Artois, Franche-Comté, Spain, the Low Countries, Sardinia, Lombardy, Tuscany, the Grand Duchy of Spoleto, Venice and Naples.

Millions and millions of subjects lay under the Caesarian City, and dozens and dozens of different cultures and idioms. Germans, Italians, Magyars, Slavs, Poles, Ruthenians and Swabian artisans and Bohemian cooks, attendants and servants from the Balkans, poor fugitives fleeing from the Turks, and above all hosts of hirelings from Moravia, who swarmed to Vienna like bees.

Of all these peoples the city that lay before us was the capital. Would we find what Atto Melani had promised us there?

Relying on the Abbot's credit, we had entrusted all our meagre savings to the girls, whom we had decided to leave in Rome to continue in their jobs as midwives, leaving them to the strict surveillance of our dependable co-tenants from Istria. We had said our tearful goodbyes, promising to return as soon as possible with us the long-awaited dowry so that they could finally marry.

However, if anything were to go wrong in Vienna, we would not have a penny, either to make our departure or to survive on. We would just have to beg and wait for death to bear us off in the freezing weather. This is what poverty can do: drive mortal beings to travel all the way across the world, and then immobilise them in its crushing embrace. In short, we had made a classic leap into the dark.

Cloridia had finally agreed to the journey: "Anything, just so I don't have to see your face covered in soot anymore," she said. The mere idea that I would at last give up the job she loathed so intensely had persuaded her to accept Abbot Melani's offer.

I instinctively looked at my hands: after days without working, they were still black under the nails, between the fingers and in the pores. The distinguishing mark of wretched chimney-sweeps.

Cloridia and the child were coughing hard, as they had done for several days. I myself was tormented by a fluxion in my chest, night and day. The bouts of fever, which had begun halfway through the journey, had gradually worn us out.

The carriage now rumbled over a little bridge that crossed one of the defence moats, and finally passed through the Carinthian Gate. In the distance I could see the green woods of Kahlenberg. The diurnal star lifted its gilded fingertips from the hill and laid them gently on my own poor person: a ray of sunlight, sudden and joyous, hit me full in the face. I smiled at Cloridia. The air was cold, sharp and immaculate. We had entered Vienna.

ಌ⊷ઉ

Instinctively I slipped my hand into the pocket of the brand-new heavy overcoat, bought on the Abbot's credit, where I kept all the instructions we needed for the journey. According to the documents the notary had given us in Rome, we would find lodgings at a certain address, where we were to present ourselves. The street name was promising: Via di Porta Coeli: Heaven's Gate Street.

In the unreal silence created by snow, the carriage proceeded slowly along Carinthia Street, which leads from the gate of the same name to the city centre. Cloridia gazed around herself open-mouthed: amid the splendid palaces with their aristocratic mantles of white and the carriages emerging from side streets, swarms of well-wrapped up serving women dawdled idly, as if it were Sunday and not the middle of the working week.

She would have liked to ask the coach driver for an explanation, but the difficulty of the language held her back.

I, however, had eyes only for the spire of St Stephen's, which I saw rising over the roofs on the right and looming ever larger. It was, I reflected, the sacred pinnacle on which the Ottomans had trained their cannons every day during the summer of 1683, while on this side of the walls, within the city I now saw was thriving, the besieged citizens had resisted heroically, struggling not only against the enemy's projectiles but also against hunger, disease, lack of ammunition . . .

The coach driver, to whom I had shown the piece of paper with the address we were supposed to go to, drew up in an elegant road leading off Carinthia Street. We had reached our destination.

I was a little surprised when, after we had stepped out, the coach driver pointed at a bell rope to announce our arrival: it was the front door of a convent.

∂∾∽

"*Uno momento, uno momento,*" said a shadowy figure in awkward Italian, appearing behind the thick dark grating beside the bell rope.

Owing to my still shaky grasp of German I had not understood that the address we were bound for was that of a nuns' convent.

On hearing our names, the shadowy figure gave a nod of assent. We were expected. Two days earlier the coach driver, during a pause on the journey, had sent a messenger ahead to announce our imminent arrival.

I unloaded our luggage with the help of the coach driver, from whom I learned that we were about to enter one of the largest convents in the city and almost certainly the most important.

We were received in a large entrance hall with little light, which we left a few minutes later to emerge into the daylight again, in the colonnade of an internal cloister: a long gallery of white stones, adorned with the images of sisters who had shown virtue to the highest degree. Following an elderly nun who seemed to be mute, but who perhaps simply did not know our language, we rapidly passed through the colonnade and reached the guest rooms. A pair of adjoining rooms had been allotted to us. While Cloridia and my son collapsed wearily onto the bed, I set about carrying our bags into the rooms with the help of a young idiot, temporarily hired by the nuns to clear out and clean up the cellars. Stooping and clumsy, but at the same time muscular and tall, the idiot was also extremely chatty and, from the tone of his conversation, I gathered that he was asking me questions about our journey and such matters. A pity that I understood not a single word.

After taking leave of the idiot with a broad smile and closing the door on him, I looked around myself. The room was very bare, but it had all one might need; and in any case it looked much better than the cellar of *tufo* we had been living in for the last two years in Rome and where, alas, we had left our daughters. I turned my eyes to Cloridia.

I was expecting a barrage of complaints, reproofs and scepticism about Abbot Melani's promises: lodging with nuns was the very worst thing that could happen to her, I knew that. The brides of Christ were the only women my wife really could not get along with.

But nothing came from her lips. Lying on the bed, still clasping our boy who was coughing in his sleep, Cloridia was gazing around herself in bewilderment, with the vacant gaze of one about to yield to the dark drowsiness of exhaustion.

Our son gave me a start. His fit of coughing was more acute than ever. It seemed to be getting worse. A moment later there came a knock at the door.

"Goat's fat and spelt flour with a drop of vermouth oil, to rub on his chest. And his head must rest on this pillow of spelt."

These words, in impeccable Italian, came from a young nun, who entered our rooms with courteous but firm solicitude.

"I'm Camilla, Chormaisterin of this convent of Augustinian nuns," she introduced herself, while, without even asking for Cloridia's permission, she arranged the pillow under the little boy's head and, pulling up his shirt, rubbed the ointment onto his chest.

"Chor . . . maisterin?" I stammered, after stooping to kiss her robe and thanking her for the hospitality.

"Yes, conductor of the choir," she confirmed in a benign tone.

"It's a surprise to hear such perfect Italian here in Vienna, Mother."

"I'm Roman, like you; Trasteverine, to be precise. Camilla de' Rossi is my secular name. But don't call me Mother, please: I'm just a secular sister."

Cloridia had not moved from her bed. I saw her peeking sidelong at our guest.

"And nothing to eat but light soup for two weeks," concluded the Chormaisterin, looking closely at the child.

"I knew it. The usual generosity . . ."

Cloridia's harsh and unexpected outburst made me flush with embarrassment; I was afraid we would soon be driven out, but the victim reacted with an amused laugh.

"I see that you know us well," she answered, not in the least offended. "But I guarantee that in this case my fellow sisters' proverbial stinginess has nothing to do with it. Spelt soup with crushed prune stones cures all fluxions of the chest."

"You treat people with spelt too," remarked Cloridia in a dull voice after a moment's silence. "So did my mother."

"And so we have been doing ever since the early days of our holy sister Hildegard, Abbess of Bingen," Camilla declared with a sweet smile. "But I'm pleased to hear that your mother appreciated it too; one day, if you feel like it, will you tell me about her?"

Cloridia responded with hostile silence.

She was truly amiable, Camilla de' Rossi, I thought, despite my wife's diffidence. She was dressed in a white habit, its sleeves lined with fine, pure Indian linen, and a hood in the same linen with a black crépon veil hanging down behind.

The face that the hood and veil left uncovered belonged to neither of the two physiognomies peculiar to young nuns (or secular sisters, it made little difference): she had neither the watery, dull eyes surrounded by pudgy pink and white cheeks like ham lard, nor the hard little tetchy eyes set in a sallow, scraggy complexion. Camilla de' Rossi was an attractive, blooming girl, whose dark, proud eyes and lively mouth reminded me of my wife's features just a few years earlier.

There was another knock.

"Your lunch has arrived," announced the Chormaisterin, as she opened the door to two scullery maids carrying trays.

The meal, curiously, was all based on spelt: flat loaves of spelt and chestnuts, cream of apples and spelt, a pie of spelt grains and fennel.

"Now hurry up," urged Camilla after we had refreshed ourselves, "you're expected in half an hour's time at the notary."

"So you know . . ." I said, astonished.

"I know everything," she cut me short. "I've already sent word to the notary that you've arrived. So come along; I'll look after your boy."

"You don't really expect me to leave my son in your hands?" protested Cloridia.

"We are all in the hands of Our Lord, my daughter," answered the Chormaisterin maternally, though as to age she could have been *our* daughter.

Having said this, she ushered us with gentle firmness towards the door.

I pleaded to Cloridia with my eyes not to offer any resistance nor to make any of her less gracious remarks about the tribe of the brides of Christ.

"Anything, if it means I don't see soot again," she merely said.

I thanked God that my consort, thanks to her hatred of the chimney-sweeping trade, had finally given in. And perhaps the young nun, who seemed to have genuinely taken our little boy's health to heart, was beginning to break down Cloridia's wall of diffidence.

When we stepped outside we found the convent's idiot leaning against the wall and waiting for us; the Chormaisterin gave him a quick confirmatory glance.

"This is Simonis. He'll take you to the notary."

"But Mother," I tried to object, "I don't know German very well, and I don't understand when he speaks to me. When we got here . . ."

"What you heard wasn't German: Simonis is Greek. And when he wants he can make himself understood, trust me," she said with a smile, and without another word she closed the door behind us.

⇛⇚

"Very generous this donation of Abbot Milani, yes, yes?"

It was with these words, spoken in diligent Italian with only Melani's name pronounced incorrectly, that the notary welcomed us into his office, gazing at us from behind his little spectacles; unfortunately it was not clear whether the words constituted an affirmation or a question.

We had arrived at the office after a short walk through the snow, during which our limbs had nonetheless grown exceedingly numb. The terrible winter of 1709, which had brought our family and the whole of Rome to its knees, had been nothing in comparison with this, and I realised that the heavy overcoats we had bought before our departure were as much protection as an onion skin. Cloridia was tormented by her fluxion of the chest.

"Yes, yes," the notary repeated several times, after bidding us remove our coats and shoes and inviting us to sit down opposite him. Simonis had remained in the anteroom.

While we enjoyed the warmth of an enormous and rich cast-iron stove coated with majolica, such as I had never seen before, he began to leaf through a file, whose cover bore words in gothic characters.

Cloridia and I, our chests bursting with silent tension, looked on as his hands riffled through the papers. My poor wife lifted a hand to her temple: I realised she was suffering one of those terrible headaches that had tortured her ever since we had fallen into poverty. What news did those papers hold? Was the end of our troubles inscribed there, or was it all just another hoax? I could feel my belly churning with anxiety.

"The documents are all here: *Geburtsurkunde, Kaufkontrakt* and, above all, the *Hofbefreyung*," said the notary at last, in a mixture of Italian and German. "Check the accuracy of the data," he added, placing the documents before me, although I had by no means grasped their nature: "Signor Abbot Milani, your bene-factor . . ."

"Melani," I corrected him, aware that Atto's signature could give rise to similar misunderstandings.

"Ah, yes," he said, after examining a page carefully. "As I was saying, Signor Abbot Melani and his procurators have been very diligent and precise. But the imperial court is very strict: if anything is wrong, there is no hope."

"The imperial court?" I asked, full of hope.

"If the court doesn't accept it, the donation cannot take effect," the notary continued. "But now read this *Geburtsurkunde* carefully and tell me if all is in order."

Having said this, he placed before me the first of four documents, which – to my no small surprise – proved to be a birth certificate bearing my name, specifying the day, month, year and place of my birth, as well as my paternity and maternity. This was truly singular, given that I was a foundling, and not even I knew when, where or to whom I had been born.

"This, then, is the **Gesellenbrief**," insisted our interlocutor, who, after gazing out of the window, suddenly seemed to be in a great hurry. "I repeat, the court is very strict. Especially when it comes to the question of apprenticeship; otherwise the confraternity could create problems for you."

"The confraternity?" I asked, not having the foggiest idea what he was talking about.

"Now let's proceed, since there is little time. You can ask your questions later."

I would have liked to say that I still had not understood what purpose all those documents (false ones, to boot) served. Above all, the notary's words did not explain what Atto Melani's donation consisted of. Nonetheless, I obeyed and refrained from commenting. Cloridia kept quiet too, her eyes glazed by the migraine and her fluxion of the chest.

"The Hofbefreyung, to tell the truth, is less urgent: I'm here to guarantee its validity. Since time is short, you could look it over in the carriage."

"In the carriage?" said Cloridia in surprise. "Where to?"

"To check that what is contained in the *Kaufkontrakt* is correct, where else?" he answered, as if stating the obvious, and he got to his feet, beckoning us to follow him.

We had entered the notary's office with a thousand hopes in our hearts, and now we were leaving it with just as many questions on our minds.

❧

We were a little surprised when the carriage that was carrying us – my wife, myself, Simonis and the notary – began to travel away from the centre of the city. We soon reached the walls and passed through one of the city gates, emerging onto a bare and icy plain.

On the journey, while my wife and I huddled in a corner against the cold and Simonis gazed out of the window with inexpressive eyes, I observed the notary and pondered. He seemed to be in a great hurry; to do exactly what, was not clear. There was no doubt that the two documents he had set before me were blatant forgeries, and came from Abbot Melani. Atto – I remembered well – was well versed in the art of falsifying papers, even more important ones than these ... This time, I had to acknowledge, his aim had been less reprehensible: he simply wanted to make the donation effective.

The notary returned my gaze: "I know what you're wondering, and I apologise for not having thought of it before. It is certainly opportune that I should at this point explain where we are going."

"About time," I thought, while Cloridia, suddenly reanimated, mustered her remaining strength to sit up and prepare herself for what the notary was about to say.

"In short, I should attempt to distract your good lady from the tedium of the journey by pointing out to her the forms, qualities and appearances of this imperial city," the notary began in a pompous tone, clearly very proud of his home town. "Outside the city walls, and all around it, is a broad level area of unpaved earth, clear of all vegetation, which makes it possible, in the event of an enemy attack, to get a clear view of the besiegers. To the east of the residential area lies the river Danube, which with generous and serpentine sinuosity flows from north to south, and from west to east, forming within its curves numerous little islands, marshes and bogs. Further east, beyond this damp, lagoon-like area, begins the great plain that stretches uninterruptedly as far as the Kingdom of Poland and the empire of the Czar of Russia. Southwards lies another flat area, leading towards Carinthia, the region bordering on Italy, whence you yourselves came. Westwards and northwards, however, the city is surrounded by woody hills, culminating in the Kahlenberg – the *Monte Calvo* or Bald Mountain as you Italians call it – the extreme point of the Alps, which rears up above the Danube, bastion of the West facing the great eastern plain of Pannonia."

Despite the notary's affable eloquence, Cloridia's face continued to darken and I myself was conjecturing with some trepidation as to the substance of the donation. If only this odd notary would come out and tell us just what it consisted of!

"I know what you're thinking," he said in that moment, suspending the orographic lesson on Vienna and turning to me: "You will be wondering about the precise nature of your benefactor's donation, and what prestige it bears. Well now, as you can read yourselves in the *Hofbefreyung*," he specified, setting one of the documents before me with great care, "Abbot Melani has procured for you – in the suburb of the Josephina, near St Michael, where we are now heading – a post as 𝔥𝔬𝔣𝔟𝔢𝔣𝔯𝔢𝔶𝔱𝔢𝔯 𝔐𝔢𝔦𝔰𝔱𝔢𝔯."

"What does that mean?" Cloridia and I asked in unison.

"Obvious: in 𝔥𝔬𝔣𝔟𝔢𝔣𝔯𝔢𝔦𝔱, 𝔥𝔬𝔣 means 'court' and 𝔟𝔢𝔣𝔯𝔢𝔦𝔱 'freed'. You have been made free to become meister, or master, by licence of the court, or by imperial decree, however you want to put it."

We looked at him quizzically.

"It's because you are not a Viennese citizen," the notary explained. "And so, given the urgent, the extremely urgent, need that the Emperor has of your services, your benefactor has generously begged and obtained from the court, on your behalf, the 𝔊𝔢𝔴𝔢𝔯𝔟𝔢𝔟𝔢𝔯𝔢𝔠𝔥𝔱𝔦𝔤𝔲𝔫𝔤," he concluded, without realising that he still had not clarified the main point.

"And that is?" pressed Cloridia with incredulous hope at the notary's unexpected words.

"The right to exercise the profession, of course! And to be welcomed into the confraternity," explained the notary impatiently, looking at us as if we were two savages – and ungrateful ones, to boot.

As I was to learn with time, the Viennese take any unfamiliarity with their language for a lack of civility and grey matter.

At the notary's sharp reaction my already enfeebled spouse fell completely silent, afraid of irritating him and so creating yet more untimely complications for Atto's long-awaited and inscrutable donation, now so close at hand.

What had I become Meister or master of? What was the profession that the Emperor was benevolently allowing me to exercise despite not being a Viennese citizen? And, above all, what services did the benevolent Sovereign require of me with such urgency?

"You will have to lead a virtuous and blameless life, carry out your duties properly and serve as a model and example to the Gesellen," he began again enigmatically. "And that's not all: as you can read in the Kaufkontrakt, or the purchasing contract, which Abbot Melani magnanimously concluded in your name, Haus, Hof and Weingarten are listed! What incomparable generosity! But here we are at last. Just in time, before twilight."

The light, in fact, was fading fast; it was still only early afternoon, but darkness falls very early in northern lands and almost without warning, especially in midwinter. Now we understood the sudden haste the notary had shown in his office.

I was about to ask what the three things listed in the purchasing contract consisted of, when the carriage stopped. We got out. In front of us was a little single-storey house, apparently uninhabited. Over the entrance hung a brand-new sign with an inscription in gothic characters.

"Gewerbe IV," the notary read for us. "Ah yes, I had forgotten to specify: yours is company number four of the twenty-seven currently licensed in the Caesarean capital and surrounding area, and is one of the five recently elevated to the prestigious rank of city companies by command of His Caesarean Majesty Joseph I with *Privilegium* of 19th April 1707. Your principal task will obviously remain that of satisfying the Emperor's urgent needs as a Hofadjunkt or court auxiliary: you are entrusted with full charge of an ancient Caesarean building which our benign Sovereign now wishes to restore to its original splendour."

At this last piece of information from the notary, Cloridia, who was trailing sullenly in our wake, under the dull gaze of Simonis, suddenly perked up and hastened her steps. My hopes revived as well: if the company Atto had acquired for us, and which I was to become master of, had been instituted by no less a person than the Emperor, and if the number of such companies in the whole city was fixed by decree, and if, furthermore, I was being put in charge – urgently! – of an imperial building, no less, then it could hardly be a trifling matter.

"So, Signor Notary," asked my wife in honeyed tones, wearing her first smile that day, "can you finally tell us what it is? What *is* this activity, which, through the generosity of Abbot Melani and the benevolence of your emperor, my husband will have the honour to practise in this splendid city of Vienna?"

"Oh sorry, signora; I thought it was already clear: Rauchfangkehrermeister."

"That is?"

"What do you call it in Italian? Master Smokebrush . . . no . . . Hearthsweep . . . Ah yes: Master Chimney-sweep."

We heard a dull thud. Clorida had fallen to the ground in a swoon.

Day the First

THURSDAY, 9TH APRIL 1711

✠

11 of the clock: luncheon hour for artisans, secretaries, language teachers, priests, servants of commerce, footmen and coach drivers.

Greedily sipping an infusion of boiling herbs, I watched our little boy at his play and at the same time leafed through the *New Calendar* of Krakow for the year 1711, which I had picked up somewhere. It was now nearly midday, and at the eating house, for the modest price of 8 kreutzer, I had just consumed the usual lavish meal of seven dishes laden with various meats, which would have sufficed for ten men (and twenty of my size), a meal that is served in Vienna every day of the week to any humble artisan, but which in Rome only a prince of the Church would be able to afford.

I would never have imagined, just a couple of months earlier, that my stomach could feel so full.

And so I now made use – as I did every day – of Cloridia's salutary digestive infusions, and sank sluggishly into my beautiful brand-new armchair of green brocatelle.

Yes, in this one-thousand-seven-hundred-and-eleventh year since the birth of Our Redeemer Jesus Christ, or – as the calendar recorded – 5,660 years since the creation of the world; 3,707 years since the first Easter; 2,727 since the construction of the temple of Solomon; 2,302 since the Babylonian captivity; 2,463 since Romulus founded Rome; 1,757 since the beginning of the Roman Empire with Julius Caesar; 1,678 since the Resurrection of Jesus Christ; 1,641 since the destruction of Jerusalem under Titus Vespasian; 1,582 since the institution of the 40-days' fast and since the holy fathers made baptism mandatory for all Christians; 1,122 years since the birth of the Ottoman Empire; 919 years since the coronation of Charlemagne; 612 since the conquest of Jerusalem under Godfrey of Bouillon; 468 since German supplanted Latin in the official documents of the chancelleries; 340 since the invention of the arquebus; 258 since the fall of Constantinople into the hands of the Infidel; 278 since the invention of the printing press by the genius of Johannes Gutenberg of Mainz and 241 since the invention of paper in Basel by Anthony and Michael Galliciones; 220 since the discovery of the New World by Christopher Columbus of Genoa; 182 years since the first Turkish siege of Vienna and 28 years since the second and last one; 129 since the correction of the Gregorian calendar; 54 years since the invention of the upright clock; 61 years since the birth of Clement XI, our Pontiff; 33 since the birth of His Caesarean Majesty Joseph the First; 6 years since his ascension to the throne; well yes, in this most glorious Annus Domini in which we found ourselves, Cloridia and I owned an armchair – well, two actually.

They had not been a gift from some compassionate soul: we had purchased them with the proceeds of our small family business and we were enjoying them in our lodgings inside the Augustinian convent, where we were still living while we waited for an extra storey to be added to our house in the suburb of the Josephina.

This day, the first Thursday after Easter, fell almost two months after our arrival in the Caesarean capital and our life now showed no traces of the famine that had afflicted us in Rome.

This was all thanks to my job as a chimney-sweep in Vienna – or, to be more precise, as "Master Chimney-sweep by Licence of the Court", 𝔥𝔬𝔣𝔟𝔢𝔣𝔯𝔢𝔦𝔱𝔢𝔯 𝕽𝔞𝔲𝔠𝔥𝔣𝔞𝔫𝔤𝔨𝔢𝔥𝔯𝔢𝔯𝔪𝔢𝔦𝔰𝔱𝔢𝔯, as it is known round here, where even the humblest ranks will not forgo the gratification of a high-sounding title. That which in Italy was considered, as I have already said, one of the vilest and most degrading of trades, was regarded here, in the Archduchy of Austria above and below the Enns, as an art, and one that was held in high esteem. Back there we were seen as harbingers of ill, whereas here people competed in the streets to touch our uniforms because (it was said) we brought good luck.

That was not all: the job of master chimney-sweep brought with it not only a social position of great respect but also an enviable income. I could even say that I know no other job that is more highly esteemed or more thoroughly despised depending on the country where it is practised.

There were no ragged chimney-sweeps here, wandering from town to town, begging for a bit of work and some warm soup. No exploited children torn from needy families; no *fam, füm, frecc*, or "hunger, smoke, cold", the three black *condottieri* that give their names to the wretched trade in the poor Alpine valleys of northern Italy.

One had but to leave those valleys behind and enter the imperial city to find everything turned on its head: in Vienna there were no roaming chimney-sweeps but only well-established ones, with all the formalities of regulation, confraternity memberships, fixed charges, (12 *pfennig*, or *baiocchi*, for a regular cleaning), official pecking orders (master, assistant and apprentice) and convenient home-cum-workshops, which often – as in my case – came complete with courtyard and vineyard.

And, to my great surprise, the Viennese chimney-sweeps were *all* Italian.

The first ones had arrived two centuries earlier, together with the master builders who had brought with them the Italian genius for architecture and building techniques. As houses grew in number and density, fires broke out more frequently, so that Emperor Maximilian I decided to hire the chimney-sweeps in Vienna on a permanent basis. In the headquarters of our confraternity there still hung on the wall, venerated almost like a sacred relic, a document from 1512: the Emperor's order for the hiring as chimney-sweep of a certain "Hans von Maylanth", Giovannino from Milan, the first of our brothers.

After a century and a half we had gained such a solid position in the city that, to practise the trade, we were issued with a licence complete with imperial permit. Since the art of chimney-sweeping had been imported into the Empire by us Italians, for two hundred years we had done all we could to keep it in our own hands. Martini, Minetti, Sonvico, Perfetta, Martinolli, Imini, Zoppo, Toscano, Tondu, Monfrina, Bistorta, Frizzi, De Zuri, Gatton, Ceschetti, Alberini, Cecola, Codelli, Garabano, Sartori, Zimara, Vicari, Fasati, Ferrari, Toschini, Senestrei, Nicoladoni, Mazzi, Bullone, Polloni. These were the names that recurred in the chimney-sweeping business: all exclusively Italian and all related to one another. And so the job of chimney-sweeping had actually become hereditary, passing down from father to son, or from father-in-law to son-in-law, or to the nearest relative, or, if there were none, going to the second husband of an eventual widow. That was not all: it could even be sold on. A rare and lucrative possession, which cost no less than two thousand gulden, or florins: a sum that very few artisans could afford! Not a day went past without my thinking gratefully of Abbot Melani's generous action.

If my fellow chimney-sweeps, back in Italy, only knew what a hell they were living in and what a paradise was to be found just across the Alps!

I was making a very good living. Each of us chimney-sweeps was assigned a quarter or a suburb of the city. For my part, I had had the good luck, through Abbot Melani's donation, to acquire the company responsible for the suburb of the Josephina, or the City of Joseph, from the name of our Emperor; this was a neighbourhood of modest artisans very close to the city, but it also included some summer residences of the high nobility, and with these alone I was able to earn more in a month than I had earned back home in my entire life.

As I was Italian, Abbot Melani had had no difficulty in acquiring the company for me. Futhermore, with his money he had acquired absolutely everything. He had only had to forge the documents – birth certificate, curriculum *et cetera* – that were necessary to prevent the confraternity of chimney-sweeps protesting to the court. To tell the truth, when I presented myself for the first time they received me rather coldly, and I could not really blame them: my appointment as chimney-sweep "by licence of the Court" did not go down well with my colleagues, who had had to sweat hard to get what had been given to me on a silver tray. I also aroused some mistrust since they had never heard of chimney-sweeps in Rome. My colleagues, in fact, all came from the Alpine valleys or even from the Ticino or the Grigioni. They accompanied me on my first cleaning assignments, to make sure that I knew how to do my job properly: Atto's money had a lot of sway in Vienna, it was true, but it was not powerful enough to make a chimney-sweep out of an incompetent fool who might one day set the whole city alight.

And so began a new life for my family and myself in the Most August Caesarean capital, where even the humblest houses, as Cardinal Piccolomini had noted with astonishment, resembled princely palaces, and where every day the gates of the massive and sublime city walls let through an unending stream of provisions: carts loaded with eggs, crayfish, flour, meat, fish, countless birds, over three hundred wagons laden with casks of wine; by evening it would all be gone. Cloridia and I gazed open-mouthed at the greedy rabble, devoted to its belly, which every Sunday consumed what at Rome it would take us a year to earn. We ourselves were now allowed a place at the table of this lavish and eternal banquet.

Atto Melani's act of generosity had come about thanks to a fortunate conjunction of circumstances: His Caesarean Majesty Emperor Joseph I wished to restore an ancient building that stood at the gates of Vienna, and needed a master chimney-sweep who would undertake to renovate the flues and overhaul the system of protection against fires, which seemed to be breaking out with increasing frequency. Shortly after my appointment, however, there had been such abundant snowfalls that I had been unable to start my work there, and, to make matters worse, part of the building had fallen in, making building repairs necessary. Today I was to visit the Caesarean property for the first time.

Just one thing was still unclear to me: why had the Emperor not appointed one of the many other master chimney-sweeps of the court, who were already responsible for the numerous royal residences?

Abbot Melani had even arranged for a small single-storey house to be purchased in our name near the church of St Michael in the Josephina, and had undertaken to have an extra storey added, an operation that was still under way: my family and I would soon enjoy the great luxury of having a house all to ourselves, with the ground floor given over to business and the upper one to our living quarters. A real dream for us, after our experience in Rome of having to share a *tufo* cellar with another family of paupers . . .

Now we could even send large sums of money to our two daughters who were still there, and we were even planning to have them join us in Vienna as soon as our new house was ready.

Atto, in his donation, had also included wages for a tutor who would teach our child to read and write in Italian, "since," he had written in the accompanying letter, "Italian is an international language and is, indeed, the official language of the Caesarean court, where hardly any other is spoken. The Emperor, like his father and his grandfather before him, attends Italian sermons, and the cavaliers of these lands have such an affinity for our nation, that they vie for the opportunity to travel to Rome and master our language. And those who know it enjoy great esteem throughout the Empire and have no need to learn the local idioms."

I was infinitely grateful to Melani for what he had done, even though I had been a little hurt to find no personal note in his letter, no news of himself, no expressions of affection, just generic salutations. But perhaps, I thought, the letter had been drawn up for him by a secretary, Atto being too old and probably too sick to see to such details.

For my part I had, of course, written a letter warmly proclaiming my sense of obligation and affection. And even Cloridia, having overcome her age-old mistrust of Atto, had sent him lines of sincere gratitude together with an elegant piece of crochet work, to which she had applied herself for weeks: a warm, soft shawl in camlet of Flanders, yellow and red, the Abbot's favourite colours, with his initials embroidered on it.

We had received no reply to our attestations, but this did not surprise us, given his advanced age.

Our little boy was now doing his best to copy into his notebook simple phrases in the Germanic idiom and in a special gothic cursive, very difficult to read, which the people here call Current.

While it was true, as Abbot Melani said, that Italian was the court language in Vienna – indeed, the sovereigns who wrote to the Emperor were required to do so in that language – the common people were much more at ease in German; for a chimney-sweep wishing to practise his trade, it was essential to learn its rudiments at least.

With this in mind, I had decided that the wages Atto had set aside for an Italian tutor should be used to pay a teacher of the local language, since I myself would undertake to instruct my son in his native language, as I had already done, quite successfully, with his two sisters. And so every second evening, Cloridia, my son and I received a visit from this teacher, who would endeavour for a couple of hours to illuminate our poor minds on the intricate and impenetrable universe of the Teutonic language. Cardinal Piccolomini had already complained of its immeasurable difficulties and its almost total incompatibility with other idioms, and this had been proved since the days of Giovanni da Capistrano; during his visit to Vienna, he had delivered his sermons against the Turks from the pulpit in the Carmelite Square in Latin; he had then been followed by an interpreter, who took three hours to repeat everything in German.

While our little infant made great strides, my wife and I were left floundering. We made greater progress, fortunately, in reading, and that was why, as I said earlier, that in the late morning of 9th April of the year 1711, in the brief post-prandial pause, I was able to flick casually (almost) through the *New Calendar-Agenda* of Krakow, written by Matthias Gentille, Count Rodari of Trent, while my little boy doodled at my feet until it should be time to go back to work with me.

Like every master chimney-sweep of Vienna, I too had my *Lehrjunge*, or apprentice, and he was, of course, my son, who at the age of eight had already endured – but also learned – more than a boy twice his age.

A little while later Cloridia joined us.

"Come quickly, they're about to turn into the street. And then I have to get back to the palace."

Thanks to the good offices of the Chormaisterin of the convent, my wife had found a highly respectable job at just a short distance from the religious house. In Porta Coeli Street, or Himmelpfortgasse as the Viennese say, there was a building of great importance: the winter palace of the Most Serene Prince Eugene of Savoy, President of the Imperial Council of War, great *condottiero* in the service of the Empire in the war against France, as well as victor over the Turks. And now, on that very day, there was to be an extremely important event at the palace: at midday an Ottoman embassy was expected to arrive from Constantinople. A great opportunity for my wife, born in Rome, but from the womb of a Turkish mother, a poor slave who had ended up in enemy hands.

Two days earlier, on Tuesday, five boats had arrived at the Leopoldine Island in Vienna, on the branch of the Danube nearest the ramparts, and the Turkish Agha, Cefulah Capichi Pasha, had disembarked with a retinue of about twenty people. Suitable lodgings had been provided for them on the island. To tell the truth, it was not entirely clear just what the Ambassador of the Sublime Porte had come to do in Vienna.

There had been peace with the Ottomans for several years now, since 11th September 1697, when Prince Eugene had thoroughly defeated them at the Battle of Zenta and forced them to accept the subsequent Peace of Karlowitz. War was now raging, not with the Infidel but with Catholic France over the question of the Spanish throne; relations with the Porte, usually so troubled, seemed to be tranquil. Even in restless Hungary, where the imperial armies had fought for centuries against the armies of Mahomet, the princes who had rebelled against the Emperor, usually chafing and combative, seemed to have been finally tamed by our beloved Joseph I, who was not known as "the Victorious" for nothing.

Despite this, in the second half of March an urgent courier had come from Constantinople bearing an announcement for the Most Serene Prince Eugene of an extraordinary embassy of the Turkish Agha, which was to arrive before the end of the same month. The Grand Vizir, Mehmet Pasha, must have taken the decision at the very last moment, as he had been unable to send a courier providing suitable advance warning. This had seriously upset the Prince's plans: since the middle of the month everything had been ready for his departure for The Hague, the theatre of war.

The Grand Vizir's decision cannot have been an easy one: as was pointed out in a pamphlet which I had picked up somewhere, in the winter it can take up to four months of hard and dangerous travelling to get from Constantinople to Vienna, passing not only through accessible places like Hadrianopolis, Philippopolis and Nicopolis but also filthy ones like Sofia, where the horses find themselves knee-deep in mud on the roads, through wretched villages in the uncultivated and unpopulated plains like the Ottoman Selivrea and Kinigli, or Bulgarian Hisardschik, Dragoman and Calcali, or fortified palankas, like Pasha Palanka, Lexinza and Raschin, crumbling border castles where the Sultan had left handfuls of Turkish soldiers to moulder away in long-forgotten idleness . . .

No, the real difficulty of the journey lay in passing through the jaws of the Bulgarian mountains, narrow gorges, with room for just one carriage at a time; it lay in facing the equally fearsome pass of the Trajan Gate, following terrible roads, deep in thick, clinging mud, often mixed with rocks, and battling against snow and ice and winds strong enough to overturn carriages. And in crossing the Sava and the Morava, the latter tumbling into the Danube at Semendria, eight hours below Belgrade, rivers that in winter have no bridges, whether of planks or boats, since they usually get swept away by the autumn floods. And then, already worn out by the journey, entrusting oneself to the icy waters of the Danube on board Turkish caiques, with the constant danger that the ice might crack – perhaps, to crown it all, just beneath the terrible pass of the Iron Gate, most dreadful especially when the water is low.

It was no wonder that, ever since the first Ottoman embassies, it had become traditional to undertake the journey during the summer months, spending the winter in Vienna and then setting out again the following spring. There had been no exceptions to this rule on the Ottoman side, given the extreme dangers of a winter journey. And in Vienna they still remembered with fear and trembling the misadventures that had befallen them, after the Peace of Karlowitz had been concluded on 26th January 1699, during the mission of the State Councillor, Chamberlain, and President of the Noble Imperial Council Lord Wolffgang Count of Ottingen, sent by his Caesarean Majesty, Emperor Leopold I, as his Grand Ambassador to the Sublime Ottoman Porte. Ottingen, who had taken far too long in preparing his journey, had not departed until 20th October, with a retinue of 280 people, sailing out on the Danube towards Constantinople, and – after reaching the inhospitable mountains of Bulgaria around Christmas – had truly, as they say, been through the mill.

Despite this, and against all tradition, the Turkish Agha had set out in the depths of winter: the Grand Vizir must have a truly urgent embassy to communicate to Prince Eugene! And this had aroused a good deal of alarm in the court and among the Viennese people. Every day they watched the shores of the Danube anxiously, waiting to hear the distant fanfare of the janissaries and to catch the first sight of the seventy or more boats bearing the Agha and his numerous retinue. About five hundred people were expected: at any rate not less than three hundred, as had always been the case for over a century.

The Turkish Agha did not arrive until 7th April, over a week late. On that day the tension was palpable: even Emperor Joseph I had considered it politically wise to give the Turks an indirect sign of his benevolence, and had gone with the ruling family to visit the church of the Barefoot Carmelites, which was in the same quarter, the island of St Leopold in the Danube, where the Turks were to lodge. When the Agha landed on the island, to the accompaniment of waving flags, resounding drums and pipes, the Viennese were amazed to discover that he had no more than twenty people in his retinue! As I was to read later, he had brought with him, in addition to the interpreter, only the closest members of his household: the court prefect, the treasurer, the secretary, the first chamberlain, the groom, the head cook, the coffee-maker and the imam, who, the pamphlet noted with surprise, was not a Turk but an Indian dervish. Servants, cooks, grooms and others had been engaged among the Ottomans in Belgrade, like the two janissaries who acted respectively as standard-bearer and ammunition-bearer for the Agha. The reduction of the retinue had meant that it had taken the Agha only two months to reach Vienna; he had set off from Constantinople on 7th February.

That morning, the embassy – entering the city by the bridge known as Battle Bridge, and then passing below the Red Tower, skirting the square known as Lugeck and the Cathedral of St Stephen – was to make its entrance into the palace of the Most Serene Prince, who for that purpose had sent a six-horse carriage, with another four horses saddled and harnessed in gold and silver for the members of his court.

I rushed out. Just in time. Before the curious eyes of the crowd, the convoy had turned from Carinthia Street into our road, led on horseback by the lieutenant of the guards, Officer Herlitska, and followed by twenty soldiers of the city guard assigned for the protection of the embassy during their entire stay. But I had to stop and press myself against the wall of the house at the corner between Porta Coeli and Carinthia Street, on account of the dust raised by the procession, the great flock of spectators and the approaching horses. First came the carriage of the Caesarean Commissioner for Victualling, which had met the Turkish embassy on the border, at the so-called Ceremony of Exchange, and had escorted it towards the capital; then – to the amazement of all – came a strange horseman of advanced, though indefinable age, who, as I gathered from the crowd, was the Indian dervish, followed by three *Chiaus* on horseback – the Turkish judicial officers, one of whom was riding on the right, with his horse being led by two servants on foot. This *Chiaus* was theatrically brandishing in both hands his letter of accreditation from the Grand Vizir, all wrapped in green taffeta embroidered with silver flowers and set on ruby-red satin with the seal of the Grand Vizir in red wax and a capsule of pure gold. To his left rode the interpreter of the Sublime Porte.

Finally we saw the six-horse carriage sent by Prince Eugene, inside which the crowd recognised, with a buzz of uneasy curiosity, the Turkish Agha, wearing a great turban, a robe of yellow satin and a smock of red cloth lined with sable. Sitting opposite him was – as

I gathered from the conversation of two little women beside me – the Caesarean interpreter. Alongside the carriage, puffing and panting and elbowing their way through the crowd, ran two footmen of the Prince and four servants of the Agha, followed by another Turkish cavalier, who was said to be the first chamberlain. The rear was brought up by other members of the Agha's household, followed by soldiers of the city guard.

I approached the Prince's palace myself. As I imagined, as soon as I reached the great front door I ran into Cloridia, who was holding an animated discussion with two Turkish footmen.

As I have already mentioned, thanks to the good offices of the convent's Chormaisterin, Camilla de' Rossi, my consort had found a job, temporary but well paid, of a certain prestige: thanks to her origins she understood and spoke Turkish quite well, and also the *lingua franca*, that idiom not unlike Italian, imported into Constantinople by the Genoese and the Venetians centuries ago, which the Ottomans often speak among themselves. Cloridia had therefore been taken on to act as intermediary between the staff of the embassy and Prince Eugene's servants, a task that certainly could not be carried out by the two interpreters appointed to translate the official speeches of the two great leaders.

"All right, but no more than a jugful. Just one, is that clear?" said Cloridia, concluding the squabble with the footman.

I looked at her questioningly: although she had said the last few words in Italian, the Turkish footman had given her a sly smile of comprehension.

"He was taken prisoner at Zenta and during his imprisonment learned a little Italian," explained Cloridia, while the man disappeared inside the great door of the palace. "Wine, wine, they're always wanting to drink. I promised that I would get a jugful for them secretly, I'll ask the sisters at Porta Coeli. But just one, mind you! Otherwise the Agha will find out and have both their heads cut off. And to think that every day the Commissioner for Victualling provides three okkas of wine, two of beer and a half of mulled wine for the Armenians, the Greeks and the Jews in the Agha's retinue. What I say is: why don't these Turks all convert to Our Lord's religion, which even allows the priests to drink wine in church?"

Then Cloridia turned towards the convent.

"Do you want me to get the wine?" I asked.

"That would be good. Ask the pantry sister to send a jug of the worst stuff, Liesing or Stockerau, which they use to clean wounds in the infirmary, so the Agha's footmen don't get too fond of it."

The great doors of the palace were closing. Cloridia ran inside and threw me a last smiling glance before the doors shut on her.

What a wonderful change in my wife, I thought, standing in front of the closed door, now that things had turned out so well for us. The last two years, full of hardships and privations of all kinds, had sapped her strength and hardened her character, once so serene and gay. But now the line of her mouth, the bloom of her cheeks, the expression of her forehead, the light in her complexion, the glossiness of her hair: everything was as it had been before the famine. Although the tiny wrinkles of age and suffering had not completely vanished from her delicate face, just as they furrowed my own, they had at least lost their leaden bitterness and were even in harmony with her cheerful physiognomy. For all this I had only Abbot Melani to thank.

The twisted and crazed thread that linked me, my wife and Atto to Rome and Vienna – I thought as I made my way to the convent's pantry – actually led in a third direction: the Ottoman lands. The shadow of the Sublime Porte hung over my entire life. And not only because eleven years earlier, when I was working in the villa of Cardinal Spada, we servants had served dinner in the garden dressed up as janissaries for the amusement and delectation of the guests, including Abbot Melani. No, everything began with Cloridia's origins: daughter of a Turkish slave, born in Rome and baptised with the name Maria, kidnapped in adolescence and taken to Amsterdam, where she had grown up, under the name of Cloridia, tarnished, alas, by the sin of trafficking her own body, before returning to Rome in search of her father, and at last finding – praise be to God – love and wedlock with my humble self. As I have already said, we had met at the Inn of the Donzello, where I was then working, in September 1683, just when the famous battle between Christians and Infidels was being fought out at the gates of Vienna, in which, by the grace of heaven, the forces of the True Faith had triumphed. And it was at that same time that I had met Atto Melani, who was also staying at the Donzello.

Cloridia had finally narrated to me the vicissitudes she had endured after being torn from her father. But she had never wished to confide anything more about her mother. "I never knew her," she had lied to me at the beginning of our acquaintance, afterwards letting fall little half-sentences, like the fact that the smell of coffee reminded her strongly of her mother, and finally cutting short my curiosity by saying that she could remember "nothing about her, not even her face."

It was not from Cloridia, but from the events of those days at the Donzello that I had learned the few things I did know about her mother: a slave of the powerful Odelscachi family, the same family for which her father had worked, shortly before Cloridia's kidnapping she had been sold to some unknown person, and her father had been unable to oppose the transaction, since he had never married her, precisely because she was a slave.

But I had never found out anything about my wife's infancy with her mother. Her face would cloud over as soon as I or our daughters showed any curiosity.

It was with great surprise that she had received the Chormaisterin's proposal to work for the Savoys as an intermediary with the Agha's serving staff. She had thrown me a dark look, indicating that she could guess who had told Camilla about her Ottoman blood . . .

And I was equally amazed, having no idea till that moment that my wife knew Turkish so well! The perceptive Chormaisterin, on the other hand, on hearing of the Ottoman embassy, had immediately thought of Cloridia for the job, already certain of her linguistic abilities; this was a surprise, since I had clearly stated that Cloridia had been separated from her mother at a very early age.

As I arrived in the convent cloisters, I only just avoided a collision with two porters as they staggered under the weight of an enormous trunk which was threatening to scrape the plaster from the walls, to the extreme displeasure of the old nun at the door.

"Your master must have packed clothes for the next ten years," grumbled the sister, clearly referring to some guest who had just arrived.

�

13 of the clock: luncheon hour for noblemen (while in Rome they have only just awoken). Court employees are already flocking to the coffee shops and performances begin in the theatres.

This day was doubly important. Not only had Cloridia begun her job at the palace of a prince, a distinguished *condottiero* and counsellor of the Emperor, but I myself was about to embark upon my task in the service of the Most August Joseph I. After the harsh winter months and a scarcely less icy start to spring, the first warm days had arrived; the snow had melted around Vienna and the moment had come to take charge of the chimneys and the flues of the abandoned Caesarean building, the task for which I had obtained so desirable an appointment: chimney-sweep by licence of the court.

As I have had occasion to mention, the harsh atmospheric conditions of the previous months had made it impossible to carry out any work in a large building like the one I had been told awaited me. Furthermore, a thaw in the upper stretches of the Danube had broken all the bridges and brought down huge quantities of ice, swelling the river and doing great damage to the gardens in the suburbs. And so some of the less envious chimney-sweeps had strongly advised me against visiting the building until the clement weather arrived.

On that beautiful morning early in April – although the temperature was still severe, at least for me – the sun was shining, and I decided the time had come: I would begin to take charge of His Majesty's abandoned property.

Seizing the occasion, the Chormaisterin had asked a small favour of me: the nun who acted as bursar at Porta Coeli wanted me to have a look, as soon as I could, at the buttery that the convent owned in its vineyards at Simmering, not far from the place I would be visiting. It was very large and contained a little room with a fireplace, the chimney of which needed sweeping. I was given the keys to the buttery and I promised Camilla that I would see to it as soon as possible.

I had already told our assistant to harness the mule and to fill the cart with all the necessary tools. I picked up my son and went out into the street. I found the assistant waiting for me, sitting on the box seat, with his usual broad smile.

A master chimney-sweep, in addition to an apprentice, must have a *Geselle* – which is to say, an assistant, jobber, or servant boy, whatever you want to call him. Mine was Greek, and I had met him for the first time at the convent of Porta Coeli, where he acted as factotum: servant, odd-job man and messenger. It was Simonis, the talkative young idiot who, two months earlier, had accompanied Cloridia and me to our meeting with the notary.

As soon as he had heard that I owned a chimney-sweeping business, Simonis had asked me if I needed a hand. His temporary job clearing the cellars at Porta Coeli was about to end and Camilla herself had warmly recommended him, assuring me that he was much less of an idiot than he seemed. And so I had engaged him. He would keep his little room at Porta Coeli until my house was ready at the Josephina, then he would come and live with me and my wife, as assistants usually do with their master.

As the days went by we had a few short conversations, if I can so term the laborious verbal exchanges between Simonis, whose grasp of reasoning was shaky, and myself, whose grasp of the language was even more so. Simonis, perennially good-humoured, would ask countless questions, most of them fairly ingenuous, intermingled with a few friendly quips. When I understood these latter, they served, at least, to put me at my ease and make me appreciate the company of this scatterbrained but gentle Greek, amid the Nordic coarseness of the Viennese.

With his corvine fringe hanging down over his forehead, his glaucous eyes fixed rigidly on his interlocutor, his facial features, which would suddenly turn grave, it was never clear to me whether Simonis followed my answers to his questions, or whether his mind was seriously obfuscated. His protruding upper teeth, vaguely rabbit-like, were always exposed to the air, covering much of his lower lip, and he held his right forearm out in front of himself, but with his wrist bent so that his hand dangled downwards, as if the limb had been maimed by a sword blow or some other accident; these features inclined one to the latter hypothesis – that Simonis was a boy of fine character and goodwill, but with very little presence of mind.

This suspicion was corroborated by my sudden discovery, one day, that my young assistant understood, and spoke, my own language.

Tired of mumbling half-sentences in German, one day, as we were cleaning a particularly problematic flue, I was about to slip and, taken by surprise, I yelled in Italian for him to help me, pulling on the rope that was holding me up.

"Don't worry, Signor Master, I'll pull you up!" he immediately reassured me, in my own language.

"You speak Italian."

"Yes," he answered with candid terseness.

"Why did you never tell me?"

"You never asked me, Signor Master."

And so it was that I discovered that Simonis was not in Vienna in search of some little job to make ends meet, but for a far nobler reason: he was a student. Of medicine, to be precise. Simonis Rimanopoulos (this was his surname) had begun his studies at the University of Bologna, which explained his knowledge of Italian, but then the famine of the year 1709 and the prospect of a less impoverished life had sent him – reasonably enough – to the opulent city of Vienna and its ancient university, the *Alma Mater Rudolphina*, on which students from Hungary, Poland, eastern Germany and many other countries converged.

Simonis belonged to the well-known category of *Bettelstudenten* – poor students, those without family support, who maintained themselves by all sorts of expedients, including, if necessary, mendicancy.

It had been a stroke of luck for Simonis that I had hired him: in Vienna the *Bettelstudenten* were not looked on with favour. Despite the frequent edicts published, vagabond students were often to be seen – together with others who joined them, but who were not really students – begging in the streets and in front of the churches and houses night and day, even during lesson times. Under cover of studying, they loafed about, pilfering and thieving. Everyone remembered the tumult that had broken out between 17th and 18th January 1706 both within and without the city, and also at Nussdorf; strict (though fruitless) investigations into this affair were still being carried out so that the culprits might be punished harshly. These students tarnished the good name of the other students and His Caesarean Majesty had issued numerous resolutions, with the aim of uprooting once and for all this lamentable practice of *betteln*, or begging – which was the word for lounging about and succumbing to vice under the pretext of study. After the tumults of five years earlier, the rector, the Caesarean superintendents and the assembly of the ancient University of Vienna had been commanded to issue a special edict giving a final warning to the *Bettelstudenten* who were roaming around and not studying: within fourteen days they had to leave the Caesarean capital. If they failed to do so they would be seized by the guards and taken *ad Carceres Academicos*, to the university prisons, where suitable punishment would be meted out. Those impoverished students, on the other hand, who daily and continuously applied themselves to their studies, had to seek a study grant in the *Alumnates* or some other means of sustenance; only those who were unable, because of the numbers, to obtain such assistance, or those who were following a particularly demanding course of study and for the moment had no other choice than to seek alms outside lesson times, would be allowed to continue in this fashion – but only for their bare necessities and until the arrival of new orders. In addition they must always carry with them the badge identifying them as true *Bettelstudenten*, which they must get renewed every month by the university and wear on their chests while begging. Otherwise they would not be recognised as genuine poor students but as vagabond students, and so be immediately incarcerated.

This explains why Simonis had offered himself as an assistant chimney-sweep: the risk of having to beg for alms to survive, and consequently ending up in prison, was always lurking.

But how that mild and simple spirit had managed to learn my own language so well and, above all, how the devil he managed to study (and at the university, no less) – these matters remained a mystery.

"Signor Master, do you want me to drive the cart, as I know the way?"

I had, indeed, only the vaguest idea where the Caesarean property lay: in the plain of Simmering, a flat area of grassland south-east of Vienna near the village of Ebersdorf. The exact name, as it appeared in the deed of appointment, was nothing if not exotic: "the Place with No Name known as Neugebäu", or the New Building. I had tried to question my workmates, but I had received only vague answers, partly of course because my imperial appointment had not made me popular. No one had been able to give me a clear idea of the building I was about to inspect. "I've never been there," said one, "but I think it's a kind of villa". "Even though I've never seen it, I know it's a garden," said another. "It's a hunting lodge," swore another, while the next one defined it "a bird enclosure." One thing was certain: none of my fellow chimney-sweeps had ever visited the place, nor did they appear to have any wish to set foot there.

It was a long way to the Place with No Name. And so I was perfectly happy to leave the mule's reins in Simonis's hands. My little boy had asked, and had been allowed, to sit on the box seat, alongside the Greek, who every so often let him hold the reins to teach him how to drive the cart. I settled myself behind them, among the tools.

My son gradually dozed off and I secured him to the cart with a rope, so that he would not fall off. Simonis drove with a firm and methodical hand. Strangely, he kept silent. He seemed absorbed.

In the open country, as we headed towards the plain of Simmering, there was no noise but the rattling of the cartwheels and the clatter of the mule's hooves.

All things considered, I reflected with a smile as I gazed absently at the monotonous panorama and yielded to the drowsiness of the middle of the day, on board the cart were three children: my little son; myself, a child in stature; and Simonis, who had remained an infant in mental capacity.

"We're here, Signor Master."

I woke up numb and aching where the tools had pressed into me while I dozed. We were in a large abandoned courtyard. While Simonis and the little boy got down and began to unload the tools, I looked around. We had entered via a large gateway; looking back I could make out the road we must have travelled along through the open country.

"We're inside the Place with No Name," stated the Greek, observing my still glazed eyes. "Through that arch is the entrance to the main building."

In front of us an archway led to a low outbuilding and gave onto another open area beyond. To our right, a little door in the wall revealed a spiral staircase. Looking upwards to the left I could see castellated walls and, to my surprise, a hexagonal tower whose roof was adorned with curious pinnacles. Everything – the tower, the gateway, the arch, the merlons – was in bright white stone such as I had never seen, and which dazzled my eyes, still heavy with sleep.

"This leads down to the cellars," announced my little apprentice.

He had been running around exploring things and had stopped in front of a blanched semicircular keep of unexpected shape, actually a kind of apse, from which there extended a long construction that could be glimpsed through the arch and which was apparently the main building.

"Good," I answered, since one always starts cleaning the flues from the cellars.

I got down from the cart and, like Simonis, armed myself with tools. Then we joined my son.

We crossed the threshold of what did in fact appear to be the entrance to a cellar and then descended a staircase. The ceiling was low, with a barrel vault, and the walls were imposing. A door at the bottom led into a great space that was completely empty: rather than abandoned, it looked incomplete, as if they had never finished building it.

While my two assistants groped the walls looking for the opening of a flue, I went ahead. Dazzled by the light outside, my pupils had not yet adjusted to the growing darkness and suddenly I found my nose pressed up against something cold, heavy and greasy. Instinctively I rubbed my nose and looked at my fingertips: they were red. Then I screwed up my eyes and peered.

It was dangling from a rope that hung from the ceiling and was swaying gently from where I had knocked it. It was the trunk of a bleeding corpse, naked, legless, headless and armless, and blackish blood was trickling from it onto the floor. It was attached to the rope by a great rusty piece of iron that pierced the body right through. It must have been flayed alive, I thought in a flash of lucid horror, since those parts that were not dripping blood were bright red, revealing nerves and bands of whitish fat.

Appalled by what I had seen, while my chimney-sweep's tools fell to the floor in a jangling clatter, with all the breath I had in my body I yelled to Simonis to run for it, bearing my son to safety without waiting for me – and then I fled myself.

I saw Simonis obeying me with the speed of lightning. Without any idea why, he lifted the little boy onto his shoulders and pelted away on his long legs. I hoped I would make it as well, even though my own legs were far from long. My hopes proved vain. I emerged into the sunlight and saw Simonis already disappearing over the horizon, lashing wildly at the mule – and then I heard it.

It was not very different from the way I had imagined it a thousand times: a tremendous bellowing, which makes men and beasts and all things tremble.

I had no time to realise what direction it came from: a powerful paw sweep knocked me sideways. I tumbled to the ground, fortunately well away, and as I rolled I heard the roar again. It was then that I saw it approaching: Prince of Terror, Mauler of Flesh; even as

I recognised the demoniacal eyes, the lurid mane, the bloody canines, I was running for my life, stumbling at every pace, moaning with terror and unable to believe my eyes. In that lonely place outside Vienna, on that frosty crisp day of early spring, in the cold north above the Alps, I was being chased by a lion.

I dashed into the little doorway immediately to my left, and with the speed of lightning I pelted down the spiral staircase. I found myself in a little open area. I heard the beast faltering for just a second or two and then come roaring after me, and I made my way into a large roofless building in search of some means of escape.

I thought I was in the middle of an incomprehensible nightmare when I suddenly found myself in front of . . . a sailing ship.

It was smaller than usual but unmistakeable. And that was not all: it was in the shape of a bird of prey, complete with head and beak, wings and tail fins, with a flag attached to these latter.

Certain now that I must be the victim of some envious demon and his lethal conjuring tricks, I leaped onto the feathery tail of that absurd vessel, with the desperate idea of yanking the flagpole from its place and using it as a weapon to ward off the lion, whose roar continued to set my flesh and all around me trembling.

Unfortunately, despite my chimney-sweep's agility and slim build, my age told against me. The animal was faster: in a few bounds it had reached me and launched itself with a final pounce onto its prey.

But it failed. It had not managed to leap high enough to catch me. Yielding perhaps to the lion's assaults, the feathered ship began to sway and its oscillations grew wider and wider. The lion tried again with a higher leap. It was no use. The more the lion leaped, the smaller it seemed to become. While I clung with all my strength to the wooden feathers, the ship was now pitching and rolling dizzily, and its bizarre sail – a kind of dome that formed the back of the bird – twisted and swelled with cavernous gulps of air.

The world was whirling frantically around me and my terror-distorted senses told me that the absurd carved bird was taking flight.

It was then that I heard someone declaim threateningly in the Teutonic idiom:

"𝔅𝔞𝔡 𝔐𝔲𝔰𝔱𝔞𝔣𝔞! 𝔖𝔱𝔯𝔞𝔦𝔤𝔥𝔱 𝔱𝔬 𝔟𝔢𝔡 𝔴𝔦𝔱𝔥 𝔫𝔬 𝔰𝔲𝔭𝔭𝔢𝔯!"

His name was Frosch, he stank of wine and the lion crouched tranquilly at his feet.

He explained that the animal loved the company of men and so, whenever anyone turned up round those parts, it had the bad habit of greeting them with roars of joy and playful leaps in its desire to lick them.

The Place with No Name, known as Neugebäu, was not just any place, he clarified. It had been built about a century and a half ago, by His Caesarean Majesty of honoured memory Emperor Maximilian II, and the only thing it retained today of its former splendour was the imperial menagerie, which was rich in exotic animals, especially wild beasts. As he spoke, he stroked the enormous lion, now fortunately listless and decrepit, which just a few moments before had seemed to me an invincible brute.

"**Bad Mustafa, you've been bad!**" Frosch kept scolding it, while the lion docilely let him put a chain round its neck and gazed sidelong at me. "I'm sorry that he scared you so," he finally apologised.

Frosch was the keeper of the menagerie of the Place with No Name. He looked after the lions, but also other animals. While he introduced himself, my legs were still trembling like reeds. Frosch offered me a sip from his flask, which he swigged from frequently. I refused: if I thought back to the bleeding corpse I might well throw up.

Frosch guessed my thoughts and reassured me: it was just a piece of mutton, put there to attract the lion, as it had just run away from him and could have gone anywhere.

Unfortunately, these explanations were offered to me in the only language the keeper knew, that guttural German, cavernous and corrupt, spoken by the humblest inhabitants of Vienna. I am reporting our dialogue as if it had been a normal conversation, instead of a confused babel, with me asking him to repeat every other sentence, provoking a series of impatient snorts from Frosch and, as he drew from his flask of schnaps (the robust liquor with which he kept up his spirits), the occasional vexed burp.

"**Italian. Chimney-sweep,**" I introduced myself in my primitive German, "**I . . . clean chimneys castle.**"

Frosch was pleased to hear why I was there. It was time some emperor took care of Neugebäu again. Now only he and the animals lived there, he concluded, waving his hand at Mustafa, who was polishing off the remains of the mutton with great gusto.

Every so often the keeper would frown at the lion, and Mustafa (the name was chosen out of contempt for the Infidel Turks) would appear to shrink, in humble contrition. The gruff keeper seemed to exercise an invincible influence over the beast. He assured me that I ran no risk now: while Frosch was present, all the animals obeyed blindly. Certainly there were some rare exceptions, he admitted in a low tone, since the lion had escaped from his control and had been wandering around freely until just a while ago.

So I was not in a terrible nightmare, I thought with a sigh of relief, while I prepared to clamber down from my mount. I had another look at it, sure that my eyes would now show me something less absurd than the sailing ship in the form of a bird of prey that I had thought I had beheld in those moments of terror.

But no. What I now saw was a mysterious object, and I would not have known whether to describe it as a monster, a machine or a ghost.

It was a cross between a ship and a wagon, between a bird of prey and a cetacean. It had the solid form of a barrow, the capacious hull of a barge, and the unblemished sail of a naval vessel. At the prow, there was the proud head of a gryphon, with a hooked, rapacious beak; at the stern, the caudal fins of a great kite; at the sides the powerful pinions of an eagle. It was as long as two carriages, and as broad as a felucca. Its wood was old and worn, but not rotten. On board, in the middle of a broad space shaped like a bathtub, there was room for three or four people, in addition to the helmsman. At the prow and stern were two rudimentary wooden globes, half corroded by time, one representing the celestial spheres and the other the earth, as if to suggest the route to the pilot. The whole ship (if it really could be defined such) was covered by a great sail, the frame of which gave it a semi-spherical shape. At the stern was the flag, which I had vainly endeavoured to pull out; it bore a coat of arms, surmounted by a cross.

"𝕴𝖙'𝖘 𝖙𝖍𝖊 𝖋𝖑𝖆𝖌 𝖔𝖋 𝖙𝖍𝖊 𝕶𝖎𝖓𝖌𝖉𝖔𝖒 𝖔𝖋 𝕻𝖔𝖗𝖙𝖚𝖌𝖆𝖑," Frosch clarified.

There was only one thing that I *had* dreamt: the ship was not hovering in the air but rested solidly on the ground.

I asked him in wonder what on earth this bizarre vehicle was and how it had got there.

By way of answer, as if fearing that the explanation would prove too long, or implausible, he rummaged in a corner of the room and thrust a heap of papers under my nose. It was an old gazette.

Nachricht
Von dem
Fliegenden
Schiffe/
So aus
Portugal/
Den 24. Junii in Wien mit seinem
Erfinder/
Glücklich ankommen.

Von neuen nach dem allbereit gedruckten Exemplar in die Naumburger Meß gesandt.
ANNO 1709.

Even in the most difficult languages, reading is less arduous than conversing. So I sat down on the ground and managed to decipher the pamphlet, which bore a date of about two years earlier:

News of the Flying Ship that successfully arrived in Vienna from Portugal with its inventor on 24th June
New edition for the Fair of Naumburg subsequent to the exemplar already printed.
Year 1709

Vienna, 24th June 1709
Yesterday around 9 of the clock the whole city was in great alarm and agitation. Every road was full of people, those who were not in the streets were at the windows, and were asking what was amiss. Hardly anyone, however, could give an account of what had occurred, people ran hither and thither, shouting and crying: the Day of Judgement is upon us. Others believed it to be an earthquake, while yet others swore that an entire army of Turks was at the gates of the city. Finally in the sky there appeared a great number of birds, both large and small, which, as it first appeared, were flying around another very large bird, and were quarrelling with it. This tumult began to descend earthwards, and everyone now saw that the cause of this chaos, which had been taken for a bird, was in fact a machine in the form of a ship, with a sail, which was stretched out above it and which swayed in the wind, and on board

of which was a man in the habit of a monk, who with several pistol shots announced his arrival.

After circulating in the sky, this Cavalier of the air revealed that his intention was to set himself down on the ground in an open space in this city, but there suddenly arose a wind, which not only impeded his project, but drove him towards the summit of the bell tower of St Stephen's Cathedral, and caused the sail to entangle itself around said tower, so that the ship became immobilised there. This event aroused a fresh clamour among the townspeople, who ran towards the square of the bell tower, so that at least twenty people were trampled in the affray.

Everyone's eyes were fixed on the man suspended in the air, but that was certainly of no assistance to him, since he was asking for help, and to that end it was hands that were needed. After observing what was happening in the city for a couple of hours, since no one could assist him, he became impatient, picked up the hammer and other tools that he had with him on the ship and set to work hammering and striking, until the top of the Bell Tower which had blocked him became detached and fell. Thus he took flight again and, after swaying to and fro for a while, with great dexterity brought his Flying Ship to earth not far from the Imperial Palace. At once a company of soldiers from the garrison of this city was sent there to take the new arrival under their protection, for otherwise the curious townsfolk would have trampled him underfoot.

He was taken to the inn of the Black Eagle, where he was able to rest for a few hours, after which he delivered some letters he had with him, and he recounted to the Ambassador of Portugal and to other Noblemen who had called to visit him in what fashion he had set off from Lisbon at six in the morning the previous day in the Flying Machine of his own invention, what great difficulties and adventures he had experienced with eagles, storks, birds of Paradise and other species, with which he had been forced to combat unceasingly, declaring that without the two shotguns and the four rifles that he had with him, and which he had had to use constantly, he would not have survived.

When he passed close to the moon, so he recounted, he realised that he had been sighted himself, which aroused a great tumult on the Moon; and since his flight had brought him very close to the Lunar Planet, he was able to see and distinguish everything and, as far as his haste permitted him, he noted that on it there are mountains and valleys, lakes *and rivers and fields, and even living creatures, and men who, so he said, have hands like men down here, but no feet, and who slide on the ground like snails, and bear on their backs a shield like that of tortoises, into which they can withdraw their whole body and take shelter. And since in this way they have no need of any dwelling space, he thought that it was for this reason that on the planet Moon there is not a single house, nor a castle. According to him, if the Kingdom of the Moon were attacked with forty or fifty Flying Ships like the one he had invented, each with four or five armed men, it could be conquered with great ease, and without encountering great resistance. It will be seen later whether His Royal Majesty of Portugal will wish to undertake such a conquest.*

I will make known with the next courier what else I can find out about this new Theseus. His Machine has been taken to the arsenal.

P.S.

I have just been informed that the so-called Flying Navigator has been incarcerated, as a Magician and Sorcerer of the first rank, and it appears that he will be burned with great urgency together with his Pegasus; this is perhaps to keep his art secret, since if it became common knowledge it could cause great trouble in the world.

I asked him if the winged sailing ship which lay abandoned in the Place with No Name was really the glying ship spoken of in the dispatch. By way of answer Frosch handed me another piece of paper. This time it was an illustration taken from an old issue of the Diary of Vienna.

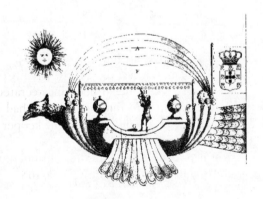

There was not the shadow of a doubt: it was a faithful drawing of the ship. It was accompanied by a short account dated 1st June 1709:

There has arrived here at the Caesarean Court from Portugal a courier with letters of 4th May and the present illustration of a device for flying, capable of travelling two hundred miles in twenty-four hours and with which war troops, letters, reinforcements, provisions and money could be sent even to the farthest lands, and in addition places under siege could be supplied with all necessities, including goods and commerce. A document has been shown which was presented to His Majesty the King of Portugal by a Brazilian priest, inventor of the aircraft. On 24th June next a trial flight will be essayed in Lisbon.

I felt a jolt in my heart: had that sailing ship really flown, as I had believed it to be doing in my desperate agitation?

It was no surprise that the ship had come from Portugal, Frosch went on to explain: just a year earlier, in 1708, the king of that country had married one of Joseph's sisters, Anna Maria. The ship had remained for a few months in the city arsenal, until the emotions aroused by its arrival had calmed down. Meanwhile the city authorities, as was reported in the gazette, had done all they could to hush the matter up. Nothing had been recounted to the Emperor: Joseph was very young, lively in spirit and enterprising; he had already become overexcited at the sight of the drawings brought to him by the Portuguese courier. He would certainly have wanted to see and study the diabolical invention, and this, in the opinion of the old ministers, was to be avoided at all costs. No one must know. The Flying Ship was dangerous, and could provoke turmoil and disorder.

I was amazed at these words: had not man dreamt for centuries of cleaving the air like a bird? It was no surprise that Frosch's gazette compared the Flying Ship to the mythical Pegasus, the winged ship from the ancient Greek sagas, and its pilot to the heroic Theseus, slayer of the Minotaur. Nonetheless, the gazette openly condemned the poor aerial wayfarer, who had even been incarcerated. I myself would have given my own soul to find out how he had flown, and where he had obtained his knowledge. I asked the keeper if he knew anything. He shook his head.

Once the matter had been hushed up, he continued, the caravel of the air was secretly transported outside Vienna, to the abandoned castle. Nobody was likely to go snooping around there. And if it were to be needed one day, it could always be salvaged.

I walked around the boat, and then boarded it, clambering up on one of the wings, which were carved in wood like the tail and the bird's head, and which served almost as gangplanks.

Overhead were ropes supported by four poles, two at the prow and two at the stern, similar to the cords one uses to hang washing. Only it was not clothes that were hung from them, but stones. They were little yellow things that sparkled, and they were secured to the ropes with little pieces of string. Not being able to reach them with my hand, I screwed up my eyes, trying to make out what material they were made of, and suddenly I realised:

"Amber. It's amber. Good Lord, it's beautiful, it looks like good quality. It must cost an arm and a leg. Why on earth have they been put there . . ."

Once again I glanced at Frosch; I could tell from his face he had no idea what purpose the stones served.

I climbed down and examined the mysterious vessel again. The curious machine, to tell the truth, was not in the pitiful state to which a prolonged exposure to rain, wind and sun might have reduced it. The wood was actually in good condition; it was as if, every so often, someone had rubbed it over with a protective oily varnish, like the one I had seen fishermen brush their boats with on the Tiber in Rome. Then I noticed that the surface of the hull was not flat and smooth, like the fishing boats. It was made up of rectilinear tubes that ran the whole length from prow to stern, as if the craft were nothing more than a bundle of pipes.

I tapped my knuckles on one of the tubes. It sounded hollow, as did the others that I tried. The tubes had moulded openings towards the prow as if they were supposed to collect something. At the stern – which is to say, at the tail end of these tubes – were trumpet-like openings, which appeared to be made to channel upwards – and so towards the sail that covered the whole boat – what was collected at the prow.

I had a look at the mast, which was still upright, at the proud prow, and at the small graceful deck. Here and there planks had been replaced, cracks patched up, loose nails fixed. Under close inspection, the small ship did not appear damaged or derelict. It was just out of commission, as if in the Place with No Name it had found a dock where it could be fixed, and perhaps also an attentive ship-boy to look after it.

"It's a small ship in every sense," I remarked, as I stroked the keel meditatively, which was not at all worn.

"Right, a ship of fools!" quipped the keeper with a coarse laugh.

At those words I gave a start.

৵৶৹

I wanted to get away. The afternoon's events had prostrated me. What was more, I was now on foot: Simonis had fled with the cart to take my little boy to safety. I had a long walk ahead of me. I would come back the next day to start work. I told Frosch so, asking him to look after the chimney-sweeping tools that I had left in the cellar when I took to my heels.

Before leaving, I gave a last look at the building we were in. As I had already noticed, it had no roof. But it was only then that I realised how enormous this space was – as broad, long and tall as an entire palace.

"What is . . . *What is this place?*" I asked in surprise.

"*The ball stadium*," answered Frosch.

And he explained (although, I repeat, it was not always easy for me to follow his idiom) that in the days of Emperor Maximilian, the founder of the Place with No Name, the ball game imported from Italy had become popular among the great lords. In this recreation the players faced one another with a sort of wooden sheath on their arms, with which they competed for a leather ball, slamming it vigorously, like cannon shots, trying to get the better of their adversaries. Frosch added with a snigger that wearing your guts out over a ball was ridiculous, and unsuited to the court of a Caesar, and a game of this sort was bound to be forgotten forever, and this, indeed, was what had happened; but in those remote times the pastime must have had quite a following, because otherwise such a generous space would not have been set aside for it.

Frosch was a wild-looking man with a big pear-shaped face, which was grey down to his nose and rubicund below the cheeks, with a greying moustache, pale eyes, a large belly and hands as large and rough as shovels. He was not likeable, I thought, but nor was he bad. He was a man to be treated with circumspection, like his wild animals: animals are capricious by nature, man becomes so through a thoughtless love of alcohol. Frosch could tame lions, but not his own thirst.

Throughout our conversation I had kept an eye on Mustafa, incredulous that such an enormous beast, however poorly in appearance, was allowed to stay outside a cage. He tore his meat to pieces, ravaging it with his fearsome fangs and claws; only an attentive eye revealed his advanced age and the lack of that vital force which, had it still been present, would have been the end of me just a few minutes earlier.

Pulling the lion by his chain, the keeper led him out of the stadium. He announced that before I set to work it would perhaps be prudent if he showed me around the place and the other beasts locked up there. He suggested that we should take a short tour, so that I would avoid any other nasty surprises tomorrow. I agreed, although with a touch of anxiety at that word "prudent", which Frosch had stressed.

"𝔑o one ever comes to check up on things here," remarked the keeper disconsolately.

Unfortunately it was very rare for an imperial commissioner to come and visit the collection of exotic animals in the Place with No Name, Neugebäu. At the court, explained Frosch sadly, this place, which had once been so splendid, had been forgotten about by everyone – at least until the advent of beloved Joseph I. Now the feeding expenses for Mustafa and his companions were paid more regularly, as were their keeper's wages, and this had made him hopeful for the future of Neugebäu. In particular, three years earlier, in 1708 – it had been the afternoon of Sunday 18th March, Frosch remembered it clearly – the Emperor, together with a great suite of ladies and gentlemen of the court, had accompanied his sister-in-law, Princess Elizabeth Christine of Brunswick-Wofenbüttel, to the Place with No Name. As his brother Charles was in Barcelona staking his claim for the Spanish throne, Joseph had represented him at the marriage celebrated by proxy between Charles and the German princess in Vienna. Then, shortly before she herself set out for Spain to join her husband, Joseph had chosen, as an act of homage, to show her the wild animals kept at Neugebäu, especially the two lions and the panther, which had only recently been acquired. This had been a memorable event in the poor keeper's forgotten life; with his own eyes he had seen His Caesarean Majesty strolling the avenues of the garden and with his own ears had heard him announce, in youthful, vigorous tones, that the place would soon be restored to fresh life. But time had gone by since then; it was already six years since Joseph I had ascended to the throne and the castle was still in a pitiful state.

"𝕸ell, 𝖜hat can 𝖜e do?" Frosch grunted sadly.

Those days were over, I asserted. Now Emperor Joseph wanted to put everything to rights again; I myself had been summoned to start inspecting the flues and the chimneys. Restoration work would soon get under way.

Frosch's eyes gleamed with something similar to joy and hope, but a moment later he was staring vacantly again.

"𝕸ell, let's 𝖍ope for t𝖍e best," he concluded dully.

Without adding anything he turned his flask upside down and noted with disappointment that it was empty. He mumbled that he had to go back and see someone called Slibowitz, or some such name, and get it refilled.

Such is the pessimistic nature of the Viennese: subjected for centuries to the same imperial authority, they are always sceptical of any good news, even when it is what they long for. They prefer to renounce all hope and prepare themselves with philosophic resignation to undergo inconveniences they consider inevitable.

As we proceeded I grew aware of a filthy and nauseating stink, and a sort of low-pitched, hostile growling. A little further on a barred fence blocked the way; beyond it was a ditch. Frosch signalled to me to stop. He led the lion forward, drew from his trousers a set of keys, opened a narrow gate in the railing and pushed Mustafa inside. Then he locked it again, turned back to me and led me into a colonnade, which looked down to the right onto a series of ditches, from which came the stink and the grunts. I shuddered as soon as I could peer down: in addition to Mustafa, the ditches held more lions, tigers, lynxes and bears, such as I had only ever seen in book engravings. Frosch was clearly satisfied by my expression, which was one of both amazement and terror. I had never thought to see so many beasts of that size assembled together. From one of the ditches, a tiger cast a suspicious and hungry look up at me. I shivered and instinctively drew back, as if trying to hide behind the railing that protected the visitor from falling into that abyss of jaws, fangs and claws. From each of the ditches rose palpable waves telling of torn flesh, bloody cravings and murderous desires.

"It takes a lot of meat every day. But it's the Emperor that pays, ha ha ha!" laughed Frosch heartily, giving me such a violent slap on the shoulder that I swayed. Two bears, meanwhile, were fighting over an old bone. Only Mustafa remained all by himself in his pit. He was ill and detested the company of his fellow creatures; he preferred to take a walk every so often with his keeper, Frosch explained.

We turned back. From one of the buildings alongside the spiral staircase I could hear an insistent and noisy chirping. I recognised it at once.

As soon as I entered the building, the chirping grew deafening. It came from birdcages, and the noise and sight instantly took me back to those happy days when I had looked after the aviaries at Villa Spada, in the service of the Lord Cardinal Secretary of the Vatican State. I was well acquainted with the feathered race, and I felt a pang when I saw how Frosch cared for the poor creatures in the Place with No Name. Instead of the commodious aviaries that I had tended at Villa Spada, the cages here were cramped and smelly, only fit for chickens and turkeys. What sunlight there was came filtering in through the door and from a couple of windows. Every specimen was in danger of suffocating, crammed together with dozens of others in the same prison. I saw species I knew, but there were many I had never seen before: marvellous birds of paradise, parrots, parakeets, *carpofori*, dwarf-birds, birds that resembled bats and butterflies, with wings of gold, jute and silk. The vast cavernous space containing the wretched cages was worthy of attention and admiration: it was a huge stable, as Frosch explained, which someone had decided to embellish with grand Tuscan columns. The upper capitals, close to the ceiling, were linked by great transversal arches, which intermeshed creating a network of vaults, in which light and dark mingled in an artistic contest of honest and decent beauty.

The poor birds, being extremely delicate (even the most robust bird of prey is so in captivity), clearly suffered from their cramped conditions. Frosch explained that these had originally been the stables of the Place With no Name and when the aviaries had fallen into disrepair, no one had troubled to build any new ones; at least in the stables the birds were sheltered from the excessive winter cold, and, as the door could be sealed hermetically, they were protected from the beech martens.

❧∾⊙

Frosch asked me whether I wanted to visit the rest of the castle now that I was here, but the sun was already sinking and I remembered that I had to walk all the way home. I was also anxious to get back to Cloridia, who – if Simonis had already recounted what had happened – would have fainted by now, at the very least.

I remounted the spiral staircase, bade him a hasty farewell and said I would return the next day.

On my way home, I gave free rein to my thoughts and my memories, which, from the moment we had left the Flying Ship, had been seething away in a corner of my brain.

Could that strange rattletrap really have flown all those years ago? The gazette undoubtedly contained details of pure fantasy, like the sightings of the inhabitants of the moon. But it was hard to believe it was entirely mendacious; the author could have invented with impunity events that had happened in far-off, exotic lands (and God alone can say how many gazetteers have done such things!), but not the arrival of an airship in the very capital of the Empire, where the gazette, although originally written for a fair, enjoyed a wide circulation.

But there was more to it than this. Frosch had described the device as a "ship of fools". This had sparked off a number of memories for me.

Eleven years earlier, in Rome, with Abbot Melani: a villa, abandoned just like the Place with No Name, which had the bizarre form of a ship (it was known, in fact, as "the Vessel"), had hosted a strange character dressed in black like a monk (just like the pilot of the Flying Ship), who had appeared before us hovering above the battlements of the villa, playing a Portuguese melody known as the *folia*, or "Foolishness", and reciting verses from a poem entitled "The Ship of Fools". Subsequently we discovered that he was not in fact flying. He was a violinist, and his name was Albicastro. He had gone off, one day, to enlist in the war. I had heard no more of him. Often, over the years, I had thought of him and his teachings and wondered what had become of him.

Now, the numerous coincidences with the ship in the form of a bird of prey and its pilot who seemed to possess the secret of flying, had brought him back sharply to my mind. The Diary of Vienna referred vaguely to a Brazilian priest, but perhaps . . .

❧

17 of the clock, end of the working day: workshops and chancelleries close. Dinner hour for artisans, secretaries, language teachers, priests, servants of commerce, footmen and coach drivers (while in Rome people take but a light refection).

Contrary to my fears, I did not find Cloridia swooning in terror. My gentle consort had left word, by means of a note slipped under the door, that she had to stay on at the palace of the Most Serene Prince Eugene. This meant, I thought, that the work of the Turkish delegation was particularly intense; or, more probably, that the Ottoman soldiery in the Agha's retinue were continuing to pester Cloridia with requests for services of varying degrees of urgency, like fresh supplies of wines.

Simonis sat faithfully waiting for me. His unchanging face showed no signs either of apprehension on my behalf or of relief at seeing me safe and sound. I was expecting him to unleash his loquacity, which had not yet found an outlet today. I was already prepared to face a barrage of garrulous questions; but no. He just told me that he had returned from the eating house, where he had taken my little apprentice for the usual lavish seven-course dinner.

"Thank you, Simonis. Aren't you curious to know what happened to me?"

"Immeasurably so, Signor Master; but I would never permit myself to be so indiscreet."

I shook my head. Defeated by Simonis's disarming logic I took my little boy's hand and told them to follow me to the eating house, where I would tell them all about it.

"Let's make haste, Signor Master. Don't forget that very soon the dinner will go up in price, from 8 kreutzer to 17; after 6 – or after the hour of 18 as you Romans say – it will cost 24 kreutzer and after 7 as much as 27 kreutzer. At 8 the eating house will close its doors."

It was true; Vienna was strictly regulated by timetables in all matters, and it was they, more than anything else, that distinguished the nobleman from the poor man, the artisan and the pen-pusher. As Simonis had just reminded me, at both lunch and dinner the same (lavish) meal had different prices according to the hour of day, so that the different social classes could eat undisturbed. And the other moments of the day were similarly divided, so that one could truly say – reversing the old adage – that in Vienna the sun was not the same for everyone.

The Caesarean city was like the proscenium of a dance theatre, on which the artists made their entrances in separate groups, strictly ranked by order of importance, and when a new line of dancers made its appearance on the stage, another left it.

However, in order that each social stratum should be able to find its own place comfortably in the day, the authorities had decided that for the humbler classes the day should begin not with the rising of the sun, as for the rest of the earthly orb, but in the middle of the night.

I had literally leaped out of bed, two months earlier, the day after our arrival in Vienna, when the stentorian bellow of the night guard had set the window-panes rattling: "𝕹𝖔𝖜 𝖗𝖎𝖘𝖊 𝕺 𝕾𝖊𝖗𝖛𝖆𝖓𝖙, 𝖕𝖗𝖆𝖎𝖘𝖊 𝕲𝖔𝖉 𝖙𝖍𝖎𝖘 𝖒𝖔𝖗𝖓, 𝖙𝖍𝖊 𝖑𝖎𝖌𝖍𝖙 𝖓𝖔𝖜 𝖌𝖑𝖊𝖆𝖒𝖘 𝖔𝖋 𝖆 𝖓𝖊𝖜 𝖉𝖆𝖞'𝖘 𝖉𝖆𝖜𝖓."

The gleaming light of dawn was actually a long way off yet: the little travelling pendulum-clock that we had bought before our departure with the credit of Abbot Melani indicated the hour of three. And it was not a mistake or a bad dream. A few moments later, the bell of the Lauds announced the start of the day from the Cathedral of St Stephen. As I would soon learn, once its imperial chimes had resounded there would be no peace: by the inflexible law of the clocks, at three in the morning the day's hard work begins. At that hour, to tell the truth, market gardeners and flower-sellers are already setting up their vegetables and plants in the baskets on the market stools. At half past three the taverns selling mulled wine and collations open up for business near the gates of the city, where day-labourers, bricklayers, carpenters, woodcutters and coach drivers take their breakfast. At four artisans and servants start work. The city gates open: milkmaids, peasants and vendors of fruit, butter and eggs swarm in towards the market squares. We chimney-sweeps, together with the roof-tilers, could be considered fortunate: in winter, because of the darkness, we never begin work before six.

In Rome, when I used to set out before dawn to reach places in the outlying suburbs, I would cross the dark, spectral city, peopled only by threatening shadows. In Vienna, by contrast, at four in the morning the city is already bustling with busy honest folk, so that one might attribute the blackness of the sky to an eclipse of the sun, rather than the early hour.

From eleven onwards, every hour is good for eating, and the last meal in the aristocratic palaces coincides with the first dinner of the humble classes. At midday, court dependants take their luncheon, and at one o'clock the nobility, who between two and three pay or receive visits from friends and acquaintances. At three o'clock clerks go back to work and school children to school. At five in the afternoon work is over and, as already said, the humble classes go to dinner. An hour later court employees dine, while theatres close their doors. At half past six the city gates close, at least until mid-April, after which they close a quarter of an hour later. Latecomers have to pay a hefty fine of 6 kreutzer. The *Bierglocke* chimes, the so-called beer bell: after it has rung no one can go and drink in the taverns, or walk the streets bearing arms or without a lantern. At seven the humble classes go to bed, while the nobles settle down for dinner; a far cry from the homes of the Roman princes, where people are still feasting at midnight!

At eight the eating houses close. The most hedonistic nobleman never goes to bed after midnight. The hours between midnight and three constitute the short night common to all Viennese, whatever their social rank.

The tumultuous Eternal City, seen from seraphic Vienna, reminded me of the menagerie of beasts in the Place with No Name. And my mind and heart turned gratefully to the image of Abbot Atto Melani, who had borne me away from there.

挈朖

18 of the clock: dinner hour for court employees.

I had finished my dinner at the eating house. The bowls and dishes that had held the seven courses lay piled up on a corner of the table, forgotten by the host. The soup of the day, always different; the plate of beef with sauce and horseradish; the vegetables variously "seasoned" with pork, sausages, liver or calf's foot; the pasty; the snails and crabs with asparagus ragout; the roast meat, which this evening was lamb, but could be capon, chicken, goose, duck or wildfowl; and finally the salad. This sequence of dishes – such as in Rome I had only ever glimpsed on the table of my patron, the Cardinal Secretary of State, many years earlier – was served, as I have already said, at the modest price of 8 kreutzer and was equally lavish throughout the year, except in Lent and the other periods of obligatory fasting, when there were still seven courses, but the meats were replaced by inventive dishes of fish, egg puddings and an array of rich confectionery.

This evening everything had been dutifully dispatched – not by me, apart from some minor items, but by Simonis. Although he had already dined with my little boy shortly before my arrival, my apprentice, who looked so lean, possessed a bottomless stomach. I myself was still so shaken by the afternoon's events that I had done little more than toy with the dishes, and Simonis had clearly taken it as his duty to spare the host the insult of having to take away dishes still laden with food.

Actually, apprentice boys had their own regular tables, when their fraternity did not possess their own private taverns and even hostels, where they would all eat together at luncheon and dinner, instead of eating with their master. The corporations of arts and trades usually had their own reserved corner in the taverns, like the tailors, butchers, glove-makers, comedians and even the chimney-sweeps. The tables were often divided: one for the masters and one for the assistants. But neither I nor Simonis liked to sit separately and, to tell the truth, the envious reception accorded us by my brother-sweeps had made us devoted customers of the eating house closest to the convent, instead of the locales favoured by the corporation.

While my apprentice so generously helped me out, I completed my far from easy account of the events of Neugebäu, omitting a great many details that would only have puzzled him inordinately. The story of the lion amused him; he was much less successful in grasping what the Flying Ship was, at least until I thrust under his nose the gazette with the detailed report of what had happened two years earlier. This absorbed him fully and, after concluding his reading with a laconic "Ah", he asked no further questions.

We returned to the convent; the Greek to go to bed, myself and the child to our nightly appointment with the digestive infusion. As we crossed the cloisters, I explained to my little boy, who was asking after his mother, that Cloridia had been obliged to stay on at Prince Eugene's palace. Suddenly my face contracted in the grimace of one drinking a bitter medicine:

"Mich duncket, daß es ein überaus schöne Übung seye, die Übung der Italiänischen Sprache, so in diesen Oerthern so sehr geübt in unsern Zeiten. Der Herr thut gar recht, dass er diese Sprache, also die fürnembste, und nutzbareste in diesem Land, mit Ihrem Knaben spricht!"

After the first instants of panic (a feeling well known to neophytes of the Germanic language), I managed to grasp the sense of the words addressed to me: *That seems to me a beautiful exercise, that of the Italian language, so widely used around here in these times. Your lordship does well to talk to your son in this language, which is the principal and most useful in this country!*"

I smiled weakly at the good Ollendorf: time had flown and the dreaded hour of our German lesson had arrived. With Teutonic punctuality our preceptor was already standing at the door and waiting for us.

ॐ✺ॐ

20 of the clock: eating houses and alehouses close their doors.

Once the torture of the German lesson was over, in which as usual my son had shone and I had suffered, we left the convent once again for our evening appointment with the rehearsals at the oratory.

I have not yet had a chance to explain that we had had to make ourselves useful to Camilla de' Rossi. The directress of the choir of Porta Coeli was an experienced composer, and for the last four years had been charged by the Emperor to write and put on four oratorios for voices and orchestra, one a year, which had earned general applause. At the end of the previous year, however, she had asked Joseph I for permission to retire and enter a convent as a lay sister. His Caesarean Majesty had therefore assigned her to the monastery of the Augustinian nuns of Porta Coeli, with the task of directing its choir. Quite unexpectedly, just a few weeks ago Camilla had been told ("on urgent notification," as she herself informed us with ill-concealed satisfaction) that His Caesarean Majesty was demanding from her another Italian oratorio in music, which was to be prepared with all possible alacrity. In response to Camilla's respectful protests, the imperial emissary declared that if the task of composing a new work was beyond her, His Caesarean Majesty would have no objections to hearing again the oratorio from the previous year, *Sant' Alessio*, which had been fully to his liking.

The reason for this insistence was a pressing one. In recent years relations between the Empire and the Church had deteriorated to their lowest point for centuries. The conflicts between Pope and Emperor were identical to those in the Middle Ages, when the Teutonic Caesars used to invade the territories of the Church, and the Popes who did not have enough cannons would retaliate by firing off excommunications. This was what had happened three years earlier, in 1708, when the troops of Joseph I – who in the inflamed atmosphere of those bellicose years considered the Pope too friendly towards the French – had invaded the Papal State in Italy and occupied the territories of Comacchio on the pretext of an old imperial right to those lands. The Pope, this time, had decided to use his cannons instead of an excommunication, and so an unfortunate war had broken out between Joseph the Victorious and His Holiness Clement XI, which had, of course, concluded with the victory of the former. At the end of this unequal conflict, the crisis had been protracted for another two years, and only now, in the spring of 1711, thanks to diplomatic efforts, was it finally drawing to a peaceful conclusion: the Emperor, of his own free will, was about to hand back the Comacchio territories. Naturally, a complete and definitive peace, like any other political strategy, required a suitable framework, such as could be afforded by a series of reciprocal acts of kindness and goodwill. And so five days earlier, on Holy Saturday 4th April, on the eve of Easter, Joseph I had been accompanied by the Apostolic Nuncio in Vienna, Cardinal Davia, and by a large entourage of ministers and high-ranking nobles, on a visit on foot to various churches and chapels in the city. The next day, Easter Sunday, the Nuncio had accompanied Joseph to high mass, both in the morning and in the afternoon, in the church of the Reverend Barefoot Augustinian Friars at the imperial palace, as faithfully reported by the gazettes. Finally, the following evening the two of them had attended the five last important sermons of Lent (which until two years earlier had included that of the most famous court preacher, the late Pater Abraham from Sancta Clara), and as they emerged they had been saluted by a triple volley of musket-fire. This had created a great stir: never before had His Majesty spent Easter with the Nuncio.

And so, to seal the happy re-establishment of relations with the Holy See, and the resolution of the Comacchio dispute, it had been decided that an oratorio should be performed immediately after Easter, in the Roman fashion, with all the trappings of scenery, costumes and action, as in the rite of the Holy Sepulchre; this marked a break with the tradition of the Caesarean court, which only called for oratorios in Lent and without any stage scenery.

Camilla had therefore been entrusted with the task of preparing an Italian oratorio, which would be symbolically attended by Joseph and the Nuncio Davia, representing His Holiness, sitting side by side.

Although no one in the court had said so explicitly, Camilla knew perfectly well that the aim of her work was far more political than musical. The *Sant' Alessio*, which in 1710 had proved so successful with numerous noblemen and people of fine perception, would be repeated this year in the Most August Chapel of His Caesarean Majesty for the ears of the Nuncio. All eyes would be on her; the Chormaisterin had set to work with a will, urgently recruiting singers and musicians from the previous year, personally choosing the replacements for those she had been unable to hire again, making sure that the ornaments of the chapel were suitable, that the musical instruments were of the finest, and making fresh copies of orchestral scores that had become faded or crumpled.

Believe it or not, in this delicate operation I myself, humble chimney-sweep, had a part to play. The oratorio required the presence of some children as extras, but it was not easy to find families willing to let their offspring out of the house at that late hour. Camilla had therefore asked us to help replenish her troop of children; given my slight stature, we were able to supply her with not just one extra, but two.

And so, in the solemn setting of the Caesarean chapel, almost every evening we attended the rehearsals of the *Sant' Alessio*, taking part when necessary in the scenes of action, and, when our participation was not required, quietly observing the orchestra players and singers as they rehearsed.

It was like being reborn into the world of singing: in my whole life I had never listened to anything other than the voice of Atto Melani singing the notes of his old master, Seigneur Luigi. By some strange quirk of fate what I was now listening to were not the arias of Luigi Rossi but those of a de' Rossi, Camilla; almost the same surname, which was now indissolubly linked in my mind to the idea of singing.

Among the motley crew of orchestra musicians, many of them well established in court circles, my little boy and I, although a little nervous on account of our ignorance of the Euterpean art, could now boast a few acquaintances. Every evening we were greeted with respect and friendly remarks by the theorbist Francesco Conti, who played several parts as soloist in *Sant' Alessio*; by Conti's wife, the soprano Maria Landini, known as the Landina, who sang the role of Alessio's betrothed; by the tenor Carlo Costa, who played Alessio's father in the oratorio; and finally by Carlo Agostino Ziani, *vice-maestro* of the imperial chapel and by Silvio Stampiglia, court poet, both of whom had a high regard for Camilla de' Rossi's music and often came to listen to the rehearsals of the oratorio.

With such high-ranking personages, who bestowed their benevolence upon us precisely because they knew us to be friends of the Chormaisterin, we could, of course, only have fleeting contacts. The only one who would engage in conversations of any length was a singer – an Italian, like most musicians in Vienna. His name was Gaetano Orsini, and he played the leading role in the oratorio. I greatly appreciated the fact that he was on very free and easy terms with us, something that his rank did not require of him in the least; he was personally acquainted with the Emperor, who held his art in high esteem and kept him on a salary among his own musicians. From the first moment I spoke to him, I felt as if I had always known him. Then I realised why: Orsini shared with Atto Melani a feature of no slight importance. He was a castrato.

I arrived at the rehearsal a little late. As I approached the door of the Caesarean chapel I heard that Camilla had already started off the orchestral players. When I entered I was greeted by Orsini's singing. The oratorio narrated the moving story of Alessio, a young Roman nobleman on the threshold of marriage. On the very day of his wedding he receives a divine command to renounce all worldly joys, and so he leaves his betrothed, goes to sea and, taking shelter in distant lands, leads a life of poverty and solitude. When he returns to Rome, disguised as a beggar, he is given hospitality at his paternal home and stays there for seventeen years without being recognised, sleeping under a staircase. Only on the point of death does he make himself known to his parents and his erstwhile fiancée.

That evening they were rehearsing the aria with dramatic dialogue between Alessio and his betrothed on the day of the uncelebrated marriage. I had just taken my place among the other extras when, introduced by the tinkling of the theorbo and the cymbals, and sustained by the concise, reasoning tones of the violins, we heard the anguishing words with which Alessio takes leave of his betrothed:

> *Credi, oh bella, ch'io t'adoro*
> *E se t'amo il Ciel lo sa*
> *Ma bram'io il più bel ristoro*
> *Mi t'invola altra beltà . . .*[1]

In the recitative that followed, she answered just as heart-rendingly:

> *Come goder poss'io di gemme e d'oro,*
> *Se da me tu t'involi, o mio tesoro,*
> *Che creda, che tu m'ami or mi spieghi*
> *E l'amor tuo mi nieghi.*
> *Conosco che il tuo amore*
> *Sta solo su le labbra e non nel core . . .*[2]

Despite his bride's distressed reply and the melodiousness of Camilla de' Rossi's music, my thoughts took me elsewhere. In my mind's eye I saw myself once again on the Flying Ship where it lay inert in the deserted ball stadium. I imagined its unknown pilot in his monk's garb, his fate shrouded in mystery: such an arcane affair, I thought, was worthy of a poem by Ariosto.

Meanwhile Alessio rejected his beloved's entreaties, and announced his final departure:

> *In questo punto istesso*
> *Devo eseguire il gran comando espresso*
> *Più dimora qui far già non poss'io.*
> *Cara consorte, il Ciel ti guardi, addio . . .*[3]

I closed my eyes. As the beautiful music of the Chormaisterin of Porta Coeli swirled around the solemn space of the Caesarean chapel, my mind resounded with the roars of the lions of Neugebäu and the screeching of the birds in their cages.

---

[1] Know, O fair one, I adore thee / And that I love you Heaven knows / But other beauty now does call me / And a more serene repose . . .
[2] Gems and gold, how can they please me, / If my love so cruelly flees me; / That you love me, you declare / And yet your love you do forswear. / You do but play the part / Of love, your lips pronounce but not your heart.
[3] O now I'm called away, / This great command I must obey, / I'm bade to stay no longer here, / Dear love, I bid thee now adieu . . .

Day the Second
Friday, 10ᵀᴴ April 1711

✠

3 of the clock, when the night guard raises his cry: "Now rise O Servant, praise God this morn, the light now gleams of new day's dawn."

The following day I woke up brimming with robust optimism, eager to return to the Place with No Name to start the job that had been awaiting me far too long, my fingers tingling with the anticipation of curiosity.

As the bell of the Lauds announced the start of the day for the humble classes, I clambered into the cart with my little apprentice and Simonis.

"This time, Signor Master, I'll take the southern road. Let's enter by the side of the gardens, away from the lions, heh heh!" said the Greek, who had been greatly amused by the account of my flight the previous evening.

While we were on our way, dawn broke. We passed a large church and then shortly afterwards we began to make out a white building in the distance, so white that the stones were dazzling in the sunlight.

When my pupils had adjusted to the glare, I saw a long set of crenellated walls punctuated with small towers with pinnacled roofs. They could have been military constructions, watchtowers or something similar, had they not been so minute and graceful, and so unusually rich in decorations that hinted at some indefinable oriental influence. Behind the wall, in the middle distance, were more buildings of imposing appearance. As we approached, I realised that the outer wall, which was of truly Cyclopic proportions, was quadrangular in form. On the longer side, the one facing the road from Vienna which we had just travelled along, the wall was interrupted by an impressive gateway, surmounted by a triple keep. We stopped and got out.

We walked through the gateway. Immediately beyond it was an open space. My little boy, who had been greatly excited on hearing

about the lion and the Flying Ship the previous evening, kept asking
where such marvels were and insisted on going to see them at once.
Simonis followed us rather absent-mindedly.

I was amazed to find myself in an enormous open space, dotted
with trees and bushes, containing another set of protective walls,
once again with towers but only at the four corners. These towers
were much larger than the ones on the outer walls; at least twice as
high, like great bell towers, and not cylindrical but hexagonal. Each
had a large domed roof, resting on a drum with windows. At the top
of each dome was a hexagonal pinnacle, culminating in a large peak,
also hexagonal. Around the dome were six more pinnacles, corresponding to each corner of the tower, and identical to the one on the
top. On each of the six façades of the hexagon were two series of
windows, on as many levels, which suggested that the towers were
compartmented and habitable.

The exotic form of the pinnacles, of their tips and of the dome
reminded me of the graceful minarets and roofs of Constantinople,
as I had seen them in the books bequeathed to me by my father-
in-law of blessed memory. I remembered that the previous afternoon, when I had arrived at the Place with No Name, I had spotted
the top of one of these towers, and that in itself had surprised me;
but I would never have imagined the wonders that extended beyond
the crenellated wall surrounding the gardens.

Why on earth, I began to ask myself, had this place been abandoned? Our beloved Emperor Joseph I now intended to restore it to
its original splendour, but why had his predecessors condemned it to
oblivion?

I was on the point of sharing these questions with Simonis, when
I decided not to break the silence, so rare in my garrulous assistant.

A little avenue, flanked by a double line of trees, led towards the
interior quadrangle. The moment I entered it my jaw dropped.

Watched over by large Turkish-style towers set at the four corners,
there lay before me a marvellous Mediterranean garden. The space
was subdivided by flower beds and lawns into four equal quadrants,
each of which was in turn composed of four smaller sectors, each one
patterned with delightful geometrical compositions. In the middle,
where the four quadrants met, was a splendid fountain in the form
of a bowl, supported by a large decorated pedestal. The enclosure,
which from the outside appeared to be a simple wall, on the inside

proved to be a magnificent loggia in dazzling white stone, with imposing columns of exquisite workmanship.

My mind was still taking in this vision when my eyes darted into the distance, towards the wall at the far side of the open space. There in front of me the colonnade opened up to reveal – sturdy and powerful – an enormous and princely castle.

Dazed by all these wonders, it took me a few moments to focus on some important details. The outer wall, the first one I had passed through, surrounded a garden that was luxuriant but uncultivated: trees and vegetation of all kinds throve in generous disorder. The interior garden – the one within the porticoed walls – still maintained the graceful forms of the beds and ornamental lawns, but they were in a state of neglect. The beds had no flowers, nor was there a single blade of grass in the former lawns. Not a drop of water danced in the air above the beautiful bowl-shaped fountain, and the walls and vaults of the portico showed the heavy marks of time.

I began to walk towards the castle. As I approached it, I thought of the name – or rather the non-name – of this place: Neugebäu, "New Building". The Place with No Name known as "New Building": a strange appellative for a complex that had been disused for years, perhaps even decades. The day before, when we had entered on the northern side, I had sensed nothing of the marvels that the place concealed. My fellow chimney-sweeps were right: what was the Place with No Name? A villa? A garden? A hunting lodge? A bird enclosure?

I studied the castle in front of me, if I could call it that. It was really a free and original work of fantasy. It had an enormous frontage hundreds of yards in length, all of it gazing triumphantly on the oriental-style gardens, but it was by no means deep; all in all it was not as large as it had first seemed, but narrow and long, like a stone serpent.

I halted. I wanted to visit the towers and I began with the one in the north-east. Inside, I found to my amazement, traces of beautiful marble and exotic mosaics, and fragments of large baths, which showed there had once been a thermal system, maybe with tanks of spiced waters and medicinal vapours. Surprised by this further marvel, I promised that I would visit the other towers later and returned towards the castle.

Curiously the building showed no oriental features, except for a gable roof, glittering with strange coruscations that made me think of the gilded coverings of Turkish pavilions. I noticed that the roof was covered with tiles of a strange, flickering colour, very different from the usual burnished brown of Viennese roofs. As I observed, my eyeballs were suddenly struck by a kind of piercing dart – then by another – and then by countless more. I shielded my eyes with my hand and peered through the slits between my fingers. What I saw astonished me: the roof of the castle, struck by the rays of the sun, glittered like gold. Yes, because the tiles of the castle of the Place with No Name were not of terracotta but of fine gilded copper. When I looked closer I could see that actually very little was left of the original covering, a prey to the ravages of time or perhaps to human greed. But what little copper remained was enough to refract the fair and blessed sunlight into sharp and powerful shafts.

The far ends of the building were closed by two semicircular keeps, which very closely resembled the apses of our churches – unexpected shapes in that generally Turkish context. It was from the eastern keep, to my right, that we had ventured into the cellars the previous day, where I had quite literally bumped into the bleeding carcass of the ram.

At the centre of the castle was the entrance staircase, which crossed a little ditch and led into the main body of the building. This was overlooked by a stone balustrade, behind which I could make out a long panoramic terrace. This main body was about a fifth of the length of the whole building; the way in was through a large doorway flanked by windows and ornamented on both sides by two graceful pairs of columns with capitals.

The castle, with its classical forms and its Christian echoes, seemed to stand in deliberate opposition, like a magniloquent northern barrier, to the pointed minarets of the towers and the warm southern air that rose from the gardens.

I looked around myself: how come no one had ever mentioned this grandiose complex to me? Was it not considered worthy to figure among the marvels of the Caesarean city?

Often, as I passed in front of the Hofburg, His Caesarean Majesty's winter residence, I had been surprised by the extreme modesty and simplicity of the building. And the summer residences were not much better: the Favorita, Laxenburg and Ebersdorf. Not to mention the extremely modest hunting pavilion at Belfonte – Schönbrunn as the Viennese call it, which had only been given the appearance of a villa since its enlargement by beloved Joseph I.

And often, as I gazed at the small graceful *casini* in the Italian style that the nobility possessed in the Josephina – Casino Strozzi, Palazzo Schönborn or Villa Trautson – I was puzzled by their architectural superiority with respect to the imperial residences! It was as if the Caesars had elected severity as the hallmark of their greatness, leaving pomp to the nobility.

And yet there had once been a time when the Habsburgs had enjoyed the marvels of the Place with No Name, a time when one of the Caesars, Maximilian II, had cultivated this Levantine dream on Teutonic land. A brief dream, so brief as not even to be honoured with a name – then nothing more. Who had left it to rot? And why?

I caught Simonis gazing absorbedly at me. Had the Greek guessed my cogitations? Did he, perhaps, have an answer to them?

"Signor Master, I have to piss and shit. Urgently. May I?"

"Yes, but not here in front of me," I answered ruefully.

"Of course not, Signor Master."

ॐ

7 of the clock: the Bell of the Turks, also called the Peal of the Oration, rings.

As Simonis walked away, wholly absorbed in his primordial needs, I heard the nearby church echo the Bell of the Turks in the Cathedral of St Stephen, inviting the distant suburbs to prayer as well. I went into a corner with my little apprentice and we knelt down for our morning prayers.

Whatever the fate of the Place with No Name till now, I meditated as I made the sign of the cross, His Caesarean Majesty Joseph I was of a different opinion from his ancestors, and rightly wanted to restore the place to its former splendour. A real stroke of luck, not only for Neugebäu, but also for me and my family, I said to myself with a satisfied smile, which I changed into a prayer of fervent gratitude to the Most High.

When the Greek returned we were spotted by Frosch. The keeper greeted us with a grunt only a shade more cordial than his usual surly *facies*. We announced that our work was about to begin and I expressed a wish to start from the service buildings; if the Emperor really wanted to make use of the place again, it was those buildings he would need even before the castle itself.

Frosch invited us to follow him, bringing our barrow with all its tools of the trade, and Simonis immediately went off to get it.

As we followed Frosch, shading our eyes with our hands against the dazzling shafts from the copper on the roofs and slowing our pace as the spectacle both enchanted and blinded us, with the cart full of tools creaking along behind us, we were greeted by a distant noise. It arose from behind the towers, behind the walls of the garden and behind the castle itself, almost as if it came from an afterworld that belonged only to the Place with No Name: the stillness of the morning was broken by the cavernous roar of the lions.

We headed to the right and passed through the service building which, as was explained to us, had in the past been a *Meierei*, or what was known in Latin as a *maior domus*, the house of the land-agent. This little building was also in a state of total neglect; through the windows, mostly shattered, we could see that weeds had invaded the interior and the roof had partly collapsed.

Passing through the archway that led out of the *maior domus* we found ourselves in the courtyard by which we had entered the previous afternoon. To the left I saw the little door that gave onto the spiral staircase. Behind it one could make out the roofs of other buildings, set lower down.

I marvelled again at the unusual nature of the place, almost like a little town with its outer walls, interior avenues, gardens and various buildings of the most singular and diverse kinds. Far different from – and far more than – a villa with its park.

Frosch led us down the spiral staircase. I noticed for the first time that it had been placed between two other buildings, set against the little upland on which the castle rose, which enabled it to dominate the surrounding grasslands. As we descended, I finally discovered, peering through the little windows that opened in the stairwell towards the exterior, the rear of the Place with No Name, facing north: there was a graceful garden in the Italian style. A central avenue led towards a large fishpond, in which waterfowl and marsh birds floated peacefully. There was nothing Levantine about those gardens; on the other side of the fishpond they opened out into Teutonic meadows, the kind loved by hunters, which stretched away in the distance towards Nordic woods, green cathedrals whose silence was punctuated by occasional bird cries, dusky spaces teeming in game, in funghi, resins and scented mosses. Far off, powerful and motionless, we could make out Vienna with its unbreached walls.

With a grunt of farewell, the keeper left us to get on with our work.

We started with a building that Frosch told us had once been the kitchen. Without too much difficulty we found the old fireplaces.

What contrasts the Place with No Name offered, hidden within its walls! So I reflected as, with my head wrapped in its canvas bag, I made my way up the first of the ducts. What mind had conceived all of this? Had it been Emperor Maximilian II, about whom I knew nothing, or a brilliant architect of his? What did this crucible of contrasts mean, supposing it meant anything? Or was it all just a mere caprice? And why, I asked myself yet again, had it been abandoned?

After carrying out a first perfunctory examination, I climbed back down to my two boys.

"There's a good deal of work to be done; it's all cracked up there," I reported to Simonis and the little one. "If the whole place is in the same condition, we had better make a map of the flues first and draw up a report on their condition. That way we'll be able to work out how many reinforcements we'll need for the job. Let's have a bite to eat now. And then we'll go on with the survey."

Having said this I sent my little boy to the cart to fetch the bag of provisions.

"Revenge."

"Sorry, Simonis?"

"Revenge is the answer to your questions, Signor Master. The Place with No Name was built for revenge, and it was revenge that destroyed it. This place is steeped in inextinguishable hatred, Signor Master."

A shiver ran down my spine at these unexpected words, which answered my unspoken questions.

"He was a follower of Christ, quite simply. And *imitatio Christi*, the imitation of Christ, was the inspiring principle of his life. But it was his fate to be born and to reign in an age when Luther's false teachings had divided the Christians, their hearts, their minds and the nations themselves," said Simonis.

"Who are you talking about?"

"Christian fought against Christian, both armed with the word of the Lord," continued the Greek, paying no heed to me, "and the greed of both camps kindled the fire of war. To the great joy of the

Infidels, the Alemannic and Flemish lands were lacerated by the divisions between Catholics and Protestants, while His Sacred Caesarean Majesty – whose authority for centuries had rested on the assembly of the princes of the Empire, but also on the investiture conferred by the Pope – struggled to defend the orthodox Christian Faith."

While I opened the bag my boy had brought me and drew out our meal, I began to understand who Simonis was referring to.

"He should not even have ascended to the Caesarean throne. Emperor Charles V, brother of his father Ferdinand I, had divided his lands before retiring to a monastery: Ferdinand I was to receive the Spanish territories, his son Philip II, Austria and the imperial crown. But the German prince-electors did not want an emperor who was so resolutely Catholic and they resoundingly called for the young Maximilian to return from Spain and be crowned. They harboured ambitious plans and believed him to be the right man."

Simonis had read on my face all the queries and cogitations that were gnawing at me; and now, while we consumed the small but restorative meal of rye, boiled eggs, sauerkraut and sausages, he talked to me of Emperor Maximilian II, the man who, one and a half centuries earlier, had been behind the building of the Place with No Name, known as Neugebäu.

From early youth Maximilian, abhorring the corruption of the Church of Rome, had been well disposed to the arguments of the Protestants. He had summoned Lutheran preachers, counsellors, doctors and men of science to the court, so that it was feared that sooner or later he himself would defect to them. His clashes with his father Ferdinand I, a fervent Catholic, had become so bitter that his august parent had threatened to block his ascent to the throne. Pressure from Catholic Spain and from the Holy See grew so strong that Maximilian had to declare publicly that he would always adhere to the official creed of Rome. But this did not prevent him from continuing to meet in private with the followers of Luther.

This aroused the hopes of the Protestant princes and of all those in the Empire who abominated the Church of Peter: would Maximilian fulfil their dream of having an Emperor no longer faithful to the Pope?

"But more pernicious than heresy itself – so thought Maximilian, who loved peace – was the war that it had unleashed. More cruel than the betrayal of a religion is the betrayal of one's own kind; and far more scandalous than the sword is the wound that it has opened."

And so, once he had ascended to the imperial throne, he chose a new path: instead of actively aligning himself with the Church of Rome, and taking part in the struggle against the heretics, he decided to serve peace and tolerance. His predecessors had been Catholics, while most of the princes of the Empire were friends of the Protestants, was that not the case? He would align himself with neither side, nor would he make any profession of faith; he would simply be Christian – of course – but neither Catholic nor Lutheran. Neither party would be able to say: "He is one of us." In the astute and ruthless century of Machiavelli, he chose to be cunning in his own way: instead of professing, he would remain silent; instead of acting, he would hold still.

And so Maximilian the Just became Maximilian the Mysterious: nobody, in the two opposing camps, could read into his heart, nobody could count him among their friends. He already knew that the Protestant princes would call him a traitor, an idler and a hypocrite. He had disappointed all those who had hoped he would inflict a hard blow against Catholicism. And yet he had not yielded, and he had preferred to carry forward his own desire for peace.

"He left all his supporters confounded," concluded Simonis.

I was confounded myself: my Greek assistant, who seemed a touch cracked, could be perfectly lucid when he chose. It was disconcerting to hear his vaguely foolish voice narrating events with such acumen! As with the Emperor he was talking about, it was never clear to which party Simonis belonged: that of the sane or that of the retarded. And it was even less clear where his talk was heading.

"Simonis, you talked of revenge earlier," I reminded him.

"All in good time, Signor Master," he answered without a trace of deference, biting into his loaf.

Maximilian's ascent to the throne, continued the Greek, had aroused great expectations throughout Europe. The ambassadors from Venice, always the most reliable in their reports home, gave assurances that he was of robust stature, well proportioned, and of good disposition. His appearance suggested a greatness and majesty that were truly regal and imperial, since his face was full of gravitas, but tempered by such grace and amiability that those who saw him were filled with reverence but also with a sense of his inestimable inner gentleness.

Those who had managed to get close to him declared that he was gifted with a lively intelligence and wise judgement. When he received someone, even for the first time, he immediately grasped their nature and their hidden temper, and as soon they addressed him, he at once understood what they were leading up to. Alongside his intelligence he also had a very sharp memory; if someone was presented to him after a long time, even a humble subject, he would immediately recognise him. All his thoughts were turned to great things, and it was clear that he was not content with the present state of the Empire. Greatly skilled in matters of state, he talked about them nonetheless with the utmost prudence. In addition to German he spoke Latin, Italian, Spanish, Bohemian, Hungarian and even a little French. The court that he had formed around himself was truly splendid; furthermore, his open and sociable character, and the competence with which he followed public affairs, had at once made him extremely popular.

"Everyone expected a long and successful reign," commented Simonis.

Maximilian the Mysterious loved beautiful things, and the sublime fruits of intellect and doctrine. His trusted counsellor Kaspar von Nidbruck, together with a host of scholars, travelled around Europe collecting valuable books and manuscripts, with which the Centuriators of Magdeburg would later write their monumental history of the Church. He had raised the University of Vienna from its decadence, and had summoned the most prestigious names of European learning to teach there: the botanist Clusius, for example, or the doctor Crato von Krafftheim, and it mattered not whether they were for the Pope or the heretic Luther.

Although he favoured peace and concord, Maximilian the Mysterious had to face war. At that time, in the second half of the sixteenth century, the Turkish threat loomed ominously in the east. The burden of defending the borders of Christendom fell on the Empire, and more especially on Vienna, dangerously exposed to the east. Only Maximilian appeared fully aware of the dreadful task facing the West, while his friends and allies proved recalcitrant: Spain shilly-shallied, the Pope promised money that never arrived, and Venice, jealous of its trade and its possessions in the East, actually made a separate peace with the Turks. The Christian and Ottoman armies finally clashed in 1566. And Maximilian was defeated; but without even fighting.

"His father, Ferdinand I, had drawn up a peace treaty with Sultan Suleiman the Magnificent that lasted eight years. In exchange for non-belligerence, however, the Empire had to pay the Sublime Porte a tribute of 30,000 ducats a year."

On Ferdinand's death, all Maximilian had been able to do was propose an extension of the agreement. But in 1565 hostilities had broken out in Hungary. Suleiman's fearsome army began to arm itself.

At the end of our meal, we continued our survey in the kitchens. Then we went upstairs again and inspected the *maior domus*. Here, as the rooms appeared to have been abandoned for a long time, we would carry out the usual test in such cases: lighting a little fire at the base of the flue and checking if any trace of smoke emerged from the chimney on the roof.

"It was then that Maximilian's destiny was fulfilled," Simonis began again, with a wry grimace as, puffing and sweating, we removed piles of rubble from the fireplace so as to be able to carry out the smoke test. "One of his diplomats, David Ungnad, informed him that in Constantinople an army of a hundred thousand soldiers had been assembled. The Emperor then bade the Imperial Paymaster, the collector of financial reserves, to spare no expense and to gather an army of equal strength."

Shortly afterwards the Deputy Imperial Paymaster, Georg Ilsung, presented himself personally to Maximilian with surprising results: thanks to his close contacts with the most powerful German bankers, such as the Fuggers, and also to his personal patrimony, he had assembled an army of eighty thousand soldiers, of whom fifty thousand were infantry and thirty thousand cavalry. He had also been promised reinforcements by the Medici in Florence, by Philibert of Savoy, Alfonso of Ferrara, by the Duke of Guise and the German electors. In Germany, Ilsung had collected great sums to pay for equipment, provisions and weapons. Innsbruck would supply locally produced helmets for defence and attack, together with Savoy horses and Italian infantry; he had negotiated with the Duke of Wüttemberg for supplies of gunpowder; and finally from Augsburg and Ulm he had obtained rifles and other weapons. Ilsung even announced that he would receive considerable financial aid from the Pope and from the King of Spain.

"Maximilian was radiant," remarked the Greek. "He promoted Ilsung to the post of Chief Imperial Paymaster, unceremoniously removing his superior. Under Ferdinand I, Maximilian's father, Georg Ilsung had already laid his hands on a great number of offices, and in this way he became the key figure in the imperial finances."

The Caesarean army left Vienna on 12th August 1566, and twelve days later pitched camp in the little town of Raab, on the Danube.

Maximilian was a man of peace, but he was not afraid to fight for a just cause, and had decided to place himself personally at the head of his troops, as Suleiman himself did, even though the Sultan was on his seventeenth campaign and he on his first.

Once they were encamped, however, the imperial army waited for events to evolve. Maximilian did not want to move. He stayed in his tent, talking to nobody. All the good cheer of their departure had vanished from his face. No one knew why. The soldiers and officers were in good spirits and were looking forward to fighting; this long wait would only depress them, and trigger off the diseases and infections typical of large camps – and sure enough they began to break out among the soldiers.

Suleiman lost no time and attacked the fortress of Szigeti, which he had long set his sights on. The imperial army at first rushed to assist the besieged city. Then, incredibly, they fell back.

The fate of Szigeti was sealed. The besieged troops launched themselves in a heroic and suicidal sortie and were massacred. The commander, Count Zriny, was beheaded and his head sent to the imperial camp.

Szigeti fell on 9th September. Then the fortress of Gyula fell. It was a disaster. All eyes were on the Emperor: a golden opportunity to triumph over the Turks and to recapture the lands of Hungary had been wasted, mountains of money had been dissipated in equipping the army, and two important fortresses had been destroyed.

Meanwhile, since the Turks seemed to have no desire to pursue hostilities, there was nothing to do but return home, just as the enemy themselves would do soon enough. Who was to blame for this failure if not the Emperor, who had refused to stir? They had long been calling him Maximilian the Mysterious; now it seemed that behind the mystery lay nothing but incompetence.

In the meantime we had almost completed our smoke test in the *maior domus*. Most of the flues had responded positively: none of them was seriously blocked, so it only remained to clean them. The story continued.

Back in Vienna, Maximilian finally broke his silence. He decided, something unheard of for an Emperor, to justify himself publicly. And he explained the mystery: when he personally examined the forces at his disposal in the Christian camp, he realised that Ilsung had lied to him: the eighty thousand men he had been promised at the beginning of the campaign were no more than twenty-five thousand, not even a third of what he had been led to believe. And the equipment was wretched: nothing like what had been promised. Not to mention the expected reinforcements, no trace of which had been seen. That was why the Emperor had chosen not to attack. Twenty-five thousand against a hundred thousand: it would have been a massacre, with the additional risk that the Ottomans, after exterminating the Christian army, would have been able to advance on to Vienna and, finding it undefended, take it in an instant.

But there were more surprises. Ungnad too had lied: some Ottoman soldiers who had been captured by the imperial troops on their way back had revealed that the Ottoman army was not especially large or well armed. Among the Turks there were many soldiers with no weapons and, above all, great numbers of young boys, terrified of their Christian enemies.

This explained Maximilian's total silence: Ilsung had betrayed him, and so had Ungnad. Whom could he trust?

"Betrayed by his own men," I remarked, surprised and intrigued by this strange story, paying no attention to the soot that was falling all around me in large clumps while I thrust my head into one of the flues to see how much stuff needed removing. "But why?"

"Wait, Signor Master, it's not over yet," Simonis stopped me. "Something else had been hidden from Maximilian, with Luciferian cunning."

This was the most important event of the whole war. It had happened even before the fall of Szigeti, on 5th September. At the age of seventy-five and suffering grievously from gout, Suleiman the Magnificent had unexpectedly left his followers in the lurch right in the middle of the military campaign: he had died.

"Died? And the Emperor knew nothing about it?"

"Nothing at all. For two whole months. And this despite the fact that David Ungnad was continually travelling back and forth between the Turks and the Christians."

The news of the Sultan's death was concealed by such an opaque veil of secrecy that Maximilian learned nothing of it until the end of October. And to tell the truth, it was this fact, even more than the fall of Szigeti, that was his ruin. If they had heard at once about the

Sultan's death, the Christian army could have taken advantage of the enemy's inevitable confusion, launched a sudden attack before they could organise themselves and almost certainly they would have achieved a great victory. Instead, Maximilian's intelligence network had kept silent. In the end Suleiman's death was revealed to him by a foreigner: the Ambassador of the Republic of Venice. Even in distant Innsbruck they had heard the news three days before the imperial camp, which was just a stone's throw from the Ottoman one.

Suleiman had actually been moribund when he set out from Constantinople; but this was something David Ungnad had not reported.

"And just think, the trick the Turks used was a puerile one: they put an old man in Suleiman's bed who imitated his voice and issued orders, following the ministers' instructions," sneered Simonis with bitter sarcasm.

The Greek was growing heated over this two-century-old tale; he may have looked like an idiot but he had a keen mind and fervent heart and this betrayal of the old emperor filled him with indignation. However, he still had not explained the reason for all this and, above all, what on earth it had to do with the Place with No Name.

"I imagine," I cut in, "that after Maximilian's public speech, the men who had betrayed him came to a bad end."

"Far from it, Signor Master, far from it. His justifications were ignored. Ilsung, Ungnad and their acolytes held the same power as before. It was as if the Emperor had never spoken. Everyone continued to blame him for the defeat. Although only whispered, condemnations of him were bandied about, and Maximilian could see them written on his own friends' faces."

"Absurd," I remarked.

"The heart of the public and of the court was too heavy with disappointment and anger to weigh the rights and wrongs of the situation calmly, or even just to listen to the facts. Maximilian's enemies knew this and took advantage of it. They subtly stirred up the people's feelings."

"But who organised it? And why?"

"Who? All of his most trusted men. Why? For revenge; the first of the long series of acts of hatred and deception that led to the building of this place, then to its repudiation, and which finally bore the Emperor to his grave."

Maximilian, Simonis went on, had become emperor only thanks to the support of the forces opposed to the Church of Rome, led by the heretical Princes. He had surrounded himself with Lutheran spirits and intellects, but only because he felt an affinity with their open and innovative minds, certainly not out of any desire to oppose or to weaken the Vicar of Christ. However, the people in whom the Emperor had placed his trust were by no means so high-minded in their intentions: they were all waiting for him to give a clear sign of rupture with Rome, something that would mark the decline and fall of the papacy once and for all. And so, the *imitatio Christi* contemplated by Maximilian went beyond his own intentions: he was betrayed and destroyed, just as the Jews had had Jesus crucified when they realised he was never going to take up the sword against Rome.

"And so the war against the Turks provided an opportunity for the heretics to avenge themselves and get rid of him," I concluded, sneezing and wiping from my face a cloud of filthy dust, released by the fall of a large piece of soot.

"It was all too easy for them: a huge number of heretical Princes supported and financed the Sublime Porte just out of hatred for the Church of Rome!"

I had already heard something similar: many years earlier, guests at the inn where I worked had told me of secret intelligence between the Sun King, Louis XIV, and the Ottoman Porte. In that case it was even worse: it was not a case of Protestant princes but of the Most Christian Sovereign of France, Only Begotten Son of the Church. The Pope had behaved no better himself, and purely for personal profit had financed the heretics. This experience had taught me that just about anything could be expected from monarchs.

"After the defeat in battle everything changed," explained Simonis, "starting with Maximilian himself."

He felt surrounded by spies, by enemies plotting to finish him off. But Georg Ilsung had been his counsellor for years, and his father's before him. He was very powerful: he had started his career working for the Fuggers of Augsburg, the family of bankers that had financed Charles V and had enabled him to become emperor by bribing the prince-electors. The Fuggers were behind Ilsung's every move. They not only lent money but even paid the Emperor in advance the tributes that the prince-electors had promised but not yet paid; and they did this at an interest rate equal to zero.

The Habsburgs were up to their eyes in debt to the Fuggers. And so Maximilian could not get rid of Ilsung that easily.

"Georg Ilsung was the fountain from which the gold of the emperors flowed," said Simonis in no uncertain terms. "If they needed money for the war against the Turks, he was the one that found it. If there was a revolt in Hungary and arms were needed, or money to pay off the leaders of the uprising, he would see to it. If a loan had to be bargained from the Fuggers, offering as guarantee the income from customs duties or the revenue of the imperial mercury mines in Idria, he was the one they turned to. If there were debts to pay, Ilsung would contact other financial backers to spread the payment of interest. If he could not find anyone, he would pay from his own pocket and patiently wait for the Emperor or his treasurers to find the time and means to pay him back."

"So he had the Emperor under his thumb."

"He could do whatever he wanted with him. In the meantime the other powerful counsellor, David Ungnad, travelled to and fro between Constantinople and Vienna, on the pretext of ambassadorial missions."

"A spy of the Sublime Porte," I guessed, without much difficulty.

"In close contact with Suleiman's financial backers," my assistant concluded.

Maximilian, he went on, felt he was in their power and wondered when they would finally cast him off. He watched with concern as his son Rudolph gradually fell into their clutches, wanting to do something about it but unable to trust anyone. He was divested of all authority, a corpse on the throne.

He had been a brilliant conversationalist, lively and sociable, full of ideas and projects. Just as the Empire had placed its hopes in him, he had placed his hopes in the future. Now he grew withdrawn, surly, and enigmatic. He no longer opened up to the pleasure of conversation; his eyes, once so lively and penetrating, had become melancholy, his voice dull and flat. The ambassadors of foreign powers reported regularly to their masters that the Emperor was no longer himself, that the reversal he had suffered at Suleiman's hands had marked him forever. A dead man, the Turkish Sultan, had defeated a living one, and had transformed him into the semblance of a dead man.

The courageous decision not to persecute the Protestant heretics, and even to accept many of them as counsellors, together now with this sad and impenetrable character, made him unpopular with his own people. By now there were those who suspected that behind this complicated man, behind his tormented nature and his incomprehensible policies, there was nothing but a confused mind.

Maximilian had never had a strong physique; now he seemed in steep decline. On the way back from the military campaign to Vienna, his old affliction of palpitations had resurfaced. He had fallen out of love with so many things that only one project now seemed close to his heart.

"He dreamed of a new building," explained Simonis, "and we are right inside that dream of his: the Place with No Name."

He was too conscientious to neglect affairs of State. But every free moment was devoted to the project of his new castle. As time went by he spent ever greater sums on it, and it was said that it became a compulsion, a sort of sweet torment: was it better to use this stone or that marble? This cornice or that frieze? In the façade, was a *serliana* better than a porch? And in the garden, what trees, what hedges, what rare varieties of roses? The indecision he had been criticised for in the war against Suleiman was now his sweet companion. The Venetian ambassador wrote to his compatriots that the Emperor had just one concern, to which he devoted himself wholeheartedly, a real obsession: creating a garden and a villa, half a league from Vienna, which when completed would be a truly regal and imperial palace.

Curiously enough, at the planning stage he turned to the same Italian architects he had summoned years ago to reinforce Vienna in view of the war against the Turks. But for the Place With No Name, these ingenious Italians did not design ramparts, ravelins and counterscarps: instead, they planned towers like minarets, oriental half-moons and Ottoman-style seraglios.

The court and the people were flabbergasted. What on earth was driving the Emperor to pay such sumptuous homage to the architecture of Mahomet?

But it was no mere caprice, no whim of a melancholy and confused spirit.

"In 1529, more than thirty years before the defeat of Maximilian, Suleiman the Magnificent had besieged Vienna. It was the first of the two great – and unsuccessful – sieges that the Infidels laid to the Caesarean city. Suleiman had set out from Constantinople accompanied by immense resources of men and money, which he had received from the many people who were hoping, either from greed or from resentment or just out of personal hatred, to see the powerful throne of Peter fall at last. The fortunes of entire families, accumulated from generation to generation, had flowed into the Sultan's coffers to finance his campaign against the Giaours, as they call us Christians. Suleiman spared no expense: during the siege he chose as his lodgings, not a military tent, but a rich and gigantic camp, almost a reconstruction of his palace in Constantinople, with fountains, water-games, musicians, animals and a harem."

To conquer Vienna, and with it the whole Christian world, did not seem an impossible enterprise, explained the Greek: just a hundred years earlier had not Constantinople itself, the New Rome, the Byzantium of the most pious Empress Theodora, Justinian's beloved consort, fallen into Turkish hands?

"That 'lascivious dancer' – as the treacherous and mendacious scribbler of Caesarea apostrophised her behind her back – with her fervent and shrewd monophysitism had won her place in paradise, and on her premature death had left a lofty testament in political and religious terms: the only unconquerable pockets of the Christian faith in Asia, against which even today the Infidels are powerless. But even Theodora had been unable to save her Byzantium from Mahomet, the Prophet who would be born less than thirty years after her death. And now the basilica of Saint Sophia, erected by Theodora herself, had been raped by the minarets of Allah. Could not the same thing happen to Vienna, the 'Rome of the Holy Roman Empire'? And then, why not, to Rome itself?"

My assistant narrated all this with some vehemence, while doing his best, with uncoordinated and awkward (but not inept) movements, to light a bundle of damp wood that stubbornly refused to ignite; and the sharpness of his voice testified to all the suffering the Greeks had undergone at the hands of their Ottoman masters.

"Instead it all went up in smoke," concluded the Greek. "Suleiman had not yet managed to overcome the resistance of the besieged city when God hurled against him a colder winter than had ever been seen before, and the Sultan had to go back empty-handed, and, what was worse, with the great risk of perishing amidst the ice storms and floods, as on the Day of Judgement. For his financial backers it spelt ruin."

It was the end of the dream. Henceforth there would be less pride and confidence in the cry, "We'll meet again at the Golden Apple!", which every new Sultan, at the end of his investiture, launches as a promise to the commander of the janissaries.

"The Golden Apple?"

"It's the name the Ottomans have used since time immemorial for the four capitals of the Giaours: Constantinople of Saint Theodora, Buda of Matthias Corvinus, Vienna of the Holy Roman Emperor and Rome of the Successors of Peter."

The Golden Apple, the allegorical name designating the four forbidden fruits of Ottoman yearning, found its incarnation alternately in the gilded domes of Constantinople, in the scintillating orbs atop the roofs of Buda, in the golden sphere surmounted by the cross of Christ that dominated Vienna from the imposing tower of St Stephen's, and finally in the mighty sphere of pure gold on the dome of the basilica of St Peter's in Rome, whose golden glow was visible even to sailors off the coast of Latium.

"And so the sultans, as soon as they ascend the throne," remarked the Greek sarcastically, "solemnly promise to lead the janissaries very soon to the conquest of those cities, almost as if this were Islam's very reason for living: to defeat the Christian world."

The first Golden Apple, Constantinople, had been conquered by the followers of Mahomet, but now Vienna had transformed the situation.

"Transformed it entirely!" I laughed. "It was a century and a half before the Sublime Porte could put together enough money to threaten Vienna again. And yet again in vain. I know the story of the siege of Suleiman in 1529: last Monday I watched the annual procession of the brotherhood of bakers, which crossed the city with music and banners, in memory of the service they rendered the city during that siege. But what does the 1529 siege have to do with your story? Is it because the families of the ruined backers were the same ones for whom Ungnad would later betray Maximilian?"

"You've guessed it, but only in part. Because there was more to it than that, much more. Do you know where Suleiman's tent was pitched during the siege, with its fountains, water-games, musicians, animals and all the other luxuries he had brought with him?"

I looked at Simonis, waiting for the answer.

"Here, on the plain of Simmering, right where the Place with No Name now stands."

At these words, I thought back to the Levantine forms of the pinnacles and domes, to the fountain, the thermal tower and the Mediterranean gardens. Still clutching a bundle of firewood, I went outside, leaving my assistant and apprentice. I gazed upwards. With the story of Maximilian's drama still echoing in my mind, my eyes roamed the sky and the towering roofs of the Place with No Name. Now I saw what had had been right in front of my eyes all this time but which I had failed to notice before: the roofs reproduced the coruscating glow of the sumptuous pavilion of Suleiman. The tiles of gilded copper once again tormented my eyeballs with their glare, and I almost felt I was admiring the sinister glitter of the Bosphorus and the glint of the scimitars that struck off the head of Count Zriny and the golden reflections of the oriental domes of St Mark's, which gazed down upon the treacherous city of Venice, which had abandoned Maximilian in the struggle against the Infidel.

Now I saw what it was, the Place with No Name, known as Neugebäu, or "New Building": not a hunting lodge, nor an aviary, nor a garden, nor a villa – no: it was an Ottoman seraglio. The towers held the treasure room, the storeroom, the small parlour and large parlour, the inner room, the walls of white marble and porphyry columns, the pages' rooms and the court guards' quarters. In each of the towers there was a reproduction of one of the areas into which Suleiman's camp had been subdivided, including the Turkish bath. And it also included the audience chamber and the law pavilion and the great room of the divan.

With this grandiose, secret parody of a sultanesque palace it almost seemed as if Maximilian, smiling ruefully, had wished not only to create a masterpiece, but above all quietly to settle the score with his Eastern enemies. At Szigeti he had been defeated by a dead sultan. At Neugebäu he had avenged himself.

Only then did I recognise the place for what it was: a castle with gleaming roofs like Suleiman's pavilion, but caged in by classical arcades and flanked on either side by two semicircular keeps, the sign of Christian apses flanking their prisoner like gendarmes. Gathered together in the main building of the Place with No Name were the two cornerstones of Europe: the heritage of the classical world and the Christian faith. They not only besieged Suleiman's pavilion, but to the south they kept watch over the gardens and the Turkish-style towers, and barred the road to the north; just so the Infidels had never succeeded in overpowering the Christian West.

The boreal meadows and woods to the north of the Place with No Name offered no scope for Levantine allusions, eloquently opening out onto a view of the Caesarean city and its ramparts, which the Infidels had never succeeded in conquering.

"This was how he got his own back on Suleiman," said Simonis, who had come up behind me with my boy, "but even more on those who had lavished gold on him so that he might move against Europe; the same ones who out of hatred for the Church had led Maximilian to the throne, and had then ditched him, laying the basest of traps for him. It was the masterly revenge of a disempowered Emperor, who did the only thing he still could do: erect an eternal monument to that original defeat of Suleiman, the wound that will never heal."

Ilsung sought with every means in his power to deprive Maximilian of funding for Neugebäu, the New Building. Already in 1564 he had got a pupil of his own hired as Court Paymaster: David Hag, who was also related to Ungnad. And so Hag became the brooding presence responsible for every single penny dispensed to the Emperor, and hence to the New Building. Every request for funding for the project met with the reply that there was not enough money, or there were other difficulties. When Maximilian managed by some stratagem to go ahead with the construction, Hag would unsettle the artisans with rumours that they would never be paid, and if they were not convinced he would stir up rivalry and jealousy among them. He also arranged for shoddy materials to be sent instead of the stuff ordered by the Emperor, so that during the construction work parts of the building collapsed. When he died, in 1599, twenty years after Maximilian, it was discovered that Hag had confined himself to marking only the Emperor's expenses in the accounts books, without ever listing the revenue destined for him."

"Not exactly the most faithful way of handling his sovereign's funds," I said ironically.

"Maximilian was probably deprived of large sums of his own money in this way," the Greek confirmed. "But even so he always found some expedient to carry on with the work, even if slowly and laboriously. And the Place with No Name, the New Building, although incomplete, became the eighth wonder, astonishing every visitor."

Failing to grasp the allegorical aims, the Turks loved and venerated the Place with No Name: for them it was nothing other than a faithful reproduction of their glorious Sultan's camp.

When Vienna was besieged again in 1683, they even took care not to damage it. There was no ambassadorial mission to Vienna that failed to visit the Place with No Name at least once. Some even pitched camp there, on the plain in front of it, the night before entering the city, in adoration of that sacred place, tearfully caressing and kissing its walls as if it were a sacred relic. When they gazed upon the seraglio, four thousand paces wide, and the sixteen corners with their towers, which dazed and confused the senses, they were moved by what they saw as a perfect imitation of Suleiman's camp.

A very different treatment, unfortunately, was meted out to the Place with No Name by the European allies of the Sublime Porte. The Kurucs, the infamous Hungarian rebels, in one of their shameless incursions six or seven years earlier, vented their rage on those poor walls. The castle was looted, defaced and burned down. That which had held out against neglect for over a century was destroyed in just a few minutes.

"After all those years! Couldn't it have just been sheer chance? Do you really think the Kurucs destroyed the Place with No Name for its symbolic value?" I asked.

"As long as there are enemies of Christianity, there will be enemies of this place, Signor Master. The hatred against the Place with No Name still rages."

I would have liked to ask him how this hatred was manifested and by whom; but at that moment Frosch arrived to see what point we had reached.

We told him that the chimneys of the *maior domus* were not in a disastrous condition, and we would be able to fix some of them immediately. But it would take us some time to draw up a map of all the flues of Neugebäu, and we could not return the next day, I said, on account of some urgent repair work that I had to carry out for clients back in the city.

After the *maior domus* we inspected some of the service buildings. We worked hard all day armed with wire brushes, butchers' brooms, ropes and counterweights, inspecting and cleaning the flues of Neugebäu; we were filthy and exhausted. But in my legs I could still feel the force that was required to satisfy my curiosity, or rather my sense of unfulfilled duty. I almost felt that the strange being, the most bizarre in the whole castle, was expecting (if an inanimate object can ever be said to expect) my visit.

I looked around myself; Frosch was nowhere to be seen. I made my way to the ball stadium.

It was still there, vigilant and motionless, but its threatening beak, so sharp and warlike, looked as if it hoped one day to cleave the cold air of the skies above Vienna again. The Flying Ship, imposing in its guise as bird of prey, rested as ever on its great belly of wooden planks, its wings spread out uselessly. Simonis walked around it several times and then leaped up inside it, taking with him my boy, who was bursting with curiosity.

Having finished his account of the Place with No Name and its builder, the Greek had reverted to his usual self, asking a host of banal questions not worth answering. Could the ship have flown up into the air thanks to its bird-like shape? And why was it a bird of prey? And if it flew again, would it not scare the lions and the other animals of Neugebäu? And could it float as well? Or would it have to be shaped like a seabird or, even better, a fish in that case?

I gave only monosyllabic answers. The discovery of the magnilo-quent symbolism of the Place with No Name and the Greek's story had filled me with doubts and questions, stirring me to a state of inward excitement, so that my work tired me out earlier than usual. In my heart there was little room left that day for the other host of riddles that made up the feathered sailing ship.

While I worked in the ball stadium with brushes and counter-weights, beginning to clean one of the half-blocked flues, I thought back to Simonis's story of the Place with No Name. He had referred to its state of neglect. And so even before the devastating raid of the Kurucs, it had been abandoned. Did that mean Ilsung and Hag had won out over Maximilian? In what way? And why had no emperor taken any interest in that wonderful place since then? I put this question to the Greek.

"To tell the truth, some Caesars, including Emperor Leopold of august memory, father of our beloved Joseph I, did plan some rather limited restoration work. But when you get down to it, no emperor has ever carried anything through, or hardly anything."

"And why not?" I asked in wonder.

"Lack of money," my assistant said with a wink, vigilant and lucid once again. "Their imperial paymasters and court paymasters always found a thousand pretexts not to finance the restoration of the Place with No Name. All of them, just like Ilsung and Hag –"

". . . because the great financial families pulling the strings behind the paymasters were still the same ones," I concluded before him.

"Exactly, Signor Master. Do you want proof? Even the tutor of the infant Leopold I, father of the present emperor, was a Fugger. They're the same as ever. And for generations they've hated the Place with No Name."

"So are they really far more powerful than the emperors?"

"It's a question of fear, Signor Master. All the Most August Caesars who reigned between Maximilian and his Caesarean Majesty Joseph I the Victorious kept well away from the Place with No Name for fear of ending up like Maximilian."

"Why, what happened to him?"

But Simonis seemed not to hear me. He had stepped outside and was examining the fading light of day.

"We must hurry, Signor Master," he exclaimed, running back in. "It's very late; soon they'll be closing the city gates!"

❧

18.30 of the clock: the ramparts close. Latecomers must pay 6 kreutzer. The beer bell rings, the wine shops close and no one can wander the streets now bearing arms or without a lantern.

Lashing the poor mule mercilessly, we managed to get through the city gates just in time to avoid paying the 6-kreutzer fine. Money saved, and immediately lost: our dinner at the eating house, because we were so late, cost us 24 kreutzer each instead of the usual 8.

On our way home, curled up as usual in the cart while Simonis and the boy sat on the box seat, with my guts churning to the jolts of the careering wheels, I thought back to the Greek's bizarre tale.

Now that I knew the story of the Place with No Name, the decision of His Caesarean Majesty Joseph I struck me in a new light and raised urgent questions: why on earth had Joseph decided to break the chain of oblivion that his predecessors had bound around Neugebäu? He must know well the sad story of his ancestor Maximilian II and the series of grudges and vendettas that had generated and undermined the parody of Suleiman's camp. He must have easily guessed, if he had not indeed learned with his own ears, that it was this murky affair that had kept his prudent predecessors away from the Place with No Name. What had given Joseph the

Victorious the impulse to intervene in a centuries-old struggle which, according to Simonis, was far from over?

I considered our beloved Emperor. What did I know of him?

Ever since my arrival I had tried to collect information on the new Sovereign's character, fame and actions, and on the expectations that the people had of him. After a life spent as the subject of popes, all of a certain age, I had found it a welcome novelty to become the subject of a young monarch with no cassock or crosier.

Numerous writings existed on Joseph I, known as the Victorious. They were all panegyrics, or stories of his infancy, of his education entrusted to the Prince of Salm (he was the first emperor not to be educated by the Jesuits, his father Leopold having yielded to the hatred that his subjects nurtured for the Company of Jesus). Then there were detailed descriptions of his marriage to Wilhelmina Amalia of Brunswick-Lunenburg, of his triumphal appointment as King of the Romans, which is the title by which the crown prince is designated in the Empire. There were also accounts of his military campaigns, first of all the siege and conquest of the fortress of Landau in the Palatinate: Joseph himself had seized it from French hands at the age of just twenty-four, in 1702 and 1704. In 1703 the French had reconquered it only because Emperor Leopold, for reasons unknown to me, had not wanted to send his son into battle.

These were the first things I remembered from all that I had read about my Sovereign, but more particularly from what I had learned at first hand from my sharp-witted fellow chimney-sweeps, who had been happy to satisfy my curiosity about the royal family with lively details, instilling in me a profound devotion to my new Sovereign.

However, I could remember nothing of any connection with the Place with No Name or its history. Or perhaps there was something: the bold beauty of the young Emperor (something truly unique in the ill-favoured Habsburg line), a mirror to his impetuous and dominating character (equally rare in that stock); Joseph's desire to impose himself on the family traditions and the consequent clashes with his father, *parvus animus* educated by the Jesuits, and the conflicts with his brother Charles, of a recondite and indecisive temperament, another product of a Jesuit education.

But I vowed that I would rummage among the various books and writings on the Emperor that I had acquired on my arrival in Vienna. I would look there for the answers to my questions.

On returning to the convent, after gulping down our sumptuous dinner at meteoric speed, I was already looking forward to immersing myself in the papers I had collected on Joseph, in search of an answer to the puzzles of the Place with No Name.

"Here I am. This evening we shall do a lesson on strolling, and on eating and drinking."

It was like a blow to the head. The person who addressed me in this fashion, just as I turned into the corridor of the guest house, was Ollendorf, the German tutor. I had forgotten: it was the feared hour of our language lesson. As he had just announced, that evening we were going to try out a conversation to learn the terms connected with walking and with food. Very unwillingly I bade farewell to my research into Joseph I and the Place with No Name.

My lack of talent for foreign idioms was exposed all the more clearly by the state of exhaustion in which I faced each lesson. That evening I was afraid that I would appear to even greater disadvantage than I had at the previous lesson, when, in an attempt to describe the best way to pay homage to a woman (kissing the back of her hand), instead of the word *hand* I had said *hund* (dog), to the great mirth of my wife and my son, and the deep disappointment of Ollendorf.

Cloridia was still at Prince Eugene's palace. I was so eager to get on with my readings on Joseph I and my cogitations on the Place with No Name that, after apologising to the teacher and offering as pretext my weariness, I begged him to teach my son by himself that evening.

I retired to my bedroom and prepared to wash, pouring water from a jug into the pot on the fireplace. As I did so I listened to my son, taking delight in his skills in German.

"*Deß Herrn Diener mein Herr, wie gehets dem Herrn?*", which is to say "Servant of your Lordship my patron, how is your Lordship?" asked the teacher, pretending that his little pupil was a gentleman.

"*Wohl Gott lob, dem Herrn zu dienen, was für gute Zeitungen bringt mir der Herr?*" "Praise be to God, to serve your Lordship: what good news does your Lordship bring?" answered the boy diligently.

I cleaned myself and was just settling down to read the heap of papers – pamphlets and other publications concerning the life and deeds of our Most August Caesar – when I heard a key rattle in the door. My wife had returned.

"My darling," I greeted her, resigning myself to a postponement of my research.

For nearly two days my wife and I had had no chance to talk, and I was curious to hear about the audience that the Agha had had with Prince Eugene. But then I saw her dejected face and dull complexion, features that clearly indicated trepidation and anxiety.

She kissed me, took off her cloak and lay down on the bed.

"So, how did it go yesterday?"

"Oh, what do you expect . . . Those Turkish soldiers, all they can do is drink. And act licentiously."

Exalted by the hospitality and courtesy extended to the Agha, the lower-ranking Ottomans had thought they could claim equal dignities, and had plied Cloridia with absurd requests.

"Unfortunately," sighed my wife, "of all the virtues that honour Christian society, the only one the Turks feel obliged to practise is hospitality. When they enter someone else's home, they think they have a right to whatever they want, because they are *muzafir*, guests, and in their religion it is God Himself who has sent them, and no matter what they do, they must always be welcome."

A virtue that contents itself with appearances, said Cloridia, is very quickly debased; and that is what happens to oriental hospitality as practised by the boorish multitude. Under the pretext of the duty of hospitality, the Ottomans, not content with the rough Stockerau wine, had raided the larder, exhausted the supplies of coffee and *acquavite*, overturned carpets, mattresses and cushions, and even broken the crockery in their debauches, taking advantage of Prince Eugene's magnanimity and the pay of the imperial chamber.

"And they stank too!" my wife said wearily. "In the Ottoman Empire no one undresses for bed, and because of the cold they're wearing the same furs they've been travelling in for months. Remember that for the Turks there's nothing more elegant than a fur coat and so they think they're cutting a fine figure dressed like this."

In Constantinople, added Cloridia, there's nothing they fear so much as the cold and so they do all they can to protect themselves from it even when for us Europeans the problem is to withstand the heat. Even in the warm rooms of the Savoy Palace the Ottomans remained wrapped up in their stinking furs and on the lookout for the slightest draught from windows and doors, which they then wanted to stop up with pieces of waxed paper. And so, while the Agha was being received with all honours by Prince Eugene, the Ottomans were bustling to and fro all over the place, making the palace servants complain; and the two groups, like hammer and tongs, had driven poor Cloridia mad, she being the only linguistic intermediary.

The last straw had come when some Armenians in the retinue had decided to light a *tandur* to sit around, with the risk of starting a fire or seriously damaging the Most Serene Prince's furnishings.

"A *tandur*?"

"A little stove full of embers and burning coal which you put under a table covered with woollen drapes that hang down to the ground. They all pull the cover over themselves, bury their hands and arms under it, and keep their bodies at a temperature that we would consider feverish. Of course this custom leads to a great many horrible accidents. And they insisted on lighting one in the palace, repeating that they're *muzafir* and so on."

That was not the end of it, continued Cloridia. When the Great Court Marshal called to greet the Agha's train, some of the Turks, wanting to show that they were perfectly familiar with the customs of us Giaours, did nothing but drink from the bottle, burping all the while, and sprawled all over the divans, believing that this was what we consider elegant behaviour. But when the Great Marshal, during the visit, spat into a spittoon on the carpet, the Ottomans gestured wildly and turned up their eyes to show how amazed they were at such barbarous conduct.

"However," I said, in an attempt to sweeten her temper, "this idea that guests are sent by God does honour to the Infidels."

"It's all show, my dear: if you call on one of them and then, when you leave, fail to pay twenty times the value of what you've consumed, your host will wait for you to step outside, losing the sacred title of *muzafir*, and stone you," she concluded.

"My poor wife," I sympathised, embracing her.

"And I haven't yet told you what happened when they heard my mother was Turkish: they pulled out a tambourine, a drum and a shepherd's whistle, and beat time faster and faster, wanting me to dance that dance of theirs with wooden spoons, all a twisting of hips and bellies, with nothing graceful about it that I can see, while what's indecent is all too clear," added Cloridia, still overcome by disgust.

"I hope at least they didn't show you any disrespect."

"Don't worry, despite all the wine I'd supplied them with, they haven't forgotten what the Sultan will do to anyone who molests a woman. And in any case that dervish of theirs, Ciezeber, was ready to remind them of it," smiled Cloridia, noticing a flicker of fear in my eyes.

"I saw him in the procession. But what's he doing in the Agha's retinue?"

"He's his imam, his priest. I just wonder why he isn't Turkish."

"I've read that he's Indian."

"So they say. At any rate he's not like the others, he behaves most worthily."

I asked her what the palace looked like inside, if she had attended the official talks, or if she had at least bumped into Prince Eugene. She told me that, as soon as he set foot inside the palace of the Most Serene Prince, the Agha was led by the master of the palace to the great staircase, and then upstairs. Here, surrounded by a great crowd of noblemen, people of rank and imperial functionaries, the Ottoman ambassador was received by two officials of the War Chancellery, who led him through the famous great hall, decorated throughout in frescoes, and then through the antechamber to the audience chamber. The Agha must have been greatly impressed by the great gathering of people, remarked Cloridia, as well as by the abundance of red velvets with ornamental gold writing that covered the walls and the armchairs. The spectacle of the great hall, of the luxurious wall-hangings and the eager bystanders reached its climax when the door of the audience hall was finally thrown open to reveal the severe face of His Imperial Eminence the President of the Aulic Council of War, His Highness the Most Serene Prince Eugene of Savoy.

Eugene was dazzling in his gold-embroidered garments, his hat decorated with a cockade studded with diamonds of incalculable value, and also displaying the Golden Fleece and his sword. He sat awaiting the Agha in an armchair underneath a baldachin of red velvet, flanked by Count Herberstein, Vice-President of the Aulic Council of War and a secret referendary and surrounded by numerous generals. The room had now filled with the great throng of noblemen, courtiers and people of note, all craning their necks to catch every detail of the conference.

"Eugene is far from good-looking," added Cloridia. "He doesn't have fine facial features, his body is too lean, but on the whole he inspired respect and deference."

As soon as he arrived before the Most Serene Prince, the Agha saluted in the Turkish manner, touching his turban three times, and then sat down on an armchair that had at once been placed opposite that of his host. The first thing the Ottoman did was to present his credentials. The Prince accepted them and immediately passed them to the secret referendary. After which a conversation was held, but neither of them had to make any concessions: the Agha expressed himself in Turkish, Eugene in Italian, which was not only the official court language but also the idiom of his family, he being a Savoy. Their words were made mutually intelligible by the Caesarean interpreter and the interpreter of the Sublime Porte; the former translated, the latter assured the Agha of the correctness of the translation. Only at the outset, Cloridia said, did the Agha formulate a sentence in Latin in honour of the Holy Roman Empire: "*Soli soli soli ad pomum venimus aureum!*", which is to say, "We have come to the Golden Apple all alone." He pronounced it carefully, reading from a document. This was interpreted not only literally – the Agha had indeed come with a retinue of just twenty people or so – but above all as a declaration of honest and peaceful intent. The Turk had come to Vienna, in short, with no ulterior motive. The paper from which the Agha had read was then personally delivered into the hands of the Most Serene Prince.

During the interview, furthermore, Eugene was seen to play with a strange metal object about two inches across, which he passed incessantly from one hand to the other. At the end, after the ritual farewells, the Agha stood up, turned round and immediately headed towards the door. Only then did Eugene, who had remained seated the whole time, stand up, remove his hat by way of salutation and then, taking care to turn his back on the Agha to show his superiority, look towards his generals. The Turk was led away by the same officers of the city guard who had conducted him thither. Reseated in his carriage between two lines of onlookers, he was taken back to his lodgings, but only to satisfy the curiosity of the bystanders, since the Agha and his retinue in fact returned that very evening to the palace of the Most Serene Prince, where they were going to stay for three days, to enjoy the most lavish and splendid treatment that the duty of hospitality imposed.

"So the Turks are staying for three days as Eugene's guests."

"That's what the Prince has decided, to pay them greater honour."

"And on Monday they'll be returning to their lodgings, at the inn of the Golden Lamb," I deduced.

"Haven't you heard the latest? The embassy isn't putting up at the Golden Lamb, as the Turkish delegations have done for a hundred years now."

"Really?" I said in surprise.

"It's still on the Leopoldine Island, in the Jewish quarter, but at the home of Widow Leixenring, which has eleven rooms, a good kitchen and a stable with a barn."

"A private house? But why?"

"It's a mystery. All I know is that the rent is paid, as always, by the imperial chamber. At the Golden Lamb they're offended, particularly because there was room for them there. And all the onlookers who were waiting for the procession outside the inn were left looking silly. The strangest thing is that Widow Leixenring's small palace is guarded like a fortress: they told me you can't get a peek at the windows even from a distance."

"So it's true that there's something serious behind this embassy. Have they come out and declared their reason for coming here?" I said, beginning to worry that we might have come all the way to Vienna to escape from Roman poverty, but at the risk of falling victims to a new Turkish siege.

With the lightning swiftness of fear, I was already seeing myself flayed alive, my wife deported (lucky her, speaking the language of those Infidels) and my son brought up in the barracks of Constantinople to become a janissary – or, worse, made a eunuch for the Sultan's harem. Meanwhile Cloridia had moved to the door that communicated with the next room. She was discreetly eavesdropping on the dialogue taking place at that moment between our little boy and Ollendorf:

"𝕲𝖔𝖙𝖙 𝖇𝖊𝖍𝖚̈𝖙𝖊 𝕰𝖜𝖊𝖗 𝕲𝖓𝖆𝖉𝖊𝖓." "Goodbye Most Illustrious Sir," the pupil was reciting courteously. Cloridia smiled tenderly on hearing his high-pitched voice.

"People are saying that this is a different embassy from the previous ones," she then confirmed, returning to me as her smile faded. "Do you want to know how many people there were on previous official Turkish visits to Vienna? As many as 400. The last time they came was 11 years ago, in 1700, and they had 450 horses, 180 camels and 120 mules. And now," she added, "arriving like this in a great hurry, almost without warning, with very few followers and a journey in the depths of winter . . ."

"So does anyone know why they've come?" I asked, feverish with anxiety.

"Certainly they know. Officially, to confirm the peace treaty of Karlowitz. And that's what the Agha discussed with Eugene in front of everyone."

"The treaty signed with the Emperor twelve years ago, when the last war with the Ottomans ended?"

"Exactly."

"And was there any need to send such an urgent embassy from Constantinople to confirm a treaty that had already been signed? They haven't made any claims or announced any hostile intentions towards the Empire?"

"On the contrary. The Ottomans have got many other matters on their minds right now: they're engaged against the Czar."

"The whole thing makes no sense. Do you think they've come for some other reason?"

Cloridia looked at me, returning the question with her eyes.

"I've asked each and every one of those drunkards in the Agha's retinue," she said then, "but do you know what they answer? *Soli soli soli ad pomum venimus aureum!* And then they laugh and they drink, so as not to say anything else. They ape their master without even understanding what they're saying."

"And the palace staff? Maybe they've picked up something from the private talks between Eugene and the Agha."

"Ah, as for that, there's been no private talk!"

"What?"

"You heard me. Eugene and the Agha have never gone off in private; they have always talked exclusively in front of an audience."

"And so they've really never talked of anything except the old treaty of Karlowitz."

"Truly inexplicable, don't you think?" she answered disconsolately. "Just think," she added, lowering her voice, "that even in the Prince's diary, there's nothing about this embassy except the sheet of paper the Agha gave him. And on the sheet all that's written is that sentence: '*Soli soli soli ad pomum venimus aureum*,' simply that the Turks have come to Vienna all by themselves."

"This is all absurd," I commented.

"Maybe this sentence conceals something we don't know," conjectured my wife. "They've explained to me that the *pomum aureum*, or the Golden Apple, is the name the Turks give to Vienna."

"Yes, I know; Simonis told me this just today," I confirmed, summarising for her what I had learned from my assistant about the history of the Place with No Name, about Maximilian II and Suleiman.

"Incredible. But where does the name Golden Apple come from?"

"Ah, I've no idea."

"Maybe it's the name that holds the key to understand the sentence," hazarded Cloridia.

Things clearly did not add up. It had been feared that the Ottomans might arrive in arms, or at any rate bringing something terrible with them. Instead, publicly emphasising that they had come all by themselves, they wanted to reassure the imperial forces as to the honesty of their intentions. But this still did not explain why they had come to Vienna in such urgent haste. And there was something else that jarred with their avowed peaceful purposes – the way they had referred to the Caesarean city, using the hardly reassuring name of "Golden Apple". The description underlined the fact that Vienna was still a target of conquest for the Ottoman Sublime Porte. It was no accident that Prince Eugene was granting them the extraordinary honour of hosting them for three days in his palace.

"And how do you know what's in your master's personal diary?" I asked with my eyes bulging, suddenly thinking of Cloridia's words.

"That's obvious: I was told by his personal manservant's wife, the one I promised to help give birth for free."

My wife, although she could not practise as a midwife, a profession which required a regular licence (like everything else here), never stopped helping women who were pregnant, in childbed or in puerperium. Her help was gratefully received, since the best obstetricians in the city, those on the same level as Cloridia, cost a fortune.

"But hurry up now," she exhorted me, "Camilla is waiting for us."

సౌ

20 of the clock: eating houses close their doors.

"Before I got married, there was nothing interesting about my life," began the Chormaisterin.

We were in the august imperial chapel, at the rehearsal of *Sant'* *Alessio*, during a break. Since only our little boy and I belonged to the troupe of extras, Cloridia did not need to be there, but Camilla de' Rossi had been so skilful in overcoming my wife's initial diffidence that she now happily accompanied us to our evening engagements, and during the break it was not rare for her to pass the time conversing with the Chormaisterin.

The breaks during the oratorio rehearsals were, for the moment, the only chances that the two women had for such chats, and the Chormaisterin seemed to value them greatly. Cloridia and I were always busy with our daily work, and for this reason could not make use of the convent's kitchen, unless we were ill. Furthermore, by the rules of Porta Coeli the nuns were not allowed to sit at table with strangers. Camilla, who was only a lay sister, was not subject to this prohibition, and was very disappointed that we did not share her meals, all based on spelt; and so she consoled herself by preparing delicious dainties of spelt for our son, which had also had the beneficial effect of restoring him to full health. This had greatly endeared our gentle hostess to my wife.

In every conversation Camilla had the amiable gift of delicately introducing the subjects Cloridia most enjoyed, *in primis* that of assisting pregnant women and looking after new mothers and babies, obviously, but also occult teachings like the interpretation of dreams and of numbers, or the art of the ardent rod or diviner's wand or whatever it is called: disciplines that Cloridia was highly skilled at, and which she had practised in her youth. Gifted with almost prophetic intuition, the Chormaisterin almost seemed to know from the outset Cloridia's tastes and inclinations, and with discreet but unfailing adroitness led the talk towards those themes.

These amiable attentions succeeded in loosening my sweet consort's tongue, so that when Camilla went on to ask her about her past, Cloridia did not bridle as she usually did but willingly proceeded to satisfy her curiosity.

That evening the conversation between the two women was in full flow when Cloridia for the first time put a few questions to the Chormaisterin: what had driven a young Roman woman, from Trastevere no less, all the way to Vienna? Did she not miss Trastevere, her *rione*? Where exactly was the house she had been born in and had grown up in? Cloridia, who knew most of Rome from her days as a midwife, had suddenly remembered a certain Camilla de' Rossi, a well-to-do shopkeeper in Trastevere, daughter of a certain Domenico da Pesaro and mother of a Lucretia Elisabetta, whom she had assisted in giving birth to her son Cintio. Cloridia would have been happy to discover that she already knew some of Camilla's relatives: you know how it is, it's such a small world . . .

"Before I got married, there was nothing interesting about my life," Camilla cut her short, showing little desire to delve into her origins, too obscure perhaps for one who now enjoyed the confidence of His Caesarean Majesty.

"Married?" asked Cloridia in wonder.

"Yes, before entering Porta Coeli I was married. But excuse me, the rehearsal has to start," she said, moving towards the orchestra players.

And thus it was we learned that Camilla, although only twenty-nine years old, was a widow.

The music began. Sweet violin strokes softly filled the vault of the Caesarean chapel, supported by the warm breath of the organ, the silvery tinkling of the lute, and the tawny tints of the violone. The soprano, in the role of the betrothed bride just abandoned by Alessio, gave voice to a mournful lament:

Cielo, pietoso Cielo . . .[4]

But immediately an angry burst of chords broke from the orchestra. The bride inveighed against her old love, and asked heaven for a weapon to punish him:

Un dardo, un lampo, un telo
Attenderò da te
Ferisci arresta esanima
Chi mi mancò di fé . . .[5]

Since the extras were not required during that passage, I had sat down to listen with Cloridia and our son on the chapel pews. Swept away by the energy of the music, I suddenly realised that with one hand I was clutching my consort's arm, and with the other the back of the bench in front of us. While Camilla's notes and the soprano's

[4] Heaven, pitiful Heaven . . .
[5] A dart, a bolt, a blow / I will await from thee, / O wound, arrest, strike low/Who broke his pledge to me . . .

silvery voice swelled in the volutes of the chapel, I thought back to the strange coincidence that had struck me the evening before: music and singing had come back into my life, and once again were associated with the name Rossi. In Rome I had come to know the arias of Atto's master, Luigi Rossi; here, the Chormaisterin Camilla de' Rossi. Could it just be pure chance? Perhaps names bring events and experiences along with them? And if so, can words therefore govern things?

While I brooded over these fleeting questions, the piece came to an end. Camilla began to instruct the singer and the players on how best to perform the passage, and to go over individual parts again; as always, the Chormaisterin was extremely eloquent and thorough in explaining just what tones she expected from the singing, what sighs from the sweet flutes, what grumblings from the gruff bassoons.

During the next pause, Camilla rejoined us. I at once urged her to continue her story. She carried on, explaining that when still very young she had married a royal court composer, a musician in the service of the Emperor's eldest son, who was the then young Joseph I.

The court composer was Camilla's music teacher, as she was already in Vienna at that time with her mother. He was Italian, and was called Francesco.

"But here in the Empire," Camilla explained, "where all names are Germanised, they called him Franz. Franz Rossi."

"Rossi? So your surname is Rossi, and not *de'* Rossi?" I asked.

"Actually it was. The noble patronymic *de'* was a generous concession of His Majesty Joseph I, just before Franz died."

Her husband, Camilla went on, had trained her in the art of singing, and more particularly in that of composition, and taken her around the various courts of Europe, where they learned the most recent musical fashions, which they would introduce into the Caesarean court on their return. In Italy they went more or less everywhere: Florence and Rome, Bologna and Venice. During the day they visited the workshops of master-lutists, explored theatres to test their acoustics, approached virtuoso singers or harpsichord players to learn their secrets, and paid homage to princes, cardinals and persons of note in return for their benevolence. At night, by candlelight, they fought against sleep, copying music to take back to Vienna for the delectation of His Caesarean Majesty's highly refined ears. Then she left us again, to go on rehearsing the orchestra.

While the Chormaisterin made the musicians try the passage over and over again, and the music swirled around the chapel, I was carried away on a sweet silent surge of memories.

Rossi! So that was the original surname of Camilla's deceased husband. Not just similar, as I had first thought, but identical to the surname of Seigneur Luigi, Atto's beloved master in Rome, the mentor of his youthful years. Luigi Rossi: the man who had taken the young castrato Atto Melani with him to Paris, conferring glory on him as the protagonist of *Orfeo*, the great melodrama requested by Cardinal Mazarin to celebrate his own greatness, second only to the supreme powers of heaven.

Almost as if in mockery of me, the soprano recited:

Cielo, pietoso cielo . . .

And once again my mind went back to those events of twenty-eight years earlier, to the Inn of the Donzello, in Rome. Not a day had gone by in Abbot Melani's company, between the four walls of the inn where I had first met him, without my hearing at least a line of Seigneur Luigi Rossi, modulated by Atto's etiolated but still passionate voice.

Meanwhile the voice of the abandoned bride trembled with anger:

Un dardo, un lampo, un telo
Attenderò da te
Ferisci arresta esanima
Chi mi mancò di fé . . .

In the parallel world of my memories, marvellous notes quivered in Abbot Melani's throat, as he sang to the poignant memory of his master (and of other things that I could not even imagine), and I, an ignorant servant boy, wondered at the sound of those ineffable melodies, never heard before or since.

"Finally we went to France, to Paris," Camilla began again at the end of the rehearsal, as we all walked back to the convent of Porta Coeli.

Since it was such a short journey to Carinthia Street from the Caesarean chapel and from there to the convent, we walked slowly to give her time to tell her story.

"But the court of France is in Versailles," objected Cloridia.

Here Camilla smiled with a touch of embarrassment.

"We didn't go to court. More than anything else Franz wanted to visit someone, the only person still alive who could tell him about a relative of his, a great-uncle, also a composer. He was very famous in his day, but he died prematurely. And times have changed so quickly that he's now forgotten. In Rome Franz couldn't find anyone who remembered him. It was only in Paris that he finally –"

"You mean Maestro Luigi Rossi, don't you? He's your relative? And it was Atto Melani that you visited in Paris, wasn't it? And that's how you met the Abbot?" I asked in an excited series of questions that already had their answer.

Just at that moment we were interrupted as we encountered a great flock of people, mostly very young.

I should have guessed it from the beginning, I reflected as I stepped around the crowd: Camilla had known Atto. It could not have been otherwise. That was why the Abbot had sent us to stay at Porta Coeli: in Paris he had met Camilla, and then they had remained in touch. Thanks to this acquaintance, despite the war between France and the Empire, he had succeeded in finding a trusted person in Vienna, the enemy capital. Had not Atto also written a letter to the Chormaisterin, expressly commending us to her care, as she herself had mentioned when we arrived? And furthermore: Franz, Camilla's deceased husband, was Luigi Rossi's nephew.

Meanwhile the group of young people were swarming into the courtyard of a house: it was an *Andacht*, one of those pious prayer meetings in front of the statues of saints and patrons, which took place everywhere in Vienna after sunset. They would sing, recite the rosary and litanies, listen to sermons and then round things off by gorging on cold meat and bread, washed down with wine; after which the couples would go off to engage in encounters of a less spiritual nature.

"When did you see Melani?" Cloridia and I asked in unison, anxious to hear about our benefactor.

"It was eleven years ago, in August 1700. The excellent Abbot welcomed us like a father, showing us incomparable benevolence and magnanimity during our whole stay in Paris. When we told him our story, he displayed a touching and delicate sensibility that won me over. I have never known anyone who can equal Abbot Melani in nobility of spirit!"

Camilla lavished praise on Atto. Well, she had been lucky, I told myself, to have seen only the Abbot's nobler sides.

"Melani told us that he had just returned from Rome, where he had attended the marriage of the nephew of the Cardinal Secretary of State. He was supposed to stay until the conclave, but a bad injury to his arm forced him to return to Paris."

As we walked on, Cloridia and I looked at each other without a word. We knew that story all too well, having lived through it with Atto – or rather, having endured it as a result of his shady intrigues. He had been stabbed in the arm, it was true, but that was certainly not why he had fled from Rome! But we let the matter drop. We certainly had no wish to fill Camilla in on the less honourable aspects of the man who, after deceiving and exploiting us for his own ends, had now become our benefactor.

"The Abbot talked to us of his master Luigi Rossi, Franz's relative."

Melani, plucking sprigs of memory from the vast wildernesses of his remembrance, with touching diligence had almost brought back to real life the figure of Seigneur Luigi for Camilla and Franz. At several points Atto had been on the verge of tears, and only the respect he bore her, a sweet fresh young lady, had restrained him. He had recounted the glory that Luigi Rossi had achieved many years ago in Rome in the service of the Barberini, and then his success at the court of the King of France; he had told them how his famous cantata for the death of King Gustave of Sweden had won him the admiration of all Europe, and how his *Orfeo*, in which for the first time the arias lasted longer than the recitatives, had renewed and transformed opera. Luigi Rossi had been a gentle spirit of fine intellect, an inexhaustible source of fresh poetry and inspired music; he had received more applause in both Rome and Paris than any Italian musician before him.

Atto, proceeded the Chormaisterin, pursuing the train of memories, shared with them not only the successes and joyous occasions from half a century ago but also the tragic ones. He told them how Seigneur Luigi had heard, while he was with Atto in France in the service of Cardinal Mazarin, that his young wife Costanza, the beautiful harpist of the Barberini, was ill. He had rushed back to Rome, and on the journey he had set to music the noble lines *"Speranza, al tuo pallore / so che non speri piu', /eppur non lasci tu / di lusingari il core"*[6] – but all in vain.

[6] O Hope, who art so pale, / I know you hope no more, / and yet the heart so sore / to rouse you never fail.

While he was still en route news reached him of his wife's death, and it was then that he composed the elegiac *passacaglia*, "*Poi che manco' la speranza*"[7].

"And this loss was to lead him slowly to the grave," concluded the Chormaisterin sadly.

She added that Atto had even shown her the handwritten *intavolature* with his master's arias. "Franz then told Abbot Melani that we were thinking of settling either in Rome or in Paris, the cities where Luigi Rossi had lived, but he advised against it strongly. He urged us to return to Vienna, saying that it was now the capital of Italian music, that in Rome and in Paris music was finished. In Rome it had been killed years before by Pope Innocent XI, who had closed the theatres and forbidden the carnival; and in addition the power of the papacy was now in decline. In Paris, now that the Sun King was in thrall to that self-righteous old plebeian Madame de Maintenon, everything, even music, had become grey and bigoted."

Abbot Melani, I reflected as the Chormaisterin spoke, knew perfectly well what was going to happen just a few months after he gave that advice. The King of Spain Charles II was close to death, and when he died his will would be opened (whose contents – O Fates! – Atto was already familiar with). He well knew that thanks to that will the throne of Spain would immediately become an object of contention, sparking off the terrible war that was to leave the whole of Europe starving, especially Italy, theatre of its operations, and France, bled dry by its own king. The Abbot's counsel, therefore, was a very shrewd one: Vienna, the blessed Caesarean city kissed by the Goddess of Opulence, was the only safe refuge.

And then, if I knew him well, it would not have escaped the attention of the Sun King's old spy just how useful it would be to have two trusted friends like Camilla and Franz in an enemy capital in wartime.

"It's been such a long time," I sighed, "since I last saw the Abbot!"

"But around that time Franz fell ill," Camilla went on. "He suffered continually from fluxions of the chest. Returning to Vienna

---

[7] Then when hope failed.

could have been fatal to him. So we went back to Italy, wandering from one court to another. My poor husband, while fearing for his own future, was worried about my fate. For this reason, in 1702, when the war of succession broke out, he decided in the end to follow Atto Melani's advice and we came back to Vienna where, if some misfortune were to condemn me to solitude, it would be easier for me to make a living."

Franz de' Rossi, her story proceeded, had immediately gone back into Joseph's service and had introduced his wife into the ranks of the royal musicians, where she swiftly earned the confidence of the future Emperor.

"Of the Emperor?" I said in admiration.

"As everyone knows, His Caesarean Majesty is a musician of considerable discernment and appreciates all those who show zeal and love in their endeavours to serve him and to satisfy his passion for the art of sounds," replied Camilla. "*Timore et amore.*"

"What?"

"It's his motto. It explains the weapons he likes to govern with: with fear and with love, *timore et amore*," the Chormaisterin spelt out clearly, with the tone of one who intends to say no more. Then she went back to the story of her marriage.

Franz de' Rossi, descendant of Seigneur Luigi, had passed away on the foggy morning of 7th November 1703 in the Niffisch Home on the Wollzeile, the Wool Street, just behind the Cathedral of St Stephen. He was only forty years old.

"I was left all alone. I had never known my father, and sadly my dear mother," she added, with a change in her voice, "whom I longed to re-embrace on my return, had died while I was away."

"My mother died far away as well," said Cloridia.

I started, and so did Camilla. My wife was referring spontaneously to her mother.

"Or at least I imagine she has died by now; who knows when, who knows where," she concluded, her voice slightly husky.

The Chormaisterin clasped Cloridia's hand tightly between her own.

"I used to have a pendant," Camilla said slowly, "a little heart in gold filigree with miniatures of my mother and my sister as a child, but unfortunately it got left behind in the house where my mother died, and there's no way to get it back, alas."

"And your sister? Where is she now?" I asked.

"I've never met her."

Although we had been walking with slow, dragging paces, and had taken every possible by-way, we had now reached Porta Coeli.

"I beg of you, don't torment yourselves with sad memories," she urged us with a smile before we separated, "there are happy things in store for you in the days to come!"

While Camilla disappeared in the direction of the dormitory, two figures emerged from the evening gloom: a young gentleman and his servant. They were heading towards the wing of the convent which held a second guest house for foreigners. The gentleman was saying to the servant:

"Remember: crows fly in flocks, the eagle flies alone."

I started. I knew that expression. I had learned it from Atto, many years ago. For the whole evening I had been thinking of him, and now he seemed to be responding. Perhaps Abbot Melani had learned that expression from Cardinal Mazarin, and so it was known to many people. Maybe that gentleman knew Camilla and had simply heard the expression from her, and she, in turn, may have learned it from Atto Melani. Enough, I was brooding too much. One thing was perfectly clear: it was one of those eternal maxims that one never forgets and is happy to repeat.

❧

Once we were in our room, while Cloridia got ready for bed, I hastened to satisfy that longing I had had ever since I returned from the Place with No Name: to rummage among the books and various writings on Joseph I that I had acquired on arrival in Vienna, to seek the answer to my doubts. Why on earth did the Most August Caesar wish to restore the Place with No Name, heedless of the chain of vendettas that surrounded the place? The sad affair of his predecessor Maximilian II and the struggles between Christians and anti-Christians that had broken out around Neugebäu had meant that for a century and a half the Habsburgs had yielded to the powerful pressure of all those who wanted this monument to Suleiman's defeat to fall into ruin. But not Joseph the Victorious. Why? What was spurring him on?

Once I had discarded the writings in abstruse German, I quickly unearthed a pair of panegyrics in Italian. I opened the first: *Applause of Fame and the Danube on the Day of the glorious Name of the Most August Emperor Joseph. Poetry for music consecrated to His Excellency the Lord Count Joseph of Paar, Great Seneschal of His Imperial Majesty*, composed by the academician Acceso Gelato on the occasion of the Sovereign's name day in 1706. I dipped into the work, which was a dialogue between the Danube and Fame:

> *Danube: Misery*
>   *Tyranny*
> *From Austria are banned;*
> *Thoughts of woe*
> *Spirits low*
> *Leave Austria's fair land:*
> *Glory's voice*
> *Shall sing so gay:*
> *And all rejoice*
> *On this great day.*
> *In the woods' dim shades*
> *On hills and in glades*
> *Let the birds raise a song*
> *Of joy and delight that shall sound all day long.*
>
> *Fame: Twixt these banks JOSEPH's fame*
> *Shall echo and sound*
> *And the waves at that name*
> *And the breeze*
> *In the trees*
> *Shall whisper their bliss all around.*

The mawkish panegyric, despite its awkward rhymes, reminded me how the devotion that had arisen in my breast for Joseph I had gradually turned into affection as I learned further details of his worth: he was naturally endowed with great clemency, heartfelt generosity, open-handed liberality and a love of justice; he was understanding, mature, resolute and made pronouncements with prudence and grace; he was unequalled in courage, and would go out hunting heedless of the weather, the season or the danger, so that even the boldest courtiers would excuse themselves from accompanying him, and he would often abandon his guards and present himself at the city gates all alone or with a single companion.

As time passed, talking to clients whose chimneys I swept, or to customers in eating houses and coffee shops, I heard more and more stories about His Caesarean Majesty's good heart. He was so open-handed, they said, that the first to ask him for a favour was the first to receive it: Joseph was incapable of turning down anyone in need. He gave everything to everyone regardless, drawing not on the imperial treasury, but on his own private coffers, so that he was often reduced to great personal privations.

But no story could outweigh the impression that I had received directly, when I saw him for the first time with my own eyes.

It was just two months earlier, in February. For the carnival celebrations they had revived the old custom of *Prachtschlittenfahrt*, the solemn sledge-ride of the Emperor and his court. In the Caesarean procession, led by Joseph himself, there were 51 sledges and over 130 people, between noblemen in sledges and servants on foot or on horseback.

The sledges were carved in marvellous shapes of swans, shells, bears, eagles and lions, but the most splendid, which had been taken on a long ride that morning with no passengers so that the people could admire it, was the one for Joseph and his consort. At the front was a wonderful piece of marquetry representing branches, an amazing work jointly created by goldsmiths, cabinet-makers and gilders; on the sides were two fauns with flutes, wonderfully life-like; to keep the imperial couple warm there were gold-embroidered ermine blankets, and at the rear were gilded standards with the Habsburg and imperial coat of arms. In the cortège there were other vehicles with likenesses of Venus, Fortune, Hercules and Ceres, concealing noble couples covered with shawls and quilts, perhaps intent on some warm, secret embrace.

After a long journey along Carinthia Street and the neighbouring thoroughfares, the procession halted in front of the Cathedral of St Stephen. Joseph got out to pray and to offer thanks to Our Lord, accompanied by his mother the widow queen Eleanor Magdalen Therese, his wife the reigning queen Wilhelmina Amalia, his two daughters Mary Josephine and Mary Amalia and his sisters Mary Elizabeth and Mary Magdalen. The imperial family, in slow procession towards the front door, graciously presented themselves to the crowd. The Caesars of the House of Habsburg consider it their duty, but also their pleasure, to gratify the people's desire to admire, approach and study them. This is another reason why the imperial family often attend public mass in one of the churches in the city or the suburbs, or march in processions, or, in Lent, follow the traditional *Via Crucis* along the so-called Kalvarienberg – which is to say, Mount Calvary – in the suburb of Hernals, where there is a church of that name.

Cloridia and I had tried to elbow our way through the crowd in the great square before the Cathedral of St Stephen, but the throng was so tightly packed we could make no headway. And so, before the imperial crowd left St Stephen's, we ran to the Hofburg, as we knew the procession would end up in its great courtyard.

Here the more far-sighted spectators had already taken up their positions: clustered together in little groups in the great open space, clinging onto columns or, if children, perched on their fathers' shoulders. I chose, at the risk of enjoying only the most fleeting glimpse, to squat down opposite the jaws of the dark portal from which the Caesarean convoy would emerge into the open space.

In the great courtyard of the palace the snow fell thickly but lightly, the roofs of the Hofburg glimmered with a spectral candour. Squeezed in among the shivering crowd of onlookers, sheltering my face from the wind, I awaited the arrival of the procession.

At last the moment came: from the great portal I heard the tinkling of the sledge bells, then there appeared a pair of footmen bearing the imperial banners, escorting the head of the parade, followed by more, and yet more. At last there emerged the first pair of white horses with fiery-red trappings, their backs adorned with imitation eagle wings, pulling the sledge where he himself, the Emperor, stood upright, heedless of the cold.

I saw him for just a few fleeting moments but they seemed endless: his august figure, just a few paces from me, impressed itself delectably and indelibly on my heart and my spirit.

The high well-shaped forehead, tawny hair, firm nose, beautiful complexion ruddied by the stinging cold, the large fleshy mouth open in a broad smile that was bestowed generously upon us, the formless crowd: all this I saw at once, and it struck my heart, already inclined to devotion, to the core. As I gazed upon him, his large eyes, glinting with the sweet azure of youth beneath the laughing curve of his eyebrows, embraced us all in a single glance. In those few instants I was able to appreciate his figure, which was not tall but perfectly proportioned, his strong shoulders and his open, decisive posture.

I was captivated, and so was Cloridia. From that moment my affection for the young Sovereign turned into passionate attachment and fidelity. Even as I gazed on him, I repeated to myself that so illustrious an heir was the perfect idea of the most heroic virtues, such as Egypt had never had in its Vexor, nor Assyria in its Ninus, Persia in its Cyrus, Greece in its Epaminondas, or Rome in its Pompey. In his reign of less than six years he had achieved twenty-nine victories in war. And with what unstinting ardour had he engaged in the famous sieges of Landau! The daring of his boldest followers appeared mediocre alongside his courage, the ferocity of the veteran soldiers seemed like inertia, and in his character there blazed a keen desire for glory, which, when instilled into the warlike breasts of the Germans, had twice hastened a victory over so considerable a fortress, defended by the obstinate courage of the most heroic French troops. Not even the Most Serene Prince Eugene had ever succeeded in conquering it! The victories of the Most August Joseph the First could only be compared with those of antiquity: of Cyrus against Croesus, in which not only had the latter been captured but the vast Kingdom of Lydia conquered; of Themistocles against Xerxes, in which he had avenged the cruel servitude of Greece oppressed by a million armed barbarians; of Hannibal against the Romans at Cannae, which had made the battlefield synonymous with defeat for centuries to come; and finally the bloody victory of Charles the Fifth on the fields of Pavia, in which Francis the First had been taken prisoner, the most courageous of that century. On closer consideration, I said to myself, now soaring to the heights of adoration, the successes of Joseph the Victorious were superior to these. After all, which of the *Romani Imperadori* could boast within the space of his Imperium such prodigious victories as those he had attained in just three years? His victories could only be compared with those of Caesar against Pompey, of Vespasian against Vitellius, of Constantine against

Maxentius, memorable and bloody battles, exemplary for the valour of the soldiers, the multitude of legions and the overpowering force of the factions.

While I lost myself in these thoughts, the long procession of sledges had all entered the courtyard of the Hofburg, illuminated by hundreds of torches, and was weaving solemn serpentines from one side of the square to the other while the people applauded and gave voice to their jubilation.

Elated with our new life in the opulent northern capital, enchanted by the snow, which did not bring in its train (as it would in Rome) the wailing figures of Indigence and Famine, and delighted by the splendour of the Caesarean court, which – unlike those of Versailles and the Papal State – was not an insult to the poverty of the people, since every pauper in Vienna received two pounds (two pounds!) of meat a week, my wife and I embraced one another.

Resurrexit, sicut dixit, alleluia!

So resounded the aria of the magnificent *Regina Coeli* composed by Joseph I, which we often heard in the churches of Vienna; and so chanted our soul, in its joy at this unexpected resurrection to new life.

Holding back tears of enthusiasm and exaltation, we impetuously gave our hearts that day to the young Caesar, incarnation of our own rebirth, in the great and unsuspected cornucopia, surrounded by hills and fertile vineyards, that was the Caesarean city.

I had given myself up to divagations and sweet memories. I returned distractedly to the panegyric:

> *DANUBE: At the flash of his Arms,*
> *FAME: At the splendour of his Glories*
> *DANUBE AND FAME: Pale flowers wither . . .*
> *DANUBE: And in spite of those Flowers*
> *To the emulous Ruler's distress*
> *The Pride of the stubborn Bavarians*
> *And Pannonians now languishes.*
> *FAME: Caesar, you who with Jove*
> *Have divided the Empire*
> *And with Mars the laurels,*
> *In the flower of your Years*

Now, that the Trumpet's sound
Invites you to rejoice,
Open your heart to Joy, and wipe away all tears . . .

Even-in these tedious rhymes there was a kernel of truth. In order to be feared, Joseph had chosen Mars, because the thought of war, whose harsh clangour was never too far from Vienna, had been a constant companion for him from his earliest years. But another divinity had to be added to the Mars of the panegyric, and that was Venus.

Joseph had encountered the Goddess of Love at a precocious age, and it could not have been otherwise, as Mother Nature had endowed him most generously. At the age of twenty-four he was handsome, strong and well-proportioned, like his robust German mother. He had no trace of the horrid jutting chin and pendulous mouth that for generations had disfigured his ancestors, including his father Leopold and his brother Charles, the current pretender to the Spanish throne. Surrounded by the deformities of the House of Habsburg, Joseph stood out like a swan among ducks.

Women (princesses, ladies of the court, simple serving wenches) appreciate a man of distinction, and he was happy to reward them at night, one by one, with the appropriate means.

And how gifted he was! Eloquent, sparkling and imaginative: he lacked for nothing. The Muses themselves had done their part, lavishing their talents on him. The King of France did not know a single foreign language; Joseph spoke six like a native. At the age of seven he wrote correctly in French, at eleven in Latin, at sixteen he could speak both languages fluently, in addition to Italian, with good pronunciation. Two years later he had mastered Czech and Hungarian. He was skilled in music and composition, and played the flute expertly. He developed his muscles with physical exercise, hunting and the military disciplines.

I picked up the second panegyric, penned by Gian Battista Ancioni: "*To Gioseppe I. King of Germany, and Roman Emperor, August conqueror. Vienna of Austria, printed by Gio. Van Ghelen, Italian Printer of the Court of his Caesarean Majesty, Year 1709*". Underneath an engraving depicting a fine bust of Joseph were the words: *Tibi militat Aether*, "Heaven fights by your side."

I flicked through it quickly and soon found a list of the military deeds of Joseph and of his generals and confederates. The author addressed the Emperor:

Comparable with those of ancient days are the present great victories achieved over the French in the fields of Hecstette by Your undefeated armies, and by those allied with You captained by those two thunderbolts of Mars, Eugenio and Marleburghio. Thanks to that undefeated Hero of Great Britain most of Flanders was conquered in the great feat of arms of Judogne, and thanks to the magnanimous spirit of Charles the Third the most extreme and arduous dangers of the siege of Barcelona were sustained with great intrepidity, and with a rare example of victory Catalonia was liberated with the precipitous flight of the terrified enemies.

But in the prodigious liberation of Turin the insuperable valour of Your armies manifested itself and the light of Your felicity blazed most clearly. Equal to the memorable constancy of the Saguntines was the great defence of that noble City, manfully sustained against French arms for a term of many months; but the fierce vigour of the repeated assaults, the multitude of troops that surrounded it, the lack of ammunition, the paucity of defenders and the difficulty of all foreign assistance, brought the defence of that strong & august City to an extreme pass. When the most sagacious Eugene, descending with Your fierce Legions to avenge like a new Belisarius with the besieged Turin all of Italy in liberty, crossing not only the horrid mountains of Germany and of Italy, but traversing with long marches the Adige, the Po, the Dora, & the most impervious regions of all Italy, forever pursued by a numerous army of the French, came with incredible dispatch within sight of Turin, and joining forces with the most valorous Duke of Savoy assaulted the entrenched armies of the French with such courage, that the ferocious assault of the Germans seemed to herald a massacre not a battle, and the confusion, fear and death were so terrible in that great deed that headlong flight, retreat and dispersion were the enemies' common thought; hence with the immense massacre and imprisonment of the French was Turin liberated, and the French troops scattered throughout Italy within the space of a few months, and with the capture of Milan all of Lombardy was taken under Caesarean arms, & very soon with incredible celerity Your arms took possession of the flourishing Kingdom of Naples, and Italy returned to its erstwhile state of long-desired liberty.

I closed the panegyric. What did these pompous writings tell me about the Most August Caesar? That the differences between Maximilian the Mysterious and Joseph the Victorious were enormous. On the one hand mildness, on the other military ardour; the elder was of a reflective temperament, the younger of a resolute nature. Joseph's life up to this point seemed all a matter of military campaigns and victories.

And yet something connected the two emperors, the young Caesar and his ancestor: after a century of oblivion the former was now disinterring his forebear and the Place with No Name, in what almost seemed a new military campaign, conducted by architects instead of generals. Looking benevolently on Maximilian's creation, Joseph was proceeding fully armed against timeless enemies, defying age-old rancour against the Empire of the Christians – rancour that had never died down, as was clear from the vandalistic raids of the Kurucs at Neugebäu just a few years earlier.

I could almost see him, spurred by the pusillanimity of his fathers, announcing to the astonished architects that, after enlarging the hunting lodge at Schönbrunn, he wished to restore the Place with No Name to its former splendour. Perhaps he would even give it a name at last.

It was at that point in my thoughts that it struck me that in my two visits to the Place with No Name I had never come across any traces of anyone else engaged in restoration work. Frosch had never mentioned the subject either, and had indeed seemed completely in the dark about the Emperor's plans. Maybe, I told myself, the architects and carpenters also preferred to wait for the thaw. Maybe over the next few days they too would turn up and start working.

Overcome by the late hour and by weariness, I promised myself that I would finish reading the papers on Joseph the First over the next few days. I did not know why, but I felt that among those old newspapers and tattered documents there may well lie the answer to my questions on the Place with No Name.

⇛

23 of the clock, when Vienna sleeps (while in Rome the foulest traffickings are just beginning).

I had been under the blankets for some hours and had not yet managed to fall asleep. I had been unable to tear my thoughts away from the Place with No Name and the Most August Sovereign, and from here my exhausted spirit had passed on to the Flying Ship and its mysterious helmsman and, finally, to Seigneur Luigi, to the arias of Luigi Rossi trilled by Atto, which I had never forgotten, and which, like nimble-footed prey, I was now tracking down, one by one, in the forest of my memories. How did that arpeggio sound, that bold modulation, and that line?

Ahi, dunqu'è pur vero . . .

Then, when memory had brought me back a full game bag, and I was already savouring an immaterial banquet of notes, rhymes and chords, my imaginary repast was whisked away by something quite unforeseen.

A noise. It came from the corridor of the cloisters. Someone seemed to have tripped up badly. It could not have been one of the nuns of Porta Coeli: the dormitory was on the opposite side from the guest house. The only thing nearby was Simonis's little room. But, as the Greek knew perfectly well, the rules stipulated that apprentices had to be in by nine or at the very latest ten o'clock, on pain of a large fine. And Simonis had always been punctual. That very evening, on returning from the rehearsal of *Sant' Alessio* I had paid him a brief visit to make arrangements for the next day, and I had found him in his room, bent over his books. The following Monday the Easter holidays would be over and the *Alma Mater Rudolphina*, the University of Vienna, would reopen its doors.

Another noise. Taking care not to waken my dear ones, I got dressed and stepped outside. I had not yet reached the cloisters when I recognised him by his voice.

"And the laurel crown . . . there it is!" I heard him whisper nervously. He was picking up a few objects, which must have fallen from a large canvas bag he was holding.

"Simonis! What are you doing out here at this hour?"

"Er . . . uh . . ."

"At this hour you're supposed to be in your room, you know the rules," I reproched him.

"Pardon Signor Master, I must go."

"Yes, to bed, and quickly," I replied in irritation.

"This evening there's a Deposition."

"Deposition?"

"I'm the barber, I must be there."

"Barber? What are you blathering about?"

"Please, Signor Master, I have to be there."

"What have you got in there?" I said, pointing at his bag, which had something moving inside it.

"Mm . . . a bat."

"A bat? Just what are you doing with that?" I asked, more and more astounded.

"It stops me falling asleep."

"Are you making fun of me? Do you want to get a fine? You know very well –"

"I swear, Signor Master, if you take a bat with you, you never fall asleep. Or you can catch some toads before dawn and dig out their eyes, then hang a flask of deer-hide round your neck with the toads' eyes inside together with nightingale meat. That works just as well, but the bat is easier . . ."

"That's enough," I said, dismayed and disgusted, dragging my bizarre assistant by his arm.

"I beg you, Signor Master. I must go. I must. Otherwise they'll expel me from the university. If you come with me you'll understand."

For the first time since I had met him, Simonis's tone was distressed. I realised that it must be something of the utmost importance. I decided that for no reason in the world could I run the risk of seeing him expelled from the *Alma Mater Rudolphina* through my own fault. And I knew very well that at that point in the night I would not get back to sleep; curiosity did the rest.

The place was an old apartment near the Scottish Monastery. According to Simonis, it was being rented by a group of his study companions. As soon as we entered I felt as if I had been hurled by a Sorcerer of Time into the wrong century. The room was full of young men dressed as ancient Romans; they wore togas and mantles, laurel crowns around their temples and leather leggings. Some of them were holding scrolls of paper, in imitation of ancient parchment. The only detail that connected the great crowd with the present day were the countless tankards of beer they were all swigging merrily. The Beer Bell, which announces the end of legal drinking time, had rung long ago, but this strange toga-clad mob seemed not to care.

Simonis emptied the bag he had brought with him, gave me some robes and took some for himself. At that moment he was spotted by a few of them and I heard a feverish murmur run round the room.

"𝕿𝖍𝖊 𝕭𝖆𝖗𝖇𝖊𝖗, 𝖙𝖍𝖊 𝕭𝖆𝖗𝖇𝖊𝖗'𝖘 𝖍𝖊𝖗𝖊!" they all repeated, elbowing one another and pointing at Simonis.

Some of the students made towards him and embraced him enthusiastically. Simonis greeted everyone with an expansive wave, to which the crowd responded with applause. With all those swishing togas, it was like being in the Roman Senate after a speech by Cicero.

I suddenly felt bewildered: Simonis the Greek, my apprentice, my underling, was the king of the evening. I thought back to his account that morning of the history of the Place with No Name and its creator, Emperor Maximilian II. My bizarre assistant undoubtedly possessed hidden talents.

As soon as he was dressed and decked out as a Roman senator himself, he was accompanied to a wooden stage in the middle of the room.

I myself had just finished putting on a toga and leggings, far too capacious for my slight build, when another excited murmur broke out. A door giving onto an adjoining room had just opened. A platoon of young men entered, apparently escorting a prisoner. In the middle of the group was a very odd individual, if only for the way he had been rigged out. He was a timid, skinny young man, who looked around himself hesitantly. He wore a hat with two enormous donkey's ears, probably made of cloth, and an even larger pair of cow horns. From his mouth hung two huge boar fangs, which must have been fixed to his teeth with some sort of paste. Otherwise he was draped in a large black cloak, which made him look both sad and awkward. He had been driven into the room by a stick, with which he was regularly beaten on the back like a beast of burden.

"𝕿𝖍𝖊 𝕭𝖊𝖆𝖓𝖔, 𝖙𝖍𝖊 𝕭𝖊𝖆𝖓𝖔!" the bystanders all cried out, as soon as the young man appeared at the door.

At once they burst into a choral song, ragged and powerful:

Salvete candidi hospites
Conviviumque sospites,
Quod apparatu divite
Hospes paravit, sumite.

Beanus iste sordidus
Spectandus altis cornibus,
Ut sit novus scholastichus,
Providerit de sumtibus.

Mos est cibus magnatibus . . .

Feeling lost amidst this seditious rabble, I went up to Simonis. I noticed at that moment that he had hung a gut string from his belt, like the ones used to play lutes, guitars or theorbos.

"It's a song to welcome the novice, telling him that they will make a real student out of him," he explained, shouting into my ear so that I could hear him over his friends' drunken voices.

"What does Beano mean?" I asked Simonis.

"Italian, I speak your language too!" butted in a tall, paunchy student, with large bright eyes, an affable face, round ruddy cheeks, and the thick dark hair of Eastern peoples.

"This is Hristo Hristov Hadji-Tànjov," said Simonis. "He's from Bulgaria, but he studied for a long time in Bologna."

"Well yes, I quenched my thirst for knowledge by imbibing at the *Alma Mater Studiorum* of Bologna," he confirmed, raising his tankard.

"Now he's gone on to another kind of thirst," joked another, gesturing at Hristo's tankard. This was a lanky fellow with shoulders like a wardrobe, who introduced himself as Jan Janitzki Count Opalinski, a Pole. "Before that he was thirsty for my sister Ida, who's a dancer."

"Shut up, you drunkard. The Beano, whom others call Bacchant," explained Hristo, after draining his beer, "is not yet a student, and so not a man either. He has asked to be admitted to the university, but his nature is still bestial, like that of a pig, a cow or a donkey. He has to show he can rise above animal passions. He's admitted into the human consortium only if he can pass the Deposition test."

"The Deposition?"

"The *depositio cornuum*," interposed another, a boy with a flowing mane of corvine hair, a fine moustache and two sharp nut-brown eyes. "This evening he'll remove his animal horns and will finally become a human being!"

"This brilliant explanation has just been given to you by a dear friend of mine," Simonis announced. "Let me introduce Baron Koloman Szupán. He comes from Varaždin, in Hungary, and has a large farm with over eighteen thousand pigs."

"Yes, and I've got eighty thousand," mocked a plump, half-bald fellow, who was introduced to me as Prince Dragomir Populescu, from Romania. "Koloman has the same name as Saint Koloman, the patron of students, but blasphemes him with his lies, and he's as much a baron as I'm the pope. Gypsy-baron, that's what he is, ha ha! If he really has eighteen thousand pigs, as he tells us, why has he never brought us a ham?"

The group of friends burst into loud laughter, but Koloman did not give up: "And what about you, Populescu, who claim to be a prince only when you're on the prowl for women?"

"Don't get worked up, Dragomir, keep calm," muttered Populescu to himself, flushing with rage and looking upwards.

"Worked up? You're as drunk as a donkey!" interjected Hristo, the Bulgarian.

"And you're a sponge in a beer barrel," retorted a good-looking man with the air of one who enjoys life, who was introduced to me as Count Dànilo Danilovitsch and who came from Pontevedro, a little state I had never heard of.

"Sorry, but how come you all speak my language so well?" I asked in wonder.

"It's obvious: we've all studied in Bologna!" answered Hristo, "and some of us in Venice as well."

"Ah, for a night in Venice!" said Opalinski wistfully.

"Ah yes, and the Italian ... women, women, women!" sighed Dànilo Danilovitsch, winking.

"The Italian women ... Don't get worked up, Dragomir!" stuttered Populescu, with dreamy eyes.

"Then came that freezing winter, two years ago, along with the war and the famine," Hristo continued, "and we all came here."

"And we've not regretted it!" Koloman concluded. "O Austria! Excellent land, irrigated with running waters, planted with vineyards, teeming with fruits and fish, and abounding in timber! And you, O mighty Danube, mightiest river in Europe, nobly born among the Swabians of the Black Forest, you make your powerful way through Bavaria, Austria, Hungary, vigorously cleave through Serbia and Bulgaria, and emerge with sixty broad arms into the Black Sea, and with your sublime waters bring grace to many superb cities, none of which is richer, more populous or more comely than Vienna!"

This was greeted with applause and, of course, a toast, which was followed by several more. From the talk and the familiar tones the students used in addressing one another, it was clear that they were all a group of comrades, accustomed to mixing beer and chatter, gross pranks and the gay *joie de vivre* of twenty-year-olds. God only knew what these fun-lovers had got up to in Bologna and Vienna. But observing the gusto with which they knocked back their beer and engaged in jokes and tricks, passing themselves off as counts, barons and even princes, I doubted that they had ever achieved anything sensible. And if one looked carefully under their Roman togas at their clothes and shoes, they all had the same blackened collars, the same patches, the same holes in their shoes. Like my assistant, they were simply *Bettelstudenten*, cheerful penniless time-wasters, much more skilled in the art of getting by than in the doctrines of science.

"Pleasant companions you have, Simonis," I said.

"You're very kind, Signor Master. Some of them come from great distances, beyond the borders of the Empire, from *Halb'Asien*, 'Half-Asia'," the Greek whispered to me, as if to excuse them.

"Half-Asia?" I repeated, not understanding.

"Oh, that's my own definition of some of the lands east of Vienna, beyond Silesia and the Carpathians, like Pontevedro, for example; lands set between cultivated Europe and the squalid steppes traversed by nomads, and I don't mean only geographically ..." answered Simonis, laying heavy emphasis on the last words.

"They all seem normal boys, just like you," I answered, still not understanding.

"Don't be fooled by appearances, Signor Master. I'm Greek," he affirmed with pride. "Some of them are divided from our Europe not

only by language and borders. The broad plains and gentle hills of
their native lands, which extend as I said beyond Silesia, beyond the
Carpathians, not only look like the landscape of the lands of the
Urals or deepest Central Asia. The similarity with those worlds so
different from our own goes much deeper."

I had no idea what the Urals or Central Asia were like, and
not having grasped the sense of these unexpected words, I kept
quiet.

The comradely atmosphere encouraged me to change the subject
and ask Simonis another question.

"Why did they all call you Barber when you arrived?"

"Now you'll see, Signor Master."

"𝕾𝖎𝖑𝖊𝖓𝖈𝖊, 𝖋𝖗𝖎𝖊𝖓𝖉𝖘!"

This command, shouted by one of the students accompanying
the Beano, hushed the whole assembly. The Greek climbed onto the
wooden platform. The Beano was escorted towards him, and he
announced in a severe voice:

"𝕻𝖗𝖊𝖛𝖎𝖔𝖚𝖘𝖑𝖞 𝖞𝖔𝖚 𝖜𝖊𝖗𝖊 𝖆 𝖇𝖊𝖎𝖓𝖌 𝖜𝖎𝖙𝖍𝖔𝖚𝖙 𝖗𝖊𝖆𝖘𝖔𝖓, 𝖆𝖓 𝖆𝖓𝖎𝖒𝖆𝖑, 𝖆𝖓 𝖚𝖓𝖈𝖑𝖊𝖆𝖓 𝖘𝖈𝖍𝖔𝖔𝖑-𝖋𝖔𝖝;
𝖓𝖔𝖜 𝖞𝖔𝖚 𝖜𝖎𝖑𝖑 𝖇𝖊𝖈𝖔𝖒𝖊 𝖆 𝖒𝖆𝖓. 𝖄𝖔𝖚𝖗 𝖋𝖎𝖑𝖙𝖍𝖞 𝖙𝖚𝖘𝖐𝖘 𝖕𝖗𝖊𝖛𝖊𝖓𝖙𝖊𝖉 𝖞𝖔𝖚 𝖋𝖗𝖔𝖒 𝖊𝖆𝖙𝖎𝖓𝖌 𝖆𝖓𝖉 𝖉𝖗𝖎𝖓𝖐𝖎𝖓𝖌
𝖒𝖔𝖉𝖊𝖗𝖆𝖙𝖊𝖑𝖞, 𝖔𝖇𝖘𝖈𝖚𝖗𝖎𝖓𝖌 𝖞𝖔𝖚𝖗 𝖎𝖓𝖙𝖊𝖑𝖑𝖊𝖈𝖙. 𝕹𝖔𝖜 𝖞𝖔𝖚 𝖜𝖎𝖑𝖑 𝖇𝖊 𝖑𝖊𝖉 𝖇𝖆𝖈𝖐 𝖙𝖔 𝖗𝖊𝖆𝖘𝖔𝖓."

"Simonis is playing the part of the Deposer this evening," whispered Koloman to me with his sing-song Hungarian accent, "the one
who leads the ceremony. He compared the Beano to a fox because
it hides in holes in the ground like schoolchildren who huddle
together among the school desks. That's why the Deposition is
also called the Baptism of the Fox. To become men we have to come
out into the open, seeking knowledge by going to university and
forgetting the world of vice and its distractions. This evening's
Beano chose his Barber himself; he's often heard about him
and admires him. He's sure to benefit from many of Simonis's
virtues."

That may be, I thought, but the whole merry mob of students
looked as if the last thing they were seeking was virtue and knowledge. Meanwhile they passed Simonis an object wrapped in a piece
of cloth. It was a piece of black fat, with which he began to paint a
fine pair of moustaches and a beard on the Beano's face. Applause
and laughter broke out, while the Beano endured it all in silence.
Simonis immediately began a short speech in German, in which the
poor Beano was exhorted to abandon his dissolute life, to turn from

vice to virtue and to abandon the darkness of ignorance by means of study.

"Now comes the Latin exam," whispered the Hungarian Koloman Szupán into my ears with a snigger.

The Beano was asked to decline the noun *cor*, which in Latin means "heart". He began to decline it correctly – nominative, genitive, dative and so on – all in the singular.

"*Cor, cordis, cordis, cor, corde, cor,*" said the Beano, spluttering awkwardly on account of the boar tusks that obstructed his mouth.

"*Numerus pluralis,*" pressed Simonis, ordering him to decline the plural.

"*Corda, cordarum, cordis . . .* ow!"

As soon as the poor Beano pronounced *corda*, which in Latin means "hearts" but also "rope", Simonis had begun to lash him with the gut string that I had seen earlier.

"𝕾𝔬 𝔪𝔞𝔶 𝔶𝔬𝔲𝔯 𝔅𝔢𝔞𝔫𝔬 𝔴𝔥𝔦𝔪𝔰 𝔞𝔫𝔡 𝔶𝔬𝔲𝔯 𝔬𝔩𝔡 𝔦𝔪𝔭𝔬𝔯𝔱𝔲𝔫𝔞𝔱𝔢 𝔫𝔞𝔱𝔲𝔯𝔢 𝔭𝔢𝔯𝔦𝔰𝔥!" he thundered as he lashed the poor wretch, who tried to cover his face and neck with his arms.

The spectators were shaking with laughter, clapping and raising their tankards to the ceiling.

Further questions and answers ensued, with crude puns that inevitably led to more whippings, and yet more guffawing from the assembly. Then they put the candidate's musical abilities to the test, forcing him to sing a students' song, which he spluttered and stammered as best he could through his boar tusks, leading to more whippings and jeering whistles.

The Beano was made to lie on the floor. Some of the students began to comb his hair cruelly, using a rough wooden brush, while others tried to force an enormous spoon into his ears, as if to clean them.

"𝔄𝔫𝔡 𝔰𝔬 𝔴𝔦𝔩𝔩 𝔶𝔬𝔲 𝔰𝔥𝔲𝔫 𝔞𝔩𝔩 𝔣𝔬𝔲𝔩𝔫𝔢𝔰𝔰 𝔞𝔩𝔬𝔫𝔤 𝔴𝔦𝔱𝔥 𝔥𝔞𝔲𝔤𝔥𝔱𝔦𝔫𝔢𝔰𝔰, 𝔞𝔫𝔡 𝔨𝔢𝔢𝔭 𝔶𝔬𝔲𝔯 𝔢𝔞𝔯𝔰 𝔢𝔳𝔢𝔯 𝔬𝔭𝔢𝔫 𝔱𝔬 𝔱𝔥𝔢 𝔳𝔦𝔯𝔱𝔲𝔢𝔰 𝔬𝔣 𝔚𝔦𝔰𝔡𝔬𝔪," recited Simonis emphatically in his role as Deposer, "𝔴𝔥𝔦𝔩𝔢 𝔶𝔬𝔲 𝔣𝔯𝔢𝔢 𝔶𝔬𝔲𝔯𝔰𝔢𝔩𝔣 𝔣𝔯𝔬𝔪 𝔱𝔥𝔢 𝔣𝔦𝔩𝔱𝔥𝔶 𝔰𝔬𝔲𝔫𝔡 𝔬𝔣 𝔞𝔩𝔩 𝔦𝔡𝔦𝔬𝔠𝔶 𝔞𝔫𝔡 𝔪𝔞𝔩𝔦𝔠𝔢."

From somewhere a carpenter's plane, a hammer and a drill were produced. Three hulking brutes leaped onto the poor examinee's back, still sore from the brushing he had just been given, and began to hammer him, plane him and drill him, first on the back and then on the stomach. I prayed that it would not end in blood.

"𝕬𝖓𝖉 𝖘𝖔 𝖒𝖆𝖞 𝕬𝖗𝖙 𝖆𝖓𝖉 𝕾𝖈𝖎𝖊𝖓𝖈𝖊 𝖋𝖔𝖗𝖌𝖊 𝖆𝖓𝖉 𝖒𝖔𝖚𝖑𝖉 𝖞𝖔𝖚𝖗 𝖇𝖔𝖉𝖞," recited Simonis solemnly while the rest of the band fell about laughing.

They made the victim stand up. They set a large bowl of water in front of him and made him soap his head, wash and dry himself with a shred of wool, swearing that he would pass to a new and more virtuous life.

But his sufferings were not over yet. Now they placed him on a chair and removed his enormous boar's fangs, tearing them from him like the most brutal of tooth-wrenchers.

"𝕬𝖓𝖉 𝖘𝖔 𝖒𝖆𝖞 𝖞𝖔𝖚𝖗 𝖜𝖔𝖗𝖉𝖘 𝖓𝖊𝖛𝖊𝖗 𝖇𝖊 𝖙𝖔𝖔 𝖒𝖔𝖗𝖉𝖆𝖓𝖙," pronounced the Deposer.

Meanwhile two students were cleaning the Beano's nails with a rough file. This, it was explained to me, was so that he should always steer clear of weapons and duels, and his fingers only consult books and manuscripts. The file was so primitive that it was really the Beano's fingertips that were being filed, causing him to beg feebly for mercy. Then they shaved the beard that had been painted on him at the beginning, but instead of soap, razor and a towel they used a brick, a piece of wood and an old canvas rag, so that at the end of the operation the poor wretch's face looked as if it had been ploughed. They then made him sit at a table and set dice and paper in front of him, to see if his immediate reaction revealed a natural propensity for the vice of gambling. The poor boy did not even move, battered as he was. They set a music book in front of him, inviting him, whenever tired from excessive study, to lighten the burden of his spirit with the art of sounds, and with nothing else. Finally the Beano was made to take off his hat with its ass's ears and horns. With a pair of old shears Simonis, performing the functions of Barber, trimmed his hair, leaving the Beano with nothing but a few scrawny, spinach-like tufts. Then they shoved his hat on again.

At that moment an elderly individual entered the room, stiff and measured in his gait, arousing an immediate murmur of deferential attention.

"It's the Dean of Philosophy," explained Koloman Szupán.

"The Dean? A professor?" I said in surprise.

"Of course! It's always the most senior professor of the Faculty of Philosophy that confers the Certificate of Deposition."

"It's an official act: if he doesn't pass the Deposition exam, the *Alma Mater Rudolphina* cannot accept the Beano," added Hristo.

Simonis came forward and gave a rapid account to the Dean of how the exam had gone and asked that the candidate should be awarded the Certificate. The Beano rose respectfully to his feet, swaying a little.

The Dean gave a slight nod, recited a few Latin formulas and gave the Beano some paternal advice. The young man was brought a glass full of dark liquid, which he drained at once, and a small pot containing white powder, which was sprinkled on his bare head, causing him to whimper in pain.

"Wine and salt," explained Hristo the Bulgarian. "They serve to flavour the Beano's words and actions with doctrine and wisdom, and to make him receptive to advice, corrections and warnings."

At this point it was a miracle the Beano was still alive. Goaded by his torturers he found the strength to recite to Simonis, in a faint voice, the ritual formula that concluded the ceremony.

"*Accipe Depositor pro munere numera grata, et sic quaeso mei sis maneasqe memor.*"

While the Deposer and the Beano embraced amid renewed applause, some of them took the hat with horns from the examinee's head and symbolically placed it on the ground: the Deposition was over. His black cloak was removed as well, and his face was finally degreased with a clean handkerchief. Amid the outburst of shouting and exultation that followed I was just able to hear Hristo's explanation.

"Now the Beano has become a Pennal. He's not a real student yet but soon will be. The Deposer from now on is his Barber."

"What does that mean?"

"If the Barber is hungry, the Pennal will fetch him something to eat. If he's thirsty, he'll get him a drink. If he's sleepy, he'll help him sleep. Whatever the Barber asks, the Pennal gives him."

I did not dare ask any further; the answer made me suspect that the poor aspiring student, despite having risen in rank, was in for a good deal more suffering and humiliation. Meanwhile a mob of spectators clustered around the neophyte, Simonis and the Dean, dispensing compliments and witty remarks.

"And when will he become a real student?"

"Oh, quite soon. The waiting time is defined by the university rules: from this evening it'll be one year, six months, six weeks, six days, six hours and six minutes."

A few moments later I was finally able to approach the poor wretch who had gone through the whole absurd performance. He was a skinny boy, whose face was contracted in a bewildered, defensive smile. A pair of glasses, with lenses steamed up by the heat of the room, concealed two round eyes, which flickered sharply, only momentarily confused by the festive hubbub to which he had been subjected. But it was only when I saw him walking that I noticed his most obvious feature: he was crippled.

Just at that moment I was distracted by the noise as the students bade farewell to the man who had honoured the Deposition with the solemnity of his presence, and who was now preparing to leave.

"Was that really the Rector?" I asked Hristo, who had come back to my side.

"Yes, of course. We're not at the philosophy faculty of Bologna! In Vienna everything is more familiar."

"What he means by 'familiar'," intervened Dragomir Populescu, taking Hristo under the arm, "is that here the university is in no better shape than this son of a bitch's family, ha ha!"

"Shut up, you old perverts, your brains are befuddled by wanking as usual," interrupted Koloman Szupán. "I'm explaining to our friend how things work in Vienna."

The university of the Caesarean city had been founded by the illustrious Emperor Rudolph IV, in the year of grace 1365; hence its name, *Alma Mater Rudolphina*. It was in the glorious early days of universities; Paris and Bologna were flooded by students eager for knowledge, ready to make any sacrifice to hear the lessons of the great scholars who taught there.

The *Alma Mater Rudophina* was no less important: such great, divinely inspired minds as Henry of Hessia, Nikolaus von Dinkelsbühl and Thomas Hasselbach (whom some accused of having for over twenty years commented on the first chapter of Isaiah without ever having understood it) had taught there.

Unfortunately, halfway through the sixteenth century, a period of decadence had set in throughout Europe: as a consequence of the Protestant schism, the favourite activity of universities was to form teams for or against the Church of Rome and to bash each other with nit-picking theological treatises.

"On Luther's side," Koloman enumerated, "if I remember rightly, there were the prestigious universities of Altdorf in Franconia, Erfurt and Jena in Thuringia, Giessen and Rinteln in Hessia, Gripswalde in Pomerania, Halle in the Duchy of Magdeburg, Helmstadt in Brunswick, Kiel in Holstein, Königsberg in Prussia, Leipzig in Meissen, Rostock in Mecklenburg."

"You've left out Strasburg in Alsatia, Tubingen in Württenberg and Wittenburg in Saxony, animal," criticised Populescu.

"And also Loden and Uppsala in Sweden, and Copenhagen in Denmark," added Hristo.

"You're as pedantic as two frigid spinsters," answered Koloman, stealing a half-empty tankard of beer from a nearby table and lifting it greedily to his lips.

"With Calvin," Koloman went on, "were Duisburg, Frankfurt on the Oder; Heidelberg in the Palatinate; Marburg in Hessia; Cantabrigum and Oxfurth in England; Douai, Leiden and Utrecht in Holland; Franeker and Groningen in Friesland; and in Switzerland, Basel."

"You've left out Dole in Burgundy, animal," said Populescu.

"For the Pope, as I was saying, the only ones still faithful were a handful of universities in Germany: Breslau in Silesia, Cologne on the Rhine, Dillingen in Swabia, Freiburg in Breisgau, Ingolstadt in Bavaria, Mainz on the Rhine, Molzheim, Paderborn, Würzburg in Franconia. But in France there were Aquae Sextiae, Anjou, Avignon, Bordeaux, Bourges, Cadruciensis, Caen, Cahors, Grenoble, Montpellier, Nantes, Orleans, Paris, Poitiers, Reims, Saumur, Toulouse, Valence. In Portugal Coimbra; in Spain, Complutum, Granada, Seville, Salamanca and Taraco; in Italy Bologna, Ferrara, Florence, Naples, Padua, Pavia, Perugia, Pisa."

"You've forgotten Krakow in Poland."

"And Prague in Bohemia."

"And Leuven in Brabant," added Hristo.

"I omitted it out of pity, because in Leuven they're impotent bigots like you two. My poor spinsters, your flaming twats have made you acid," answered Koloman, grasping Populescu, pulling out his trouser belt and pouring the rest of his beer into his codpiece. A savage brawl broke out among the three of them, which soon died down as they were all laughing too much to fight.

In the days of the religious disputes, continued Koloman as soon as the three had returned to a semblance of restraint, Vienna was no longer listed among the seats of universal wisdom. The Caesarean city had to fight other enemies: the constant threat of the plague, the Turkish danger forever at their gates and above all the chronic penury of the public coffers, which was reflected in the niggardly endowments of the university. The professors were paid late, sometimes not for months, and with letters of exchange rather than cash. The best teachers had begun to abandon the Viennese university, their places being taken by mediocre or even third-rate colleagues. These latter did not even use the title of professor, and often had never even earned it, but were simple *doctores*. The continual to and fro of teachers, always on the lookout for a more tempting post, year after year had ended up throwing the whole system into chaos. The courses were watered down, the textbooks grew shoddier by the year and everywhere knowledge was considered worthless. During the Thirty Years' War, which about half a century earlier had brought the whole continent to its knees, the culture and good behaviour of the students had suffered too. In 1648 the heir to the throne, Ferdinand, son of Emperor Ferdinand III and child prodigy, had decided to give a good example by matriculating at the *Alma Mater Rudolphina*: and so, at the age of just fifteen, he became the first Habsburg to enrol at the university. But it did not last long: six years later Ferdinand was to die suddenly of smallpox, leaving the throne to his younger brother, Emperor Leopold, who was much less gifted than him. And so the students soon went back to their coarse, shameless ways, abandoning themselves to revels and dissipation rather than the pursuit of doctrine and intellect. Fights and duels were the order of the day; showing no fear of God the young scholars smashed up inns, manhandled guards, attacked and robbed harmless passers-by – and, of course, persecuted Jews. The university and its members nonetheless preserved many of the privileges that the Empire had granted them from time immemorial, and so students who had been found guilty of murder and other grave crimes would be pardoned, or would easily manage to escape trial. Even in peaceful Vienna, it was not unusual to stumble across the corpses of students.

They had learned little from the good example given ten years earlier by Emperor Joseph I himself, who – no less gifted in intelligence and learning than his predecessor Ferdinand, his father's brother – had chosen to matriculate at the *Alma Mater Rudolphina*.

There was only thing that counted at the university of the Caesarean capital: pleasure.

"When we organise the Depositions and other feasts, everything works perfectly. The Rector always comes and respects all the ancient traditions," concluded Koloman, now completely drunk. "He's a great man, the Rector, honest, sincere and upright."

"You've forgotten that he's very likeable," Populescu butted in, raising his tankard for the umpteenth time.

"And that he's a jolly good fellow," concluded Hristo, failing to stifle a fine hops-scented burp.

Day the Third
SATURDAY, 11TH APRIL 1711

✠

7 of the clock: the Bell of the Turks, also called the Peal of the Oration, rings.

Headache, shaky limbs, muddy mouth. The riotous night spent with the students had robbed me of those lively forces so essential for a fresh start to the day.

The bizarre ceremony of the Deposition had finished around two o'clock. When I got back to Porta Coeli (of course I had a copy of the keys to the gate) I was in a state of feverish excitement, which kept me awake almost till dawn. Yielding to the friendly insistence of Simonis's friends, during the ceremony I had ended up accepting a tankard of good beer myself, which had been followed by a second, and then a third. To avoid the effects of the carousal, Simonis and his study companions had each knocked back a glass of vinegar and had wrapped a cloth soaked in freezing water around their pudenda. Infallible remedies, they claimed, but I had not been persuaded. And I had been wrong: although I had avoided total inebriation, I woke up with all its symptoms.

When I opened my eyes, roused by the Bell of the Turks, Cloridia was already at work in Prince Eugene's palace. Our little boy must have already gone off to work with Simonis. That morning we had two urgent jobs in the Josephina area, cleaning flues. Simonis and my son would be there on the spot already, waiting for me with all the tools. The idea was that I would work with them for a while and then let them finish on their own, while I went to see the work that was being done at our own house, situated not far away, as the master-builder had been wanting to consult me about it for a few days now. However, it was not too late, and after saying my prayers there was still plenty of time for me to have breakfast.

As usual my consort had left a little bread and jam near the bed, and something interesting to read. Whereas in Rome hearing or reading the news (always full of murders and acts of violence) would leave me feeling anguished and dismayed, in Vienna I often enjoyed leafing through the gazettes, and it was also highly recommended by Ollendorf, our German teacher, as a way to fill those deplorable gaps in my learning.

Unfortunately (for him), in Vienna there were only two gazettes, and the older of the two was Italian. To be precise, it was *written* in Italian. As I have already had occasion to mention, it was called *Corriere Ordinario*. It came out every four days from van Ghelen, the Italian court printer, and had been founded by Italians about forty years earlier. It was of little use for the purposes intended by Ollendorf, but much more enjoyable to read.

I thought back to the evening spent with the students, in which I had spoken Italian almost the whole time. Simonis's friends had all studied in Italy – in Bologna and in Venice – and they still felt nostalgic for those days. To feel really at home, I said to myself joyfully, in Vienna you just had to speak Italian. Glowing with pride in my origins I picked up the *Corriere Ordinario*.

As I idly leafed through it, I thought how hard life must have been for Abbot Melani in Paris. I knew from his stories, and from the *vox populi*, that in France the Italians had almost always been despised, hated and persecuted. The famous Concino Concini, Louis XIII's Italian favourite, had been executed after his removal from office, after which the Parisians had taken his corpse, cut it into pieces and eaten it. Then along had come Cardinal Mazzarino (or Mazarin), a truly Italian schemer, who had imported our country's music and theatre into Paris. The excessive power he had accumulated, and the arbitrary way he had used it, had made him unpopular with everyone. During the Fronde, Italian artists had been subjected to all kinds of cruelties: Jacopo Torelli, the stage designer of *Orfeo*, had almost been lynched by the mob, despite having Frenchified his surname into Torel, while Atto himself and his master Luigi Rossi had had to flee Paris. After the Cardinal's death, the Italian musicians had been packed off back to Italy. Having driven them out, the French had been very happy to replace them with their own Jean-Baptiste Lully (forgetting that his real name was Giovan Battista Lulli, and he was from Florence). So just what would the French say if they ever saw Vienna?

The Italians here were not only numerous, well respected and influential. In Vienna, quite simply, it was like *being* in Italy.

Ever since my arrival I had been very pleased to discover that the corporation I belonged to, the chimney-sweeps, was in the hands of my fellow countrymen. But that was only the start of it. Everything, every corner, every living being that did not belong to the vulgar mass, seemed to speak my language. Among Viennese gentlemen one conversed, dressed, courted, handled money, preached, planned, wrote and read in Italian. Letters were dictated, goods bought and sold, friendships made, loves and hatreds formed using the idiom of Dante and Petrarch. We Italians were admired, much sought after, and, if not loved, certainly respected. At court our tongue was actually the official language.

As I meditated along these lines, taking a complacent pride in my origins, at the foot of the bed I spotted the German-Italian phrase book that Atto Melani had given me. It had been printed in Vienna, but its author, the tutor of the imperial family Stefano Barnabè, was an Italian friar. Even the works in German by the court preacher, the barefoot Augustinian Abraham from Sancta Clara, were printed by the *Italianissimo* typographer Viviani. We had St Francis, Dante and Columbus, the discoverer of America; we were a people of saints, poets and navigators. Why be surprised that Vienna's first newspaper was also our work? I began reading.

The first correspondence was from Lisbon, and reported tumults in the Kingdom of Portugal. Despite the war, the news had arrived quite quickly: the article was dated 23rd February, just a month and a half ago. It was followed by a report on the meetings of the parliament in London and news on the war from Saragossa in Spain, where Joseph I's brother, Charles, was competing for the throne with the French Philip of Anjou, the grandson of Louis XIV. I skipped to the second page where, after leaving aside sad military news from Aslan in Crimea and Danzig, I at last found something interesting:

Tuesday 7th April, third feast of Easter. The most August Sovereigns with the Serene Archduchesses their Daughters, and the customary entourage proceeded after luncheon to visit the Church of the Barefoot Carmelite Fathers in the suburb of the Island of St Leopold; and there they attended the Vespers and Litanies.

The Turkish Agha having arrived here on the same day with a retinue of about 20 Persons, he was provided with lodgings in the aforesaid Suburb of St Leopold on the Bank of the closest Branch of the Danube; and the day before yesterday at midday he had an audience with the

> *Serene Prince Eugene of Savoy, who to this end had sent a 4-horse*
> *Carriage for six . . .*

There followed a description of the audience, up to the leavetaking between Eugene and the Agha. All this was well known to me since I had either been present myself or had heard Cloridia's account of it. The anonymous chronicler provided just one new detail:

> *And now it is said that the aforementioned Most Serene Prince Eugene*
> *is preparing to leave for the Low Countries, to initiate the operations of*
> *the Campaign against France.*

As I have had occasion to say, it was well known that Prince Eugene was longing to leave for the front again. Now it seemed that having received the Agha with all honours he had decided it was time to set off.

There followed some reports from Madrid on the appointment of major generals and brigadiers, and then lesser news from Paris and the Low Countries.

While I put the *Corriere Ordinario* back on the ground, another bundle of papers slipped from its inner pages. Cloridia had been concerned about my German, and had also bought the *Wiennerisches Diarium*, or the Diary of Vienna, the city gazette in German which every three days or so reported the latest events. It was, essentially, the paper the good Ollendorf wanted me to read. Like the *Corriere Ordinario*, the Diary of Vienna was today's issue; Cloridia must have bought it as usual at Rothes Igel, the little palace of the Red Porcupine, in Tuchlauben, or at the Portico de' Tessutari, where the gazette was on sale.

I began to work my way painfully through the first item. Screwing up my eyes and drawing on my scanty resources I managed to make out that on Wednesday, three days earlier, the Emperor had appointed as member of the Secret Council the Count of Schönborn, otherwise known as Hugo Damian, Lord of Reichelsperg and Hepenheim, Count of Wiesenthaidt and Old Biesen. Pleased at having grasped at least the gist of the article, I went on to the second page. Here an account was given of the arrival of the Turkish Agha. Not wishing to attribute too much importance to the dreaded Ottomans, they had compressed the news into just ten lines, while the appointment of Count Schönborn as Secret Councillor took up twenty-five.

There followed various reports from Hungary, from Poland and Russia (the Czar was preparing for war against the Tartars), from

Naples (earthquake in the city of Reggio), from Rome (Cardinal Gozzadini blessed the Bishop of Perugia). I then read news of the war in Spain (the French General Vendôme was withdrawing with 4,000 infantry and 1,500 cavalry towards the Dauphiné) and many other items from every part of Europe. As time was now pressing, I passed quickly to the last pages. Here were bulletins that the Viennese read avidly: the list of people of every rank who had arrived in or departed from Vienna, and that of the new baptisms, weddings and deaths. I myself often enjoyed glancing through this section, looking for names I knew, such as my clients, but today there was no time. I was just about to drop the *Wiennerisches Diarium* onto the floor alongside the *Corriere Ordinario* when my eye fell on the bulletin of new arrivals in the city, and on one name in particular:

> Den 8. April 1711.
>
> Schotten-Thor. Herr von Paratn / komt
> von Stockdorff / log. in seinem Hauß.
> Herr Milan / Kayserl. Post-Maister / komt
> auß Italien / gehet ins Post-Hauß.

My eyes remained glued to the page of the gazette. I cast another glance at the second announcement: *Herr Milan*, "Il Signor Milani" if translated into Italian, "Official of the Imperial Post, coming from Italy, alighted at the Post Station."

"Il Signor Milani." Milani?

It was as if all the bells in the city were sounding the fire alarm. Surprise was mixed with disappointment: after immersing myself for so long in the Italian conquest of Vienna, I had stumbled on this priceless item not in the Italian newspaper but in the Viennese one.

I got dressed at lightning speed, dashed out of the room slamming the door behind me and rushed towards the convent gates. Where was the Post Station? Could it be on the Wollzeile, the Wool Road, as I seemed to remember? I mentally prepared a question for the first passer-by I should encounter, cursing my awkward German: "Excuse, I look for Post Station . . ."

I ran into the street, my breath steaming in the cold morning air, and immediately turned right into the Rauhensteingasse. It may have been the icy breeze but at that moment everything came together in my head: the memory of the previous evening, when we had met a young man talking to a servant outside the convent, the proverb about eagles and crows that I had overheard; and before that the two porters carrying a heavy trunk full of clothes to the convent; the thought that Porta Coeli had a second guest house, round the corner, right on the Rauhensteingasse; the announcement in the *Wiennerisches Diarium*; finally, as I ran headlong into the side road, like a ray of sunlight cutting through the fog, that voice:

". . . and later we'll go and look for the boy."

I smiled at "the boy", something I had not been for a while now, and tripping on the cobbles in my haste, and perhaps also from a sudden whirling dizziness, I found myself staring upwards. Gazing down at me was a pair of curious dark glasses above a large, lead-whitened nose, in a face half concealed by a large green cloak and a black hat. I did not recognise him, but I knew it was he.

By his side, the young man from the previous evening stared at me in surprise.

"I'm . . . I'm here, Signor Abbot," I stammered.

ॐॐ

11 of the clock: luncheon hour for artisans, secretaries, language teachers, priests, servants of commerce, footmen and coach drivers.

The sudden encounter with Abbot Melani was followed by an exchange of warm, brotherly greetings.

"Let me embrace you, boy," he said, patting me on the cheek and running his fingers over every part of my face. "I can't believe I've found you again."

"I can't believe it either, Signor Atto," I answered, quelling my starts of surprise and tears of joy.

Between my first and my second encounter seventeen years had passed, and between the second and this last one another eleven. For a long time I had been sure I would never see him again. But now Atto Melani, prince of spies, secret shadow behind the intrigues of half Europe, but also my irreplaceable leader in life and its adventures, was here in flesh and blood before my eyes.

At each meeting it had been he who had sought me out, and each time from afar, from his own Paris. Eleven years earlier he had surprised me in Rome, emerging from nowhere like a sharply delineated shadow in the July sunlight, as I hoed the gardens of Villa Spada, and he had taken a sly relish in my amazement. Now he had joined me here, in remote Vienna, in the frosty Habsburg spring, where I had been resurrected to new life thanks to his benevolence.

"Tell the truth," he said, masking his emotion with irony, "you were not expecting to see old Abbot Melani round these parts."

"No, Signor Atto, even though I know anything can be expected of you."

After our embraces we had to separate: I explained to the Abbot that my obligations at the Josephina could not be postponed, that duty called me, alas. We would meet up again later that day to pick up the threads of our friendship.

So we fixed a meeting later, near the Cathedral of St Stephen.

Abbot Melani knew all too well what sort of work I was doing in Vienna, since it was he who had procured me the job. However, when we met again a couple of hours later, he could not refrain from raising a handkerchief to his nose as soon as he caught the smell of soot from my chimney-sweep's clothes.

"There's no one nosier than a nun," he then began to grumble. "Let's keep away from Porta Coeli and look for somewhere quiet where we can chat at leisure."

I could tell him just the place. Knowing the Abbot, I had foreseen his request and had already dropped in at the convent to leave a message for Cloridia and Simonis with the address. There was a coffee shop not far away, in Schlossergassl, or Road of the Locksmiths, a place known as the Blue Bottle. It was certainly not a place frequented by the aristocracy, but neither by the rougher elements of the rude populace, and games of cards or dice were forbidden there, being considered pastimes for blasphemers. The middle classes went there, always after lunch; so you would encounter self-important court functionaries, their moustaches still dripping with boar's gravy, or dignified governesses on amorous trysts, if it was too cold to lurk in the thickets of the Prater. One certainly did not go to coffee shops to be in society! Every table, every discreet nook and corner was practically a separate niche, which could be used for meetings with friends, confidants, lovers or for the solitary rite of reading. Nobody talks in coffee shops, everybody whispers; the Viennese know the art of discretion, and you will never find anyone's eyes rudely fixed on you, as so often happens in Rome. The arrival of two or even three people at the next table does not disturb even the most cantankerous lover of solitude. I have been there and can testify: no one knows the true meaning of peacefulness until they have visited a Viennese coffee shop. In any case, at that hour the middle classes had not yet taken luncheon, and so the place was practically deserted.

As soon as we entered, Abbot Melani was recognised as a customer of distinction thanks to his clothes, and when we were seated a pretty girl with olive skin and jet-black hair served us swiftly. It was coffee, but I did not even notice what I was drinking, my spirit was in such turmoil. We were sitting at a table for four. Shielded by his black lenses, Abbot Melani introduced me to the young man in his company: it was his nephew Domenico.

"So, do you feel settled in this city?" he asked with an imperceptible grimace, which, like the ingredients of a successful pudding, mingled formal curiosity, allusive complicity with my new prosperous status, a desire to be thanked for the generous gift he had bestowed on me, plus the secret intention modestly to decline such thanks.

We had just taken off our cloaks and overcoats, and for the first time I was able to observe the man I had been waiting to meet for eleven years. Contrary to his usual preferences in matters of clothing and colours (red and yellow tassels and ribbons everywhere), Abbot Melani was soberly dressed in green and black. Behind the dark lenses that concealed his pupils, a strange novelty on Atto's face, I noticed his drawn features, his sagging skin, and the furrows of time vainly coated with a piteous shroud of white lead. Twenty-eight years earlier in Rome, at the Inn of the Donzello, I had first met the mature Abbot; at Villa Spada there had appeared before me a sprightly old man; now in the Caesarean city he struck me as decrepit. Only the cleft in the middle of his chin was there where I had left it; the rest had yielded to the scythe of time, and if not entirely decayed, it was gently withered, like an old prune or a fallen leaf. Only his eyes, which I remembered as triangular and sharp, escaped my assessment on account of his dark glasses.

I looked at him hesitantly, unfurling a broad smile. My heart was brimming with gratitude and I did not know where to begin.

"Domenico, will you please hang it up," said Atto, handing his walking stick to his nephew.

It was at that moment that I took in the fact that, when we entered the place, I had seen Abbot Melani offer his arm to his nephew in order to avoid tripping on the entrance stairs, and that, once inside, he had let himself be guided step by step so as not to knock against the chairs and tables.

"I have to tell you that thanks to your generosity," I said at last, "and only thanks to that, Signor Atto, we are properly settled."

As I concluded my predictable response, the steed of my thoughts had set off at a gallop: earlier, as we approached the coffee house, had I not seen Atto avoiding obstacles by waving his stick close to the ground, from left to right?

"I'm pleased to hear it. And I hope your children are all well, and your good lady wife," he answered amicably.

"Oh certainly, they're all very well – the little one, whom we brought with us, as well as the two girls, whom we've left in Rome for the moment, but we hope soon . . ." I said, while this new conjecture thrust itself forward. I did not dare ask about it.

"Praise be to heaven, just as I had hoped. And congratulations on the little boy, who had not arrived yet when we last met," he remarked, as amiably as before.

Meanwhile the pretty waitress had come up to offer us the gazettes: she had guessed we were Italian.

"Read the *Corriere Ordinario*, signori! Or the the Diary of Vienna," she said, carefully spelling out the titles of the two newspapers in their respective languages and offering us a copy of each.

Domenico made a gesture of refusal. Atto let out just one heartfelt exclamation. "If only . . ."

It was then that I cast a last dismayed look at his glasses and was sure of it. Atto was blind.

"But forget about your thanks," he added straightaway, turning to me, without my having said a word. "It is I who owe you an explanation."

"Explanation?" I repeated, still distracted by the discovery of his distressing condition.

"You will naturally be wondering how the devil Abbot Melani managed to get into Vienna when there is a war with France, and all French enemies, and even their goods, have been banned from the Empire on account of the war."

"Well, to tell the truth . . . I suspect I know how you managed it."

"Really?"

"It was in the newspaper, Signor Atto. I read it there, in the list of travellers who have arrived in town. It helped that you are Italian.

I realised that you passed yourself off as an intendant of the imperial posts, signing yourself, as you sometimes do, as Milani instead of Melani. I imagine that you made it seem that you had arrived from Italy, using a passport that had been forg–"

"Yes, that's it, very good," he interrupted, breaking me off as I uttered the most compromising word in my whole speech. "I asked the good Chormaisterin of the convent of Porta Coeli not to let a word get out about my arrival here, I wanted to surprise you. But I see that, contrary to your old habits, in Vienna you read the newspapers – or at least the *Wiennerisches Diarium*, which is a very well-informed paper. The Austrians are like that, they love being in the know," he added with a tone that revealed a combination of fear of the enemies of France, admiration for their organisational skills and vexation at their talent for espionage.

"So you too read the column with . . ."

"My dear Domenico, who also knows German," he said, gesturing towards his nephew who continued to remain silent, "sometimes illuminates the darkness into which God has chosen to plunge me," he recited, alluding to the fact that it was now Domenico who served as reader for him.

Atto Melani's arrival in the city really was quite incredible: coming from the enemy city of Paris, he had managed to penetrate the capital of the Empire with impunity. And the border controls were extremely strict! There had always been a rigorous mechanism for checking up on new arrivals and on dangerous individuals: foreigners, spies, saboteurs, bearers of disease, gypsies, beggars, rogues, dissolute characters, gamblers and good-for-nothings. Ever since the Turkish threat had become a constant one, and particularly since the last siege in 1683, Emperor Leopold I, father of the present Caesar, had tightened all controls. There were regular censuses on all those living within the walls, excepting soldiers and their families. Everyone who had anything to do with travellers and visitors was subject to careful checks. Owners of apartments, landlords, hotel-keepers, hosts, coachmen: nobody could transport, host or feed anyone without reporting all data on the person to field-marshals, burgomasters, magistrates, commissioners for streets or districts, security commissions, culminating with the fearful Inquisitorial Commission. Anyone who secretly took in strangers, even for just one night, risked serious trouble, starting with a hefty fine of six imperial *Talleri*. To prevent foreigners from getting through the city gates unchecked, by simply changing from a long-distance carriage into a city wagon, coachmen, postillions and trap-drivers were all subject to checks. And that was not all: to deter hardened offenders, two secret stations were set up for anonymous denunciations against suspicious travellers and their accomplices, one in the Town Hall in Via Wipplinger, the other at Hoher Markt, the High Market.

Despite all this, Abbot Melani had quietly entered Vienna.

"How on earth did you elude all the checks?"

"Simple: they made me sign the *Zettl*, that sheet where they register your details, and I passed through. And I signed in my usual way: I had no intention of changing my name into Milani. I know I sometimes write hastily, but it was they who read it wrongly. In these cases the best strategy is not to hide at all."

"And no one suspected anything?"

"Look at me. Who is going to suspect a blind, 85-year-old Italian, obliged to travel in a litter?"

"But an 85-year-old blind man surely can't be a postal intendant!"

"Yes, he can, if he's retired. Don't you know that here in the Empire you keep your titles until you die?"

Then he began to touch my face, as he had done when we first met, to rediscover with his fingertips what he still preserved in his memory.

"You have been through a good deal, my boy," he remarked, feeling the furrows delved in my forehead and cheeks.

He gripped my hands, still hardened by the calluses and chilblains I had brought from Rome. He said nothing.

"I'm sorry, Signor Abbot," I managed to say without taking my eyes from his face, while all the words of gratitude – and even of ardent filial love for the decrepit old castrato – died in my throat at the sight of those two impenetrable black lenses.

He stopped fingering me, tightening his lips as if to repress a grimace of sadness, at once concealed by the cup of coffee that he raised to his lips and by an affected little gesture as he adjusted his black lenses on his nose.

"You will be wondering why I am here, apart from the pleasure of seeing you again, a pleasure which, at my age and with the serious ailments that trouble me, would not have sufficed to over-rule the doctors. To the very last they tried to prevent me from leaving Paris to face such a long and dangerous journey."

"So . . . you came for some other reason," I said.

"For some other reason, yes. A reason of peace."

And he began to explain while the coffee, sweetened with a touch of perfumed *lokum* (a sort of gelatinous Turkish nectar, which unlike honey does not spoil the taste of beverages), flowed through my stomach and veins and I was finally able to enjoy the warm sensation of having rediscovered the scoundrel, impostor, spy, liar and perhaps even murderer, to whom I owed not only my present prosperity but also a thousand teachings that had lightened my existence, either through my acceptance or – more often – through my rejection of them.

Melani's story began with the events of two years earlier: 1709 and its cruel winter had been dire not only in Italy, as I myself knew all too well, but also in France. It had been the most terrible year of Louis XIV's entire reign. In January all the roads and riverbanks were frozen, sudden deaths were carrying off both the rich and the poor in great numbers. Many of those who ventured forth through the country, on foot or on horseback, died from frostbite. The churches were full of corpses, the King had lost more of his subjects than if he had been defeated in battle. Even the King's confessor, Father La Chaise, had died of cold, on the short journey from Paris to Versailles. Atto himself had stayed shivering in his bed the whole month. The troops were ill-paid and the officers, unless supported by their families, fought unwillingly. The bankers no longer paid in gold coins and ready silver, but in notes from the mint known as currency notes. All letters of exchange and other payments were made with these notes, and by order of the King, if anyone demurred over them, or wanted to change them into gold or silver ("real money and not waste paper!", exclaimed Melani), they were only exchanged for half their nominal value.

In April famine struck. The city was besieged by swarms of poor peasants who were dying of hunger; no one could leave Paris without the risk of being robbed and killed. The people were exhausted, famished and desperate. At the end of the month there was almost a general uprising: in the church of St Roch a pauper, who had been begging in church, was arrested by a group of archers. As the transgressor (even though unarmed) resisted arrest, the archers beat him to death in front of the shocked congregation. The people then rose up and tried to lynch the guards, who only escaped by taking refuge in a nearby house. Meanwhile the flame of revolt had been kindled:

hordes of enraged citizens came to St Roch from all over Paris, and the tumult lasted for hours and hours before being finally quelled.

In May the famine merely multiplied the number of tumults; the only bread available was as black as ink, and cost over a Julius a pound! On market days there was always the danger of the whole city rising up.

In June the city's coffers were exhausted, there was no money except for the war, and yet even the soldiers no longer received any wages and had to get their families to send them money.

When the cold season returned, the frost killed all the olive trees, a vital resource for the south of France, and the fruit trees turned barren. The harvest was wiped out and the storehouses were empty. Corn, which came cheap from eastern and African ports, was continually plundered by enemy fleets, against which France had very few ships. The King had to sell his gold plate for a mere four hundred thousand francs; the richest lords in the kingdom had their silverware melted by the mint. While Paris only ate jet-black bread, in Versailles the King's table was furnished with humble oat-bread. But in the gazettes not a single word was said about all this grinding poverty, thundered Atto; the newspapers contained nothing but barefaced lies and bombast.

"You will have wondered what your dear old Abbot Melani was up to in Paris," he said sadly. "Well, I suffered from hunger, like everyone else."

The Sun King had realised by now that he had to make peace with his Dutch, English, German and Austrian enemies at all costs. But his overtures, addressed to the Dutch by diplomatic paths, were scornfully rejected over and over again.

"No one must know," whispered Atto Melani, leaning towards me, "but even the Marquis of Torcy humbled himself in an attempt to obtain peace."

Torcy, who was considered abroad as the principal minister of France, left Versailles for Amsterdam under a false name and turned up at the palace of the Grand Pensionary of Holland, who learned to his amused surprise that this great enemy was humbly waiting for him in the antechamber to sue for peace. He turned him down. Torcy then made the same request to Prince Eugene, commander of the imperial forces, and to the Duke of Marlborough, leader of the English army. They too turned him down. The French then tried to bribe Marlborough, again without success. The Sun King was finally reduced to the unthinkable: he sent a letter to the governors of his cities and to the whole population, in which he endeavoured to justify his conduct and the terrible war that was bleeding the land dry.

"Really?" I said, amazed at Atto's last words, never having heard anything about the Most Christian King other than how arrogant, scornful, implacable and cruel he was.

"This war has changed many things, boy," answered the Abbot.

"Including the greatest king in the world?" I asked, citing the definition of the Most Christian King that I had heard from Atto thirty years earlier.

"*Le plus grand roi du monde*, the greatest king in the world, yes," he repeated in a tone that was new to me, adding to the sugary tinkle of those words a dose of vinegary scepticism. "Which is the greatest king in the world? The proud Sun or the sober and patient Jove? The bloody barbarous *condottieri* or the best Caesars of the Roman Empire? And in truth, whose mind does not marvel at the contemplation of Caesar's military ardour, Augustus's royal arts, Tiberius's profound and arcane mind, Vespasian's economy, Titus's amiable virtues, Trajan's heroic goodness?" Atto proclaimed heatedly. "Who does not admire Hadrian's various and manifold literature, Antonine's clemency and equity, Marcus Aurelius's wisdom, Pertinax's strict discipline, Septimus Severus's fierce and versatile simulation? What can I say of Diocletian's nobility of spirit, Great Constantine's sublime piety and victorious fortune, Julian's perspicacious spirit, Theodosius's tolerance, religion and parsimony and the many virtues and high prerogatives of the other Roman emperors? It was these virtues that made them eternal in the grateful memory of the human race, certainly not the blood spilled in military campaigns!"

I could not understand what Abbot Melani was leading up to.

"Much could be said to commemorate the majesty of the laws, the gravity of the senate, the splendour of the equestrian order, the magnificence of the public buildings, the riches of their treasury, the valour of the captains, the number of the legions, the maritime armies, the royal tributaries, and Africa, Europe and Asia held under the will of one single man. But if the sovereignty of the Roman Caesars' imperial rule lasted a thousand years it was due less to blood and martial valour than to good sense and the gift of reason, of true freedom and of righteous rules of living bestowed upon the subjugated peoples."

It had certainly not been, I reflected, the policy of the Most Christian King to bestow freedom and righteous rules of living on his conquered peoples: his first concern was to put everything and everyone to fire and the sword. He had even done so in the Palatinate, although it was the birthplace of his sister-in-law. I had never heard Atto Melani lavish such praise on virtues of government so remote from those of his sovereign; indeed, I had always heard him seek to justify the dubious conduct of the French.

"In like fashion was Deioces exalted to the throne of the Medes," continued the Abbot. "Venerated for his rectitude, he was called to settle their differences with fairness. Similarly, Rome, when still unregulated and fierce, called Numa Pompilius from the Sabines as their ruler, his only known merit being the austere and religious severity of his habits. And what other aim did the ancient republic have than the universal peace of its peoples, and the eradication of barbarism and blind brutality, perennial sources of vices, and wasteful ravagers of human concord and civil life? It was thus only fair that an empire founded on reason and on true valour, governed by the rule of honesty, whose aim was peace among its peoples, and in which each member was granted free access to dignities and to honours, should still be universally venerated as legitimate and holy, and its leader be recognised and obsequiously adored as the living oracle of reason and of true valour. The legitimate heir of that ancient Roman Empire is the Holy Roman Empire of the German nation and your Most August Caesar Joseph the First, the Victorious."

"Your words surprise me, Signor Atto, but I cannot but agree with you. The wisdom of the Caesars of the House of Habsburg spared Vienna the insult of the famine that raged throughout Europe," I declared.

"Remember, boy: no praise is more befitting to an Emperor than that of virtue: true nobility is nothing if not virtue ingrained in a family, passed on from father to son," Melani pronounced solemnly. "Without virtue the royal family is destined to perish and with it the whole kingdom. The Habsburgs will sit on the throne of the Hofburg much longer than the lineage of the Most Christian King in France."

I could not believe my ears. Was this the voice of Atto Melani, the faithful servant of His Most Christian Majesty, the secret agent of the crown of France, whom I had always seen blindly serving his king, even at the cost of tarnishing himself with appalling crimes? Now of all times, in the middle of a war?

"The French care for nothing but appearance, and at that they are true masters," he went on. "His Most Christian Majesty has created around himself the grandest, costliest and most magnificent of spectacles. He has outdone every other monarch in the splendour of his court, and the trumpets of glory and fame have sounded for him every day. His cannons have pounded half Europe, his money has corrupted every foreign minister. The tentacles of France have extended everywhere, but to what end? Now its body is like a beached octopus: empty, flaccid and rotten."

He adjusted his black glasses on his nose, as if to insert a pause that his impatience barely accepted.

"How much has all that glory cost France? How many peasants have died of hunger to pay for their king's cannons and ballets? In France they waste as much as 250 thousand silver scudi on the court, a third of the state's budget, while in Austria they spend less than 50 thousand. They drove my friend Fouquet from the ministry of finance and slandered him; but it was only then that the public finances truly collapsed, with the court now spending three times as much as it did in the days of Louis XIII, and the kingdom in ruins! So who is the thief?"

He fell silent and wiped a bead of sweat from above his lips. Then he replaced the handkerchief in his pocket with hasty annoyance.

"Ah, my dear! I wish I could roll up the surface of the world like a carpet and drag the adversities of Paris right here, before your eyes. Then you would see it all for yourself: people dying of hunger, desperate citizens, bakeries assaulted for a crust of bread, riots brutally crushed. You would see families selling their meagre possessions to survive, war widows prostituting themselves for their family's sake, children begging in the streets, newborn babies dying of cold. Is this glory? Everything is falling apart in Louis's kingdom. The Horsemen of the Apocalypse are four in number, but only one, the white steed of War, is galloping at such speed. One day you will come and see me in Paris, at Versailles. That is when you will appreciate the greatness of Vienna."

"Of Vienna?"

"The French adore show, and at Versailles everything is show," sighed Atto. "In that false universe, everything revolves around the

Sun King and his radiance. Any mortal being can walk quite undisturbed into the gardens, the royal palace, even the royal apartments: only His Majesty's little room for private meals is private. You can see him take lunch and dinner or attend his morning *levée*, when he wakes up with his breath still rancid from the previous evening's partridges. When he comes out from mass, there are so many people waiting for him you would think you were in some square in Paris. And between the Tuileries and the Louvre there are only supposed to be a few authorised courtiers; instead there's such a crowd of carriages, idle strollers and domestic servants that one might as well be at the fish market. There are so many people bustling around the royal palaces, both inside and outside, and they behave so shamelessly, that in order to reduce the number of thefts in the Royal Chapel the death penalty is supposed to be in force. Wholly absurd, since no one is ever executed. At lunchtime any parasite can worm his way into the rooms, maybe chatting with His Majesty's nephew, and sit down at the table of the great master of the house, or at that of the chamberlain, of the almoner, that of the court preachers or the King's confessors. Amid this drunken bedlam, where idle chat and extravagance have free rein, while you bow in some corridor as the golden salt cellar is carried towards His Majesty's table, you will be surrounded by gossip about lovers and the sodomitic adventures of this or that person. If you are ill, you can let yourself by touched by the King during the *toucher*, when he touches invalids with the same hand that throughout his life has penned orders for invasions and the butchering of entire nations. If you have an important friend, you can take part in the *débotté*, when His Majesty graciously allows his boots to be removed: foolish rituals which he now uses for his own glorification, but which go back centuries, to the days of the Valois. And over these years, while the courtiers have quarrelled among themselves for the most prestigious position, for a higher salary or just out of mutual hatred, and have dared to mock the sovereign who tolerates them, France has been bleeding itself dry with the cost of the war and sinking ever deeper into its present inferno. On the other hand, in Vienna . . ."

"In Vienna?" I repeated again, amazed to hear Atto praising the enemies of France.

"Can you not see with your own eyes? In France it is waste that reigns, and in Austria parsimony. There adultery is the rule for every sovereign, and here faith to one's consort. Only servants enter the Emperor's bedchamber, and not every passing flatterer. He does not have himself portrayed in a chariot crushing all those that resist him, nor does he order operas from that bootlicker Lulli showing himself dressed up as Perseus, slaying dragons and conquering princesses. Instead, Leopold, the father of the present Emperor, had himself portrayed in the act of bowing down before the power of the Lord, thanking Him for removing the plague from Vienna."

In his decrepitude Atto Melani was experiencing the bitter defeat of his king's arrogant and overbearing ideals, and with it the failure of an entire life, his own, spent in the arduous (and all too often humiliating) service of France.

The French who had visited the imperial treasure chamber here in Hofburg, Melani went on, had gone guffawing back to France, to tell the Most Christian King how little – in comparison with the treasures of Versailles – the jewels of the Habsburgs were worth.

"They laugh and say that the gallery and the five cabinets are full of cheap trinkets or little more. Among the paintings there are just a few Correggios that are of any value; the jewel cabinet is ridiculous, apart from one piece, it seems, a large bowl hollowed out of a single emerald, so valuable that only the Emperor is allowed to touch it; not to mention the great clock cabinet, which only has one item in any way special: a mechanical crab, whose movements seem so natural that you can hardly tell it from a real one; the agate cabinet is adequate, with a few fine larger pieces, and some vases of lapis lazuli, while the coin cabinet is incredibly feeble: no coins of value and everything set out haphazardly. And the last cabinet, so they tell me, only contains absurdities like little waxen images and ivory toys, suitable for a child of five!" exclaimed the Abbot with his eyebrows raised in wondering arches.

However, the French, Atto commented, changing tone, would have done well to withhold their contempt, since the frugality of these great Caesars had been entirely to the benefit of their subjects, while in France people were dying of hunger.

"In Vienna there had never been any room for favourites and adventurers like Concini, black souls like Richelieu, profiteers like Mazarin, traitors like Condé, crafty concubines like Madame de Maintenon: in the Caesarean court only the ministers chosen by the Emperor hold posts of command. The great noblemen here have served the imperial house for centuries, they are not treacherous serpents. It is not only the treasure chamber but the whole palace that is modest, and there are half as many servants as in Versailles. Displays of splendour and great palaces are left to the noblemen; the Emperor only needs decorum, tradition and religion. He leaves the government of the regions in the hands of the great families; in exchange they accept his primacy. Here there are no plots, poisonings, luxuries, obscure magic rituals, and all the indecencies that dishonour Versailles, which, if I were to tell you about . . ."

"Yes," I agreed, "you spoke to me about them years ago, as you also told me about the calumnies against Superintendent Fouquet, and the black masses of Montespan, the King's lover . . ."

"Ah, that woman . . . But have I really told you all these things already?"

Melani's memory was beginning to fade. No wonder, now he was well over eighty-five.

"Yes, Signor Atto, both in the Inn of the Donzello and at Villa Spada."

"What a memory. Most fortunate. Whereas I am good for nothing now."

"Uncle, don't talk like that," intervened his nephew Domenico for the first time. "Pay no attention," he said to me. "He likes to complain. Thank God, he is much better than he seems."

"If only the Most Christian King would grant me the freedom to leave Paris! I would go straight back to my home in Tuscany," moaned Atto disconsolately. "I'd be fine, down there, in Pistoia, among my relatives, on my estate at Castel Nuovo. I bought it years ago, and I've never seen it yet. I've even furnished it with a portrait gallery: the King, the Connestabilessa, the two cardinals, the Dauphin and the Dauphine with the King on horseback between them . . . I sent the four small ovals with Galathea that were in the Villa of the Vessel and which Abbot Benedetti bequeathed to me, and I've had them hung at an angle above the four small windows in the gallery. But I have to make do with imagining the effect from my nephews' letters! And if I stay in Paris I'll be reduced to poverty, with no real money but those notes from the mint that are mere waste paper! The city is full of them, 150 million *livres*, they say, because in the rest of the kingdom nobody wants them. They're the work of the devil and the ruin of France; if you change them for Italian money they give you less than half, so that even the slightest outlay for my smallholding costs me a fortune, and I've not even been able to afford iron hoops for my wine barrels . . ." Here Atto sobbed. "I've reached the point of banking on the King's lottery which they play on St John's Day, and begging God to grant me a win that I can spend entirely on Castel Nuovo. But the King will not let me go; he says he's grown up with me, that he cannot do without Abbot Melani, and if I insist he gets angry and sends me away, and each time I make all those awful journeys to Versailles to implore him to let me return to Italy, and they're terrible on my poor old bones . . ."

"Move from Paris to Tuscany? At your age?" I said in amazement.

"What did I tell you?" said his nephew, with a wink. "He took all the hardships of the journey here from France like a twenty-year-old."

"Do not exaggerate, please, Domenico," said the Abbot irritably.

The nephew may have been exaggerating; but the fact remained that the old castrato was sitting calmly in front of me after having travelled across the windy plains, through the snowy mountain passes, over the frozen rivers that separate cold Paris from freezing Vienna. All this without the precious gift of sight and, what was more, after crossing the border under the false name of a modest functionary of the imperial post. To carry off this trick he must have hidden his blindness and given up the privilege of travelling in a litter in addition to a whole series of comforts and luxuries that would have aroused suspicion. The art of lying, I told myself, repressing a smile, would be the last gift to abandon Abbot Melani's weary spirit . . .

Even so I was astonished to hear of his financial problems: Abbot Melani must have made great sacrifices to pay for my post as master chimney-sweep complete with house and vineyard!

"Signor Atto, it must have cost you a fortune to send me here, I really had no idea . . ."

"Forget it, forget it," Melani waved away my concerns. "Let's get back to us. As I mentioned, I'm here on a peace mission. But now let's pay and leave."

He gave a slight circumspect shake of his head as if to indicate that it would be more prudent not to talk here.

"Let's go for a walk," he announced, "and you will listen to what I have to say to you. Only when walking can we be sure there are no unauthorised eavesdroppers."

Domenico summoned the waitress with a nod and she helped Atto get to his feet and put his coat back on. After this she kindly put a good piece of chocolate decorated with marzipan into his hand, and the old Abbot munched it without waiting to be asked twice.

"My compliments, excellent service," Melani praised her, happily leaning on the young woman's soft, delicate arm and backing up his words with a generous tip.

We set off towards St Stephen's and then towards the Street of the Red Tower.

On 11th September 1709, Atto started up again, the tremendous Battle of Malplaquet was fought. The French left eight thousand dead on the field. The allied forces, led by Marlborough and Eugene of Savoy, lost twenty-one thousand, but even so the victory was theirs. Immediately afterwards they besieged and conquered the fortress of Mons, and managed to hold those of Tournai and Lille.

The following year, 1710, began for France with another series of military defeats. The enemy was penetrating into the heart of the kingdom; there was even a second front opening up in the south, where, with the help of the Duke of Savoy, Prince Eugene's cousin and Lord of Piedmont, the enemy forces of Marshal Mercy were threatening to enter. June saw the fall of Douai, Béthune, Aire and Saint-Venant. The allies began to plan a raid as far as Paris. On every front France was defeated. In Spain the French were badly defeated at Saragozza in August. In Germany, France's unfortunate ally, Bavaria, was dismembered by the Emperor and given in fief among his relatives. The electorate of Cologne, another ally of Louis, had already been annihilated. In Hungary the rebel magnates, whom France supported with the aim of wearing down the Empire in the East, were defeated by Joseph I; their leader Rakoczy was broken forever, his party ruined.

The two crowns, as Atto called France and Spain, were in pieces. The Kingdom of France had no money, no army, no food, and was on the verge of total collapse, exposed to the unprecedented incursions of its enemies. The Kingdom of Spain, which Louis XIV had endeavoured against the rest of Europe to keep in the hands of his grandson Philip of Anjou (this was the reason for the war), had also been crushed. Trade had been wiped out, the countryside devastated, the population exhausted or killed, the country split in two by a fratricidal war between the supporters of France and those of its enemies.

"At this point Louis XIV is no longer asking for peace: he is imploring it," stated Atto, as we turned into Wool Street.

The Most Christian King of France had begun new secret negotiations with the enemy powers in the Dutch city of Gertruidenberg, but his envoys were still treated with contempt. The conditions demanded by the allies were deliberately absurd: the Most Christian King should forcibly drive his own grandson Philip from the throne of Spain within two months. And so the war continued. A new hope of peace had come from England: power struggles among ministers and the crown were weakening the party of the Duke of Marlborough and strengthening those who were tired of squandering money on the war and were seeking peace.

"In January, just three months ago," whispered Atto Melani with extreme circumspection, "an unknown priest, a certain Gautier, a secret envoy of the English, presented himself to the Marquis of Torcy offering to negotiate a separate peace. Since then secret negotiations have been opened with the Earl of Oxford and the Secretary of State, St John."

"But didn't you say that the English were negotiating with France along with with the Empire and Holland in that city . . . in Gertruidenberg?"

"Shhh! Do you want everyone to hear?" Atto hushed me. Then he answered almost inaudibly: "The peace talks of Gertruidenberg have failed. Now the English are negotiating unbeknown to the Empire and Holland. Anything is allowable in war, even this. But it won't be much use."

"Why?"

He stopped and turned towards me, as if he could see me.

"Because here in Vienna is the man who is impeding peace. His name is Eugene of Savoy. For his own personal interests he wants to continue the war at all costs, and the Emperor listens to him. But I will convince His Caesarean Majesty to change his mind."

"The Most Serene Prince Eugene is impeding the path to peace?" I exclaimed in surprise.

"What would Eugene of Savoy do if the war were over? He would go back to being what he was before: a half-blood Italian born and raised on French territory, where he was so cruelly mocked and derided that he had to run away, dressed as a woman, no less. He was only accepted here in the Empire because the Austrians, in war, are utter dunces."

I was stupefied. I had heard nothing but panegyrics for Eugene. In Austria he was a genuine national hero, second only to our beloved Emperor Joseph the Victorious. We resumed our walk.

"His lucky day is 11th September: the day his mother was welcomed at the court of Paris, where she would meet her husband. The same day as the Battle of Zenta, in which Eugene won his first great triumph against the Turks. And the same day as the Battle of Malplaquet, in which our hero destroyed the French armies of Marshal Villars."

I could not understand why Atto insisted on talking to me about Eugene of Savoy. It was true that, although he was a hero venerated throughout the Empire, I knew very little about him. I was aware, but only because I had heard it from Atto himself, that his mother was a cruel and wicked woman: Olimpia Mancini, niece of Cardinal Mazarin, who had procured for her a rich marriage with a cadet of the Piedmontese Dukes of Savoy. I well remembered what Atto had told me all those years ago about the perfidious Olimpia: Mazarin's scheming niece had even plotted against her sweet sister Mary, the first love of the Most Christian King, whom I had had the honour of meeting through Atto in Rome eleven years earlier.

I also knew that Eugene had been despised by Louis XIV and for this reason had fled Paris when young. But apart from that I knew very little about the man who was considered in the Empire the greatest general of all time, the inscrutable military genius whose life's mission was war, who was ready to sacrifice all to it.

"Eugene is as indispensable to this cowardly people as a dog to a flock of sheep. Find someone over here, with the exception of Emperor Joseph I, who deserves to be called a soldier! Who drove the Turks from Vienna in 1683?" continued Atto, warming to his subject. "I'll tell you: the great Polish king John Sobieski, the Bavarian Maximilian Emanuel, the French Charles of Lorrain, the Palatine Louis of Baden, the Italian Pope. He was there too, Eugene of Savoy, even though he was only twenty. Everyone, in short, except the master of the house: the late Emperor Leopold . . ."

We were now slowly crossing Carinthia Street, on our way back to the Blue Bottle.

"I know, I know, Signor Atto, you told me when we first met. The Emperor had left Vienna."

"Left? Say rather that he had cut and run in a blue funk . . . but let's get back to ourselves," Atto said. "As I was saying, this wretched war would have been over long ago if Eugene of Savoy were not hindering peace."

It would not even have broken out, I wanted to answer back, if *someone* had not forged the will of the previous king of Spain . . . But that was an old story, and the past cannot be changed.

"Do you really accuse the Most Serene Prince of such base intentions?" I asked. "Do you seriously believe he would put the whole of Europe to fire and the sword and constantly risk his own life just for the sake of personal glory?"

"Dog Nose was born . . . sorry, I mean, Eugene was born in 1663, boy. He's the same age as you: forty-eight. I saw him grow up and believe me, he has no life outside of war. He *is* war. And I can't blame him."

"Why did you call him Dog Nose?"

"Oh, it's just a comic name that his old playmates gave him. Not very well brought-up lads. You see, Eugene's upbringing was, let's say, lacking in some respects," said Atto in a curiously embarrassed tone. "As a boy he fell in with disreputable company, and the military life was the best remedy. At the age of fifteen they had even given him a priest's tonsure, but he was already thinking of becoming a soldier. When His Most Christian Majesty refused to give him charge of a regiment, he fled from France disguised as a woman of the people, to come and realise his dream of war here, in the Empire."

Atto Melani was now talking like a river in spate, but I still could not understand why he persisted in expatiating on Prince Eugene, and my attention was flagging. Instead I was pondering on the latest events: when had he come to Vienna? Two days ago, the 8th, to be precise. And when had the Turkish Agha arrived? The 7th. What a coincidence: just a day apart. Atto Melani, agent in the service of the Most Christian King; the Turks, traditional allies of France. What were the odds? Both coming to Vienna on account of Prince Eugene.

I had known Melani for thirty years. I knew all too well that if something momentous was stirring and Atto was in the neighbourhood, he was bound to have a hand in it. Could the Agha's mysterious embassy have been brought about by some obscure manoeuvre of the Abbot's? I was almost half a century old, as Atto well remembered, and he was eighty-five. It was not so easy to hoodwink me now; I would keep my ears open.

In any case, that was why Atto had "suddenly" remembered his debt to me and had sent me to Vienna . . .

Once again he needed me – poor helpless being that I was, but still affectionate and idealistic – to weave his plots! Benefactor indeed!

I was swaying to and fro, like a felucca adrift, tossed on the currents of contrary feelings. What a generous man Abbot Melani was: instead of vanishing from my life, he had made me prosperous. What a profiteer Abbot Melani was: instead of sending me to Vienna he could perfectly well have given me a piece of land in Tuscany as he had promised! By now my two girls would both be married, instead of waiting on the outcome of my new life in the capital of the Empire. On the other hand, if he had not needed me in Vienna, would he not have left me to rot in Rome in my *tufo* cellar?

Under the weight of these thoughts my expression had grown baleful and my footsteps heavy and circumspect, when Abbot Melani's words at last caught my attention again:

"What nobody remembers is that the Savoys by tradition are great traitors."

"Traitors?" I said with a start.

"They reign over a duchy straddling the Alps, which is not large but extremely important from a strategic point of view. It's the gateway into Italy for the two crowns, the French and the Spanish. And they have shamelessly exploited this, continually switching alliances. How many times in Paris have I been left with no letters from Italy because the Duke of Savoy had suddenly taken it into his head to arrest all the couriers passing through his states! There has never been any way to check these recurring acts of high-handedness, which amount to little more than blackmail, nor to neutralise the family's outrageous acts of treachery."

We had returned to the Blue Bottle. Atto was cold, and wanted to conclude our conversation somewhere warm. We entered and took our seats.

Eugene's great-grandfather, he continued, Duke Charles Emmanuel I of Savoy, in his reign of almost fifty years had managed to switch sides three times. First he had married the daughter of Philip II of Spain; then he had passed over to the French side, hoping they would help him expand his dominions in Italy; then he had gone back to the Spanish side. His son Victor Amadeus I had married a French princess, Christine. When he died, the widow, to keep her power, had to fight not against some foreign power but against her husband's brothers, who treacherously wanted to depose her.

One of these, Thomas Francis, was glorious Eugene's grandfather. He too had married a French princess and seemed hell-bent on defending the Kingdom of France, even settling for a certain period in Paris.

"Then came the usual *volte-face*: he set off for Flanders, entered the service of the Spanish enemy and announced to his relatives that he wished to devote himself heart and soul to the struggle against French power," said Atto, with a mixture of irony and disgust.

Eugene's other direct relatives did not shine for their moral qualities, nor for their physical ones. His uncle Emanuel Philibert, the firstborn and thus the heir to the duchy, was deaf and dumb. His aunt Louise Christine, who had married the Margrave Louis Ferdinand of Baden in Paris, suddenly rebelled against her husband, refusing to follow him to his lands in Germany, on the pretext that in France their only son would receive a better education (her husband, a cousin of Eugene's, responded by simply carrying the child off to his homeland). Eugene's father, finally, was not a traitor and had perfect hearing and speech, but had married Olimpia Mancini, Eugene's mother, a perfidious, scheming woman, suspected of numerous poisonings.

"Splendid lineage, the Savoys and their wives," concluded Atto, "ambitious, traitors, deaf mutes and poisoners."

"I don't understand: how can Prince Eugene have come from such a family?" I asked in bewilderment. "He is known as an upright man, an untiring *condottiero*, and a faithful subject of the Emperor."

"That is what the people say. Because they do not know what I know. And what I know will enable me to stop the war."

He instinctively moved his head, as if he could still look around himself. Then he said to his nephew:

"Domenico, are there any snoopers here?"

"I don't think so, Signor Uncle," answered the young man, after glancing around at the nearby tables and the rest of the coffee house.

"Good. Now listen," he turned back to me. "What I am about to tell you, you must reveal to nobody. No-bo-dy. Clear?"

Although worried by this brusque change in tone I agreed.

Atto pulled from his jacket a piece of paper folded in four, which concealed a letter. He opened it and set it before me. The text was in Italian.

Desiring ardently to testify to Your Majesty my humble devotion and my keen yearning to act in such a manner as to put an end to a conflict that has troubled all Europe so gravely and for such a long time, I consign this present missive to a trusted person so that You might be informed of my offer, and take the decisions that will seem to you most befitting and necessary.

As is common knowledge, Spanish Flanders has for many years been greatly troubled by disputes and wars, and being as it is in need of true and secure leadership we consider that assigning that land to the House of Savoy in our person would be the most potent means to free that land and its people from such dire suffering.

Such a decision would, with immediate and irrevocable effect, lead the war towards settlements closer to the legitimate desires of Your Majesty and of the Most Christian King of France, on account of the gratitude that such a measure would necessarily arouse.

Confirming myself a most humble and devoted servant of Your Majesty, and with the ardent desire to be able to contribute to the re-establishment of peace, as well as to the precious service of Your Majesty,

Eugenio von Savoy

"This obviously is a copy. The original is in the hands of the King of Spain, Philip V, to whom it was addressed," whispered Atto.

He closed the letter and replaced it with great speed in its hiding place, bestowing a complacent little smile on me. Even without seeing me he must have guessed my stupefied and confused expression.

"The matter arose at the beginning of the year," he went on almost inaudibly.

An anonymous officer had gone to the Spanish court in Madrid, over which reigned Philip of Anjou, grandson of the Sun King. The anonymous officer had succeeded in getting the letter delivered to Philip, and had then disappeared. On reading those lines, the young king of Spain had been thunderstruck.

"If I've understood properly," I said, "with this letter Eugene is proposing an agreement. If Spain hands him its possessions in Flanders –"

"You call it an agreement," Atto interrupted me. "The correct name is treachery. Eugene is saying: if Spain promises to award me the hereditary possession and government of its territories in

Flanders, then out of gratitude I will abandon the Empire and its
army. The Emperor, deprived of his valiant commander-in-chief, will
undoubtedly accept an armistice, which France desires intensely,
and the path towards peace negotiations will be open."

I kept silent, bewildered and disturbed by the tremendous revelation. I did not like the turn the conversation was taking.

Philip, continued Atto, had immediately transmitted a copy of
the letter by confidential paths to Versailles, where only two people
had read it: the Sun King and his prime minister Torcy.

"Let me tell you," said Atto, "that I myself have the honour of
reporting to Torcy all the arguments, even secret ones, that foreign
diplomats do not wish to present to His Majesty in official audiences. In short, they still make intensive use of my services at court.
And so His Majesty and Minister Torcy decided to entrust me with
this mission."

"You mean your peace mission?"

"Exactly. The young Catholic King of Spain and his grandfather,
the Most Christian King of France, cannot accept such a barefaced
offer of betrayal. But they can take advantage of the situation, and
achieve the same result: peace. That's why they decided to send me
to Vienna to inform the appropriate authorities of Eugene's treachery.
In this way the imperial army will find itself effectively without a
leader, and the path towards the armistice will be open."

"Inform the appropriate authorities?" I stammered, guessing
where the conversation was leading.

"Certainly: the Emperor. And you will help me."

The terror I suddenly felt must have been painted so clearly on
my face that Atto's nephew asked me if by any chance I wanted a
glass of water. Now it was clear why Atto had forced me to listen to
all that preamble about Eugene of Savoy. I wiped a few beads of
sweat from my forehead, as gelid as the flowing Danube under its
crust of winter ice. In the confusion that swirled around my brain,
where the Turkish Agha was weaving enigmatic dances first with
Abbot Melani and then with the Duke of Savoy, one thought
outweighed all others: Atto had once again ensnared me in one of his
fateful intrigues.

What could I do? Refuse outright to help him, and maybe arouse
his ire, with the risk that he might revoke the gift he had bestowed
on me or that he might commit some indiscretion and reveal me as

his accomplice? Or take the risk, and try to satisfy him, maybe in as uncommitted a fashion as possible, hoping that he would leave Vienna very soon?

One thing was certain: the donation that had made me wealthy was not a reward for the services I had done him in the past, but for those that he was expecting from me over the next few days.

"Holy heaven," I sighed, my voice choking, as I myself began to look around to see if anyone was listening in, "and how do you think I can help you?"

"It's simple. My cover as an intendant of the imperial posts cannot hold out for long, here in the city. If I tried to present myself at court I would be recognised as a French enemy, and cut into pieces like a sausage. We'll need some kind of shortcut to reach the Emperor."

He leaned forward again, to whisper even more tremulously: "In the same street as the Porta Coeli there lives a person who is close to the Emperor's heart. She is a girl aged just twenty, named Marianna Pálffy. She's the daughter of a Hungarian nobleman faithful to the Emperor and she is Joseph's lover."

"Lover? I had no idea . . ." I said in consternation.

"Of course you had no idea. These are tempting items of gossip that the Viennese do not confide to foreigners; but French agents ensure that they reach Paris. Joseph found lodgings for her in Porta Coeli Street, on the suggestion of Eugene, whose own palace is next door. She lives, to be precise, in a small building owned by a nun from Porta Coeli, Sister Anna Eleonora Strassoldo, a noblewoman of Italian origins, who is now headmistress of the convent's novitiate. She can also serve as a means to reach the Pálffy woman," he replied, in the most casual of tones.

I felt crestfallen: that was why Atto had found lodgings for himself and for me at Porta Coeli! The convent was right at the heart of the web of intrigue that he was busily weaving between Eugene's palace and the house where the lover of Joseph the Victorious lived. I felt like telling him that I had understood his design, but I did not have time to open my mouth. Atto had already asked his nephew to hand him his stick and was now standing up.

"I'm going for a stroll. Let's not go out together again, people might notice. You stay here, if you want to enjoy the warmth a little longer. I'll contact you when it's time to act."

I was quite prepared to stay there by myself, sitting at the table, dazed and disconsolate, when the door of the coffee shop opened again and a new arrival took Atto and his nephew by surprise. At the entrance to the Blue Bottle stood Cloridia.

"I got your note at the Porta Coeli," she said to me – and then she saw *who* was with me. At first she could not believe her eyes.

"Signor Abbot Melani . . . Signor Abbot Melani! Here?"

𝕰𝕺

Unlike the previous occasions when they had met, Cloridia broke into a broad and heartfelt smile on seeing Atto. She was full of generous affection and thanked him profusely for the gift that had finally brought us comfort and prosperity. The Abbot responded to Cloridia's words with great tact and equal friendliness, and when she expressed her sorrow at his loss of sight, Atto even seemed to be touched. Time had left its marks on both their faces, but had sweetened their characters. Cloridia found a withered, fragile octogenarian, and Atto a mature woman. While they were still exchanging affectionate words, the door opened yet again. It was Simonis. He humbly greeted Cloridia, Atto and Domenico; Abbot Melani, catching the unpleasant smell of soot, raised his handkerchief to his nose again.

"We must hurry," my wife announced. "In a moment he'll be leaving Prince Eugene's palace. We can follow him."

"Who?"

"That Ciezeber, the dervish. I saw some strange things at the palace today. And after what the Agha said to Eugene, we had better try to get things straight."

"What did the Agha say to Eugene?" put in Atto.

"A strange phrase," answered Cloridia. "He said that the Turks have come here all alone to the *pomum aureum* . . ."

"It's a complicated story," I said to Melani, trying to interrupt my wife, who still knew nothing of my suspicions about Atto and the Turks. "I'll tell you about it later."

"*Pomum aureum?*" asked Atto, clearly very interested in all that was going on in Eugene's palace, "and what does that mean?"

"The city of Vienna, or perhaps the whole Empire," answered Cloridia, who had failed to catch my numerous stern looks advising her to say nothing.

"Very interesting," remarked Atto. "I don't think one often hears a Turkish ambassador express himself in such imaginative terms. It almost sounds like a coded message."

"Exactly!" said Cloridia. "The expression *pomum aureum* clearly indicates Vienna, but why specify that the Turks have come here all alone? Who could have come with them? To understand that we need to know where this expression 'Golden Apple' comes from."

"If you like," put in Simonis, "I can help you solve the problem."

"And how?" asked Atto.

"I can get some student friends of mine to examine the case. They're all very sharp young men, as you know," he said, addressing me. "All you need do is offer a suitable cash reward. It wouldn't be too expensive; they don't expect much."

"Perfect. Excellent idea," Cloridia pronounced.

I could not protest: we were not short of money, after all. The situation had slipped from my control.

"Now let's go, quickly," urged my wife, "otherwise the dervish will get away from us."

We made hastily towards the door, abandoning Atto Melani and Domenico in the coffee shop, instead of being abandoned by them as had been the earlier plan. As I bade them a hasty farewell, I saw the surprised and slightly bewildered expressions on their faces.

As soon as we stepped outside, a freezing gust of wind impelled us on. We were just about to reach Porta Coeli Street when Cloridia held me back:

"There he is, he must have just left the palace," she said, pointing at a dark figure of unusual build.

"Simonis, go back to Porta Coeli and carry on with the afternoon's cleaning rounds with our boy. As for me and Cloridia, I don't know what time we'll get back."

The pursuit began.

Ciezeber had a large white cloak, a long, grizzled and unkempt beard, and a grey pointed felt cap wrapped around by a green turban. He had a hunting horn by his side, a bag on his shoulders and in his hand he held a stick with a sort of large iron hook at the top. His demeanour, despite his advanced age, was grim and wild. I would not have cared to meet him in a lonely spot. His tattered clothes, pale, deeply furrowed face, emaciated figure and fierce brutish features gave him the appearance of a cross between a priest and a vagabond.

He seemed totally unaware of the curiosity of the passers-by, who at every corner turned round and gazed at him in amusement. He was moving at a swift pace away from Porta Coeli, measuring his stride with his stick, in the direction of the church of the Augustinians.

"Curse it, Cloridia," I said as we followed him, "what made you talk about the Turks and the Agha in front of Atto? Didn't it strike you that he might have come here for some shady dealings, as is usually the case?"

I explained that Abbot Melani had arrived in Vienna at almost the same time as the Turks, and that it might not have been just a coincidence.

"You're right," she admitted, after reflecting for a moment. "I should have been more careful."

It was the first time in her whole life that my intelligent and acute consort, able to foresee, calculate and assess everything, and to analyse and connect every event, had ever had to admit to an oversight. Could it be that with age the implacable blade of her acumen was losing its edge?

"Do you know something?" she added contentedly. "Ever since we stopped being poor and started to enjoy your Abbot Melani's gift here in Vienna, I've finally learned how to be careless."

Ciezeber had meanwhile walked all the way down Carinthia Street and was about to leave by the gate of the same name: the gateway to the south, the same one by which Cloridia and I had first entered Vienna on our arrival.

The pursuit was not without its difficulties. On the one hand Ciezeber was easy to distinguish even at a distance, thanks to his headgear and clothing. On the other hand, the flat landscape of the suburbs to the south of Vienna makes it difficult to follow anyone without the risk of being spotted.

As he made his way through the Carinthian Gate the dervish drew a number of amused remarks from travellers and merchants, who were passing through in their carriages, but he remained wholly indifferent and did not vary his pace. Along the way Cloridia explained certain details of Ciezeber's clothing.

"The kind of horn he has is sounded by dervishes at fixed hours every day, before prayers. The stick is used to support his head in the brief moments he devotes to rest, but actually it's an instrument of spiritual training: dervishes love to rest their chin on the large hook at the top of the stick and close their eyes; but the stick holds him up only when the hook is completely still. If the dervish really falls asleep, the hook sways, the stick falls down and wakes him up."

"Almost an instrument of torture, I'd say."

"It all depends on your point of view," smiled my wife. "The fact is that these dervishes, as my mother told me, can do some really bizarre things."

After leaving the Carinthian Gate, we had crossed the dusty clearing known as the Glacis which surrounds the ramparts of Vienna, and we had crossed the city's lesser river, called the Wienn, from which some say the Caesarean city derives its name. The dervish proceeded at a good pace, making his way towards the suburb of Wieden, beyond which stretched long rows of vines, a pleasant expanse of green as far as the eye could see. We left Nickelsdorf and Matzesdorf behind, and we came in sight of the external fortifications, the so-called Linienwall, erected just a few years earlier by Italian experts.

Still following the dervish we passed through the gate in the defensive walls, thus leaving the city's territory altogether. Our pursuit continued in the open countryside, along the road that leads from Vienna to Neustadt.

All around us were ploughed fields, with just the occasional building. We kept walking behind our man for a good hour, often at the risk of losing him: outside the walls there were no palaces or houses to conceal us, so to avoid detection we had to stay at a good distance. As I have already said, his tall stature and unmistakable Turkish turban made him recognisable from a long way off. Luckily I knew the road well: it was the same one I had travelled along with Simonis and our little boy to get to the Place with No Name.

In the meantime Cloridia told me what she had seen at Eugene's palace that day.

"Today Ciezeber received a visit from a mysterious individual. For some very, very shady business."

"A mysterious individual?"

"Nobody was able to see him. He entered by some back door, and left the same way. But I was lucky: not only did I discover he was there, but I managed to find out that he was not Viennese, and perhaps not even Christian."

Things had gone this way. Cloridia had accompanied a servant girl to the palace as two members of the Agha's retinue wanted to purchase some fabrics from her. They were bargaining in one of the rooms on the first floor, when Cloridia, through a chink in the door, saw a strange, evil-smelling figure stealing up the stairs, wrapped in a filthy overcoat which carefully concealed his face. He was accompanied by one of the Ottoman soldiers who usually escorted the dervish. As the servant girl seemed perfectly at ease in her negotiations (one of the two Turks interested in her fabrics spoke a little German, and above all knew how to count and was familiar with the value of the coins), Cloridia found a pretext to leave them and managed to identify the room to which the mysterious individual had been taken. Once the girl and the two Turks had come to an agreement, my crafty little wife went to spy on what was going on in the mysterious visitor's room.

"I immediately identified Ciezeber's voice. In addition to him there were at least two other Turks present. Obviously they were talking in their own language. Then there was that strange filthy man, the mysterious guest, who expressed himself in a language I did not know – it could have been European or Asiatic. He had a hollow, stammering voice, but I don't know whether it was due to age or some speech defect. The strange thing is that, although the individual words were incomprehensible, the general sense of what he was saying was fairly clear."

"And what was he talking to the dervish about?"

"About a head. The head of a man. The dervish wants it at all costs."

"Good heavens," I exclaimed, "they're planning a murder! And who are they going to kill?"

"I'm afraid I didn't catch that, maybe they'd already said it before I arrived. It's probably someone important, or at least I got the impression that that's how the dervish and his two companions consider him."

"And the head – when are they planning to . . . to obtain it?"

"That's what Ciezeber was asking the visitor, and insistently. The visitor promised to set about it and to get news to them by this evening or tomorrow."

My mood, already dampened by my awareness that I had become a pawn in Abbot Melani's conspiracy, became even more depressed. Cloridia and I had guessed correctly: the Turkish embassy had come to Vienna not for diplomatic ends, but for some shadowy and bloody design.

Our pursuit continued. We had long ago left Matzelsdorf behind with its poetic little houses, among which welcome taverns lay concealed, and the Linienwall. We had started along the road towards Simmering. Every so often the land rose slightly, affording us a distant but impressive view of the city, surrounded by its powerful walls.

Ciezeber maintained a steady rhythm in his walking, without ever hesitating at the crossroads; he seemed to have no doubt about his final destination.

"When we started out you said you knew where he was heading," I reminded Cloridia.

"At the end of the conversation with the mysterious guest I heard Ciezeber announce that he was going to a distant lonely place. A wood, I'd say, since there's no shortage of them around Vienna."

We looked at each other: a wood, for example, like the one at the Place with No Name. Which, by now it was clear, was where we were heading.

Soon the fields gave way to the green shades of oaks and larches, spruces and red beeches, which clustered together around the Place with No Name. We took a path that made towards a little hill near Maximilian's manor, from which the house could clearly be seen. At every step the vegetation grew thicker.

No one who has not seen them can imagine how rich and blessed the Viennese woods are. When you finally leave the vine-clad hills and orchards behind and immerse yourself in the dense sylvan foliage of the basin of Vienna, it's like being received into the soft lap of a tender mother, who comforts her children, still choking from the dust of the city, and consoles them with gently caressing leaves and sweet birdsong, cushioning their footsteps with velvety leaves and dewy lichens.

It was that season of early spring when the forest floor delights the eyes with its emerald green, and a pungent culinary aroma tickles your nostrils and your imagination. What stirs these feelings is a herb, whose name I did not know then, which fills the Viennese woods in April, and whose spicy effluvium makes you think that every nook conceals a dish of river trout with herbs, or a stuffed leg of pork.

We made our way into the forest on the heels of the dervish, who was still unaware of our pursuit. After another half-hour of walking, Ciezeber finally came to a halt in the very depths of the woods.

Beyond him, through the tree trunks, we could make out the imposing white shape of the Place with No Name. It was as if he had chosen that corner of the forest precisely because it was so close to Maximilian's creation. After all, was not the Place with No Name, known as Neugebäu, dear to the Turks? We hid behind the trunk of a large fallen tree and watched.

After setting his bag down on the grass and taking out some curious tools, he arranged them on a carpet on the ground. He did not look around himself: he seemed certain that he was all alone.

He bowed deeply towards the east, with a grave, impenetrable face. Then he sat down. After pausing with his eyes closed, he stood up again and went and knelt down in front of the carpet where his tools were lying and kissed the ground. Then he put his hands on the implements, as if in blessing, pronouncing some incomprehensible formula in a low voice. Finally, rising yet again, he took off his cloak and goatskin coat. He stood there, half-naked, his chest both skeletal and firm, heedless of the cold.

He pulled out two bracelets with rattles from the bag and slipped them onto his ankles. Then from inside the coat he took a long dagger whose handle was decorated with bells and he stepped barefooted onto the carpet, among the tools. Up to now he had remained perfectly calm and composed. But now he gradually grew animated, as if by the effect of some internal fire: his chest swelled, his nostrils dilated and his eyes began to roll in their orbits with extraordinary speed.

This transformation was accompanied and stimulated by his own singing and dancing. After beginning with a monotonous recitative, Ciezeber soon grew louder, passing onto lilting shouts and cries, to a feverish rhythm set by his swiftly tapping feet, and the rattling of his anklets and the tinkling of the bells on the dagger handle.

When the rhythm became frenzied, the dervish repeatedly lifted and lowered the arm that was holding the dagger as if, stirred by some alien force, he was not even aware of his own movements. A convulsive spasm shot through his limbs. He was now shouting so frenetically that we could hardly hear the rattles and bells. Then he began to jump, executing such prodigious leaps and continuing all the while with his stentorian singing that the sweat streamed down his bare chest.

It was the moment of inspiration. At first he seemed to cast a rapt glance at the distant expanse of white stone of the Place with No

Name. Then, brandishing the dagger, which he had never abandoned, and the slightest shake of which set the numerous bells jangling wildly, he stretched his arm out in front of himself. Then, suddenly bending it with great vigour, he thrust the dagger into his cheek, so that the tip penetrated his flesh and appeared inside his open mouth. Blood gushed from both sides of the wound, and I raised my hand as if to ward off the horrifying spectacle.

The dervish bowed down, pulled out the blade and, licking his hand, washed his wounded cheek with saliva. The operation lasted just a few seconds, but when he raised his head and turned in our direction, all traces of the wound had vanished.

Then Ciezeber sat down again with his eyes closed for a few moments. Standing up once more, he began the same performance all over again, and this time wounded his arm, which he medicated in the same way. Once again, the wound vanished.

The third ritual bewildered and horrified me even more profoundly. After rummaging among his utensils, Ciezeber armed himself with a great curved sabre. He gripped it by both ends, placed the concave side of the blade on his belly and with a gentle oscillatory movement made it penetrate his own flesh. At once a purple line stood out on his dark, shining skin, black blood trickled down his legs, staining the rattles on his ankles. As he inflicted this torment on himself, the dervish smiled. Cloridia and I gazed at each other in appalled astonishment.

Swaying slightly, Ciezeber bent down over his tools. He picked up a little box with an ornamented top and opened it. In his hand he held a small piece of dark material, like a crust of bread. Then he extracted from the heap of tools a sort of small pointed knife, and began a strange oration, with his mouth half open.

"It's as if he were reciting the psalms," I whispered to Cloridia.

"Indian psalms, though," she answered.

The psalmody lasted quite a while. Every so often Ciezeber would break off, open his eyes and address the two objects he held in his hands in a strange amorous tone, and then start chanting again.

At last the bizarre ritual ended. The dervish medicated the long cut on his belly with saliva; all traces of suffering vanished from his face and body and the wound seemed to heal almost instantaneously. After replacing the dagger, rattles and anklets, gathering together the heap of tools and rolling up the carpet, the dervish got dressed again and set off calmly back towards the city.

We left our hiding place. I walked towards the spot where he had carried out his horrifying rituals. On the grass, drops of blood could be seen that had run off the carpet. I bent down to touch them, and they stained my fingertips. Still uncertain of what I had seen, I tasted them. It was definitely blood.

What on earth had happened? Had my eyes not seen properly? Had the blood not really come gushing out? Had my hands not really touched it and my mouth not tasted it? I thought back to all the performances I had seen by famous conjurers who flocked into Vienna for the annual markets, but I could remember nothing that bore any resemblance to what I had just witnessed. We had been observing an extremely primitive and simple being – and, in addition, he had thought he was on his own. So there could be no tricks.

Disturbed by the awful spectacle, I listened unenthusiastically to what Cloridia told me about the feats dervishes are capable of.

"My mother often told me: they can cut off any limb, even their own head, and heal it at once as if nothing had happened. It seems they possess natural secrets – or rather, supernatural ones, which come down from the ancient priests of Egypt."

"How come the Agha brought an Indian dervish to Vienna?"

"I have no way of knowing that. But perhaps he was summoned to carry out an important task, one that could not be entrusted to a Turkish dervish."

"Aren't the Turks good dervishes as well?"

"Who do you think a dervish is?" asked Cloridia with a little smile.

"Well, when I saw them mentioned in the books about the Sublime Porte and its customs, I imagined they were monks with a vow of poverty, pious Muslim mendicants, in their own way holy men, subject to a fairly austere rule, subject to some kind of sacerdotal hierarchy, who carry out charitable duties or sacrifices."

"Nothing could be less like a Turkish dervish than your fantasy figure," my wife said sarcastically. "Any Turk can be transformed instantly into a dervish, so long as he puts round his neck or onto his belt some kind of talisman, a stone picked up near Mecca, a dry leaf that's fallen from a tree overshadowing a saint's tomb, or any sort of thing. There are dervishes who wear a goatskin like a pointed cap on their heads, and this singular ornament is all they need to prove incontrovertibly their right to the title of dervish and the veneration of the faithful."

The Turkish dervishes, my wife went on, live by begging and are ready to turn to theft whenever people do not prove generous enough. Like every good Turk, they have wives whom they leave in their native villages while they go on their eternal pilgrimages, taking a new wife whenever they feel lonely, and abandoning them as soon as they reacquire their taste for the vagabond's life. Sometimes, after a few years, a dervish will return to the wife he remembers most fondly. If she has waited for him, the couple will get back together for a while; if she has found some better option or has not been patient enough, she will apologise as best she can and need not fear any resentment on the part of the dervish.

"This is the Turkish dervish," concluded Cloridia, "an idler and an impostor who will sometimes turn to brigandry, when circumstances permit it. Dervishes worthy of the name are something quite different – for example, the Indians like Ciezeber."

Dervishes of this kind, explained Cloridia as we made our way back to Vienna, are much sought after: they can heal men and animals miraculously, they know how to cure sterility in women, mares and cows, they can find treasures hidden in the earth, and drive out evil spirits haunting flocks or girls. They have the power to intervene in anything of a magical nature.

"Their mysticism makes them capable of feats like the ones we've just seen," concluded my consort, "but it has nothing to do with fidelity to the Prophet. In fact, their orthodoxy is often questionable and they are suspected of being indifferent to the Koran."

Unsettled by the spectacle that Ciezeber had offered us, and disconcerted by what Cloridia was recounting, I could only come up with pointless questions:

"Just what were those objects he held while he chanted? And how do you think Ciezeber manages to pull off those miracles?"

"My darling," she answered patiently, "I know something of the dervishes but I can't explain the secrets of their rites."

"I don't see what all this has to do with the head that Ciezeber wants to get hold of at all costs, nor with the Agha's visit. And I don't understand whether he came here, right in front of the Place with

No Name, for a specific purpose: this is a sacred place for the Turks," I said, thinking back to Simonis's story of Suleiman's tent.

"I'll settle for having no opinion. In some cases, it's the only way not to make a mistake," Cloridia said peremptorily, as we made our way back, savouring the luscious garlicky smell of the wild herbs that grow in the underwood.

☙❧

17 of the clock, end of the working day: workshops and chancelleries close. Dinner hour for artisans, secretaries, language teachers, priests, servants of commerce, footmen and coach drivers (while in Rome people take but a light refection).

When we got back to Porta Coeli Street, Cloridia went to Prince Eugene's palace to see to some matters she had left unresolved before we started following the dervish. At the convent I found Simonis who had just finished cleaning all the soot off our son, and who was setting off with him to the nearby eating house for their evening meal. I joined them, and over dinner I told my assistant about Ciezeber's gruesome rituals in the woods. However, the difficulty of making Simonis understand what I had seen and the series of idiotic questions that he then asked soon made me regret I had said anything about it. I began to wonder just why the Greek could at times be so lucid and at others, like this moment, so totally doltish.

"Tomorrow we'll get on with our work at Neugebäu," I announced, to change the subject.

"If I may, Signor Master, I'd like to remind you that tomorrow is Sunday. If you wish, I can certainly work, but it is also *Weisser Sonntag*, which is to say *dominica in albis*, and I think that if some guard should find us . . ."

Simonis was right. The next day was Sunday, *dominica in albis* to be precise, and by law anyone found doing *opera servilia et mercenaria* would be subject to financial and even corporal punishment and confiscation of goods, since – as the imperial edict declared – working on a holy day aroused divine wrath and therefore paved the way for plagues, wars, famine and pestilence.

"Thank you Simonis, I had forgotten. Monday then."

"I'm sorry to remind you, Signor Master, that on Monday lessons begin again at the university, the Easter holidays having finished."

"You're right. I hope you have found someone to follow the lessons for you again."

"Of course, Signor Master: my Pennal."

"Your . . . what? Oh yes, that lame boy," I said, remembering the Deposition I had attended.

"Yes, him, Signor Master; his name is Penicek, I'm his Barber and he's entirely at my beck and call. However, I'm afraid I'll have to attend in person the university's reopening ceremony at least. But I'll do all I can to avoid any inconvenience."

I nodded. I was really lucky to have found Simonis as my assistant chimney-sweep. He worked from morning to night, disregarding regular hours, festivities and the thousand and one legal opportunities that Vienna offered every day and every week to stay off work.

To my amazement and dismay I had discovered, soon after moving there, that in the Caesarean city there were no more than 250 working days a year, with interruptions as regular as they were absurd. First of all there were the so-called "blue Mondays", which is to say the Mondays when, on one pretext or another, the Sunday break was extended. To these were added countless different activities, like the annual markets, which often went on for weeks and gave people the right to take days off to attend them, and pilgrimages, which could also last a whole week. And all these absences from work had to be fully remunerated!

"I've been wanting to tell you, Simonis, that I'm satisfied with you and with your work," I said to the Greek as I meditated on these matters.

"Thank you, Signor Master, I'm honoured," he answered deferentially, his mouth full of onion and chamois sauce.

I had good reason to thank my assistant! In all that chaos of festivity, Simonis used the great number of university holidays to devote himself wholeheartedly to his work as a chimney-sweep under my authority. There were very few days when I had to do without his labour, and even then it would never be for more than a few hours: like Maundy Thursday, the previous 2nd April, when the *Herren Studenten* (as it said in the summons) were called to the ritual washing of feet in the chapel of the Caesarean college; or next 25th April, feast of St Mark, when they would accompany the great procession from St Stephen's to St Mark's and back again.

When I had told our few acquaintances that we were about to leave for Vienna, they had looked at me as if I were mad: you're going off to the cold, among those doltish sausage-eaters! After being there just a few months, I had a strong suspicion – or rather, the certainty – that it was the Romans who were the dolts.

"Signor Master," put in Simonis, stemming the stream of self-satisfaction that was swelling in my breast, "I've let my student friends know about your interest in the Golden Apple. I took the liberty of arranging a brief meeting here, so you can tell them what you need and instruct them personally. Dànilo Danilovitsch, however, sent me a note a short while ago asking to meet us at midnight: maybe he already has some information."

Cloridia came into the eating house on her way back from work at Prince Eugene's palace. It was clear from the expression on her face that she was deeply upset.

"Oh, my husband, if you only knew what happened to me today," she began, taking a seat and draining my glass of wine in a few gulps.

Then she smiled at our son, who was gazing across the table at her with a worried expression. She leaned over to give him a kiss and fondled his hair. Then she asked Simonis, who had already eaten, to take the boy back to the convent in time for his German lesson; she and I would join them shortly.

Cloridia wanted to report some grave circumstance to me, but was afraid of our son's reaction. When Simonis and the boy had gone, my wife dropped her motherly smile and pressed my hand between hers, which were damp with cold sweat.

"What's the matter?" I asked in alarm.

"Thank God that Monday is my last day working at the palace; the Agha will be received by Prince Eugene again, but then he'll go back to his lodgings on the Leopoldine Island. On Tuesday Eugene will leave for The Hague. The end of the job will mean the end of my pay, but no matter. If what happened to me today were to happen again, it could all get very nasty."

"Get very nasty? Why, what happened?"

"That foul creature . . . the one who promised to get the head for the dervish."

"Yes?"

"He was at the palace again. I met him twice. The first time was on the servants' staircase, with his Turkish companions. If you could have seen how he eyed me! I saw his face at last, if you can call that bundle of leathery scraps a face. He stared at me with bloodshot eyes, and his grey, suspicious pupils bored into me like grappling hooks. I walked away quickly, but I had the impression his eyes were still on me. I'm afraid he guessed something; let's hope that later, when I saw him the second time, he didn't realise I was spying on him."

"And why did you have to spy on him?" I exclaimed, horrified at the thought that my sweet spouse might end up a target for a head-hunter.

After her first encounter with the hooded man, Cloridia had been acting as interpreter between the Agha's major-domo and one of the palace cooks, when out of the corner of her eye she had seen this monstrous individual again, this time walking up the palace's main staircase. He had a furtive air and would have got by unobserved if Cloridia had not happened to open the door of the room she was in just as this creature was going up to the second floor. Intrigued by his cautiousness, Cloridia had slipped away from her interlocutors and silently followed him.

"I was scared, but it was worth taking the risk. Maybe the hooded man was going to have another talk with Ciezeber," explained my courageous little wife.

But the unknown figure continued to wander around the palace in perfect solitude. He must have been well informed: it was the hour when the staff was usually concentrated downstairs, between the kitchens and the service rooms, and there was no one about in the corridors on the first and second floor. After quickly exploring some rooms on the second floor, the furtive figure went back to the lower floor.

Here, explained Cloridia, in a room that looked onto Porta Coeli Street, some large bookcases were being set up: "They say that Eugene intends to fill them with a great collection of books, and to this end he's already planning to buy a great number of printed volumes and manuscripts as quickly as possible."

As the carpenters had not yet finished their work on the book-cases, some wooden chests had been temporarily placed on the empty shelves, whose contents were unknown to everyone, except Eugene and his collaborators. The hooded individual, acting with feline swiftness, entered this future library unchallenged.

Not being able to enter herself (and above all not wanting to do so), Cloridia tried to work out what he was up to by putting her ear to the door. First she heard a scuffling noise on the left-hand side of the room. Then a tinkling of coins, as if someone were picking up handfuls of them and dropping them into a bag. Finally, footsteps approaching the door.

The individual then emerged from Prince Eugene's future library and slipped away along the corridors of the palace, probably planning to leave by some service door.

As soon as she was left alone, Cloridia entered the library. On the shelves were several large wooden chests of various shapes and sizes. The individual could have searched any number of them but only one drew her attention: its lid was not properly closed, perhaps because it was defective, so that the light-coloured wood of its interior was visible.

Raising the lid, Cloridia found a dusty jumble of objects: heaps of old gazettes, military maps and drafts of letters. Apparently all things of little value, which Eugene must have put there temporarily, until the library should be ready. Although she only had a few moments to spare, Cloridia groped around the bottom of the chest and her fingers felt something cold and metallic, which emitted the same tinkling sound she had heard a few moments earlier. She peered more closely into the chest and made out a small heap of strange metal fragments of irregular shape.

"I took one of them, have a look."

My sweet spouse had hesitated a while before pocketing the strange object, which after all did belong to the Most Serene Prince, but since there were a great many of these strange metal fragments bearing effigies of coins, it would not make much difference to take just one of them, for the moment at least. There would be plenty of opportunities for her to replace it. In the meantime we could work out just what the devil it was, and why this mysterious individual had apparently carried off a heap of them.

I turned it round in my hands.

"It's blackened with age, but it's undoubtedly silver," I remarked.

"Exactly. And if you look at the top edge, it looks like the rim of a plate. A silver plate."

In the middle was a round engraving, on which a nobleman's coat of arms could be discerned: a lion's foot on a striped field. Above it, next to a raised border, were the words:

LANDAV 1702 IIII LIVRE

At the four corners the lilies of France had been stamped.

"What on earth is it?" I asked, bewildered.

"Ah, don't ask me."

"It looks very much like a coin; it says '4 livre', and *livres* are French liras. And at the corners are the lilies of France. But it looks as if it hasn't been coined at a mint, but with some rudimentary contraption."

"Perhaps it's a forged French coin," said Cloridia.

"It wouldn't fool many French people, I'd say."

"Landau is the German city where Emperor Joseph won two battles, if I'm not mistaken," said Cloridia.

"Exactly, in 1702 and 1704. But this is definitely not a commemorative medal. Firstly, because medals of that sort don't look as shoddy as this. Secondly, because it has lilies, a French symbol, not an imperial one."

At that moment we had to break off; Simonis was back. We showed him the strange coin, asking him if he could throw any light on it.

"Never seen anything like it. I know that Landau is an important German fortress in the region of the Palatinate, and our beloved Emperor besieged it and captured it twice. But what this piece of silver is, I've no idea."

The discussion was very short, because at that point Simonis's student friends turned up. There was the whole group: "Baron" Koloman Szupán from Varasdin, the Romanian "Prince" Dragomir Populescu, the Pole Jan Janitzki Count Opalinski, the Bulgarian Hristo Hristov Hadji-Tanjov, and, to complete the set, the Beano – or rather the Pennal – of the Deposition, the Bohemian Penicek, who limped over to stand servilely behind his Barber, Simonis.

"Thank you for coming to lend us a hand," I began, inviting them with a gesture to sit at our table.

"Always at your service," Hristo Hristov Hadji-Tanjov, the Bulgarian, said at once.

"Don't be fooled by appearances, Signor Master," said the Greek, as if to reassure me, "you can rely on us. Right, Hristo?"

"Of course, dear Simonis," said Hristo, drawing breath as if in preparation for a long speech. "Students are the noblest stock of the human race! We are the most valuable treasure, the quintessence of mankind, gold among the baser metals, the gem set in the gold. In the world we are like the wise man among idiots, like man among the unreasoning animals. We are the ornament of the city, the laurel crown of parents, blessed children of the gods, favoured scions of wisdom, pillars of knowledge and of the land!"

This aroused the first of a long series of clappings and whistles of approval.

"It's only that invert Populescu who has no pillar," remarked Koloman Szupán, provoking a general outburst of laughter.

"And you have two, one outside and one inside," retorted Populescu.

"No smuttiness, you idiots, there's a lady here," warned Simonis, politely gesturing towards Cloridia, who actually seemed highly amused by these fatuous jokes.

Hristo continued his harangue.

"And what else? We are princes and stars of the world, and all eyebrows should now arch in amazement. I have no doubt that many of our enemies will turn up their noses, but anatomists report that the limbs, veins, flesh and bowels are the same in all men: true nobility resides in the brain and not in so-called noble blood. In ancient Egypt only scholars had a noble title. The Roman Emperor Antoninus Pius, highly cultured and of temperate habits, preferred to give his own daughter in marriage to an impoverished philosopher rather than to a rich imbecile."

"He could have given her to Koloman, who's poor but also an imbecile," joked Populescu.

"Or to you, a pederast and an imbecile," replied Koloman.

"Don't get worked up, Dragomir, keep calm," grunted Populescu to himself.

"Silence, my good friends, let me finish! Students are to the city what the thumb is to the hand. We should be called angels for our friendliness, since being free and easy is an angelic virtue. Where do civility and humanity flourish, if not in universities? There, even more than in courts, since courtesy in the ignorant is spiced with manifest hypocrisy. We students are the genuine carbuncle, which outshines all other gems; we are the emerald and sapphire of the city, which, with their vivid pleasing colours stimulate the eyes of all spectators: how splendid it is to see these sons of the Muses stroll up and down the city, a feast for the eyes, unlike the vulgar, puffed-up footsloggers! And we will not mention all the indescribable adversities a poor student has to face from early youth to the end of his life! Sources of fear, exhaustion and headaches ... I will just say that students are the most precious of noblemen, a crown *contextam splendidissimis virtutibus, gemmis longe pretiosioribus!*"

"Come off the high horse!" Opalinski retorted.

"I said we are a crown enriched with the most splendid virtues, and with gems that are even more precious! Does that suit you, ignorant dolt?" Hristo snapped back. "And that's all I have to say."

The Bulgarian's disquisition and his final quip aroused a great burst of applause from his companions, in which Cloridia and I politely joined. "Let's hope for the best!" I thought to myself, eyeing the troop of scholarly roisterers.

I gave a brief account of the mysterious sentence "*Soli soli soli ad pomum venimus aureum!*" which the Agha had pronounced at the audience with Prince Eugene, and I promised them a suitable reward in money. However, on the advice of Simonis, to whom I had recounted everything, I omitted the fact that Cloridia had heard the Agha's dervish plotting to cut someone's head off. According to my assistant, if I told them that detail, all the money in the world would not suffice to keep them there: they would all take to their heels at once. I also left out the fact that the Most Serene Prince had kept the paper containing this sentence, given to him by the Agha, in his personal diary, no less; I was ashamed to reveal that Cloridia had pried into his private papers. Prince Eugene, to tell the truth, deserved much worse, given the treachery revealed in the letter that Abbot Melani had shown me. But I certainly could not spill such a secret to a whole horde of students.

These high-spirited students all came from the lands east of Vienna. They had suffered under the Ottoman yoke and had a great hatred for that people.

"Turks: beasts dressed up as men," whispered Populescu with disgust.

"Pennal! Do your Turk's face," ordered Simonis.

Poor Penicek mimed an expression that was idiotic and ferocious at the same time.

"No, Pennal, that's Jan Janitzki, *Count* Opalinski," sniggered Hristo, miming grotesque haughtiness.

"Go and get buggered by the Turks, Hristo Hadji-Tanjov Junior," Opalinski defended himself, "seeing that they adore eunuchs like you."

The jeering and scoffing against the Sublime Porte and the coarse civility of its subjects went on for a while. I saw Cloridia's face darken. Simonis's companions did not know that my gentle consort had a Turkish mother. When she returned from her job at Eugene's palace, she herself had described the baseness of the Ottomans. But no one likes to hear their own folk scorned by others.

To distract them, I told them about the mysterious hooded creature in filthy rags who had stared so threateningly at Cloridia.

"He must have been Turkish too," sneered Dragomir. "Their women dress so dreadfully that your radiant beauty, Monna Cloridia, must have literally blinded him."

I saw my wife cheer up a little at this unexpected compliment.

"But you hear so much about their harems . . ." protested lame Penicek, who had probably approached very few women in his life.

"Right, because you get taken in by their boasting; the Ottomans are great at inventing cock-and-bull stories about the supposed wonders of their country. But have you ever entered a harem?"

"Well, not yet . . ."

"It's nothing more than a filthy den, all darkness and confusion, pestilential and full of smoke. Imagine black, peeling walls, wooden ceilings with great cracks, everything covered in dust and cobwebs, greasy torn sofas, tattered curtains, candle grease and oil stains everywhere."

Turkish women, went on Dragomir, have no mirrors, which are rare in Turkey, so they put on all sorts of frills at random, unaware how ridiculous they look. They make excessive use of coloured powders, for example putting blue intended for the eyes under their nose as well. They help each other to put their make-up on and, since they're rivals, they give each other the worst possible advice. They dye their eyebrows with so much black that they paint huge arches on their forehead from the bridge of their nose right up to their temples, or, even worse, draw a single long line right across their forehead.

"The effect of all this make-up, combined with their idleness and filth, makes Turkish women quite revolting," remarked Populescu with a grimace.

"Just when did you become an expert on Ottoman harems?" said Koloman Szupán in surprise.

As if that were not enough, continued Populescu without answering him, every woman's face is made up in such a complicated way that it is considered a work of art that is too difficult to wash off and redo every morning. The same for their hands and feet, painted in shades of orange. So they never wash, fearing that water will cancel the rouge. What makes the harems even dirtier are the numerous children and the maidservants, who unfortunately are often negresses, who live there with them.

"The negresses rest on the same divans and armchairs as their mistresses, with their feet on the same carpets and their backs resting against the same wall-hangings! Ugh!" exclaimed Dragomir.

"Do you find negresses so disgusting?" sneered Koloman. "I'm amazed you have such a delicate palate . . ."

"I'm not like you, who would go with a monkey," retorted the Romanian.

Populescu added that as glass is still a novelty in Asia, most windows are closed with oiled paper, and where paper is hard to get they solve things by doing away with windows altogether and make do with the light that comes down the chimney, more than enough for smoking, drinking and beating rebellious children, the only pastimes Turkish women engage in during the day.

"The harems, in short, are hermetically sealed, artificial caverns, heated by stifling cast-iron stoves, and full of unkempt women and badly behaved children!" concluded Populescu with a coarse laugh, clutching his neck with both hands to mimic the sense of suffocation.

"There's nothing to laugh about," put in Cloridia unexpectedly, having listened in silence to Populescu's whole description. "There's no air in the harems, it's true, but the poor women don't realise it, and actually stay for hours in front of the fire: the poor things are locked up the whole day, hardly ever moving, and they always feel cold. My mother was Turkish," she revealed calmly.

This unexpected information cast a sudden damper on the spirits of the jovial crowd.

"Anyway, you have all my compassion: I didn't know you were a eunuch," added my wife, turning a broad smile on Dragomir. "You know, don't you, that entrance to the harems is strictly forbidden to all men, at least those worthy of the name . . ."

At this point, she got up and left, leaving them all crestfallen.

When the meeting was over, I rejoined Cloridia and our son at the convent, where I subjected myself to the torture of the German lesson, which had been brought forward since the next day was Sunday. My wife and I did not do too badly, although our minds were on quite other matters. That evening the subject we were dealing with was travel.

"𝕲𝖔𝖔𝖉 𝖘𝖎𝖗, 𝕴 𝖆𝖒 𝖍𝖊𝖗𝖊 𝖙𝖔 𝖆𝖕𝖔𝖑𝖔𝖌𝖎𝖘𝖊, 𝖋𝖔𝖗 𝖎𝖓 𝖒𝖞 𝖉𝖊𝖕𝖆𝖗𝖙𝖚𝖗𝖊 𝕴 𝖉𝖎𝖉 𝖓𝖔𝖙 𝖆𝖈𝖖𝖚𝖎𝖗𝖊 𝖆 𝖑𝖎𝖈𝖊𝖓𝖈𝖊 𝖋𝖗𝖔𝖒 𝖞𝖔𝖚𝖗 𝖌𝖔𝖔𝖉 𝖘𝖊𝖑𝖋."

"𝕲𝖔𝖔𝖉 𝖘𝖎𝖗, 𝖜𝖍𝖊𝖗𝖊 𝖓𝖔 𝖔𝖋𝖋𝖊𝖓𝖈𝖊 𝖜𝖆𝖘 𝖎𝖓𝖙𝖊𝖓𝖉𝖊𝖉, 𝖓𝖔 𝖆𝖕𝖔𝖑𝖔𝖌𝖞 𝖎𝖘 𝖓𝖊𝖊𝖉𝖊𝖉."

"𝕿𝖗𝖚𝖑𝖞, 𝖌𝖔𝖔𝖉 𝖘𝖎𝖗, 𝕴 𝖆𝖒 𝖌𝖗𝖊𝖆𝖙𝖑𝖞 𝖔𝖇𝖑𝖎𝖌𝖊𝖉 𝖋𝖔𝖗 𝖙𝖍𝖊 𝖍𝖔𝖓𝖔𝖚𝖗."

And so on. Ollendorf made us repeat a series of formulas that were as elegant as they were of dubious utility to a chimney-sweep and his family.

❧

20 of the clock: eating houses close their doors.

The orchestra had struck up the introduction to Alessio's aria. The main part was played on the lute by Francesco Conti, a good friend of Camilla de' Rossi, who wove his arpeggios against the background of a dark melancholy murmuring of strings.

We were inside the Hofburg, in the Most August Caesarean chapel, at the rehearsal of *Sant' Alessio*. The notes had the power to relax my sweet wife and to calm her fears after the unpleasant encounter at the Savoy Palace.

With just a few eloquent gestures of her forearm the Chormaisterin contained the threatening mass of the violas, softened the impassioned violins and opened the way to the timid lute. Then Alessio intoned the wise verses with which he tried to console his former betrothed, whom he had abandoned many years before, and who now, having found him again, still did not recognise him.

> *Duol sofferto per amore*
> *Perde il nome di dolor*
> *Cangia in rose le sue spine*
> *Più non ha tante ruine,*
> *Più non ha tanto dolor . . .*[8]

While the touching melody softened our hearts and minds, I thought back over the events of the day. Ever since Atto Melani had arrived in the city, even before I had met him or even merely learned of his presence, my calm and satisfying Viennese life had become chaos: first of all, the adventure among the lions of the Place with No Name and its absurd Flying Ship, then the arrival of the ambiguous Turkish embassy, which clearly harboured dark designs (starting from Ciezeber's awful plan, to chop some poor wretch's head off). Then the arrival of Atto himself, who wanted to involve me in an international espionage plot against Eugene of Savoy (the Serene Prince who was so generously employing my wife Cloridia!). And should I call him Eugene of Savoy or Dog Nose? Had Atto let that nickname slip out accidentally or on purpose?

After eleven years I had just re-encountered Abbot Melani and I was already quietly cursing him.

> *Duol sofferto per amore*
> *Perde il nome di dolor . . .*

Finally there had been the discovery that Ciezeber possessed disturbing magic powers, which he employed in obscure and bloody rituals. As if that were not enough, the dervish was engaged in shady business with some individual who was supposed to bring him somebody's head and who seemed to be menacing Cloridia. Even in my family something new and strange had occurred: my wife, who had never said a word about her past and about the Turkish mother who

---

[8] *Pain suffered for love | Loses the name of pain | Turns to a rose each thorn | It feels no need to mourn | And feels no more the pain.*

had brought her into the world, had suddenly opened up and begun to talk about these matters. To the point of proffering extremely useful information on dervishes and their powers.

Meanwhile the voice of Landina, Conti's soprano wife, who was singing the role of Alessio's fiancée, responded to her betrothed without knowing it was he:

> *Se dar voglio all'Oblio*
> *La memoria di lui, cresce l'affetto*
> *E se cerco bandir dal cor l'oggetto*
> *Di rivederlo più cresce il desìo.*[9]

What would have happened, I wondered, if in the wood of the Place with No Name Ciezeber had discovered that Cloridia and I were trailing him? Given his powers, I could only shudder and imagine some tragic and gory finale. And if I did not lose my head through some sorcery of the dervish's, I was likely to end up being tried and beheaded for plotting against Eugene, supreme commander of the imperial army – and, what was worse, acting in league with a French secret agent, even if he was blind and decrepit. On calmer reflection, there was no guarantee that the letter in which Eugene sold himself to the French would have the effect Atto hoped for: had not Ilsung and Ungnad, the two treacherous counsellors of Maximilian II, remained coolly in their posts even after the Emperor had discovered their imposture? All things considered, the encounter with Mustafa, the old lion of the Place with No Name, had been just a mild foretaste of the mortal dangers I would encounter in the days to come.

"Master Chimney-sweep, you look pale and thoughtful today."

"Who's there?" I turned round with a jerk, my heart in my mouth.

The voice that had made me start so violently was that of Gaetano Orsini, Camilla's jovial castrato friend, who sang the role of Alessio.

The orchestra had paused for a break, Orsini had come over to exchange a few words and I, absorbed in my dark apprehensions, had noticed nothing.

"Oh, it's you," I sighed in relief.

"I should have said: pale, thoughtful and very nervous," he corrected himself, patting me on the back.

---

[9] *If I endeavour to efface | His memory, then my affection grows | And if my heart to him I try to close | My yearning for him grows apace.*

"Forgive me, it's been an awful day."

"Yes, for everyone. Today we had to rehearse for hours in the afternoon as well; we're all very tired. But you just have to grit your teeth, or on the day of the performance we'll make fools of ourselves in front of the Nuncio. And the Emperor will give us all a hiding, hee hee."

"Including poor Camilla," I added, struggling to match Orsini's good humour.

"Oh, not her, of course. No, definitely not," he added with a curious little laugh.

"Oh no? Special clemency for the Chormaisterin of Porta Coeli?"

"Don't you know? Our friend is a very close confidante of His Caesarean Majesty," he said, lowering his voice.

I fell silent for an instant, exchanging a bewildered glance with Cloridia.

"So far Camilla has composed an oratorio per year for the Emperor," Orsini went on. "That makes a total of four oratorios, and she has never wanted to be paid. It's a real mystery why, all the more so since His Caesarean Majesty spares no expense when it's a matter of the court chapel. He's kept on all 76 of his father's players and has even hired several others, especially violinists, so that there are now actually 107 of us, something unheard of in Europe. Not to mention the opera theatre that was inaugurated three years ago. After the Ottoman siege 28 years ago, Vienna never really had one worthy of the name."

Under Joseph I, Orsini went on, Vienna had become the capital of Italian opera, both serious and light, and also of harlequinades, pantomimes, ballets, shadow puppetry, marionettes, tightrope-walkers *et cetera et cetera*. Opera, in particular, was of a higher quality than anywhere else in Europe: fourteen or more performances a year, all featuring the most famous names among singers, composers and instrumentalists.

"All strictly Italian," Orsini said with pride.

This gave some idea of the artistic heights achieved thanks to the magnanimity and exquisite taste of His Caesarean Majesty. He himself was as skilled in the musical arts as he was in those of war, and during his leisure hours, when there was no urgent state business, he would sit down at the harpsichord or pick up the flute or try his hand at graceful compositions. These included a fine *Regina Coeli* for solo soprano, violin and organ and a number of virtuoso operatic arias in the style of the Italian Alessandro Scarlatti. The personal talent of our young and beloved Caesar, together with the great number and high quality of his performers, encouraged every kind of experiment, so that the instruments were often used in new and surprising ways. In this way the Josephine Chapel, as the chapel of the Caesarean court had been renamed in honour of the Emperor, was famous for its innovations, unparalleled elsewhere in Europe.

"But despite all that, our mysterious Chormaisterin has never wanted a florin from the Emperor. Even before entering the convent she always found a way to make a decorous and honourable living."

"Oh yes, it's true," Cloridia and I both nodded, pretending to know what Orsini was referring to.

"She travelled through all the small towns of Lower Austria, healing hundreds of invalids, in accordance with the dictates of the Rhineland abbess, St Hildegard. Even the priests who had been called to administer extreme unction would consult her. They would have her hurry to the bedside of a dying invalid, she would indicate the most suitable treatment – always based on spelt, I believe – and in less than two days there would be a miracle: the dying man would eat, walk and leave the house on his own two feet."

"True, she achieved excellent results with our son too," I agreed.

"Yes, but here in Vienna Camilla only treats friends. The university comes down hard on anyone who practises the art without a degree in medicine."

"I know all about that," confirmed my wife, who could not practise the profession of midwifery except secretly.

"Anyway, now everything has turned out nicely for our Chormaisterin," said Orsini. "When the Emperor asked her to settle permanently in the capital, rather than accept payment she told him that she no longer felt able to compose and asked permission to enter a convent. His Majesty placed her in the Porta Coeli, which is the richest and most liberal of all the monasteries in this city."

"Liberal?" said Cloridia in surprise. "But isn't it an enclosed order?"

"In theory, certainly," laughed Orsini. "However, they can receive any female visitors they want and in their cells they play at Hombre, by permission of the abbess, which is very easy to obtain. They're always guzzling those little delicacies that the kitchens turn out, especially those sugar figures, which they keep on hand to nibble at whenever they feel peckish."

"Now that I think about it," I said, "I've noticed that the grating is not much of an obstacle: you can easily put your head through it, and anybody who's just a little thinner than average could squeeze right through."

"I've seen visitors with my own eyes go up to the grating and kiss the nuns' hands, and they didn't pull back – on the contrary, they stretched their hands out through the bars without any hesitation!" added the young castrato.

"I'm glad for the Chormaisterin that life at Porta Coeli isn't too hard," remarked Cloridia.

"But that's certainly not why the Emperor put her there: it's so that Camilla can console the little Pálffy . . ." he concluded in a cheerfully allusive tone. Then he pulled an apple from his pocket and began to munch it.

The little Countess Pálffy! That morning, thanks to Atto, I had learned that she was the Emperor's lover and that she lived in Porta Coeli Street as well, very close to the convent. The very person that Abbot Melani wanted to use to deliver to the Emperor the letter that revealed Prince Eugene's treachery. I pricked up my ears and smiled with complicity, to induce the musician to continue.

". . . and so His Caesarean Majesty's carriage turns up at the oddest hours in Porta Coeli Street, collects someone and takes that person to the Hofburg," trilled Orsini insouciantly, as if he were saying things everyone knew. "The people think that it's Eugene of Savoy inside, summoned by Joseph to discuss urgent matters of war. Actually it's his confidante Camilla, if the Emperor has something to confide. Or, if he feels like doing something other than talk, it'll be Marianna Pálffy inside, hee hee."

I was joining in Orsini's umpteenth little burst of laughter, but Cloridia stopped me at once by squeezing my arm: Camilla was approaching. Although her face was tired and full of apprehension, she greeted us with her usual affability.

"I see that you've as good an appetite as ever, even at this hour of day," she said smiling at Orsini, who held his half-eaten apple in his hand.

"The fruit of the tree of good and evil," Orsini joked back. "I've finally decided to taste it."

"Don't say that," answered Camilla, suddenly serious.

"It was just a joke: I've already tasted it many times," said Orsini, still jocularly.

"Cavalier Orsini, I told you not to use those words," Camilla retorted, with unexpected harshness.

Orsini and I looked at each other in embarrassment.

"They are expressions from the Scriptures," added Camilla, perhaps realising that she had gone a little too far. "I beg you not to use them inappropriately."

"I didn't foresee that I might offend you," Orsini justified himself.

"You don't offend me, but the Scriptures. And what is needed is prudence, not foresight. The latter is the divine gift of the wise . . . But please excuse me, we must continue our work," she said in evident embarrassment, making her way with bowed head to the front of the orchestra, a clear sign that the interval was over.

❧

When we got back to the convent, exhausted after a day full of novelties and surprises, we went straight to bed. Cloridia fell asleep in my arms at once; but although thoroughly worn out, I just could not close my eyes.

A thousand questions swirled around my mind, each linked to the next like the beads of a necklace made of mysteries. Why had Camilla de' Rossi not told us she was friends with the Emperor? Out of discretion, perhaps. But why did she refuse payment for her compositions, and choose instead to withdraw into a convent?

And also: Camilla had seemed anguished, but what was the reason? I could understand that she did not wish to waste a whole half-hour with us, as she usually did. But why had she not addressed a single word to us? And there were plenty of things we could have said to one another! After all, just the evening before, Atto Melani had taken up lodgings in the convent.

Camilla, as Atto himself had confirmed, had known for some time that the Abbot was coming to Vienna, but at his request she had kept the secret. That was why she had told us earlier, with a sibylline smile, that in the days to come, "happy things" were in store for us. But what did Camilla know of the motives that had brought Atto to the Caesarean city? The Abbot had not said a single word about this. Did the Chormaisterin find nothing strange in the visit of the old castrato, from the enemy country of France, no less? Did she not know that Melani was a spy by profession?

No, no, she probably did not know, I told myself. Atto must have concocted some credible cock-and-bull story. Probably he had told her that he wanted to see me again at all costs before he died. Maybe he had used the theatrical tones that he could adopt so effectively to his own advantage ... And Camilla had fallen for it.

But the questions doubled and multiplied, as in a game of mirrors. Why did Atto not use Camilla to deliver Eugene's letter to the Emperor? Did he not know that the Chormaisterin was a friend of Joseph's? No, probably not. Otherwise he would not have set off on the trail of Marianna Pálffy, without even referring to Camilla. I myself, after all, had learned of the friendship between Joseph and the Chormaisterin only by chance, thanks to Gaetano Orsini's chattering.

What should I do? Pass on that valuable information to Atto, or keep it under my hat? It would be very easy for Camilla to get Prince Eugene's letter to the Emperor. But what would happen if Atto, as I suspected, was acting in league with the Turks? Would I not then be exposing His Caesarean Majesty to some dangerous plot? I could even be accused of being an accomplice!

No, it was better to say nothing to Atto. Indeed, I should keep a close watch on him (which was not as difficult as it would have been in the past, since he was now an old man). But above all, I should try to conceal from him the fact that the means of contact with the Emperor, which he was seeking so desperately, was just round the corner – indeed, inside the very convent where he was sleeping.

If only Atto knew how easy it was to communicate with the Emperor! From the conversations of my brother chimney-sweeps, my clients and the customers of inns and coffee houses, I knew that, for all the splendour of the young Emperor's deeds and despite my own profound devotion, he had within himself old griefs and deep wounds, and these had been scarred over by a sort of acerbic ingenuousness. It was this that could serve Abbot Melani as a breach: if he could but obtain an audience with the Emperor by means of Camilla, he would definitely succeed in making himself heard, and probably in obtaining what he hoped for. Which would be all to the good if

Atto's intentions really were directed towards peace, as he claimed. But it would be all to the bad if he were in fact acting in league with the Turks for illicit ends.

Joseph the Victorious was born with the lively spirit, the majesty and the generosity of a great monarch. He was capable of grand gestures, he could persuade the irresolute and move the indifferent. He was impatient, impetuous, rapid in his decisions, ardent and spontaneous. But he would listen to the most insignificant complaints, make promises that he could not possibly keep and he was at times incapable of saying no.

This weakness, so well-hidden and insidious, was due to a cruel trick of destiny: he had been born to a man who was his exact opposite.

His father Leopold had been pious, timid and bigoted; Joseph the Victorious was audacious, self-confident and cordial. Leopold had been prudent, reserved, phlegmatic, indecisive, constant and moderate; Joseph exuded energy from every pore. At the age of just twenty-four he had gone into battle against the French, commanding the army himself, and had conquered the famous fortress of Landau. He had been known ever since as Joseph the Victorious. His father Leopold, by contrast, when the Turks approached Vienna in 1683, had at once taken to his heels.

The young Joseph, the firstborn and thus destined for the throne, had clearly felt a vocation for ruling from the very beginning. He loved his people, and was loved by them in return. But he also expected obedience from his subjects, and so had chosen as his Latin motto: *Timore et amore*, "with fear and love", thus declaring that in his rule he would use two of the most powerful passions.

His father, on the other hand, had become emperor by chance: as a young man he had been groomed for the priesthood, because the throne was reserved for his elder brother, who then died of a disease. Reigning had been nought but a burdensome duty for him, to be carried out with patient slowness. It was no accident that his motto had been *Consilio et industria*: "With commitment and wisdom". He had been brought up by the powerful Jesuits, who had mastered his impressionable soul. Instead of making religion his guide, Leopold had made blinkers of it. Being of a timorous character, his very faith was faltering, and he was obsessed by superstitions and omens; he was afraid of magic and the evil eye. Convinced that he was cultivating the virtue of patience, he let himself be maltreated even by the beggars he received at court.

Joseph was religious, of course, but he detested the conniving Jesuits. He swore to himself that as soon as he ascended to the throne there would be no more room for them at court.

Out of laziness and in order not to lose his own flatterers, his father had for decades kept a grossly swollen court and government, full of useless, time-wasting ministers, all overpaid and litigious. Joseph could not wait to throw them all out and replace them with people he trusted – young men, efficient and competent. The ministers knew it (Joseph had even founded a kind of parallel palace, the so-called Young Court) and detested him.

His father's continual rebukes, upbraiding him for his amorous excesses, only worsened matters. In the end, his father banned him from participating in affairs of state. He did not understand and could not tolerate this son who was so different from him, and so similar to his great enemy, the Sun King: splendid, victorious and concupiscent. Leopold preferred mediocrities to wits, old people to young, bunglers to specialists, cowards to heroes. How could he ever have loved his own firstborn child?

And in fact he loved another: Charles, the younger son.

Charles was the perfect incarnation of all the mediocre qualities that put Leopold at his ease. Joseph was impetuous; Charles, educated by the Jesuits, was measured. The elder was attractive, the younger barely passable. Joseph gave his opinion at once, and was garrulous; Charles hesitated, and so kept quiet. Joseph laughed, and made others laugh. Charles was afraid of being laughed at.

They had both come from the same womb, but one was born to rule and the other to be part of the flock. Charles could perhaps have lived with his brother without too much antagonism, but the seed of rivalry was sown between them by their own father, who never concealed the fact that he preferred the younger. On his deathbed, at the very last moment, he hastened to insert a few clauses favouring Charles to the detriment of Joseph, just when the latter was excluded from politics.

And so Joseph felt mortally offended, and Charles hated him because he believed that he deserved the throne: did not his father say he was the better man? The younger son, a gloomy, rancorous spirit, had not been brought up as a younger son, but as a future king – of Spain. And now he was unable to resign himself to the fate of being left without a crown on his head.

The two brothers had not met for eight years: Charles had left for Spain in 1703 to compete for the crown against Philip of Anjou, grandson of the Most Christian King, and he had never been back to Vienna. But there had been a thousand occasions of friction: first the question of dominion over Milan and Finale, then the administration of Lombardy, and finally Naples, where they incited their protégés against one another. Even though Austria and Spain were separated by entire nations, armies, seas and mountains, Charles thought of his brother with envy every day, every hour, every single moment. A fine legacy Joseph had been bequeathed by his father, I thought: the enmity of his ministers, the rivalry of his brother and that strange juvenile ingenuousness, which could only expose him to danger: for example, the machinations of Abbot Melani.

Cogitating in this fashion, I got up from bed and tiptoed towards my papers: all possibility of sleep having evaporated, I was curious to continue reading those papers that I had collected on my beloved Caesar, and which I had promised myself I would finish reading as soon as possible.

I did not only want to find the answers to my questions about the Place with No Name; now that Abott Melani intended with my help to bring Joseph I the proof of Eugene's treachery, my Sovereign filled my thoughts more than ever.

I began to leaf through the writings in German. I came across an account of his wedding:

𝕻𝖔𝖒𝖕𝖔𝖘𝖊𝖗 𝕰𝖎𝖓𝖟𝖚𝖌 𝕴𝖍𝖗𝖔 𝕶𝖔̈𝖓𝖎𝖌𝖑. 𝕸𝖆𝖞𝖊𝖘𝖙. 𝕵𝖔𝖘𝖊𝖕𝖍𝖎 𝕽𝖔̈𝖒𝖎𝖘𝖈𝖍: 𝖚𝖓𝖉 𝕳𝖚𝖓𝖌𝖆𝖗𝖎𝖘𝖈𝖍𝖊𝖓 𝕶𝖔̈𝖓𝖎𝖌𝖘 / 𝖊𝖙𝖈. 𝕸𝖎𝖙 𝕴𝖍𝖗𝖔 𝕸𝖆𝖞𝖊𝖘𝖙𝖆̈𝖙𝖙 𝖂𝖎𝖑𝖍𝖊𝖑𝖒𝖎𝖓𝖆 𝕬𝖒𝖆𝖑𝖎𝖆, 𝕽𝖔̈𝖒. 𝕶𝖔̈𝖓𝖎𝖌𝖓 / 𝕬𝖑𝖘 𝕶𝖔̈𝖓𝖎𝖌𝖑. 𝕲𝖊𝖘𝖕𝖔𝖓𝖘 / 𝖊𝖙𝖈. 𝕾𝖔 𝕯𝖊𝖓. 24. 𝕱𝖊𝖇𝖗𝖚𝖆𝖗𝖎𝖏 1699. 𝖟𝖜𝖎𝖘𝖈𝖍𝖊𝖓 4. 𝖚𝖓𝖉 5. 𝖀𝖍𝖗.

As I ran my eyes over this description, overladen – as was always the case with Teutonic gazetteers – with boring details, I remembered other gossip I had heard around town. Joseph was so sweetly ingenuous in his behaviour, so youthfully spontaneous, so nobly candid! It would be all too easy for a sly trickster like Abbot Melani to gain the young Sovereign's trust, expressing himself in perfect Italian and concealing the fact that he had been sent by the French. And what if Atto were in league with the Turks?

Only after Joseph had taken a wife (he had married the German princess Wilhelmina An ...a of Brunswick-Luneburg) had Leopold allowed him to concern himself with affairs of state again. But by then the young man had earned the hatred of his father's ministers.

On 5th May 1705, after a half century of rule, Leopold finally died. The position of the Empire was extremely grave: war was raging against France and its allies, entire armies were ready to invade Austrian soil. Taxes were collected haphazardly, the country's finances were in a disastrous state, the imperial chamber on the verge of bankruptcy. The army was disorganised, the militias badly armed and the men undisciplined. There was a risk of losing all control over the imperial territories (rebellious Hungary, the troubled regions of Italy, never-peaceful Bohemia).

During Leopold's funeral a Jesuit, the court preacher Wiedemann, dared to admonish Joseph: only a prince educated by the Jesuits, he thundered, could hope to reign happily and successfully.

Joseph refused to be intimidated; he sent the Jesuit into exile and confiscated the two thousand printed copies of his speech. Then he warned the other Jesuits who resided at court: from that moment they would not be allowed to interfere in political matters. After this he sacked, one after the other, the incompetent ministers and functionaries his father had cherished, and replaced them with new men, fresh and eager to serve him. The only one who was not dismissed was Eugene of Savoy. The new ministers chosen by Joseph were not all little lambs. There were plenty of quarrels and rivalries, but thanks to his charisma he knew how to treat them and how to settle disagreements.

The young Caesar set about the long, arduous work of economic recovery, without losing sight of what could improve, even minimally, the daily life of his subjects, starting with Vienna. And so, among the many initiatives, he ordered the city's streets to be cleaned regularly; he organised the drainage system; he made it obligatory to register deaths promptly in the suburbs as well as in the centre; and he had a theatre built for the common people near the Carinthian Gate, where they put on popular comedies of the old Viennese tradition, which derived from the even older Italian Commedia dell'Arte. Finally, from the city's arsenal he picked out 180 Turkish cannons, which had been left as spoils of war after the siege of 1683; a foundry was to transform them into the glorious new bell of the Cathedral of St Stephen, the largest and most beautiful that had ever been seen in the capital and Caesarean residence, Vienna. This work was to be presented and inaugurated on this coming 26th July 1711, the propitious thirty-third birthday of Joseph the Victorious.

At this point I came across a "Prognostico cabalistico Prototipo", a horoscope of Joseph: *Horoscopus gloriae, felicitatis, et perennitatis, Joseph Primi, Romanorum Imperatoris, semper Augusti, Germaniae, Bohemiae, Hungariae, &c.&c. Regis.*

It had been compiled with arithmetical calculations on the basis of the Holy Scriptures by *Doctor saluberrimae Medicinae* of Padua Josepho Wallich, *olim* Hertzwallich, in 1709. The prophecy, written in Hebrew, Latin, Greek, Chaldean, Syrian, Cabalistic, Rabbinic, Jerusalemite, Polish, Italian, French and German, was crystal-clear:

> *Joseph First, Emperor of the Romans, forever August, Father engendering Heirs for the Peace of Kingdoms and Provinces, and all his days will be victorious.*

The prophecy had proved true. In that year 1711, after six years of rule, the anathema of the Jesuit Wiedemann seemed to have been definitively disproved. The financial and military situation had greatly improved. The people loved and feared Joseph, as he had wished: *Timore et Amore.* Now that his father's memory had been effaced, he felt in charge of his kingdom. But under the surface of this new state of affairs, the old ministers nurtured their undiminished hatred, longing for revenge. And no less poisonous, in distant Spain his brother Charles's rivalry throbbed like a living thing: a vicious force lying coiled under the unextinguished ashes of hatred.

Here it was again, I thought – hatred; the same terrible passion that had marked the fate of the Place with No Name and its builder, and which had frightened the predecessors of the Most August Emperor. Now, perhaps, I had the answer to my questions: Joseph the Victorious was used to overcoming obstacles. He claimed for himself alone the right to inspire fear: *Timore et Amore . . .*

However, at the end of the previous year, something else had come along to arouse apprehension among his subjects. The almanac of the *Englischer Wahrsager*, or the English fortune-teller, in its forecasts for the year 1711, had declared:

> Man hört von ungemeiner Plage:
> am Käyserhof grosse Klage.
> Käyserlicher schneller Fall
> Gibt weit und breit den Widerschall;
> Viel Böses wird dadurch gestifft,
> So einen felicem Staat betrifft.

The dire prophecy had spread around the city with the speed of lightning. I had heard it from my fellow countrymen as soon as I arrived in Vienna, and I had rushed to get hold of the Italian version:

> *A canker now appears:*
> *The palace floods with tears.*
> *The swift imperial fall*
> *With thunder does all ears appal;*
> *A great Evil is perpetrated,*
> *A* felix *State is lacerated.*

The English fortune-teller's almanac spoke of a "swift imperial fall" that would cause floods of tears and tear asunder a prosperous nation: how could one not fear for the House of Habsburg and for *felix* Austria, as the land that hosted me was known? Luckily there came the *Warschauer Calender*, the Almanac of Warsaw, to counter the pessimism of the English fortune-teller, calming the fears of the people with its prophecy written in clear letters:

> Oesterreich
> Wird die Letzte auf der Welt seyn

This too was quickly published in Italian:

> *Austria*
> *Will be the last in the world*

People's fears were assuaged and soon forgotten. But since the beginning of April a strange atmospheric phenomenon had been noted: on certain days the sun rose not with its usual golden hue but tinged blood-red. I myself, on my way to work, had often noticed this curious occurrence with amazement. Some attributed it to natural causes, but the Viennese shook their heads, muttering that it was an

ill omen: innocent blood would be spilled in the Archduchy of
Austria.

As if that were not enough, another bizarre and grim episode
confirmed people's fears.

The Emperor was visiting the church where his beloved friend
the Prince of Lamberg was buried – the inseparable companion of his
hunting adventures and procurer of young lovers. Joseph I asked a
minister where Lamberg's tombstone was. The minister answered:
"Your Majesty, right beneath your feet." This was interpreted by the
young Emperor as an omen that he himself would soon join his
friend.

This lugubrious episode was soon on everyone's lips in
Vienna, and some compared it to the *Presagium Josephi propriae mortis*,
the biblical episode in Genesis, where the patriarch Joseph
foresees his own death and the fate of his loved ones, telling
his brethren: "And Joseph said unto his brethren, I die: and God
will surely visit you, and bring you out of this land unto the land
which he sware to Abraham, to Isaac, and to Jacob." And people
remembered too how Jacob appeared in another portent, because
everyone knew that Emperor Ferdinand I had foreseen in a
dream that he would die on St Jacob's day, and so a doleful chain of
whispers passed around the city, full of references to famous
presages of death taken from the Bible, from history or just from
legends.

I went back to bed, thinking over the words pronounced that
evening by the Chormaisterin. Foresight, she said, is the divine gift
of the wise.

ॐ

*23 of the clock, when Vienna sleeps (while in Rome the foulest trades
begin their traffickings).*

I had finally dropped off when there came a discreet knock at the
door.

"𝔚ho's there? 𝔚ho wants me?" I exclaimed in German, jumping out
of bed. I had been dreaming that I was having a lesson with Ollendorf
and in the excitement of this unexpected awakening I repeated
phrases that I had just learned, parrot-fashion, from him.

"Signor Master, it's me."

It was Simonis: I had completely forgotten the appointment we had at midnight with Dànilo Danilovitsch, his Pontevedrin companion.

Just a few minutes later we were in the street. My sense of the cold was exacerbated by sleepiness, and I would have gladly stayed in my soft bed. Luckily, to alleviate the torture of this nocturnal excursion there was a carriage waiting for us. It was actually an uncovered wagon – or, to put it simply, a cart. A modest vehicle, one of those used to transport people to places close to the city. On the box was Penicek, whom I greeted with amused surprise. When we were aboard, Simonis explained this unexpected presence.

"Our Penicek drives a wagon to maintain himself as a student."

He reminded me that the *Bettelstudenten*, on account of the Rector's edict, risked being locked up in the academic prison if they were found begging without a monthly permit, which was extremely difficult to obtain. He added that the cart we were in was an example of an old *Fliegenschutz* – an uncovered vehicle with just a cloth by way of protection against insects.

"And is Penicek employed by someone with a licence, as you are?"

"Well, you see, Signor Master, it's not always possible to find a regular job like the one you were so kind as to give me. Let's say that Penicek is . . . outside the rules."

"What do you mean? Doesn't he have a permit to transport people or goods?" I asked, vaguely alarmed.

"Well, officially, no."

"He's unauthorised? How can he be? I know that they're very strict in checking up on travellers. They inspect all coach drivers and I know that they have to file information on everyone they transport!"

"It's true, I'm afraid," admitted the Pennal. "My trade is full of spies, but also of inspectors who are, let's say . . . tolerant!" He turned and winked in a knowing fashion.

"Penicek," added Simonis, "is, so to speak, tolerated by the authorities, as happens with others. You just have to make a little 'offering' . . . and this way of working gives you a number of advantages. You explain, Pennal."

"Well, yes, Signor Master," Penicek said, as the old cart went creaking through the deserted city-streets. "First of all, as I'm not included among the *Kleinfuhrleute*, the small-scale transporters of people, nor among the *Großfuhrwerker*, who do the heavy transporting, I don't pay taxes, and they don't confiscate my cart and horses for court journeys, or for carrying cannons when war breaks out. I'm not obliged to help get rid of rubbish or, in the winter, snow. If I don't want to, I don't even have to get dirty carrying coal, or breaking my back between Vienna and Linz. I just do trips between the city and the suburbs, and that's more than enough for me. The heavy transporters have for some time now been obliged to own at least eight horses and four carts. Last year hirers of horses joined in the same confraternity as the small coach drivers. And so now they have to decide which rules to abide by. Everything's getting so complicated – I have no wish to be involved! I've got my little animal, my four wheels and my shed in the Rossau area. It cost me just two *soldi*, and when I want to quit I can sell the whole lot. Of course, I have to be careful: if I have an accident, and they find out that I was drunk, I'd not only be fined heavily but I'd get into a lot of trouble. The important thing is to be very careful all the time."

Despite his subdued air, I thought, this Penicek clearly knew his way around.

"Simonis," I asked my assistant, "you came into my service to earn some money, while Penicek is a coach driver. But I imagine Danilovitsch, as a count, is kept in his studies by his family."

"Yes, he's a count, he belongs to one of the most illustrious families of Pontevedro – which, unfortunately, is a little state that's totally bankrupt. To restore his nation's credit Dànilo did try his luck with some rich widows in these parts, but it all came to nothing."

"Too bigoted!" Penicek shook his head, holding the horse's reins. "He should have tried in Paris: plenty of merry widows there . . ."

"Unfortunately with this wretched war he couldn't," the Greek explained. "And so now to make ends meet he's forced to carry out a rather dishonourable trade: spying."

I gave a start: after Atto Melani, another secret agent?

"Not in the sense you fear," Simonis added at once. "He's a legal spy, an authorised one."

He explained that the previous Emperor, Leopold, Joseph I's father, had been a pious, modest, upright and moderate spirit. He had shunned all excesses and cultivated prudence, patience and parsimony. And since Austria, as I well knew, was kissed by the Goddess of Opulence and even the lowest subjects could live like kings, in order that noblemen should not be confused with labourers, princes with woodcutters, ladies with servant girls, Leopold had divided society into five classes: he set down rules on the luxuries that each class was permitted to have. Only noblemen and cavaliers were exempt from these rules, holding special privileges.

"Yes, I've heard of these five classes," I objected, "but ever since I've been here no one has ever asked which one I belong to."

"Perhaps it's because you're a foreigner, and no one has thought of checking up on you. But for the Viennese it's a very serious question."

For each class there were detailed rules setting out just how much they were allowed to spend on clothing, eating, public appearances, marrying and even dying.

"I don't understand: who makes sure that all these rules are respected?" I asked.

"That's obvious: the inhabitants of Vienna themselves. And the students above all."

Leopold had instituted a kind of vice squad: a body of spies who infiltrated weddings, parties and even private homes to check that no citizen violated the law. Dànilo Danilovitsch was one of these.

"Students, who are always short of money and have quick minds, are among the best spies," remarked Simonis.

Authorised spies had a right to a third of the fines levied on transgressors, and so it was to be expected that they would carry out their duties diligently. However, it was not always easy; how could they know, for example, whether a dress cost thirty, fifty or two hundred florins? And so tailors, furriers and embroiderers were hired as well, and they were expected to denounce (under the threat of being punished themselves) clients who ordered clothes not permitted to their respective class. In the same way, legions of cooks and larder servants (known as "pan-peepers") were enrolled to denounce their gluttonous masters. Carpenters reported orders of luxury items of furniture, cloth merchants those of sumptuous textiles, painters blew the whistle on clients who asked for oversized portraits. Excessive opulence in carriages was denounced by coach drivers and postilions, and so on.

It got to the point that there was no corner in Vienna without a lurking spy, staring at people as they passed and at their boots (were the heels too high?), their faces (French face powder?) or the ladies' false moles (too numerous on the left cheek?). The result of this proliferation of spies was that suspicion reigned in the kitchens, people looked daggers at one another in tailors' shops, and in carriages the travellers eyed the attendants as if expecting a stab in the back. Those who were spied on (who obviously took their revenge by spying on others in turn) had to lock their larders to hide an extra piglet, or their cellars to conceal their padded armchairs, or they had to bury their youngest daughter's gold ring in the garden. Besides, who could possibly remember all the prohibitions? On feast days jewels and coiffures were not supposed to cost more than six hundred florins for the first class, three hundred for the second, from twenty to thirty for the third, from fifteen to twenty for the fourth and four kreutzer for the fifth. A wretched, illiterate fieldworker of the fifth class had to be careful not to own towels costing over a florin and thirty kreutzer, scarves and hats over a florin, and not to order meals or banquets for over fifteen florins, or five florins if for children, and woe to anyone who overspent by a single cent. You practically had to live with your nose buried in a notebook full of figures, only raising your eyes to check if your neighbour had broken some rule so that you could denounce him.

Life had become hell, which was certainly not what Leopold had wanted for his subjects. But above all, the Viennese, who have a natural sagacity and like to live peacefully, had realised that what they could get from spying on people was worth much less than the freedom they had lost. All the more so, since noblemen, ministers and high prelates, exempt from Leopold's prohibitions, continued to stuff themselves, to throw parties and to dress up just as they liked. Indeed, it was fashionable to be round-bellied (a mark of prestige and wealth); topped by the tall curly wigs then in vogue, these bellies gave the ruling class an unmistakeable pear shape.

"So how do you explain," I objected, "that in the peasants' homes in the suburbs, where you and I go to clean their chimneys, we see cutlery in carved ivory, magnificent ceramic plates, curtains and tablecloths with wonderful lacework, ornamented glasses, luxurious armchairs and stoves decorated with refined craftsmanship? You've seen it all yourself: even the country cottages always have full larders, and the smells that come from the oven make you faint with hunger."

"Things have greatly improved," said Simonis.

Tired of all this spying, he explained, the Viennese had begun to turn a blind eye on their neighbours' offences. Leopold, who had issued the first decree in 1659, had had to repeat it in 1671, in 1686, in 1687 and twice more, because his citizens by now turned a deaf ear, and smart people had found ways to get round the rules by circulating luxury goods under the names of more modest articles.

"So you'll easily understand, Signor Master, that when the old Emperor Leopold died, after reigning for fifty years, the Viennese heaved a great sigh of relief. And spies like Dànilo began to earn a little less than before, because things had become more tolerant, especially with Joseph who is the exact opposite of his father – he loves luxury, beauty and splendour."

"How do you know that Dànilo is a spy? Isn't it supposed to be a secret trade?"

"Signor Master, nothing escapes the trained eye of a student. And we're his companions: there are too many of us for him to get away with anything under our noses."

"It's certainly not an activity that confers any honour on a student, that of Dànilo Danilovitsch; particularly on a count, even if he is as poor as a church mouse," I remarked sceptically.

"But Dànilo is a Pontevedrin count, Signor Master, and Pontevedro is in half-Asia, you remember?" he answered with a sly smile. "Just like this donkey, my Pennal. Isn't it true, Penicek, that you're a half-Asiatic beast? Nod, Pennal!"

Poor Penicek turned and nodded towards us.

"More, Pennal! And look happy!" the Greek rebuked him.

Penicek obeyed and began to jerk his head affirmatively, smiling idiotically the while.

"Yes, Simonis, I remember that you referred briefly to Half-Asia during the Deposition," I said, watching this performance rather uneasily, but not wanting to interfere as it was a student matter. "You said that the lands on the borders of Asia, like Pontevedro, are very different from ours, I think."

"In them European culture meets with Asiatic barbarism," answered Simonis, turning serious, "Western ambition with Eastern indolence, European humaneness with the wild and cruel conflict between nations and religions. Signor Master: to you or me, who are Europeans, it would sound not only alien, but unheard of and incredible. With those people you can never trust in appearances. But now we must break off, Signor Master: we're here."

We got down from Penicek's cart and made our way up a stone staircase. It led up to a large open area at the top of the city walls, looking over the Glacis, the open plain that surrounds the city and separates it from the suburb of the Josephina.

"We've often met here, Dànilo's companions, and . . . strange, I can't see him." Simonis looked in all directions. "He's usually very punctual. Wait, I'll go and look for him."

Dànilo Danilovitsch had chosen for the meeting place a secluded spot on the city ramparts. The fortified walls were almost entirely accessible; unfortunately they were notorious for the shady dealings that took place there at night. The soldiers of the city's garrison took advantage of the darkness for secret wine trading, and also for encounters with the numerous young women of loose morals who traded their own bodies on the ramparts. But that evening was so cold, with a freezing wind mercilessly lashing the ramparts, that no soldiers or prostitutes were to be seen.

Simonis had been away for a good quarter of an hour now. What the devil had happened? I was about to go and look for him when I saw his shadowy figure emerging from the darkness.

"Signor Master! Signor Master, run, quickly!" he whispered in a choked voice.

I ran with my assistant to the terrace of a nearby rampart, where a vague dark shape was stretched on the ground.

"Oh my God," I moaned when I recognised the shape as a human body, and its face as that of a large, bulky youth: Dànilo Danilovitsch.

"What's happened to him?" I asked, panting from the shock and the fear of being involved in a murder.

"They've stabbed him, Signor Master, look here," he said, opening the greatcoat. "It's soaked in blood. They must have stabbed him at least twenty times."

"Oh my God, we must get him away from . . . What are you doing?"

I stopped. Simonis had pulled a little flask containing liquid from his pocket and was holding it under Dànilo's nose.

"I'm seeing if he sneezes. It's rue juice: if he sneezes, the wounds aren't fatal; if he doesn't react, it means there's nothing we can do."

Unfortunately the young Pontevedrin did not move.

"My God . . ." I moaned.

"Shhh!" the Greek silenced me.

Dànilo was saying something. It was a weak gasp, and as the breath left his mouth, turning into vapour in the cold air, it looked as if his soul were deserting him.

"Zivio . . . Zivio . . ." he muttered.

"It's a Pontevedrin greeting," explained Simonis. "He's raving."

"The Apple, the Golden Apple . . . the forty thousand of Kasim . . ." the student added.

"Who stabbed you, Dànilo?" I asked.

"Let him talk, Signor Master," Simonis interrupted me again.

". . . the cry of the forty thousand martyrs . . ." he went on raving.

Simonis and I looked at each other in desperation. It seemed that Dànilo had just a few moments of life left.

"The Apple . . . Simonis, the Golden Apple . . . of Vienna and the Pope . . . We'll meet again at the Golden Apple . . ."

It sounded like a farewell.

It was the Greek who then urged the dying man:

"Dànilo, listen! Resist, curse it! Who did you talk to about the Golden Apple? And who are the forty thousand of Kasim?"

He did not answer. Suddenly his breathing grew faster:

"The cry . . . of the forty thousand, every Friday . . . The Golden Apple in Constantinople . . . in Vienna . . . in Rome . . . Eyyub found it."

Then his breath was cut short, he stretched his neck upwards and opened his eyes as if a celestial vision had appeared to him in mid-air. Finally he had a spasm, and his head, which we were holding up more out of pity than for any useful purpose, fell back. Simonis compassionately lowered his eyelids.

"Oh my God," I moaned, "how are we going to carry him away?"

"We'll leave him here, Signor Master. If we carry him away the guards will stop us and we'll get into real trouble," said Simonis, standing up.

"But we can't, he must be buried . . ." I protested, thoroughly shaken.

"The garrison will see to it tomorrow, Signor Master. Students drink a lot at night, they challenge one another to duels. In the morning they often find corpses," said Simonis, tugging me by the lapel, while the wind grew stronger on the bastions and almost howled in our ears.

"But his relatives . . ."

"He didn't have anyone, Signor Master. Dànilo is dead, and no one can do anything right now," said Simonis, dragging me down the staircase that led away from the bastions, while what had seemed mere wind became a tempest, and on Vienna, unexpectedly, there began to descend, merciful and gentle, the white benediction of snow.

Day the Fourth
SUNDAY, 12 APRIL 1711

✠

Like a sleeping giant, the Place with No Name lay quietly under the blanket of the snow. As I crossed the great garden with its hexagonal towers, myriads of immaculate flakes pirouetted earthwards in a graceful dance. There was no wind, the air was sharp and still as in a memory. The pinnacles of the towers, like minarets, were adorned with fantastic pearly caprices.

As I approached the front of the manor house, I had to shield my eyes against the blinding glare of the alabaster stone, intensified by the reflecting snow and milky-white sky. I turned to the right, went beyond the *maior domus* and reached the courtyard of the main entrance. Here I went down the spiral staircase that led to the cages where the wild beasts were held.

The snow came down on my head like a blessing, everything gleamed as in heaven. Even the naked trees, with their claw-like, crooked branches seemed softened by all this whiteness. As I descended the spiral staircase I caught glimpses through the windows of the fish pond in the garden north of the Place with No Name, sealed by a light stratum of ice, as opalescent as almond paste and as crisp as a biscuit.

I reached the lion cage. Frosch was waiting for me.

"𝕸ustafa has escaped," he announced. "𝕳e went into the ball stadium and disappeared."

How could that be? I let him lead me to the stadium, wondering whether Frosch had had one too many drinks again, and had forgotten where he had left his favourite lion.

"𝕿here, that's where it happened."

He pointed to the Flying Ship, lying as ever on its belly in the middle of the ball stadium. In the whirl of events in the last few hours I had almost forgotten its existence.

I looked back at Frosch, my doubts clear from my expression. A lion does not disappear just like that.

But since the guardian of the Place with No Name continued to point towards the old airship (if it had in fact ever flown), I decided to have a look.

"𝔍𝔣 𝔐𝔲𝔰𝔱𝔞𝔣𝔞 𝔰𝔥𝔬𝔲𝔩𝔡 𝔱𝔲𝔯𝔫 𝔲𝔭 𝔠𝔬𝔪𝔢 𝔞𝔫𝔡 𝔥𝔢𝔩𝔭 𝔪𝔢 𝔞𝔱 𝔬𝔫𝔠𝔢," I told Frosch.

I walked all the way around the Flying Ship. Nothing. On the snow there were indeed the old lion's paw prints, but they disappeared just where I was standing, next to one of the two large wings.

So I climbed up on the wing, went aboard and began to explore the living quarters in the middle of the ship. It was at that moment that it all started.

At first it was a slight pitching, then a vigorous shudder, which increased rhythmically. It was as if the tail and wings of the Flying Ship were radiating powerful jolts through the wooden structure, and these were passed on to the rest of the ship, making it creak. Suddenly the vibrations ceased.

Frosch gazed at me attentively, but without any surprise. The ship was rising.

Instinctively grabbing hold of a wooden handrail, I saw the prominent walls of the ball stadium dropping away, and the horizon broadening, and the roof of the Place with No Name coming towards me, and the indistinct glimmer of the winter landscape bursting open, like the gates of heaven, and the blessed light of the sky pouring in on all sides – around, above and below me. The Flying Ship, at last, had taken flight again. I heard the creak of the tiller. I turned round and saw him: the black helmsman was gazing straight ahead, as he steered the ship through the airy billows with a confident hand. But he soon left the tiller, which continued to move by itself, as if governed by an invisible spirit, bending down and reappearing with a violin. Skilfully handling the bow he modulated the first notes of a motif I knew. In that instant I recognised him: it was Albicastro, the violinist I had met years ago in the Villa of the Vessel, and the music was the Portuguese *folia* he was always playing.

And I realised that it was true, the gazette Frosch had shown me had not lied: two years earlier that old craft had indeed flown, and had circled the bell tower of St Stephen, brushing against the pinnacle on which was perched the Golden Apple. And its mysterious helmsman was no Brazilian priest, but none other than

Giovanni Henrico Albicastro, the Flying Dutchman and his Phantom Vessel, as Atto Melani, petrified with terror, had called him the first time we saw him, apparently held in the air by his mantle of black gauze above the Vessel's crenellated walls.

But now that my eyes were ranging over the gardens of the Place with No Name, the snow-covered plain of Simmering, and the distant roofs of Vienna and the spire of St Stephen's, and even as I walked up to Albicastro who was playing his *folia* and smiling at me, and I wanted to re-embrace him, everything ended. Behind me I heard a new juddering, a sort of dull, hostile growling. "I should have guessed it: he was hiding in here," I said to myself in a flash of intuition, as I turned round and suddenly felt his warm, inhuman breath upon me. Mustafa growled once, twice, thrice, his right paw lashed out at me and his claws struck my cheek, ripping it to shreds. Before it all ended, another yell – mine – rose desperately, and at last I woke up.

No one could jerk me out of this nightmare but myself, and I had managed it. The sheets were soaked in sweat, my face was as hot as Mustafa's breath, my hands and feet as cold as the snow in the dream. It was not enough for the Place with No Name to fill my thoughts during the day; now it had to invade my nights as well. It was as if Neugebäu had too many secrets to be classified among the reasonable things of this world.

Cloridia had already got up with our little boy and had gone out. They were undoubtedly waiting for me to go to mass. Praise be to God, I thought; prayer and communion would save me from the aberrations of nocturnal shades once and for all.

જ્જ

5.30 of the clock: first mass. From now on the bells will ring in succession throughout the day, announcing masses, processions, devotions. Eating houses and alehouses open.

As I got ready, I heard a gentle rap of knuckles on our door. A discreet hand had slipped a note under it. Atto was summoning me urgently: we were to attend morning mass together at St Agnes in Porta Coeli, the convent's church.

The sudden April snow shower, rare but not impossible in Vienna, had covered the whole city and the suburbs with a thick and graceful mantle, just as in my dream. I set off with Cloridia and our little boy towards Via Rauhenstein, or Road of the Rough Stone, the street that ran alongside the convent, where the main entrance to the church of St Agnes was. We found Atto and Domenico waiting at the entrance to the nave. I noticed with surprise that the Abbot, although wearing different clothes from those of the day before, was once again dressed in green and black, almost as if he had refurbished his entire wardrobe with just those two colours.

Already shivering from the sudden drop in temperature, we took our places among the pews on the left.

"𝕿𝖔𝖉𝖆𝖞 𝖜𝖊 𝖆𝖗𝖊 𝖈𝖊𝖑𝖊𝖇𝖗𝖆𝖙𝖎𝖓𝖌 𝖙𝖍𝖊 𝖋𝖎𝖗𝖘𝖙 𝕾𝖚𝖓𝖉𝖆𝖞 𝖆𝖋𝖙𝖊𝖗 𝕳𝖔𝖑𝖞 𝕰𝖆𝖘𝖙𝖊𝖗, 𝖆𝖑𝖘𝖔 𝖐𝖓𝖔𝖜𝖓 𝖆𝖘 '𝖂𝖍𝖎𝖙𝖊 𝕾𝖚𝖓𝖉𝖆𝖞' or *Quasi Modo Geniti*," began the celebrant. "𝕿𝖍𝖊 𝕲𝖔𝖘𝖕𝖊𝖑 𝖜𝖊 𝖜𝖎𝖑𝖑 𝖍𝖊𝖆𝖗 𝖎𝖘 𝕵𝖔𝖍𝖓, 𝖛𝖊𝖗𝖘𝖊 20, 𝖆𝖓𝖉 𝖎𝖙 𝖙𝖊𝖑𝖑𝖘 𝖔𝖋 𝖙𝖍𝖊 𝖉𝖔𝖚𝖇𝖙𝖎𝖓𝖌 𝖔𝖋 𝕿𝖍𝖔𝖒𝖆𝖘."

Within my temples the memory of Dànilo's death was hammering away; I had described it in detail to Cloridia as soon as I got back to Porta Coeli. It hardly needs saying that the episode had thrown us both into a state of deep anguish. The student's final words suggested that the murder had been committed by the Turks. Dànilo had been about to tell us of the first results of his research into the strange question of the Golden Apple.

"Today," the priest went on, "marks the end of the celebrations of the holy passion, death and resurrection of Our Lord Jesus Christ, which began three weeks ago with Black Sunday, known also as *Judica*, when, as cited in John's Gospel in chapter 8, the Jews stoned Jesus. There then followed Palm Sunday, when, as we read in Matthew's Gospel chapter 21, Jesus entered Jerusalem. Last Sunday, Holy Easter, we read the account of the resurrection of Our Lord as handed down to us by the Evangelist Mark. On Easter Sunday we read Luke, 24: the walk to Emmaus; on Tuesday, *idem*, Jesus among the children. All telling of joy and happiness."

But what was the meaning of the arcane words that Dànilo had muttered in his death throes? Only vague recollections of what he had learned? Or obscure anathemas that his murderers had hurled at him before killing him? Cloridia and I were deeply worried that someone might connect Dànilo's death with me and Simonis, and that we might somehow get involved in a trial.

"It is no accident that the next four Sundays all have names of great jubilation and hope: *Misericordia, Jubilate, Cantate* and *Rogate*. And do not forget the miracle of forgiveness and love that took place centuries ago in this very convent and from which it took its name

Himmelpforte, Heaven's Gate (in Latin, *Porta Coeli*): when the sister doorkeeper erred and fled with her confessor, the Blessed Virgin took her place, assuming her appearance. And only when the sinner returned in penitence did the abbess learn of the substitution and the Virgin reveal herself, blessing the sinner, and disappearing before the astonished eyes of all the nuns. Rejoice and hope in the clemency of the Most High!" concluded the priest.

It really was time to hope, I told myself, swayed by the words from the pulpit. Nobody had yet come looking for us, at home or elsewhere. If all went well, as my assistant had predicted, Dànilo's death would be written off as the result of a drunken brawl, or a settling of scores among minor criminals. The exequies would be taken care of by some merciful charitable confraternity.

During the religious service Atto asked Domenico to look first this way, then the other, and then back again. He was looking for someone, and I knew perfectly well whom. At the end he asked me.

"Has she come?"

"Who?" I pretended not to understand.

"What do you mean, who? The Pálffy woman, curse it. On some pretext Domenico got one of the nuns at Porta Coeli to describe her to him. She told us that she often comes to St Agnes for the first mass. But there's no one here who matches the description."

"I can't help you, Signor Atto," I answered, while someone in the pew behind shushed us, muttering disgruntled remarks about the usual prattling Italians.

I looked upwards. In the gallery sat the nuns, while the lay sisters were at the front of the nave. I also saw the Chormaisterin: bent over her kneeler, she was praying fervently, raising her face to the holy crucifix and then to the statue of the Blessed Virgin of Porta Coeli. I stared more attentively: from the way her shoulders shook I would have said that Camilla was weeping. The evening before she had struck me as tense and nervous. Cloridia remarked it too, and looked at me inquisitively; I answered with a show of dumb perplexity. I had no idea myself what was agitating our good friend.

At the door Atto and Domenico waited a little longer for the Emperor's lover to appear, or at least a young woman corresponding to the description they had received of her, but in vain.

Another possibility, said Domenico, was that Countess Marianna Pálffy might go to the nine-thirty service, the mass for the nobility, in the Cathedral of St Stephen. There was nothing for it but to arrange to meet there, in the hope of better luck.

There was a little time before the service began and so we lingered in the convent church. Cloridia and I were looking around for Camilla; we were hoping to be able to speak to her and to find out what was upsetting her. Meanwhile Atto had asked Domenico to escort him towards the headmistress of the convent's novitiate, who, he hoped, would lead him to Pálffy.

"Suor Strassoldo?" said Atto with great urbanity, using Italian since the nun's surname was Italian.

"*Von* Strassoldo, please!" brusquely answered the sister – a thin, middle-aged woman with small, menacing blue eyes.

Atto was caught off-guard: omitting the patronymic "von", which testified to the Strassoldo family's noble blood, was not a good start.

"Please excuse me, I –"

"𝔜ou are excused, but so am 𝔍," von Strassoldo cut him off. "𝔍 have many things to see to and 𝔍 don't speak 𝔍talian. 𝔍'm certain that the 𝔠hormaisterin will be able to help you in anything you need." With that she turned and walked away, leaving Abbot Melani and Domenico flustered and above all humiliated, since other nuns had been present at the short conversation. Not even with a blind man had the tetchy mistress of the novitiate sweetened her manners.

"Signor Abbot," I whispered in his ear, while the other nuns moved away, "people behave differently from the way they do in Italy, and perhaps in France too. When they don't welcome a conversation, they cut it short."

"Oh, forget about it," Abbot Melani interrupted me, extremely irritated. "I understand perfectly: that silly old woman of Italian origins does not like her old compatriots. They're all the same, people of that sort: after just one generation they pretend they don't remember where they came from. Just like the Habsburgs and the Pierleoni."

The latter name was entirely new to me. What had that Italian surname got to do with the glorious Habsburgs, the Emperor's family?

"Don't you know who the Pierleoni are?" asked Atto with a cruel little smile.

According to official historiography, he explained, the Habsburg Empire was born from the ashes of the Roman Empire, which had died out on account of the barbarian invasions of Goths and

Longobards. Thanks to his heroic valour, Charlemagne drove the Longobards from Italy and was acclaimed Roman Emperor. Subsequently, thanks to the undefeated virtue of the German Otho the Great, the name, insignia and authority of the Roman Empire passed down to the most glorious Germanic nation, and at present they rested with the Austrian lineage of the Habsburgs, the resurrected progeny of the Caesars.

"But this is the balderdash that historians peddle," hissed Atto, throwing a malevolent glance in the direction of Strassoldo, "because nobody wants to dig up the truth on the origins of the Habsburgs."

The history of the Habsburg emperors began with Rudolph I, who ascended to the throne in the year of Our Lord 1273. All were agreed on this point.

"But what happened before that day," said Abbot Melani, "nobody knows."

According to some scholars, the origin of the Habsburg blood should be traced back to to a certain Guntram, whose son around the year 1000 was supposed to have founded a castle of the name Hasburg, which is to say Habsburg. Others traced it back to a certain Ottobert, around 654. Still others to Aeganus, the royal house-steward of France, who had married Gerbera, daughter of St Gertrude.

Other scholars answered indignantly: not a bit of it, the Habsburgs descend from the royal blood of the Merovingians. Prince Sigebert, son of Dietrich of Austrasia, in the year 630 had received the county of the Alemans from the King of France, and his successor Sigebert II had assumed the title of Count of Habsburg. It was from his son Pabo of Alsatia, after nineteen generations, that Rudolph I was finally to descend.

Most certainly not, thundered scholars even more learned than the previous ones: the Habsburgs descend from Adam.

The dynastic series (which included the kings of Babylon, of Troy, of the Sicambrians, kings and counts of France, kings of Gaul, kings of Austrasia, dukes of Alsatia and of Alamannia, counts of Habsburg and of Ergau) according to these scholars was as clear and limpid as the sun, although a little patience was required to read it all through: Adam, Seth, Enos, Cain, Mahalel, Iared, Enoch, Methusalem, Lamech, Noah, Chus, Nimrod, Cres, Coelius, Saturn, Jupiter, Dardanus I, Erichthonius, Tros, Ilus, Laomedon, Antenor I, Marcomir, Antenor II, Priam I, Helenus, Diocles, Bassan, Cladodius

I, Nicanor, Marcomir II, Clogius, Antenor III, Estomir II, Merodacus, Cassander, Antharius, Franco, Chlodio, Marcomir III, Clodomir, Antenor IV, Ratherius, Richimerus, Odemar, Marcomir IV, Clodomir IV, Farabert, Hunno, Hilderich, Quather, another Chlodio, Dagobert, Genebald, another Dagobert, Faremond, yet another Chlodio, Meroveus, Childeric, Clodoveus the Great, Clothar, Sigisbert or Sigebert, Childepert, Theodopert, another Sigisbert, yet another Sigisbert, Ottbert, Bebo, Robert, Hettopert, Rampert, Gunstramo, Luithardo, Luitfrido, Hunifrido, another Gunthram or perhaps Gunstram, Belz, Rapatus, Werner, Otto, another Werner, Albert the Divine, Albert the Wise and finally the usual Rudolph I.

Of course, in this reconstruction the names of many kings appeared several times, with uncertain spellings (Bebo or Pabo? Gunstramo or Gunthram? Sigisbert or Sigebert?), and nothing was very clear at the end of it. What was good, however, was that the competing scholars, worn out, had given up rebutting one another.

But there were other researchers, the most learned and unstinting, who objected: did Rudolph I not descend from Albert the Wise? Well, Albert the Wise descended from Alberto Pierleoni, Count of Mount Aventine, member of an ancient and illustrious Roman family. Having moved from Rome to Switzerland, Alberto Pierleoni had married the daughter of Werner, last count of Habsburg, thus founding the dynastic line, Habsburg-Pierleoni. The Roman family went back to Leone Anicio Pierleoni, who died in 1111, of highly noble blood because he descended from none other than the Roman Emperor Flavius Anicius Olybrius.

"Unfortunately, the theory of their descent from Pierleoni, which was very fashionable under Leopold, Joseph I's father, proved suicidal," sneered Atto, still furious at being humiliated by Strassoldo.

The Pierleoni, as other experts observed, were a rich and powerful family but had been tarnished by some extremely embarrassing affairs. It included cardinals and bishops but also grasping and unscrupulous merchants and bankers, who maliciously financed the Holy See with the aim of making it an accessory to simony, so they could blackmail it and turn it into their own profitable backyard. A Pierleoni was elected pope under the name of Gregory VI in 1045, but it was then discovered that he had shamelessly bought the papal seat from his predecessor, Benedict IX. This reached the ears of Emperor Frederick III, who descended upon Italy, forced Gregory VI to resign and retire into exile in Germany, where the ex-Pope then died, surrounded by general scorn.

Another Pierleoni was elected pope in 1130 under the name of Anacletus II, but on the day of his election another cardinal was appointed pope under the name Innocent II, causing a grave schism that created anguish and torment throughout Christianity (Anacletus was to quarrel with five more popes). In addition, according to other rumours, the Pierleoni family (who, like so many medieval Roman families had their own private army and fortified castles in the middle of the city, and regularly went to war against rival families) were actually of Jewish blood: their forefather, a certain Baruch, was a Jew who had converted to Christianity, and the legend according to which some popes had been secretly Jewish was based on the true story of the Pierleoni. In addition, the Jews were far from popular with Emperor Leopold I, father of Joseph I the Victorious, and he had confined them in a ghetto on the other side of the Danube, the Leopoldine Island, just where the Turks had pitched camp during the siege of 1683.

"In short," concluded Atto, taking me by the arm and cackling, "the glorious Roman family from which the imperial blood of the Habsburgs is supposed to descend was composed of popes, long disliked by most people in Vienna; of Jews, disliked by Emperor Leopold I; and by Italians, disliked by everyone: you saw how that idiotic Strassoldo woman behaved."

Meanwhile Camilla de' Rossi had come up to us and Cloridia had addressed her. The two women were now talking animatedly in front of a small group of young novices. I went up to them, taking Atto by the arm. We came into earshot just as my wife was answering questions from the novices, who were very curious about us, a family of strange Italians who had come to Vienna from the distant city of the Pope. Camilla was acting as interpreter from German to Italian and vice-versa.

The young women (all of excellent families and very well-behaved) asked about Rome and its splendours, the Pope and the Roman court, and finally wanted to know about the life we had led there, as well as our past. I listened with a touch of anxiety, since Cloridia had to conceal the stain of the infamous profession she had practised during her troubled adolescence.

"I don't remember anything of my youthful years," she replied, "and besides my poor mother was Tur . . ."

Just as she was about to reveal her mother's Eastern origins, I felt Atto start and his wizened hand clutched my arm. I saw Camilla de' Rossi's eyes open wide and she broke in brusquely: "Now my dears, it's time to get to work, we've talked long enough."

As soon as the little group of nuns had moved away, Camilla took Cloridia's arm and, approaching me and Abbot Melani, she explained the brusque end to the conversation.

"A few years ago, in the church of St Ursula near here, on the Johannesgasse, Cardinal Collonitz baptised a young Turkish slave who belonged to his lieutenant, the Spaniard Gerolamo Giudici, and assigned her to this novitiate. At once a revolt broke out in the convent, because the nuns, who were all of noble descent, were afraid that Porta Coeli would lose its good name. Giudici insisted and the dispute was taken as far as the Emperor and the consistory, who found for the nuns: the young Turkish woman was refused entrance."

Actually the poor girl was terrified of being locked up in a convent, continued Camilla. Fearing that sooner or later Giudici would succeed in finding one for her, one night she managed to run away. Despite long and careful searches, nobody could discover where she had fled, or with whom.

"As you can understand, my friends," Camilla concluded, "certain arguments just cannot be touched on here."

Collonitz. The name was not new to me. Where had I heard it before? I was unable to answer this. At any rate, the message was clear: if anyone at Porta Coeli were to discover that Cloridia was the daughter of a Turkish slave, we would probably be forced to leave the place in an instant.

A quarter of an hour later, after a short walk through the snowy streets, while Cloridia was at the palace, I went with Atto and Domenico to the Cathedral of St Stephen, in search of Countess Pálffy.

At the nine-thirty service here the atmosphere was very different from St Agnes. First of all, it needs saying that while the three p.m. weekday vespers only brought in a handful of old women and a few beggars, late-morning Sunday masses were so crowded that one had to go from church to church to find somewhere to sit.

In the square outside the church, dazzling with the fresh snow, was one of the typical beggars you will find in front of every Viennese church every day of the year. Dressed in a light blue skirt, she had a little box for alms fastened to her waist, which she shook as people passed her on the way into church. When we approached she leaped as if possessed and shouted to the crowd: "Come and be blessed! Come and be blessed!" Abbot Melani and Domenico were quite startled. The nine o'clock rosary had just finished and the priest was about to give the benediction. There was a sudden rush into the cathedral, and we found ourselves dragged along in a stampede of stomping, sliding, slush-encrusted boots, which bespattered the atrium with mud and snow. Those few people who gave no signs of wanting to enter the church were berated by the beggar with curses and insults.

"Here in Vienna Sundays are truly hallowed, it seems," remarked Atto, stamping his feet free of snow once inside, while his nephew rearranged his hat and cloak, which had been unsettled by the horde of eager churchgoers.

"Not only Sundays," I explained with a slight laugh, as I adjusted my own clothes. "Every day, here in St Stephen's alone, there are eighty masses and three rosaries. The Franciscans celebrate thirty-three masses a day at regular intervals, and in the church of St Michael there's one every quarter of an hour."

"Every day?" said Atto and his escort in amazed unison.

"I counted them up myself," I went on, "and I worked out that every year, just in the Cathedral of St Stephen, they celebrate over 400 pontifical offices, almost 60,000 masses, over a thousand rosaries, and about 130,000 confessions and communions."

Without counting benedictions, I concluded, as Atto and Domenico listened in astonishment: there were always a few in one or other of the over hundred churches and chapels in the city, so that more than once the city authorities had asked the priests to agree on regular schedules for everyone, to save the people running randomly from one church to another in spasmodic search of a blessing.

Once inside the church we realised that high mass was under way, and the service was being celebrated at a dozen altars simultaneously. Where could Countess Marianna Pálffy be hidden, if she were there? The enterprise was becoming complicated.

As we made our way down the nave, I looked all around myself. Noblemen and ministers with powdered wigs had their backs turned to the altar and were exchanging tobacco, reading letters and recounting anecdotes from the newspapers. Leaning against the columns of the aisle, they observed and remarked upon new fashions or beautiful women, the gigantic dimensions of St Stephen's guaranteeing confidentiality and safety from prying eyes. The individual altars were meeting places, and even had their own nicknames to distinguish them: "𝕷𝖊𝖙'𝖘 𝖒𝖊𝖊𝖙 𝖆𝖙 𝖙𝖍𝖊 𝖜𝖍𝖔𝖗𝖊𝖘' 𝖆𝖑𝖙𝖆𝖗," people would say; or "𝖆𝖙 𝖙𝖍𝖊 𝖇𝖆𝖐𝖊𝖉 𝖈𝖆𝖐𝖊," "𝖆𝖙 𝖙𝖍𝖊 𝖋𝖑𝖔𝖗𝖎𝖓𝖘' 𝖘𝖖𝖚𝖆𝖗𝖊," "𝖆𝖙 𝖙𝖍𝖊 𝖜𝖊𝖓𝖈𝖍𝖊𝖘' 𝖑𝖆𝖓𝖊," "𝖆𝖙 𝖙𝖍𝖊 𝖗𝖆𝖒𝖕𝖆𝖗𝖙 𝖈𝖔𝖙𝖙𝖆𝖌𝖊𝖘". These were all indecent allusions to the fact that these altars were favourite spots to meet women of loose morals; the poor priests could do nothing about this and were often jeered at by the women.

This immoral behaviour was so deeply rooted that some religious services had been given abusive nicknames: the 10.30 mass in the church of the Capuchins was referred to openly as the "𝖜𝖍𝖔𝖗𝖊𝖘' 𝖒𝖆𝖘𝖘", and the one at 11 o'clock in St Stephen's as the "𝖑𝖔𝖆𝖋𝖊𝖗𝖘' 𝖒𝖆𝖘𝖘".

But the harlots and their clients were not the only plagues of the cathedral: this morning as ever (and this was Sunday *in albis*!) the church was crowded with all manner of people and animals and goods: bumpkins and crones stood around with piglets under their arms, or even tubs full of squawking chickens, geese and ducks; lazy noblemen had themselves carried in sedan chairs right up to the altar, and their equally idle servants then parked the chairs inside the church, too lazy to go and wait outside.

In short, the high mass was like a gigantic fairground: a constant profane bustle, with a *sottofondo* of endless babbling.

His Caesarean Majesty, by means of an imperial licence, had appointed commissioners whose job it was to walk around the church and threaten to fine or arrest anyone disturbing the services with idle chatter or inappropriate behaviour. The revenue from the fines was distributed among the poor. However, these sanctions made no difference. As the circulars of the episcopal consistory complained, in St Stephen's the people persisted in gathering in groups, gossiping, swearing, blaspheming, walking to and fro, knocking back liquors and engaging in blatant mercenary activities, mocking, vilifying and even threatening those who warned them to respect the sacred temple.

At the end of the mass we waited outside again, observing the congregation as they left the church, mingling with the crowd of Sunday strollers. "Domenico," said Atto, "even if it's cold I want to go for a short walk . . ."

"Wait, Uncle."

Atto Melani's nephew was standing on tiptoes, as alert as a bloodhound. He was observing a group of three young women, and in particular a very tall one with fiery red hair, bundled up under a small hat that was too flimsy for the weather.

"It's her, Uncle, I really think it's her. She's going back home."

"Let's follow her, damn it. Boy, come with me," said Melani, addressing me.

The three young women were heading towards Carinthia Street, and were walking against the flow, pushing their way through the crowd of Sunday strollers all converging on the centre of the city. We followed the three girls at a reasonable distance, not wishing to give the impression that this bizarre trio (consisting of a blind old man, a midget and only one person of marriageable age, Domenico) was trying to force its attentions on three pretty young maidens.

"As soon as they slow down, go and introduce yourself," Atto ordered Domenico, "and give her the letter."

"Which letter?" I said with a start, thinking of the letter in which Eugene had offered to betray the Emperor to the French.

"Just a note with a humble request from two Italian cavaliers seeking the honour to be received by the Countess, and offering her our services."

A propitious occasion presented itself just a few moments later. The three young women paused to exchange a few words with an elderly nun, who then continued on her way. The three girls lingered on the spot for a few moments. Domenico walked up to them and with a graceful bow introduced himself. He was a handsome young man, fresh-faced and well-mannered, with a gentle, pleasing voice. He must have chosen the right words, because we saw Pálffy's face, which had a slight tinge of sadness, brighten at the compliment he offered. I wondered what hidden worry she had. The little group exchanged a few amiable words. Domenico was about to put his hand into his waist-coat pocket, perhaps his fingers were already touching Atto's note.

But a familiar noise had been growing louder by the instant. A splendid two-horse carriage, clanking and rattling, was heading straight towards the trio of young women and Domenico. The postillion made a gesture of salutation to the Countess, who responded immediately, taking her eyes off Atto's nephew. The carriage had now pulled up, the doors opened and the three women prepared to climb in. I described to Atto what was happening.

"The note, has he given her the note?" asked Abbot Melani, frothing and thrusting his face forward like a tethered steed.

At that precise moment two footmen climbed down from the carriage and helped the Emperor's lover to climb in. As she stepped onto the footboard, Domenico handed her the note. She took it in her hand, but with a very courteous gesture gave it straight back to him without opening it. In the meantime, still holding Atto by the arm, I approached them. An instant before she disappeared inside the vehicle, I saw Pálffy's face tense up as she gave way to a discreet and subdued fit of weeping. The carriage moved off, Domenico gave a timid wave, but no response came from within.

"Curse it," said Atto, gnashing his teeth when his nephew told him the outcome of the encounter. "These twenty-year-old lovers are always ready to burst into tears and never understand a thing. We won't find another occasion like this so easily."

❧

13 of the clock: luncheon hour for noblemen. The middle classes enter the coffee houses, and performances begin in the theatres.

As he took his leave, Abbot Melani bade me meet him again at lunchtime: we would eat again in some public place. I explained that it would be better to meet before one o'clock, because in Vienna only noblemen eat after one, and prices go up steeply.

"Good to know," he answered. "So let's *not* meet before one o'clock. I like to share my table only with people of my own rank."

When the time came I took him and Domenico to an eating house near the Hofburg. We arrived just in time: it had started snowing again.

I asked at once if we could be seated at one of the more secluded tables. The *cantiniere* came up and rattled off the rich list of dishes of the day, which included Styrian, Polish, Hungarian, Czech and Moravian specialities, and for just a few extra pence some exotic ones: pomarances, oysters, almonds, chestnuts, pistachios, rice, muscatel grapes, wine from Spain, Dutch cheese, Cremona mortadella, Venetian sugared almonds and Indian spices.

We gave our orders and we were soon served a tender veal fillet, a coal-baked pink trout and succulent fritters with cream. As always, the quantities were far beyond the needs of any normal human being. As soon as they tasted it, Atto and his nephew were pleasantly surprised.

"I didn't know people ate as well as this in Vienna. Are we in some special place?" asked Domenico.

"We're in an eating house like a great many others. But I have to say that even in the lowest tavern here you'll be served the most fragrant soups, the crispest fries, the most savory roasts," I said warmly, proud of my adopted city. "All food in Vienna is of high quality, and always of the finest; every ingredient is as fresh as a rose, every portion generous, every dish freshly cooked. And all at decent prices."

"And in Paris all you can get are rancid cakes, rock-hard bread and fish from the age of Abraham!" exclaimed the Abbot, with a bitter sneer.

I was overjoyed with Atto Melani's amazement and I told him in precise detail all the gastronomic specialities of the heavenly soil he had the honour of treading. Actually, what I was really hoping was to lower Atto's guard and so make him ready to answer the questions I would put to him shortly about the death of Dànilo Danilovitsch. I knew Melani, and were I to subject him to my questions directly all I would get would be sly, hypocritical and misleading replies.

If the wealth of a nation can be measured by its food, I began solemnly, addressing my two wondering fellow-diners, then in Austria it was as if King Midas had passed by, transforming everything into gold. A normal family of three eats half a kilo of meat a day, something unimaginable in Rome.

As I held forth in this fashion, with Atto and his nephew looking more and more dazed, their attention was gradually distracted by an increase in noise from the neighbouring tables.

It was the less poetic side of the gastronomic passion that characterised the Caesarean capital.

Domenico looked around himself and soon his perplexed eyes fixed on the other diners in the restaurant: there were those who were using their napkins to blow their noses, scratch their heads or mop their brows; those who were swigging their wine, gurgling it in their throats and letting it dribble down their chins and necks; those who kept pouring out wines for their neighbours and digging their elbows amicably but forcefully into their stomachs if they did not knock it straight back; those using their forks to drag the heaviest portions of roast meat from a central tray to their plates, leaving an embarrassing trail of grease across the tablecloth; those licking their plates or scraping them with their fingernails; those sneezing or coughing loudly, spraying their neighbours with phlegm; one who was spitting; one who had burned his tongue with a boiling morsel and was roaring with pain; and finally one who had finished and was surreptitiously bundling up the leftover food in his napkin.

The expression on Atto's nephew's face was one of consternation. He threw an interrogative glance at me, which I pretended not to catch. He did not know that the Viennese lack of table manners had become the subject of sermons for the great Augustinian preacher Pater Abraham from Sancta Clara, and that other eminent authors had issued patient rebukes to the faithful, instructing them to behave less bestially at mealtimes!

"Domenico, I hear shouting. What is the matter?" asked Atto, picking at his trout.

At one of the central tables a highly embarrassing scene had taken place. A spit of roast meat had been served straight from the oven. One of the diners, wishing to remove the ash from a haunch of pork, had blown hard on the spit and the burning embers had ended up in the eyes of a woman sitting opposite. Her husband had demanded immediate redress from the guilty party. As their spirits were all heated with wine, a small altercation had broken out, which the staff had struggled hard to quell. Unfortunately before they did so the offended woman's husband had succeeded in plunging the scorching spit into his adversary's backside, which he had run off to medicate.

"Oh, it's nothing, Signor Uncle, a slight disagreement," said Domenico, not wishing to expose the less dignified side of the Viennese culinary passion, whose virtues I had just extolled.

"A friendly exchange of opinions," I said, trying to back up Domenico's lie, even though Atto was not fooled.

"These Viennese and their city are as vulgar as I have heard them to be in Paris," he said, not concealing the smug satisfaction he took in being able to disparage them. "They may be extremely rich, but their streets are as tangled as a ball of wool, and they're so narrow that the façades of the palaces, which deserve admiration, are difficult to see . . . though, of course, that does not matter much to me, since I have lost the gift of sight. I appreciate far more the squares of Vienna, where I can walk without any inconvenience, since they're all paved with very hard stones, are they not?"

"The stones are so hard that not even the heaviest wheels of the country carts can harm them," I confirmed.

"As I thought. But there remains the fact that as the roads are so narrow, the rooms are extraordinarily dark and, what is most annoying, there is no building that is inhabited by only five or six families. Highly distinguished ladies, and even ministers of court, are separated from the apartment of a cobbler or a tailor only by a partition wall, and there is no one who lives on more than two floors of a palace: one for himself and the other for the servants. The owners of the palaces rent out the rest to anyone who asks, and so the great stone staircases are always as dirty and shabby as the streets. But then of course you don't see the dirt: the buildings are too high, the streets are dark and very little light gets in through the windows. Of course, I can see nothing in any case, alas, but that is what they say in Paris about Vienna. Can you confirm it?"

"You're not wrong – it's often like that, Signor Atto," I agreed, overwhelmed by his sudden baleful outburst. "However, I would just point out that the interior of the houses –"

"I know, I know," the old castrato broke in. "I've heard that once you've climbed the stairs, there is nothing more astounding than the rooms where the Viennese *beau monde* live: a series of eight or ten great spacious rooms, with doors and windows all richly carved and gilded, furniture and ornaments of a quality rarely found elsewhere in Europe even in the most princely residences, tapestries from Brussels, gigantic mirrors with silver frames, beds and canopies with damask and velvets of fine taste, great paintings, Japanese porcelain, enormous chandeliers in rock crystal . . ."

While Atto rattled on, I thought of the occasions when my work had brought me into the homes of the wealthy. Amazing the power of Parisian gossip! Atto was blind, but it was as if he had seen everything with his own eyes. He was clearly torn between admiration and envy for the enemies of France: the previous day, when he arrived, he had been full of praise for Vienna, the Caesars and their restrained opulence, and he had lashed out against the arrogant dissipation of the French, which had brought the country to ruin. But now, envy at all this wealth was stirring him to more venomous and defamatory judgements. Old Abbot Melani was becoming somewhat self-contradictory, I thought with a smile. Unless . . . I was struck by a doubt: suppose Atto had not been sincere the previous day? Suppose he had extolled the good sense of the emperors and the prosperity of their capital city only to avert any suspicion that he might have come to Vienna to plot in league with the Turks? I decided to try an open question:

"Signor Atto, what do you think of the Agha's mission? What do you think he's trying to obtain from His Caesarean Majesty?"

"That is what I would like to know myself. It could help me greatly in my – or rather in *our* mission. The suburbs of Vienna, I was saying . . ." he added, returning to the previous subject and biting into a cream-fritter, "like your Josephina, are exquisite. I wonder how often you yourself have paused to admire that jewel, the Vice-Chancellor's summer villa, Schönborn, from the outside. Yesterday we went for a walk around it, before going to the theatre. They even talk of it in Versailles. And what a garden! And what enormous orange and lemon trees, all in gilded vases! At least that's how my nephew described it to me."

Domenico nodded politely. I returned to the attack, this time with a fairly explicit provocation, hoping to stir Atto into some revealing reaction.

"Of course, it would be very convenient for France," I said, "if a new conflict were to break out between the Empire and the Turks: His Caesarean Majesty would have to engage his armies in the East as well. It would be a great relief to the Most Christian King."

"I really don't think that can happen," answered Atto blandly. "After the treaty of Karlowitz the Eastern waters are peaceful. The Turkish embassy that has just arrived has no other aim than to remind people that the Sultan is still alive, and it strikes me as a purely theatrical gambit."

He had contradicted himself. Just a moment before he had said that he had no idea what the motive for the Ottoman embassy was and that he would like to know more.

"By the way," he added, changing the subject yet again, "as I mentioned, yesterday afternoon we went to the theatre. They told me that Marianna Pálffy adores comedies, and I hoped to meet her. We took a box for four people; the ticket was very cheap, a ducat. The theatre was dark and the ceiling too low, but I've never laughed so much in my life! Thanks to the description my nephew gave me, of course."

I made no reply to this idle chatter, but Atto went on regardless:

"It was a comedy in which Jove assumes the guise of Amphitrion in order to go to bed with his wife Alcmene. But mostly he runs up a series of debts in his place, and for most of the play we see poor Amphitrion being pursued by his creditors. Idle nonsense, with bawdy jokes that wouldn't be tolerated from a fishwife in Paris, ha ha."

Atto persisted in ignoring my questions about the Agha's embassy, which was the hottest news of the day in Vienna. It was so blatant that it became suspicious.

"Fashion is terrible here as well, isn't that right Domenico?" he continued to ramble.

"Yes, Signor Uncle."

"Sadly I am denied the light of day, dear nephew. In such a large city I can't even observe the attire of the inhabitants, but I'm not missing much. I know this very well because Domenico reads to me from the Parisian gazettes just how awful the fashion of the Caesarean court is if compared with that of France or England. The only thing they have in common is that ladies wear skirts. Otherwise, Viennese fashion is monstrous and against all common sense. Here even the richest fabric is embroidered heavily in gold and a dress only has to be costly to be admired, no matter whether it's in good taste or not. On other days, people just put on a simple cloak and whatever they want underneath. Isn't that true, dear nephew?"

"Yes, Signor Uncle," repeated Domenico.

I was beginning to lose patience.

"For example, here in Vienna it's considered especially beautiful to have as much hair as an average-sized barrel could contain. And so ladies have enormous scaffoldings of starched gauze set up and fixed to their heads with ribbons. Then they put them on their heads, resting on round rods, the same ones, the same ones that our dairy-maids use to hang buckets of fresh milk on, and they cover this whole infernal contraption with false hair, which everyone here considers extremely elegant."

"Signor Atto –" I tried in vain to interrupt him.

"Then, to hide the difference from real hair," he went on regardless, "they sprinkle the whole contrivance with pounds of powder and wind it round with three or four strings of diamonds fixed with enormous brooches of pearls or other stones, red, green or yellow.

And then, with this paraphernalia on their heads, they can barely move! You can imagine how this outlandish way of dressing brings out the natural ugliness that nature chose to confer on women here, to match their sour, crabbed characters. They told me in Paris that there's no liveliness here, everybody is stolid and phlegmatic and no one ever gets excited, except over questions of ceremonial. That's where the Viennese expend all their most frenzied passions. But is it true?"

"Not so far as I've noticed," I answered, irritated by the stream of insults that Atto was directing at my adopted city; if he had such a bad opinion of it, I would have liked to say, why had he sent me here?

"And yet I have looked into the question and at the post station I heard that a little while ago two carriages crashed into one another in a narrow street and the ladies inside refused to agree to reverse and give way to the other, since they were both of the same rank. They spent almost the whole night listing their own titles and merits to prove that the other should reverse and soon enough their yells could be heard in the neighbouring streets. It seems they even woke the Emperor, who had to send his own guards to make them stop, and the only way they could resolve things in the end was by pulling both carriages back at the same time and sending them on their way by alternative routes," he concluded with an impertinent little laugh.

All I could do was try the final thrust:

"Signor Atto, there's been a murder," I suddenly said.

At last Abbot Melani's chatter came to a halt.

"A murder? What are you saying, boy?"

"Last night. A friend of Simonis, my apprentice. Simonis had asked some of his friends, whom I'd met, to look into the question of this strange Golden Apple that the Turkish Agha talked about in his audience with Prince Eugene."

"I remember it perfectly. And so?"

"Last night Simonis and I had an appointment with one of these students, on the ramparts. His name was Dánilo, Count Dánilo Danilovitsch. We found him on the point of death. They had stabbed him several times; he died in our arms."

Abbot Melani took his blind eyes off me, turning mournful and worried at the same time.

"It's a very sad affair," he said after a few moments of silence. "Did he have any family?"

"Not in Vienna."

"Did anyone see you while you were tending to this Count Dánilo?"

"We don't think so."

"Good. So you shouldn't get involved in the matter," he said with a note of relief in his voice; if I were to be drawn into the enquiries, someone might follow the thread and arrive at him, an enemy spy.

"Did you say his name was Danilovitsch? That isn't a German name. Where did he come from?"

"From Pontevedro."

"Ah, well, they're not civilised people. Count indeed! Pontevedro! They're little more than brutes, rough people . . ."

Abbot Melani seemed to see things just like Simonis, who had coined the term "Half-Asia".

"I'll bet that to support himself in his studies he took on some fourth-rate job," added Atto.

"Spying. He denounced anyone who broke the laws on modesty in dress for money."

"A spy by profession! And you're amazed that someone like that, a Pontevedrin what's more, should end up stabbed? Boy, it's always sad of course, but there's nothing surprising about this death. Forget all about it," Melani said decisively, apparently not remembering that he too was a spy by profession.

"And suppose it was the Turks? Dànilo was looking into the Golden Apple. While he was dying he whispered some strange sentences."

Atto listened with interest to what the poor student had muttered before breathing his last.

"The cry of the forty thousand martyrs," he repeated thoughtfully when I had finished, "and then this mysterious Eyyub . . . It sounds like the ravings of a poor wretch in his death throes. Dànilo Danilovitsch may have found out something about the Golden Apple, but it all seems quite clear to me: the Turks have nothing to do with it, your friend ended up just as one might expect a Pontevedrin spy to do."

The meal with Atto left me with a sense of sour uneasiness on two accounts. Abbot Melani had avoided my questions about the

Turkish embassy too openly, somehow, as if the event were of no interest, and instead had subjected me to an annoying series of irrelevant reflections on Viennese customs. Too cold a reaction, I said to myself, for such a consummate diplomat as Atto, drawn to all intrigues and secrets, to any item of news on the political front.

The second reason for concern was the way he had dismissed the death of poor Dànilo Danilovitsch. Just why, although he listened with interest to the last words Dànilo had uttered before dying, had he chosen to draw all suspicion away from the Turks?

Atto announced that in the afternoon he would try to approach Countess Pálffy once again. I made no reply. Let him handle it by himself, I thought.

I had to go with Simonis to an important meeting: his study companions were going to to get together to report the information they had gathered on the Golden Apple.

❧

A short while later I was in Penicek's trap, alongside Simonis. I was beginning to appreciate that my assistant had at his disposal a docile Pennal, even though lame, with a means of transport thrown in. Simonis had a slave: something that not even I, who fed him, could boast.

We began the journey in total silence. The memory of Dànilo's last moments weighed on us. It was easy to deduce that the death had been due to Dànilo's dangerous activity as a sycophant, as Abbot Melani had at once affirmed. But the suspicion that the poor wretch had been killed on acount of what he had learned about the Golden Apple, although not supported by any definite evidence, was in our minds and, drop by vitriolic drop, was injecting remorse into our hearts. I caught Simonis gazing at me absorbedly.

"You still haven't asked me, Signor Master," he said, forcing himself to smile, "what jobs my companions do to support themselves in their studies so that they don't end up in the academic prison for illegal begging."

The Greek was trying to tear down the curtain of doleful silence.

"You're right," I said, "I know hardly anything about them."

Overwhelmed by all that happened in the last few days, I had asked my assistant very little about his friends. Given poor Dànilo's ambiguous occupation, and Penicek's irregular one, I was both curious and diffident as to the kinds of jobs they might be engaged in.

"Koloman Szupán is the richest of all," Simonis informed me, "because he's a waiter. As you already know, our Pennal here present is a coach driver. Dragomir Populescu has little time to earn a crust of bread; he spends all his time with women. He tries it on with all of them, but with very little success. Koloman hardly ever tries but always succeeds."

"Oh yes? And how does he do that?"

"He has what you might call extraordinary means at his disposal," said Simonis, with a slight smile. "The word has spread among young Viennese women, who focus on the essentials and who are always very, very satisfied with Koloman. If you're lucky, Signor Master, soon we'll have proof."

"Proof?"

"It's three p.m. and at this hour Koloman is always hard at it. He has extraordinary vigour; every day at this hour he has to give free vent to his energies, otherwise he gets sad. If he doesn't have a fine wench to hand, he's liable to climb the first window he sees, wherever he is, and make his way across roofs and eaves to find some willing beauty. I've seen him at it with my own eyes."

We had reached a modest little house near the ramparts. After ordering Penicek to wait for us outside, the young Greek knocked. A young man opened up, saying at once:

"He's upstairs, he's busy."

Simonis answered with a knowing smile. When we were inside he explained that the whole house, a small two-storey building, was rented to a group of students, who were all intimately acquainted with each other's habits. In the narrow hallway we sat down on an old bench, close to the staircase leading to the upper floor. I had hardly had time to shake the snow from my cloak when a cry came to us from upstairs.

"𝔄aaaahhh! 𝔜es, like that, again . . ." cried a girl's voice.

"We won't have long to wait, Koloman knows we can't arrive late," whispered Simonis, winking at me.

"𝔜ou're an animal, a beast . . . 𝔄gain, go on, please!" continued the Teutonic woman imploringly.

But Koloman must have heard we had arrived. We heard his voice offer some tactful objection. The discussion continued for a while and then grew more animated. Suddenly we heard a door slam violently, the same woman's voice insulting Koloman and then footsteps descending the stairs. We saw the young woman (quite pretty, blond hair gathered at the back of her neck, plain but new clothes) running towards the door, foaming with rage. Before stepping outside, ignoring our presence, she turned back towards the staircase and shouted a last epithet at Koloman:

"𝔜ou're just a miserable 𝔥ungarian waiter, you deformed beast!"

She slammed the door so hard that the whole hallway shook.

"The usual Viennese refinement," said Simonis with a soothing smile.

Just then our friend came downstairs, buttoning his shirt with an expression halfway between embarrassed and amused.

"Actually I'm a baron, the twenty-seventh Koloman Szupán of my family, to be precise, and I only work as a waiter to support myself while studying," he said as if the young woman were still there. "Excuse the rather unedifying scene, but the Viennese are like that: when you have an engagement and are obliged to speed things up, they lose their tempers and turn unfriendly. Whereas in Italy . . ."

"Women are more patient?" I guessed, while Koloman put on his cloak to go out.

"In Italy I never speed things up," smiled Koloman, slapping Simonis on the back and walking towards the door.

The Pennal's trap set off again slowly, plodding along the road with its soft mantle of snow towards Populescu's home: the same apartment where two days earlier I had attended the scene of the Deposition. It was here that the group of students had agreed to meet: each of them had sought information about the Golden Apple, and they would undoubtedly have some news to give us. Unfortunately, what might have been an enjoyable get-together among students had become an emergency meeting. Word of Dànilo's tragic death must have spread throughout the university, but obviously it was his friends who had been most affected by it. Koloman Szupán himself, after that first moment of cheerfulness, grew taciturn. To drive away sad thoughts, just as Simonis had done with me a moment earlier, I tried to strike up a conversation on the journey, and asked him if he was satisfied with his job as a waiter.

"Satisfied? For the moment, I thank God that Lent is over," said Koloman, mopping imaginary sweat from his brow.

"Why's that? I thought that in Lent waiters in inns worked less than usual, since you can't eat meat and so the diet must be lighter."

"Lighter?" Koloman burst out laughing. "In Lent you have to sweat twice as hard to do all those complicated fish recipes! Roast eel with lard; pike in sour cream; baked crabs with parsley-roots stewed in oil with lemon and oyster sauce; roast stockfish with horseradish, mustard and butter, not to mention roast beaver . . ."

"Roast beaver? But that's not a fish."

"Tell that to the Viennese! And you have to catch them, the furry wretches. Good job there are also Luther's eggs.

"Luther's?"

"Yes, the ones Luther will never eat. They're the Lenten eggs. They call them that as a joke, because Catholics eat them to abstain from meat, while the Protestants laugh and eat whatever they want. Then there's fish."

During the Lenten penitence, explained Koloman, in the kitchens of Viennese inns you'll find an unimaginable quantity of fish, and of an even greater variety than in Italy. Even among the mountains of the Tyrol there were those, like the famous doctor Guarinoni (yet another Italian), who advised people not to overdo it with all the things on offer: fish from streams, rivers, lakes and the sea, from the most unlikely places; from the Hungarian lake of Balaton, from Bohemia, Moravia, Galicia, Bosnia and the Italian coast of Trieste. From Venice special mail coaches brought heaps of oysters, sea-snails, mussels, crabs and clams, frogs and turtles, and other speci-alities arrived on special swift convoys even from Holland and the remote North Sea.

"I know they're placed under blocks of ice but don't ask me how on earth they get here still fresh after such a long journey; I've never understood it," added Koloman.

As it was a tough job to abstain from meat until Easter, and as water is always water, during Lent the menus would contain, along-side the fish and crustaceans, otters and beavers! All served roasted and eaten with great relish.

Abraham from Sancta Clara was quite right, I thought, when he said that in Vienna no animal of land, air or water can be sure of not ending up on the table.

"These Viennese," Koloman added, "didn't curb their appetites even when the Turks were breathing down their necks."

"What have the Turks got to do with it, Koloman?"

He explained that during the famous, dramatic and glorious siege of 1683, which has gone down in history, the Viennese never lost their appetite and relish for good cooking. While the city risked being conquered and razed to the ground, groups of Viennese, including women and children, would leave the fortress at night, at great risk to themselves and their fellow citizens, to go and buy bread from the Turks.

"From the Turks? And they sold it to them?"

"They had some really poor soldiers who needed the money. And in the Turkish camp they were never short of bread."

Those found guilty of such trafficking were punished in the respective camps, both by the Christians (three hundred whip-lashes) and by the Ottomans. However, Koloman explained, there was no way to put a stop to it. And in Vienna there was also the problem of thirst.

"Of course, water . . ." I remarked.

"No, there was always water. It was wine they'd run out of."

As the gourmet always prevailed over the soldier in the Viennese spirit, entire cartloads of wine were often intercepted, which had been brought down from the surrounding countryside, and which stole their way into the city at night. Sometimes unthinkable things would happen, like the occasion when the besieged Viennese, while the battle was raging, managed to get hold of an entire herd of over a hundred bullocks, from behind the Turkish lines (how this was managed was a mystery).

I heard with ill-concealed disappointment this behind-the-scenes insight into the great siege. How far removed from my grave meditations on the heroic resistance of the Viennese! Things had apparently been quite different.

"Not exactly the unblemished, fearless heroes of legend," I remarked dazedly.

"Oh, they were fearless all right. But they had plenty of blemishes: of wine and fat, on their collars and shirt sleeves," laughed Koloman.

Just think, he concluded, that during the siege in 1683 there was even someone in the city who had treacherously passed on a very valuable piece of information to the Turks: within the stronghold civilians and soldiers were no longer collaborating; the Viennese were exhausted and wanted to surrender.

"It was 5th September. Hardly anyone knows this story, which could have changed history. For some mysterious reason the Turks did not attack at once, and what a stroke of luck that was! Six days later reinforcements arrived and the Christian armies won."

But I knew why the Turks had not attacked Vienna at once: I had discovered it twenty years earlier in Rome with Abbot Melani. But it was a highly complicated story and if I told it to Koloman, he would not believe me.

By now we had arrived. Shaking the snow from our boots and our clothes, we were welcomed in by Dragomir Populescu, who was waiting for us with Jan Janitzki Opalinski. They greeted us with an anxious, anguished air. This time Penicek came in with us, and made his greetings, as awkwardly and ponderously as ever, with his ugly little eyes like a bespectacled ferret.

"I have news," said Opalinski at once.

"So have I," added Populescu.

"Where's Hristo?" asked Koloman.

"He was busy. He told me he'd be a little late," answered Simonis. "In the meantime we can start."

"But Koloman, what are you doing here at this hour? Have the good ladies of Vienna all stood you up today?" sniggered Dragomir, with a hint of bitterness in his voice.

"On the contrary. But you always leave them so horny, with your little sparrow's twig, that it just takes me three minutes each to make them come."

"Don't get worked up, Dragomir, keep calm ..." muttered Populescu, clenching his fists.

"That's enough joking," said Simonis. "Dànilo is dead, and we all have to be very careful."

They all fell silent for a moment.

"Friends," I spoke up, "I thank you for the help you're giving me on the question of the Golden Apple. However, after your companion's death, I won't blame you if you want to go no further."

"But perhaps Dànilo was bumped off by someone taking revenge for one of his acts of spying," muttered Opalinski thoughtfully.

"It may even have been one of his fellow-countrymen from Pontevedro," Populescu said in support. "They're real beasts there, not like where I come from in Romania."

"After all, he's certainly not the first student to end up murdered," added Koloman.

And they all competed in bringing up sad cases of students of the University of Vienna who had died violently for the most varied reasons: in duels, surprised while stealing; involved in smuggling *et cetera et cetera*.

"And they were all from Half-Asia," whispered Simonis to me with a significant glance, as if to underline the particular inclination of those people for an iniquitous life.

"Perhaps these Turks have nothing at all to hide," ventured Opalinski at last.

"Well, yes, it strikes me as strange that the Agha should have pronounced those words publicly, if there was anything secret behind them," said Populescu.

"Perhaps he wanted to send a coded message to someone, confident that anybody who was not in the know would not get suspicious," conjectured Koloman.

"That doesn't sound a great idea to me," answered Populescu.

"But they're Turks . . ." laughed Simonis.

The Greek's quip set them all laughing. I was almost tempted to tell them that I had seen the Agha's dervish carrying out horrifying rituals, and especially that Cloridia had heard him plotting to get someone's head, and that was why we were investigating the Golden Apple. In fact, none of those who had attended the Agha's audience, as Cloridia had done, had had the slightest suspicion and they had all interpreted the phrase "*soli soli soli ad aureum venimus aureum*", or "we've come here all alone to the Golden Apple", as a declaration of peaceful aims.

I guessed that the enthusiasm of those boys was strengthened by the mirage of the money that I had promised as a reward. But now Dànilo was dead, the game was turning dangerous, and perhaps it was right to talk. But Simonis, guessing my doubts, signalled to me with his eyes to keep quiet. And once again, like a coward, I did so.

Having no more to say about the sad end of their Pontevedrin companion, we started to talk about the Golden Apple.

Populescu explained that he had met a beautiful brunette, who served in a coffee shop. At first he had tried to ensnare her for base, seductive ends, but then he had thought it worth exploiting her acquaintance to ask a few questions about the Golden Apple, since the coffee shop owner came from the East.

"A brunette?" I said, surprised. "I thought that as students you would go searching in libraries and archives."

Simonis's companions explained that there was nothing to be got from books, other than information on the Imperial Apple or Orb, or the Orb of the Celestial Spheres, distant relatives of the Golden Apple.

"The Imperial Orb, as I'm sure you all know," explained Opalinski, who was very erudite, "is constituted by the terrestrial globe surmounted by the cross of Christ. The Archangel Michael holds it in one hand, while with the other he grips a cross in the form of a sword and hurls Lucifer into hell for his crimes of envy, pride and vanity against the Most High. It's no accident that in Hebrew the name Michael means: 'Who is like God.' That's why the Imperial Orb became the Caesarean emblem, given to the Holy Roman Emperors during their coronation as a symbol of the person destined by God to govern and protect the Christian people from evil. It derives in turn from the Orb of the Celestial Spheres, a representation of the sky surrounding the terraqueous orb. The Orb of the Celestial Spheres was a symbol of power as well: for the Romans and Greeks, it was an attribute of Jove, King of the Gods."

"What nonsense!" Populescu broke in. "Terracqueous orb, indeed. Everyone knows that in ancient times they thought the earth was flat."

"That just shows how ignorant you are," retorted Koloman Szupán, a great friend of the Pole. "That's the usual propaganda to make us think that today we're more evolved, intelligent and modern than in the past. And you've fallen for it."

"Quite right, Koloman," approved Opalinski. "The Greeks and Romans knew perfectly well that the earth was round; just think of Parmenides and the myth of Atlas, who holds the terracqueous orb on his shoulders. And even in the despised Middle Ages they all knew it. Did St Augustine not say that the earth is *moles globosa*, which is to say a ball? Apart from Cosmas Indicopleustes and Severianus of Gabala, only Lactantius went round saying that it was flat, but in his day no one believed him. But unfortunately some dunces with professorships dug up the ravings of Lactantius and passed them off as the ruling doctrine of the Middle Ages."

"Bah, historical nonsense," the Hungarian said, spitting on the floor.

"In any case," Populescu resumed, "the story of the Golden Apple is exclusively Turkish, and has been handed down by word of mouth alone. My brunette, as I was saying . . ."

"From mouth to mouth . . ." sneered Koloman. "The erudite Dragomir enjoyed an oral encounter with his brunette!"

"Are you just jealous because you couldn't think of anything better than asking those queer friars?" retorted the Romanian. "By the way, they send their greetings to you. They told me they have unforgettable memories of you."

"Don't get worked up, Dragomir, keep calm!" snarled Populescu, infuriated by the quips from the duo of Koloman and Opalinski.

The story of the Golden Apple as related by the young woman, he continued, was as follows:

"When the new sultan is crowned in Constantinople, they follow a very detailed ceremonial. The Sovereign is carried in a procession to a sanctuary outside the city: the tomb of Mahomet the Prophet's standard-bearer, the *condottiero* who conquered Constantinople, seizing it from the Christians. Here they make him put on a belt with the holy scimitar. Then he re-enters Constantinople and passes on horseback in front of the barracks of the janissaries, the Sultan's élite guards, where the commander of the sixty-first company, one of the four companies of archers, hands him a goblet full of sherbet. The new sultan drinks the entire contents of the goblet, then fills it with fragments of gold and hands it back, shouting: *Kizil Elmada görüsürüz!*, which means, 'We'll meet again at the Golden Apple!' It's an invitation to conquer the Christian West, whose churches are actually crowned by the Imperial Orb of Archangel Michael, or the gilded sphere surmounted by the cross of Christ, first and foremost the golden ball of the Basilica of St Peter. That's why Dànilo also mentioned Rome."

"But we knew most of this already," I objected. "What we really want to know is why the Golden Apple has that name. Otherwise we'll never understand why the Turks talked about it to Eugene of Savoy, and why they said they came *soli soli soli*, which is to say all alone. And we'll never truly understand what Dànilo said before he died."

"Just a moment," Populescu protested. "I haven't finished."

The story actually began, he explained, in the year 1529, during the first great siege of Vienna by the Turks. The date was familiar to me by now: in that year the armies of Suleiman the Magnificent had set up their general headquarters on the plain of Simmering, where Maxmilian was later to create the Place with No Name.

"As everyone knows," said Populescu, "after the long siege Suleiman's army had to give up the idea of conquest and go back home because of an exceptionally early and harsh winter, and the cold was too much for the Ottomans in their tents."

Suleiman then pointed out to his men the bell tower of St Stephen's, which could be seen very clearly from the Turkish camp. The Sultan could have given the order to destroy it by cannon fire, but instead said: "This time round we have to renounce the conquest of Vienna. But one day we will succeed! On that day, the tower you see will become a minaret for Mahometan prayer, and alongside it will rise a mosque. For this reason I want the tower to bear my own sign as well!"

And so Suleiman had them make a massive ball of pure gold, big enough to hold three bushels of grain, and sent it to the Viennese, offering an exchange: if they hoisted the ball to the top of the bell tower of St Stephen, Suleiman would refrain from destroying it by cannon fire. The Emperor agreed, and the ball was placed on the top of the tower.

"That is why Vienna has been known ever since as the Golden Apple of Germany and Hungary," concluded Populescu.

"But I found out something else," intervened Opalinski. "I questioned an Infidel stableman of Ofen, which is to say Buda in Hungary, who in turn had spoken to the interpreter in Agha's retinue, Yussuf, also from Ofen."

There was a murmur of approval, mixed with concern: one of the group had succeeded in getting information directly from the feared Ottomans.

"It wasn't easy," Janitzki stated. "At first he was very diffident. He didn't speak a word of Italian or German, and only understood a little *lingua franca*, the Ottoman jargon imported to Constantinople by Venetian and Genoese merchants."

Opalinski had approached the Infidel stableman, invoking Allah several times by way of greeting, in order not to arouse any suspicion, and had then started with the questions: but the other man had not been taken in and had asked at once:

"Say, Turque, who be you? Be Anabaptist? Zuinglist? Coffist? Hussite? Morist? Fronista? Be pagana? Lutheran? Puritan? Bramin? Moffin? Zurin?"

"Mahometan, Mahometan!" Jan had given the obvious answer to his diffident interlocutor, concerned to know whether he was of another religious faith.

"Hei valla, hei valla," the stable-keeper said, seeming a little reassured. "And what your name?"

"Giurdina," lied Opalinski.

"Be good Giurdina Turk?" the stable-keeper asked, with one finger raised, wanting to make certain of the Pole's loyalty to the Sultan.

"Ioc, ioc," he reassured him.

"You not be plotter? You not be cheat?"

"No, no, no!"

At which point the Infidel had started up:

> To Mahomet, for Giurdina,
> I will pray both morn and e'en-a
> I will make a Paladina
> Of Giurdina, of Giurdina,
> Turban give, and sabre-ina,
> Galley too, and brigantina,
> For defence of Palestina,
> To Mahomet, for Giurdina,
> I will pray both morn and e'en-a.

This was the traditional greeting in *lingua franca*, indicating complete trust in the interlocutor. From now on Opalinski could ask any favour he wanted from the Infidel stable-keeper.

"Tch," Populescu snorted impatiently with a touch of envy. "You've made it quite clear how learned you are and we admire your infinite knowledge. Now please get to the point!"

According to what Opalinski had learned from the Agha's interpreter, thanks to the good offices of the stable-keeper, as soon as Suleiman's army left Vienna, Ferdinand, the Emperor's brother, had a holy cross placed on top of the ball. When Suleiman heard this, he flew into a rage and announced a new invasion. And so, putting enormous pressure on the Sultan's coffers and those of his financial backers (already ruined by the failure of the siege), the Turkish army in 1532 invaded Styria and ravaged it. Luckily, once again he failed to enter Vienna; in fact, he did not even get there: the fortress of Gün in Styria, and its heroic commander Nicklas Jurischitsch, although fully aware they faced a certain and horrible death, chose to resist to the bitter end and so, paying with their own lives, they succeeded in saving the capital. The imperial army commanded by Charles V in person arrived and drove Suleiman back, inflicting on him a loss of ten thousand men.

"It was truly a fortunate year, that 1532," sighed the Greek Simonis, delighted at the account of the defeats of the hated Ottomans. "The imperial forces, commanded by the Genoese Andrea Doria, freed Patrass from the Turks along with other cities in southern Greece. Ah, what glorious times! Rejoice, Penicek!"

And Penicek, obedient as usual to the commands of his Barber, began to laugh.

"But not like that," Simonis upbraided him, "with pleasure and satisfaction!"

So Penicek mimed contentment: he nodded and shook his fists in a pathetic little performance while they all mocked him.

"More!" ordered the Greek.

Penicek got to his feet, continuing the same gestures, until Opalinski, sniggering, gave him a thwacking kick in his behind. The poor Pennal, who was already lame by nature, fell heavily to the floor.

"He knows Italian as well," I observed.

"Yes, but he's not part of our little Bolognese group. He studied at Padua, this dunce, and you can tell!" sneered Opalinski.

However, the Emperor, Opalinski went on, when Penicek, thoroughly humiliated, took his seat again, judged it wiser to remove the holy cross from the golden ball and to make a peace treaty with the Sultan. Ever since then the ball has been the symbol of Vienna for the Turks, and their objective.

"Just a moment, there's something wrong here," I objected. "Simonis, you told me that for the Ottomans the Golden Apple means not only Vienna but also Constantinople, Buda and Rome. But if I remember correctly, Constantinople was conquered by the Turks several centuries ago."

"Yes, in 1453," answered Koloman and Dragomir in unison; clearly between one amorous adventure and another they had found the time to learn a few historical dates.

"And so long before Suleiman besieged Vienna, in 1529," I remarked. "Simonis, you explained that the Golden Apple indicates the objective of the Ottoman conquest. So why indicate Constantinople as the Golden Apple, if that name only came up during the later siege of Vienna, when Constantinople had already been conquered?"

"Simple: because in Constantinople too there was a gilded ball," Koloman intervened. "As you know, I asked the monks, who always know everything. In the Augustinian monastery I spoke to an Italian monk, who was evangelist and confessor to the Turkish prisoners of war who had asked to convert to the True Faith."

According to what the monk had told Koloman, it all went back to an ancient Byzantine legend, when the ancient statue of Emperor Constantine used to stand in Constantinople. Some claim that the statue was of the Emperor Justinian. Whichever it was, the statue, all gilded, stood opposite the imposing church of St Sophia, on a great column. In his outstretched left hand the Emperor held an orb, also of gold, and pointed it threateningly towards the East.

It was a kind of warning to the people in the East. It was intended to signify that he, the Emperor, held power, symbolised by the orb, in his hand and they could do nothing against him. According to some the orb was surmounted by the holy cross: an Imperial Orb, therefore, rather than a Golden Apple."

Other Turkish prisoners, continued Koloman, had told the monk that the statue in front of St Sophia was of the Madonna, not of Justinian or Constantine. It stood on a green column, and in her hand the Madonna held a miraculous stone of red garnet, as large as a pigeon's egg. They say that the stone was so splendid it lit up the whole building, and travellers came to see it from every country, also because at the foot of the green column the holy remains of the Magi had been buried. But during the night of the birth of the Prophet, as the Turks call Mahomet, the statue of the Madonna collapsed.

"And the garnet stone?" we all asked.

"The monk told me that according to some people it's now at *Kizil Elma*, which is to say the Golden Apple. Others claim it was stolen and taken to Spain. Yet others say it was walled up in the side of St Sophia that looks towards Jerusalem."

We looked at one another, a little confused.

"I still don't understand," I declared. "And it's not clear who Eyyub and the forty thousand martyrs were, the ones poor Dànilo talked about."

"Maybe some Pontevedrin rubbish, which has nothing to do with the Golden Apple," conjectured Opalinski.

"We'll have to get more information," said Populescu. "Maybe my brunette at the coffee shop can help us: you know, she told my fortune!"

"Does she read hands?" asked Koloman.

"No, coffee grounds. For the first time I saw how it's done."

The young woman had served Populescu a good cup of boiling coffee, telling him not to drink it all, but to leave a little at the bottom. And then our friend followed her instructions: holding the cup in his left hand, shaking it three times he stirred the mixture up again, and then drained the contents into the saucer, and finally passed the cup to the Armenian woman. After scrutinising and interpreting the vague shapes that the coffee had left at the bottom, the young woman gave a clear and unequivocal response.

"The trumpet, rectangle and mouse came up," said Populescu, all excited.

"And what does that mean?" asked Opalinski.

"The trumpet indicates great changes on account of a new love."

"It's true, love changes people," Koloman mocked him. "You're always so much like yourself that not even your fingernails grow!"

"Very witty. Then the rectangle: it means great erotic activity, and that hits it right on the nail."

"Why, have you been raped?" asked Simonis.

"Cretin. You should have seen how my little one looked at me, while she explained the rectangle to me. It was as if she were saying: you'll see what we can get up to . . ."

"All right, Nostradamus," said Koloman with a sceptical smile, "and the mouse?"

"Well, that's the least favourable of the three signs but, judging from the rubbish you come out with, that's right on the nail as well. In fact it means: watch our for your friends."

"But you haven't got any!" exclaimed Koloman, while the whole group burst into ferocious laughter, which was the last straw for Populescu.

"Laugh away, but I hope my little brunette in the coffee shop .. ."

"Hope away, she'll never go with you," sneered Koloman.

"Nor with you: she hates the stink of armpits."

಄

17 of the clock, end of the working day: workshops and chancelleries close. Dinner hour for artisans, secretaries, language teachers, priests, servants of commerce, footmen and coach drivers (while in Rome people take but a light refection).

We took our leave of Koloman and Opalinski, not without paying them for the work carried out so far, and then took some rapid refreshment with Penicek and Dragomir in a nearby taphouse (chicken soup, fried fish, mixed dumplings, boiled meat, roast capon and wild cockerel). Then I prepared to travel back to Porta Coeli.

Instead Simonis surprised me with an unexpected piece of news:

"We must hurry, Signor Master, Hristo might already be waiting for us," he said, inviting me to climb back onto Penicek's cart and ordering the Pennal to set off towards the great space of the Prater.

"Of course, Hristo. But didn't you say that he would join us at the meeting?"

"You must forgive me this little lie, Signor Master. As you saw, he didn't come. But it's not that he couldn't. The fact is that he didn't want to talk in front of everyone."

"Why on earth not?"

"I don't know. I saw him briefly this morning and he told me that that's what he preferred, because there is something he finds suspicious."

"And what is it?"

"He didn't tell me. But he did mention that he thinks the real meaning of the Agha's sentence is all hidden in the words *soli soli soli*."

"And why?"

"He said that's it to do with checkmate."

"With checkmate?" I said with a mixture of surprise and scepticism. "In what sense?"

"I've got no idea. But if I were you I'd trust his instinct. Hristo is a real philosopher of chess."

Hristo Hristov Hadji-Tanjov, explained Simonis, had a passion for chess, and he supported himself by playing matches for money, which he always won. Vienna at night was the undisputed kingdom of gamblers. All over the city people pitted themselves against lady luck – in coffee shops, luxurious establishments and dingy taverns.

The cart jolted: Penicek had suddenly switched direction.

"What's up, Pennal?" asked Simonis.

"The usual: a procession."

It was the Oratorian Fathers of St Philip Neri. That was why Penicek had abruptly changed his route and gone down a side street: if we had been spotted by the people in the procession, we would have had to stop, kneel down and wait patiently for the Holy Sacrament to make its slow way past us, and so risk arriving late at our meeting with the Bulgarian.

"Hristo usually plays at the inn called the Green Tree, in Wallner Street," said Simonis. "A fine inn, always very crowded."

He explained that it was frequented not only by artisans, merchants and common folk, but also by irreproachable aristocrats with noble names and clergymen of exemplary reputation, all eager to be robbed blind by professional players of dice, cards, bassette, thirty-forty and trik-trak, and, last but not least, chess.

"Most of them come from your country, Italy, and they're the best, including the chess-players: Hristo often tells me about a certain Gioacchino Greco, a Calabrian, who, in his opinion, is the greatest player of all time. They too only play for money, lots of money," added Simonis.

We were interrupted once again. Penicek's vehicle had given another jerk.

"And now what is it?" asked my assistant severely.

"Another procession."

"Again? What's going on today?"

"I've got no idea, Signor Barber," answered Penicek with the utmost deference. "This time it's the Brotherhood of the Immaculate Conception. They're all heading towards the Cathedral of St Stephen."

I leaned out and before our vehicle set off down the side street, I had time to see the participants' afflicted faces and to hear their fervent voices raised in song.

Every night, Simonis went on, entire estates would change hands, ending up in the pockets of Italian adventurers, leaving behind a trail of tears, desperation and suicides: gold, land, houses, jewels, and, for those who had nothing else to offer, even hands or eyes.

"People bet their eyes? What on earth do you mean?"

"Such things are unknown to those who work honestly, Signor Master, and who stay at home at night, instead of hanging around places of entertainment. Well now, to curtail certain excesses, an ancient communal ordinance of 1350 is still in force which forbids anyone who has run out of money but who still wants to offer a pledge, to bet on his own eyes, hands, feet or nose. There are people who have done it. And who have lost. That's partly why about fifteen years ago Emperor Leopold had to re-declare his condemnation of gambling, as a sower of poverty and despair."

While Simonis was explaining the mysteries of Viennese night-life, the progress of the cart was interrupted by a great gathering.

"Pennal, what the devil is it this time?" asked Simonis.

"Forgive me, Signor Barber," he said, in a humble tone. "I just wasn't able to avoid this procession."

"What's going on today?" I said in amazement; even on a Sunday, and even in such a sanctimonious city as Vienna, it was unusual to have so many processions all so close together.

"It's the corporation of the smiths and knife-grinders this time. And they're on their way to the Cathedral of St Stephen as well," Penicek told us.

"There must be a great prayer-meeting there. Do you know anything about it, Pennal?" asked the Greek.

"Nothing, I'm afraid, Signor Barber."

The road was indeed barred by the arrival of a holy procession, announced by the insistent sound of a bell and preceded by two road-sweepers, who were shovelling the snow into piles on either side of the road to make way for the Holy Sacrament. In accordance with Viennese custom, we all had to get out and kneel down for a minute making the sign of the cross and beating our chests, like all the passers-by around us.

"Curse it, we'll be late," moaned Simonis, as the cold of the snow penetrated our bones.

Meanwhile the procession advanced, led by the priest who was holding up the Holy Sacrament. I noticed quite a few faces in tears in the crowd. Next to me a group of young men had seized someone of their own age by the scruff of the neck and thrown him to the ground, forcing him to kneel. In the Caesarean city, Protestants (the poor wretch must have been one) on such occasions were officially only required to take their hats off; but in fact they were often forced to kneel down like all the others. It was said that once an incident of this sort had befallen the Ambassador of Prussia, so that the imperial court had been obliged to issue a formal apology.

The delay was getting worse: because of the procession other carriages had stopped, and the passengers had knelt down inside them. The people kneeling on the ground glared hostilely at them. If we had been in the suburbs, where manners were rougher than in the city, the passengers would probably have been forced to get out and prostrate themselves on the ground.

At the same time (this I knew from experience) at the sound of the bell all the occupants of the houses nearby would have stopped working and knelt down, making the sign of the cross and beating their chests.

Even a puppet theatre, which just a minute earlier had been offering one of its scurrilous shows, had become magically petrified: as the Holy Sacrament passed by, the street artists had all been transformed into devout worshippers.

As soon as the tail of the religious procession had passed on its way, everything and everyone went back to their previous activities, as if nothing had happened.

"I can understand losing at cards or dice, which have always led to ruin," I said, turning to Simonis once again, as soon as the cart had started up again, "but chess? Who would let himself be fleeced by a chess player?"

"Hristo will definitely be able to tell you more about that than me. But everyone knows that chess, of all ludic pastimes, is the most sublime and elevated. Many claim that for its subtlety, chess is the only game suited to princes. You may have heard that among the Viennese nobility it's beoming fashionable to take lessons in the science of chess playing, just as they used to do with music, philosophy or medicine."

I recalled that in the living rooms of the houses of the rich, when inspecting their chimneys, I had almost always seen chessboards of exquisite workmanship, finely inlaid or even in beautiful coloured stone.

"Today the best chessboards are made in Lyons, in Paris and Munich," added my assistant. "And before the war broke out, they used to import the most beautiful specimens here. Chess is

becoming a game for the rich. Hristo often has the chance to teach
chess to pupils who pay well. When he accepts games for pay, the
challenger is very often a wealthy young man. So, all in all, he does
pretty well."

"But professional players like Hristo must lose occasionally."

"We students are protected by special legislation. In an ancient
privilege brought in by Duke Albrecht, around 1267, it was established that a student when gambling can only lose the money he has
on him, and not a penny more, and he cannot give up his books or his
clothes. In addition the win is only valid if there's a guarantor who
administrates the players' winnings. And since Hristo plays without
a guarantor, on the rare occasions he does lose, he cites this law,
which his opponents don't know about. And he doesn't pay. But if
the loser is not a real cavalier, and suspects he's been tricked, he
could try to get his revenge."

By now we had reached the Leopoldine Island, on the other side
of one of the branches of the Danube, the area where the house
stood that was going to host the Agha's embassy the next day. After
travelling down a long tree-lined avenue, we crossed a bridge over
another canal separating the Leopoldine Island from the generous
open stretch of the game reserve known as the Prater.

What Hristo wanted to tell us must be genuinely hot stuff, I
thought, for him to fix an appointment all the out way here in this
intense cold.

As we crossed the bridge, leaving on the right the villa of the
noble family Häckelberg and on the left the Löwenthurm property,
we were faced by the immense stretch of the Prater.

On the opposite side of the bridge we stopped. We were alone.
Simonis and I got down from the cart, while Penicek remained on
the box and nodded when my assistant ordered him not to move
until we returned.

The winter weather had driven everyone into their houses and
emptied the roads, especially in this corner of the city close to cold
forests and damp, grassy meadows. There was no sign of any of the
numerous boys from the Leopoldine Island who would come out to
the Prater at every snowfall, entering secretly by some gap in the
fence, to play on their sledges.

"The entrance is barred," I remarked, pointing to a large gate
that must be the way in.

"Of course, Signor Master, this is an imperial game reserve. Come along, follow me," he said, inviting me to walk alongside the fence towards the right.

"But once Cloridia and I entered by this very gate and walked around here for a whole day," I objected as we walked along.

"The gamekeepers often close an eye to respectable-looking couples. But in general common people are barred from entering: only His Caesarean Majesty, dames and cavaliers, imperial councillors, chancellors and functionaries of the court chamber are allowed in. It was Maximilian II who made the Prater the great reserve that it is today, joining together a number of separate plots of land. Some of these areas, for example, belonged to the convent of Porta Coeli. The nuns owned half Vienna."

"Yes, they've still got that vineyard at Simmering, not far from the Place with No Name."

"Here at the Prater," my assistant went on, "Maximilian also created the great tree-lined avenue you must have seen on your previous visit."

So, I thought, we were once again following in the footsteps of Maximilian II, the lord of the Place with No Name. Maybe it was a sign of destiny.

At last Simonis stopped, pointing to a spot where a wide gap in the fence, hidden by a bush, made it possible to slip through.

"The children of the Leopoldine Island use these gaps to go and play in the Prater. And my friends and I use them too, when we need a little privacy," commented Simonis.

No sooner had we slipped through than we were greeted by an idyllic and unreal landscape. The reserve was entirely covered by a blanket of snow. The tips of the trees thrust upwards into the milky immensity of the celestial vault; the snow seemed to have been transfused into every object, so that the green earth and blue sky were embraced in the blankness of a pure and opalescent coitus. In that fantastical world, pheasants, deer and bucks lay hidden, prey to the Emperor's venatic passion.

"Strange," said Simonis looking around. "Hristo should have been here ages ago. That damned procession, I don't know whether we're late or he is."

"There are tracks here," I observed after we had waited for a few minutes.

In the mosaic of scuffled marks and scrapes on the ground by the unauthorised entrance, some human footprints could be seen, clear and fresh. The snow was getting thicker.

"What do you think, Simonis, could they be his?"

"Judging by the size of the foot, Signor Master, they could well be."

So, with the incessant snow making it harder and harder to see anything, we began to follow the tracks.

There was not much time; soon the snow would obliterate them. The footprints headed to the right and joined a long path flanked by a double line of trees: the great avenue which, as far as I knew, ran all the way through the Prater to the Danube. But almost at the beginning there was a fork to the left.

"He didn't go left or right," declared Simonis, observing the traces, "he went between the two prongs, through the woods. And do you see that the footprints have got wider apart?"

"So he started running."

"So it seems, Signor Master."

No place, in the snow, is as beautiful as Vienna. Trees, hills, bushes, lawns, mossy rocks: the Prater was a single immaculate expanse. In the distance, much further than we could see, I knew that the branches of the bending Danube flowed, sinuous and seething.

Since ancient times the river Danube has been considered the prince of European rivers, and one of the world's pre-eminent rivers. It is no surprise that Ovid compares it with the Nile of Egypt, and it should be noted that, along with the smaller Po in Italy and the Thames in England, contrary to the nature of all flowing water in the world, it flows eastwards: only in Hungary does it turn briefly towards the west, and in Misia, it bends slightly northwards, thus, as already noted, impeding – thank God! – the westward march of the Ottoman peoples. The Danube was also an important source of sustenance for the Caesarean city. There were numerous landing places for the commerce of wines and foodstuffs, as well as numerous smaller harbours for the transportation of people and for fishing. One of these wharves, for example, lay in a canal that divided the Prater from an island known as the Embankment. It was there that Cloridia and I, during a Sunday stroll we had taken months earlier in the Prater, had engaged in laborious chit-chat in German with some boatmen.

The snow and wind were increasing in intensity. Pluvial Jove and the Wind Rose seemed to have been sharpening their wits upon one another, in a combined effort to recreate January conditions in April. The wind was blowing straight into our eyeballs, and we had to shield our faces with our hands in order to proceed without stumbling.

"Can you see anything?" I said to Simonis, almost shouting over the roar of the wind.

"There's something ahead. On the ground."

A bag. An old cloth shoulder bag, half-buried in the snow, containing something heavy, hard and square, the size of a plate. Brushing away the flakes that had settled on the bag, we opened it: there, wrapped in a red rag, was a large chessboard in solid wood, with its base reinforced by a plate of inlaid iron, and a little pouch full of small, finger-sized objects.

"Signor Master, it's Hristo's chessboard."

"Are you sure?"

He opened the pouch. He pulled out a black pawn, and then a knight painted in peeling white: they seemed to be a microcosmic representation of the white mantle of snow and the black of the wizened bushes that embroidered the Prater in two-tone lacework.

"They're his chess pieces. He always uses these in his games," said Simonis, as I picked up the poor abandoned bag and its contents.

"Let's go on," I exhorted him, though I was beginning to look over my shoulders by now.

The last stretch, still flanked by snow-shrouded trees, was almost all uphill. We puffed and panted our way upwards, numb with cold. By now Hristo's tracks (if they really were his) were covered in snow. The last prints vanished just before a small hill that rose in front of us, whose gradient was even steeper than the slope we had just struggled up. From its top there must be a view of the Danube.

"Let's go back," I proposed. "I wouldn't like . . ."

A noise, distant but quite distinct in the muffled silence of the snowfall, made the words die on my lips.

Simonis and I looked at each other: there were footsteps on the snow. Immediately, the noise stopped. The snow and the small whirls of flakes driven by intermittent gusts of wind limited visibility to a few paces.

Without saying a word, Simonis made a sign that we should climb
to the top of the hill. With our heads bowed and our backs bent, as
if we were trying to hide in fields of corn, we clambered up as fast as
possible. As soon as we got to the top, thanks to a favourable flurry
of wind, the view opened up miraculously on the thousand isles of
the bend of the Danube, and I thought back to a book I had read in
Rome, before we set off on our journey to Vienna, in which I had
learned that the springs of the glorious river are at Donaueschingen,
in Germany, where its calm, limpid waters emerge from the mysterious depths of the Black Forest, which the ancients called Sylva
Martiana, and then spout forth from a cemetery lying in the territories of the counts of Fürstenberg. And while my eyes took in those
celebrated waters, which had travelled over four hundred leagues on
their way here from Germany, I almost forgot what we were doing up
on the top of that hill, and I only just heard Simonis's voice saying:

"Signor Master, Signor Master, come here, quickly!"

Hristo's body was lying face down near a tree, his head squashed
in the snow. We had to pull with all our strength to extract the head,
as it had been pressed with inconceivable violence into the bottom
of a hollow, which had somehow been dug into the fresh snow. Just
below the nape of his neck, we found that a deep knife wound had
soaked his back with blood. But that had probably not been fatal; for
this reason they had pushed his face into the hollow until his heart
and lungs had given out.

When we turned him over his face was a mess of blue and white
blotches. It looked as if he had only been dead for a while, a very
short while.

"Curse it! Poor Hristo, my poor friend, what have they done to
you?" said Simonis, in a mixture of perturbation, anger and grief.

Hristo Hadji-Tanjov, the chess-playing student, had ended his
young life in the snow-covered fields of the Prater: he would never
see Bulgaria again.

I got to my feet. As if to console me, a vision in complete contrast
presented itself to my eyes: three small sledges, probably left there
by a group of playmates, tied to a tree and ready to be used in next
winter's snow. While Simonis prayed in a low voice, I made the sign
of the cross myself, wondering whether the Lord was showing us the
sledges, an innocent relic of childish pleasures, to console us in the
midst of our worldly pains.

"What shall we do?" Simonis asked at last.

Hristo was at least twice as tall as me, and one and a half times as broad. Carrying him was clearly impossible.

"We'll have to bury him in some way," I remarked. "Or . . . just a moment."

I had spotted something. While they were suffocating him, Hristo had thrust one hand into the snow, and it was lying outstretched and half frozen. The other hand, his right one, was still clutching his belly. Perhaps, as they attacked him and forced him to the ground, he had not had time to free himself. In that right hand I had seen something. I got closer and, trembling convulsively, I forced the fingers open and extracted the object. Now Simonis was next to me. I handed it to him.

"A chess king. The white king," he observed.

"So while they were following him, Hristo left the chessboard on the ground, the one we found earlier, with the other pieces. He just kept this white king in his hand. But why?"

"I don't know," answered Simonis. "But now that I think of it, whenever he played an important match, if he couldn't make up his mind about a move, he would always turn over in his hand one of the pieces that his adversary had already taken. I've often watched his companions playing. There are some players who scratch their heads, others who tap their feet under the table, and others who fiddle with their noses. He would release his tension on the pieces already taken. Once, during a match, I saw him hold a knight in his hand for almost an hour. He played with it obsessively, continually passing it from one hand to the other."

"And so today, before being followed, he was already holding the white king," I concluded. "As he ran away he certainly didn't have time to put it back in the bag, and it stayed in his hand right up to the end. But why did he have it in his hands? He wasn't playing a game."

At that moment we heard it again: the same scuffling of feet. Then a shot: a bullet whistled very close to us, burying itself in the snow. Two shadows darted from the trees. We took to our heels without a single glance at one another. Simonis was already running towards the Danube when I suddenly made him change direction.

"Over here!" I yelled, gesturing towards the sledges.

Just a few seconds later we were on the slope of the hill and could hear the pursuers' steps close behind us. My sledge was scarcely bigger than a toy, but for that very reason, with just the barest minimum of its surface resting on the snow, it shot downhill like a bullet. In front of me I could see Simonis, thanks to his greater weight, descending even faster. Suddenly I saw a trunk ahead of me, twice as broad as my sledge. I swerved to the right, braked slightly with my feet so as not to roll over in the snow, but there was already another bush in front of me; miraculously I dodged it, leaning to the left.

Only then, as I regained speed, did I look back. Carefully avoiding the tree trunks, one of the unknown men was still following us, but he was proceeding uncertainly on that rocky, snow-covered slope.

My sledge ran into a rock protruding from the ground (April snowfalls are never as abundant as February ones), and I cursed as I jerked it free, darting a backward glance as I did so and seeing that my advantage over my pursuers had diminished.

My sledge got stuck again, this time on a stretch of ground where the snow was too shallow. I got off and began to run. I had lost sight of Simonis, who had gone much further down the hill. Behind me I heard our pursuers' voices. I turned and saw that they too were splitting up – one was continuing to follow me, while the other was going after Simonis.

Praying that they would not understand Italian and that the Greek would hear me, I shouted: "Simonis, to the right, towards the canal!" I could have turned to the right as well, and shared my fate with Simonis. Instead I decided to keep straight on: ahead of me the slope continued, and I had seen that by going downhill I was able to outstrip my aggressor. I could no longer hear his footsteps behind me. Suddenly a boom broke the silence of the Prater: the Turk, if that was what he was, had fired again. The bark of a tree to my right shattered into a thousand splinters. My enemy, clearly exhausted by the chase, had decided not to face me with cold steel: he hoped quite simply to blow my brains out. I began to zig-zag, trying to put as many trees as possible between his pistol and my back. How long would my shoes hold out? I had lost all feeling in my fingers, and from my ankles down I was half-frozen; I could no longer even swear that I was wearing anything on my feet.

Another shot above my head, and a branch exploded into fragments. The man was cursedly fast at reloading his pistol. Each time he did so he lost ground, it was true, but not enough, on account of my short legs.

Meanwhile I had reached the path that led back to the Leopoldine Island. There were fewer trees, and we were now in the open. Neither I nor my assailant was running any longer: worn out by our exertions, we dragged ourselves along on legs that were half-dead. It was at that point that the fourth shot – the decisive one – rang out. Before falling flat on my face in the snow, I felt the impact clearly in my back, just as I started along the path which, if I had had any breath left in my lungs, would have led me out of the Prater, towards safety.

Reanimated by his success in hitting me, the man was soon standing over me. As I tried to get to my feet, he pushed me down. He sat on my chest, trapping my right hand with his knee and my left with his hand. With his other hand he pulled a knife from his pocket. I was squirming like an eel, and with another backward thrust I would have managed to free myself, but he was too swift for me, and it would only take his well-honed blade (so I thought in those last instants when I thought he would stab me) one thrust to finish me off. Perhaps, I reflected with the strange rapidity that thoughts come to one at such crucial moments, Simonis at that moment, in some other part of the Prater, was suffering the same fate. Out of the corner of my eye I saw the red bloodstain from the wound in my back spreading on the snow.

There was a handkerchief over his face, so all I could see were two dark deep eyes glaring down at me; the rest, from the mouth down, was carefully hidden. His pupils bore into mine while the knife rose in the air, ready to deliver my death.

It was at that point I heard, as if in a dream, that voice:

"Stop!"

Just a few feet away from us stood Penicek.

My executioner hesitated just an instant, then left his prey and began to run in the direction from which we had come.

We did not even try to follow him, unarmed as we were. He had decided to avoid an unequal fight, but he still had the pistol with him: if he had time to reload, and above all if he knew we had not the slightest means of defence, we would be in a very tight spot.

"All well?" asked Penicek with a look of dismay, as he came limping up to me.

"My back, the wound in my back," I answered mechanically, as I got to my feet.

He looked at me and zealously ran his hand over my back.

"What wound?"

"From the pistol! He shot me!"

Then I looked at the ground. The scarlet blotch on the snow, which I had taken for my blood, was just the red cloth that Hristo Hadji-Tanjov's chessboard had been wrapped in.

Hristo's former tool of the trade had flown from the bag to the ground during the struggle with my faceless aggressor. I touched my back: it was unhurt. Then I realised. I took the bag from my back: it had indeed been struck by the pistol shot. I bent down on the ground and picked up the red cloth with its contents. The red cloth was also perforated. I drew out the chessboard, whose metal base was slightly dented. The bullet had been parried by the plate of ornamented iron. Hristo Hadji-Tanjov's chessboard had saved my life.

"Where is Signor Barber?" asked Penicek, in a worried voice.

"He ran towards the Danube," I answered, exhorting him to follow me. "We must run and help him. He's being chased by another man – I don't know whether he's Turkish or Christian. How did you find us?"

"I heard the pistol shot and realised you were in danger. I followed your tracks in the snow," he said as we started off again. "But what's happened to Hristo?"

When I had told him everything, Penicek turned pale with horror. Meanwhile we headed towards the point where I had separated from Simonis.

We found no sign of my assistant. We continued looking for quite a while, anguished at the lack of tracks and the fear of finding Hristo's murderers on our heels. I was half frozen, and prayed that my toes were not frost-bitten.

We finally reached the little landing stage on the canal between the Prater and the island known as the Embankment. Some small boats for transporting people and animals were lying on the sand, just a few feet from the water of the Danube. But there was no sign of Simonis. We were about to go away when we heard the cry:

"Signor Master!"

"Simonis!" I exclaimed, running towards him.

He had been hiding under one of the upturned boats, sheltered like a tortoise by its shell.

"The villain was still hunting me down until just a few seconds ago," he told us, still panting with fear and exhaustion. "I was sure

.he was about to find me, but then he must have seen you coming. He went off in that direction," he said, pointing more or less to the same spot where my pursuer had vanished.

"They must have met up again to leave the Prater together," deduced the Pennal. "Obviously they didn't want to leave by the same gap we used."

I explained to Simonis just how Penicek had saved my life.

"Are you wounded, Signor Master?" asked my assistant.

I explained in detail how things had gone, showed him poor Hristo's chessboard and the iron plate dented by the projectile.

"Now let's get back, before those two change their minds and return," I urged them.

Once more we trudged across the frozen meadows of the Prater, leaving just three pairs of footprints in the snow. Hristo's poor shoes, which should have scored the soft snow with us as well, were instead being ravaged by the beak of a crow.

昆昆

20 of the clock: eating houses and alehouses close their doors.

"You can't understand the importance of Landau unless you look at a map," said Atto, sketching an imaginary Europe in the air with his ancient, bony hands.

Once back at the Porta Coeli, I felt a burning need to talk with Abbot Melani, to tell him everything, to seek consolation for the doubts and regrets that were gnawing at me, but above all to look into his eyes to study his reaction. I wanted to understand whether Atto had anything to do with Hristo's death, or whether the chess player and his companion Dànilo had paid the penalty for their dishonourable trades.

And so, with my face still smeared in muddy slush, my limbs half-frozen and the chill of the young Bulgarian's death – for which I myself was perhaps to blame – still upon me, I knocked at Atto's door.

His nephew opened the door, his face crumpled, his voice hoarse and his body racked by serial sneezing; he was suffering from a severe cold.

He observed my pitiable state in some puzzlement, particularly at that hour. Melani was already in bed.

"Forgive me, Signor Atto," I began, "I didn't think –"

"Don't worry. I lay down out of boredom. An eighty-five-year-old man, blind, in a convent. What do you expect him to do but go to bed with the chickens?"

"If you want to rest, I'll leave."

"On the contrary. I was looking for you an hour ago. That blessed Countess Pálffy: I kept watch on her front door all afternoon, and nothing happened. She may be the Emperor's lover but she lives like a nun. Nothing like Madame de Montespan . . . These Austrians are so virtuous, even the adulterers! Virtuous and boring."

"Signor Atto, I have serious news. Hristo Hadji-Tanjov, another of Simonis's friends, is dead. They stabbed him and suffocated him in the snow."

I told him about the tremendous adventure we had had in the Prater, and how I myself had only just escaped death. He listened without saying a word. As I talked, Domenico listened in amazement and made the sign of the cross, wondering to himself where we had ended up, in Vienna or in hell.

At the end Atto asked: "What was this Hristo's surname?"

"Hadji-Tanjov."

"Ha . . . what?"

"Ha-*dji*-taniof, he was Bulgarian."

He raised his eyebrows superciliously, as if to say, "I might have guessed."

"Half-Turkish, in short," he remarked dismissively.

"Why?"

"I see you're not very strong on geography, or history. Bulgaria has been under the Ottoman yoke for four hundred years, in Rumelia, as the Turks call the European part of their empire."

I was staggered. So Hristo was a subject of the Sublime Porte.

"And how did he earn his living? Did he love dangerous trades as well, by any chance?"

The question, asked in that tendentious tone, caught me off guard.

"He was a chess player. He played for money."

Atto Melani was silent.

"I know, gambling is not without its risks," I admitted, "but this is the second time that one of my assistant's study companions has been murdered, and once again – strangely enough – just when he was about to meet me. And what's more, his murderers fired at me.

Why would they have done that if Hristo's death had nothing to do with the Turkish Agha?"

"Simple. Because they were afraid you had seen them. Maybe they're in Hristo's chess circles and they're scared of being tracked down. Any more stupid questions?"

"My questions may be stupid, but you don't seem very bothered by the mortal danger I was in."

"Listen, with the Pontevedrin's death, there seems to be no doubt that it was a settling of scores. And Hadji-Tanjov also died because he took some wrong step – made a wrong move, I should say, given his passion for chess. You make sure you don't make any wrong moves. I will weep for you most sincerely, but if it's your own fault, you must weep for yourself."

"You really have nothing else to say to me?"

"No, I haven't. But if you're really looking for the person to blame for this, look in the mirror: anyone who makes an appointment with you ends up dead," he declared, with a sardonic laugh.

I insisted no further. The news that Hristo was an Ottoman had filled me with doubts. Baleful Abbot Melani refused to take the death of these young students seriously, and my urgings only made him clam up. If I wanted to get anything out of the moody old castrato, this was not the way to go about it. But I was now too tired to think.

While Domenico helped his uncle to to emerge from under the blankets and sit up on the bed, I pulled out a piece of cloth from my pocket to wipe my face and I dropped the piece of blackened silver that Cloridia had taken from Prince Eugene's palace.

"What's that thing?" asked Atto at once, with a twitch of his eyebrows, looking in my direction.

I gazed in wonder at his vigilant eye.

"My blindness improves a little at night. Thanks to the treatment with the myrobolans, the gerapigra and the fact I sleep barefoot in all weathers," he explained. "In any case what I meant was, what was that tinkling I heard?"

He groped for his dark glasses on the bedside table. His nephew handed them to him and he put them on. I explained the circumstances in which Cloridia had found the object and placed it in his palm.

"Interesting," he remarked. He held it and seemed to study it closely with his fingertips.

"Sit down beside my bed. And tell me exactly what's engraved on it," he said.

I described in detail the two sides and read the inscription.

"*Landau 1702, 4 livres?*" he repeated with a slight smile, "and Prince Eugene had it in his hand during the audience with the Agha? I see, I see."

"It looks almost like a rudimentary commemorative coin of the first conquest of Landau by the Most August Emperor, in 1702," I commented.

"More than that, my son, much more."

Landau, began Atto, was the nerve centre at the heart of Europe, right in the middle of the continent, equidistant from Berlin, Hamburg, Vienna, Milan and Paris. It stood in the Palatinate, in the south-west of Germany, just above Italy and right next to Austria, but for decades it had been in the possession of the Sun King: it was the blade that France pointed at Germany's underbelly and Austria's hip.

Given its great strategic importance, more than twenty years ago Louis XIV had entrusted the most brilliant of his engineers, the famous Vauban, with the task of strengthening its fortifications. At once a suspicious fire had reduced three-quarters of the city's private houses to ashes, and Vauban had found it easy to transform the town into an armoured and impregnable stronghold.

It was the beginning of 1702, and the War of the Spanish Succession was already raging in northern Italy. Everyone was expecting hostilities to start up on German soil as well.

At the end of April the Empire's troops began to surround Landau and occupy all the access routes to the city. On 19th June the imperial troops dug their trench. Eight days later, 27th July, a colossal boom was heard: the imperial army was giving a martial salute as Joseph, the then twenty-four-year-old King of the Romans, the Empire's crown prince, arrived in person.

The French commander of the citadel, Melac, at once sent a herald to the enemy camp, preceded by a trumpeter, with a message for the King of the Romans: in addition to respectful compliments on his arrival, they asked him to indicate where he would pitch his tent, so that they could avoid hitting it with their cannons.

"What do you mean?" I said in surprise. "Did the French really offer to spare the leader of the enemy troops?"

"Do you know how to play chess?"

"No."

"Well, in chess the king, supreme leader of the enemy army, is never killed. When the hostile pieces have forced him into a corner with no way out, checkmate is declared, and the game is over. The defeated king has to capitulate, but does not die. That's what happens with real sovereigns too: they are not killed. Their peers and generals know and respect the ancient military customs."

But Joseph, he went on, valiantly turned down Melac's offer: "My tent is everywhere, shoot wherever you like. And save thou thy labour, gentle herald, come thou no more here. Tell your commander they shall have no other answer, I swear, but these my joints; which if they have as I will leave 'em them, shall yield them little."

Then he turned to his own men, dismayed and worried at the risk their commander-in-chief had chosen to run: "When I bestride my horse, I soar, I am a hawk. My horse is pure air and fire, and the dull elements of earth and water never appear in him, but only in patient stillness while his rider mounts him. And no one, not even the French dogs, can shoot a hawk."

In the days that followed Joseph visited the trenches, while the musket balls whistled all around him. A chamberlain of honour suggested that he should not endanger his precious person. He cut him short: "Let those who are afeared go back."

On 28th July he had the army line up for battle, after examining their equipment himself. On the night between 16th and 17th August the citadel was attacked. The French resisted heroically three times. But in the meantime the coffers of Landau's garrison had been depleted. Melac did not hesitate: he paid from his own pocket.

"What do you mean?"

Atto brandished the strange piece of blackened silver I had given him.

"It's another case of the good conventions of war that I was talking about. A true commander will never allow his men to fight without being paid. Domenico, please, could you adjust the cushion behind my back?"

"Of course, Uncle."

Melac therefore had the silver plates from his own dinner service broken up, and by makeshift means they printed the coins of Landau on them. They were rough, wretched fragments, each one of a different shape – rectangular, square, or triangular, like the pretend money in a children's game.

"The metal stampings, done half by a French goldsmith and the other half by a German, weren't all the same either. But each of those coins not in circulation was worth more than gold, boy," said Atto, staring at me gravely, "because they were the offspring of the noble rules of war."

"So this coin-like object was the money for Melac's soldiers. A fragment of his silver dishes!" I said, amazed at the ingenuity of the idea. "That's why it's so irregular. So it's a war souvenir: that's why Prince Eugene has a whole collection of them. He must really value them if he still keeps one in his pocket."

During the siege in 1702 Joseph took part in the most dangerous assaults, serving as an example to everyone and exposing himself selflessly. He was charitable to the wounded, he grieved with the widows and consoled the orphans of the fallen. The soldiers were incredulous when they saw his luminous dashing figure amid the cannon smoke, his sword always raised, his long tawny hair, freed from his wig, besmirched with the dust of battle and he, King of the Romans, heedless of fatigue, of danger, of blood, forever to the fore.

The imperial operations were coordinated by Margrave Louis of Baden. Among his subordinates was an Italian, Count Marsili.

"Count Luigi Ferdinando Marsili, is that right? I know that name," I said. "I think I bought a couple of his treatises some time ago, one on coffee and one on phosphorus, if I'm not mistaken."

"That's he. A great Italian," declared Atto.

The Margrave was slow and awkward at manoeuvring men, and unlike Marsili did not know the refinements of trench warfare, the use of explosives or the technique of sappers. For two months no progress had been made, they had suffered great losses and the French resistance seemed invincible. A French army under General Catinat was approaching; if Landau was not conquered soon, they would be crushed. Marsili, who could not bear to see his men die one by one, let Joseph knew about the mistakes made by the Margrave of Baden. They must reinforce their cannons and mortars, he said, and improve their aim. Joseph inspected the lines in person and showed confidence in Marsili: he would follow his advice. Louis of Baden foamed with rage. Marsili promised that Landau would be taken within a week.

Joseph then discovered what no general had had the courage to explain to him: the troops were tired, disheartened and frightened. Capturing Landau seemed an impossible enterprise to them, and if Catinat's army of liberation arrived it would be a disaster. We need more men – Joseph heard people murmur around him – there are too few of us.

The day before the final engagement, the King of the Romans left his generals and mingled with the troops, amid the simple infantry. He heard a soldier complaining again: the French are a tough proposition, we need more men to win. So Joseph climbed on top of a cannon and spoke to his men on an equal footing.

"Soldiers, subjects of the Emperor, listen to me! What's he that wishes we were more? If we are mark'd to die, we are enough to do our country loss; and if to live, the fewer men, the greater share of honour. God's will! I pray thee, wish not one man more. Rather proclaim it, through my host, that he which hath no stomach to this fight, let him depart; his passport shall be made and crowns for convoy put into his purse! We would not die in that man's company that fears his fellowship to die with us. Tomorrow will be the day of the Battle of Landau. He that outlives this day, and comes safe home, will stand a-tiptoe when the day is named, and rouse him at the name of Landau. He that shall live this day, and see old age, will yearly on the vigil feast his neighbours, and say, 'Tomorrow is the day of Landau:' Then will he strip his sleeve and show his scars and say 'These wounds I had on Landau's day.' Old men forget: yet all shall be forgot, but he'll remember with advantages what feats he did that day. Then shall our names, familiar in his mouth as household words – Joseph King of Romans, Fürstemberg, Bibra, and Marsili – be in their flowing cups freshly remember'd. This story shall the good man teach his son, and the Day of Landau shall ne'er go by, from this day to the ending of the world, but we in it shall be remember'd; we few, we happy few, we band of brothers. For he today that sheds his blood with me shall be my brother; be he ne'er so vile, this day shall gentle his condition: and gentlemen at home and safe a-bed shall think themselves accursed they were not here, and hold their manhoods cheap whiles any speaks that fought with us upon the Day of Landau!"

His words had gradually risen to an exultant cry and all around the King and his unsheathed sword the soldiers were applauding and laughing and weeping with emotion. Joseph then turned with a

smile to the infantry soldier who just a moment earlier had been
bewailing the lack of reinforcements: "Thou dost not wish more
troops, dost thou?"

"God's will! My liege," he replied, raising his fist with tears in his
eyes, "would you and I alone, without more help, could fight these
foul French curs!"

"But was Prince Eugene there?" I asked the Abbot, deeply
stirred.

Atto had broken off for a moment, wearied by his long narrative,
and was sipping a glass of water. He put the glass down on the table
but did not answer me.

"That night, the night before the final battle, no one slept,
neither the imperial troops or the French," he went on. "Now enter-
tain conjecture of a time when creeping murmur and the poring dark
fills the wide vessel of the universe. From camp to camp through the
foul womb of night the hum of either army stilly sounds, that the
fixed sentinels almost receive the secret whispers of each other's
watch: fire answers fire, and through their paly flames each battle
sees the other's umber'd face; steed threatens steed, in high and
boastful neighs piercing the night's dull ear, and from the tents the
armourers, accomplishing the knights, with busy hammers closing
rivets up, give dreadful note of preparation. Proud of their numbers
and secure in soul, the confident and over-lusty French do the low-
rated imperials play at dice; and chide the cripple tardy-gaited night
who, like a foul and ugly witch, doth limp so tediously away.

Nor does Joseph sleep. The officers offer him their company but
he refuses and leaves his tent: "I and my bosom must debate awhile,
and then I would no other company."

He borrows from a field assistant a hooded cloak that conceals
his face and explores the camp, pretending to be an ordinary
captain.

The poor condemned imperials are exhausted. Their gesture sad
investing lank-lean cheeks and war-worn coats presenteth them unto
the gazing moon so many horrid ghosts. But the royal captain of this
ruin'd band, he who soon shall be Joseph the Victorious, walking
from watch to watch, from tent to tent, goes forth and visits all his
host, bids them good morrow with a modest smile and calls them
brothers, friends and countrymen. A largess universal like the sun his
liberal eye doth give to every one, thawing cold fear, that mean and

gentle all, behold, as may unworthiness define, a little touch of Joseph in the night.

Still hidden in his hood, he lingers with a group of infantry soldiers. One of them says: "Tomorrow perhaps we will die, but the King of Romans need not fear anything: he is surely asleep calmly in his tent. He will fight as well, but is not as we are."

Then Joseph replies: "I think the King is but a man, as I am: the violet smells to him as it doth to me. His ceremonies laid by, in his nakedness he appears but a man. Therefore when he sees reason of fears, as we do, his fears, out of doubt, be of the same relish as ours are."

Then as dawn approaches, he is left all by himself: "Upon the King! let us our lives, our souls, our debts, our careful wives, our children and our sins lay on the King! We must bear all. O hard condition, twin-born with greatness, subject to the breath of every fool, whose sense no more can feel but his own wringing! What infinite heart's-ease must kings neglect, that private men enjoy! And what have kings, that privates have not too, save ceremony, save general ceremony? And what art thou, thou idle ceremony? What drink'st thou oft, instead of homage sweet, but poison'd flattery? O God of battles! steel my soldiers' hearts; possess them not with fear; take from them now the sense of reckoning, if the opposed numbers pluck their hearts from them. Not today, O Lord, O, not today, think not upon the fault my forebear, Charles the Fifth, made in compassing the sacred crown imperial! He did make expiation, abdicating and becoming then a monk. And every day I have the holy mass said for his soul, and churches and monasteries have I and my good father had erected so the abject stain of moneylenders' loot shall be washed clean from the imperial crown. O why is it not dawn? The day, my friends, and every other thing await my nod. Tomorrow will I trot a mile and leave in my grim wake a road paved with French faces."

The voice of Abbot Melani, almost a new Homer, was trembling with weariness and passion.

Dawn breaks, finally they fight. Yet another assault on the stronghold is beaten back. But it is clear that Landau is about to yield. Their spirits are as broken as their bodies, all that every soldier wants is to put an end to the combat, and to seize the neck of the French enemy and cut his throat, and rape his wife and burn and sack his house. As in every real war, man is turned to beast, and the beast goes in search of men.

Then Joseph appeared alone, on a horse, before the walls of the citadel, as close to the wall as he could get while remaining out of shooting-range. Unsheathing his sword he cried out:

"Therefore, you men of Landau, take pity of your town and of your people, whiles yet my soldiers are in my command; whiles yet the cool and temperate wind of grace o'erblows the filthy and contagious clouds of heady murder, spoil and villainy. If not, why, in a moment look to see the blind and bloody soldier with foul hand defile the locks of your shrill-shrieking daughters; your fathers taken by the silver beards, and their most reverend heads dash'd to the walls, your naked infants spitted upon pikes, whiles the mad mothers with their howls confused do break the clouds!"

At the top of the ramparts Governor Melac appeared on horseback. He listened in silence. Terror had gouged dark furrows in his face.

"What say you then," concluded the King of the Romans. "Will you yield, and this avoid, or, guilty in defence, be thus destroy'd?"

On 9th September Melac raised the white flag. The next day came the capitulation, which was followed by the exchange of prisoners. By 11th September it was all over.

As promised, Joseph held his soldiers back: the city's inhabitants had not a hair of their heads harmed. An imperial soldier who had stolen a pyx from a church was immediately hanged by order of the King himself, who attended the execution impassively, even though the condemned man was one of his dearest soldiers. The mothers, who the night before had heard Joseph's threatening words, and in the darkness of their homes had swooned, clutching their babies to their breasts, knelt down to kiss the imperial insignia. The French evacuated the city the next day; Melac, defeated, had to parade past the King of the Romans: "Great King" was the salutation addressed to him by the French governor, grateful to him for having spared them the terrible violence that frenzied troops always wreak after every siege.

Marsili had predicted that, as a result of his astute moves, Landau would yield within a week. But thanks to his brilliance and to the greatness of the young monarch, it had taken even less time: four days had sufficed.

Atto paused. He had run out of breath. In my collection of writings on Emperor Joseph, I had found several accounts and panegyrics on his deeds at Landau, but unfortunately they were all in German and written in the Teutonic style, with an abundance of boring details and a total lack of anecdotal matter. Abbot Melani's tale, by contrast, had catapulted me into the feverish heart of the battle and revealed the spirit of my own sovereign.

I could hardly believe the admiration and even the love for the young Caesar that breathed forth from the old castrato's words. Until then I had never heard him glorify any other monarch than his own Sun King!

"Signor Uncle, at this hour you should be asleep," Domenico told him.

On his return to Vienna, Atto started up again, paying no attention to his nephew's words, great festivities were held. In the city a great procession was immediately formed, making its way to the church of St Stephen, where a solemn *Te Deum* was celebrated. In the New Market Square a column was solemnly erected in honour of St Joseph, protector of Austria. Even Leopold and his wife, those august parents with whom the young King of the Romans had always had difficult relations, were radiant at the triumph of the imperial arms.

Before that victory, Joseph had just been a promising crown prince. After Landau, and thanks to the help of Marsili, he became a hero.

"But before that there was already a hero," observed Atto. "His name was Eugene of Savoy, the victor of the great Battle of Zenta, the scourge of the Turks. Now in the contest for glory there was an adversary with an unassailable advantage: he was handsome, and he had a crown on his head."

In Vienna Leopold's ministers were furious. They knew very well that Joseph could not wait to drive them all out and replace them with his own trusted men. The only way to stop him was to put pressure on his father Leopold. The manoeuvre proved successful. The following year, 1703, when Joseph asked his father if he could go back to war, permission was denied. The ministers' pressure on Leopold had worked. Eugene, too, who was still resentful at having been put in the shade by Joseph, had done his discreet best to make sure that the King of the Romans did not return to the war. Hostilities continued in the Rhine area, and soon there came bad news: the French had besieged Landau and finally reconquered it.

"So Prince Eugene had a hand in it! But it's absurd," I remarked. "Were he and the others not afraid that losing the war might be worse than giving honour and glory to Joseph?"

"The powerful are always ready to destroy the world in order to keep their own positions," answered Atto. "And at that moment, with a weak emperor like Leopold, no one was more powerful than his ministers, starting with Prince Eugene."

This brought us up to 1704. The military season was already well under way, autumn was just round the corner and the forces of the Empire and its allies wanted at all costs to close the year with an important victory. They decided to stake everything on Landau, to recapture it from the enemy. On 1st September the young King of the Romans finally arrived. In the end, and only after much tribulation, his father Leopold had agreed to let him depart for the front. On the battlefield he was greeted by Eugene of Savoy and the commander of the Anglo-Dutch allied troops, the famous Marlborough, great friend of Eugene. Now that the hero of the siege of two years earlier had arrived, they were no longer at centre stage. They were sent to the river Lauter, to provide cover for the operations, while the Margrave of Baden greeted Joseph before Landau with twenty-seven battalions and forty-four squadrons.

Once again the leader of the besieged French garrison, Laubanie, offered not to aim his cannons at those places where Joseph would be lodging or visiting, and once again the King of the Romans answered that he was perfectly safe, and would go wherever he wanted without telling anyone.

"Joseph the Victorious never knew it perhaps, but in that second siege of Landau the rule of checkmate was once again respected," said Atto, "and in the noblest manner."

"What do you mean?"

"A certain Count Raueskoet, one of Joseph's hunting companions, presented himself at Versailles, explaining that in his preparations for battle, Joseph used to go hunting close to the French lines without any escort. It would be child's play to capture him. His Majesty scornfully rejected the proposal and immediately expelled the traitor from France, and even warned the imperial troops of Raueskoet's treachery. Remember, boy: checkmate yes; assassination among sovereigns and princes of equal rank, never."

The battle began, even harder and bloodier than the two that had preceded it. This time winter came early, they fought in the cold, in the rain, in the mud. On 27th September the French tried to effect a sortie, but unsuccessfully. Four days later the imperial heavy artillery (carried to the front through the mire with great difficulty and heavy losses of men) began to pound Landau. A hail of fire was unleashed upon the fortress, but the French held out tenaciously. Eugene of Savoy was furious: Landau should have been taken in five or six weeks, he wrote to Vienna from his tent: instead things were dragging out while the French went on the rampage in Italy.

"But maybe there was a more serious reason for his agitation," said Atto. "He and Marlborough had been pushed to one side by Joseph. They had lost their place of honour."

In the end the bloodshed was horrific, the fortress of Landau only yielded after nine weeks of relentless cannon fire and assaults. The commander Laubanie lost his sight in both eyes, and would die two years later from his wounds, which never healed. The French garrison surrendered, once again throwing their arms down at Joseph's feet. The young heir to the throne had shown that he could retrieve the situation with his presence alone. His first victory had made him a young hero, with his second he had become a model for all soldiers. Winter had come, the military campaign of 1704 had concluded with an important victory, the English and Dutch allies could go back home satisfied. In Vienna the victory bells rang out again, and Eugene nursed dark, malicious thoughts of resentment. And suppose Joseph were to become the new rising star of the war, effacing the legend of Prince Eugene, which had been spreading throughout Europe? But the year after the recapture of Landau, things changed. Emperor Leopold, Joseph's father, died. It was not wise for the new young sovereign to leave Vienna and to set out for war, since he did not yet have any male heirs (his little son, Leopold Joseph, had died in infancy). Eugene remained commander-in-chief of military operations, and the fate of the war lay in his hands for the next three years.

The silent contest between the Sovereign and his general started up again in 1708. The Queen of England asked that Eugene should be sent to fight in Spain, where Charles, Joseph's brother, was unable to get the better of the French armies of Philip of Anjou, the grandson of the Most Christian King who had ascended to the Spanish throne. The imperial troops in the Iberian peninsula were captained by Guido Starhemberg, on whom fortune did not always smile. Eugene chafed at the bit: he knew he was superior to Starhemberg, and in his place could win great glory and honour.

There began a feverish back-and-forth with the English allies, but the imperial forces were adamant: the Prince of Savoy could not travel so far from Austria. Eugene had to put up with it, and hold his peace.

The silent war was repeated in autumn 1710. Once again there was a plan to send Eugene to Spain, but His Caesarean Majesty was still opposed to it, and it came to nothing. Eugene gave vent to his feelings among his friends, using allusive, indirect words. "Could it be that Stahremberg has not done all that was expected of him?" he asked ironically. And he revealed that with his own eyes he had seen Joseph arrive at the conference of ministers holding the paper nominating Eugene as commander in Spain, but he had rejected the idea without even referring to it. Joseph was not wrong: he was thinking of the safety of the Empire.

Twice with Landau, and twice again with Spain, Joseph had trampled over the pride and ambition of Eugene of Savoy. The loser had kept silent and obeyed; he had no choice in the matter. But what would happen if the secret competition, evident only to the two rivals, continued always to the advantage of one of them? And what connection was there with the strange coin that Cloridia had come across so fortuitously in Eugene's palace?

"That coin is the symbol of Landau," concluded Atto, "the first serious defeat that Eugene had to swallow. And it shows that the Prince of Savoy has not forgotten the affronts that Joseph has inflicted on him. Not a single one."

Caressing the coin in his fingers, Atto gloated. Once Joseph read Eugene's treacherous letter, the path to peace would be very short.

"If only we could get close to that little Pálffy woman," he grumbled impatiently, while he was seized by a great yawn, urging him to slip once again under the blankets, into the arms of Morpheus.

❧

Back home, on the other side of the convent, Cloridia came to greet me.

"My love," she said, stretching her arms out to me, "it's been a terrible day."

"You don't know the whole of it."

"What do you mean?"

I told her what had happened. At the end we stood there, both trembling, appalled at the violence that had broken out around us. I told her about the coin of Landau as well.

"I've a story connected with that."

"Really?"

"You're not the only one who's had a bad experience. Today at Prince Eugene's palace I was followed."

"Followed? Who by?"

"By that monstrous fellow who stole the coins of Landau. I kept coming across him. I would go to the kitchen and see him following me at a distance. I would go back to the first floor, and he would turn up from some nook or corner. I would go away and then find him just a few minutes later behind me. I'd go here, and so would he; I'd go there, and so would he. It was enough to drive me mad. If you could only have seen him ... The last time he even walked in a half-circle around me, and then showed me his sharp brown teeth in a frightful smile. Ugh! – like a hellish dream. At that point I ran back home."

"But who is he, what does he want?" I exclaimed in agitation. "He promises the dervish a decapitated head, then he stares at you, follows you around, steals Prince Eugene's coins ... What's the link between all these things?"

"All I know is that a man with a face like that is capable of anything. Including what they did to Hadji-Tanjov."

But we still had not heard the most serious news of the day.

To cheer ourlseves up we went into the cloisters to see our little boy playing there, and then we went into the convent church. Unnerved by all the evil that had been unleashed around us we felt the need to collect our thoughts in prayer before the Most High and to plead for grace and protection.

As soon as we stepped within its cold, incense-laden half-light, we found the church full of the nuns of Porta Coeli. They had all gathered together to recite the holy rosary. We were a little surprised: that late hour was certainly not a time of prayer at the convent. We made the sign of the cross and, settling in a corner at the back, we

joined fervently in the oration, supplicating divine help and praying
for the souls of the two poor murdered students.

After the holy rosary came the moment to implore the Blessed
Virgin of Porta Coeli. We gradually realised that an indistinct
murmuring was acting as counterpoint to the nuns' litany, and we
soon made it out as the sound of sobbing. Our eyes wandered in
search of its source and fell upon the Chormaisterin, prostrate
beneath the statue of the Blessed Virgin of Porta Coeli, to the left of
the altar, her breast shaking convulsively. Our feeling of puzzlement
suddenly turned to utter incredulity and bewilderment.

"*Pro vita nostri aegerrimi Cesaris, oramus,*" we heard the nun who
was leading the prayers cry.

Those words struck us like a gust of icy wind: "Let us pray for the
life of our Emperor, gravely ill," the nun had said. I hoped for an
instant that I had misunderstood, but the grief and anguish with
which Cloridia lifted her hand to her forehead sadly confirmed that
I had heard correctly. So the Emperor was ill? The Most August
Caesar, our beloved and radiant Joseph the First, was in mortal
danger? What had happened? And how on earth had we not heard
anything? But there was no way for us to find out any further details
at that moment: we had to wait until the end of the oration.
Those moments that separated us from a fuller explanation seemed
interminable. And then the church emptied at last and Camilla,
rising to her feet, turned towards us. As soon as she saw Cloridia she
embraced her.

"Camilla . . ." murmured my consort on seeing the young face
disfigured by grief.

She motioned us to follow her: she had to put out the candles.
The tiny flames were mirrored in Camilla de' Rossi's tear-streaked
cheeks, and she continued to clutch Cloridia's hands in a vain effort
to repress her sobs.

In town everyone had been talking about it since that morning.
At first it had circulated as a vague rumour, then the word had
become more insistent, until, like a bolt from the blue, orders were
issued for public prayers to be offered every hour and for exposition
of the blessed sacrament both in the public Caesarean chapel and in
the Cathedral of St Stephen. In the Caesarean chapel the various
members of the court had followed upon one another from hour to
hour: the tribunals, the ministers, the grandees, the cavaliers, the

dames and other people of noble rank. And similarly, in the cathedral, orations had begun in the afternoon attended by Monsignor the Bishop Prince in person and the chapter of the cathedral; and then the religious orders, confraternities, schools, arts, trades and hospitals had come in procession, with great throngs of the common people, who, with anguished devotion and zeal, had implored divine intercession.

Prayers had been going on in all the other parish churches inside and outside the city. Special couriers had even been sent throughout the Archduchy of Austria above and below the Enns, to announce the Oration of the Forty Hours, so that – as the public announcement stated – His Divine Majesty might be pleased to grant longer Life and happy Government to this Most Clement and Most August Monarch of ours, for the consolation of his faithful Peoples, and for the benefit of all Christianity in these grave and dangerous circumstances of War, which involved the whole of Europe.

Even Ottomans and Jews residing in the Caesarean city had called for extraordinary days of prayer and fasting and had distributed special alms.

The Emperor was ill. For some days he had been in bed, isolated from everything and everyone; no one could approach him. And not because Joseph the Victorious was unable to hold a conversation, or to preside over the conference of ministers, but because his illness was contagious. And mortal. The doctors' diagnosis seemed clear: smallpox.

"Like Ferdinand IV . . . just like him," sobbed Camilla.

Within my breast, as on a racecourse trampled by the hooves of maddened horses, dire portents were galloping towards their own incarnation.

My thoughts ran to Ferdinand IV, the young King of the Romans carried off by smallpox fifty years earlier. The firstborn of Emperor Ferdinand III and elder brother of Leopold, he had suddenly died at the age of just twenty-one. I had read the story of Ferdinand, a child prodigy, in the books I had bought on my arrival in Vienna. It was on his magnificent gifts that his father had set his hopes of reviving the Empire after the ill-fated Thirty Years' War. This blow had fallen at such a delicate moment that the House of Habsburg had even risked losing the imperial crown. France had immediately taken advantage of the situation to block Leopold's election as Emperor and he had been forced to pay out huge sums of money to the Protestant princes to get himself elected, and had had to renounce solemnly before them any intention of going to assist the Habsburgs in Spain in their war against France. And so the French-Spanish war had ended with the defeat of Spain and King Philip IV had been forced to give the hand of his daughter Maria Teresa to Louis XIV rather than to Leopold. And it was that very marriage that had given the French their right to the throne of Spain, which was at the root of the present War of the Spanish Succession. In short, if Ferdinand had not died so prematurely and unexpectedly, the Bourbons of France would not have become related to the Habsburgs of Spain and so the war of succession would not have broken out.

The young Ferdinand, despite enjoying excellent health and rare good looks, had been swiftly carried off by smallpox. When the older people recalled that bereavement of the imperial family, which had led to so many other past and present bereavements, they trembled: Joseph was not yet *geblattert* – which is to say he had not yet had smallpox.

Now it had happened.

"The first symptoms began five days ago. Until today the thing had been kept secret. I myself only heard about it last night," said the Chormaisterin, her voice still hoarse from weeping.

And so we learned that on Tuesday 7th April Joseph the Victorious had dined with his mother and had been affected by a slight headache. A minor nuisance, which disappeared the next day, so that on Wednesday morning the young Emperor had decided to devote himself to his usual hunting trip. On his return he had complained of a strong constriction in his chest, trouble in breathing and strange pains all over his body. Suddenly he had been seized with a fit of vomiting, expelling a considerable quantity of pituitary matter. The doctor had been summoned, and he had attributed the sickness to excessive eating during the Easter celebrations, and for that evening he had prescribed shredded hyacinth with some species of buds.

The night had been troubled. The morning of the next day, Thursday 9th April, Joseph had been seized with another violent fit of vomiting, regurgitating viscous, ill-digested matter, followed by pure bile in quantities equivalent to several spoonfuls. The slight headache had returned, but above all he was afflicted with great pain shifting between the abdomen and chest, and finally settling in his loins. Joseph the Victorious, a young man, robust and vigorous, a most courageous soldier, was to be heard screaming like a child. Fortunately, his urine and pulse were normal, and so an enema had been applied – an insufflation of water and salt, which had proved highly beneficial. But the pains had continued until the evening, together with the screams. The enema had been repeated, bringing on copious bilious excretions, and an eye powder had been prescribed (in accordance with Aristotle's well-known instructions), as well as a powder of native cinnabar. In the evening his pulse had begun to quicken, and at one in the morning he had begun to grow decidedly feverish.

While Camilla talked, like a lugubriously tolling bell, a date was thrumming in my mind: 7th April. On that day Joseph's illness had begun, but also the Turkish Agha had come to Vienna. And that was not all: the next day Abbot Melani had arrived in the city.

"Are you absolutely sure it's smallpox?" I asked Camilla.

"That's what they're saying at the moment."

"How is the Emperor now?"

"Nobody knows. All information about the last three days is kept strictly private. But . . . where are you going?"

ॐ

"Eh? What are you saying?" mumbled Abbot Melani from beneath the blankets, his tongue still thick with sleep.

"You're acting the innocent? I knew it!" I shouted, beside myself.

I had come crashing into Atto's apartment like a Fury. I had hammered frantically on the door (the nuns' cells were all at some distance, after all) and Domenico, jumping out of bed in alarm, had opened up to me, convinced the city must be on fire at the very least.

"The Turkish Agha arrived in Vienna just a day before you, and you pretend you know nothing about it! Once again you had it all planned, you and that dervish!"

"Dervish? I don't know what you're talking about," said Atto, sitting up in his bed.

"Signor Uncle . . ." Domenico tried to interpose.

"Yes, the dervish in the Turkish retinue, that Ciezeber, who slices himself up with his disgusting rituals and then heals himself as if nothing had happened. Nice people you go around with, Abbot Melani! And you're conniving with the dervish to get the Emperor's head. Ah, now you put on your astonished look! You didn't think I knew, did you?"

Uncle and nephew fell silent. This gave me courage and I went on:

"You, Abbot Melani, you say you came here to force the Empire to make peace. You waved that letter under my nose from the traitor Prince Eugene, who wants to sell himself to France, but you kept quiet about the other manoeuvre, the more important one, which removes the main obstacle in this war: the Emperor! His Caesarean Majesty Joseph I has no sons. If he were to die, the heir to the throne would be his brother Charles, who for the last ten years has been fighting to wrest the throne of Spain from Philip of Anjou, the Sun King's grandson. If Joseph died, Charles would have to come straight back to Vienna to become emperor, and that would be the end of the war. Eugene has betrayed his side by now: even if the Empire wanted to, it no longer has a king to set up in Spain, nor a general. The throne of Madrid would be left permanently to your sovereign's grandson. A perfect plan! That's why the Emperor is sick. Smallpox, my foot: it was you French, in league with the Turks as usual, who poisoned him."

"Is the Emperor sick? Smallpox? What are you saying, boy?"

"And the sickness, strangely enough, started with the head . . . the same head that the dervish was plotting to get. Or is that just a coincidence? But who could believe that! Not me, that's for sure, knowing you as I do, alas! But how could you do it? At your age, do you have no fear of God?" I asked, my voice broken.

"I don't know where you –" protested Atto, who had put a hand to his belly, while his face contracted.

"And don't think that I've forgotten that Philip of Anjou was proclaimed King of Spain thanks to a forged will. And it was you who forged it, eleven years ago in Rome, under my nose!"

"Signor Uncle, you shouldn't allow him –" said Domenico.

"Such a generous reward – I don't think!" I went on with renewed fury. "You found me a job and a home here in Vienna so that you could exploit my loyal service yet again, and then skip out at the right moment, as you did twice in Rome! This time it's an even dirtier game: get the Emperor assassinated, a young man not yet thirty-three! That's why you made me rich. You wanted to buy me. But you won't succeed, ah no! This time you won't

get away with it. There's no price for the life of my king! I'll go
back to Rome and starve in the *tufo*, but not before I've done all
I can to impede your dirty plans. It'll have to be over my
dead bou͵!"

"Good heavens, boy, you don't . . . Domenico, please!" implored
Atto, pressing his hand to his belly with a grimace and making as if
to get up.

"Signor Uncle, here I am," said his nephew solicitously, rushing
to hold him up and lead him behind a curtain, where there was a seat
for his bodily needs.

Here Abbot Melani had an attack of colic, the so-called gravel
sickness, accompanied by discharges of diarrhoea and by a robust
venting of piles or haemorrhoids, or whatever they are called. I
suddenly found myself without an adversary, and in a state of great
embarrassment. I offered my assistance, but Domenico rejected it
from behind the curtain with a sulky grunt.

"The Emperor . . . the poison . . ." I heard Atto gasping.

"Signor Uncle, you're losing a lot of blood, you must drink your
citron juice."

"Yes, yes, quickly, I beg you . . ."

Domenico drew aside the curtain and signalled to me to
support the old Abbot for a few seconds, who was sprawling
awkwardly on the seat. For the first time I saw his castrato's pudenda.
Atto, paying no attention to me, continued to moan, while his
volcanic intestine gave no sign of settling, nor the piles of ceasing to
gush forth. His nephew rushed away and poured a few drops from a
little flask into a large glass of fresh water, which he handed to
his uncle.

"Well, I think that . . ." I blathered, getting ready to take my
leave.

But Domenico thought that I wanted to continue with my accusations and from behind the curtain he yelled:

"Have you no pity for a poor old man? Do you want to kill him?
That's enough now. Go away, go away!"

࿇

Thus dismissed, I crossed the convent in a daze and dragged myself
to my bed, where Cloridia was still sitting up, in a light doze. She
had tried to stay awake for me, but had been overcome by weariness.

And so I was left to writhe in solitary despair and doubt. I collapsed on the bed, with my head between my hands. Ever since we had heard the fateful announcement in church I had not had a single second to reflect: so was the Emperor about to die? It seemed a nightmare; but sadly there were too many signs that I was not dreaming. That same Sunday, had not my assistant and I encountered as many as three processions heading towards the Cathedral of St Stephen, while Penicek's cart took us to our appointment with poor Hadji-Tanjov?

I saw Hristo's chessboard on the table. I ran my fingertips over the dent which, by blocking the projectile, had saved my life.

The evening before, I reflected, we had all noticed the Chormaisterin's inexplicable nervousness during the rehearsal of *Sant' Alessio*, when she had lashed out at poor Gaetano Orsini with such unusual irritation. Camilla had chosen an extremely melancholy and gloomy aria for the rehearsal and had then talked of omens: now I realised that she had been brooding over grim presentiments of death. She had been thinking of the Emperor, who had lingered at the tomb of his friend Lamberg, and undoubtedly also of the sombre prediction of the English divine and the anathema of that treacherous Jesuit, Wiedemann, and probably of countless other signs, since there was no shortage of people wishing for the death of His Caesarean Majesty. How could one blame her? Twenty-eight years earlier, as a servant boy in the Inn of the Donzello in Rome, with my own eyes I had read in an astrological gazette a correct prediction of the death of a sovereign: the unfortunate consort of the Most Christian King.

No, unfortunately it was not a bad dream, I moaned, as I opened the chessboard. One question tormented me above all others: what lay concealed in Abbot Melani's heart and mind? He had arrived in Vienna on the same day that the Emperor had fallen ill, and just one day after the Agha's arrival. Atto had come to play France's game on two different boards. On the one hand, to expose Eugene's treachery, putting him out of action once and for all, without even granting him the Low Countries, as he had asked. He had confessed this to me openly. On the other hand, the more radical solution: to assassinate Joseph I. Just how the two things were linked to one another was not entirely clear to me, but what did that matter? The Abbot himself had taught me years ago: it is not necessary to know everything, but just to understand the sense of what happens. And the sense of it all – I had grasped that all too well. With all the experience I had accumulated alongside the scheming castrato, I just needed to put two and two together. This time it had not been necessary to wait for all the misadventures to come to fruition for me to work it out; I had not discovered Melani's game only after his departure, but just twenty-four hours after first meeting him again. I was getting better at this game, I told myself with bitter sarcasm.

And yet it was also true, on the other hand, that my accusations seemed to have upset Atto greatly. But I should not let myself be fooled, I told myself: he had always pretended in front of me, even at the most dramatic moments. I had even seen him sobbing over the death of his dearest friends, only to discover later that he himself had been involved in it up to his neck! I must not forget that Atto had come to Vienna on the very day that the Emperor had felt the first symptoms of his illness. The same thing had happened in the past: twenty-eight years earlier Melani had turned up at the Inn of the Donzello on the same day that the aged French lodger had mysteriously died...

The baleful castrato had always used me as a pawn, as if I were of no more importance than the poor white pawn I now held in my hand, a helpless meal for the treacherous black bishop – the scoundrel of an abbot.

Poor me: I had become a master chimney-sweep, and the owner of a cottage and vineyard in the Josephina, only thanks to Atto Melani! If his plot were to be discovered, I would end up on the scaffold alongside him. After putting my life and my family's livelihood at risk, now the old castrato might easily drag me with him to death! But he was a venerable old man of eighty-five: the executioner, after all, would only be anticipating the grim reaper by a few days or weeks. Whereas I was in the full flush of life and had a family to support! I suddenly felt giddy and began to shake with fear.

I clutched the black bishop tightly in my other hand, almost as if I could thus strangle Abbot Melani, crush him, make him miraculously vanish from my life.

I looked at our child, serenely asleep, and then at Cloridia's sweet face. I cursed the castrato and his intrigues, so eager to unsettle their dreamless sleep! And what about my two girls, who had stayed in Rome and were longing to join us? What would their wretched fate be, when they heard that their father had been condemned for high treason and hanged like a common malefactor, or beheaded, or even (and here my shudders became uncontrollable) drawn and quartered on the terrible wheel?

With overpowering remorse, I confessed that I had brought these ills on my family by myself. What an unworthy husband and father I had proved! A poor insipid foot soldier, just like the white pawn I now clutched in my hand and whose head I would have liked to rip off with one bite out of sheer rage.

Oh, my Cloridia, the bold, enchanting and learned courtesan of twenty-eight years ago, who had set my boy's knees a-trembling! To what wretched fate had I consigned that lovely complexion of gleaming dark velvet which contrasted with her luxuriant Venetian blond curls, which framed those large black eyes and the serrated pearls of her mouth, that rounded yet proud little nose, those lips smiling with a touch of rouge just sufficient to remove their vague pallor, and that small but fine and harmonious face and the fine snow of her bosom, intact and kissed by two suns, on shoulders worthy of a bust by Bernini? I had met her when she was more sublime than a Raphael Madonna, more inspired than a motto of Teresa of Ávila, more marvellous than a verse of the *Cavaliere* Marino, more melodious than a madrigal of Monteverdi, more lascivious than a couplet by Ovid and more edifying than an entire tome of Fracastoro.

What had I done to her? Widow of a gallows bird! To begin with I had not been a bad husband, I told myself: to unite herself with me she had abandoned prostitution, into which she had been cast by the foul and secret events that I had uncovered when we met in the Donzello Inn. Yes, but afterwards? We had lived in the little house purchased by my father-in-law, not by me, and until two years ago we had lived on the income of the small farm he had bequeathed to us. I had worked hard at Villa Spada, it was true, but what about the fame that Cloridia had won as an excellent midwife, to the great financial benefit of the whole family?

What a good-for-nothing I must be, since in three decades I had been unable not only to guarantee my Clorida prosperity but even to spare her the insult of poverty and finally the loss of the property inherited from her father. And yet she had not stinted herself: she had given herself to me wholly, remaining ever-loving and faithful, giving birth to three children, bestowing on them with her womb the gift of being, and with her breast the gift of well-being.

At the end of all this reasoning, the trial I had been conducting against myself concluded with a conviction.

I looked again at the black chess bishop. I had to admit it: if he had not arrived, the black Abbot Melani, to save us from poverty, at this hour we would still be in Rome, in the jaws of hunger, our little boy perhaps already dead from cold after yet another hard frost, myself dead from a fall from a roof, or, worse, burned alive in a chimney fire. Who could say? It is true that with his donation Atto had been fulfilling a promise, I considered with wavering spirit; but if I had never met him, would I not in any case have fallen victim to the famine of 1709 and the decadence of the Spada family, for whom I had been working?

Vienna and Rome, Rome and Vienna: suddenly the hidden thread of my existence unravelled in my mind. Twenty-eight years earlier, while the future of Europe was being decided in Vienna, in that small inn in the centre of Rome, just a few yards from Piazza Navona, the meeting with Abbot Melani had changed my life forever. He had trained me in the ruses and stratagems of politics, of state intrigues, in the dark *facies* of human existence. He had pulled me prematurely from the blind ingenuousness to which I would otherwise have been destined. Revealing to me the evil of this world, he had caused me (although that had not been his purpose) to flee it, to abandon my vacuous youthful dream of becoming a gazetteer and instead to withdraw into a world constituted by the important things of existence: my family, the love of my dear ones, a modest and virtuous life, marked by the fear of God.

But over the course of time, in order to achieve his ends he had tricked, exploited and deceived me. I had been his docile and unconscious instrument, and I had helped him to set in motion machinations favouring the King of France. He had got what he had wanted from me: help, advice, even affection.

Everything now seemed changed, and even to have turned into its opposite. I was no longer the ingenuous little boy of our first meeting, nor the young family man he had met on his return to Rome. I was a mature man of forty-eight, hardened by a life of labour. In the Vienna that had played such an important part in our first adventures, almost three decades earlier, I had finally found the reward for all that Atto Melani had taken from me with his empty promises. My God, did it all have to end tragically on a gallows?

Having given vent to panic, rage, a thousand regrets and torments, just like a duck flapping his wings dry on leaving a pond I now shook off all reminiscences and pondered on the present. The old castrato's fainting fit had not seemed faked: with my own eyes (and not least with my nose...) I had had clear evidence of the pitiful state he had been reduced to by the news of the Most August Caesar's illness. And in any case, had I not heard Atto describing in passionate tones the heroism of Joseph the Victorious? And even earlier, the very day we had met at the coffee house of the Blue Bottle, had not Atto himself painted in gloomy colours the wretched end of France and the failure of the vainglorious reign of Louis XIV, while he praised Vienna and the Habsburgs? Those had not been the speeches of an enemy of the Empire. Unless . . .

Unless he had made all those speeches deliberately to deceive me and allay any suspicions I might have.

I did not yield to sleep – rather, I almost fainted when, after dropping Hristo's chessboard, a little piece of paper emerged from its false bottom:

> Shah matt
> checkmate
> the King is enclosed

Day the Fifth
Monday, 13ᵀᴴ April 1711

✠

It was midnight when, with lightning speed, I dashed to Simonis's room.

"We must find your companions," I exhorted him, waking him from a deep sleep, "and at once. I'll pay them and tell them to leave off their enquiries: it's too dangerous."

I told him about the Emperor's sudden illness, about my suspicions that he was being murdered (but I omitted Atto's probable involvement), and I showed him the little piece of paper written in poor Hadji-Tanjov's own handwriting.

"The King is enclosed," the Greek read slowly, and I could not tell whether his tone was one of distraction or concentration.

"Do you understand, Simonis?" I asked, wondering whether at that moment I was speaking to the usual idiot or the alert student I had discovered over the last few days. "Hristo told you that the solution of the sentence was in the words *soli soli soli*, and that it was linked to checkmate. Now with this piece of paper we can finally understand the meaning of Hristo's words: 'checkmate' comes from 'shah matt', which I imagine is Persian, since chess, unless I'm mistaken, comes from that part of the world."

"And 'shah matt', according to what Hristo wrote here, literally means 'the King is enclosed'," concluded the Greek.

"Exactly. I think Hristo, playing one of his chess games, had an intuition and understood something that links the Agha's statement with the Emperor."

"Aren't you getting ahead of yourself? Are we sure that 'the King is enclosed' refers to His Caesarean Majesty?"

"Just use your brain," I said impatiently, "who else could it be? The Agha came to Rome, he uttered that strange sentence, his dervish wants someone's head, Joseph the First just happens to fall ill . . ."

"How can you be sure they're poisoning him? And suppose it were really smallpox?"

"Trust me," I answered curtly.

I would have liked to say, "When Abbot Melani's around, nothing happens by chance and above all nobody dies a natural death."

"But what's the link between *soli soli soli* and 'the King is enclosed'?"

"Well, we don't know that yet," I admitted, "but I know enough already not to want any more students on my conscience. I'll tell your companions what Cloridia heard from Ciezeber. I want to be sure they drop this business and that none of them takes it any further, even just out of curiosity."

Simonis grew thoughtful.

"All right, Signor Master," he said at last, "we'll do as you wish. This matter concerns you. Tomorrow I'll start looking for my friends to tell them that you –"

"No, look for them now. At once. Right now those boys are running the risk, without knowing it, of ending up like Dànilo and Hristo. Who shall we tell first, at this hour?"

"Dragomir Populescu," answered my assistant, after a moment's reflection. "With the job he does, the night is his world."

�❧

Saint Ulrich, Neustift, the Jägerzeile, Lichtenthal and the lands of the chapter of the cathedral: we were rapidly combing all the zones in the suburbs where music and dancing took place. Thanks to Penicek's mysterious connections – Simonis had got him out of bed and forced him to drive us in his cart – we had passed through the city gates by paying a mere "offering", as he called it, to the guards.

Simonis had already hinted that Populescu scraped the barest of livings, and that night he revealed to me the list of his various occupations.

"A cheat at cards and billiards, and a specialist in rigging all forms of gambling: dice, bowls and so on. And in his spare time, an unauthorised violinist."

"Unauthorised violinist?"

The Greek explained that dancing and music were not such an obvious and innocent pastime as one might think. Pater Abraham from Sancta Clara had thundered against them in his sermons: "*It is*

well known good habits can by good strings be ripped: chiefly in dances, where
leap as you may, one's honour oft is tripped."

For about a decade now, for reasons of public decency and
morality, the authorities had been trying to impose limitations on
dances: two years earlier the municipal council had even asked the
Emperor to abolish them. An exception was made for weddings,
during which violins were allowed to play until nine or ten p.m., but
no later. However, these rules were not respected; indeed, there had
been a wild outbreak of *Geigen und Tanzen*, those dances to the merry
sound of violins, especially in the suburbs.

In the meantime we had visited a dozen places with orchestras
and dancers: there was no sign of Populescu.

In the beer halls, Simonis continued as we drove on to the
next tavern, the town council had even forbidden dancing entirely,
on the pretext that the instruments played in such places (reed-
pipes, colasciones or mandoras) did not deserve the name of musical
instruments, and the customers – people *vilioris conditionis*, of vile
condition – under the influence of beer, violins and dancing,
abandoned themselves to unmentionable liberties and abominable
practices.

In the end, however, since these prohibitions achieved very little
(even the Emperor was in favour of greater freedom for innkeepers,
dancers and musicians), they had introduced a tax on dancing; as
Austrian wisdom has it, what cannot be forbidden must be taxed.

Everyone was taxed, except the noblemen, so long as the balls
they gave were free of charge. There was a tax on weddings, baptisms
and all the various local celebrations *et cetera*. The owners of taverns,
beer halls and such like had to pay five florins a year. In addition,
places of entertainment within the city walls, on the occasion of
public festivals, had to pay thirty kreutzer per musician, and a full
florin for private parties! The result was that people played and
danced in secret, or declared fewer musicians than there actually
were. The Office of the Court Treasury sent inspectors out but the
innkeepers would not let them in and even threatened them. Even
the musicians had to pay something: to play they had to have a
licence. The fine for unlicensed musicians was six florins.

"So one of our Dragomir's thousand trades is that of unlicensed
musician," said Simonis, who seemed, as he chatted away, to have
forgotten how urgent our search was.

While my assistant explained the secrets of Populescu's nightlife, we visited the umpteenth tavern, asking the owner and customers in vain if they had seen him around. As we left the place, where about twenty clients were dancing to the sound of a small orchestra, we saw the host talking in the doorway to a couple of individuals, who looked like officials or secretaries. In the middle of the conversation, the host (a corpulent and rather grim-looking man) suddenly spat into the face of one of his two interlocutors, and then slapped him repeatedly. He then summoned a couple of robust young men from inside the tavern, on whose appearance the two officials immediately took to their heels.

"Another fruitless inspection," confirmed Simonis with a smile.

We had now toured all the places likely to hold dancing, but had found no trace of Populescu.

"Strange," said Simonis seriously, "I was almost sure we would find him in one of these places . . ."

Then I saw him clap his hand to his forehead.

"How stupid of me! Of course. At this hour he'll be at the Three Bumpkins! Quick, Pennal!" he ordered.

"Are we going to the Three Bumpkins? The one in the Neubau suburb?" asked Penicek.

"Exactly, that one," answered the Greek.

"What is it?"

"A bowling alley."

"At this hour?" I asked in amazement. "You can't play bowls at night!"

"You're quite right, Signor Master, but you need darkness to rig the long alley," answered my assistant nonchalantly. "And so our good Dragomir, or the gallant gentleman who commissioned the task, will go there tomorrow and win, and so will all his gambling accomplices."

"Everyone knows Dragomir in the gambling world, especially the crooked part, heh heh," sniggered Penicek, turning towards us while with his reins he steered the cart towards a small bridge.

"Shut up Pennal! Who said you could open your mouth?" the Greek snapped.

Humbled and contrite, Penicek turned his face back towards the dark road.

"But how much can he make?" I asked in some doubt. "I've seen bowling alleys in noblemen's gardens, it's true, but unless I'm mistaken, bowls are generally considered a pastime for ordinary people. And playing the violin at the weddings of common people can't earn him that much either."

"That's the point. Populescu supplements his income by occasionally spilling the beans to the guards, letting them know who's dancing, playing or gambling without a permit, or without paying taxes."

"He sells himself to his own enemies?" I asked in surprise.

"Obviously when he's not the one playing or organising the game or the bet . . ." Simonis winked at me.

Since public gambling houses were forbidden, explained the Greek, individual games were subdivided into legal and illegal ones. Games of skill, such as chess, were almost always allowed, while the greater the role of chance, the greater the prohibitions.

"The bans have nothing to do with morality: they just serve to keep the social classes divided, as usual," said Simonis ironically. "You can never win that much with gambling. And so you won't get any *nouveaux riches*. To make a lot of money, luck by itself isn't enough – you need merit. Or rather, you have to be rich already: the nobles don't pay taxes on gambling."

Dice were often forbidden, bowling and cards went up and down. What made it difficult to enforce the bans was the fact that from the feudal age on, in order to elude inspections the names of the games and sometimes even some of their rules were constantly being changed, or the games that were allowed – games not played for money – were often turned into games played for money. And so the list of forbidden games was always getting longer, in an endless race between the law and the sharpest players, said Simonis, laughing with relish. Once again I had the impression that my assistant was more concerned to tell me about these aspects of Viennese life than to find Populescu. But maybe I was mistaken, I told myself.

As with dancing, in the end the law gave up and chose to make money from the situation rather than to forbid it. Forty years earlier an all-inclusive "entertainment tax" had been introduced, the revenue of which was to go towards the city's prisons.

"The easiest to tax are the bowling alleys," remarked Simonis, "because they can't vanish. But Dragomir has to be very careful every time: as you've already seen, the hosts can be very vindictive. Woe betide any informer they catch."

The taxes on card games, on the other hand, were almost impossible to collect.

"That's why last year they made yet another attempt to tax all games."

After a long series of surveys, Simonis explained, they had decided on the following plan: a tenth of the winnings must be paid into the public coffers. The organiser of the game had to buy certain ivory game tokens from the *Oberamt*, the communal office, and these would be changed into cash for the winner after a tenth had been detracted from it. This was paid to the *Oberamt*, which as a reward gave half to the organiser of the game, explained Simonis, strangely inspired by this account, which was so punctilious that it reminded me of the stories in the German-language gazzettes, abounding in details.

"Needless to say such an intricate procedure fell apart in just a few months. All over Vienna people laughed: 'Cards aren't like music: you can play cards in silence!'"

And so they had fallen back on the Viennese penchant for snooping.

"And that's Dragomir's most profitable trade," said my assistant, "organising secret games, crooked gambling, forbidden dances, mass dives into the Danube, and then denouncing the whole thing and getting a reward."

"Dives?"

"Of course, you won't know about that, Signor Master, because you only got her a few months ago and you haven't yet admired a Viennese summer . . ."

You see, Simonis went on, open-air bathing had been very fashionable for about ten years in the Caesarean city, despite the fact that it had been forbidden since the last century. Almost every day you would see children and adults of both sexes bathing stark naked in the various branches of the Danube and in the Wienn, the city's other river. And it did not only take place in secluded spots, but in the very centre, among the houses and along the crowded streets. Amidst the city bustle you would suddenly see someone strip off and, leaving his clothes on the side of the road, he would cheerfully dive in, immediately followed by other passers-by, in an effort to cool down. It scandalised respectable ladies, irritated gentlemen and did great harm to the education of children, who found themselves confronted by the unedifying spectacle.

"In the summer Dragomir goes along, strips off, dives in, shouts 'Ah it's lovely!', and as soon as he's got a number of passers-by to imitate him, out he gets and off he goes to the guards to tip them off and get a reward."

"Another spy, like Dànilo. Even worse," I said.

"Half-Asia . . ." whispered Simonis into my ear.

"Populescu won't make many friends, with this trade."

"Oh, on the contrary, he has a lot of friends. They're the ones who don't know about his double-dealing: dupes waiting to be fleeced."

We had reached our destination, in the suburb of Neubau. We left Penicek on the box and approached the entrance of the Three Bumpkins. It was completely dark.

"It's closed," I said

"Of course. The little jobs that Dragomir does are very . . . unoffical. We'll climb over the gate."

It was a tavern with a fine garden equipped with two alleys for bowls. We patrolled them. They were deserted. The Greek frowned.

"The Seven Yards!" he commanded Penicek when we got back to the cart. Then he turned to me: "It's the city's shooting range, along the Als, just outside the western ramparts."

"Finding Populescu isn't as easy as you thought," I said.

The Greek was silent.

Nor was there any sign of our man at the Seven Yards.

"We'll look for him elsewhere," announced Simonis as we made our way back to the Pennal's cart. "We'll search all the bowling alleys he uses."

"Why are you so sure we'll find him there?" I asked doubtfully.

"After the snow the weather looks more promising. Over the next few days, as soon as the weather gets a little warmer, Viennese citizens will come pouring out as usual, driven crazy by their city's eternal cold. And Dragomir will be waiting for them with open arms . . ." he laughed.

The Greek was right. In many countries bowls are the people's favourite amusement in warm weather; even too much so, as Pater Abraham from Sancta Clara rightly complained: "In summer the common people go swarming into the gardens and bowling alleys where they indulge in swearing and cursing and fighting and bickering."

"But how many bowling alleys are there in and around Vienna?" I asked, to get some idea how much more travelling we were in for.

I was extremely tired, and already a little sorry that I had not waited until the next day, as my assistant had suggested.

"Six hundred and fifty-eight short alleys, or circular ones, and forty-three long ones."

"My God! And how do you expect to find him?" I exclaimed, afraid that the Greek had succumbed to a bout of idiocy.

"Don't worry, Signor Master. Apart from the two we've already visited, Populescu is a regular customer of just one other alley. We'll find him there for sure. But if you're tired we can put it off till tomorrow."

"No, let's go on."

"Pennal, get this old crock moving and we'll go to the alley . . . the Golden Thingie, what's it called? Ah yes, the Golden Angel," ordered Simonis.

"The Golden Angel? The one in the east, on the Landstrasse, opposite the Gate of the Stoves, where the Commorrers, the Stullweissenburgers, the Neuheußlers, the Bruggers and the Altenburgers all call?" asked Penicek, listing the coach drivers from the various cities of the Archduchy of Austria, the Empire and beyond, who evidently ended their journeys to Vienna in this tavern.

"No, the other Golden Angel, the one in the north, in the suburb of Währing."

"Ah, I've got it. It's on the Alstergasse, isn't it?"

"Exactly."

We inspected the fourteen short alleys and the long alley of the Golden Angel, but with no luck: everything was draped in the desolate silence of the night.

"I could have sworn he would be here," said my assistant gloomily, as we climbed over the fence on our way back to the cart.

"My God," I exclaimed disconsolately. "First we found Dànilo dead, then Hristo. And now, God forbid . . ."

"Just a second! Could it be that I remembered wrongly?" Simonis said suddenly, as he climbed into the cart. "Perhaps the place Dragomir always hangs out at is the Golden Moon, or something similar. Pennal!"

"Perhaps Signor Barber means the Golden Moonshine, in Wieden," stammered Penicek deferentially.

"Yes, yes, that's it," exclaimed my assistant.

Driving Penicek's poor horse to the point of collapse, we visited the seventeen short alleys of the Golden Moonshine; the fifteen short ones and the long one of the Golden Deer on the Leopoldine Island, across the Battle Bridge, where travellers from Leipzig and Nuremberg arrive; and then the Golden Ox, where the Nurembergers lodge, together with the Schlasckwalters, the Planners and the Neuhausers; the Golden Eagle, terminus for the coach drivers from Silesia; the Golden Ostrich, arrival point for postillions from Breslau, and for the Neusers and the Iglauers; the Golden Peacock, hostel for the Poles; and even the Golden Lamb, where the Pennal's fellow-citizens lodged, the coach drivers from Prague; without counting a whole host of other alleys with gilded names. Penicek himself drew on his expertise as a driver, taking us to all the places he knew: in the south, in the suburb of Wieden, opposite the Carinthian Gate, we inspected the Golden Capon, where the Venetian coach drivers stayed, and the Golden Amber, where the drivers from Villach stayed. It was all in vain: the name of the correct inn was buried in Simonis's memory, and it seemed to have got blocked.

I was in a grim mood and trembling with anxiety for Populescu's life. If he had been murdered, the number of corpses on my conscience would have risen to three. Because now I was sure of it: Dànilo Danilovitsch and Hristo Hadji-Tanjov had been killed on account of their investigations into the Golden Apple.

Weariness finally won out over these funereal conjectures. I closed my eyes. Luckily I managed to sleep a little in the cart between one place and the next. Having searched all the places with gold in their names that we could remember, we took Penicek's suggestion to visit other taverns, where travellers came from outside Vienna: for profiteers like Populescu, foreigners are always the ideal dupes. So we went back to Wieden to inspect the Basket of Coal, where coach drivers from Graz, Marburg and Neustadt called; and then to the Black Goat on Landstrasse, a haunt of traders in oxen from Hungary; and finally, in the suburb of Rossau, opposite the Scottish Gate, where Penicek himself had a stable, we looked in at the Black Amber, the arrival point for people from places in Lower Austria, like Passau, Crems, Wachau and others, and the White Lamb, where sailors from St John, from Greifenstein *et cetera et cetera* landed.

At these last few stops, to tell the truth, I let Simonis go and search, while I continued to doze.

"Aren't you sleepy?" I asked my assistant, while Penicek himself nodded off placidly on the box.

"I have my bat with me, Signor Master," he answered, pointing to his little shoulder bag.

"What? Oh yes," I said, remembering the strange remedy against sleepiness that my assistant had adopted on the night of the Deposition. "But won't it suffocate, shut up in there?"

"It's used to it. And anyway it's asleep now!"

"Ah."

ॐ∽ॐ

"Talk of the devil!" exclaimed Populescu the moment he saw us.

I heaved a sigh of relief. At the Golden Crown, on the Leopoldine Island, we had finally found the Romanian. After rigging the bowls and the hard clay of the alley, he was getting ready to go. I was about to tell him about the danger he was in, but Populescu got in before me: he had some important new things to tell us about the Golden Apple. There was just one problem: his informer, with whom he had fixed a meeting, had not turned up. He jumped onto Penicek's cart, inviting us to accompany him to an address not far off.

"Let's go to the Hetzhaus, Pennal. And hurry, by God," he ordered him cheerfully, and then turned to me. "Don't worry, the last time I found him easily. He's a Romanian boy, like me, but he comes from an area of beggars, in the mountains, nothing like my part of the country," he was keen to clarify, lifting the palm of his hand to show that he came from far more civilised lands. "There's Romania and Romania: I was born on the Black Sea, and I'm a prince!"

"Yes, of course, your highness," said Simonis, winking at me, amused by his "half-Asiatic" companion's clarification.

"The boy's father was taken prisoner of war by the Turks," Populescu went on, "and knows a lot about their legends. He promised he would give us some useful information."

"How useful?" I asked doubtfully.

"He says he knows where the Golden Apple comes from, and where it ended up."

"Listen, Dragomir," I interrupted him, "I have to speak to you. You must stop . . ."

But the Romanian had not heard me. We had already arrived. Populescu got down from Penicek's cart and signalled to me and Simonis that we should wait.

My assistant addressed me in heartfelt tones:

"If I may be allowed, Signor Master, before you speak to Dragomir and tell him to stop his investigation, it might be better to wait and see what his informer has to say about the Golden Apple. We're almost there. I wouldn't want my companion, after he hears that the Agha's dervish is plotting a murder, to run off right now."

I was silent for a moment.

"You could be right," I agreed then. "After all there are four of us. I don't think Populescu is in any immediate danger."

Simonis looked at me in silence, waiting for my last word.

"All right then. I'll speak to him afterwards," I concluded.

Simonis said nothing. He seemed relieved.

It was still the middle of the night, and we were still on the Leopoldine Island, outside the Tabor Schantz. The Pennal had parked his cart near a strange building, which I had never heard of before: the Hetzhaus, or "House of Incitement". It was a tall wooden building of a circular shape, from which, despite the late hour, there came an infernal clamour of human shouting and animal cries.

"What's going on in there?" I asked Simonis.

"Have you never heard of the Hetzhaus, Signor Master?"

"Never."

At that very moment Populescu returned.

"It's full tonight. Come with me, it'll be quicker if we do it together."

The Pennal, as usual, waited outside for us. We made our way to the entrance, where a huge, ogre-like man stopped us:

"Spectators or owners?"

"Don't you recognise me, Helmut?" answered Populescu, "I'm looking for Zyprian."

The ogre replied that he had seen our man about an hour earlier. However, he did not know if he was still around, and he let us through. I looked at Simonis questioningly.

"You'll understand everything in a moment, Signor Master."

The entrance was a simple low and narrow corridor leading towards the middle of the wooden building. As we advanced, the din grew even louder and I was able to distinguish its two principal noises: men yelling and poultry squawking. Finally we emerged into a large amphitheatre, illuminated by a great number of torches. On the ground level there were a number of compartments, in which animals were caged; when the grating was lifted they came out into the arena and fought. Next to the grating was the spectators' entrance and large containers for dogs.

A heaving mass of individuals was swarming around the centre of the arena, yelling and gesticulating. The noise was now deafening, and was accompanied by a stifling stench of beasts, sweat and urine. The crowd, all male, was made up of rough burly types, peasants and louts.

"Welcome to the Hetzhaus," said Simonis, pointing to the scene at the centre of the amphitheatre, while Populescu asked someone for information. We moved towards the centre of the show. A group of quarrelsome-looking brutes passed in front of us, greeting Populescu with cheerful coarseness.

At that moment, peering through the crowd, I finally saw what it was that held the attention of the swarming crowd. In the arena two large cocks were massacring one another with sharp pecks, incited by the spectators' furious yells, amplified by the echo created in the building's hollow space. Just then, the larger of the two cockerels firmly seized the other's neck with its claw, pinned its head to the ground and with its beak pitilessly pecked it. The crowd cheered, spurring the two creatures on – one to kill, the other to die – with equally bestial fervour.

"So Simonis," I asked him, "what does 'spectators or owners' mean?"

"Spectators are the ones that come here to bet," said Simonis, as I watched the bloody spectacle, "owners are the ones that own the animals they bet on."

In the meantime Populescu had rejoined us.

"It's no use, I can't find out if the boy is still here or not. We'll have to look for him. He's easy to recognise, because he only has one eye, the left – the other is covered by a bandage. He's a boy aged thirteen, as thin as a rake and almost as tall as me."

As Populescu moved away again, greeting strangers to left and right, I asked Simonis: "What does Populescu get up to in the Hetzhaus?"

"He scrapes together a little cash by cheating mugs with rigged bets. The Hetzhaus was opened a few years ago by two Dutch traders, and is very successful. In Vienna animal fights have been in fashion for over a century, and there are lots of people who live by betting on them. The boy we're looking for, even if Populescu won't say so openly, is undoubtedly one of the little tricksters that hang around these places. Now let's split up, keeping an eye on each other: whichever of us sees the little squinter first must signal to the others."

Left on my own, I studied the place. All around, the numerous barred cages held animals of every sort: in addition to cocks, there were dogs, bulls, oxen, wolves, boars and hyenas, and their yelps of angry fear made the place sound like one of the circles of hell. The cages were set out in radial fashion, and from each one the animal inside could be unleashed and led straight to the combat. It was as if some wicked enchanter had transformed Noah's ark into a place of slaughter. At the entrance, ignoring the yells and yelps, the stink and the blood, a salesman was cheerfully peddling bread, sausages and cheap Schwechat wine.

Meanwhile the larger cock had finished massacring its rival, which was carried off half-dead from the arena. The owner of the winner picked up his beloved pet and held it high to the jubilant acclaim of the audience. I saw gold and silver coins changing hands, filling the winners' eyes with joy, and the losers' with rage.

At that moment, above the uproar of the gamblers and their beasts, I heard a shout:

"It's him!"

I looked up. Populescu was pointing at a figure moving swiftly and almost invisibly through the forest of legs, arms and rustic faces. I saw him clearly: a pale, thin face, the right eye blindfolded. I tried to intercept him, but taking advantage of the obstacle of a small knot of people the boy managed to dodge past me and to flee towards the exit. We all three chased after him, pushing aside anyone in our path, and just a few seconds later we were in the street. By the time we got outside, as was to be expected, the boy had been swallowed up in the dark. The massive Helmut, who stood on guard at the door, had just glimpsed him darting by.

"Curse it," hissed Populescu, his breath steaming in the cold night air.

"And now?"

"Zyprian lives a long way off, in the suburb of Wieden," he answered. "He won't get back till dawn. He'll have had to find some place to shelter in. But I know there's another place he hangs around in, near here, where he sometimes acts as pimp. He won't expect me to know about it, because it was one of his hustlers that told me about it, and not him. Pennal, curse it, what are you waiting for to get this cart moving?"

This place looked quite different. We were now in the elegant square of Neuer Markt. In the centre, gleaming amid the half-darkness, stood the monument to Joseph the First, Victor of Landau. A large opulent place of entertainment spilled light not only from its ground-floor windows but also from those on the first floor. Next to the street entrance was a life-size wall painting of a be-turbaned Grand Turk holding, as was the fashion in coffee houses, a steaming cup of coffee and beckoning people in. A number of luxurious carriages were parked nearby, whose owners – noblemen and high court functionaries – were being expensively entertained within the building.

"This is the Mehlgrube. It's the most elegant place for anyone looking for nocturnal enjoyment," said Populescu. "It has the best billiard tables, the best card players, the best music and the best whores in the city. People drink and dance even at this time of night, despite all the rules. The more successful a place is, the greater the laws it can break: there's all the more money for bribing magistrates."

On the upper floor the notes of the orchestra were almost drowned by the laughter and clatter of the dancers. A piece in three-quarters time had just finished, greeted by rapturous applause.

"Did you hear?" snorted Populescu. "People are no longer happy just to dance 𝕷änðler or 𝕷angaus: now they all want this strange dance from who knows where, called 𝖂al𝖟er, or something similar. And yet doctors say that this waltz is too fast and immoral, it can lead to overheating and illness, and even to early death. If you ask me, in a couple of years people will have forgotten all about it."

While Populescu went off in search of Zyprian, Simonis had to answer my questions.

"Dragomir acts as a factotum for the professional swindlers. While they play cards, he peeks at the hand the dupe is holding, a poor fellow who has no idea he's playing with two or three tricksters. If they play billiards, he makes sure the victim gets given a cue of poor quality, which is guaranteed to make him lose, or every so often he switches the cue ball with a faulty one, so that the poor sucker's decisive shots all go wrong."

In the meantime Dragomir had returned, looking exultant.

"I've found him. They're keeping him warm for us."

Through a little door that gave onto the road he led us into the cellar, at the bottom of a short staircase. Just one dim lamp illuminated a little room full of wine and beer barrels, where we found the one-eyed boy sitting at a table. He was being watched over by a paunchy fellow, who had dull, half-closed eyes but looked imposing and threatening. He was even larger than the ogre Helmut who had stopped us at the entrance to the Hetzhaus. His arms, I calculated, were as thick as my thighs.

"He helps me to get my clients to pay up," Populescu explained, pointing to him with a knowing smile, filling a flagon of wine from one of the small barrels.

The young Zyprian looked more angry than frightened, and gazed at us with his one eye like a caged animal. He at once assailed Populescu with a stream of abuse; the latter answered him in the same language.

"He says he won't talk, and that he doesn't remember anything," explained Populescu, draining his flagon. "Earlier he promised to help me. Then he started saying that these things are sacred for the Turks, that you shouldn't ask too many questions, otherwise their god might get angry and punish us. But I pointed out to him that promises must be kept. Otherwise Klaus will step in," he said, nodding to the brute next to Zyprian.

"Among themselves," Simonis whispered into my ear, "Half-Asiatics are particularly cruel."

Zyprian spat on the ground as a mark of contempt. Populescu gave a sign to Klaus, who gave Zyprian's left cheek a resounding slap. The impact was so violent that the boy tottered on the chair.

"Go to hell," he hissed in German.

"Don't get worked up, Dragomir, keep calm," muttered Populescu to himself. "Klaus, again," he ordered.

This time three backhanders were delivered. The first made the victim shake again, the second made him lose his balance, and the third knocked him to the floor. Klaus hit without any style, but efficaciously. Zyprian bore up.

"You'd better leave us for a while," Populescu said to us. "We're going to have to use strong measures."

I shivered and looked at Simonis, who jerked his head as a sign that we should take Dragomir's advice. We went and sat down a little way off. A few moments later we heard Zyprian's first screams, followed by Populescu's burps, as he knocked back another flagon of beer.

"Half-Asia," muttered the Greek, shaking his head.

"I don't think that has anything to do with the violence," I objected. "You talk as if they were the outcasts that live in the Americas: now those really are savages."

"These are no better, Signor Master. An old Pontevedrin joke says that a peasant, at the gates of heaven, is offered whatever he wants, on condition that his neighbour, who's still alive, will get twice as much. 'Take out one of my eyes,' answers the peasant with a malicious smile. There, that's how people in Half-Asia treat each other."

From Zyprian's screams it really did seem that Populescu was giving orders for not just one but both of his eyes to be taken out.

"Believe me, Signor Master, in those parts men live like wild animals," the Greek said heatedly. "Don't be fooled, there's nothing heavenly or idyllic about the wildness of lands like Pontevedro; it's a state of utter darkness, of obscure, foggy and bestial crudeness, an eternal cold night, beyond the reach of any ray of civilisation, any warm breath of human love. It's neither day nor night there, just a strange twilight, possessing neither our culture nor the barbarism of Turan, but a mixture of both: Half-Asia!"

"𝕿hat's enough, for the moment," we heard Dragomir Populescu order the brute, who had just set his knee on the boy's stomach and was preparing to hit him again.

Simonis and I approached. I was shocked by the coldness with which Dragomir Populescu, a student with an unsuspected double life, had set the thug on the poor child. Obviously it was not the first time that our companion had had someone beaten up; only one who belonged to the sordid criminal world, I thought, could deal so casually in violence and bullying. Cheats, tricksters, pimps, spies and fornicators. Simonis was not wrong: although his companions might call themselves students, they were anything but lovers of letters and sciences.

Zyprian's resistance seemed to have been broken. The boy was lying on the ground with a blood trickling from his lower lip and a dark ring swelling round his eye even as we watched. He mumbled something under his breath.

"Louder," ordered Populescu, pouring his beer over his head.

Zyprian kept quiet. At another signal from Populescu, Klaus gave him a kick in his ribs.

The boy moaned and turned on his side.

"Aren't we overdoing things?" I interposed.

"Shhh!" Populescu hissed at me. "Now then, Zyprian, what can you tell us about this Golden Apple? My friends are here for you."

Zyprian began talking in his own language again, this time slightly louder. To make his mutterings intelligible, Dragomir translated them simultaneously into Italian, stopping every so often to ask him to repeat words that he had not pronounced clearly on account of his swollen lip.

"Everyone talks about the Golden Apple, the secret of all power. Everybody is looking for it, but no one knows where it's ended up. One day in Constantinople the sheik Ak emseddin had an idea: he exercised his gift for visions, and identified the spot where Eyyub, Mahomet's standard-bearer, who died during the victorious siege of the city, must be buried."

"Eyyub!" declared Populescu, turning to us with a look of triumph. "It's the name pronounced by Dànilo before he died! And so he's the standard-bearer of Mahomet that my beautiful brunette in the coffee house was telling me about . . ."

Together with Sultan Mehmed and three men, the story went on, Ak emseddin dug for three days. At last, at a depth of three cubits they found a large green stone, with an inscription in Kufic letters that said: "This is the tomb of Ebû Eyyub El-Ensârî". Underneath the stone they found the corpse of Eyyub, wrapped in a saffron-coloured shroud. His face was so beautiful and holy that it looked as if he had just died. In his blessed right hand he held a Mühre."

"A what?" interrupted Simonis.

"For men of no understanding," went on Zyprian's tale, "it's just a small spherical object, like the little balls they use to flatten paper. But for anyone kissed by the benediction of true knowledge, it is infinitely more: it's a stone with magical forces of divine origin."

"But is this Mühre the Golden Apple?" I asked.

"The Mühre is formed in the head of a snake of royal blood," Zyprian's muttering tale continued, in Populescu's translation, "and it is actually solar matter. It is protected by seven layers of skin, which drop off one by one. And so it has to be kept in a dark nook, where no ray of sunlight can enter, and it must be covered in gold. If even a single bead of sunlight enters, the Mühre flees into the heavenly spheres, towards the matter it is related to."

This was not all. According to what the poor boy told us, every so often clutching his head in pain, the old emperors of Byzantium, or Constantinople, had a shiny stone on their crown as rulers of the world; this stone had been taken from the chamber of Nebuchadnezzar, the founder of Babylon. It had been given to him by the Magi. Nebuchadnezzar, to defend his conquest magically, had had countless signs drawn throughout his kingdom, in the shape of a snake.

"This was because the Cosmos-City itself was surrounded by a snake, which imitated the snake that surrounds the whole earth," explained Zyprian.

And he recounted that Alexander the Great, when he was searching for the fountain of life in the land of eternal darkness, had placed a splendid stone on the tip of his spear: in the West they said that he had obtained it at the gate of the earthly paradise; in the East, however, the wise men said that Alexander and his vizir Sûrî had reached the City of Copper built by Solomon. This stone then became the Golden Apple.

"Just a moment, Dragomir, just a moment. I'm getting lost," I protested, rubbing my eyes, as if seized by a terrible headache.

"I haven't changed a single word the brat said," Populescu defended himself, pouring himself another flagon.

The boy went on, and explained that Hüma, the bird of paradise, had revealed to Solomon the origins of the precious stone known as Mühre.

"In the Fourth Heaven there's a mountain of golden sand, on top of which stands a splendid palace. The dome of this palace consists of the stone rings of all the men of power who governed the world before Adam. After subduing the earth, they yielded to the ambition of wishing to conquer the heavens and become gods. And so the Angel of Death went to meet them and asked for their rings back. In the dome of the heavenly palace the only one missing is the last ring, the one that closes the dome. That's what the Mühre is formed from."

Simonis and I looked at each other in amazement. Zyprian's revelations led in contrasting and extremely intricate directions.

"In my opinion, this Mühre is the garnet stone from the statue of the Madonna of St Sophia, as Koloman told us," remarked Simonis.

"But it could also be the golden ball that Suleiman had them mount on the bell tower of St Stephen's, as Jan Janitzki said," added Populescu.

"Let's ask him where Eyyub got the Mühre from," I said.

"It was in the centre of the world. Eyyub stole it to hand it over to the future conquering sultan," was Zyprian's answer.

"The centre of the world must be Constantinople," explained Populescu, "since these are Turkish legends."

"And now where is the Mühre?" I asked.

"Nobody knows."

"And Kasim's forty thousand? Ask him if he knows about the forty thousand martyrs."

The boy unwillingly muttered a few words.

"He said: the forty thousand martyrs shout on Friday," translated Dragomir.

"But Dànilo already told us that before he died," I said.

Populescu asked Zyprian again.

"To be precise, they shout on Friday evening. He knows nothing else."

The last answer, which verged on stupidity, was not encouraging.

"Ask him if the words *soli soli soli* mean anything to him," I suggesed.

Zyprian, who in the meantime had sat down again, wiped the blood from his lip. On hearing the question he shook his head and spat on the ground. Klaus clenched his fist and with a glance sought instructions from Dragomir Populescu, who indicated he should let the boy go.

"I don't understand any of it," remarked Simonis, as we left the cellar and walked towards Penicek's cart. "A lot of the information tallies, but none of it makes any sense. It's not clear whether the Golden Apple is this Mühre, and whether the Mühre is the ball of the statue of the Madonna, or of Justinian or Constantine, or the one on the top of St Stephen's, depending on the various versions. Zyprian says it actually came from the centre of the earth, and even from Alexander the Great, from the Fourth Heaven and from Solomon's ring. Whatever it is, if this ball of solar matter, as he calls it, was kept in Eyyub's tomb, the Agha's phrase 'we have come alone to the Golden Apple' makes no sense anymore."

"I don't understand it either," Populescu answered him, in the voice of one awash in beer, "but there must be a reason why the Turks talked about the Golden Apple to Prince Eugene."

"I say we should look into this Eyyub, Mahomet's standard-bearer: it can't be an accident that Dànilo spoke his name before he died," the Greek suggested, climbing onto the cart.

"No, our Dragomir mustn't investigate anything at all now," I intervened, casting an angry glance at my assistant and pulling out the money to pay Populescu. "Nor must your other companions, because –"

"Well said!" exclaimed the Romanian, breaking into a broad smile at the sight of the coins. "I agree with you. For the moment we've learned enough. This evening I've got a date with my beauty at an *Andacht* on the Kalvarienberg, and this money is just what I need, thanks!"

"Be careful, Dragomir," I tried to speak to him, handing him the money. "There's something you should know . . ."

"I'll be very careful! She says she's a virgin," he laughed, "but I have a couple of tricks to see if that's true."

He was drunk. Not an ideal condition for hearing and, above all, for understanding what I had to say to him. We made him get up onto the cart with us.

"Yes, but now listen: the Agha's dervish . . ." I tried to start off.

"The dervish? That spinning top in the white skirt?" he sneered, and then he burped. "I'll be lifting different sorts of skirts this evening! I don't give a damn whether the dervish is a virgin or not, ha ha! But my dark-haired chick from the coffee house . . . Heh heh, just listen to me: I'll get her to drink *Armoniacum* salt with spring water, and if she's not a virgin, she'll piss herself, ha ha! And I've also got carbonised roots of ephen – or celeriac or whatever you want to call it – to put under her nose: if she's not a virgin, another piss! Just imagine what a fool she'll feel, ha ha!"

I felt dispirited. Dragomir's coarse laughter was soon joined by that of my assistant, and if that were not enough, he ordered the Pennal to laugh as well.

"Of course, it's a real pity if she's not a virgin," declared Dragomir, with fussy exactitude, "but at least I can be sure of getting my oats, and without too much of a fuss! Ha ha!"

The cart pulled up. We were outside Populescu's house. Before I could open my mouth, he opened the door and got out.

"Just a moment, Dragomir," I called him, "there's something you should know . . ."

"A thousand thanks, Signor Master," he laughed, totally drunk, bowing several times and waving the little bag of coins in the air before entering the front door.

"Off you go, Pennal!" ordered Simonis.

"No, wait!" I protested. "Simonis, I hardly said anything!"

"He's drunk too much. He wouldn't have understood anything. If you like, you can talk to him this evening – he said he has a date with that girl at an *Andacht*, on the Kalvarienberg."

"Well, I have no choice now," I said resignedly. "I'm worn out, and we haven't managed to warn any of your three companions. I wonder if we shouldn't have looked for Koloman or Opalinski first, instead of Dragomir."

"They were both at home. Sleeping."

"What?" I said furiously. "So why did you advise me to start with Dragomir?"

"It wouldn't have been polite to wake them up: they're not under my orders, like the Pennal."

I was silent, overcome by amazement. It was too idiotic an answer, I thought, to come from a half idiot.

❧

5.30 of the clock: first mass. From now on the bells will ring in succession throughout the day, announcing masses, processions, devotions. Eating houses and alehouses open.

On our way back to Porta Coeli, the roads began to come to life. From bread shops, inns and sweet bread bakeries there came wafting the smell of chocolate – the same smell that will unexpectedly tickle your nostrils (the only city I know where this is true) in the middle of an alleyway, a garden, or a crowded avenue, like mystic manifestations of the afterlife.

Snow-white milkmaids, ruddy bakers, whistling musicians and lazy footmen came into the streets and began to swell the ranks of the humble toilers, while the noblemen, still in bed, breathed sluggishly in the coils of sleep.

Proceeding cautiously so as not to knock down some careless shop boy, Penicek's cart was turning from Carinthia Street into Porta Coeli Street, and I had already glimpsed my Cloridia standing outside the door of the nunnery, when I realised something strange was happening.

I knew she would be worried by my long absence, and so I had stood up in the cart and was waving to her festively when I saw a shadowy figure emerge from nowhere and grip her arm. Cloridia yelled.

The memory of what happened in the next few moments, and the great agitation that overwhelmed all of us, is still hazy to me. However, I will try to describe those whirling moments as faithfully as possible.

We were not more than twenty paces from Porta Coeli. Simonis leaped down from Penicek's cart and ran to assist my spouse. I tried to do likewise, even though I knew my stride to be much shorter. However, the nag that was pulling the Pennal's cart, sensing danger, lost its head. The cart tottered and I stumbled as I jumped out, and went crashing to the ground. I looked up at once and saw more clearly the shadowy figure that had attacked Cloridia. He was now backing away as Cloridia hurled insults at him. From his clothing I realised immediately who it must be: the hooded man, the friend of Ciezeber the dervish, who had so menacingly dogged Cloridia at Prince Eugene's palace.

Simonis was almost upon him, but the individual had already taken to his heels, vanishing into the ash-grey haze of dawn. Cloridia was on the ground, terrified and weeping. Simonis lost valuable seconds in checking that she had not been wounded in any way. Then, while I moved forward half-limping, my assistant set off in pursuit again, and I followed him. The hooded man could not escape us.

The passers-by watched this early morning chase incredulously: from the windows they urged us to catch the thief (although he was not one), and one or two sleepy-looking youths even gave signs of joining in the chase, although they desisted almost immediately. Running all the way down Porta Coeli Street the hooded man first reached the circle of the ramparts, then turned left along the Seilerstätte road and then down the lane behind the convent of the Augustinian nuns of St James. Simonis was hot on his heels, but I had worked out a better move: I took the parallel street, the Riemergasse, which, unlike the other route, which twisted and turned, ran straight as a die. Although I was by no means a fast runner, I reached the confluence between the two arteries at the same moment as Simonis and the hooded man.

And so it was that when the two burst out of the lane, I appeared in front of the pursued man. The monstrous face loomed up ahead of me and, even as we laid hands on my wife's unknown aggressor, I realised to my immense surprise that I knew him and that he knew me.

As he came lurching towards me, in shape halfway between a mole and a stone marten, he goggled at me and then grinned bestially, opening his arms to enfold me in a lurid embrace. But Simonis fell upon him from behind, and we all went crashing into a nearby cart of fruit and vegetables, knocking it over along with its owner and sending a torrent of apples, cauliflowers, turnips and radishes cascading over the pavement in a thousand directions, like drops of quicksilver escaping from an alchemist's alembic and slithering across the ground in a crazy bid for freedom.

A great blow to my temple set my head reeling. While the shouts of the bystanders and the desperate greengrocer deafened the whole street, I struggled to come to my senses, eager to see and understand what was going on. I saw the hooded man's face leering down at me, while the arms of three or four robust passers-by held him tight. With his yellowing teeth and treacherous grey pupils, he continued to smile at me:

"I am surprended to find Your Illustriosity here in Vindobona, very live and kicksome."

"Ugonio?!?" I exclaimed with difficulty, before losing my senses from the blow.

Hunter of relics, catchpoll in the service of the sects of beggars, hardened swindler involved in every disreputable affair in the Holy City: it was not the first time that Ugonio had burst in upon my life.

Our first encounter had been in the underground tunnels of Rome, when, twenty-eight years earlier, I had met Abbot Melani. He was a *corpisantaro*, a raider of "holy bodies" or sacred relics. I had then bumped into this bizarre individual eleven years ago, again on the occasion of Atto's visit to Rome: at that time the *corpisantaro* was working for the secret companies of beggars. There was not actually any direct relationship between Melani and Ugonio: it was simply that the Abbot's shady affairs were inevitably tangled up with the subterranean and sordid world in which the latter wallowed.

"How stupid of me, I should have realised," I murmured, as soon as I came to my senses. "Ugonio is from Vienna."

The *corpisantaro* came from the capital city of the Empire, and that was why his grip on our language was so precarious.

My body was now held up by four robust arms, and I was assisted towards the convent of Porta Coeli. The blow that had laid me out had come from the greengrocer's cart, which had hit me right on the head as it overturned. I could hear my rescuers commenting on what had happened, and inveighing against Ugonio. At the side of the street, a double row of spectators was gazing as I staggered past, preceded by Simonis and by a cluster of people who were pushing and shoving the *corpisantaro*. They were busily collecting the testimony of Cloridia, so that they could hand Ugonio over to the authorities to be tried. I stared at him.

His disgusting appearance, which Cloridia had described, was well-known to me. He had the same drab, wrinkled and flabby skin, grey bloodshot eyes, crooked hands and cankered nose, all wrapped in a filthy greatcoat with a cowl. Although his age was hard to guess, the years had taken their toll on him too: previously Ugonio had been repellent; now he was also hoary. But he was clearly in good physical shape: it had taken two of us to bring him down, after an exhausting chase.

Eleven years earlier, to help the Abbot and me, the *corpisantaro* had aroused the enmity of the most powerful beggars in Rome, and had had to flee from Rome, and from Italy itself. I could still remember his blood-caked face and his bandaged hand, when he had come to Villa Spada to take his leave of Atto and me. He had told us then that he would retire here, to the city where he had been born.

I asked to be set on my feet: I could now stand up unsupported. I summoned Simonis. When my assistant was assured that my condition was satisfactory, I explained that not only did I know our prey, but that this individual, however unsettling in appearance, had certainly not intended any harm to my wife.

"Are you sure, Signor Master?"

"Leave him to me. And send away all these people. As you speak good German, explain that it was a quarrel between me and this man, and that it's all been resolved amicably. I'm not going to press charges against him."

"Actually, if I were you, I would . . . But all right – as you wish, Signor Master."

Simonis had some trouble in convincing the people around us, but in the end we managed to get them to leave us and to avoid any intervention by the city guards. Now came the most difficult part: to explain everything to my wife.

❧

"Is he still here? Why haven't you taken him straight to jail?"

We were in our lodgings in Porta Coeli. Cloridia was gazing at Ugonio in fear, holding our little boy tight in her arms, like a hen with its chicks.

"The fact is that you don't know him, but he knows you," I explained, as I invited Simonis and Ugonio to sit down.

My assistant looked at the *corpisantaro* with a mixture of surprise, disgust and diffidence, and he took care to sit as far as possible from him. Every so often he gave a discreet but marked sniff, as if to see if it really was his coat (as indeed it was) that gave off the stale smell that was rapidly filling the room.

"He knows me? Since when?" asked my sweet consort suspiciously.

I explained who Ugonio was, that he was a rogue, undoubtedly, but that when required he had proved trustworthy and had given incontrovertible proof of his loyalty.

Eleven years earlier, when Cloridia and I were working in Rome, in Cardinal Spada's villa, he had broken into his house secretly several times. He had first seen Cloridia's face then, and he knew that she was my wife, while Cloridia had no idea of Ugonio's appearance. At Prince Eugene's palace he had looked at her several times, intently, not with any hostile motive but because he was not yet sure that he had recognised her. In the end he had become convinced that she was my wife. That morning he had decided to present himself. He had approached her in front of Porta Coeli, hoping to be recognised, but Cloridia had reacted with fear. He had tried to hold her by the arm, and those who had witnessed the scene, including me, had taken it for an attack.

"I see," Cloridia said at last, forcing herself to smile.

"Ugonio can be trusted," I repeated, "if you take him the right way."

"So why does he trade in people's heads? And why did he steal the Landau coins from Prince Eugene?" asked Cloridia, scowling suspiciously again.

"He'll tell you himself, if he doesn't want me to press charges, as I could do," I said, looking meaningfully at Ugonio.

The *corpisantaro* started.

"First of all: the Landau coins you stole are part of your usual trade, aren't they?" I asked.

Amid the shapeless mass of Ugonio's features his yellow-brown pointed teeth displayed themselves in an expression that was a mixture of surprise, disappointment and childish satisfaction at his skilful and nefarious theft of the coins.

"I do not dispute the accusement of Your Lordliness," he replied in his clumsy, catarrh-filled voice. "But decreasing the scrupules so as not increase one's scrupules, I would like to assurify your married lady, the wedded spice and consortium of Your Highfulness: I, yours truthly, this identifical person of myself, never, not even for a split century, did I dream of harmifying a head on her hair."

"What did he say?" asked Simonis in bewilderment. As a non-native speaker of Italian he had trouble in following Ugonio's verbal convolutions.

"𝕿𝔥𝔢 𝔱𝔥𝔢𝔣𝔱 𝔬𝔣 𝔱𝔥𝔢 𝔠𝔬𝔦𝔫𝔰: 𝔞𝔩𝔩 𝔯𝔦𝔤𝔥𝔱, 𝕴 𝔠𝔬𝔫𝔣𝔢𝔰𝔰. 𝕭𝔲𝔱 𝕴 𝔫𝔢𝔳𝔢𝔯 𝔱𝔬𝔲𝔠𝔥𝔢𝔡 𝔱𝔥𝔢 𝔤𝔬𝔬𝔡 𝔩𝔞𝔡𝔶, 𝔫𝔬𝔯 𝔱𝔥𝔬𝔲𝔤𝔥𝔱 𝔬𝔣 𝔡𝔬𝔦𝔫𝔤 𝔰𝔬," the *corpisantaro* translated rapidly, his mother-tongue being German.

"Yes, I gathered this," I agreed. "You just wanted to introduce yourself to Cloridia, though there were certainly more elegant ways of going about it. Now tell me: are you working for Abbot Melani?"

Ugonio again seemed taken aback by this.

"I ignorified completely, and also wholesomely, that Abbot Melani had taken abodance here in Vindobona," he answered after a moment's silence. "But to be more padre than parricide, I can confide that, negating the true with sincerity, I do not comprend the insinulation that Your Pomposity makes against me"

Simonis raised one eyebrow, puzzled again.

"𝔐𝔢𝔩𝔞𝔫𝔦: 𝕴 𝔨𝔫𝔬𝔴 𝔫𝔬𝔱𝔥𝔦𝔫𝔤 𝔬𝔣 𝔥𝔦𝔪," Ugonio translated with a grunt.

"Oh yes?" I pressed him. "So why were you plotting with the Agha's dervish to cut some poor innocent man's head off? Who is your victim? Maybe someone high up, very, very high, even *too* high up?"

A heavy silence fell on the room. Very soon I would find out if my suspicions about Abbot Melani's journey were well-founded. Ugonio, stunned, said not a word. I returned to the attack.

"The Emperor is ill. Very ill. They say it's smallpox. They say. But I suspect there's something else behind it. It just so happens the illness started with his head – *with his head*, I say. Do you know anything about it?" I asked threateningly.

Ugonio stood up. His murky grey face looked flushed, and (if his sallow complexion had allowed it) almost crimson.

"I can testiculify to Your Imminence my profundest facefulness. Not to be a rustic physician, I swear and curse to you, from the fundaments of my heart, my full allegiance. To make things crystal-clean: I am not in the know of nothing about his Scissorian Majesty and his pathogenic indisposability. For the other tissue, about the dervishop I cannot spill even a single pea, because . . ." And he broke off.

Simonis and I exchanged glances: this time my assistant had understood everything. Ugonio's face was even more purple. He swallowed and finished the sentence in German:

". . . because otherwise they'll cut me into pieces."

"You don't imagine that I'll be satisfied with this lie," I answered in a harsh voice.

The *corpisantaro*'s face seemed on the point of exploding. He had met me in Rome when I was the timid boy servant in a fourth-rate inn. Now I was a mature man, I knew life and its hardships. The old *corpisantaro*, who had shown he still had plenty of life and vigour in him, surely had not expected to be grilled so intensely.

"The head you talked to Ciezeber about," I said clearly and menacingly, going right up to him, "now you'll tell me *whose it is.*"

By way of reply Ugonio, with a gasp of lacerating terror such as I had never heard from him before, leaped to his feet and staggered towards the door in an improbable attempt to flee. He was of course immediately caught by Simonis, who, as he grabbed him by his coat, caused a curious tinkling sound to come from the *corpisantaro*. At a sign from me the Greek opened his coat (not without a grimace of distaste) and we saw, hanging inside it, something I well knew: an enormous iron ring to which were tied dozens, nay hundreds, of old keys of every shape, condition and size. It was Ugonio's secret arsenal, his precious key ring.

The *corpisantaro*, who spent more time underground than above, often needed to penetrate the subsoil by way of cellars, warehouses or doors barred by bolts and locks. To solve the problem ("decreasing the scruples so as not increase one's scruples" he had specified) he had devoted himself from early days to the systematic bribery of servants, maids and valets. Knowing full well that the masters of villas and houses in possession of keys would never in any circumstances have let him have a copy, the *corpisantaro* had bartered with the serving staff for the duplicates of keys. In exchange, he would let the servants have some of his precious relics. Of course, Ugonio had been careful never to give up his best pieces, even though he had had to make the occasional painful sacrifice, like a fragment of St Peter's collarbone. But he had managed to get hold of the keys to the cellars and foundations of the palaces of much of Rome. And the locks to which he did not have keys could often be opened with one of the many other keys of a similar kind.

Now the ring was more than twice as large as when I had last seen it on him: in addition to the Roman keys there were now the keys to all the cellars of Vienna. And that was no small achievement: as Cardinal Piccolomini had observed three-hundred years earlier, the city's cellars are deep and spacious, giving rise to the saying that in Vienna there are as many buildings below as above ground.

"If you don't confess straightaway, I'll tear all your adored keys from you and throw them away," I threatened.

Ugonio began to whimper and said that if that was how things were he could tell me some more about the matter, but not until tomorrow. He repeated several times that he would rather go straight to hell than talk now, and he would prefer a thousand times to rot in the terrible imperial dungeons, where – he well knew – he risked being tortured and having his limbs mutilated. It would still be far preferable to the horrifying fate that would await him if he revealed to us the secret of his pacts with the dervish.

Ugonio's terror was practically a confession. I had no doubt about it now: it was Atto who had tracked Ugonio down and hired him; he was the link between the Abbot and the Turkish embassy. Atto had known the *corpisantaro* for thirty years. He had learned how valuable he was for certain shady dealings. And he also knew how to make the best use of him without being swindled. Had the decrepit old castrato really hoped, I thought with a smile, that I would never find him out?

"All right. Tomorrow morning here, then. Let's say at nine: I've got a cleaning job at Porta Coeli – immediately afterwards we can meet. In the meantime, for surety, I'll keep hold of these," I said at last to Ugonio, taking from his overcoat the ring with the keys, to keep as hostages. "I'll give them back when you show up again."

Ugonio desperately stretched out his hooked hands towards the ring. Then he lowered his head: if he had had the slightest idea of doing a bunk, now he knew that it would cost him his precious keys.

"Now listen carefully, Ugonio. We saw Ciezeber performing strange rites in the wood," I announced, glancing meaningfully towards Cloridia, who was caressing our son's head, as he was clearly scared.

My wife went out, taking the boy into the cloisters, to spare him from hearing this grim conversation.

I started up again, recounting the arcane rituals that we had seen the dervish performing, right up to the point when Ciezeber had pulled out his little knife from his bundle of things and the small mass of dark stuff. At the end I fixed my pupils questioningly on Ugonio's. He was still highly offended by the loss of his key ring and drummed his yellow, claw-like fingers on the table nearby. Then he said:

"I cannot furnish Your Presumption with any furtherances. My dealifyings with the dervishite are only on businesses, and wholly licit swindlifications. But I was able to identificate the little knife and the black objection that Ciezeber extricatified in the forestal woodiness, and which you have descripted with such claret."

"So you know what I'm talking about?" I said, taking heart.

"Undoubtfully. I had notified the peculiarousness of the dervishite's paraphernations."

"And so? Did you work out what that stuff was for?"

"To be more padre than parricide, I can ensure you, after careful exanimation, that they are instrumentations of an insanitary purpose."

"They've got something to do with diseases?" asked Simonis.

"𝔄re you deaf, by any chance?" asked Ugonio impatiently, casting a longing look at the key ring I still held in my hands.

"Ah, they're medical instruments," I muttered in disappointment.

"I confirmate."

How had I failed to think of that? Cloridia had even told me that some dervishes were also healers. And what we had witnessed in the wood near the Place with No Name must have been a mystic ritual to confer greater power on their treatments. In the dervish's operations I had sought a trace of the poison which, under the false name of smallpox, was killing the Emperor; now I discovered that it was the exact opposite, a therapeutic intervention.

I was stuck midstream. I had not yet managed to find any proof of my suspicions with regard to Atto Melani, the Ottoman embassy and the secret poisoning of Joseph I. And yet I had to find something: I had to *do* something, damn it, I repeated to myself as I observed Ugonio and wondered how to proceed. If by ill chance someone were to discover Atto Melani, the enemy agent, I would end up on the gallows with him. The mystery of the head remained unsolved, and this – by now it was clear – was the key to everything, but I still had to find a way to drag the truth out of the *corpisantaro*. There was another path, which might lead to the truth.

"Ugonio, have you ever heard of the Golden Apple?"

He caught his breath. He was not expecting that question.

"It is a complicable and horrendiful story," he said at last.

According to Ugonio, the whole thing had begun three years earlier. As we already knew from Frosch, in 1708 a sister of Joseph the Victorious, Anna Maria, had married the King of Portugal, John V. After a few months, the young Queen had heard from the ladies of her new court of a strange popular belief. Spain's war of succession, which was raging throughout Europe, would only be won by the Empire if the original Golden Orb or Apple of Justinian, which guaranteed the supremacy of the Christian West, were to be placed on the tallest spire of the most sacred church of the Caesarean capital – which is to say, the bell tower of the Cathedral of St Stephen: substituting, that is, the sacrilegious orb created and mounted on the bell tower by Suleiman. In some mysterious fashion Justinian's Golden Orb had ended up in Spain, and then had gone on to Portugal. That was not all. Emperor Ferdinand I had had a holy cross placed on top of Suleiman's orb after a rather disconcerting episode: as soon as the Sultan had abandoned the siege of the Caesarean capital, there had appeared in the sky, in full daylight, none other than the Archangel Michael, who, with the blazing tip of his unsheathed sword, had engraved in letters of fire a mysterious message at the top of the spire, on the pedestal supporting the sacrilegious orb.

"The Archangel Michael is the very figure who traditionally holds the Imperial Orb in one hand, while he drives out Lucifer with his sword in the shape of the holy cross," I said in amazement, recalling Koloman Szupán's tale.

"Exactly," said Ugonio.

The *corpisantaro* went on. Seven times the Archangel pointed his sword at the pedestal, and seven were the words he engraved there. The sparks from his sword were seen by a multitude of the faithful gathered in the square before the Cathedral of St Stephen. They testified without a shadow of a doubt to the truth of the miraculous event, and the Emperor at once sent two labourers to the spire to make a faithful copy of what the Archangel had written there. The two labourers were carefully chosen among the illiterate, so that no one apart from the Emperor would be aware of the secret. What they delivered to him troubled him to such an extent that he spent the whole night praying in the Caesarean chapel, prostrate, with his face to the ground, and the next day he ordered that the holy cross of the Redeemer should be placed immediately on top of the sacrilegious orb, thus transforming it into the Imperial Orb of the Archangel Michael. Ferdinand I chose never to confide to anyone what the Archangel had written, and took his secret with him to the tomb. After his death several attempts were made to send someone up there to read the message on the spire, but various misfortunes rendered all attempts vain: one person tumbled from the tower, another was blinded by a sudden flash from the sky, another one fell, *et cetera et cetera*. It was even rumoured that a priest of the Cathedral Chapter, on a night of full moon, had ventured up there, but nothing further was heard. The story related that the Archangel's message concluded with an express imposition of silence.

These tales of the Golden Apple and the Archangel Michael were reported to Joseph I's sister, the new bride of the King of Portugal. And so it was that a flying Ship had set out from Lisbon, equipped with a highly secret system of propulsion and driven by a mysterious and unidentified figure, whose mission it was to put the true Golden Apple in its place, on the highest point of St Stephen's, and at the same time to read the Archangel's mysterious message.

Simonis and I exchanged glances: Ugonio's tale tallied with the accounts of the students. Hristo, Populescu, Koloman and their friends had established that, according to the legends, the Golden Apple was the symbol (but maybe something more) of the power of the West. They had learned that the mysterious object dated back to Justinian; that it had been buried in Constantinople with Eyyub, Mahomet's standard-bearer; that it had then ended up in Spain; that during the first siege of Vienna, Suleiman had had another one made. And finally, that Ferdinand I had had a holy cross placed on Suleiman's orb, which had enraged the Sultan. And recently, we ourselves had read in Frosch's gazette that the Flying Ship had arrived in 1709 from Portugal, steered by a person nobody knew, and that it had got stuck – it just so happened – on the spire of St Stephen's. These things could not just be coincidences.

There was something else that tied in curiously with these events, which only I knew about: the mysterious flying helmsman, mentioned in the Diary of Vienna as a presumed Brazilian priest, in fact had all the characteristics of the strange individual I had met in Rome eleven years earlier, during my second adventure with Atto Melani: the violinist Albicastro, who, it just so happened, always played the same melody known as *folia*, a dance that originated in Portugal.

"Let's sum things up," I said. "While all these strange things are happening in Portugal, the Agha is received by Prince Eugene and tells him *soli soli soli ad pomum venimus aureum*. Meanwhile, your Ciezeber plans to chop off –"

"Just a momentum."

Ugonio asked me to repeat the sentence that the Turkish ambassador had pronounced in front of Eugene of Savoy.

"It is an indicative phraseology, incontrovertebrate and plauseworthy."

"What?" asked Simonis.

"He says the Turks' message is perfectly clear," I translated.

There was no doubt, the *corpisantaro* declared with conviction: the Ottomans, too, had come to Vienna to get back the Golden Apple. Only in this sense had they "come to the *pomum aureum*", as the Latin phrase used by the Agha said literally.

"It may be so," I admitted, "but why did they declare it to Eugene?"

"I ignorify that," Ugonis merely said, shrugging.

"And where is the Golden Apple now?"

"I have besought it highly and lowly and with undefaltering faststeadness. Some insinufy that the driver, before they threw him into deep dudgeon, snuggled it into the Flying Ship. Misluckily I have not catched a glint of it there. The guardian and his feline ferocities are too snoopivigilant."

"So where is it?"

"To be more padre than parricide, I hope to be able to beseek it more caringfully. I'm also doing my utfulmost to get a deacon of the cathedral to speak: he is obsessified with sacred relishes. Tomorrow, in exchange for a *corpus santus* he will perhaps belch forth the Archangel's phrase."

"That's the way. Give him Adam's apple core," Simonis scoffed.

My assistant and I had hardly any time to discuss the encounter with the old *corpisantaro*; a few minutes after he had left, the Chormaisterin herself came and knocked at our door. She had heard what had happened, since her sisters had told her about the attack on Cloridia, the subsequent chase and finally the chaotic arrest of Ugonio. I explained how things had gone, taking care to play down my relations with the *corpisantaro*. I said he was a minor thief I had met long before in Rome, whom I had decided to forgive as a compatriot. Much more important was the news that Camilla herself gave us:

"Let us all thank the Lord," she declared with a sigh, "the Emperor is much better. His illness seems to be progressing well, the doctors foresee that in a few days' time His Majesty will not only be out of danger but restored to full health."

The public prayers that had begun the day before throughout the city, and especially in St Stephen's, had had an effect. For this reason they would continue to recite the sacred orations for another six days, that heaven might grant in full the imperial subjects' prayers. But in particular they had commenced the oration of the Forty Hours, which had which had recited a few years earlier when Archduke Charles, Joseph's younger brother, had fallen dangerously ill; on that occasion, too, the illness had passed with the help of God. The oration could only be done by men, it lasted a week and prayers had to be recited six hours a day, in shifts which were divided (it hardly needs saying) by social classes. On the first day, the Sunday that had just passed, the imperial family had started the prayers. Today it was the turn of the nobility, then the five social classes would pray, obviously during working-hours: from eight to eleven and from three to six. The oration would be concluded by us artisans and traders with all our employees. The women, during this period, were exhorted to pray in church as fervently as possible.

We all rejoiced at the splendid news. Simonis and I embraced poor Camilla, who had been suffering so grievously until that moment and who was already preparing herself for the long prayer vigils that awaited her for the whole week. We had not slept and nor had we had breakfast, but the news revived our spirits and our senses.

"Today is Monday, Simonis."

"To work, Signor Master," answered my assistant, with his slightly foolish smile that always inspired such confidence.

Work, of course. But we both knew that what was really calling us was the mystery of the Golden Apple. The key to our doubts awaited us at Neugebäu, in the Place with No Name.

ॐ॰॰ॐ

7 of the clock: the Bell of the Turks, also called the Peal of the Oration, rings.

The road was finally clear of snow. The news of the improvement in the poor Emperor's health was, I thought, truly welcome. But the dark shadow of misfortune and death that those days had cast over us was far from dissipated. As we trudged along I still pondered on the terrible end of Hristo and Dànilo Danilovitsch, and the suspicious origins of the illness of Joseph the Victorious – and such unexpected facts as the revelation that Hadji-Tanjov was an Ottoman subject. Not to mention the highly mysterious indications left by the Bulgarian student of a link between *soli soli soli* and checkmate . . .

The nocturnal quarrel with Abbot Melani had yet to be settled; my suspicions were far from allayed. Sooner or later Atto and I would talk again, and then perhaps I would get a clearer view of his shady conduct. It was true that he had been taken seriously ill when I accused him of conspiring for Joseph's death, but that could have been the perturbation of a guilty man caught red-handed, rather than that of an innocent man wrongly accused. Or again, it could have been a skilful performance to get out of a tight spot, playing the part of the guileless innocent: I was all too familiar with the prodigious acting skills of the old hypocrite, impostor and trickster.

That day at Neugebäu it was not only the riddle of the Golden Apple that awaited us, but also a great deal of work. I was afraid that I would not be able to get the full benefit of Simonis's assistance: he had to go back to town to take part in the ceremony to mark the return to lessons after the Easter holidays.

"Don't worry, Signor Master," he reassured me. "The celebration is in the afternoon."

"In the afternoon? And the lessons?"

"They don't start till tomorrow. Otherwise there would be more people absent than present."

"And why would that be?"

"The students here get the most out of all holidays. They will have been revelling and feasting, eating and drinking right up until dawn. Today the student body of the *Alma Mater Rudolphina* will be snoring peacefully in their beds, sleeping off their hangovers. That's why they wisely postpone the reopening ceremony until Monday afternoon, and lessons until Tuesday."

We stopped for a break in the vineyards that Porta Coeli owned at Simmering. We identified the buttery and cleaned the flue, as we had promised the Chormaisterin. It was a spacious room, so that we could not resist the temptation to draw off a little wine and go and drink it in the commodious room where the fireplace stood.

As we continued on our way, it struck me that on my two previous visits to the Place with No Name I had seen no trace of any other artisans. Nor had Frosch, the gruff watchman at Neugebäu, made any mention of other artisans, workers or architects in the manor house or in his gardens. Indeed, Frosch had seemed totally in the dark as to the imminent restoration work ordered by the Emperor. Perhaps, I told myself, the architects and carpenters had preferred to wait until the thaw. Over the next few days maybe they would come along as well and start their operations, but it still struck me as strange, and I made a note to myself to ask Frosch about it.

After the unexpected snow of the previous days, the countryside now seemed to show the first timid signs of the new season. The unseasonable snow was already melting, the sharp air and thick morning mists were definitely yielding to the rays of the day star and to the cold crystalline air of the Viennese spring.

We came in sight of the Place with No Name just as dawn was shyly caressing its pure white walls. Wielding immaterial paintbrushes, a fiery ray tinged the towers with pink and gold, daubing them with the first patina of dawn light. As soon as the last traces of mist lifted, brilliant rays struck the roofs of the castle, the spires of the corner turrets and the peaks of the great hexagonal towers, scattering the reflections of the copper tiles in all directions. Sharp and powerful, refracted by the roofs of the Place with No Name, the fair and blessed light of the sun shimmered throughout the plain of Simmering. With a murmur of wonder, we immediately lifted our hands to our brows in order not to be blinded by the dazzling light; every bush, every blade of glass, every single stone seemed to be overwhelmed by that magnificent and almost unbearable vision. It was as if the castle, suspended in the grassy plain, were being annihilated by fire and, at every instant, freshly recreated, ready for a new ineffable combustion. What a striking contrast, I thought, between our journey shadowing the obscure Ciezeber along this same road and the overwhelming splendour of this vision.

"Look!" exclaimed my little boy, pointing towards the sun.

Fighting against the light, I fixed my eyes for a moment on the day star.

"It's blood-red, it's blood-red again," I observed with dismay.

Simonis did not remark on the bizarre phenomenon that had manifested itself repeatedly over the last two weeks and which was feared as a sign of ill omen.

With our hands still shading our eyes, we slowed down as the spectacle both enthralled and blinded us. At that point, above the creaking sound of the cart carrying our tools, we heard a distant sound of salutation. It came from behind the towers, behind the garden's encircling walls and behind the castle itself, almost as if it issued from a Beyond that belonged only to the Place with No Name: in the still undisturbed dawn peace, the cavernous roar of the lions resounded again.

This time we entered by the West Gate, the one we had left by on our last visit. Crossing the main courtyard, in front of the façade of the castle, I cast watchful glances around myself, remembering with a shiver my adventure with Mustafa.

Our first thought, obviously, went to the Flying Ship. But we were disappointed; no sooner had we arrived in the ball stadium than we found Frosch wandering around restlessly. He was taking food to the birdcages, opposite the stadium, and every so often he threw pieces of meat to the wild animals in the ditches. The watchman gestured towards a hole low down in the wall of one of the ditches: it was a small tunnel, barred by a simple little gate. It was what remained of the underground passages that once made it possible to escape, when necessary, from the Place with No Name and to re-emerge in the surrounding countryside.

While Frosch chattered away, Simonis and I exchanged knowing glances: we would have to wait for a more suitable moment to inspect the Flying Ship. In the meantime, to work.

While we lifted the tools out of our cart and got ready for work, I asked Frosch the question I had pondered on our way from the city: whether we were in fact the only people – artists, labourers or artisans – who had turned up at Neugebäu to start the restoration work.

"𝔒f course you're the only ones. 𝔚ho else would dream of working here?"

I answered that the imperial chamber paid generously for this kind of work, and there was no reason why carpenters, painters, bricklayers or decorators should not be happy to honour the ancient and glorious manor house with their labour.

"𝔒h they would honour it willingly enough," said Frosch with a laugh, "if they were not afraid."

"𝔄fraid of what? 𝔒f the lions?" I said in surprise.

Frosch burst into noisy laughter, and asked me who could possibly be frightened of poor old Mustafa, the only ferocious beast at Neugebäu that was ever allowed out of its cage. My face flushed a little with anger; Mustafa had frightened me, sure enough, when I had met him for the first time. His paws and teeth were not made of feathers or wool, after all. Suddenly Frosch grew serious again and said almost inaudibly:

"𝔑o, no, nothing like that: they're afraid of the ghosts."

This time it was my turn to smile, showing my scepticism. Frosch paid no heed, and explained in all seriousness that – according to what the people said – for decades now at Neugebäu strange presences had been manifesting themselves, making the place inhospitable and frightening.

"𝔈veryone knows about the spectres of 𝔑eugebäu," he added, "but they pretend not to know. 𝔍f they're asked about it, they look the other way."

He moved off for a moment, in search of a little millet to distribute to the birds. From the birdcages behind the old stables we could hear them squawking.

Left on my own I remembered that, when I had asked my fellow chimney-sweeps about the Place with No Name, none of them had offered to accompany me to the place, and indeed they had pretended not to know the old mansion at all, although it must be familiar to all inhabitants of Vienna.

But another memory, a more remote one, made me even more pensive. Eleven years ago in Rome, during my previous adventure with Abbot Melani, in the deserted villa of the Vessel I myself had had an experience of immaterial presences, whose nature I had never been able to ascertain. I had reflected on this just a little earlier, that same morning, on hearing Ugonio's tale: had not the mysterious pilot of the Flying Ship from Portugal, in his monk's habits, whom I had learned about from the old gazette that Frosch had shown me, reminded me of the black violinist, named Albicastro, who had appeared to hover over the battlements of the Villa of the Vessel and who had played the Portuguese melody of the *folia*?

And now from Neugebäu, the forgotten mansion, came another unexpected reminder of the abandoned villa of the Vessel. What was this allusion, this echoing chime between two places and two experiences so distant from one another in time and in space?

In the meantime Frosch had come up to me again. I certainly could not share all my cogitations with him, and confined myself to asking him if he knew any more details about the ghosts of the Place with No Name.

He said that the son and successor of Maximilian II, the unhappy Emperor Rudolph II, had been a fanatical occultist. Forever surrounded by astrologers and alchemists, for years and years he had spent huge sums acquiring rare materials, retorts and alembics, and hiring magical consultants, in the attempt (pursued in vain by legions of alchemists) to give life to the famous and mysterious Philosopher's Stone.

I asked him why he had called Rudolph "unhappy"?

"𝕰𝖛𝖊𝖗𝖞𝖔𝖓𝖊 𝖐𝖓𝖔𝖜𝖘 𝖙𝖍𝖆𝖙!" he exclaimed. "𝕭𝖊𝖈𝖆𝖚𝖘𝖊 𝖔𝖋 𝖍𝖎𝖘 𝖋𝖆𝖙𝖍𝖊𝖗'𝖘 𝖉𝖊𝖆𝖙𝖍."

It was perhaps because of the calm that reigned in the plain of Simmering, and the privacy that the large isolated mansion guaranteed him, that Maximilian's son had chosen the Place with No Name as his laboratory, setting up there a well-equipped secret alchemical workshop.

"𝕴𝖙 𝖜𝖆𝖘 𝖉𝖔𝖜𝖓 𝖙𝖍𝖊𝖗𝖊, 𝖎𝖓 𝖙𝖍𝖊 𝖇𝖆𝖘𝖊𝖒𝖊𝖓𝖙," said Frosch, pointing at the doorway to the round keep on the east side of the mansion, where we had entered on the previous occasion and I had bumped into the bleeding sheep carcass.

The watchman added that when Rudolph carried out his nocturnal experiments, people on the plain of Simmering had been able to see, through the single little round window of his alchemical workshop, the iridescent flames of the alembics with which Maximilian's successor invoked the occult forces of the elements.

"𝕿𝖍𝖊𝖗𝖊 𝖆𝖗𝖊 𝖌𝖍𝖔𝖘𝖙𝖘 𝖙𝖍𝖊𝖗𝖊, 𝖇𝖚𝖙 𝖙𝖍𝖊𝖞 𝖆𝖑𝖘𝖔 𝖈𝖆𝖑𝖑 𝖎𝖙 𝖙𝖍𝖊 '𝖜𝖎𝖙𝖈𝖍𝖊𝖘' 𝖐𝖎𝖙𝖈𝖍𝖊𝖓'," said Frosch, with a little ironic smile, making it clear that the fear everyone felt for that place was as strong as its spectres were evanescent.

"Signor Master, the boy and I are ready," Simonis interrupted us. He had put on his working clothes and had selected all the tools necessary for the job at hand.

I had a special task for my boy: I told him to keep an eye on Frosch, and to let us know if he went away. We would take advantage of his absence to visit the Flying Ship.

Obviously I was tingling all over with the desire to inspect the Flying Ship. But now, after Frosch's words, the Place with No Name had been graced by yet another mystery. As we worked away amid the dust of the chimneys and flues in the kitchens of Neugebäu, completing the job we had begun on the previous occasion, Frosch's words continued to echo in my mind.

The keeper of the lions had referred to Maximilian's death and to the son who had succeeded him, the unhappy Rudolph II. Curiously, it was at Maximilian's death that Simonis's tale had broken off during our last visit to the mansion of Simmering: it was then that my assistant had suddenly remembered that the gates into Vienna were about to close and we had had to rush back to town.

I told him what Frosch had just recounted about Maximilian and his son Rudolph. He paused briefly; he was scraping encrusted brick dust off a large iron palette knife. He wiped his cheeks and forehead with the back of his hand, and it was as if with the particles of coal and dust a thin layer of skin fell from his face, and my assistant Simonis, the penniless young man with a vaguely idiotic smile, the listless and slightly retarded student, turned back into the acute connoisseur of imperial history that he had revealed himself to be over the last few days.

"The lion keeper wasn't lying to you, Signor Master; the Viennese really do believe that there are ghosts in this place. And it's true that Rudolph, Maximilian's son, was an alchemist, occultist and a very unhappy person. But Frosch didn't explain why this came about. As you well know, this place doesn't have a name."

"Right. Which is why it's known as the Place with No Name."

"But you also know that it has a nickname: Neugebäu, which means 'New Building'."

"Of course, I know that."

"Well, don't you find it strange? Such an impressive place, and two non-names: 'Place with No Name' and 'New Building'."

"I thought that Maximilian had died before he found a definitive one," I answered.

"No, Signor Master. There are residences, like Schönbrunn for example, that received their names even before the first stone was laid. Neugebäu would never be baptised with its real name: it had to be guessed."

"Guessed?"

He wiped a bead of sweat from his brow and started cleaning the palette knife once more, which had fallen from his hands in the meantime and got dirty again.

The construction of the Place with No Name, explained Simonis, in his tortuous, long-winded fashion, was the riddle whose solution would be revealed as work proceeded. Only when it was completed would the mansion and its gardens reveal, to those who knew how to look, their true nature. Its name would burst spontaneously from the eyes and lips of those who had guessed the metaphor.

And then the *vox populi* would call it "Suleiman's Tent", or "The Ruin of the Turks", "Maximilian's Revenge" or even "The Triumph of Christ", depending on the inclinations and acumen of those who would visit it.

But Maximilian had died too soon. His jewel had been left incomplete, and therefore anonymous: it was simply "the new building", and therefore a Place with No Name.

"Maximilian's death, Signor Master: all the events that followed had their origin there."

In 1576, the year the Emperor died, Neugebäu was not yet finished. The main body, in particular, did not have its interior furnishings: the long gallery on the ground floor, which in the designs was intended to hold an antiquarium, a gallery of wonders to amaze the world. It was to have contained statues, displays of weapons, paintings, tapestries, coins, works in gold and porcelain. The great Jacopo Strada – the brilliant Italian antiquarian whom Maximilian had engaged at great cost, and who was famous for having conferred glory and splendour on the greatest palaces in Munich – was to have collected them. When this last part had been completed, Neugebäu would be ready to be presented to the world.

However, with Ilsung and Hag breathing down his neck, as Simonis had already recounted, the Emperor was having problems in finding the money.

The previous year Ungnad had returned from Constantinople after a two-year sojourn there, and shortly afterwards the Turks (it just so happened) had once again begun to threaten the borders of the Empire. The Diet of Regensburg, the assembly of all the princes of the Empire, urgently needed to be convened. On 1st June Maximilian set out from Vienna to superintend the meeting. Like the first session he had presided over ten years earlier, it was a diet of crucial importance: it was essential that the princes, both Catholics and Lutherans, should rediscover a form of unity or the Turks would prevail.

Maximilian confided to his acquaintances that he intended to be present no matter what, even should it cost him his life. Prophetic words. The imperial caravan made its way up the Danube. The weather was bad, and so was the Emperor's mood. He confessed to his counsellors that if he had not found the strength to start his journey just then, maybe he would never have set out at all. He was indisposed, and felt weak at times. He opened the diet on 25th June; after the initial speeches he himself addressed the assembly. His hearers were impressed by the eloquence with which he described the Turkish threat, which loomed ever closer and ever more formidable. An agreement must be found, if the whole of Christendom was not to be overwhelmed. Negotiations began at once among the Protestant and Catholic princes and the Pope's legates. There were long, tortuous and exhausting discussions. Maximilian seemed worn out again. He complained that the air of Regensburg did not suit him, and wished he were back in Vienna.

At the end of July he was seized with haemorrhoidal pains. The month of August went by without any problems, but in the night between the 29th and 30th he had a severe attack of calculosis accompanied by tachycardia, which continued until 5th September. On that day, amidst severe pain, he expelled a calculus the size of an olive pit.

"The 5th of September was a fateful day, Signor Master. If you remember what I told you, on that same day ten years earlier Suleiman had died without Maximilian hearing anything about it. And in the days that followed there had come the military defeat against the Turks which had ruined his fame and prestige forever."

From 5th September Maximilian's condition grew visibly worse. The tachycardia persisted, his breathing grew laboured, his appetite vanished. A fit of palpitations lasted for ninety consecutive hours. Everybody, except doctors and imperial counsellors, was forbidden to approach the bishop's house, where Maximilian was staying. The bells were forbidden to ring. The Emperor was in his fiftieth year: a critical age, said the doctors. Over the next few days he would have colic, difficulty in breathing and stomach pains. He slept badly, and this made it difficult for him to recover.

Meanwhile his old personal doctor was called for, the Italian Giulio Alessandrino, who on account of his advanced age had retired and was living in Italy. But at the same time, those attending on Maximilian began to talk about a strange woman. She came from Ulm and was called Magdalena Streicher.

"She was a healer, according to some. Others called her a charlatan," said Simonis with a sharp edge to his voice. "At first no one was against her visits. Perhaps because the idea came from someone highly influential: Georg Ilsung."

"Ilsung?" I said in amazement, "Ilsung the traitor?"

Yes, Simonis repeated, it was he who recommended that this charlatan woman should be hired. He assured everyone that she was able to solve the most difficult cases, ones that had baffled official medicine. Princes and court dignitaries all quickly agreed: they had heard good things about this woman, and some even claimed to have been treated by her, and successfully.

Our inspection of the kitchens had finished. Simonis stood up, and for the umpteenth time he dropped the palette knife, which ended up on my poor right foot. My assistant apologised. As we gathered our tools and prepared to enter the mansion itself, I noticed once again how awkward Simonis's movements were, and what a contrast they made with the sharpness of his storytelling and the adroitness of his nocturnal activities.

There were three Simonises, I thought as we made our way into the interior of the mansion. The first was the Simonis of every day: a rather foolish student, with a silly expression, slightly squinting eyes, a dopey smile and clumsy movements. Then there was the second Simonis: he still had the doltish expression, but beneath his half-lowered eyelids his mind (as in his stories about Maximilian) darted about nimbly and sinuously. Finally there was the determined, courageous and even cruel Simonis, who bullied the poor Pennal and led me around nocturnal Vienna in Penicek's cart facing mortal dangers. The face of this last Simonis, the third one, had no trace of the foolish expression. I still trembled at the thought of the bullet that had been fired into my back in the Prater, miraculously repelled by Hristo's chessboard. What memory did he have of the terrible dangers we had faced together, of Dànilo's last gasp, of Hristo's frozen corpse? His face showed nothing.

As to the existence or not of a fourth Simonis, the Simonis who pretended to be an idiot and like a puppeteer pulled the strings of the first three just as he wished, I could not yet form an opinion. I thought I had caught just one fleeting glimpse of him since we first met: the previous night, after taking leave of Populescu. But finding no reason for such behaviour, I had instinctively shelved the suspicion.

And so, from the anonymous kitchen spaces lying outside the main body of Neugebäu, we made our way towards the mansion. As we approached we were at once caught up in the dark, sombre atmosphere of those walls, which contrasted so sharply with its white stone, its airy gardens and its lofty, soaring towers.

As we crossed the eastern courtyard, leaving the *maior domus* to the left, Simonis went on with his story.

As soon as she arrived in Regensburg, Magdalena Streicher, the mysterious healer, went to converse with Maximilian, who nonetheless rejected her treatment: he was still waiting for his trusted Italian doctor, Giulio Alessandrino.

On 14th September the invalid's condition inspired greater optimism. But over the weeks he had made a number of dietary errors: he had eaten sour fruit and drunk frozen wine. He complained of heart trouble and he was never free of an insidious cough for more than an hour or two. His pulse was weak and irregular.

Maximilian granted no audiences, but he had enough strength to work: every day he summoned his secret imperial council and dealt with the most important matters. On 26th September Giulio Alessandrino, on whom they were all pinning their hopes, finally arrived. But while the Italian was on his way, the charlatan woman had been given a free hand, and she had started to administer her own treatment to Maximilian. The invalid was immediately entrusted to the care of Giulio Alessandrino, but then for mysterious reasons he was consigned once again to Streicher. This toing and froing between the experts had disastrous consequences. Ever since the charlatan had started treating him at the beginning of October, Maximilian's condition had worsened to such a point that they were all expecting him to die. When they approached his bed, they would hear him murmuring heartrending phrases: "Oh God, no one can know how much I suffer. I beg you, Lord, let my hour come."

On the afternoon of 6th October he fell unconscious, and for a moment they all feared he was dead. But he regained his senses and vomited a great quantity of catarrh. Over the next few hours, against all expectations, he slept well and long. Meanwhile his son Rudolph had been summoned from Prague, with the task of attending the final conference of the diet in his father's place.

After a beneficial night's sleep between 6th and 7th October, thanks also to the treatment of Giulio Alessandrino, Maximilian seemed restored to health. He received the Ambassador of the Grand Duke of Tuscany and the Ambassador of the Republic of Venice, who found him much improved. He spoke aloud the whole time, and was only disturbed by a slight difficulty in breathing and tachycardia. His cough had almost disappeared.

This improvement seemed to stabilise. Plans were made for the patient to set forth on 20th October on his way back to Austria. On 10th October, however, Maximilian had a relapse, and so, on the night of the 11th, despite Alessandrino's protests, Ilsung brought the charlatan back onto the case. The Emperor felt pains in his upper left abdomen; the woman diagnosed pleurisy and brought in a great number of remedies, the sad effect of which would be seen shortly after. Finally, Maximilian's former personal doctor, Crato von Crafftheim – whose services had been dispensed with because he was old and sick, and above all Protestant – was also consulted. "A great deal has been done up to now," whispered Crato, pointing at the woman from Ulm in front of the court, "but nothing right."

At one in the morning Rudolph and other dignitaries and court officials were summoned. Now it was clear that the end had arrived. The Empress, who had spent every hour close to her husband and had never left his bedside for the last three days, was awoken at five by the Duchess of Bavaria, Maximilian's sister, who was relieving her. About to go to mass, she then she returned and tearfully embraced her husband, who had had another heart attack in the meantime.

The Empress could not bear the distress and was carried away unconscious. Doctor Crato was once again admitted to visit Maximilian. He took his pulse in his fingers, but the Sovereign interrupted him: "Crato, there's no more pulse." The old doctor still pressed his fingertips, and found a feeble throb. He moved away and confided to those present: "This is the limit of human help. We can only hope in divine help." The charlatan had disappeared in the meantime. No more would be heard of her.

I interrupted him: "Are you telling me that Streicher poisoned him on Ilsung's instructions?"

"There was no poison. To kill a sick man you just need to get the treatment wrong," answered Simonis with a slight smile.

Death was imminent by now. One great question remained: would Maximilian the Mysterious, who had never made a clear choice between the Church of Rome and that of Luther, die as a Catholic or a Protestant?

"Whichever choice he declared," explained Simonis, "would be a deathblow for the unity he longed for among Christians."

In his final hours, relatives, priests and ambassadors gathered around his bed. They tormented him right up to the last moment, begging him to take the Catholic sacraments of confession and extreme unction. He surely did not want to declare himself a Protestant?

Maximilian, weaker and weaker, held out and gave no answer. Finally the Bishop of Neustadt was brought to the bedside. The Bishop insisted and grew heated, raising his voice. "Not so loud, I can hear perfectly," answered the dying man. But the Bishop went on, until he was almost yelling.

"Not so loud," repeated Maximilian for the last time. Then his head dropped and he breathed his last. It was a quarter to nine on the morning of 12th October, his saint's name day.

"He was dead, but he had won his last battle. Refusing the Catholic sacraments, but without proclaiming himself a Protestant, he had defeated those who wanted to take advantage of his final moments. Maximilian had rejected the corruption of the Church of Rome, but he had not given himself over to the Protestants, who supported the Turks and wanted the Empire to move away forever from the Catholic religion. His Lutheran enemies, backed by the traitors Ilsung, Hag and Ungnad – the same ones who had elected him and who were now killing him – were left empty-handed."

"But why had they decided to kill him just then?"

"Because it was clear now that Maximilian would not become a puppet in their hands. He had not agreed to recant the Catholic faith, and he had fought against the Turks as long as he could. He was no longer of any use to them. Perhaps his successor would be more pliable. When Maximilian set off on his journey and arrived on Protestant soil, no moment could have been more suitable to make a clean end of things."

In the meantime we had begun our inspection and audit of the chimneys in the large rooms on the ground floor of the mansion. We had entered by the great front door, which Frosch had kept open for us. What we found was a large room with a ceiling of triple height, where our voices echoed as in the nave of a church. The floor had once been muddied by the boots of Maximilian the Mysterious; there his heart had rejoiced on seeing a column finally set in place, a moulding hoisted onto the wall, a wall plastered properly.

A large window opened in the opposite wall, giving onto the northern gardens. In the walls to left and right two large doors led into other rooms. Everything in that enormous cubic space was bare: the walls, the floor, the ceiling. For those desolate walls Maximilian the Mysterious had desired impressive paintings, trophies, statues and tapestries.

"You see, Signor Master? There's nothing. Plans, hopes, desires: everything crushed in the coils of the conspiracy between Ilsung, Ungnad and Hag."

Turning around, we saw through the doorway the spires of the hexagonal towers rising above the wall that separated the courtyard of the mansion from the gardens. From the point where we were standing Maximilian must have had a sweeping view over his immense project, while the workers and craftsmen laboured away. The tale proceeded.

While Maximilian was dying, his young son Rudolph was delivering the closing speech of the diet at the town hall of Regensburg. The text had been drawn up urgently by his moribund father: it was Maximilian's final effort. In the previous years he had seen his son's mind gradually yielding to the mental torments of the educators imposed by his enemies, so that now the heir to the imperial throne was a frail being in the hands of Ilsung and his acolytes.

As he stood there before the princes of the Empire and the Pope's legates, holding the pages in his hands, Rudolph was approached by a messenger, who whispered into his ear that Maximilian had passed away. He listened impassively, as if it were the blandest of news. Then the young Rudolph, who now knew he was Emperor, continued reading, and his voice never trembled. He knew that if he lost control of the session the princes who were his father's enemies would take advantage of it to stir up trouble and sabotage his election to the Caesarean throne.

The session finished in good order; Rudolph had won the battle fought in his throat. But the inner turmoil of these moments and the other momentous matters that awaited him were bound to have their effect.

Rudolph asked the princes not to leave Regensburg and summoned them for the following day. He would have to inform them of his father's death; till then the imperial court would keep its secret. An autopsy was carried out, and the innards were interred in a copper case in the cathedral of Regensburg.

While David Ungnad set out again calmly for Constantinople, where he would remain for two more years, Maximilian's final journey began: the saddest, darkest and most painful.

At the moment of his death it had not been decided where he would be buried. He had chosen Vienna; instead they decided on Prague.

"And why was that?" I asked in surprise.

"Maximilian had twice kept the great Suleiman outside the sacred walls of Vienna, and with him the enemies of Christ: by way of revenge Maximilian himself was to be kept forever far from the dear land that he had saved from the insult of Mahomet."

"So it was actually a *post mortem* revenge?"

"The hatred of certain people knows no end."

I shivered while the Greek proceeded with the tale. A funeral procession, led by Rudolph, would take the body from Regensburg to Prague, travelling for hundreds of miles over the lands of the Empire in the grip of winter. At every halt the coffin must be greeted solemnly by the local authorities. The procession would be grand and awe-inspiring. The imperial family, the courtiers, pages, footmen, trumpeters, organists, drummers, officers, cooks, quartermasters, councillors and chancellors, even the carriage-drivers and boatman who were to transport the cortège: everyone, their ashen faces framed by white ruffs, would be wrapped in dark cloaks and black vestments, urgently procured from the markets of Augsburg and

Nuremberg, together with massive supplies of candles, cutlery, blankets, imperial insignia, banners, standards, horses, not forgetting a final stock of priests and choristers.

But right from the outset fate was against them: the city council, made up of Protestants, refused to escort the procession out of the city, or to light their way with lanterns. Their enemy was dead: let him go to the devil by himself.

Finally the cortège set off. The coffin was loaded onto a boat that headed down the Danube. The winter set in: rain, wind and snow made the roads impassable, causing injuries and wearing out the horses. The procession struggled onwards. In each city they reached, fewer and fewer subjects came from their homes to honour the corpse of this Emperor who had been too mysterious.

The procession straggled and trudged through the winter landscape. Amid the howling gale, within the stone-cold coffin, dragged awkwardly by creaking carts, by hacks half-dead from exhaustion, by frostbitten hands, scorned by the welcoming committees, led hither and thither like a burden with no destination, Maximilian the Wise was an unloved, shelterless and peace-denied body: he was now the dead man with no homeland.

It was January 1577. It had taken three months for the funeral cortège to arrive in Austria, at Linz. It was hoped that they would reach Prague in eight more days. But a fresh blizzard began to rage, blocking the road they had intended to take. They had to change their route, staying in isolated castles, continually losing their way and re-finding it with difficulty.

When the funeral procession reached Bohemia, the few who turned out to greet it were not even sufficient to carry the coffin. They finally arrived in Prague on 6th February, almost four months after Maximilian's death. But their misadventures were not over yet. The *Castrum doloris*, the funeral baldachin set up in the church of St Vitus, was not yet complete. The ceremony had to be postponed; many declared that they would not be able to attend, even including two archdukes of the House of Habsburg.

The funeral rites were at last celebrated, and the procession made its way through the streets of Prague. Finally there was something of a crowd: it was led by the papal legate, the Ambassador of Spain, the Ambassador of the King of France, Hungarian magnates, the Ambassador of Ferdinand, the Archduke of the Tyrol and

Maximilian's brother. Then came the princes of the Empire, envoys from Austria, from Silesia, from Moravia, priests and laymen, in addition to numerous knights, bishops, abbots and Jesuits, who had come flocking from all around.

The bier that held the sarcophagus was of dark, knotty wood. The shroud was crimson against a gold background, with six glittering imperial coats of arms. Behind the sarcophagus marched Rudolph, his sallow face hidden by a black, ankle-length cloak, his nervous hand clutching his sword hilt at his belt. He was followed by his brothers Matthias and Maximilian, who were also cloaked and armed with swords. Then came the papal legate in a broad-brimmed hat with green tassels, holding a large white candle in his joined hands, kept warm by pearl-studded gloves. More candles, enlivening the procession with shining points of light, were held by the princes of the Empire, who followed in the procession. Some of them were weeping, and the rain washed away their tears. In the grim multitude, groups of noblemen bore the holy imperial crown, the crown of Hungary and those of the other lands of the Empire, glittering tremulously like stars in the wintry night sky. After the procession of men came another: that of the horses. The first was Maximilian's steed, sadly swathed in a dark cloth with the imperial coat of arms. Then came the horse of the Empire, which was the most richly adorned, surrounded by banners and standards. Finally there were the Barbary horses of Silesia, of Spain, of the Tyrol and of France, all with lowered eyes, drooping ears and unsteady gait, as if they too wished to pay their tribute of tears.

The procession arrived in front of the church of St James, in old Prague, just beyond the town hall. The sarcophagus was crossing a road between two pharmacies, where the faithful have always gone to worship the relics of the body of St John Chrisostomos. Suddenly someone, to stir up trouble, threw coins among the common people observing the procession. The tactic proved entirely successful; with eager shouts the mob hurled themselves on the coins and fights broke out. The soldiers forming the armed escort ran down the side streets to reinforce the head of the procession; the scuffles and the clash of weapons raised the alarm: "Treachery! Treachery! It's Antwerp again!" shouted the spectators, perched at the windows, on the gutters and ledges, alluding to the recent massacres of Catholics in Protestant lands.

The pallbearers began to panic, the coffin lurched, Maximilian's rotten bones were about to fall to the ground. Those who continued to resist witnessed grim omens; underneath the sarcophagus there inexplicably appeared an enormous and hideous sow. The pallbearers tried to drive it away with their lighted torches, but in vain, and so they fled in terror, convinced it must be a diabolic apparition, while the animal vanished as suddenly as it had appeared.

Rudolph, pale and trembling, was left on his own. While everyone abandoned him, the young man stayed beside his father's sarcophagus and was about to draw his sword. But one of the courtiers, perhaps a ghost from who knows where, held his arm, preventing him from unsheathing the weapon. Rudolph turned round but saw no one. He was now expecting to be stabbed in the back, but at that moment mounted archers came to his assistance.

The people from the procession were now fleeing in chaos down the back streets, through the mud and slush. Violence broke out. Madness had seized Prague, and the people's hatred against the clergy was let loose; anyone wearing a cassock was hunted down like a dog. Everyone was fleeing. The fastest were the bishops, abbots and Jesuits: they leaped from the bridges into the freezing waters of the river, ran into homes, into cellars, were caught by the owners of the houses, knocked about and kicked out. The dean of Hradschin fell into a cellar breaking his leg, and a canon and two abbots came crashing down on top of him, and all of them were at once beaten out of the house by the women there. One of the three sought refuge in a nearby tavern, but was thrown out amid insults. In the fury people pushed aside their neighbours, fell or were knocked down and trampled into the mud, the horseshit, and finally killed.

"The traitors had cast their net everywhere," remarked Simonis. "The folly of those days in Prague was the poison they had injected into the body of the Empire. It was a dress rehearsal for what they could have done later. And it was a sign of the curse they had cast on Maximilian."

As they rushed through the streets of Prague, terrorised by the thought of the Protestants, the priests threw off their cassocks in order to run faster and were left half naked. The Father Superior of the convent of Our Lady Mother of God was struck down by a blow to the face with a halberd and a Viennese Jesuit was found with his skull smashed in. The Bishop of Olmütz, battered and tattered, slipped into a shop and begged the owner on his knees not to betray him; he even offered her a hundred florins but was kicked out all the same. A soldier attacked the Bishop of Vienna, stealing his precious crozier studded with pearls and gems, and beat his servant mercilessly, while the Bishop ran for his life, abandoning his holy ornaments. Even the Archbishop of Prague, who previously had walked with great difficulty, ran off like a hare.

It was two hours before calm was restored. Slowly the fugitives reappeared and formed a straggling train behind Maximilian's bier. But the new procession was dirty, ragged, trembling and as grey as the leaden skies that hung over the city. The participants no longer had precious stoles and pearl-adorned gloves; the gold- and silver-embroidered caps were buried in the mud or in the pockets of the jackals. There was only half the number of priests, the singers had disappeared, and the procession moved forward in total silence. Some were limping, most were looking nervously over their shoulders and to their sides. No one dared to comment on the shameful behaviour of a few moments earlier. Everyone asked in vain what had sparked off this pandemonium, and why it had ended as quickly as it had begun. The sermon in the church of St Vitus at Hradschin lasted only half an hour. After the holy service the young Rudolph made his way to the altar to bestow his alms, with a great white candle held solemnly in his hands.

Everyone's eyes were fixed on him, and they were all seeking an answer from him. How had he been scarred by the events of Regensburg and Prague? The people observing him did not know it yet, but that nightmare had inflicted the final blow on his psyche, already so sorely tried by his father's enemies: henceforth he would be Rudolph the Misanthrope, Rudolph the Indolent, Rudolph the Mad.

"After his first years of government," declared Simonis, "everyone understood that his intellect was clouded, obsessed with magic arts and alchemy, consumed by fears and phobias. As time passed Rudolph locked himself up in secret laboratories of necromantic arts, and gave heed to the lowest and unworthiest of his own servants. And in the end he soiled even this place with these absurdities."

"So it's true that he had an alchemical workshop here at Neugebäu as well."

Simonis nodded gravely. "Rudolph was mad, but, what is worse for a Caesar, he was also, sadly, ridiculous. He had seen too many

horrors in his youth. And so he preferred to spend his evenings star-
gazing, instead of using his eyes and judging for himself."

Going against his father's will, Rudolph moved the capital: from
Vienna the sweet the court was transferred to Prague the magical,
Prague the obscure, Prague the diabolic. It was here that the disgrace
of Maximilian's funeral had taken place, it was here that Rudolph
would lose his senses.

In August 1584 two English magicians arrived in Prague: Jan
Devus (but he was called John Dee) and Edward Kelley. Devus,
Queen Elizabeth's astrologer, was preceded by his fame as a wise
man. He conversed with spirits after summoning them with a magic
mirror, a globe of quartz he said he had received from the Archangel
Uriel. It was not clear whether he was an impostor or was actually
possessed. Kelley wanted to be called Engelander (but his real name
was Talbot) and appeared to be a vulgar swindler; his ears had been
cut off (the punishment for forgers in England) and he covered them
with his long greasy hair. He had a corvine nose, mouse-like eyes and
a base, greedy expression.

The two men charmed and wheedled and swindled their way into
court, extorting money with astrological predictions, remedies
against sickness, vague promises to find the philosopher's stone.
Rumours arose: they were spies and rabble-rousers, sent by Queen
Elizabeth to undermine the Habsburgs' power in the region. Or
contrariwise, their ugly appearances were deceptive: they were real
enchanters. But what difference did it make? The devil is English,
people say.

Like crazed magnets, Devus and Engelander attracted legions of
warlocks, necromancers, dark wizards, alchemists and spagyrists.
Prague opened up its soft, dark underbelly; the forces of darkness
were welcome, the Emperor's feeble mind threw wide the gates, and
the fetid wind of the magical arts swept in triumphantly.

The people were confused, the noblemen let themselves be
swindled, the slimy English pair grew rich rapidly and finally wormed
their way into Rudolph's confidence. The Emperor was also obsessed
with astrology; he asked all those who visited him to bring their own
horoscopes with them. If the astrologers gave a negative verdict, the
visitors were driven out. Rudolph spent crazy sums on talismans,
elixirs, amulets and panaceas. He never stirred a finger, even with
women, if he suspected that the person in front of him was born

under an evil star. Everyone took advantage of this and bribed his councillors to gain access to him. Anyone could deceive the Emperor.

Pious Maximilian's son was first fond of Devus, then drove him out because the Papal Nuncio scented the stench of black magic. That left him with Engelander, who was even worse, spending his time guzzling, bullying and drinking. He bought a house next to that of a certain Dr Faust, an expert in the dark arts (black magic and the printing press) who was said to fly over Prague mounted on a horse with dragon wings and to have made his way from his own village of Kutna Hora (Gutenberg in German) to Germany, to invent printing. Engelander was hot-headed; during a duel he killed a nobleman, and Rudolph took advantage of this to lock him up in a tower: he wanted to extort the secret of the philosopher's stone from him with hard imprisonment. The Englishman refused, tried to escape, fell into the moat of the fortress and broke his leg, which was replaced with a wooden one. No-Ears thus became Wooden-Leg. His wealth was swallowed up by his creditors, and Rudolph did not want him anymore, but he still believed him to be the custodian of countless secrets, loved him and hated him. Sent back to prison, Engelander tried to escape again; he broke his other leg and committed suicide.

In Prague, the diabolic city, the revenge plot of Ilsung and his companions had been fully accomplished: Rudolph was now a prey to hallucinations and fits of anger; he saw plots and conspiracies on all sides and sought death himself several times. What was worse, his madness was to survive him: his bastard son, the bloody Don Giulio, obsessed with hunting, always surrounded by packs of wild dogs, a beast among beasts, often drunk and reeking with the stench of the skins he liked to tan himself, passed from a passion for the chase to a passion for tormenting animals, and then for torturing men and women, until, in a mad night of love and slaughter, he ended up killing and cutting to pieces his own lover, the defenceless daughter of a barber in the village to which he had retired. He was declared mad and locked up in the castle of Krumau, where he later died, probably assassinated.

I said nothing, overwhelmed by the terrible story. I had been gripped from start to finish by Simonis's words. From one of the windows I cast a glance out at the immense gardens of the Place with No Name.

"As you can imagine, Signor Master," concluded Simonis, "with Maximilian it wasn't only his son's brain that fell into ruin, but also

Neugebäu. Since then no one has ever done any work on these gardens, this villa or the menagerie. But without maintenance gardens die, walls crumble and animals are no longer acquired. How much longer can all this go on? Joseph I is the first Emperor to have wanted to save this place. May God grant him his wish."

From the great entrance hall we passed into the room on the left. Here too the bare walls, the time-worn floor, the great windows that opened onto the sky and the immense vault above our heads, which transformed our voices into a chorus of echoes, seemed to warn the visitor of the greatness of the Place with No Name, an uncompleted glory still awaiting its moment.

While we explored the walls of the great room, in search of the flues, a date was nagging at me: the 5th of September, the day Maximilian had begun to succumb to death. As we had made our way towards one of the students' meetings, Koloman Szupán had recounted that on that same date, during the great Turkish siege of Vienna in 1683, from within the city a traitor had informed the Ottomans that Vienna was in its last throes, and could be conquered at once. But that day also figured in the memories of my first adventure with Atto, twenty-eight years earlier: it was on 5th September in the distant year of 1661 that Nicholas Fouquet – the French finance minister and Atto Melani's friend, whose destiny would be bloodily fulfilled in Rome in the inn where I worked, and where I had met Atto – had been arrested. The day of Fouquet's arrest was also the Sun King's birthday: the greatest and most powerful sovereign in Europe had been born on 5th September. And Suleiman's death: again, 5th September.

That date, the fifth day of the ninth month of the year, seemed to sound a fateful knell in the history of Europe, but also in my own life. The Sun King, Emperor Maximilian and Sultan Suleiman, Fouquet, Vienna, Rome and Paris: these imposing names all seemed to be swirling around me, a mere nothing in the great theatre of human affairs, as if my destiny were mysteriously bound up with theirs. Or was this just the delusion of a poor chimney-sweep?

Having completed my work in the room to the left and in the identical, mirror-image one on the right, we passed through the door that led beyond the second of the two rooms. Suddenly the pure cold air of the wintry countryside lashed our faces: we had emerged onto the great terrace overlooking the northern garden. There was a broad view over the plain of Simmering, the surrounding countryside, the distant walls of Vienna and, even further off, the hazy green of Kahlenberg. The terrace was supported on Cyclopic stone columns, hewn from entire blocks: sculptural marvels. Above our heads, the high vault of the terrace was ready to receive the enormous frescoes that Maximilian must have imagined, maybe conceived, perhaps even sketched in pencil with his Italian artists, and which had never been realised.

High up on the great walls of the terrace there hung a horizontal line of stone ox skulls of splendid workmanship. These skulls, horrid and solemn, set something stirring in my memory. What did they remind me of? And at once I realised: Rome, twenty-eight years earlier, during my first adventure with Abbot Melani. In the underground passages beneath the Holy City we had visited a strange island where we had found precious Roman remains, amid which Atto, a great connoisseur of ancient things, had recognised a taurobolium: a pagan religious image, dear to the worshippers of the god Mithras, depicting a scorpion and, more significantly, a bull. Another echo, I thought, another thread linking past and present. The Place with No Name continued to cast subtle allusions around me, like a tangled web I had to unravel.

I looked out again at the great terrace and the view that could be enjoyed from it.

"Everything is grand here," I sighed, "and on a scale I've never seen before. It's like the Villa Medici in Rome, and at the same time also like a Venetian villa, and then . . . well, I imagine Versailles to be a bit like this," I said, gesturing to the gardens and the fountains that extended to north and south of the mansion, behind and in front of us.

"I don't know what Versailles is like," answered Simonis, "but anyone can understand what a great jewel Neugebäu could have been, instead of being condemned to oblivion."

It was just then that I heard a curious noise coming from the west wing of the mansion. It was halfway between a trumpeting and a roar, and I could not have said whether it was mechanical or human in origin, or whether it came from above or below. I instinctively turned to Simonis, but my assistant had already gone back inside and had not heard anything. From the large interior room my little boy had called to us: he had been looking for us everywhere in the enormous spaces of the mansion. He had at last seen Frosch walking away from the eastern entrance; the old guard had been heading towards a cottage some way off. It was the moment we had been waiting for.

ॐ∙ॐ

Lying lazily on the ground, which was still frozen, the Flying Ship seemed to be patiently awaiting the arrival of spring. I quickly climbed aboard to reconnoitre, using the large raptor's wing, and then I jumped down again.

"We have to search methodically," I said to Simonis. "I'll explore the keel, you start inside."

While Simonis rummaged through the cockpit I remained on the ground to explore the exterior of the ship, exhausted by the work we had been doing in Neugebäu and nervous about Frosch's possible return. I was looking for the Golden Apple in the worst of spirits. The embassy of the Turkish Agha, the ambiguous position of Eugene of Savoy, the outcome of the war, the deaths of Dànilo and Hristo, Abbot Melani's journey, the dervish Ciezeber, the Emperor's sickness, Ugonio's strange manoeuvres, even the Flying Ship itself: everything revolved in some way around the mystery of the Golden Apple. It was imperative that we get to the bottom of this matter. If we did not clear up these secrets, everything would remain shrouded in impenetrable fog, and maybe I would stay entangled in Abbot Melani's manoeuvres without even realising it. There was no choice: we had to find the Golden Apple, or at least discover what had happened to it.

Spurred by these reflections, my poor blackened fingers scraped desperately at the freezing wood of the ship, in search of a crack, a hiding hole or a drawer that would finally reveal the symbol of power over the West.

"If only we could understand just what happened to this wretched thing . . ." I muttered to myself, uncertain whether to address a plea to the Almighty or to let off steam by cursing.

At that moment the Flying Ship juddered slightly. This was followed by another light tremor, like a jolt that shook the strange bird-shaped craft from its tail to the tip of its beak. I thought that it was Simonis's movements in the cockpit that had provoked these oscillations. I looked up, but the Greek was sitting calmly and fingering the seats, to see if they concealed a false bottom. If it had not been an inanimate object I would have been tempted to stare hard at the Flying Ship's eyes, to see if they moved . . . And at last I did so. The two lifeless wooden eyeballs had the harmless expression of all stuffed creatures.

I climbed on board myself. As soon as I had done so, I felt another strange vibration.

"Signor Master, did you feel that?" Simonis asked me, when I reached the prow.

I did not answer. Something else had caught my attention. Something wrong. I looked out of the cabin: the ground had become . . . too low down. If I were to leap down now, I would break my leg. How could that be?

Then came a new perception: no longer that of the air coming towards me, but rather of my cheeks cleaving the cold wind of the plain of Simmering; they themselves had become small, trembling vessels. And then a crazy, inexplicable conviction: that underneath the Flying Ship an immense wave, a sort of powerful volcano, was exerting a propulsive force skywards, and we were just above it.

"What's happening, Simonis?" I asked at last, dimly realising that the same bizarre thoughts were in both our minds.

Everything came to a sudden head: the sensation of a volcano erupting beneath our buttocks, our cheeks being jerked backwards, the ground dropping. My heart began to hammer hard, and I thought back to the dream I had had a few days earlier, the mad dream in which I had risked being eaten by Mustafa, in which I had foreseen precisely what was now happening: the Flying Ship was taking off.

☙❧

How will I ever explain or describe those moments to my grandchildren? And yet one sensation was perfectly clear to me. It was as if the laws of nature, mastered by some benign sorcerer, had chosen to grant us our wish to find the Golden Apple, and tremendous ancient forces, capable of overturning the world, had been revived for us, and like mystic handmaids had clustered to form a circle, or rather a chalice, and were lifting the Flying Ship higher and higher. My little child, down below, was gazing up at us in dismay: was it possible that his father was escaping into the heavens?

"Simonis, I . . . I felt the ship moving beneath me, the first time I climbed aboard, to escape from Mustafa, but I wouldn't believe it!"

I almost yelled to my assistant, as if these words could explain the impossible.

As we ascended, the great terrace of the Place with No Name seemed to plunge downwards, but it was we who were climbing, and far below my son reacted with a mixture of laughter, tears and shouts. After a few exclamations of surprise and horror, Simonis now fell silent. I looked downwards, assessing the fatal dive we were soon bound to make, and I prayed.

But we did not fall. Like a young bee greedy for pollen, a powerful and mysterious force continued to suck us upwards. We were now twice as high as the roof terrace of Neugebäu. We felt like the highest thing in creation, higher than the hills, than the mountains, maybe even than the clouds themselves. While the wood of the old ship creaked beneath our feet, as light and dry as a cuttlebone, my head began to spin, stifling my cries of wonderment and fear, and I joined my hands in prayer, since *Deus caritas est* (this grave concept is given us by the Lord with his miracles!); and if God created the world out of love, those ancient divine forces, which had now been unleashed to grant us the exhilaration of flight, perhaps wished to free us for a few instants from the tyranny of matter, and to teach us and welcome us at last into their wild recklessness of love.

"Signor Master, we . . . we're flying! Like a bird – or rather, like an angel," Simonis said at last, his voice choking, making the sign of the cross over and over again.

As the wind whipped through my hair, I admired the boundless view over the plain of Simmering, and in the distance I could see, as on an architect's drawing board, the suburbs of Wieden, the Danube, the Leopoldine Island, even the distant Josephina, with their almost invisible inhabitants, and I laughed and cried in a mixture of fear and madness: perhaps the same folly that, they say, unhinges the mind in the high mountains, when the air is too thin.

Between one prayer and another I murmured those famous lines of the Divine Poet that refer to a magic air vessel: I did it for Cloridia and our children. As I saw the gardens of the Place with No Name become as small as a kitchen garden, its towers shrink to childish toys, the great fish ponds contract to miserable wells, Frosch's lions turn into mice, I asked the Poet for protection, and recited under my breath:

Guido, I would that Lapo, thou, and I,
Led by some strong enchantment, might ascend
A magic ship, whose charmed sails should fly
With winds at will where'er our thoughts might wend,
So that no change, nor any evil chance
Should mar our joyous voyage; but it might be,
That even satiety should still enhance
Between our hearts their strict community

And then I saw the clouds sailing below us, and, much as father Dante had done, I wished that my wife and our children were on the ship, and that we could always remain together with those dearest to us.

. . . and here always talk about love.

"Look, Signor Master, look at the city!"

The Caesarean city, its ramparts, its towers, its steeples, the spire of St Stephen's: even at that distance, everything seemed to be flattened on the ground and to become our slave. Simonis, as white as a sheet, was torn between his desire to gaze out and enjoy the view, and his instinct to crouch down in the middle of the ship in order not to fall.

Meanwhile we had ceased to rise.

"Maybe we'll go down now," I muttered in a hoarse voice, desperately gripping the seat.

But I was wrong. No sooner had I uttered those words than my cheeks and forehead felt the cold rush of air coming straight at me. The Flying Ship was now proceeding, as a sailor might have put it, full speed ahead.

"It's going towards Vienna," I shouted, torn between dismay and exaltation.

❧

As fields with fruit trees, cottages and vineyards slipped beneath us, I realised I was trembling from head to foot. The temperature was freezing up there, as if we had climbed a mountain. Powerful gusts of wind lashed through our chimney-sweeps' overalls, and also through the ship, which offered us no shelter. Goaded by the wind, the craft juddered and creaked.

"How can this be, Signor Master? What's keeping us up?" asked Simonis repeatedly, and I could answer with nothing but dumb amazement.

Then, once the crazy exaltation of the first minutes of flight had died down, we noticed a strange phenomenon. Above our heads, in the ship, were the four guy ropes I had observed the first time I visited the Flying Ship. From the ropes, as I remembered, hung numerous fragments of amber, but now the precious yellow stones were completely transformed. They were no longer dead matter: the gems vibrated, as if an invisible energy were stirring them, and they were resonating in harmony with it. A light rustling noise came from the amber stones, a sort of faint poem of sounds.

I touched one. It immediately stopped vibrating. Then, just an instant later, it started again. I touched the rope with the tip of my finger. The cable was completely motionless, and showed no sign at all of agitation. It was as if it were secretly transmitting some form of invisible vitality, coming from the tail of the Flying Ship, which was transmitted to the fragments of amber, and the intense impulse that it conveyed made them chirp with the celestial music. Was this the force that made the ship fly? And if so, how? What sublime engineer and musician had managed to compel a secret force to serve an equally secret motor, and to turn it into a prodigy? He must have been greater than the famous Leonardo, than Bernini, and even than Heron, who had succeeded in forcing the doors of a temple open by lighting a fire somewhere else entirely.

But other details seemed inexplicable. As I have already mentioned, the hull of the Flying Ship did not consist of simple planks with smooth surfaces, but of polished tubes, which formed a huge bundle whose extremes were, at the stern, the tip of the tail, and at the prow, the bird's head, which acted as figurehead. Well, those wooden pipes, which had seemed lifeless and inert when I examined the Flying Ship on the ground, now seemed to be the channel for a current of air, an interior gust or flow, which, like that of the pieces of amber, radiated from the tail of our aircraft towards the prow. Whether this current was of air or of some fluid, it was impossible to say: all that issued from the tubes was a kind of lowing noise, like the sound that can be produced by rolling up a sheet of paper into a tube and shouting into it.

At the prow, enigmatic and impassive, the Flying Ship's hawk's head cleft the air of the sky above Vienna like a real and living bird. Above the cabin, and therefore above the ropes that held the pieces of amber, the bellying sail that gave our ship almost the appearance of a sphere, flapped cheerfully as it was buffeted by the wind. At the stern, the flag of the Kingdom of Portugal, lashed by the gusts of the upper air, flapped proudly and seemed in a hurry to get somewhere.

"Why?" I asked the aged airship, fingering its age-blackened boards, "why did you choose this day after all this time? Why with us on board?"

The bird's head, at the prow, continued on its way undaunted.

"Maybe, Signor Master, I don't know ... but ..." shouted Simonis, trying to outdo the din coming from the tubes of the craft.

"Go on," I urged him, terrified and at the same time disheartened, while the Flying Ship described a great curve to the right, and seemed to want to head towards the bends of the Danube. Then it resettled towards the left. For a moment we slightly lost our balance and had to hold on to our seats. My heart pounded with the force of a fusillade.

"It's as if the ship took off just to grant us our wish!"

"I would have been happy to stay on the ground!" I replied.

In part I was lying; under the mantle of panic I could feel a sense of absurd euphoria at being one of the few, the very few, men (indeed, who else was there?) to have ever flown.

"I meant another wish!" shouted Simonis again. "To find the Golden Apple! Isn't that what we want, and what we wanted when the ship took off?"

I fell silent, bowing my head, partly because of the strong wind, partly because I was ashamed to admit that I shared that totally irrational thought with Simonis, the foolish student (if that is what he was). I, too, had thought, or rather I had *felt*, that the Flying Ship had unfurled its wings for us, in response to our wish to discover the secret of the Golden Apple and settle its final fate. It was as if our own willpower had set in motion some arcane mechanism, some ancient hidden force, which had been awaiting this moment of reawakening for a precise purpose: was not the Golden Apple, according to Ugonio, the reason the ship had been built?

Penetrating the secret of the Golden Apple, as we wished to do, would probably lead us to solve many other questions connected with it, if not all of them: the outcome of the war, the fate of the Emperor, and with it the fate of Europe itself and of the world. Supposing that objects had free will, was this what the Flying Ship wanted as well? If so, our fear and the risk we were running would be of some use. I was overcome by an excess of emotions and I could not restrain myself. "O majestic ship of the celestial air," I said in a low voice with my hands clasped, while the freezing wind whipped my forehead and neck, "I don't know if I will come out alive from your belly. But if I do, and if you really wish what we wish, use your power justly and be for us the Ark of Truth, of Redemption and of Justice. So arrange things that the Golden Apple shall lead us from the labyrinth where we are lost."

We were now flying through that portion of the sky over the curves of the Danube. I could see the Prater (and with a sudden pang I saw Hristo's livid, snow-crushed face again), and the series of curiously named muddy islets around which the river weaves its way: the Stone, the Walkway, the Valley of Tabor, the Old Stove, the Port of Hunters and finally the Embankment, not far from that path in the Prater where my life had been saved by a Bulgarian chessboard.

Simonis and I pointed out to each other places and districts in the city. As if we were bending over a geographical map, we competed in identifying the monastery of Porta Coeli, my house in the Josephina, and then the walls of the Caesarean Palace, this or that rampart in the walls, the city gates, villas and gardens in the suburbs, the great expanse of the Glacis or the little suburb of Spittelburg. We could clearly make out even the distant gate of Mary Help of Christians in the Linienwall and the road towards Hietzing. The great wall of the Linienwall was so clear that it might have been visible from much higher up, said Simonis, perhaps even from the moon.

"O Ark of Redemption and of Justice," I said with tears in my eyes, as I counted one after another the gardens of Lichtenthal, the villas of Rossau and the gate of Währing, "O Ark of Truth, if you deserve this name, which of my few merits made you choose me for this feat? Were you not deterred by my many weaknesses as a man and a sinner?" And even as warm tears coursed down my chilled cheeks, I smiled at Simonis, and he was crying himself and smiling at me, and not even his foolish face, his untrimmed fringe and protruding teeth could conceal his and my perturbation: we wanted a god of the air that we could kneel to, but we were confronted only by a mystery.

"Signor Master, suppose someone down there sees us?"

"Let's hope not, otherwise they'll put us in prison as they did with the man who brought the ship from Portugal. If anyone does see us, let's hope they take us for a flight of geese, or that they think they're seeing things."

"If they take us for geese they'll shoot us. Goose stew is a favourite dish here in Vienna," said Simonis with a strained smile.

Then he exclaimed:

"Look, Signor Master, a cloud is coming towards us!"

Instinctively we shielded our faces, as if that vaporous cotton wool could hurt us. Obviously nothing happened, except we found ourselves immersed in its unreal white haze.

In Rome the sky is of gold and lapis lazuli, perfumed and rounded, and the clouds are always high and distant. In Vienna the light and tint of the sky express plainness of spirit, linearity of thought, a love for things noble and ancient, the typical inclinations of that people. The clouds are almost always low, the firmament is periwinkle-blue. The ship leaned slightly to one side, tracing a broad semicircle to the left.

"We're circumnavigating the city," I deduced.

The Flying Ship was gradually steering its prow back towards the Place with No Name.

We completed the short flight back from the city to Neugebäu without saying a word. When our ship began to descend towards the stadium, we were almost sorry that the secret gods of the sailing ship had decided to take their leave of us. It all ended in the calmest and neatest fashion, as if the invisible pilot who had been steering the ship by our side wished to round things off with a neat display of his prowess. We saw Frosch's little mice gradually turn back into lions and tigers, the puddles of the Place with No Name grow into fish ponds, and the mansion shed its toy-like appearance and reassume its majesty. The Flying Ship landed without any trouble, as if it were always doing this, right in the centre of the stadium, almost in the exact same spot from which it had taken off. The ship settled on the ground with a dull thud, as if the vital force that had animated it had suddenly vanished. My little boy had been watching us on our homeward journey for a while now, and as soon as we stepped to the ground he burst into a welcoming clamour of tears and laughter. My legs, sorely tested, trembled as if I had been fasting for a week; when I leaped from the ship I almost fell headlong to the ground.

Not knowing what to say, I hugged my child and, as if returning from a simple donkey ride, I said: "Well, that's that done."

એન્જ

Frosch had not yet returned from his patrol outside the Place with No Name. He might have seen the Flying Ship take off; it was probably better to go straight back to town, so that he could not know for sure that we had been aboard the ship.

"You never know," I said, urging Simonis and my boy towards the door out of Neugebäu, "no one can guarantee that Frosch wouldn't tell on us. I've already risked my life twice in this place: with Mustafa and with this Flying Ship. I'd rather not end up in prison."

In just a few minutes we had collected all our equipment and were on our way back to Porta Coeli. As we left the Place with No Name, still dazed by what had happened and still suffering from that dizzy feeling that hits you when you come back to land after a long voyage, my son continued to bombard us with questions. It was only by a miracle that I heard the same curious noise, halfway between a trumpet and a drum, that I had first noticed on the great terrace of Neugebäu. But I was still too befuddled by our recent experiences to pay any heed to it.

એન્જ

17 of the clock, end of the working day: workshops and chancelleries close. Dinner hour for artisans, secretaries, language teachers, priests, servants of commerce, footmen and coach drivers (while in Rome people take but a light refection).

When we got back to Porta Coeli it was too late for Simonis to take part in the re-opening ceremony at the university.

"Anyway there will be a second unofficial ceremony this evening, organised by us students," he told me. "God willing, I won't miss that one."

"I could come with you, to look for Populescu and the others."

"Certainly, Signor Master, if you wish."

Despite the many events of that day, I had not forgotten that I wanted to put the Greek's three surviving companions on their guard and to tell them to proceed no further. With Dragomir, to tell the truth, I had already tried the previous night, but the Romanian had been too drunk to understand a single word, and so now we were looking for him again, in the hope of finding him sober, or at least of finding Koloman Szupán or Jan Janitzki Opalinski.

On the journey home we had chosen not to talk about our adventure in front of the little apprentice. I asked my assistant to take him to dinner. Meanwhile, with my stomach still taut from my aerial journey, I rushed to see Cloridia.

I had had no opportunity to spend any time with her since the previous evening, when, in the convent chapel we had learned the sad news of the Emperor's illness. The events that had followed had overwhelmed me: my rage with Atto, my visit to Simonis, the wanderings in search of Populescu, the encounter with Ugonio, the happy news of Joseph I's improvement and finally, while she was at work, my absurd flight on the winged Portuguese ship at Neugebäu. Now I surely had the right to spend a little time with my wife and to tell her all that had happened! I was already thinking that I might take her with me to the Place with No Name to show her the Flying Ship and ask for her advice, since she was never astounded by the supernatural. Cloridia might be able to explain what had happened to me.

Now my little wife was once again all for me, I thought exultantly. Her stint at the palace of the Most Serene Prince must have finished that morning. After a new audience with Eugene, the Agha and his retinue would have returned to the palace of the widow Leixenring, on the Leopoldine Island. The Prince of Savoy was to set off tomorrow for the war at The Hague, in the Low Countries.

"My love," I called out as I opened the front door.

There was no reply. I looked for her in the bedroom – no sign. Cloridia was not there. Maybe they had kept her back at the palace of the Most Serene Prince, I said to myself. I was crossing the cloisters, heading back towards the porter's lodge to ask the nun there if she had seen her come home, when I heard:

"It was so long since I had felt any discomfort, except for the weakness in my sides and my legs, that it struck me as strange last night to have an attack of colic – and one that lasted for several hours. I felt some relief after taking a large glass of fresh water with citron, which has been my usual remedy for over thirty years now. There is no worse torture than gravel: calculi and urine retention. It's a terrible illness, and if it had happened to me on the journey I would have died in some inn. And what was worse, it was accompanied by painful intestinal discharges."

It was Abbot Melani's voice. He was telling someone about his collapse the previous evening, when I had burst so furiously into his room. He was coming in my direction, perhaps to go for a short walk in the cloisters with his nephew. I decided not to let him see me: I did not want to risk being dragged into any more of his intrigues. I hid behind a column.

"And so I suppose," Atto's voice continued, "that this mishap struck me because two days ago I took two mugs of chocolate that the Signora Connestabilessa sent me some time ago from Madrid. The Chormaisterin to whom I showed them told me that they were not high-quality chocolate. Alas, I'm blind now and I didn't notice anything strange in the taste. I swear that I'll never go through this again, and as long as I live I'll never touch chocolate again!"

I grew pale. So Atto was still in touch with the Connestabilessa Colonna! I knew that name well: she was Prince Eugene's aunt, sister of his mother Olimpia Mancini. The Connestabilessa's name was Maria, and eleven years earlier she had been the Abbot's accomplice in the intrigues in favour of France, which had led to the outbreak of the War of the Spanish Succession.

I also noticed that Melani, talking with his unknown interlocutor, attributed his malaise of the previous evening not to the news of the illness that threatened the life of his Caesarean Majesty, but to . . . a cup of bad chocolate. He was certainly not making an excuse: no one could be ashamed of having been taken ill at the grave news that had shaken and distressed the whole city. And so all the elements in his defence came tumbling down: the accusation of plotting with the Turks to have Joseph poisoned had provoked no reaction in Abbot Melani.

"My head still feels very weak, so I know I must take a rest and I mustn't tire myself out as I have been doing until today. The March moon has always been fatal to me and I committed the imprudence of setting forth on a journey in that very month – and what's more, to come to this freezing place, while in the rest of the civilised world it's already spring!"

Atto, worn out by his eighty-five years, was inveighing against the long Viennese winter.

"Well, my dear, I'm so glad that you have accepted my proposal. Deprived as I am of the gift of sight, and with Domenico confined to bed by that awful cold, you are my salvation."

"It's a pleasure, Signor Abbot, and I thank you once again for your generous remuneration."

I was dumbfounded. It was my wife's voice.

It did not take me long to understand. Atto's nephew had fallen ill and the old castrato had suddenly found himself without assistance. He was travelling incognito in a foreign land – even worse, in the enemy's land; who could he have turned to if not my trusted consort? By a stroke of luck, furthermore, Cloridia had just finished her term of service at Prince Eugene's palace. My wife had obviously been very happy to accept the offer from Abbot Melani, who, as I had just heard, had clearly hired her on generous terms.

So I grumpily bade farewell to the idea of any intimacy with my wife this evening. Curse Melani! We did not need his money: I was already earning enough myself, and I even had enough left over to send to our daughters in Rome. I had wanted to be able to relax a little with my wife at last, and instead she had been whisked off by the old castrato. My anger at this unwelcome surprise made me even more distrustful of the sinister Abbot.

Crestfallen, I went off to have dinner at the tavern, where I joined Simonis and my little apprentice. I arranged with the Greek that later he would pick me up to go and see the students' post-paschal ceremony.

On the way back to the convent, my little boy said he urgently needed to urinate. As usual with children, it is wisest not to keep them waiting in such circumstances, lest they should wet themselves. So I judged it best to go swiftly into a narrow, dark side street off Porta Coeli Street. While my son relieved himself, I heard:

"So how did it go?" said a voice in Italian, which I immediately recognised.

"As you can imagine, it wasn't easy, effendi," answered the other, in a foreign accent. "But in the end we managed it – when they saw your money, they gave in."

"How much did it cost?"

"All that you gave me, effendi."

"What?!"

"They sold their master's heart. There's no price for such a thing, effendi."

These words were spoken by a man dressed in the Armenian fashion, in the classic turban and cloak. His interlocutor was Atto Melani. Cloridia was not there.

The Abbot was standing, leaning on his stick, in the recess of a palace in the dark street. I saw the Armenian hand him a small coffer, which he opened to touch its contents carefully. Atto held out a little bag.

"Here is your reward. Farewell," he said, moving furtively in the direction of the convent.

"May God bless you, effendi," answered the other man, bowing several times in the direction of the Abbot after quickly checking the contents of the bag.

Atto walked slowly in the direction of the convent, staying close to the wall so as not to get lost and feeling the way ahead with his stick, to avoid tripping up. Bold behaviour, I thought, for Abbot Melani to venture out into the street, blind and alone; the business he had with the Armenian must have been very important!

The master's heart: one did not have to be a genius to understand what this shady transaction was all about, or *whose* heart it was! One just needed to put two and two together! Not only had Atto Melani arrived in Vienna at the same time as the mysterious Turkish embassy, just when the Emperor had fallen ill: now I had actually caught him in secret consultations with an Armenian – which is to say, a subject of the Sublime Porte! What was more likely than that he was one of the Armenians in the Agha's retinue, maybe a minion of the dervish, Ciezeber, who wanted the Emperor's head? This time the Armenian had mentioned the heart: fine metaphors these Easterners had for their misdeeds! Strip away the poetic flourishes and the meaning was clear: do away with His Caesarean Majesty.

That crazy castrato, I moaned, would drag me with him to the gallows! And we would be joined by that madman Ugonio. I had to run back and tell Cloridia what I had just seen and heard. She must give up that new job with him at once.

When I got home I saw that my wife had preceded us.

"*Wohlan! Come along now!*" Ollendorf addressed us, when I opened the front door.

It was the evening appointed for our German lesson and Cloridia had started without us.

As soon she saw us she broke into a broad smile. She asked Ollendorf to continue the lesson with just our little boy and led me swiftly to the bedroom.

"You'll never guess what news," she exclaimed radiantly as soon as we had closed the door behind us.

She told me all about her new job working alongside Abbot Melani.

"What do you think? This way you and I can spend more time together!" she concluded.

I answered with a forced smile. Suddenly my courage failed me. Poor Cloridia: every time Melani had turned up in my life, I had neglected her to go in pursuit of intrigues and misadventures. Now that *she* could finally spend the day with Atto, I was supposed to tell her to keep as far away from him as possible. What was worse, the mere thought that to spend time with my wife I would have to put up with the old spy's company made me feel sick.

"Darling, I'm afraid it's not possible," I began to say, hugging her close.

"What's not possible?" she said acidly, drawing away.

She did not yet know the gravity of the situation and I had spoiled her mood. I started my explanation from the very beginning. I told her of my suspicions about the Emperor's illness and the Abbot. And also of the furious accusations that I had hurled against him the previous evening and his subsequent collapse. I ended with the episode I had witnessed just moments earlier.

"For these reasons, dear, you must leave Abbot Melani alone. Tomorrow you'll tell him that you can't work for him," I concluded. "Anyway, before accepting you might have consulted me: you knew that his sudden arrival here in Vienna had struck me as suspicious right from the start."

"Is that all?" she asked in surprise. "What you've just told me seems a very good reason to stick close to him and keep an eye on him."

"But we could get involved . . . And in any case," I added with a touch of impatience, "haven't you reproached me all these years for letting Melani drag me into terrible danger? Now that it's your turn you don't seem to be so keen on staying away from him."

"My love, I told you before we came to Vienna that the Abbot was up to his old tricks again, but you wouldn't listen to me. And in a certain sense, you weren't wrong: now we're doing fine and I wouldn't go back to Rome and our hungry life there for anything in the world. As for your Abbot's shady dealings, accept it, we're already in it up to our necks. In fact you should be happy that this time it's I who will be keeping an eye on him: you never notice anything and you regularly fall into his traps. Trust me."

She was right, I am sorry to say. There was nothing for it but to trust in my wife's shrewdness. It was a good thing she was always so courageous.

"Just listen to what a clever little boy we've got," she said, putting her ear to the door.

The young pupil was diligently spelling out:

"𝕹𝖆𝖈𝖍 𝖉𝖊𝖒 𝖎𝖈𝖍 𝖉𝖊ß 𝕸𝖔𝖗𝖌𝖊𝖓𝖘 𝖆𝖚𝖋𝖌𝖊𝖘𝖙𝖆𝖓𝖉𝖊𝖓 𝖇𝖎𝖓, 𝖘𝖔 𝖑𝖊𝖌𝖊 𝖎𝖈𝖍 𝖒𝖎𝖈𝖍 𝖆𝖓, 𝖈𝖆𝖒𝖕𝖊𝖑𝖊, 𝖚𝖓𝖉 𝖜𝖆𝖘𝖈𝖍𝖊 𝖒𝖎𝖈𝖍, 𝖚𝖓𝖉 𝖙𝖍𝖚𝖊 𝖒𝖎𝖈𝖍 𝕲𝕺𝖙𝖙 𝖉𝖊𝖒 𝕳𝖊𝖗𝖗𝖓 𝖇𝖊𝖋𝖊𝖍𝖑𝖊𝖓, 𝖚𝖓𝖉 𝖓𝖆𝖈𝖍 𝖉𝖊𝖒 𝖎𝖈𝖍 𝖒𝖊𝖎𝖓 𝖔𝖗𝖉𝖎𝖓𝖆𝖗𝖎 𝖌𝖊𝖇𝖊𝖙 𝖛𝖊𝖗𝖗𝖎𝖈𝖍𝖙𝖊𝖙 𝖍𝖆𝖇𝖊 . . ."

"After I have got up in the morning, I get dressed, I comb my hair and I wash, and I commend myself to God, and after I have said my ordinary prayers . . ."

My wife hugged me; in this sweet conjugal embrace all my tension suddenly evaporated and like a river in spate I poured out my heart to her. I recounted all the recent events, giving an awe-inspiring description of the journey on board the Flying Ship and telling her about the Golden Apple that it was supposed to have carried from Portugal to Vienna, with the aim of placing it on top of the spire of St Stephen's.

Cloridia, as always when faced with a supernatural or at any rate inexplicable event, reacted naturally and practically:

"Why don't you try and exploit the Flying Ship?"

"How?"

"To spy on the Turks, for example. Today they left Prince Eugene's palace and went back to their lodgings in the house of the widow Leixenring on the Leopoldine Island. It would be interesting to have a look through their windows."

"But I'm not a sailor, I don't know how to navigate a ship – let alone a flying one!" I protested. But the niggling notion of such a move began to stir at the back of my mind. "By the way, today they had their farewell audience with the Agha, didn't they?"

"Yes. Prince Eugene is leaving tomorrow for The Hague," Cloridia confirmed.

"Did the Agha say anything else that was strange?"

"Nothing at all. And I don't think I saw anything that was remotely suspicious. The dervish wasn't there."

❧

I still had a little time before Simonis would call to take me to the students' post-paschal ceremony, where we would find his companions. I started tidying up my papers and I came across the two treatises by Count Luigi Ferdinando Marsili, the man who had brought to Europe the recipe for drawing the piquant beverage from the coffee plant, but more particularly the Italian who, during the first siege of Landau, had been favoured by Joseph I over the inept Margrave of Baden and who had enabled the Emperor to conquer the citadel in just four days. To tell the truth, I had scarcely glanced at them since buying them. But now, after Melani's gripping account of Landau, I was curious and wanted to embark on a more careful reading of the treatises written by this valiant compatriot, which – in the editions I owned – also contained exhaustive biographical data on the distinguished author.

And so I discovered, with no little patriotic pride, that Count Marsili was a man of refined understanding and acute spirit, always ready to take on mental as well as physical challenges. In his youth he had made keen studies of mathematics, philosophy and natural sciences, and had been the disciple of some of the most brilliant minds of the day, like the famous Marcello Malpighi. He had enriched his senses and his intellect by visiting Venice, Padua, Florence, Rome and Naples: an artistic and intellectual journey that only the scions of the wealthiest and most illustrious families could afford. As a member of the retinue of the Ambassador of the Most Serene Republic of Venice he had visited the glorious and remote city of Constantinople, observing the Turkish army, on which he had then written an essay, revealing its character and organisation. On his trip to the Orient he also carefully studied the coastal waters and shorelines of the lands he traversed, even studying the underwater flora and fauna, which resulted in further learned publications. This enterprising spirit cost him dearly: infected by the plague, he had to return to Venice for treatment, and his father, on account of the frequent visits he paid him, also fell victim to the disease and died of it. In 1682, only twenty-four-years old but fully mature, he decided to embark on a military career in the service of the Empire.

With humility he rose through all the ranks: simple soldier, corporal, sergeant and finally captain.

It was 1683 and the Turkish siege was raging at the gates of Vienna. Marsili was one of the defenders of the city. Wounded and captured by the Ottomans, he avoided certain execution by casting off his uniform and documents and passing himself off as the servant of a Venetian merchant: thanks to his previous trips to the East he knew a little Turkish and managed to fool his prison guards. They medicated him with ox dung and salt, and he ended up as a slave in the Turkish camp at the gates of Vienna, where he suffered mistreatment and torture. He was assigned to a coffee shop, his task being to grind the beans and offer them to purchasers (in the Ottoman camp every sort of luxury was available, even artificial fountains to give a sense of pomp and opulence). Just like any other slave he was sold to two visiting Bosnians who hoped to make a profit by reselling him to the merchant whose servant Marsili had – mendaciously – claimed to be. And so negotiations began with Italy; friends and relatives in Bologna paid two hundred florins and so freed him.

He came back to Bologna from Vienna on foot. He arrived in the city at two in the morning, the left side of his body semi-paralysed, his legs swollen, his right arm wounded and dangling, one eye tumefied and swollen with tears, his skin burned by the sun. He had lost his hair, and he covered the baldness as best he could with a wig. But as soon as he had recovered some of his strength, he returned to Vienna, to Emperor Leopold, to report what he had learned of the Turkish army. They put him in charge of the imperial cannon foundry. He immersed himself in the study of military engineering and with great skill he created the fortifications of the fortresses of Esztergom and Visegrád. Then he returned to the war zone and took part in the siege of Buda, in which he revealed his unfailing military talent: he drew a map of the city, planned the conduct of the siege, selected the building materials and personally chose the utensils for the sappers. As soon as Buda was conquered, his soldiers pillaged the city. He, meanwhile, although wounded in one arm, wandered through the smoking rubble in search of the famous library of the King of Hungary, which he had long dreamed of exploring (alas, he was to find only a few volumes).

He was not a simple man of arms: for Marsili the art of war was the handmaid of knowledge and of right thinking. War, for him, was less and less an exercise in cruelty and more and more a chance to observe and understand. He studied the course of the Danube, revealing its every secret detail, publishing the results in a lavish scientific volume. He discovered an ancient bridge, hitherto unknown, constructed by Trajan, and many other Roman remains. As soon as the military operations gave him a little breathing time, he applied himself to the study of wave motion, of the riverbed and of the winds. He observed and scrupulously recorded numerous species of fish, of aquatic birds and of mineral stones. He summarised his observations in notes, illustrated tables and maps. He knew that the art of war was always advancing; to keep up with it, one had to follow developments in all subjects: geography, medicine, engineering, politics, diplomacy and even economic science. "Idiots believe," he said scornfully, "that soldiers are destroyers of the fine arts, ememies of literature and ultimately that they are people who profess something wholly barbarous, believing that they do nothing but burn, pillage and kill, without realising what art and what study are required to reap rewards from this profession and what profits the human republic derives from it. Many who have sons or brothers with no aptitude for study say: we will send them to war. In so doing they malign the nobility of war."

In 1699, when the imperial troops had to sign the peace of Karlowitz with the Ottomans, he was invited to take part in the negotiations: he was the only one able to make detailed suggestions for the new borders that the peace treaty was to establish. During the pauses in the negotiations he tirelessly inspected the territories of Croatia and Hungary destined to be divided with the Turks, without neglecting his scientific observations: he ordered his soldiers to collect the local species of mushrooms, complete with the clods of earth; this led to another treatise.

On his return to Vienna he was rewarded with the title of General of Battle. But another war had already broken out: the one for the succession to the throne of Spain, King Charles II having died without leaving an heir. The first theatre of operations to which he was assigned was none other than the siege of Landau, where he would emerge victorious, along with his emperor.

But at this point I had to break off: there was a knock at the door.

಄

"What a noble creature the student is, has been sufficiently well proven. But the nobler he is, the more he is exposed to disadvantages, misfortunes and dangers!"

Simonis and I were attending the students' ceremony for the recommencement of university lessons. My assistant's knock at the door had brusquely torn me from my admiring contemplation of the life and feats of the valiant Count Luigi Ferdinando Marsili, my compatriot.

We arrived right in the middle of the inaugural speech, delivered by Jan Janitzki Opalinski, who was standing on a ramshackle table in what appeared to be a damp cellar:

"In youth the student must put up with great disappointment and hard blows from dull rod masters who thrash these tender young plants instead of treating them with sympathy and benevolence, and so impede their full blossoming. As Horace says, and even more eloquently the scholar Dornavio Anitympanistas, they treat students in the manner of an executioner and so repress the free workings of the spirit."

Applause broke out.

"It is commonly said – we heard it said by our own rector at the ceremony today – that there are six mortal dangers for students: drunkenness, anger and idleness; and then constant lechery and the pursuit of prostitutes, which is said to be fatal to the soul, to weaken the understanding and memory, to dim one's sight and to cause shaking in the limbs; and finally post-meridian slumber, which is said to be fatal to good temper. False, it's all false! And whoever says such things has no love for us, nor any understanding of our delicate nature."

The cellar was crowded with students right up to the ceiling. They were nearly all *Bettelstudenten*, poor students. Some of them still bore on their chests the much-coveted university badge which allowed them to beg in order to support themselves in their studies. In one corner, a rickety table with miserly slices of black bread and a scanty collection of chipped glasses gave an idea of their straitened circumstances. The only thing that flowed in abundance was youthful merriment.

"Opalinksi is there making the speech. But how are we going to find the others in this mob?" I asked Simonis disconsolately.

"We'll just have to try. Along with poor Hristo, Jan Janitzki Opalinski is one of the most erudite students I know. It's no accident that he's Polish – Poland is a beacon of Christian civilisation facing Half-Asia. Jan is perhaps the best orator in the whole *Alma Mater Rudolphina* – when he talks the students all listen entranced," answered my assistant. "When Janitzki finishes, you can talk to him. We'll ask him about the other two. He should at least know where Koloman is, they're great friends."

"What are truly insidious and fatal to students' health" continued the Polish student, as we elbowed our way through the crowd – "are other factors, wrongly considered virtues. First of these are the long vigils of study and meditation, which consume every humour of the body, desiccate the limbs and organs and, according to Hippocrates, leave food and drink raw in the stomach. The body undergoes a wasting process known as marasmus, your breath grows shorter and tuberculosis wells up. Elucubration is an oppressor of health, especially at night, when the smoke of oil lamps clogs the air. It is not necessary to read a great deal to be good students, but to read what is useful, and not continuously but with order and method. Otherwise you grow pale, your body begins to itch in several places, your eyes burn and your expression becomes bovine and absent."

"Look, there's Populescu over there!" I said, suddenly spotting the imposing bulk of the Romanian.

"Where?" asked Simonis, stepping in front of me to have a look himself.

When he moved, Populescu was no longer there.

"Damn it, we've lost sight of him," I groaned.

"Signor Master, let me look for him. I'll do a tour and report back to you."

He was right. With my short stature I could hardly see anything: I certainly could not compete with his bird's-eye view. I crouched down on a step descending to the cellar and waited for the Greek to get back to me after he had found his companions.

"Most harmful to the health of us students," the speech continued, "is perpetual sedentariness, which clogs the veins and arteries, squeezes the bowels so that they emit too much bile, makes the body grow sour, forms stones in the kidneys and turns the face yellow and black."

"It is extremely beneficial to bathe and dive in the beautiful rivers of this blessed city," Jan concluded, "to smoke tobacco, and to drink wine and beer. It is not so harmful to health, if not indulged in to excess. You can drink as many as three times: the first as a toast to health, the second to friendship and the third to favour sleep."

His final words aroused even heartier applause than his earlier ones, accompanied by shouts of approval, whistles and even a few belches.

At the end of his speech Opalinksi climbed down from the table that had served as a platform and came towards us.

"You've come to see if your old Jan is busying himself with the Golden Apple, haven't you?" he said. "Don't worry, I've not forgotten you. In fact I have important news."

"And what's that?" said Simonis with interest.

"I've discovered who the forty thousand martyrs of Kasim are, the ones poor Dànilo mentioned before giving up his spirit to Our Lord God."

When Sultan Suleiman moved to attack Vienna and was defeated, Janitzki narrated, just two hours later there fell a famous nobleman named Kasim Beg. He was from Voivodina, a land near Hungary, but, like many rebels from over there, he had found no better way to vent his hatred against the Empire than by adopting the religion of Allah. Kasim had been given the task of distracting the Christian army, which was pursuing the Sultan. Suleiman's order to him was to ravage all the territories across the Danube, exterminating and setting fire to every village. The trick succeeded. In order to defend the lives of at least the women and children, whom Kasim's soldiers were slicing up like sausages, the Christian troops lost sight of Suleiman, who thus managed to escape with the rest of the army. Kasim, instead, paid dearly for his crimes. Together with his forty thousand men he was massacred by the Christian soldiers, enraged by his cruel treatment of the helpless. Ever since then the Muslims have considered Kasim's forty thousand as martyrs for the faith.

"It is said that on Friday nights on the site of the battle one can still hear their war cry: 'Woe to you! Allah! Allah!'" concluded Opalinski. "Even today you can still see the remains of statues representing young soldiers, erected to commemorate the forty thousand martyrs."

"And so Dànilo Danilovitsch's last words refer to this story," I said with disappointment.

"Yes," said Opalinski. "I'm afraid our poor companion was repeating in his agony what he had just learned: Kasim, Eyyub and so on. Nothing secret, at least apparently not. But my investigation isn't over, quite the contrary –"

"No, Jan, thank you very much," I cut him short. "Leave off. This story of the Golden Apple is becoming too dangerous."

"Dangerous?" he repeated, with a vaguely sceptical air.

And so I told him about the dervish's disturbing transactions, but the Pole did not seem troubled.

"Here's some money as a reward for your services," I said, handing him a little bag. "I want to warn the others as soon as possible," I concluded. "Do you know where I can find them?"

"Koloman was serving as a waiter here this evening, but I don't know which room he's working in," answered Opalinski, weighing the bag with satisfaction. "Dragomir went off almost immediately."

"And the Pennal?" asked Simonis.

"Haven't seen him."

ತ⊷⊗

We had no choice but to go and find Populescu, at the *Andacht* on the Kalvarienberg, where he had told us he was to meet his brunette. Then we would look for Koloman Szupán.

Simonis and I took leave of one another. We agreed that we would meet up at nine o'clock in a place to be agreed on. The Greek would let me know where: he had to find Penicek, so that we could go there in his cart.

Even in the excitement of the last few hours, I had not stopped thinking of the events of the day. Images of the flight over Vienna on board the Flying Ship rolled ceaselessly through my mind. And Cloridia's idea kept buzzing in my head even more insistently: to try and exploit the powers of the winged boat. If we could learn how to steer the ship, we could turn it into an invincible instrument in our favour. We could spy on the Turks through the windows of the palace where they were lodging on the Leopoldine Island, as my combative wife had proposed, but we could also fly over the Hofburg, where the Emperor was lying ill, victim of some obscure plot, and, who knows, maybe even descend to look through the windows . . . No, no, I told myself, my imagination was running away with itself.

But it would do no harm to find out a little more about this whole matter. And so I decided to take advantage of the authority that Simonis had over the Pennal, and asked that he be entrusted with a small mission: to gather information about the history of attempts at human flight as fast as he could.

However, we would not be able to give the Bohemian student any reason for this task: if we told anyone what had happened in the Place with No Name, we would be taken for madmen.

"All right, Signor Master," Simonis finally agreed. "I won't tell him anything, and I'll order him to bring the results tomorrow morning."

We separated. There was another matter that required my urgent attention.

જ્જ

20 of the clock: eating houses and alehouses close their doors.

Trumpet blasts and drum rolls filled the vault of the Caesarean chapel, while the bass voice intoned melodious lines:

> *Sonori concenti*
> *Quell'aure animate,*
> *Spiegate, narrate*
> *Le gioie del cor*[10]

Camilla de' Rossi was conducting the orchestra with a grave face, absorbed in countless cares. I was attending the rehearsal of *Sant' Alessio* seated in my usual place, and already the events of the last few hours were skittering about in my heart and in my mind: the nocturnal excursion on the trail of Populescu, the touching account that Simonis had given me of the death of Maximilian, the incredible journey on board the Flying Ship...

But I had no time to meditate any further. This brief restorative interval was interrupted as Abbot Melani came up, resting on Cloridia's arm, and hovered over me.

I glared at my wife, and she responded by rolling her eyes to heaven, as if to say, "There was nothing I could do."

---

[10] *With harmonious sounds | Animate the air | Explain, declare | The heart's joyous stories.*

Since Cloridia had started looking after him, Atto had become as fretful and capricious as a little boy. Instead of staying at the convent of Porta Coeli in the company of poor Domenico, who was still ill, he had demanded and had been allowed to attend the rehearsal of the oratorio. I could imagine his real motive: after my outburst the previous evening, he wanted to talk to me at all costs. As usual, the old castrato was going to come up with some cock-and-bull story to counter my accusations and dismiss them. I was all too familiar with this procedure. It had always happened like this in the past: on every occasion he had managed to allay my justifiable suspicions, playing with me like a puppet and fooling me completely. It would be interesting to see the expression on his face if he found out that I had witnessed his dealings with the Armenian! And that I had met Ugonio! What absurd story would he invent to justify himself?

He was a Siren, wily old Abbot Melani, and I was Ulysses. And so this time I would not listen to a single one of his beguiling words. That was the only way I could be sure of not getting snagged again on the hook of his lies like a simpleton.

"After all, Signor Abbot is a musician," said Cloridia, to justify their arrival, referring to Atto Melani's former career as a singer.

With a skilful manoeuvre, Abbot Melani somehow managed to get past Cloridia and sit down beside me.

"Over the last few days I've lost a lot of blood from the piles," Atto whispered to me, sounding like a victim.

I did not turn round.

"A few years ago in Paris," he added, "the change in the weather and the thaw caused a great turmoil in the humours of my body. In the morning I had gone to pay my respects to the Lord Marquis of Torcy and I was obliged to go straight back home without seeing him."

I remained impassive.

"You know, I'm used to it by now, and it doesn't bother me too much. And I always wear this little ring here on my finger, which they say is good for piles. The Grand Duke of Tuscany sent it to me."

Atto waved the ring that he wore on his little finger in front of my nose.

"But after a bleeding, when I have a bowel movement it hurts, and these are the worst pains. They torture and weaken one."

He wanted to stir my compassion. I continued to pretend not to hear.

"I've suffered a great deal," he insisted. "It was five months since my piles last bled. And then I applied leaves of Juno, which softened the varicose veins and, thank God, finally caused them to break. To stop the bleeding I used powder of thalictrum."

The bass, against a background of brass and percussion, continued his rumblings:

Con gare innocenti
Di voci erudite . . .[11]

"Signor Atto, you're disturbing the rehearsal," I whispered in annoyance into his ear, terrified at the thought of drawing the attention of any of the musicians.

"Unfortunately I've run out of it now," Melani went on imperturbably. "The French called it *argentine*. Do you think you could get some for me? I need it urgently, alas: as soon as I sit on the seat for a bowel movement, the piles come flushing out in clusters, two or three at a time, like cherries, I don't know if you can picture them."

. . . Cantate, ridete
Le glorie d'Amor[12]

The contrast between Atto Melani's anatomical descriptions and the sweetness of Camilla de' Rossi's music was unbearable. Luckily at that moment there came the break. I took advantage of it to get up and escape from the Abbot's company. He tried to stand up as well. I ordered him, with a sharp glance at Cloridia also, not to move from his seat. And then I moved away quickly.

Almost at once I ran into Gaetano Orsini, who greeted me with his usual joviality.

"How are things, my dear friend? Is your family well? I'm glad to hear it."

"My compliments to you," I said deferentially.

"A friend of mine is having problems with his chimney. Can I promise him you'll drop by one of these days?"

"Of course, I'm at your service, and his as well. Would it be one of my fellow workers who didn't do his job properly?"

---

[11] With innocent rounds / Of learned voice.
[12] Sing and rejoice / At all Love's glories.

"Who can say? From what I've heard, every time he came he was as drunk as a lord – he doesn't remember anything either, ha ha ha!" chortled Orsini.

He gave me the address, a small palace near the Coppersmiths' Slope. I promised that I would see to it as soon as possible.

"Do your best," he urged me. "My friend was a gentleman of the chamber of the late Cardinal Collonitz, the hero of the siege of Vienna."

"Hero?"

"Yes, in 1683, during the final battle against the Turks, Collonitz always managed to find money to provide food for the people and to pay the soldiers. How he did it, no one knows. And he was always in the front line, saving souls and rescuing orphans. He was made a cardinal in 1686 for his heroism. He died four years ago."

In 1686: so Collonitz was appointed cardinal by Pope Innocent XI, Benedetto Odelscalchi, whose sinister plots I know all too much about. My deceased father-in-law had worked for the Odelscalchi. Now I remembered: it was my father-in-law who had mentioned the name of Collonitz to me. He was one of their right-hand men at Emperor Leopold's court.

"I beg you to remember me most warmly to my friend. His name is Anton de' Rossi."

I noted the coincidence but said nothing.

When Orsini had left me, I saw Abbot Melani approaching swiftly on Cloridia's arm.

"Nothing I can do about it, he won't stay in his place," whispered my wife, rolling her eyes to heaven again.

I silently cursed the Abbot and my own consort.

"Signor Atto, you've arrived most opportunely. I wanted to introduce you to Gaetano Orsini, the soprano who's singing in the role of Alessio. Come with me," I said.

I was trying to get rid of him by palming him off on the good-natured and talkative Orsini, who was a castrato like the Abbot and might distract him from his purpose of sticking close to me all evening.

"No, for heaven's sake," the Abbot said with a start.

"I'll introduce you as Milani, intendant of the imperial post, of course," I assured him in a whisper. "Our dear Chormaisterin certainly won't betray you, will she? And Orsini isn't exactly the sharpest of –"

"I see that in thirty years I haven't managed to teach you anything
at all! Is it possible that you're still taken in by appearances?" hissed
Atto in exasperation. "Instead of tormenting yourself with disgraceful
suspicions about me," he added acidly, "you would be wiser to keep
a closer eye on those around you."

Of course Camilla would keep the secret, Atto explained, but had
he not told me many years ago that you will find the worst spies
of all among musicians? Was not trafficking in notes and pentagrams
almost synonymous with espionage and secret messages? The
name of Melani was all too well known among musicians: in his
day he had been one of the most famous castrati in Europe.
Presenting him falsely as Milani, he was convinced, would not
protect him from the suspicions of one for whom lies were practically
his daily bread.

Had he not told me, when I first met him, about the guitarist
Francesco Corbetta, who under the pretence of concerts acted as a
secret courier between Paris and London? At the same time we had
also stumbled across the secrets of musical cryptography which had
been most skilfully employed by the celebrated Jesuit scientist
Athanius Kircher, who had used scores and pentagrams to hide state
secrets of tremendous gravity. And I should be aware that the famous
Giovan Battista Della Porta in his *De furtivis litterarum notis* had illustrated numerous systems by which messages of every kind and
length could be concealed in musical writing.

He was right. I had not reflected on this but now I remembered
it well. The Abbot had described very clearly just how talented and
skilful musicians were at espionage, like the famous John Dowland,
Queen Elizabeth's lutist, who used to hide coded messages in the
manuscripts of his music. Had that not been the trade practised
throughout Europe by the young castrato Atto Melani?

I had always regarded Camilla de' Rossi's orchestra with a mixture
of sympathy and innocence. But really I should have looked on them
very differently: behind every violin, every flute and every drum
there could be concealed a spy.

"So why on earth did you come to the rehearsal?" I demanded
sotto voce, looking around myself, suddenly afraid that we might be
overheard.

"If I keep my mouth shut nothing will happen. And you already
know the answer to your question: I have to talk to you. Seriously.

After what happened the other night, when you made all those horrible accusations against me, you and I have to clarify matters. If you will give me a proper chance."

"I haven't got time now," I answered curtly.

I looked at Cloridia. On her face I saw neither approval nor blame, but just an ironic half-smile.

Having once again turned my back on Abbot Melani, leaving him with my wife, I went up to Camilla. The Chormaisterin's face was tired and drawn.

"Good evening, my dear," she greeted me affably.

After exchanging a few desultory remarks I decided to say: "I came across the name of a certain Anton de' Rossi, a gentleman of the chamber of the late Cardinal Collonitz. Was he by any chance a relative of your late husband?"

"Come now, my name is the commonest in Italy. The world is full of Rossis," she said amiably, before announcing to the musicians, with three handclaps, that the break was over.

She was right, I thought, going back to my place, the world is full of Rossis.

But what a strange coincidence, all the same.

చాలా

When the rehearsal of the oratorio was over, I went to say goodbye to Cloridia. I had received a note from Simonis in which he told me to meet him at the Blue Bottle coffee shop. I explained to her that I had to go to the Kalvarienberg in search of Populescu.

"Who, that Romanian who bragged about knowing the Turkish harems?" asked my wife, recalling Dragomir's boasts, which she had cut short by calling him a eunuch.

"That's the one. I want to tell him –"

"You're going to the Blue Bottle, boy? It's close by, good, good. Monna Cloridia, you'll take me there, won't you? A good hot coffee will do me the world of good."

It was Abbot Melani. He had risen from his seat and rejoined us. I did not bother to protest. I just noticed that, when he was anxious about something, he did not allow his blindness to get in the way.

Cloridia entrusted our son to the Chormaisterin, asking her to put him to bed, and we set off.

On the short journey I explained why I was looking for Populescu: I was afraid for the safety of Simonis's companions and I wanted them to leave off their investigations into the Golden Apple.

"So you really believe," interjected Atto with a chortle as we entered the coffee house, "that those Slavic daredevils are in danger because of senseless Turkish legends?"

Simonis was already sitting at a table in the coffee shop waiting for Penicek. He was surprised to see me arrive with other people. I explained that the Abbot had just come for a cup of coffee and then he would go back to the convent, accompanied by Cloridia. Atto did not protest.

"On the Kalvarienberg we'll also find Koloman Szupán," the Greek informed me. "I met him coming out from work and took the chance to tell him that you wanted to speak to him and pay him. He said he'll definitely come along."

Unlike the previous occasion, when I had entered the coffee house with Abbot Melani just after our first encounter, the place was now full of people. There small groups of cavaliers engaging in friendly conversation, a few elderly gentlemen with books, and waiters bustling between the tables and the kitchen, clearing away plates and cups and tidying up after customers.

"You're a lucky man, so young and strong. Judging by your voice, at least," began Atto, sitting down beside the Greek. "My health is very shaky in this changeable season."

"I'm very sorry, I hope you recover soon," my assistant answered laconically.

"But the greatest burden is my age," added Atto, "and the piles that torture me ceaselessly. Especially the other night, when I thought I was going to die."

Poor Simonis, I thought, now it was his turn to listen to Atto's endless whining about his aches and ailments. I hoped that Penicek would arrive soon.

"A few years ago," Melani went on, "the change in the weather and the thaw caused a great revolution in the humours of my body, just like now. I went out one morning to pay my respects to a dear friend in the country and I was forced to go back home without seeing him."

Atto was repeating to Simonis what he had already told me during the rehearsal of *Sant' Alessio*, but this time he omitted the name of the minister Torcy and anything else that would betray him as a French spy.

A grim-faced fat woman, who usually sat at the cash desk, came to take our orders.

"A pity," whispered Atto when she had gone. "From the voice I think she's not the nice waitress we had last time, who so kindly gave me the chocolate scoop with marzipan. Is that right, boy?"

"No, Signor Atto. I don't think she's here today," I answered, after looking around in search of the girl's raven hair.

It's really true, I thought with a smile, old people turn into children again. Ten years ago Atto would never have been softened by a scoop of chocolate offered by a simple waitress.

The grim-faced cashier came back almost immediately and served us first with a scowl and then with coffee, cream and the classic Viennese brioches.

"The bleeding from the piles kept me stuck to my seat for the rest of that day," Melani continued, sipping his hot coffee and nibbling at a pink *lokum* to sweeten the bitter Asiatic beverage, "and I would almost have suffocated had I not reached the seat in time and so not had the chance and the freedom to abandon myself to the effort that nature was making to heal me. And when nature had finally taken all the blood it thought necessary from me, I recovered. The doctor almost proclaimed it a miracle, attributing it to the effect of my good constitution, because, although I can no longer read or write with my own hand, God has granted me the great gift of preserving my mental faculties at the age of eighty-five, which is what I turned on the 30th of last month."

While Atto harangued us on his haemorrhoids and on the miracles of his longevity, I whispered into Cloridia's ear:

"I beg you, my love, try and persuade the Abbot to go to bed as soon as possible. I don't want him in the way."

"Are you afraid of falling into his net again?" she smiled. "Don't worry, this time he can't fool you: I'm here! He won't catch me out, the dear Abbot. What is important is that you must never be left alone with him."

I grew morose. Great confidence my wife had in me. Although I had to acknowledge she had good reason for it, I had never been able to bear that annoyingly maternal way she had of rubbing my nose in my shortcomings. I withdrew into myself and said not a word.

"What is this thing, a *croissant*?" asked Atto, placing his hand on the tray next to his cup and fingering the warm brioche.

"Here, in the Archduchy of Austria, below and above the Enns, it's called *Kipfel*," Simonis expounded learnedly. "They say it was invented about thirty years ago by an Armenian coffee house owner, a certain Kolschitzki, on this very spot, at the Blue Bottle, to celebrate the liberation of Vienna from the Ottoman Half-Moon. That's why they're shaped like crescents."

"Are we in an Armenian coffee shop?" asked the Abbot.

"Here all the coffee houses are in the hands of Armenians," answered the Greek. "They were the ones who first started trading in it. They have an exclusive imperial privilege."

"Have you ever seen them? A most singular people," I said provocatively to Melani, thinking back to his secret encounter with the Armenian.

"I've heard about them," he said, hastily thrusting his nose into his warm infusion.

Armenians and coffee: gazing at Abbot Melani's aquiline profile adorned with the dark glasses that gave him the appearance of a bewigged old owl, I thought back to the past.

Once again Vienna took me back to Rome. Once again the Habsburg city shot forth a shaft which plunged deep into my memory, into my recollections of twenty years earlier. Everything led back to my youth, to that inn near Piazza Navona where, as a modest scullion, I had first met Abbot Melani and my Cloridia. The inn had often hosted parties of Armenians, accompanying one of their bishops on a visit to the Eternal City. Shy as I was, I used to observe those exotic prelates and their retinue without daring to ask any questions, hovering about them curiously and deferentially, but I knew that on their way to Rome they must have stopped off in Vienna. And I remembered very clearly their long black vestments, their manner both circumspect and devout, their olive skin, their ash-grey eyes and the strange perfume that wafted about them, rich in spices and coffee.

In Vienna I then discovered that the black Asiatic beverage and the Armenian people were inseparable. I loved now and again to thrust my nose into those dark but welcoming places, where they read gazettes, smoked, played chess or billiards. Sometimes, grateful to the Lord for the financial comfort I was enjoying in Vienna, I would treat myself to a steaming cup, absent-mindedly leafing through the gazette (the Italian one) in the hope that no one would address me, forcing me to resort to my pitiful German. Every so often I would look up and cast a fond glance at the Armenians, individuals with Turkish features who were reserved, industrious and silent; I was grateful to them for inventing the coffee shop, the unique and ineffable boast of the august city of Vienna.

There was no sign of Penicek yet. The delay was beginning to unnerve us.

"This little ring here, they say it's good for the piles," I heard Melani say at the end of my cogitations, as he showed Simonis his be-ringed hand. "Putting it on the little finger of my right hand and clasping it continually with the other hand. A niece of mine sent it to me . . ."

Niece, indeed, I thought with a little laugh; during the *Sant' Alessio* he had told me that the Grand Duke of Tuscany had given it to him. He was getting more and more prudent, Signor Abbot . . .

"I hope it works," Atto went on. "It's also good for toothache and headaches, if you put it on the little finger of your left hand."

"Megalleh Tekuphah."

We turned round. It was a little old man with wild eyes who had spoken; he was sitting hunched over a nearby table.

"You've been struck down by the Megalleh Tekuphah, the cursed blood of haemorrhoids," he repeated, addressing Melani. "You are a cursed being."

We looked at one another in astonishment. Atto gave a start.

"Tekuphah means rotation, like a spinning ball, or the sun completing its orbit from morn to eve, until it comes round again in the morning."

With some relief, we exchanged meaningful glances: our interlocutor was clearly a touch deranged.

"His blood shall be on us and on our children, says Matthew the Evangelist. Jesus Christ was crucified, they used four nails to fix him to the cross, and the blood of the Tekuphah is none other than the blood of Our Lord that gushed from his holy wounds: in fact it gushes out four times a year."

"My God, the man is blaspheming," exclaimed Abbot Melani in a muffled voice, making the sign of the cross.

While Cloridia administered a glass of water to Atto to calm his agitation, we turned our backs on the moonstruck orator and tried to resume our conversation. But none of us could think of anything to say. I looked around for another free table, but the café was packed full.

There were four Tekuphah a year, the imperturbable old man continued, one every three months. The first in the month of Tischri, when Abraham on Mount Moriah was to sacrifice his son Isaac at the will of God. He already had the knife in his hand and was about to slit Isaac's throat. And so God saw that Abraham would do anything to obey him, and the angel of the Lord came straight from heaven and said: 'Lay not thine hand upon the lad, neither do thou anything unto him.' Abraham did not kill his son, but he had made a cut on his neck from which a few drops of blood fell.

"For this reason every year in this month the drops of blood that fell from Isaac's neck spread throughout the world, and everyone must take care to drink no water unless they have first put an iron nail in it."

The other Tekuphah was in the month in which Jephtha was to have sacrificed her only daughter, and for this reason every year all the waters are turned to blood. But if you throw in an iron nail, the Tekuphah will do no harm. The third Tekuphah was in the month of Nissan, when according to the Scriptures the waters of Egypt were turned to blood. For this reason every year at this time it is believed that all the waters become blood, but if you throw in an iron nail, nothing evil can happen. The fourth Tekuphah was in the month of Tammus. At this time God ordered Moses to speak to a rock so that water would gush from it. The rock did not obey and Moses struck it with his stick. Because the rock only let out a few drops of blood, Moses struck it a second time, and at last water came out.

"And so every year, at this time, all the waters turn to blood," concluded the old man. "This is the most dangerous Tekuphah – so much so that some claim that even the iron nail can do nothing against it."

"That's enough now!" I said, seeing the octogenarian Abbot Melani ashen-faced and Cloridia deeply concerned.

I looked around again for the waitress who had served us a few days earlier, but in vain. However, I spotted the coffee shop owner. I signalled to him that the old man was importuning us. But he pretended not to see me and went on serving the other tables.

"Never forget to put an iron nail among the food and on the dishes you eat from!" the madman warned us, "otherwise the blood of the Tekuphah will suddenly appear in all sorts of ways: in jars of lard, as happened in Prague to my parents, who were terrified and threw the whole jar into the water; in saucepans of water or in pitchers of butter. And from there it will leak into you and make its departure from your backsides!"

"Curse indeed. Piles are a natural illness," gasped Atto, looking at us with a strained smile while his hands trembled visibly. "I confess that it is due to the over-rich food I ate in my youth."

"You are lost in the mazes of error!" thundered the other man. "The Jews do not eat unhealthy foods, they are forbidden all dishes that are said to lead to bleeding. This is why with the force of Divine Law they forbid the pig and the hare, whose meat offends health, floods the heart and obscures the intellect. But it is they who are most grievously struck down by the Tekuphah, because they cruci-fied the son of God and his blood is upon them. My father bled every four weeks. I do not, but only because I converted to the True Faith and always carry an iron nail with me."

As he said this, with a wild grin he plucked a nail from the cup of coffee he was drinking, and waved it before our amazed eyes.

At last, like a saviour from heaven, we saw Penicek arriving.

"The tremendous Tekuphah is about to pour down upon you and your eyes will cake with blood," the old man hissed as we paid and rose to our feet.

❧

The image of the patron saint hung in a corner of the courtyard, sitting on a throne. It was illuminated by numerous candles and adorned with green branches. All around was a throng of worship-pers: mostly clerks, mothers and old people; the inhabitants of the neighbourhood. Some were singing hymns at the top of their voices, others were mechanically muttering the rosary. We looked around. There was no sign of Dragomir and Koloman.

We found seats for Cloridia and Abbot Melani, who had not yet fully recovered from the crazy old man's chilling words and had refused outright to return to the convent. Then we walked away from the statue of the saint. In the rest of the large courtyard, hardly touched by the flickering candlelight, there were the other worship-pers, younger and more numerous, who were celebrating the saint's feast day in very different ways. Moans, not liturgical hymns, filled the air; and instead of the murmured litanies, little grunts.

"This is just where we should find those two," sneered Simonis.

In every corner of the courtyard our eyes beheld unspeakable things going on, things that – although passionate – had very little to do with the faith, and even less with the divine office.

I had already heard of this. The area around the church of the Kalvarienberg, or Mount Calvary, in the suburb of Hernals, was the favourite place for men and women, under cover of the evening *Andachten*, to engage in their operations of mutual conquest;- the church itself had come to be known as "The Foyer", like the foyer of theatres, where young people get up to all sorts of things. It was said that on the Kalvarienberg in Lent the same things happened as in summer in the Aurgarten, the well-known resort of debauchery on the banks of the Danube.

"Oh, pardon," the Greek apologised at that moment. Seeking his companions in a gloomy corner he had thrust his nose a little too closely into the manoeuvres of a semi-clad young couple.

"Populescu said he would come here with his brunette," I said, "but Koloman Szupán didn't. Shouldn't we look for him outside? Maybe he's waiting for us in the street."

"Someone with Koloman's gifts is not going to forgo an *Andacht*," my assistant answered with a complicit smile.

He was right. Shortly afterwards we found the Hungarian student, hard at work in a dark gap between two bushes:

"𝕬𝔞𝔞𝔞𝔥𝔥𝔥𝔥! 𝔜𝔢𝔰, 𝔩𝔦𝔨𝔢 𝔱𝔥𝔞𝔱, 𝔞𝔤𝔞𝔦𝔫 . . . 𝔜𝔬𝔲'𝔯𝔢 𝔞𝔫 𝔞𝔫𝔦𝔪𝔞𝔩, 𝔞 𝔟𝔢𝔞𝔰𝔱 . . . 𝕬𝔤𝔞𝔦𝔫, 𝔤𝔬 𝔬𝔫, 𝔭𝔩𝔢𝔞𝔰𝔢!" moaned the voice of a Teutonic girl.

"It's him," said Simonis without any doubt. "I don't know how he does it, but Koloman always gives them pleasure in exactly the same way. When you've heard one, you've heard them all."

"There's no mistaking a real friend," I said, with awkward irony.

"No, we won't find Dragomir in here," said Koloman, tucking his shirt back into his trousers. "He'll be in one of the chapels on the Via Crucis, along the main street. That's the only place where it's dark enough to disguise his miniscule twig, ha ha!"

So we rejoined Cloridia and Abbot Melani and went out into the street again – the Kalvarienbergstrasse, or the Street of Mount Calvary. It was lined all along with little chapels representing the Mysteries of the Passion. They too provided opportunities for the two sexes to indulge their base instincts. In order to take advantage of this profane custom, at the foot of the Kalvarienberg were clustered countless little booths selling hot sausages, sugar figurines and croissants with hot cream. After the *Andachten* the couples would flock into the restaurants in the area or to the south, in the suburb of Neulerchenfeld.

The first chapels we inspected, peering into their pitch-black interiors, were all, needless to say, occupied. None of them contained Dragomir.

"He must be of a very religious temperament, your friend," remarked Atto, hearing that we were passing from chapel to chapel, unaware of what was going on in them.

Cloridia led him a little further downhill (the road sloped noticeably), so that he would not hear the moans of the couples. I saw them enter and take a seat in a chapel, one of the few unoccupied ones.

"There he is at last!" exclaimed Koloman, peering into the gloom of yet another aedicule, after we had passed a few empty ones.

We had found Populescu – or rather, we had caught him in the thick of it. It was lucky Cloridia was not with us: Dragomir was standing with his back to us, his trousers down, his body leaning forward. Beneath him, in the darkness, it was possible to imagine his amorous conquest.

"He's hiding here so as not to show how tiny his little pin is. It's no use, Dragomir, your friend will realise all the same," sniggered Koloman.

It was then that we heard the shouts. It was Cloridia, calling for help.

We all rushed towards her. Abbot Melani was lying awkwardly twisted on the steps of the chapel he had entered just a moment before with my wife, and there was a dark pool spreading around him.

"Signor Atto, Signor Atto!" I yelled, catching him under his armpits.

"The Tekuphah, the curse . . ." he suddenly gasped, putting his hand to his chest.

He was alive, fortunately. But in the darkness to which our eyes had now grown accustomed we were able to see that his head and face were striped with black blood.

The seconds that followed were, to put it mildly, frantic. What had happened, who had struck him, how could it have happened in front of Cloridia? While Simonis and Koloman helped me to lay Atto Melani down on the floor of the chapel, I looked at my wife, who was paralysed with fear.

"I . . . I don't know . . . suddenly, the blood . . ." she repeated.

In our eyes and in our minds we could hear the prediction of the old madman in the coffee house.

I suddenly felt a shiver run down from my head to my shoulders, like a warm tingle of horror. Was I about to pass out from fear? I passed my hand through my hair. It was sticky and greasy. I looked at my palms: more blood. I felt faint.

"Just a second," put in the Greek.

He pushed me aside firmly and extended his hands to where I had been standing, as if to see if it were raining. It was indeed raining: thick, black treacly drops were dripping down on us from the chapel's ceiling.

"It's the blood. It's coming from here," said Simonis, looking at the palms of his hands, horribly spattered.

Then he beckoned Koloman, who was thinner than him, to climb onto his shoulders.

"There's something stuck up here," said the Hungarian, running his hands over the ornamental cornice above our heads, along the internal perimeter of the little temple. "Like . . . a little cage."

Finally he pulled from the cornice a kind of iron fretwork box. We opened it.

Inside, immersed in a foul puddle of gore, lay a poor limp rag, reduced to a condition in which no man would ever wish to show it to a woman. Only the two spheres, which God had conceived for procreation, still seemed to preserve a touch of dignity. The rest was spongy, shrivelled flesh, wretched tatters of hair and skin, crudely dissected by some rough blade, all deformed and unrecognisable like a death mask.

Koloman immediately turned round, struggling to contain his disgust. Simonis and I were almost hypnotised by this spectacle of senseless ferocity. Who would ever dream of so absurdly mangling a virile member?

Meanwhile Abbot Melani, to whom Cloridia was repeating over and over that it was not his blood and that he was perfectly fine, was gradually recovering from his fright.

"Hell," remarked Koloman, his spirit reviving, "I knew it's better not to joke with these Teutonic misses. Dragomir must definitely see this stuff," and he went back towards the chapel where Populescu, like all the other couples, had clearly been too preoccupied to be distracted by Cloridia's agitated cries.

We remained standing around the little cage with its revolting contents. Everyone was too upset to speak. Cloridia could not take her eyes off the macabre container with its severed pudenda. She grew thoughtful. Suddenly, to the surprise of everyone, she found the door and opened it. Then she lifted the container and stroked its bottom, as if her fingertips might catch something that the darkness concealed from our eyes.

The Hungarian reappeared almost immediately, his face deathly pale, his eyes staring wildly.

"We must get away, at once, all of us," he said in a strangled voice.

"What's the matter, Koloman?" I asked him.

"Dragomir wasn't . . . We thought he was . . . there was nobody there with him, nobody, nobody . . ." he said with the first tears streaming down his face.

Our inspection took just a few moments.

Cloridia had cleaned up Abbot Melani's head as best she could, and he, leaning on his stick and on my wife's arm, looked at the corpse without saying a word. I stared balefully at the old castrato. Nothing could shake my feeling that he knew more about this than he was letting on.

"Away, come away from here," I said. I looked around and took Cloridia's hand and gripped Abbot Melani under the armpit, while Simonis seized Koloman by the arm, ordering him to stop crying, or else we would be noticed.

We began to walk down Mount Calvary Street, resisting the temptation to run and trying not to show our faces when we met the rare passers-by.

Until some couple in heat discovered it, Dragomir Populescu's corpse would remain there, as we had seen it shortly before: the trousers lowered, his torso leaning forward. Underneath his lustful body, however, there was no concubine, but three pointed candlesticks, the sort they stick Easter candles on. Some robust hand had thrust them hard into the chest and heart of the poor Romanian student from the Black Sea.

More black blood was slowly soaking his thighs and trousers, seeping from the stump of lacerated flesh where once his sex had been.

❧❦

We joined Penicek again, who had been waiting for us at the bottom of the street. While the cart set off, Simonis told him briefly what had happened.

"Half-Asia!" the Greek muttered by way of conclusion.

"And suppose it had been the Turks?" I asked.

"Asia or Half-Asia, it's all the same."

"Signor Barber, if I may be so bold, we must get rid of Populescu's body," intervened Penicek, "otherwise the guards will find this whole story a little too atrocious. A *Bettelstudent* does not die like this. They might carry out some serious investigation."

"You're right, Pennal," agreed Simonis, "we can't run the risk of being involved. We also knew Dànilo. We saw him die."

"You're talking as if you were the murderers," objected Cloridia.

Simonis responded with silence, staring at us with his slightly foolish eyes. Was it not he who had set his friends off on the trail of the Golden Apple? And was it not Cloridia and myself, I thought, who had started off the whole story, alarmed by the strange embassy of the Agha? Furthermore we had said nothing to Simonis's companions about Ciezeber's plot. If they had learned in time that the Turks wanted someone's head, and especially that this someone was in all likelihood the Emperor himself, at this hour they might still be alive.

I decided that the moment had come to tell Koloman Szupán about the dervish. Obviously I omitted to say that I had known this for days and had said nothing. The Hungarian was terrified. He knew well, coming from where he did, what the Infidels were capable of.

Penicek interrupted us, offering to get rid of the remains of Populescu with the help of two cart drivers, unlicensed like himself, whom he could trust.

"You won't make it in time. Some couple will spot something first and raise the alarm," I said, shaking my head.

"But they live just round the corner," insisted Penicek. "Trust me."

Having said that, without even waiting for any sign of assent from me or from his Barber, he pulled up the cart and climbed down, slipping into a doorway with all the speed that his crippled leg would allow him. When he came back, two shadowy figures emerged with him, who set off quickly in the direction of Mount Calvary.

"Don't get worked up, Dragomir, keep calm! Coolness and . . . sang-froid!" chortled Penicek with a macabre humour that was quite out of place, while his colleagues prepared to carry out their melancholy offices.

"Shut up, you filthy Pennal!" Simonis snapped indignantly, whacking him on the neck.

Once we had started moving again, Penicek now driving quietly on the box seat, conjectures started to fly freely.

"It's clear to me," began my assistant. "The girl Populescu had arranged to meet was the death of him."

"It's the same one Dragomir had asked about the Golden Apple. But it can't have been her," objected Koloman. "She wouldn't have had the strength to skewer him with those candlesticks."

I looked at Atto Melani. He was sitting beside me, with his head leaning backwards. He had been well wrapped up by Cloridia, who was talking encouragingly to him in a low voice, asking him how he felt, but getting no answer. The Abbot's eyes were half closed; he seemed half asleep, but I knew the old fox of a castrato. I knew that he was listening to everyone and pondering within himself.

"Say it, I dare you: you think this death is just another coincidence?" I whispered into his ear.

Atto gave a slight start, but kept quiet.

Koloman meanwhile went on: "I would say that it's the work of at least two men, probably her relatives, and also to hide that little cage so high up –"

"It's a *tandur*," Cloridia interrupted him.

"What?" I asked, not remembering where I had heard that name.

"I've examined it carefully. The container of your companion's severed pudenda is an Armenian *tandur*."

"Armenian?" I said with a start.

"Yes, it's a kind of little stove for warming yourself."

Now I remembered. Cloridia had mentioned it to me when she came back from the audience with the Agha. It was a little stove full of cinders and burning coal to be placed under a table covered with woollen drapes that hung down to the ground. The Armenians would pull the blanket up around themselves and put their hands and arms underneath to keep warm.

"So it must have been the Ottomans!" I exclaimed. "You yourself, Cloridia, told me that some of the Armenians in the Agha's retinue insisted on lighting a *tandur* to sit around, at the risk of setting the palace on fire."

On hearing the Agha's name again, Koloman Szupán grew pale with terror and, wringing his hands, asked Cloridia in a stammering voice whether she was sure of what she said and what the devil a *tandur* was exactly.

While my consort replied, I thought back to the Armenian who had met Abbot Melani, and the obscure traffickings between the two of them and the little bag of money that the castrato had put into his hands at the end.

"It was the Armenians, Signor Atto," I repeated to him in a low voice so as not to be heard by the others, looking at him with spite, "the Armenians of the Agha, to be precise. Doesn't this tell you anything? Perhaps they have an accomplice: someone who gave them money, a lot of money, for this murder."

The old Abbot remained silent.

"At last we have the proof that it was those cursed Ottomans. And if they did away with Dragomir, they also murdered Dànilo and Hristo," I insisted.

Melani did not move a muscle. He seemed to be dozing. I started up again:

"You wanted to talk to me to proclaim your innocence: you've been chasing me all evening. Now I'm here to listen to you, come on! How come you have nothing to say to me now?"

Atto turned towards me and behind his black lenses I saw him furrow his brows, almost as if he wanted to strike me down with his blind stare. He pursed his lips, perhaps to hold back words that were ready to burst from his mouth.

He was so stubborn, the old castrato. He just refused to accept the evidence: I was no longer the simpleton he had left at Villa Spada eleven years earlier, whom he had been sure of finding again in Vienna. But above all he could not resign himself to the fact that he had lost that edge, that dialectic agility, and that promptness of response that had always enabled him to fool me. And so he preferred to shut himself up in obstinate dumbness.

"That Populescu was Romanian," he whispered at last. "If you weren't so ignorant of those lands, you would know that Romania too is under the dominion of the Sublime Porte. At any rate, Turks, Armenians, or Romanians, it makes no difference to me. I have nothing to do with it."

"We're dead, we're all dead."

Mortifyingly silenced by Abbot Melani's reply, I reflected on my ignorance and on the unexpected prospects that were opening up before me. At that moment Koloman began to repeat the same words of terror over and over, his eyes staring, his hands compulsively clutching the celery stalk between his thighs, almost as if he were afraid that by some evil trick it too might end up as a chopped ingredient in a *tandur* stew.

"Just a moment," Cloridia stopped him, "we can't be sure that it was the Agha's Armenians. Populescu's girl was Armenian herself."

My wife's statement, pronounced in a tone free from all doubts, pulled me from my cogitations and threw us all into amazement.

"How can you say that with such certainty?" I asked.

"Because Populescu boasted he knew the Turkish harems."

"Right, and you called him a eunuch," I recalled, thinking with a shiver that Cloridia had proved prophetic: on Mount Calvary Dragomir had indeed been emasculated.

Thinking back to it, she went on, Dragomir Populescu's talk about the harems could only have come from an Ottoman woman, but not a Turkish one.

"First of all, Dragomir couldn't have seen a harem because, as I said, men are not admitted, except eunuchs; secondly his description could only have come from someone who had lived in a harem, not just visited one."

In addition, Cloridia added, the Armenians were a people subjugated by the Turks and so were often servants, and they told the simple truth about the harems because they hated their masters. The details of the rouge also made it clear that Dragomir's source was a woman, and the contempt for the negro servant women suggested she was Armenian. The Armenians, in fact, despise the negroes, whom they consider subhuman, and they detest having them as workmates.

"Populescu's pudenda," concluded Cloridia, "could have been placed in the *tandur* as a warning to leave Armenian women in peace."

"It's not possible," I protested. "Dànilo, Hristo and now Dragomir. They were friends and all three of them have died within a short space of time. It is not just a coincidence."

"But it's a fact," objected Simonis, "that Dragomir had announced that he wanted to carry out some tests to see if his girl was chaste or not."

"What were these?" asked Cloridia.

"He was going to make her drink water with *armoniacum* salt and inhale powdered ephen roots. If she wasn't a virgin, she would pee herself."

"Your friend was just asking for it!" exclaimed my wife scornfully. "I'm not surprised his girl emasculated him!"

"Clear proof that the girl was not chaste," remarked Penicek.

"Shut up, Pennal!" Simonis rebuffed him with irritation.

"What an imbecile Dragomir was! How could he trust an Armenian?" gasped Koloman, his voice choked with apprehension.

"Why?" I said in surprise.

"They're not people to be trifled with. Don't tell me you don't know: their coffee shops should be avoided like the plague. All of them. Even idiots know that Armenians are the most treacherous and lurid individuals of the whole human race. They're two-faced double-dealers, children of Satan, snakes in human form."

Koloman recalled a historic event he had told me about earlier: during the great Turkish siege of Vienna in 1683, a week before the final battle, there was a serious act of treachery. From inside the city someone had informed the Ottomans that Vienna was at the end of its tether and could be conquered immediately. The army wanted to resist but there were only five thousand soldiers left. The citizens were ready for an armistice with the Turks, to put an end to the hardships of the siege and to ward off the risk – in the event of defeat – of being massacred. The controversy between soldiers and civilians had not yet been resolved and on 5th September it was a highly delicate moment when either side might end up prevailing. Amid the general confusion the city guard on the ramparts was slackened. It was just then that the traitor carried out his dirty work: he sent the Turks a package of confidential letters containing descriptions of the split between civilians and soldiers, so that the Turks could easily deduce that this was the best moment for their attack. The villainous spy was the servant (whose name nobody knew) of a merchant, known to the Viennese as Doctor Schahin. Fortunately, despite this valuable information the Turks decided to wait a little longer. In the meantime reinforcements joined the Christian armies, which then triumphed gloriously in the decisive battle of 12th September.

"And so?"

"The traitors, Schahin and the nameless servant, the ones who injected into the suffering limbs of the besieged city the deadly poison of treachery, were two Armenians."

He explained, in excited tones, that the Armenians originally inhabited a remote kingdom between Turkey and Persia, which was subjugated by the Ottomans. They began their journey westwards from the Crimea, sometimes from Constantinople itself, the capital of the Turkish Empire, and swarming across Poland and Galicia they finally reached Vienna. They hated the Turks, who oppressed their small and ancient kingdom, and from whose yoke they wished to free themselves. For this reason many of them travelled back and forth between Vienna and the Ottoman Porte, acting as spies for the Empire. But as soon as they could, they would take advantage of the trust that the noble Council of War granted them, and would sell themselves to the enemy.

They were capable of the boldest enterprises, and of unprecedented feats; disguised as merchants, interpreters, couriers, they would undertake to carry out acts of sabotage, defamation and assassination for their masters. They would lead whole caravans into the desert for weeks, without any fear of hunger, thirst or fatigue, and they remained active until old age. They could handle explosives, and were skilled in medicine and also in the secret arts of alchemy. Poison was a docile instrument for them. In exchange for their services, they received by imperial decree the licence to open coffee shops or to practise as court couriers, travelling freely between the Empire and the lands of the East. In the lands between Poland and the Empire there rose villages populated entirely by Armenians, where they governed themselves with their own laws and their own judges. They were not subject to customs duties and, moreover, having the monopoly of the office of translating and interpreting, they actually controlled the flow of trade in its entirety, not only from east to west, but also from north to south. Thanks to these advantages they grew rich on the worst kind of trafficking.

An Armenian named Johannes Diodato, a great friend of that Schahin who had betrayed the city during the siege of 1683, had rushed into the remains of the Turkish camp the day after the liberation of Vienna to sell the abandoned weapons of the losers, and after the conquest of Ofen he had speculated on the slave trade.

"The notorious Georg Kolschitzky himself, the founder of the
Blue Bottle coffee shop," declared Koloman with concern, "is said to
have gone calmly back and forth across the enemy lines during the
siege bearing dispatches – he operated as a spy of the imperial forces
against the Turks, but almost certainly also vice-versa."

In Ottoman lands they purloined silver coins and smuggled them
into the Empire. About thirty years earlier, thanks to the protests of
the Viennese traders, they had reached the point of expelling almost
all of these dubious figures.

"But the war council always needs them and in the end they
managed to get back in," explained the Hungarian student.

"And the coffee shops?" I asked.

They were nothing more, Szupán explained, than places where
the wicked Armenians trafficked in secret and sycophantic messages,
corruption and intrigues. They seemed to be untouchable: whenever
they aroused scandal and the waters grew too troubled, they would
go off to Constantinople, but they would come back, with impunity,
just a short while later. They married among themselves to cement
their business alliances. But since they were evil-hearted, they
would sometimes ruin one another, denouncing the treachery of
friends and relatives to the Emperor.

I listened in utter amazement. Those beautiful shops, their inef-
fable peace, the smell of coffee . . . All this, according to Koloman
Szupán, concealed levels of deceit and treachery that the fair face of
Vienna would never make one suspect.

"If there's any intrigue or speculation to be done," continued
Koloman, "nothing will stop the Armenians."

Not only were they as elusive as eels. It was even difficult to
identify them: you might have always called one of them by the
exotic name of Schahin, the betrayer of the besieged city in 1683,
but you would then discover that his real name was Kalust Nerveli,
or Calixtus or Bonaventura, and his friend Diodato also answered to
the name of Owanes Astouatzatur. Others did not even have a
surname, like the mysterious Gabriel, from Anatolia, who in 1686
with a dreadful explosion blew up the powder magazine inside the
castle of Ofen, or Buda, so that the imperial forces regained it from
the Turks after over a century.

"And we were imbeciles too," concluded Koloman Szupán.
"Dragomir told us that his girl worked in a coffee shop. Those

places are always in the hands of Armenians. It was natural that she should have been one. We should have thought of it and warned him."

"Populescu did describe her as dark in appearance," agreed Simonis.

"And he told us that the brunette had heard about the Golden Apple from her master," I added, "who must therefore have been an Armenian coffee shop owner."

I broke off. While I was speaking, my mind repeated two words mechanically, "brunette" and "coffee", as if in search of some hidden meaning.

At last I found it. I stared at Cloridia with my mouth open.

"What are you thinking?" she asked.

"The Blue Bottle . . . When we last went there – do you remember Signor Atto? – we were served by a brunette, the one who offered you the chocolate scoop."

"The coffee shops of Vienna, if they're all Armenian as you said," objected the Abbot with irritable scepticism, "will be full of dark-haired waitresses."

"But if it's as I say it is, if that waitress who served us is the same one that Populescu had an appointment with here at Mount Calvary, then the talk about the Tekuphah that we heard at the Blue Bottle could have been a threat addressed to us."

"Yes, it's possible," agreed Simonis. "Perhaps he was related to the girl, and already knew who we were."

"And the fat woman who served us the coffee scowled at us," I insisted.

"What, that old fool's gibberish a warning? Never," Melani said scornfully.

Atto adopted an air of indifference, but I had seen him almost die from fear not long before, when the curse of the Tekuphah, *alias* poor Populescu's blood, had dripped onto his head. Now he simply wanted to divert my suspicions from his unmentionable dealings with the Armenians.

ॐ०॰॰

At Porta Coeli I helped Cloridia put the old castrato to bed. In the adjacent room, Domenico was snoring laboriously, afflicted by his cold.

Just before bidding Atto goodnight I could not restrain myself:

"Are you still convinced that Dànilo, Hristo and Dragomir died one after the other, just a few hours apart, purely by coincidence?"

"I haven't changed my mind. I still think that they were not murdered because of their investigation of the Golden Apple. But take note: I have never said that their deaths are not linked to one another."

Day the Sixth

TUESDAY, 14 APRIL 1711

✠

7 of the clock: the Bell of the Turks, also called the Peal of the Oration, rings.

"Man has always dreamed of being able to soar into the airy heights, of avoiding the ineluctable fate of his mortal species, which can only attain heaven by divesting itself of its earthly raiment."

"Get to the point, stupid Pennal. We've got no time to waste. Isn't that right, Signor Master?"

I would have liked to go to the Coppersmiths' Slope, to repair the chimney flue of Anton de' Rossi, former gentleman of the chamber of Cardinal Collonitz, and also friend of Gaetano Orsini. Instead, I had barely had time to finish the jobs I was already committed to: I had been working for no more than three hours when Cloridia sent for me. She needed my help. She had to go and see the wife of Prince Eugene's first chamberlain. The woman was about to give birth, and as a good midwife my consort took care to check up on her as often as possible. Since she clearly could not take Abbot Melani with her, she was leaving him briefly in our charge.

And so at that early hour in the morning, Simonis, my little apprentice and I, in the company of Atto and Penicek, were sitting in the Yellow Eagle, an alehouse in the Greek quarter, not far from Porta Coeli. The poor cripple was expounding the fruits of his research to us: following my assistant's instructions the previous evening, the Bohemian student had at once asked the other students for material that might throw light on the great mystery of flying, and at dawn, as soon as the libraries opened, he had proceeded to look for books on the subject. Simonis and I were quite certain that we had not dreamt it. The Flying Ship had indeed taken off and lifted us high into the skies over Vienna. We were now eager to know whether, as Cloridia suggested, we could exploit the art of flying. The information gathered by Penicek, I hoped, would provide the answer.

We had said not a word either to the Bohemian or to Abbot Melani about what had happened on the Flying Ship, since there was a very real risk of being thought mad. And in any case I did not trust Atto.

Simonis had suggested the Yellow Eagle, in the Greek quarter, as a suitable place to talk about this curious subject, which might attract the attention of prying ears. This place, close to the meat market, was also known as the Greeks' Tavern, since many of its customers hailed from that community. Abbot Melani, despite his blindness, had sensed that we were in a place not entirely befitting his rank.

"Only low people," I explained, "come to alehouses."

"Why is that?"

"There's nothing the Viennese are so keen on as class divisions. It's no accident they don't play billiards here. And all you'll see on the gaming tables are dice and German cards."

"Anyway, let's get back to the question of flying," I said, addressing Penicek.

"I don't understand. Why have you asked this clever young man to instruct you on such a strange subject?" asked Atto.

"Oh, it's nothing important," Simonis answered, "it's just for an exam at the university. Go on, Pennal."

"All right, I'll try and be quick," stammered the poor young man humbly.

Noticing the disappointed expression on our faces after these stories that were at least two centuries old, Penicek hastened to add that he had succeeded in finding something more recent. Indeed, this was the most interesting part of his whole account, and at the centre of it – as ever – there was an Italian: a Jesuit priest.

His name was Francesco Lana. He was born in Brescia in 1631 into a noble family, and at the age of sixteen he had entered the Society of Jesus, embarking on a serious career of study and research in the field of mathematics and natural science. His lively intelligence and tireless commitment took him to numerous Italian cities, and then led him to a career of teaching, whereby he earned the esteem of scholars and men of learning in every country.

In Brescia, at the age of thirty-nine, he published his masterpiece: the treatise entitled *Prodromo, or an Essay on Some Inventions*, in which with unrivalled acumen he tackled a number of scientific questions, including the project of a vehicle capable of flight.

This jolted us from the state of semi-lethargy we had been cast into by Penicek's previous prattle.

Lana's project, he explained, was based on a simple observation: air has a clearly determined weight, although much inferior to that of the other elements, and if a body is lighter than the volume of air that it moves, then it will rise. Consequently, if by means of a simple pump the air were to be removed from a pair of large and very light spheres, constituted for example by a thin sheet of copper, then they would become lighter than the surrounding air, and rising from the ground they would be able to lift a small craft.

"Something like a . . . Flying Ship!" I remarked.

"Indeed, that's exactly what the Jesuit called his idea," said Penicek, showing us a copy of Lana's design, which he had taken from an illustration in his treatise.

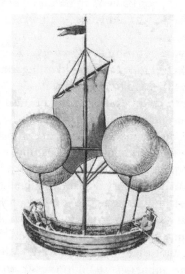

"And . . . did this ship ever fly?" asked Simonis.

Actually, explained the Pennal, the ship described in the *Prodromo* was never even built. Some claimed that the Jesuit had himself decided to give up the plan, fearing that whoever piloted the ship might endanger his own and other people's lives. Lana had confined himself to an experiment with a small model of the ship in the courtyard of a palace belonging to the Jesuits in Florence. But nobody knew whether the little model had actually flown. The Italian priest was in any case reluctant to create his flying ship, because he was sure that it would immediately be used for military purposes. And nobody could get him to change his mind. Under the weight of all his great intellectual work, the Jesuit died in 1687 aged only fifty-six, without his ideas ever having been put into practice.

Simonis and I exchanged a glance of suppressed disappointment. Four-fifths of Penicek's account consisted of useless anecdotes and remote happenings, and in the only part of it that bore any relation to what had happened to us – Francesco Lana's flying ship – all he could give us was the vaguest information.

"I had to end up with a stupid Pennal from Prague!" muttered the Greek in annoyance, miming despair by running his hands through his hair.

"One last question," I said, silencing my assistant with a jab of my elbow, not wanting poor Penicek to be totally intimidated. "Once it had taken off, just how would Francesco Lana's ship have been able to steer itself?"

"There's no word of this in the *Prodromo*. They say that Lana had thought of a system of ropes that could influence the stability of the craft. He is even supposed to have tried it out in the little model he experimented with in the courtyard of the Jesuits in Florence, but this is just rumour: nothing specific is known."

Simonis swore under his breath, cursing himself, the Pennal and even the glorious institution of the Deposition, which had lumbered him with this bumbling student from Prague.

The two students took their leave. Simonis ordered Penicek to keep rummaging through the papers he had collected to find something more useful, and then to go to the *Alma Mater Rudolphina* to follow some lessons on his behalf and to bring him the notes at the convent. My assistant then went off to work with my son again: they had a few small cleaning jobs to do in the suburbs. Unfortunately it was a little too far to take the old Abbot in the cart: the journey would break every bone in his body. And so, alas, I was left alone with Atto.

"Now, can't we talk about something a little more serious?" he started as soon as the others had left.

I would have done anything to get out of this conversation, but I had already eluded Abbot Melani the previous evening, during the rehearsal of *Sant' Alessio*, and then again at the Blue Bottle. Populescu's death had thrown the whole group into fresh turmoil, but now there was no way of avoiding things.

I was determined not to be made a fool of again. A thousand times the maleficent castrato had succeeded in getting what he wanted out of me by deceit, only to turn his back on me afterwards. But this time I would not fall for it: his excuses would neither move nor persuade me.

"Boy, I have a mission to carry out," he began.

"That does not concern me. The mission is yours, not mine. You have rewarded me for the services I rendered you in Rome. Well, that was what you had promised to do, wasn't it? The account is settled. I owe you nothing else. And I don't intend to get mixed up in political affairs that do not concern me. You are a subject of the Most Christian King; I am a subject of the Emperor. France is an enemy of the Empire, and I wish to have nothing to do with it. If I can do something for his Caesarean Majesty, I will. But not in league with you."

"You don't trust me," he answered. "I had gathered this a while ago. But don't you understand that I need you? And not just because I'm old and blind, and good for nothing now. Thanks to you, in the past, I have managed to pull off the most difficult of missions."

"Of course," I said with a sardonic little laugh, "but thanks to lying. You lie. You have always lied. On each occasion you have done just what you wanted: you always had a secret plan in mind, and you took great care not to tell me the truth. You have always used me as your pet slave."

"It's not true, I have never meant to do anything of the sort," he protested keenly.

"But the facts are there to prove it, Signor Atto. When we met I was just a little boy, and you, with your shameless gift of the gab –"

"Do you want to make me ill again?" Atto interrupted me, a tragic expression on his face.

"Cut the pathetic performance," I replied angrily, getting up. "Try not to gobble so much chocolate next time!"

"So now you're spying on me?"

"Stop it, both of you!"

It was Cloridia's voice. She had come back, breathless and panting, and she stood there holding a piece of paper in her hand.

"Cloridia, try and understand, the Abbot and I –"

"First read this."

She opened the paper and thrust it into my hand. It was a pamphlet, one of those gazettes folded in four, not published on any

regular basis but only for extraordinary events. I read it straight
through and at once changed colour. Then I translated it for Abbot
Melani. He leaned against the back of his chair, as if suddenly the
weight of his years had become unbearable.

The Grand Dauphin, the firstborn son of the Most Christian
King, was seriously ill. The pamphlet did not say so clearly, but as
with Joseph the illness could be fatal.

The heir to the throne of France had smallpox.

કુન્ઝ

The entire universe had turned upside down in front of my eyes.
Some mysterious force had so arranged things that the two main
contenders in the war of succession to the throne of Spain – France
and the Empire – had been struck down by the same mortal illness.
On one side it had struck the young reigning Sovereign, on the other
the heir to an old king, who could not have long to live.

They called it smallpox, but it mattered little what name it was
given: a fatal claw had lashed out at the two greatest contenders in
the War of the Spanish Succession. Could it be a coincidence that
the Emperor of Austria and the heir to the throne of France should
have both fallen ill at the same time, and right in the middle of a
terrible war that had thrown the whole of Europe into turmoil, with
a disease showing the same symptoms? Obviously not. Now I was
more positive than ever that a deadly poison was carrying out its
slow, insidious and murderous task.

But what part was Abbot Melani playing in all this?

Atto had come to Vienna to conspire with the Turks against the
Emperor. It was no accident that he had arrived just a day after the
Agha and after Joseph I had fallen ill. But the Abbot could not have
poisoned the Grand Dauphin of France: you do not change your
master at the age of eighty-five.

I looked at Atto and, as if he could feel my eyes on him, he turned
towards me. It was no longer the face of a decrepit old man that I
saw but a skull, as if Atto were already a corpse: ashen pallor, half-
open mouth, teeth protruding on account of his sunken withered
cheeks, blue lips and eye-sockets. The Kingdom of France risked
losing the successor to its throne, and maybe countless others after
him, and perhaps it would end up like Spain, which was now being
torn asunder by the forces fighting over its spoils . . . All these fears

I saw passing over the yellow parchment of his forehead, visible under the carefully daubed white lead of his make-up.

My suspicions about him suddenly collapsed like a house of cards. Atto was not poisoning anyone, and so his arrival at the same time as the Turkish Agha was just a coincidence . . . Whatever dark force was now pulling the strings of life and death in Vienna and Versailles, it was certainly not controlled by Abbot Melani.

Cloridia looked at me gravely and caressed my hand: she guessed my thoughts. Melani asked me to step outside the alehouse, just me and him. My consort nodded; she would wait for us at Porta Coeli.

The Abbot and I walked towards the nearby meat market. The road was full of people, and every so often a carriage trundled by. We just needed to talk with a little prudence in order not to be overheard by any passers-by.

He remained silent. I looked at him as he walked, leaning on my arm and his stick: he was panting laboriously, almost as if he did not have enough breath. From the rapid pulsations in his scrawny neck I guessed that his heart was palpitating feverishly and depriving him of breath. I was afraid he might collapse.

"Signor Atto, maybe we should go back to the convent."

He came to a halt. He passed his trembling hand behind his dark glasses, over his half-closed eyelids, as if to wake himself from a bad dream. Then he straightened his bent back and let out a long sigh. His forehead was furrowed now, but he seemed to have regained strength.

"One day, a long time ago," he said in a grim voice, "I explained that there are two types of forged documents. The first, the genuine forgeries, just recount balderdash. The others are the forgeries that tell the truth," he said at last.

"I remember, Signor Atto," I said. Did he mean to say that the pamphlet with the news from Paris could be a forgery?

"The forgeries that tell the truth have been drawn up for a beneficial purpose: to divulge, even in the absence of authentic proof, a true piece of news. The forgeries of the first kind are simply mendacious and nothing else. However, that does not necessarily mean that they might not have been produced for a good purpose as well."

This ambiguous speech surprised me a little. What was Abbot Melani leading up to?

"Well," he went on, "in the last few days you've come up against a document of this latter kind."

I gave a start.

"A forgery, which was, however, drawn up with praiseworthy intentions," he explained, "from a desire for peace."

When he added this, my mouth dropped. I was beginning to understand.

"I didn't want to tell you this, curse it," he whispered with vexation, tapping the pavement with the tip of his walking stick.

"The letter that tells us that Eugene wanted to betray the Empire . . . you mean the letter that is at the heart of your mission. It's a forgery, isn't it?" I asked, my voice cracking with incredulity and surprise.

"Let me explain, boy," he said, squeezing my arm a little tighter.

Much of the story that Atto had told me was, in fact, true. It was true, that is to say, that at the beginning of the year an anonymous officer had gone to the Spanish court of Madrid, over which reigned Philip of Anjou, grandson of the Most Christian King. It was true that the anonymous officer, before disappearing into thin air, had succeeded in passing to Philip a letter, from which it transpired that Eugene of Savoy was ready to sell himself, in exchange for a large recompense, to the French enemy. And finally it was true that on reading those lines, the young Catholic King of Spain had been flabbergasted.

But then Atto told me what had followed. Philip had had a copy of the letter sent to his grandfather, the Sun King. The French sovereign had been equally amazed. But his minister Torcy had also examined the letter, and reacted quite differently.

"Torcy said that Eugene would never have written such a letter. In his opinion the Prince of Savoy would never have been so ingenuous as to offer himself to the enemy, jeopardising all that he had so laboriously achieved by serving the Empire: fame, power, wealth . . ."

The minister of the Most Christian King was convinced that it was a trap set by Eugene himself, a trick very much in keeping with the *condottiero*'s twisted, indirect mind: if the French were to contact Eugene, responding positively to the offer contained in the letter, he would at once denounce a plot against himself, orchestrated by some conspirator in Vienna in league with the enemy.

"And was Torcy right?"

"Yes and no. The letter is indeed a forgery, as he said. But it was not commissioned by Eugene, who is actually in the dark about this whole story."

"And so who . . ."

I paused, holding my breath. We looked at one another for some long seconds. I raised my eyebrows interrogatively. Atto's silence was as clear as a written admission.

"I had hoped," he went on, his eyes lowered, "that the French secret agents in Vienna would get that letter to the Emperor. I was already prepared to come here myself, to superintend the operation. But the whole thing was blocked. Unfortunately Torcy had persuaded His Majesty to do nothing about it. I have never seen eye to eye with that minister: far too circumspect."

At that point, Atto explained, there was nothing he could do but come to Vienna himself and deliver the letter to Joseph I – or, more precisely, to someone who would be able to pass it on to him, like Countess Pálffy.

"Does France want peace? I am seeking to obtain it," he said, "and if no one gives me the means, I make shift as best I can."

Those words were followed by another silence, broken only by the sound of our feet on the paving stones, the shouts of a group of young boys chasing one another, the subdued laughter of young ladies out strolling and the clatter of a carriage turning a corner. This silence between me and Atto said it all: the decline of Abbot Melani, his last desperate attempt to influence political events, the indifference of the King (attentive, however, to the suggestions of his ministers), the solitude of the old counsellor of the crown, his impotence and his refusal to accept defeat.

"Of course, foreign ministers still seek me out to obtain secret audience with His Majesty, and to talk of particularly reserved matters – it is difficult to find a trustworthy and esteemed go-between at court," said Melani, with a fresh surge of pride. "But it's something quite different to make one's own advice reach the King's ears, and persuade him of the best thing to do."

Matters were clear: Atto, the King's trusted servant, was still a good channel for people seeking an audience with the Sovereign or his ministers. But his opinions, at court, were no longer heeded. With the forged letter from Eugene he had once again endeavoured to write a chapter of European history, as he had successfully done in the past. But this time he had had to play a direct role in the game: no one at Versailles paid attention to the old castrato anymore. To put his plan into effect, he had first needed to find a skilful calligrapher (eleven years earlier I had met such a person in his service) to produce the forged letter from Eugene, and then make it reach the King of Spain.

I already knew Abbot Melani's technique: it was the same as eleven years earlier, when he had had a forgery made of the will of the dying King Charles II, the last of the Spanish Habsburgs. That forgery had enabled a French Bourbon to sit on the Spanish throne. On that occasion who had taken the paper with the false signature all the way to Spain? I had met her myself: Atto Melani's old friend, the Connestabilessa Maria Mancini, aunt of Eugene of Savoy, former lover of Louis XIV and for a long time a French spy in the Spanish court. I had had first-hand experience (and had been an unwitting instrument) of her and Atto's secret machinations on behalf of France, and also of the ambiguous mishmash of amorous affairs, politics and espionage that conjoined Maria Mancini, Atto and the Most Christian King. I had seen then just how casually Atto and his friends practised the art of forgery. And only the day before, talking with Cloridia about the bad chocolate that had made him ill, Atto had let it drop that he was still in touch with Maria Mancini.

It was ironic. Eleven years earlier the three of them – the Abbot, the calligrapher and the Connestabilessa – had been the devisers of a forgery, the last will and testament of the King of Spain, that was to light the fuse of war.

And now the same three characters wanted to redress that colossal error, and the only scheme they could come up with was to repeat, step by step, exactly the same procedure: to produce and take to Spain a second forgery, the letter from Eugene, so as to put an end to the conflict that had devastated Europe and, what was worse, had brought France to wholly unforeseen ruin.

But this time they had failed: the fuse once lit could not be extinguished; the course of events, now hurtling forward at an apocalyptic gallop, could not be bridled a second time. And so the decrepit old castrato had had to drag his tired limbs all the way to Vienna to get a copy of the forged letter into the Emperor's hands, hoping thereby to create such a scandal that Eugene, the enemy of peace, would be divested of all authority.

"The great French ministers of the past, my friends, are all dead, even those much younger than me," he said bitterly, to explain why no one listened to him at court anymore. "There are no longer the

Pomponnes, the Chamillarts, the de Lionnes, the Le Telliers. I was truly in their confidence. The only one left is that suspicious cur Torcy, who, it just so happens, is the son of Colbert, the Serpent. I can never get Torcy to pass on even the briefest note to His Majesty, let alone a memorandum, like the ones the Most Christian King used to receive from me regularly. Today anyone who wants to do anything good for France has to make shift for himself. And that is what I have done, boy. In your opinion, is Prince Eugene's reputation worth more than peace?"

The question was rhetorical, and I did not answer. I was reflecting bitterly on something quite different.

In the past it had always been I who had uncovered (when already too late) Atto's lies, and the secret games he had played with my unwitting help.

This was the first time, in the thirty years I had known him, that I had had the honour of hearing Melani confess directly to his own intrigues. It was a sign that the times had changed, I thought, and the old Abbot did not belong to this new age. Atto was the only survivor of a vanished era: his longevity, far from granting him repose and recompense, had condemned him to sip the bitter chalice of defeat and oblivion.

Fate had made a toy of him. Just twenty-four hours before the unwitting Abbot set foot in Vienna, the Turks had arrived and the Emperor had fallen ill. A coincidence? No: this was a slap in the face from destiny. In this new era Atto was simply irrelevant; it made no difference whether he was here or not. In the great fresco of the world, Abbot Melani no longer figured.

I looked with compassion at the poor old man, whose services were no longer required by anyone. He turned his face to me and I thought I saw a grimace of wounded pride, almost as if his eyes had perceived my pity.

"Signor Atto, I truly . . ." I tried to rally him, seeking consolatory phrases, but they just would not come to my lips.

Melani halted me with a dejected wave of his hand, as if to say, "Don't bother." We walked on in silence for a while, arm in arm.

"Now that the Dauphin is also on the point of death, everything is clearer," he said at last. "Something or someone is plotting against both France and the Empire. Something or someone that is above everything, since the Sun King and Joseph the Victorious are mortal adversaries in the war that is tearing Europe to pieces."

"Don't you think that the Dauphin is really sick with smallpox?"

"And do you think the Emperor is?" he snapped back, with bitter sarcasm.

There was no need to say another word. Now that the Grand Dauphin was lying ill, Atto revealed his thoughts: he too had never believed that Joseph the Victorious had smallpox.

"To pass off poison as a contagious disease is child's play: not only the arch-doctor at court, Monsieur de Fagon, but all the other doctors of the royal family are totally without experience of such illnesses," explained Atto, "because as soon as a house is found with smallpox or any other contagion, they are forbidden to go near it, for fear that they might infect a royal prince. Common sense would suggest that in such cases they should consult those doctors in Paris who treat such illnesses daily."

"Maybe they have done."

"They never do," he said with a meaningful smile.

"And so the same thing could have happened at the Caesarean court!" I said, aghast. "The Emperor's doctors might have just as little experience of smallpox as those of the Grand Dauphin."

I had at once suspected that behind Joseph's illness lay the sinister and secret work of the poisoner, but to hear it directly confirmed by Atto's voice sent shivers up my spine.

I could well understand the colic that had seized the poor Abbot two days earlier. It was nothing to do with chocolate from the Connestabilessa! He had collapsed on hearing the news of the Emperor's illness: the worldly-wise old spy had immediately understood that evil powers, as yet unidentified, were at work, and that France, not being among them, was exposed to the same dangers. In certain games – I had learned this myself – if you are not among the killers, then you will undoubtedly end up among the victims.

"Boy," he whispered, suddenly halting and gripping my shoulder, "I was about to succeed, all by myself, in bringing to an end a European war that has raged for eleven years! A group of conspirators, all in league with one another and highly organised, can do much more, and with great ease."

"The Turks!" I exclaimed, and told Atto about the strange machinations of the dervish with Ugonio.

"Ugonio?!?" cried Atto, on hearing the *corpisantaro*'s name.

I explained the circumstances in which I had found him.

"Of course, now I remember; the filthy creature is from Vienna. The world is very small," he concluded, shaking his head almost incredulously. "After all these years I wouldn't mind seeing him again – or rather, meeting him again," he corrected himself sadly, alluding to his blindness.

From Melani's surprised reaction I had the confirmation (if I really needed it after his confession) that he was in the dark about everything. I had got it all wrong: the Abbot could not have known anything about the shady dealings between Ugonio and Ciezeber.

I explained that Cloridia had heard them plotting to get someone's head. The Abbot listened in a tense silence. While I talked I watched him closely, but his black lenses prevented me from fathoming his innermost secrets. I also reminded him of the mysterious phrase pronounced by the Agha before Prince Eugene, and finally I summed up the strange Ottoman legends about the Golden Apple.

"Only one thing puzzles me," I concluded. "What do the Turks have to do with the Grand Dauphin's sickness? The Sublime Porte has always been allied with France . . ."

"That does not matter. What matters is the method."

"What do you mean?"

"The Ottomans, by themselves, would be nothing. Over the centuries, they have always been the military arm of the West, directed against the West itself. Two hundred years ago the King of France, Francis I, suggested to Suleiman the Magnificent that he should attack the Empire in Hungary; the suggestion was taken up, and successfully. In Italy the city of Florence summoned Mehmet II to its aid against Ferdinand I, King of Naples. Venice, to drive the Portuguese, her trading rivals, out of the East, made use of the forces of the Sultan of Egypt. And there are scores of Italian military engineers who have offered their services to the sultans, as long as they were well paid. When Philip II of Spain set out to conquer Portugal, in order to mollify the neighbouring King of Morocco he gave him an estate, thus placing Christian lands in the hands of the Infidels, and he did this with the aim of dispossessing a Catholic king. Even Popes Paul III, Alexander VI and Julius II, when it struck them as opportune, called on Turkish help."

I had heard many of these unedifying examples three decades earlier, in 1683, from the same Abbot Melani. Just one episode was missing from the list, and I could understand why he had omitted it:

in that very year 1683 the Most Christian King had secretly supported the Turks when they threatened Vienna.

"The Ottomans are the ideal instrument. In my long life I have seen many of them, including bandits and malefactors."

I had no difficulty in believing it; who could say how many shady deals Atto had engaged in with the Infidels at the behest of his king . . .

"Some of these bandits had faces enlivened with expressions of brutal passion," Melani went on. "There was no prostration; it is not enough to have a soul, you also have to feel the divine guest's presence to suffer when it declines, to be ashamed, upset and dejected. Christian criminals, thank God, usually bear on their foreheads signs of their struggle, even if a lost one, against their own perversity. Even the air of triumph that sometimes brightens the face of a hardened criminal, is it not a sign of this struggle? Among the Ottomans, however, the criminal is not a man whose character is any different from that of a wise man. The Turkish bandits had a more confident stare than I did as I looked at them. I could not help but see in them men whose nature was different from ours, men who truly did not know the Christian meaning of the words virtue and vice. No Christian is ignorant of the distinction between vice and virtue; anyone who does not understand it is outside Christianity, and indeed outside simple human nature. But from my dealings with Ottomans, I realised unfortunately that in the bosom of a civilisation almost as ancient as the Christian one, but founded on completely different bases, such a phenomenon existed: the man without a conscience!"

Atto's words left me utterly dismayed. I now felt in my body a piercing fear of the Turk, as one dreads a hurricane which destroys people and things but is totally unaware of what it does. As he said, without a conscience. The Abbot was right: the Turks had always been pawns in the hands of the West. Had not Simonis told me that poor Maximilian II, the father of the Place with No Name, had been a victim of the treachery of the Protestant princes, who had incited the Ottoman armies against the Empire? And what had Maximilian's councillor, Ungnad, been up to, if not scuttling between Vienna and Constantinople, manoeuvring the Turks so as to favour the intrigues against the Emperor?

"But precisely because the Ottomans are bloodthirsty people, with an inclination for wars of conquest," I objected, "it's easy to see that they want to invade Europe."

"Bloodthirsty people, with an inclination for war, you say?" asked the Abbot, resuming his walk. "I could tell you things about the Ottoman Empire that you don't even imagine, and which would change your mind at once. Do you know what the derebeys are?"

"The dere-what?"

Like all empires, Atto explained, the Ottoman Empire was based on a feudal system. The Grand Sultan, absolute Sovereign, was represented in the provinces by a network of rulers, who were, however, far from loyal: the derebeys.

"They are restless, ferocious lords, forever in revolt against the Sultan. They seize control of the collecting of taxes, which are supposed to be paid to the Sultan; they refuse to respond to the central government's conscription call, instead enlisting troops for their own personal armies; they have their own standards and wear their own uniforms; and they often go to war against the Sultan himself."

Almost all of Asia Minor was subdivided among a small number of such derebeys. Not to mention the mountain territories, Atto went on, where again nobody answered the conscription calls.

"In the Giaur-Daghda not a single mountain dweller wears the uniform or pays a single para, which is the fortieth of a piastra, to the Sultan's treasury."

Whenever the Sultan tried to reduce them to obedience, the inhabitants of the valleys would all flee to the mountains, leaving the enemy army to wander over their abandoned lands, or they would pour out *en masse* to confront the Sultan's men, twenty-five thousand mountaineers against a thousand soldiers, which was enough to put an end to hostilities and re-establish peace with Constantinople. At least until the next recruiting drive or the next tax collection, when the war would inevitably start up all over again.

"The Ottoman empire has many such peoples. This shows how absurd it is to claim that the Turks are ready to invade the neighbouring nations. The very opposite is true: they have huge internal problems, which would make any act of external war highly inadvisable. The desire to expand at all costs into Europe, as they have done, threatening Vienna, Venice or Hungary, while just a few miles from Constantinople their empire is wholly ungovernable, means that their main aim is not the preservation of the Ottoman Empire, but the destruction of those faithful to Christ and their lands."

"But don't you think that is inevitable? They're different from us, incompatible by birth with the Christian religion."

"That isn't true either. Countless Christians live in Constantinople and carry on their trades there freely. But I'll go even further. Suleiman the Magnificent, like his predecessors, chose the highest ranks of the Ottoman state from the *devsirme*, the so-called 'harvest': the nursery of fifteen thousand Christian children who were kidnapped every year on his orders in Rumelia, the European part of the Ottoman Empire, for example in Hungary. These children were then brought up in Constantinople, because he secretly believed they were more intelligent than the Turks."

From this "harvest" they then chose the ones who would join the janissaries, the elite and highly trained army corps. The janissaries were therefore all Christians by birth, and had not a drop of Turkish blood, also because originally they were obliged to remain celibate, and so had no offspring: year by year the old members were replaced by kidnapping new children. When they arrived in the territories of the Muslim empire, the children were carefully studied from a physiognomical point of view: depending on their facial features, which revealed this or that inclination, they were sent to serve in the Sultan's private palace, in the state administration or in the army, among the janissaries.

"But I imagine that the highest-ranking dignitaries, the ones closest to the Sultan, were Turkish," I objected.

"On the contrary. The Grand Vizier, or the prime minister, subordinate in authority only to the Sultan, has hardly ever been Turkish, and not even Muslim. Of the forty-seven Grand Viziers who succeeded to the Porte between 1453 and 1623 only five were of Turkish origin: the others included eleven Albanians, six Greeks, a Circassian, an Armenian, a Georgian, ten Chaldeans and even an Italian. And Ibrahim Pasha, the famous Grand Vizier of Suleiman the Magnificent, was not Turkish but Venetian."

"Venetian?"

"Certainly! He was born in the territories of the Venetian Republic. That is why I say: the destructive power of Mahomet in reality does not exist, it is a creation of the West, turned against the West itself."

These words made me thoughtful: Atto's explanations tallied with what Simonis had told me about Maximilian and his struggle against Suleiman the Magnificent. Had not the fire of Ottoman aggression against the Empire, according to my assistant, been lit by the German Protestant princes and their secret emissaries, Ilsung, Ungnad and Hag? After seeking in vain to convert Maximilian to Lutheranism, they had taken their revenge by unleashing the Turkish armies against him.

"But the financiers of the siege that Suleiman laid against Vienna in 1529 were from Constantinople," I objected.

"And where do you think they came from, if not from Europe? Families of merchants who had moved to Constantinople for the greater freedom they could enjoy there in trading. There have never been any Turks so rich that they could choose to bleed themselves dry for the sole pleasure of seeing the Sultan take up arms against the Holy Roman Empire."

I was surprised. It was hard for me to think that beneath the Turkish turbans, the distinctive mark of Mahomet's fearsome followers, more Christians were concealed than Turks.

"With Joseph and the Grand Dauphin," Atto went on, "we are faced with two assassination attempts in which the victims are fortunately still alive. To solve the case, we must presume the instigator is someone manipulating the Turks and capable of striking at the highest level. But who?"

The Abbot now indicated that he was tired. I suggested returning to the Golden Eagle.

"Better to rest here, by the side of the road," he answered.

The old spy was forever afraid of eavesdroppers, I thought. I led him to a staircase leading up to a small building set back from the road, which appeared to have been closed for years. I cleaned the dust and dirt from the steps as best I could and helped the Abbot to sit down.

There are a thousand people who might desire these deaths, Atto continued in a low voice, each one for a different motive.

"The maritime powers, Holland and England, are interested in weakening the two greatest contenders in the conflict, the Empire and France, to prevent whichever of them wins the war from gaining a position of supremacy. If the anti-French alliance won the conflict, and Joseph's brother Charles ascended to the throne, the Habsburgs would hold Europe in a vice-like grip from east to west, from Vienna to Madrid, becoming far too powerful a giant."

"That's exactly what the English and Dutch want to stop France from becoming," I remarked.

"Precisely, and you don't change your mind after eleven years of war. Now they have almost reached their objective: to make France powerless. The country is already on its knees financially. In addition, the grandson of the Most Christian King has not proved as pliant to his grandfather's wishes as was feared. It is rumoured that he is even thinking of proclaiming a formal renunciation of the throne of France, just to finish the war. There is only one last step: to deprive the Most Christian King of an heir who might disturb their plans to weaken France."

"How could the Grand Dauphin disturb them?" I said in surprise. "From the gazettes it's clear that he doesn't have his father's strong temperament."

"That is all outward show, as with his mother, the deceased Queen Maria Theresa of Habsburg – may the glory of God be upon her. He is a man of few words and has made it clear that he has no wish to interfere in political and military matters. But it is not from want of experience, but rather on account of the great respect and deference he has for His Majesty. France and the whole of Europe would suffer a great loss if the Grand Dauphin were to die, because if he ever becomes king, his reign will be a golden century for his own people and for those of other states: "For, unlike his father," and here the Abbot pronounced his words very carefully, "ambition would not lead him into any enterprise prejudicial to the general peace, as he is a prince of justice, of prudence and fairness, full of humanity and charity towards the poor."

"And why should such a good, peace-loving sovereign be a source of trouble for the maritime powers?"

"The power of Holland and England is based on large-scale commerce throughout the world, which makes its greatest profits through war."

"I thought war was the ruin of commercial transactions."

"Small transactions, certainly. But large-scale trafficking thrives on the weakening of nations. The Lord God gave man the possibility to live on an earth fecund with fruits. But when the fields are made barren by the raids, fires and ravages of war, the people fall into the hands of speculators and usurers, who make them pay for their goods fifty times what they are worth! Peasants can no longer rely on the efforts and skill of their own hands to survive; they need money, a great deal of money, to buy for its weight in gold what in peacetime they used to produce for themselves with no difficulty. Without money one can no longer do anything, even in the remotest village. You don't know how many have grown immensely rich thanks to war! Take the Thirty Years' War, which broke out under a century ago. The usurers of then are the powerful of today. And when it was kings that incurred debts, those vultures were even rewarded with noble titles."

From a wily and unscrupulous castrato to a moralising old codger: what changes life can bring about, I reflected while Atto talked. Now the Abbot was even railing against the aristocracy. His arguments were quite different from those I had heard from him twenty-eight years ago; they almost sounded like the grumblings of my late father-in-law, who had been a Jansenist.

"With a king like the Grand Dauphin," Melani went on, "France would finally emerge from its downward spiral of arrogance and destruction; England and Holland want the opposite to happen. The country must continue to degenerate, the court must be hated by the people. It annoys them that the Most Christian King has adult sons and grandsons; the ideal would be if there were no heir, or if he were a baby, which amounts to the same thing. It would not be like the days when the Most Christian King ascended the throne, aged just four: then there were the Queen Mother, Anne of Austria and the Prime Minister, Cardinal Richelieu and later Cardinal Mazarin, who defended the country from any interference by other potentates. Now there is no longer a queen, nor a prime minister. Louis XIV has taken everything into his own hands. After his death a regency would leave the country at the mercy of the first scheming meddler, who might just happen to be sent by England or Holland to set off a mine under France's backside."

But there was more to it than that, continued Atto:

"There has been a rumour going round since February that Joseph I is thinking of proposing to France that Spain should be divided, so as to leave his brother Charles at least with Catalonia and its capital Barcelona."

"Really? That would solve the Spanish question."

"Quite. But you know what it would really mean? That the two major contenders, France and the Empire, would lead the peace process, and the destiny of Europe would remain in their hands, as has been the case for centuries. This is just what England and Holland do not want: the commercial powers are planning to sweep away the old world order and create a new one under their auspices. No, France and the Empire must not make peace, it must be imposed on them. On conditions set by England, above all, and Holland."

"So you think that Joseph I is not going to find favour with England and Holland, no matter what he does."

"Exactly. War or peace, the Empire, France and Spain must no longer be arbiters of their own destiny. The English and Dutch want an end to national sovereignties. That's why they entered the war, and why they cannot wait to carve up the possessions of the Spanish Crown in the New World. A rich, boundless, virgin land, with no law or morality: sharp-eyed merchants as they have always been, they know perfectly well that whoever dominates it will rule the world. And they have no intention of leaving it to the Spanish, French or Germans."

"So you say it's for these reasons," I summed up at the end of Atto's harangue, "that the two maritime powers are plotting against His Caesarean Majesty."

"It's a possibility. But it's not the only one."

There was a second hypothesis: a motive within the Empire.

"You know that Charles and Joseph detest each other," said Atto. "They have always done so, ever since their father set them against each other, favouring the younger over the elder. Nature made them different, the family made them enemies. And ever since Joseph became emperor, Charles has hated him even more profoundly, he himself being forced to fight for his throne."

If Joseph were to die, Charles would lose an uncertain crown, that of Spain, for one that was perfectly secure and far superior: that of Emperor, in Vienna.

"Joseph has only two daughters; his only son died as a child. If he died, Charles would succeed him. Does that not strike you as a slight motive for murder?"

But that was not all. During his short life, Joseph had left a formidable trail of hatred and envy.

"The Jesuits hate him: when he ascended the throne he at once excluded them from government, and was quite brusque about it. You may have heard about the threatening remarks a Jesuit made to Joseph as soon as he ascended the throne, and Joseph had him expelled. But his father's old ministers also hate him: even as a boy Joseph fought them mercilessly, until he finally became emperor and drove them all out. All except one. But he hates Joseph too."

I knew who we were talking about.

"Signor Abbot, you have already shown me a letter from Prince Eugene, and it was forged."

"Yes, but everything else I told you – about Landau, Eugene, his jealousy of the Emperor, his fear of being cast aside when the war finishes – is true."

"And if Joseph really comes to an agreement with France to carve up Spain, leaving his brother Charles with Catalonia, there will be peace."

"Exactly. And there's no way that Eugene can make the young but inflexible emperor change his mind. And so our prince, at the age of forty-eight, will have to submit to the decisive temperament of an emperor aged just thirty-three. If he is really implicated in the poisoning of His Caesarean Majesty, I have to admit that he has made his calculations very carefully: unlike Joseph, Charles has a weak character and will not stop him from pursuing the war, even without the support of England and Holland. And when this one dies down, there will always be another one. One war is as good as another for Prince Eugene; he will always need a war from which he can reap honours and power, at least until he retires from old age. But it's a game that Joseph will no longer tolerate."

"True," I agreed, "the Emperor is making peace with everyone, even with the Pope, who is on the French side."

"Quite. Believe me for once, now that I've even confessed the truth about that letter. The moment has come for everyone to show their cards."

"I've always done that with you."

"Yes, *you* have. But Eugene is one who does not know what a straight line is. He is twisted, oblique, sinuous. Like all those of his race."

"What race?"

He rolled his eyes to heaven, as if entreating the Most High to grant him the strength to keep quiet.

"It doesn't matter," he said evasively. "What I am anxious to make you realise is that Eugene's military envy – which is all one with his craving for glory and power – is a real scourge. It was born long before him, and will die after the last soldier."

"But one doesn't kill out of military envy, least of all one's own sovereign!" I protested.

"It's obvious you know no history. I could give you scores of examples, starting with ancient Athens, where this unhealthy and underhand passion has led to the best commanders of the fleet being put to death unjustly," said the Abbot, lifting the palm of his hand to emphasise the great worth of these captains. "It brought the city to defeat in the Peloponnese War, it led to the destruction of the walls of the Piraeus and finally to ruin."

At that moment a group of passers-by, seeing Atto's outstretched hand and his blind man's glasses, took my working clothes for those of a beggar and casually tossed us a coin.

"What was that?" asked Melani, at the tinkling sound.

"Nothing. A few coins slipped out of my pocket," I lied in embarrassment.

"What was I saying? Ah yes. Mind, we are only making conjectures to identify which of the various suspects is really plotting against the Emperor: to work out whether it's England and Holland, or Charles, or the Jesuits, or the old ministers, or Eugene. As for military envy, leaving aside the numerous *exempla* from history, I would rather talk to you about a case closer to our own days: Count Marsili. Do you remember?"

It was odd that Atto should mention Marsili. Just a few hours earlier I had been reading of his feats until interrupted by my assistant's knock at the door.

"Of course I remember," I answered. "The Italian who suggested the winning strategy to Joseph, denouncing the errors of Margrave Louis of Baden."

"Exactly. The continuation of that story will make you realise what role military envy might be playing in Joseph's fatal disease: since it – envy, that is – almost always kills."

A few years before the siege of Landau, narrated Atto, Marsili had taken part in the siege to free Belgrade from Turkish occupation.

There the first incident took place. General Guido Starhemberg, in order to impose his own personal strategy, caused grave loss of life among the imperial troops. The 59th Infantry Regiment was almost wiped out. For too long now the imperials had been wearing themselves out pointlessly around the fortress. Marsili openly criticised Starhemberg's strategy, even though the latter was superior to him in rank. And Marsili did not spare his subordinates either: he demanded swiftness, discipline, parsimony in expenses (quite a few officers took advantage of the availability of military money to pocket a few "tips"). He had one of his lieutenant-colonels locked up for insubordination;

this man then denounced him for tyranny and had him removed from the service. Only at the end of the conflict did he obtain justice.

"In battle Count Marsili had always demanded fidelity, honesty and courage from every soldier. But he courageously denounced his superiors if they made mistakes that cost human lives."

"Bold," I remarked.

"And very dangerous. Fortunately, his enemies could do little or nothing against such a valuable officer: no one knew the territories where the war against the Turks was being fought as well as he did."

With the capture of Landau the military star of Joseph the Victorious was in the ascendant, continued Abbot Melani. It was before him that the French garrison laid down their arms, but a good share of the glory fell upon Marsili. By now he was considered the greatest expert in fortifications and sieges in the Caesarean camp. He knew the secrets of every military school, be it French, German or Italian. He had even won the sympathy of the troops, whom he had treated so strictly, and that of his fellow officers, who recognised his loyalty and impartiality. Because dishonesty, like ignorance, is an offence to the nobility of war.

But the Margrave of Baden foamed with rage at the way Marsili had denounced his shortcomings directly to the King of the Romans. This Italian had not only shamed him, but was also insufferably cultivated, honest and virtuous. Just who did he think he was?

The Margrave soon found a way to avenge himself. In December that same year, 1702, the French were threatening the Austrian fort of Brisach on the Rhine, vital for control over Breisgau. The Prince ordered Marsili to go to Brisach to help another Italian, Marshal Dell'Arco, in case this latter (a strange and equivocal excuse) should fall ill. The Margrave of Baden knew perfectly well that Marsili and Dell'Arco were on very bad terms, and that together they would achieve very little.

There were 24,000 French besiegers. The Brisach garrison had only 3,500 men, Marsili was told; in fact they were even fewer. He found ill-armed men, half-broken cannons, no sappers or miners (indispensable for the defence of a fortified place), and not even any water in the moats to keep the besiegers out. He wrote at once to the Margrave of Baden that the situation was desperate, but received no answer. So he set about strengthening the fortifications, but at once quarrels arose with Dell'Arco, and shortly afterwards Marsili was put under arrest for six weeks. Money ran out, and the troops, who were no longer being paid, complained. So he tried to obtain a loan on the nearby market of Freiburg; the attempt failed, and consequently he had a lead coin struck on the field, which was distributed to the soldiers. Marsili guaranteed it with his own personal property.

"Just as Melac, the French commander of Landau, did!" I interjected.

"As every true commander will and must do in such situations," replied Atto gravely. "That also explains why officers must belong to noble and wealthy families: nobility can reach where others cannot."

It was the second half of August 1703. The resistance of the small garrison was heroic, but the French were gaining the upper hand, thanks to the leadership of the Duke of Bourgogne and above all that of Marshal Vauban, the Sun King's great military engineer.

"The one who had fortified Landau?"

"The very same. And he had fortified Brisach too, when it was under French control, and knew it like the back of his hands."

The imperial officers had lost all hope now, but Marsili was unflagging: with his own hands he fixed the artillery pieces, designed mines and barriers and kept all those who still wanted to fight close about him. Dell'Arco summoned a war council; the officers no longer hoped for any relief and decided unanimously to surrender. Only Marsili was determined to preserve their honour. The French must grant his garrison military honours – he thundered in front of the other officers – a drum roll and flying colours. Everyone must know that Brisach had been lost with honour. On 8th September 1703 the imperial troops, exhausted, filthy and bleeding, left their fortress, parading with heads held high, while the French stared in disbelief: was it really this handful of scarecrows that had pinned them down for all these months? Someone whispered to the conquerors that the true soul of these wild men was Marsili, who was just as ragged and weary as all the others, but whose reddened eyes gleamed with the rage of defeat; it was clear that he would have fought on and on, if he had only had the right companions, curse it! Because cowardice, like ignorance, is an offence to the nobility of war.

But the worst was yet to come. Released with the other officers, he rejoined the ranks of the imperials, and at once the war tribunal was convened.

"The war tribunal?" I said in surprise. "Why?"

"Dell'Arco, Marsili and the other officers were indicted for having surrendered."

"But what else could they have done? They were a tenth the number of the French."

"Listen."

Very swiftly, on 15th February, the sentences were issued: Dell'Arco was to be beheaded, Marsili to lose his rank and military honour. Three days later, Dell'Arco was executed at Bregenz, in the public square, like an ordinary criminal. Marsili had his sabre symbolically broken. He survived, but was forever dishonoured. The crowd's rage, and above all the Margrave of Baden's desire for revenge, were placated: it was no accident that the other officers had their sentences suspended.

It was then and only then that Marsili – the courageous Marsili, who, after enduring hellish imprisonment on the Turkish field, after being tortured and wounded, after dragging his bleeding body to Bologna, had desired above all else to return and serve his emperor; Marsili, who had never bowed his head before the envy, malice and meanness of his fellow soldiers; Marsili, who had won on the field the esteem and gratitude of the King of the Romans, the future Joseph I; Marsili, the scholar and scientist, the Bolognese nobleman who could talk on easy terms with the common soldiery; he who, every evening, wore his fingers away counting the dead that day, while the other officers drank and laughed and gambled away the money stolen from the garrison's funds – it was then and only then that Marsili understood: all that had been needed to annihilate him, the man who had kept tens of thousands of French troops in check, was the envy of one man, one on his own side: the Margrave of Baden.

"Oh, military jealousy, what horrors you are capable of!" exclaimed Atto mournfully. "Oh, soldier's envy, how atrocious your crimes are! Oh, officer's rancour, how shameful your wicked actions, all craven, all secret, all perfect! How many unwitting combatants have you sent to death by deceit? How many courageous captains have you locked up in military prisons, replacing them with idlers and cowards? How many sergeants have you slaughtered treacherously in the ditches of Lombardy, in the snow of Bavaria, in the cold ford of a Hungarian river, so that you might hang on their rivals' breasts the medal of infamy? The Margrave of Baden is not the real criminal. It is you, military jealousy, the faceless monster that broke the career and life of Count Luigi Ferdinando Marsili, dishonouring him and turning him into a renegade. You are the monster that kills by shooting in the back, that vilifies the upright, promotes the inept, detains provisions, provides incorrect information about the enemy, sends faulty weapons to the front, denies relief to the besieged, reports lies to headquarters. And so, battle after battle, war after war, you crush the valiant to the ground, devouring their spoils, while you fondly prop up the weak shoulders of the spiteful, the petty and the cowardly: they invoke you and with your aid they seek the ruin of the good."

Atto fell silent. The old castrato had, of course, never fought, but his voice vibrated with the contempt of one who had understood all the cruelty of war. Questions were already rushing to my lips.

"You said Marsili is a renegade. Why?"

"That's what they called him, because later he commanded the Pope's army, even though at the trial of Bregenz he had sworn he would never fight on the same side as the enemies of the Emperor. But the oath had been extorted from him by force: how could it be considered valid? And he said yes to the Pope because he was from Bologna, and therefore a subject of the Pope. The French and the Dutch had offered him a post as general, but he had refused to fight for those enemies that had killed so many of his comrades. Despite this, His Most Christian Majesty invited him to Paris and presented him at court with all honours: 'Count Marsili, who served the House of Austria for so long and who was so unjustly degraded over the question of Brisach; how grave this injustice is, I know all too well.'"

My cheeks had flushed with anger, pity and compassion on hearing Marsili's absurd and cruel fate. Was that how his loyalty to the Empire was rewarded?

Abbot Melani, meanwhile, was struggling up from our improvised seat. His legs were stiff. I handed him his stick and helped him to his feet.

"But, Signor Atto," I objected while we resumed our slow stroll, "you attribute to the Most Serene Prince of Savoy the same base passions as the Margrave of Baden. But so far, apart from a forged letter, you haven't been able to produce anything more than suppositions. Even the coin of Landau, which Eugene held in his hand during the audience with the Agha, well, what does it prove? Nothing. Couldn't it be that it reminds the Prince of his beloved sovereign's most beautiful personal victory rather than an affront to his own reputation as a soldier? Everyone knows with what exemplary fidelity Eugene has served the Empire so far. He might be frustrated at having been overshadowed twice at Landau, and at not being able to go and fight in Spain because of Joseph's opposition, but you must admit it's very difficult to believe that the Prince of Savoy is conspiring against the life of his sovereign out of military jealousy or from fear that peace will deprive him of his power."

"It's not only ancient history that you don't know, but also the race of those like Eugene."

"Oh come on now," I protested, "you referred earlier to this presumed race. Why don't you speak clearly for once?"

"Oof! I didn't want to face this question. But since the stakes are so high, may God forgive me . . . It's only fair that you should know. Besides it is not our fault if Eugene is a . . . how can I put it?" he hesitated.

I stayed silent, waiting for the word.

"A woman-man," he said at last with a slight sigh, as if a weight had been lifted from his shoulders.

"A woman-man?" I said in amazement. "You mean that he too . . . that they've cut . . . I mean . . ."

"No, no! What are you thinking of?" exclaimed Atto. "He . . . he loves men!"

His irritation at my misapprehension had finally given the Abbot the gift of clarity. He was telling me that the Most Serene Prince Eugene of Savoy was a sodomite.

"The minister of war? The most valiant general in the Austrian army?"

"Here in Austria this matter has been kept more or less secret," he went on, "but in Paris everyone knows it."

"You're lying," I tried to argue back. "Eugene of Savoy may be ambitious, as you say, envious of his Emperor, but not a . . ."

Then I too hesitated. Standing in front of me was Atto Melani, famous castrato. A poor unsexed being, robbed of his virility by the cruel choice of his parents. After his early youth, in which he had been a successful singer, he had undoubtedly known the shame of sodomy, the sorrow of mockery, isolation, loneliness and sadness.

He must have understood my embarrassment at once, and he spared me, going straight on with his explanation.

As Atto had hinted the first time he had spoken of it, Eugene's youth had been a disaster. He had grown up at the Hôtel de Soissons, the Parisian residence of his paternal family, a splendid building where there was no shortage of comforts, amusements and games. But his parents had left him to vegetate amid governesses and nurses, without providing any upbringing, attention or love. His mother was a famous schemer, obsessed with court intrigues and the power games at Versailles, a suspected poisoner who had eventually been banished from the kingdom on this account. She certainly had no time to waste on little Eugene, the last of her many children. His father was too weak a character to make up for his consort's errors, and in any case he had died prematurely (she was, indeed, suspected of having poisoned him). The boy grew up under the influence of his older brothers and sisters and other debauched young aristocrats, all arrogant and spoilt, with no guide to teach them any authority or decorum. The children thought they could do anything, and indeed nothing was every forbidden them. Instead of teachers and preceptors, all they had were footmen and butlers. There was no such thing as study: just playthings, toys and games. They knew no limits, no fear of God.

"If the nurses and house tutors dared to remind them that they must not break a certain object, or that a certain game might be dangerous, or that certain words were contrary to the dignity of good families, they were merely derided, mocked, insulted and even spat upon," said Atto.

After their early years as thoughtless hooligans, Eugene and the young reprobates entered puberty. Everything was transformed; mischief and playfulness were tinged with quite different colours.

"The handsome lads began to lust after the beautiful girls, and the girls to look for their equals," explained Abbot Melani.

With the same unreasoning wildness of their early years, they now played quite different games. Their bodies no longer thrilled over a stolen toy, a lunge too far with a wooden sword or a foolish prank, but for quite different things. Their mouths, which had till then been used for singing and talking, now also knew how to kiss. Idleness fuelled the flames.

And so, whereas previously the humble servants had tried to prevent the children from coming into contact with each other lest they should get hurt, now, when there was contact, they preferred to turn their backs and leave them to it, because they did not have the right words (and above all the courage) to prevent the little princes and princesses from giving and taking what they wanted.

The games were for two, but also three or four. There was always an audience; the onlookers and participants were always ready to change places. To ensure a greater variety of games, the couplings were free, and knew no limits of gender or of position. The days were long, their energies still wild, and their scruples non-existent.

"Boredom due to excessive wealth often leads down strange paths, and I hardly need go into details. These are things we all know. By hearsay, of course," clarified Atto, in a grave tone.

When it was cold, they played their games at home. All they required was a curtain, a dark corner, a space under the stairs, and satisfaction was guaranteed for two or more, as the case might be, without standing on ceremony. If there were women, fine. Otherwise they managed without.

"And it's absurd for the French to call this thing 'the Italian vice'," said Abbot Melani, suddenly growing heated. "It's the same hypocrisy the Italians use when they call syphilis 'the French sickness': a stupid attempt to pass off one's own failings on another. Let us be clear about it: is not France the homeland of that vice? The race of women-men was born there, in the land of Vercingetorix. Do not the French symbolise their homeland with a cock? Well then, I say, what creature better reflects the foolish, overblown arrogance of the French sodomites?"

He had turned indignant, had Abbot Melani, against France and its inverts: he, a naturalised Frenchman and an invert by castration (but I well knew that a woman had been, and was still, the love of his whole life). It was as if in old age Atto suddenly detested all that had been precious to him throughout his life: the kingdom of Louis XIV, who had made him rich and influential, and his castration, which had opened to him the doors of opera and the great world (Atto had been born the son of a poor bell-ringer). The greatest slanderers of sodomites, I thought, are the sodomites themselves, who know their innermost nature better than anyone.

At that point he began to reel off the golden book of the pansies of France, as if he had been waiting for this opportunity for years:

"Everyone knows about Henry III of Valois. But we also know every detail of Louis XIII, father of His Most Christian Majesty. Gaston d'Orléans, His Majesty's uncle, had the same vice. Monsieur, His Majesty's brother, was a collector of *mignons*, or of little boys."

I was speechless. Grandfathers, uncles, brothers: the Most Christian King of France, according to Atto, was surrounded by perverts.

He went on to list a series of characters; all, he claimed, well known in France: the Gran Condé, the Cavalier of Lorraine, Guiche, d'Effiat, Manicamp, Châtillon . . . And many relatives of Eugene: his elder brother Philippe, his two cousins Ludovique and Philippe Vendôme, the Prince of Turenne and the young François Louis de la Roche-sur-Yon, recited Atto, leaving me free to imagine that sodomy went hand in hand with incest.

All those noble names were forever engaged in an obscene ballet of ephebic and virile love affairs, in defiance of nature, religion and decency. They were mad nights, those of the Parisian debauchers, sleepless nights scented with the oils they rubbed all over their bodies before lying down together, nights spent choosing this or that feminine garment, trying on skirts, bracelets and earrings in front of the mirror . . .

" 'The Italian vice' they call it!" he repeated, as if this were what most enraged him. "In what Italian court will you find such foul frenzies? Indeed, in what European court? In England there have been just two cases, both well known: Edward II Plantagenet and William III of Orange, who was Dutch. But the former descended directly from the beautiful and depraved Eleanor of Aquitaine, and the latter's maternal grandmother was Henriette of France, sister of Louis XIII. Exceptions, therefore, in which French blood prevailed. But at the court of France, when you try to draw up a list of the depraved, you always end up losing count. Madame Palatina was right when she said that nowadays the only ones who love women are men of the lowest ranks! And there is no point in making subtle distinctions, as the Parisians do, between the effeminate and the sodomites. In mud, water and earth become a single thing."

While Atto inveighed in this fashion, I found myself reeling from shock after shock: even William of Orange, the *condottiero* whose feats I had learned of during my first adventure with Atto, almost three decades earlier, had belonged to the race of women-men!

In Paris, about forty years earlier, his story proceeded, the Cavalier of Lorraine, a well-known sodomite, and his worthy friends Tallard and Biran had founded nothing less than a secret sect of unnatural love. The members vowed never to touch women again – not even their wives, if they were married. The new initiates agreed to be "visited" by the four Grand Masters who ruled over the confraternity, and they swore an oath of secrecy about both the sect and its "rituals".

The coterie was so successful that it attracted new candidates almost daily, even of illustrious name. For example the Count of Vermandois, illegitimate son of Louis XIV and of Madame La Vallière, who had the privilege of choosing which of the four Grand Masters would "visit" him.

"The other three took it badly, because Vermandois was really very good-looking," said Atto with a touch of embarrassment in his voice, which betrayed the involuntary preferences cultivated by the young castrato many years earlier.

While Atto talked, I gradually saw more deeply into his innermost self. And I perceived the relief with which the Abbot was living the last stage of his life: decrepitude. He was now finally free from the effects of the mutilation that had precluded him from enjoying the love of women. Extreme old age, which extinguishes all carnal fire, had buried all traces of effeminacy amid the castrato's wrinkles, just as it had sapped the virility of his contemporaries. Even the white lead of his face, the carmine and the moles on his cheeks were not as exaggerated as in former days; the Abbot applied them now as did all gentlemen. And he was no longer bedecked with tassels or red and yellow ribbons: Melani always wore dark clothes, as befitted an elderly man.

At the ripe age of eighty-five, in short, Atto was a little old man just like so many others. And he was savouring the pleasure of finally railing against the woman-man he had once been.

"So you say that the father, uncle, brother and a son of His Majesty the King of France are notorious inverts . . ." I said, almost incredulous.

"Exactly. For years his brother went from one boy to another, and the King pretended not to notice. As if it were perfectly normal for him, too."

The question was in the air now. Atto anticipated it:

"Well," he said in a grave voice, "with regard to His Majesty, may God forgive me, similar abominations have also been whispered. But they were just attempts to convert him – sorry, to pervert him. They did not succeed, fortunately."

Sodomy, observed Atto, is the direct offspring of beauty: was it not born in ancient Greece, when philosophers considered the company of young men sublime, because they were even more beautiful than maidens? Well then, amid that whirl of forbidden games, secret passions and unmentionable experiments into which the whole of Paris had flung itself, Eugene always found himself alone: he was ugly.

It was that time of life when young people blossom: their eyes open, their lips become tumid, their breasts plump and firm, their shoulders robust, girls' hips grow round and those of boys solid. Poetry becomes flesh, and seeks other flesh.

Eugene's face, which had never been attractive, opened out like a piece of dried, cracked mud. His nose turned up, while his mouth sagged; his cheeks, neck and body wizened like an old biscuit; his eyes, instead of tapering, remained round and dark. His hair, amid all his friends' soft fair curls, remained flat, lifeless and corvine. And lastly he was small: the puniest of the whole gang.

"Have you ever seen Eugene close up?" asked Abbot Melani.

"No. Cloridia told me that his face is a little strange, not very attractive."

"Not very attractive, you say? As a boy his nose was so short that his two upper fore-teeth were always uncovered, like a rabbit's. He always huffs through his open lips, because he can't close them."

When Eugene's transformation was complete, a new name was ready for him. With that misshapen face, he now became Dog Nose to his friends.

And it was a double humiliation that they inflicted on him, when they took advantage of his lack of strength and sodomised him in the kitchen or on the service stairs, with the serving women pretending not to see; they would then run away, mocking him with that atrocious nickname. He too had joined the race of women-men.

"Look carefully at the portraits of Eugene you see around the place. Yes, they've flattered him. The eyes aren't his, nor the nose or the mouth. But the painters and engravers knew nothing of his vice, and that's why they made no attempt to eliminate that look of a hysterical old hen: the raised eyebrows, the disgusted expression, the over-rigid, upright bust. All typical marks of the invert," said Abbot Melani with a note of ostentatious disgust.

"As is the often the case with inverts, his character, torn between guilt and shame, grew duplicitous like that of a woman. He learned the feminine arts of dissimulation, oblique language and allusion. He is sullen and harbours grudges for ages. You yourself have had a clear demonstration of this: the old coin from the siege of Landau. He must have procured it from one of the participants at the siege, since he had to leave the field free for Joseph, and did not take part in the final assault. He preserves it secretly like a dagger steeped in poison: it reminds him of the day when military laurels were snatched from him by the young Joseph. An isolated event, but still a sign that his glory as a general is fragile and subject to the whim, but even more to the worth, of his sovereign."

I listened in astonishment and thought: Eugene, the castigator of the Turks at Zenta; Eugene, the conqueror of Northern Italy; Eugene, the victor of the massacre of Höchstädt . . . What abyss of vice and perdition had spawned the greatest man of arms in Europe? I now understood why days earlier, during our first conversation, Atto had let slip the cruel name, Dog Nose, which Eugene's companions had saddled him with: the Abbot never lost sight of the dark past of the Most Serene Prince of Savoy.

"To save our hero from bad company, as I have already told you, it was decided he should be launched on an ecclesiastic career: on a trip to Turin, his mother had him receive the priest's tonsure."

It was the official act of renunciation of the world and of all earthly passions. But when Dog Nose returned to Paris and saw his friends again, he fell into his old ways. The planned ecclesiastic career was abandoned?

"In that period he earned new nicknames," said Atto with a malicious little smile, "all very witty: Madame Simone, or Madame L'Ancienne, which is to say, Madam the Elderly – perhaps because, when he dressed up in female clothes, his wrinkled face made him look like a little old woman."

"He dressed up in female clothes?" I stammered.

"Of course! Don't you remember what I said a few days ago? Even when he escaped from France to come and place himself at the service of the Empire he disguised himself in female clothes," sneered Atto. "His mother and his aunt, too, when they fled from Rome to abandon their husbands, dressed up as young men. But a woman dressed as a man is by no means as twisted and ridiculous as a man in petticoats."

"I don't understand. If Eugene really is effeminate, how do you explain that he became the great general that he now is? War isn't for sissies. The Prince has fought the toughest and bloodiest of campaigns, he's been in the thick of assaults, gunfire and cavalry charges. He's led sieges, attacks, retreats . . ."

There's nothing surprising, answered Atto, about a famous general belonging to the race of women-men. There have been scores of them among the great French military leaders: Turenne, Vendôme, Huxelle, Condé and many others. In these cases, the soldier's manly virtue was deliberately transformed into that kind of coarseness that loves to treat men as women, because it is only in them (in their beards, in their muscles, in their stench) that they find their own rough inspiration reciprocated and satisfied. The Marshal of Vendôme, a descendant of King Henry IV of France and a war hero, was an inveterate drinker and smoker, a filthy overbearing braggart, who shared his bed with his dogs and thought nothing of pissing in it. Even as he talked and gave orders to his subordinates he would calmly defecate in a bucket, and then, after passing it in front of his adjutants' noses, he would empty it and use it to shave. The hardships and atrocities of war were perfectly in keeping with his bestial nature. Such men became lovers of men precisely because they were soldiers. Eugene's case was quite different, however.

"Dog Nose is not depraved because he's a soldier. On the contrary: he became a soldier because he's depraved."

Then he cleared his throat, as if his very vocal chords were reluctant to tackle such a difficult argument.

"He is one of those sodomites who have not freely chosen their wretched condition. Had he been able, he would willingly have avoided being effeminate. But something, while he was still at a tender age, threw Eugene unceremoniously into the ranks of women-men."

Now the Abbot was finding it hard to talk. Until now, from the height of his eighty-five years, he had chosen to forget that he himself had been of that unfortunate stock. However, now that he had to talk of the carnal violence that Eugene had been subjected to as a child, he could dissimulate no longer: such acts were all too similar to the painful castration that had been inflicted on Atto Melani's childish flesh. And the memory made his voice tremble.

On the brink of twenty, Dog Nose felt useless, dirty and empty. His siblings and his youthful companions had derided, humiliated and raped him. These people, the only friends he had in the world, loved to abuse him because he was the smallest and ugliest in the whole group. To escape this condition, Dog Nose had only one option: to turn things on their head. He came from the lowest perversion: to save himself, he had to switch to the greatest virtue. The hardest and most dangerous.

"He stopped dressing up as a woman and dressed up as a soldier instead. In that way he would become someone else, someone he probably would rather not have been, but he was forced into the role, in order to cease being Dog Nose or Madame l'Ancienne. So he couldn't take religious vows? Then he would take military ones: Dog Nose became a Priest of War."

He asked Louis XIV for the command of a regiment. The King, who despised him, refused. And so Eugene fled from France and went over to the enemy. He placed himself at the service of the Empire, where he obtained the command and soldiers he desired. From that moment on his religion became war, and only war.

He would grow merciless, unfeeling and brutal: more masculine than a real man. No one would ever know his true nature. He would not write private letters. Ever.

"His missives have often been intercepted, but they are always disappointing. His correspondence deals exclusively with political and military matters. Eugene does not know feelings, human relations or the impulse of passions: only duty."

And duty, as he conceived it, was simple: to kill as many enemies as possible. In war he would always refuse armistices, in peace he would seek conflict. In his wish to be sent to the most dangerous fronts, to obtain means and money for his armies, he did not hesitate to argue bitterly with the Emperor: first with Leopold, then with his son Joseph the Victorious.

Time wrought another transformation. The Priest of War became the Captain of Death. When he was in command, the fight was always to the death. In this way, his name would never be associated by anyone – least of all by himself – with tranquillity, love or peace. He had known peace at the Hôtel de Soissons, and had seen that it led to vice.

He would never have lovers of the female sex; if they came his way, he would use them as a smokescreen. Women did not in fact disgust him, but the Captain of Death had very different things on his mind. In the meantime the perverse tendencies of his youth would be forgotten: his old companions in depravity had every reason to hope so.

As the years went by, he counted whizzing cannonballs in their thousands, he saw soldiers dying like flies, the countryside ablaze, mothers and fathers weeping over their slaughtered children, entire nations reduced to ruins. But if there was ever any chance of achieving peace, or even just a truce, he would reject it with all his might. The Captain of Death had to trample every last trace of Madame l'Ancienne into the mud of the trenches.

Sometimes he would attract some young night guard into his tent and share moments of reciprocal intimacy. And then, for just a few instants, Eugene no longer knew who he was: Captain of Death, Priest of War, Dog Nose or Madame l'Ancienne? But the next day, with his well-polished marching boots pulled on tight, everything was as it had always been.

"Now you know the real reason why Eugene of Savoy does not want the war to end," concluded Atto, exhausted by this unsettling explanation. "I tried in some way to make you understand all this the first day we met again. But now you have – how can I put it? – a more complete picture. Eugene has no idea how to face peace. What could he do without braids on his jacket? He would instantly be turned back into his old self: Madame l'Ancienne. He hates peace, because he is afraid of it. He's not fighting against Louis XIV, but against himself. And the war continues unabated."

"Joseph's new strategy – peace with the Pope and the Hungarian rebels, the division of Spain with France –"

". . . might have driven Eugene to take extreme steps," the Abbot anticipated me. "Dog Nose would therefore be assassinating the young *condottiero* who stole the limelight from him at Landau; and also the Emperor who prevented him from winning military glory in Spain; and finally the man who could one day force him to return to Vienna, to cease fighting, and to become Madame l'Ancienne once again. Finally, in his own body, Eugene is suppressing his own childhood companions at the Hôtel de Soissons: those who stole his innocence."

"But I still don't understand: we have too many culprits. England and Holland; Charles, Joseph's brother; the Jesuits; the ex-ministers; and Eugene of Savoy. Which one of them did it?"

"It's not clear to me either. Partly because it is only England and Holland that have a definite interest in the Grand Dauphin's death, while I don't see how this could serve any of the others. We need to keep a close eye on these Turks and understand just what this dervish, who plays with his neighbour's head, is up to."

"That reminds me! I was supposed to meet Ugonio half an hour ago!" I exclaimed, looking up at the rich façade of a small palace in front of us, on top of which stood a magnificent blue and gold clock, showing the hour as 9.30.

ॐ

The sister had knocked at my door in alarm: the man asking for me had come at nine on the dot. She had never seen him before and he had a menacing appearance. The poor woman did not know where to turn: Cloridia was out, having been urgently summoned to Prince Eugene's palace. The wife of the first chamberlain was giving birth. And so the nun had asked the strange visitor to come back later.

Since he had refused to give his name on both occasions, I asked the sister for a brief description; a few words sufficed to tell me who it was.

After trying to explain things to her in my pitiful German, I asked Simonis, who turned up at that moment with my son to get new orders from me, to tell the nun that there was no need to be alarmed. She could admit the monstrous individual without any fear, since I knew him and he was perfectly harmless, despite his unusual appearance. Then I sent my little boy to play in the cloisters.

"I humpily offer Your Enormity my most obscene respectables," Ugonio began unctuously in a subdued and catarrh-filled voice.

Then he saw that Atto was present and launched into further salutations.

"I see with the uttermostful pleasuredom that the His Lordliness the Abbey is in excellentitious healthiness. To be more medicinal than mendacious I complimentate Your Highfulness on his most refineried comportment."

He now took in the fact that Atto was blind and expressed his sorrow with some perfunctory expressions, assuming a highly affected expression of grief.

"But I recognised you at once," replied the Abbot, lifting his handkerchief to his nose in response to the disgusting stench given off by the *corpisantaro*'s greatcoat.

On his back Ugonio bore a large bag of filthy and ancient jute, which seemed to be crammed with a great number of vile, stinking objects.

"No idle chatter," I said brusquely. "What news do you have?"

The news was abundant and extremely positive, explained the *corpisantaro*: as he had promised during our previous encounter, he was now free to reveal the nature of his mysterious relations with Ciezeber.

"So go on."

"I must deliver to him a swindlification of excessing rarity and worthfulness."

"We know that," I answered icily, "it's the head of a man."

The *corpisantaro* seemed petrified: how did we know that?

Then he gave a quiet grunt, as if by way of confirmation. The story he went on to relate, which I will now try to repeat as faithfully as possible, sounded truly bizarre and implausible. Afterwards, however, my research substantially confirmed it.

The story began in 1683, during the last and most famous siege of Vienna by the Turks.

It was the Turkish Grand Vizier, Kara Mustafa Pasha, who had wanted the attack on the imperial capital. He had proposed it to the Great Sultan, had led the army in person and had been disastrously defeated. The responsibility was entirely his; after the debacle, his fate was sealed.

Before setting out for war, Kara Mustafa had been so certain of victory that he had promised to bring the Sultan the head of Cardinal Collonitz, who had always been one of the most active fomenters of war against the Turks. To win the divine favour of Mahomet, before setting out on the military campaign, the Grand Vizier had had a sumptuous mosque built in Belgrade.

After the defeat, the Sultan had not forgotten his subordinate's promise, and took pleasure in turning it against him with savage sarcasm.

"He played a most abominimous and nauseafull trickery on him," Ugonio said with coarse glee.

On 25th December 1683, the birthday of Our Lord and therefore dear to Cardinal Collonitz (this was the first cruel irony), around one in the afternoon, three high court dignitaries presented themselves in Kara Mustafa's apartment in Belgrade, led by the Agha of the janissaries, together with some robust individuals. Kara Mustafa, taken aback, asked what they might want at that hour, and whether anything serious had happened. In the midst of the group of dignitaries he saw the severe face of the Capigi-Bachi, the Sultan's Grand Master of Ceremonies, and he deduced that the dignitaries must bear orders from the Great Lord. The Agha of the janissaries announced that a decree had been issued by the Sultan; as he drew it forth, four brutes leaped at Kara Mustafa's neck.

The Grand Vizier was strangled with a rope and then beheaded: the same end (the second cruel irony) that he had sworn for Cardinal Collonitz. Following the ancient Turkish custom, the skin and flesh were then stripped from his face and head. To be certain of his lieutenant's death, the Sultan had them deliver to him the skin of his face, stuffed with cotton and spices. The stripped skull, along with the body and the rope, was buried (the third tremendous irony of the Sultan) in the mosque in Belgrade built by Kara Mustafa, as a perpetual warning to the subjects of the Sublime Porte who failed in their duty.

"But then the Sultan was confunded by a most discomboboling and gastflabbering contangency," concluded the pestiferous scoundrel.

The Sultan did not imagine that just five years later, in 1688, Belgrade would fall into Christian hands. After a fierce battle, under the command of the Prince-Elector of Bavaria and the Duke of Lorraine, the imperial troops succeeded in breaking into the city and taking control of it. As the Jesuit fathers were the first to intone the *Te Deum* after the victory, the mosque of Kara Mustafa was entrusted to two of this order, whose task it was to turn it into a Catholic church. The pair were the confessor of the Duke of Lorraine, Father Aloysius Braun, and the missionary father Francis Xavier Beringshoffen.

One night disturbing noises were heard in the mosque, as of a pickaxe bashing the walls, and objects being smashed. Braun and Beringshoffen, terrified by the thought of ghosts, at once summoned a group of soldiers to find out who could be in the building at that hour. The two trembling fathers entered the mosque with the soldiers, shakily holding a holy water sprinkler and lanterns out in front of themselves, followed by the armed men. They found that it was not ghosts that were disturbing the nocturnal quiet but men of flesh and blood: it was a group of seven musketeers, enlisted in the Christian armies that had just reconquered Belgrade. The musketeers, surprised and frightened by the ambush, explained that they had fought hard during the assault on the city, and some of them had been wounded, but they had missed out on the sharing of the spoils.

Winter was on its way, and they did not even have the money to buy warm clothes. However, they had learned from a friend that Kara Mustafa had been buried in that mosque, along with many objects of great value, including luxurious winter garments, which would just suit the seven poor musketeers. They had not thought twice and had broken into the mosque, profaning the tomb of the Grand Vizier.

Fearing that the two priests would be angry at the covert violation of the mosque, which legally belonged to the Society of Jesus, the seven soldiers offered to hand over to the Jesuits everything they had found in the tomb of Kara Mustafa, including the most unexpected object: his head.

At that point Ugonio rummaged in his lurid jute bag and pulled out an object the size of a melon, wrapped in a greyish cloth. He unwrapped it: we all instinctively jumped back, even the Abbot.

It was a human head covered in a layer of silver. However, the features could be discerned: a high forehead, a long aquiline nose rather like that of certain Jews, narrow eyes, traces of beard on the cheeks, and a typically Turkish frown transformed by violent death into a contorted and desperate grimace.

"Then that is . . ." I hesitated.

". . . the head of Kara Mustafa," Atto completed, aghast.

"So that's the head Ciezeber wanted from you!" I exclaimed.

Ugonio offered me the exhibit, which I examined with a mixture of curiosity, disgust and reverence, happy to leave it in the *corpisantaro*'s claw-like hands.

In that face covered by an accretion of silver, in its grimace of suffering and torment, lay all the tragedy of the last siege of Vienna: Kara Mustafa's mad plan of conquest, the bloody battle, the final defeat of the Ottomans and the tragic death of the Grand Vizier who had dreamed of crushing Christianity. How many deaths in battle was just one of the wrinkles of that pain-wracked face worth? How many miles of military march had it seen? How many tears of widows, wounded men and orphans were condensed in just one of the tears wept by the dying Kara Mustafa? The patina of silver, which was intended to protect this remnant of human flesh, actually made it a perpetual monument to the vanity of things.

Out of the corner of my eye I watched Atto as he listened to the story, as astonished as I was, hidden behind the protective cover of his blind man's glasses. How many such interrogations I had seen him carry out, years ago! But now it was I who held the cards: I was not just a fully rounded adult, but also a man marked by experience. Old Atto, I thought with a bittersweet mixture of pride, vindictiveness and compassion, was at that age when even the boldest paladins become peons.

But I shook off these thoughts and returned to the present.

"Why were you so afraid to tell us this story?" I asked Ugonio. "How did you think that Ciezeber might hurt you?"

"Decreasing the scruples so as not increase one's scruples, I have sworn and cursed not to blabber anything of the task the dervishite has consigned me. The Ottomaniacs desiderate most lustily and lechily the noggin of the Great Visionary. They think it will prevent all misfortunations: it will help them to organise a most cudgelsome and slaughterous army, and to spiflicate Vienna with much pervertitude and ravishment."

I learned with amazement that the Turks thought that they could obtain from the head of a dead man what he had failed to achieve when alive. But what bewildered me was the new picture that was forming after Ugonio's revelations. When my Cloridia had overheard Ciezeber demanding someone's head at Eugene's palace, it had had nothing to do with assassination, let alone the feared regicide, but merely concerned the theft of Kara Mustafa's head. The dervish had hired Ugonio on account of the *corpisantaro's* long experience in trafficking relics and mortuary objects, and not for any homicidal project.

And I had thought the life of the Emperor himself was at stake!

The *corpisantaro* meanwhile concluded the story of the decapitated head. From Belgrade the two Jesuits had brought Kara Mustafa's head to Vienna, where they delivered it – thus bringing the vengeance full and ironic circle – to none other than Cardinal Collonitz. On 17th September the Cardinal deposited the trophy in the city's arsenal. Twenty-two years had passed since then.

"And how the devil did you get hold of Kara Mustafa's head? How did you know where it was?"

"I conductified a painstoking investifigation, and then committed a most blackguardsome and mischieving burgledom," explained Ugonio.

The *corpisantaro* had succeeded not only in discovering that Kara Mustafa's head was held in the city arsenal, but also in stealing it. But then, I said to myself, had I not seen him in Rome carrying out dozens of such nefarious enterprises?

Ugonio, he himself explained with ill-concealed pride, had made rather a name for himself among collectors in that sector. While in the Holy City it was saints' relics that were most profitable, here in the Caesarean city the market was dominated by anything connected with the two sieges, especially projectiles from the Ottoman cannons. The *corpisantaro* listed a series of desirable items of booty, like the stone weighing 79 pounds that had been fired from the Leopoldine Island in 1683 and which, complete with commemorative inscription, was still embedded in the façade of the Neustädter Hof, a palace not far off, which ran from Press Street to Crab Street. Or the three cannonballs almost half a rod in diameter, also lodged in the walls, complete with commemorative plaque, of the house known, naturally enough, as House of the Three Balls in the nearby quarter of Sievering. Or the famous Golden Ball, fired by the Turks on 6th August 1683 and still embedded in the façade of a corner house in the square known as Am Hof, a tavern that belonged to Citizen Councillor Michael Moltz, who had had the ball gilded and had named the house At the Golden Ball. Or again the Turkish ball that could be admired in the saloon wall of the Golden Dragon alehouse in Steindlgasse. But the Eszterházy buttery, in Haarhof, was also full of sacred Turkish relics, as the defenders of the city in 1683 had often refreshed themselves there with a glass of good wine; not to mention the rare objects left by the great Polish King Sobieski, when on 13th September 1683, the day after the victory over the Ottomans, he had personally recited the *Te Deum* in the Loreto Chapel. And to conclude, declared Ugonio, now slavering at the mouth, the relic of relics: in the Romanesque chapel of the Scottish Church there was the oldest Marian statue in Vienna, dating from four centuries earlier, which was said to have miraculously extinguished the fire that had broken out in the early days of the 1683 siege.

These, it was fairly clear, would be the next victims of the *corpisantaro*'s rapacity. While Ugonio listed them avidly, I groaned to myself.

Once again I found myself floundering midstream. And so the head belonged to Kara Mustafa, Ciezeber's rituals had purely therapeutic aims and Abbot Melani was a poor old man reduced to attempting a feeble forgery, which had failed almost immediately: but the Emperor was ill and so was the Dauphin!

This might matter to Atto, but it was of very little concern to me. Now that the Abbot had confessed that he no longer counted for anything on the European chessboard, I could finally heave a sigh of relief; there was no longer any risk of my ending up on the gallows for high treason. But no – I said to myself, suddenly on the rack again: someone, after all, must have murdered Dànilo, Hristo and Dragomir, Simonis's student companions! If the Bulgarian and the Romanian, as the Abbot had said, were subjects of the Sublime Porte, Atto himself, the previous evening, had not been able to rule out the possibility that the three deaths were linked to one another.

One thing was certain: we had not yet discovered what was hidden behind the Agha's Latin phrase. It could not be an innocent phrase, as everyone had interpreted it during the audience at Prince Eugene's palace: since then there had been three deaths, and all three victims had been carrying out research into the Golden Apple. That was not all. Hristo, before dying, had confided to Simonis that in his opinion the riddle of the phrase lay in *soli soli soli* and it had to do with checkmate, or "Shah matt, the King is enclosed", as I had read in the note found in his chessboard. But what did it mean? To find that out, would we have to start our research all over again, this time focusing on chess? Three students were dead already, the Emperor was ill: time had run out. The path indicated by the Bulgarian really looked like a dead end.

Although the Abbot considered the strange tales about the Golden Apple nonsensical legends (and how could one blame him?), they were the only clue we had to the real meaning of the Agha's phrase. We needed to take a different tack.

I pulled out Ugonio's precious ring of keys, which he instinctively tried to grab with his gnarled hands, uttering a muttered exclamation halfway between a curse and a cackle.

"Not yet," I commanded, jerking back the tinkling metal ring.

The *corpisantaro* drilled me with his bloodshot little eyes.

"Tell me what your plans are for the next few hours," I bade him.

"I must insinufy myself into Eugene's palace," he answered without losing sight of the key ring, "to deliverate the noggin of the Grand Visionary to the dervishite."

"Once you have handed over Kara Mustafa's head to Ciezeber you'll have no more to fear, I gather."

The *corpisantaro* did not answer, thus providing mute confirmation.

"Fine. So if you really want to get your keys back, there's just one small step you need to take. It's clear there has been an unfortunate

misunderstanding. Our previous pact is no longer valid. We thought
we were dealing with a plan for a murder, but it turns out to have
been, well, an archaeological mission: the search for Kara Mustafa's
head. You realise that we had to wait quite a while just to discover
that you had nothing important to tell us. These are setbacks that
call for serious reparation. We have to reconsider our agreement: I
will give you back the keys when you find out what words are written
on the spire of St Stephen's, where the Golden Apple once was!" I
said, remembering that Ugonio was working on a deacon at the
cathedral to get information on the subject. "I'm sorry, but only then
will our accounts be settled."

Ugonio answered first with lively protests ("It is an adulterous
swindlification, treacherish and duplishitous!" he yelled, rising to his
feet), but seeing that Atto and I were adamant, and observing
Simonis's muscles, he gradually became more submissive, settling
down to a cantankerous capitulation. He had no choice: we held all
the cards. In fact, we would never have denounced him: with all the
murders that had happened around us, Atto and I had as little desire
to approach the city guard as he did. But he could not know this, and
wanted a quiet life.

"I know it perfectfully, and in most pedantical detail!" Ugonio
suddenly exclaimed, looking up with a determined air, his eyes fixed
on his beloved keys.

"Ah yes?" I said diffidently.

"We are all ears," said Abbot Melani, who had remained thoughtful
throughout. "Begin by telling us who you heard it from."

"I . . . I was informatised. The peas were spilt to me by . . . um, a
secretary of the burgermister."

"A secretary of the burgomaster? When and how, for goodness' sake?"

"To be more padre than parricide, it was two years, six quatrains,
thirteen inches and half a lustrum ago, in a secret and most confiden-
tiable meeting," he answered, promptly putting his hand on his
heart by way of oath.

"That may be. But just yesterday you didn't know it. And what
are the words?"

"Er . . . hum . . . *Quis pomum aureum*," began the *corpisantaro* with
his index-finger solemnly raised as if to recite a speech by Cicero, "*de
multiis cognoravisti . . . etiam Viennam multorum turcarum . . . talis mela-
mangiaturpaternosteramen.*"

Before finishing the sentence in an almost incomprehensible mumble, the *corpisantaro* had hesitated as if he found it hard to remember.

"Can you repeat that?" asked Abbot Melani, taken aback by this disjointed sentence.

Ugonio took a deep breath, as if preparing for a three-day apnoea.

"*Quis pomum aureum, de multiis ignoravisti . . .*" he began to say.

"Previously you said *cognoravisti*, not *ignoravisti*."

Ugonio gave a foul, yellow-toothed smile, which combined sympathy, clemency and a touch of good humour.

"If I am grillified too closefully, I misremember everything sometimes always."

"You've also forgotten, it seems, that the Archangel Michael only wrote seven words. You told me so yourself, don't you remember?"

"Mmm . . . ye-es . . ."

"That's enough, Ugonio," I interrupted him. "I can see that there's nothing else for it."

I got up and opened a little cupboard where I kept several of my chimney-sweeping tools. I chose a large pair of pincers and made as if to break open the key ring.

"No-o-o!" yelled the *corpisantaro*, throwing himself upon me. He was at once seized by Simonis's strong arms.

"Keep your ridiculous lies to yourself," I warned Ugonio. "I must know whether there is really anything written where the Golden Apple used to be, and what. If you don't give me any proper help, I'll break the ring and throw all your precious keys one by one into the Danube."

"You've won. This evening all right?"

"So soon? If you try and fool me again . . ."

After delivering the head to the dervish, Ugonio had something else "urgentitious and appeteasing" to carry out, he explained with a greedy smile: probably one of his lurid traffickings. After that, he announced importantly, he would devote himself heart and soul to the Archangel Michael's message; he had an appointment with the deacon of St Stephen's and he counted on coming straight back to us then with good news.

"Ah yes," I remembered, "the relic collector. Don't fob him off with anything obviously fake, otherwise say goodbye to any revelations about the Archangel."

"And to your keys," added Simonis, with a laugh.

So we agreed on another meeting at the convent at dinner time, at 17 of the clock. After that, I explained to Ugonio, I would be busy with the rehearsal of *Sant' Alessio* in the Caesarean chapel.

Ugonio urged us a thousand times to be there ready and waiting with his keys. His "business" could not survive another minute without his beloved key ring, which opened up all gates; his activity as *corpisantaro* risked total financial collapse. He was old and tired, he whimpered, and had to collect enough resources for the few days that were left to him.

He calmed down only when I swore solemnly on the Bible that I would guard the keys like pieces of pure gold.

After replacing the head in his jute sack, his own face made even greyer, more flaccid and wrinkled by his failure to recover the keys, Ugonio left our rooms, bestowing on them by way of parting gift the same stale stench that I remembered from twenty-eight years earlier, when I had first encountered his shadowy figure in the lugubrious tunnels of subterranean Rome.

As soon as the room was free of his mephitic presence, I replaced the key ring in the cupboard that I had chosen as its hiding place. At that very moment I saw a slip of paper twirl down to the floor in capricious spirals. I picked it up.

It was a little sheet of paper, which had been stuffed inside the key ring until that moment. As a result of all the to-and-fro movement of the ring, it had finally detached itself and in graceful swirls had come to rest at my feet. I opened it up.

"Well, well," I murmured.

"What is it?" asked Atto.

It was a memorandum: Ugonio's sordid criminal enterprises, the cream of his depraved and brutal existence, written as a precaution in Italian (or rather, Ugonio's Italian), lest the note should end up in anyone else's hands. The first lines referred to the previous days:

Thursday – extort shopkeepers.
Friday – swindlificate nun.
Saturday – Court: bear false witnessification.
Sunday – Distribute forgified coins.
Monday – Return stealified swaggery to blind orphan, but extortify ransom.
Tuesday – Theft in church: bribify priest

The notes left one in no doubt of the *corpisantaro*'s regular nefarious practises: extortions from shopkeepers; a fraud practised on a young nun; perjury before a court of justice; trafficking in forged money; restitution, on payment of a ransom, of goods brazenly purloined from a poor blind orphan; theft in a church, after purchasing the priest's acquiescence. Nothing new, in short: the usual outrages to be expected from this creature of the underworld. But what could one say of the note for the following day?

Wednesday – Decapitated head of Hüseyin Pasha to the dervish.

I should have guessed it! The head Ugonio intended to deliver to Ciezeber was not the precious (to the Ottomans at least) head of Kara Mustafa, but that of a certain Hüseyin Pasha. Whoever he was, his skull was certainly not the one the dervish was expecting. For all his magic arts, he was about to become the dupe of the fraudulent tricks of a simple *corpisantaro*.

As soon as I read the note to Abbot Melani, he was as amazed as I was. But imagine our surprise when, at the very end of that sequence of infamies, I read aloud two expressions, one in Latin, which referred beyond all doubt to someone well known to us:

Wednesday afternoon- Al. Ursinum. Two hanged men.
Then – Deacon of St Stephen's.

It was too much. I tossed the note into Abbot Melani's hands, as if he could have deciphered it (and to tell the truth, probably spurred by his impossible desire to read it, he snatched at the scrap of paper with singular alacrity).

I rushed to the door and then into the street, in pursuit of the *corpisantaro*.

It was too late. By the time I reached Porta Coeli Street, Ugonio had already vanished. I went as far as Carinthia Street, turned back and explored the side roads: nothing.

Back at the convent, I reported my discovery to Abbot Melani.

"Al. Ursinum? Of course, it's perfectly clear."

Ugonio had become especially nervous when his collection of keys had been confiscated. With it he had also lost his weekly memorandum, in which he revealed that the head he wanted to palm off on Ciezeber was not that of Kara Mustafa, but some quite different person. The dervish had threatened Ugonio with reprisals should he not keep his assignment secret; one can only imagine what would happen if he were to discover he had been cheated.

But it was the word "Ursinum" that was most deeply worrying: it could only indicate the Latinised name of Gaetano Orsini, the castrated protagonist of *Sant' Alessio*. And the abbreviation "Al." obviously stood for "Alessio": the name of the oratorio in which Orsini played the role of protagonist. Less clear, but by no means secondary, was the identity of the two hanged men.

What on earth did Ugonio have to do with Orsini? What could a professional sneak thief have in common with a celebrated tenor, a friend of Camilla de' Rossi, who was actually close to the Emperor? Did the two have an appointment, or even some secret agreement?

Perhaps, quite simply, Orsini was another collector of relics, I told myself, and Ugonio had an appointment to sell him one of his "rare pieces". But in that case why would the *corpisantaro* have been so reluctant to tell us about it? With a covetous expression, he had defined his next engagement, after the delivery of the head to Ciezeber, as "urgentitious and appeteasing": if he had nothing to hide, he would have said whom he was meeting. I had just informed him that I went to the Caesarean chapel every evening for the rehearsals of *Sant' Alessio*, so he knew very well that I was acquainted with Gaetano Orsini!

No, Orsini and Ugonio were hiding something. It was as if the devil and holy water were being mixed together, light and dark, nothing and everything. Or maybe it was all too predictable: wasn't the musical world traditionally a den of spies? Was it not obvious that spies should get together with swindlers? Yes. But who were the two hanged men? We had just heaved a sigh of relief over the head the dervish had demanded, and along came two more corpses!

"So Ugonio is in league with Gaetano Orsini, that beggarly Sant' Alessio," exclaimed Melani. "Damnation! And just think we had the filthy *corpisantaro* in our hands just a moment ago."

"He won't abandon his keys, Signor Atto," I consoled him. "As soon as he comes back we'll question him closely on the contents of the note."

Looking shattered, the Abbot sank more profoundly into his armchair. I sat down as well. The sudden shift of perspective brought about by the revelations of the old trafficker in relics had left us speechless.

The *corpisantaro* had explained things most convincingly: the dervish was not interested in anyone's death, but in the head of Kara Mustafa. So if there was no shadow of a Turkish plot, who had done away with Dànilo, Hristo and Populescu?

It was a fact that no proof existed against the Turks. There remained Dànilo's last words just before dying: the young Pontevedrin had clearly stated the name of the elusive Eyyub and of the no less mysterious forty thousand martyrs of Kasim.

But it was possible, I told myself at last, that the poor dying man had been simply delirious, and had been senselessly repeating the results of his research into the Golden Apple. Perhaps Dànilo too had come across the legends whereby the Golden Apple was supposed to have entered the tomb of Eyyub, as we had heard from Zyprian.

Like a ray of sunlight capriciously refracted on the troubled surface of water, everything was multiplying in a thousand directions, its contours and outline becoming blurred. Was the riddle of the Ottoman embassy now somehow mixed up with the mysterious bond between Orsini and Ugonio? And did it have anything to do with the Emperor's illness? After all, Atto had told me that musicians were all spies; he himself was a living example! And did that also apply to the Chormaisterin?

At that moment there came a knock. It was Penicek. At the porter's lodge they knew the Bohemian cart driver and let him through without any trouble. He stuttered that he was looking for Simonis: he had come, as promised, to provide more information on human flight and he also had to hand over the notes he had taken on the lessons that he was following on behalf of his Barber. He was accompanied by Opalinski, the Pole.

☙❦

"Brontology . . . stilbology . . . nubilogy?" I stammered in bewilderment.

"They are philosophical doctrines one can use to investigate the most mysterious phenomena of nature," said Simonis rather mechanically, as if he were parroting a university lesson.

Nubilogy, in particular, according to Penicek, suited our case. I turned to Atto to ask if he had ever heard of it, but the old Abbot, overcome by weariness, had dozed off.

"And what is it?" I asked Simonis.

"It's a science that studies, how can I put it, the interventions and influences of air on bodies, so that they perform a certain sort of motion, which ... I don't know how to put it ... You explain, Pennal!" ordered my assistant.

Limping forward, the Bohemian opened a bag full of books and laboriously and fumblingly placed the volumes on the table before him.

"Watch where you put your clumsy feet!" Simonis snapped, the Pennal offering him his only chance to vent the fears of the last few days.

"I'm truly sorry, Signor Barber," he humbly apologised.

Poor Penicek then confessed: not knowing how to proceed with his research into the subject of flying, he had turned to Jan Janitzki Opalinski, who, as everyone knew, was extremely knowledgeable and had been happy to help him out.

"I don't know why you are so keen to know if a wooden ship can rise into the air," Opalinski then began, stepping forward, "but it is a much debated issue."

There was, continued the Pole, a learned professor of natural science who had answered the question. As was always the case in Vienna when there was a technical problem to face, it was an Italian who came to our aid: his name was Ovidio Montalbani, and he had taught for a long time at the University of Bologna. In academic circles he was very well known for having published books of unprecedented doctrinal profundity in which he investigated the most abstruse and obscure fields of knowledge: calopiedology, charagmaposcopy, diologogy, athenography, philautiology, brontology, cephalogy, stilbology, aphroditology and above all nubilogy.

I gave a glance at the first of the books that the Pennal had piled up on the table.

Some pages were marked by little strips of paper. I opened at one of these markers and read:

This Aristotelian anathimiasis, which is none other than a smoky mist which has risen into the air, according to Pliny, and the watery concave vapour of which Metrodorus held discourse, and the Air swollen with Anaximenes, when it is coined in clouds, then still under a fluxile form it becomes visible within the penetrated body of the air, which for this reason appears under a troubled turgidity that is itself also swollen ...

I raised my eyebrows in wonder. Rather than a book of natural science it seemed to be a riddle. I went on to the next bookmark, and tried again:

> *The total figure of cloudy bodies of the circular, or more appropriately elliptical, air, which might appear, as can be seen, an aggregate of infinite, partial, highly variable and varied circumscriptions. It must conform itself in accordance with the figure of its local and conservative space, which is circular, or elliptical . . .*

"Damn it, this is totally incomprehensible," I exclaimed impatiently, giving the book to the Bohemian.

Penicek received the book still open at the page where I had read this last passage, adjusted his glasses on his nose, read through these lines, and finally, with a contrite air, passed it to Opalinski, who, after reading it through, declared: "It's perfectly clear."

"What's perfectly clear?"

"Summarising very roughly, clouds are not made of a particular substance, but of a certain vaporous mist. Since air is mobile, this mist can be lifted and moved."

"But I know this!" I protested.

"Well, Signor Master," replied Opalinski, remaining unruffled, "at this point another work by Montalbani might be useful to us, the *Brontology*, which examines with most fertile acumen all the secrets of thunder, lightning flashes and thunderbolts. But as time is short, it will be better to consider directly the work of another author, a compatriot of Montalbani, master of great science and doctrine, the most learned and glorious Doctor Geminiano Montanari."

He picked from the pile a tattered little book with a curious title and handed it to me:

THE FORCES
OF **AEOLUS**
PHYSICAL-MATHEMATICAL
DIALOGUE

I turned it round uncertainly in my hands.

"And so?" I asked, not even bothering to try to read it.

Opalinski took the book back and opened it at one of the usual strips of paper, then handed it back to me.

"It's one of the most exquisitely erudite books of the great master," he informed me.

I looked. There were two illustrations that were, for once, very clear:

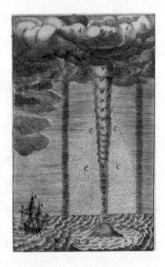

"Here, do you see? This is the ship, and the whirling current of a vortex is approaching. These vortices, also known as waterspouts, can flatten homes, churches, bell towers or even lift entire buildings with all the people inside."

Then he pointed at the second picture.

"You see? Here the sailing ship has been picked up and – whish! – carried up into the sky."

Simonis looked at me in utter amazement.

"I know about whirlwinds," I said, "and their devastating effects." Opalinski and Penicek nodded.

"A thousand thanks, Jan, for your valuable help," said the Greek, looking highly satisfied. "Signor Master, may I leave you a moment?" he asked. "I'll just take my friends to my room and come straight back."

I nodded.

"And you, take your hat off, idiotic Pennal! Say goodbye properly to Signor Master, you grinning ape!" he said, cuffing the poor cripple on the head. The latter humbly and contritely bowed several times, supporting himself awkwardly on his lame leg.

A few minutes later my assistant was back.

"In short, Signor Master," he began, smiling radiantly, "the Flying Ship could have been taken and lifted into the air by one of those whirlwinds or vortices or tornadoes or whatever they're called, which can swallow up entire fleets, lift them up, transport them to some other place and set them down on the ground, without the crew being harmed at all."

"Yes, and the Flying Ship is much smaller and lighter than the vessels that sometimes get lifted by waterspouts," I added thoughtfully.

The Greek nodded with satisfaction.

"But . . ." I objected, "was there any wind, when we took off from the ball stadium?"

Simonis was silent.

"I don't think so," I answered myself.

"No, there wasn't," he confirmed, already less self-assured.

"Were there any great gusts, or any especially swirling currents?" I insisted.

"Well, no. No, there wasn't anything like that," he admitted.

"So it is highly improbable that the Flying Ship rose into the air because of a whirlwind," I concluded.

"Highly is the right word, Signor Master, very good," Simonis complimented me.

I said nothing for an instant, to be sure that my assistant had no other arguments. He had not. With a tinge of melancholy I looked at the pile of books Opalinski had gathered together. My assistant was picking them up to replace them in Penicek's cloth bag.

"Just one question, Simonis: why does Jan Janitzki understand what's written in those books and you don't?"

"Simple, Signor Master: he studies."

I was about to ask him what he did do at the university, but I refrained; he had already explained all too clearly what the real occupations of Viennese students were.

When the Greek had closed the door behind himself, I turned towards Atto. He was still snoring, with his head bent awkwardly and stiffly to one side.

He was lucky! Old age deprived him of the strength needed to face distress, and consigned him into the oblivious arms of Morpheus. In the past he would have racked his brains ceaselessly over what was happening, just as I was doing. I was at a loss. Nothing seemed to make any recognisable and logical sense, but at the same time I could not afford to overlook anything and risk losing the thread of my actions and ending up involved in some disaster. Having escaped a death sentence for espionage on behalf of France, I now risked being accused of complicity in a series of murders, or of shady manoeuvres against Prince Eugene and his Ottoman guests.

And I thought: Cloridia and I had arrived in Vienna to turn our lives around. We had left the city of popes with all its illusions: Rome the turbid, Rome the duplicitous, Rome the cold stepmother, heedless of its children. In the Caesarean city we had felt we were breathing pure, fresh air. But now the carriage of our existence seemed to be mired once again in the marsh of suspicion, ambiguity and deceit. Even the diabolical Abbot Melani, sheltering behind his dark glasses, could hardly keep up with matters.

Oh, Flying Ship, I suddenly said to myself, oh Ark of Truth, did you raise me to the heavens only to delude me? I had fled the mud of Rome; I was once again trudging through the murky swamp of the possible.

৯০৭

11 of the clock: luncheon hour for artisans, secretaries, language teachers, priests, servants of commerce, footmen and coach drivers.

"They start at three in the morning with a soup containing three eggs and spices. At five, cream of three eggs and chicken soup. At seven, a couple of fresh eggs. At nine, egg yolk soup with spices and a good few pancakes, plus a goblet of aromatic wine from Traminer. At midday roast capon and other birds, wild cockerel and wine, with assorted types of bread. At one o'clock a couple of baked cakes and more wine. At three, a snack with roast capon, a dish of fried fishes, with wine, bread and mixed dumplings. At five a good egg pie, with wine. For dinner: from five to six courses, including boiled and roast meat, freshwater fish. At seven another good chicken soup. At nine a frying pan full of baked cakes, bread, wine and assorted loaves. At midnight, another egg yolk soup with spices. Can you believe it?" exclaimed Cloridia.

The first chamberlain's wife had given birth to a beautiful boy. My gentle consort had just returned from Prince Eugene's palace. Now she could take up her post with Abbot Melani again and relieve me of my duties. As Atto was snoring, my wife recounted the birth to me. Immediately after delivery, the mother had begun, after the Viennese fashion, to gorge herself on every possible delicacy.

"I said to her: do you really want to guzzle all that stuff? It's not a calf you're suckling. Do you know what she replied? That where she comes from, in Lower Austria, new mothers eat much more. Immediately after birth, what with snacks, luncheons and dinners, they stuff themselves 24 times in 24 hours. Not to mention the parties after the baby's born: to celebrate a birth it's considered an offence to the guests to consume anything less than 110 pounds of lard, 60 of butter, from 1,000 to 2,000 eggs, 120 pounds of bread-crumbs and an entire barrel of aromatic wine from Traminer."

While Cloridia chattered away, all afire as she always was after a successful delivery, my mind was on other things. The first chamber-lain's wife: it was she who had told Cloridia that Prince Eugene kept the piece of paper with the Agha's mysterious utterance in his personal diary.

It was true that the Turks now seemed to have little to do with the Emperor's illness, but if we wanted to know just what the Agha's phrase concealed, perhaps all that remained was to have a look at the paper on which it was written. At this point anything was worth trying.

I waited for my wife to conclude her rant and I went on to tell her, in a low voice so as not to wake Atto, what had happened so far that day: the Abbot's confession, Kara Mustafa's head and the rest.

"I had thought of that myself," Cloridia said at the end. "Perhaps the phrase needs to be interpreted in a different way. Perhaps it's a secret code, or maybe the paper the Agha read from, the one he gave to Eugene, contained something else."

"Do you think you could get hold of that piece of paper from your new mother, even for just an hour?"

"I told you, I had already thought of that!" she answered, and pulled it from her pocket.

I had no wish to enquire with what promises (or subterfuges) and at what risk Cloridia had obtained it from the first chamberlain or from his wife.

"I must give it back this very evening. Prince Eugene writes in his diary every day after dinner."

"Speaking of that, wasn't he supposed to leave for The Hague today?"

"He's put it off."

"Why?"

"Nobody knows."

"Maybe because of the Emperor's illness," I suggested.

"Could be. But His Majesty is continuing to get better. Whatever the reason, Eugene takes his diary with him when he's at war. We're lucky that he hasn't left yet."

She handed the piece of paper to me. In the centre of it, in the uncertain handwriting of a Turk, lay the famous phrase *soli soli soli ad pomum venimus aureum*. Nothing else.

"May I?" asked Simonis at that moment, drawing near.

He scrutinised the paper carefully, taking it to the window to examine it better in the daylight.

"Signor Master, if you have no other orders for me today, I could perhaps help you to find out whether this piece of paper conceals anything."

"We'll go the Place with No Name tomorrow. This matter is more urgent. But what do you plan to do?" I asked with some curiosity.

"In my room I have just what is needed."

A moment later we were all in Simonis's room. There we found Penicek, zealously scribbling away in the Greek's notebooks, and Opalinski intent on copying the notes for himself.

"Have you finished, Pennal?" asked Simonis brusquely.

"At this very moment, Signor Barber," he stammered. "Here, I've made a fair copy of everything."

"Good," declared my assistant, after giving a quick glance at the lame Bohemian's work. "And don't you ever dare to give me a rough copy of the notes again, do you understand?" he reprimanded him severely.

"Yes, yes, Signor Barber, forgive me, Signor Barber," said the Bohemian, his head bowed.

"A Pennal from Prague I had to end up with," grumbled my assistant to himself, while he rummaged through the books in his trunk.

He pulled out a tiny volume, then he went to fetch a chair for Cloridia. I picked up the book. The title page was decidedly spare in its details:

> *Doctoris Henrici Casparis Abelii*
> 𝔖𝔱𝔲𝔡𝔢𝔫𝔱𝔢𝔫 𝔎𝔲̈𝔫𝔰𝔱𝔢

Which is to say "Artifices of the Students" by Doctor Henry Gaspar Abelius. No date or place of printing, nor even the printer's name. It was no more than forty or so pages. I opened it. There was no preface, no letter to the gentle reader, and not even a dedication to some respectable patron. It was divided into short chapters. I dipped into it.

"𝔖𝔢𝔠𝔯𝔢𝔱 𝔞𝔤𝔞𝔦𝔫𝔰𝔱 𝔴𝔬𝔲𝔫𝔡𝔰 𝔣𝔯𝔬𝔪 𝔴𝔢𝔞𝔭𝔬𝔫𝔰," I read slowly in my laborious German.

"Here, Signor Master," Simonis said quickly, snatching the book from me and opening it at another page. "This is the part that interests us: 'How to do invisible writing and make it reappear.'"

"Magnificent!" exclaimed Cloridia. "Just what we need. How does it work?"

Opalinski looked up inquisitively.

Simonis explained the arduous and dangerous task we were embarking upon.

I was afraid that the Pole might get alarmed and go rushing off. But he did not. As I had already noticed the previous evening, Janitzki did not seem particularly alarmed by the deaths of his fellow students.

"So now," concluded Simonis, "we finally have the chance to discover whether the Agha's phrase conceals a secret or not. If we don't find anything on this piece of paper either, it means that the Turks have nothing to do with the matter. And so our three companions did not die on account of their investigations into the Golden Apple."

"You can rely on my help," answered Opalinski.

"So," the Greek went on to read, "here it says that to make writing invisible, you have to put *acqua fortis* in the ink, but this often results in yellow stains."

According to Doctor Abelius's little book, Simonis went on, others write with strong *vincotto* mixed with straw ash, as is explained even more clearly in *Weckeri Secretis*, which we did not have.

"If necessary we can send the Pennal to go and get it," the Greek stated imperiously.

"Um, what would that be?" asked Penicek timidly.

"The *De Secretis* by Alessio Pedemontano, translated from Italian into Latin by Jacob Wecker – everyone knows it!" Opalinski mocked him, once again in a good mood.

"Ass of a Praguer!" raged Simonis, cuffing the poor Pennal repeatedly and noisily.

The Polish student, as Simonis had said and as I had observed myself, was extremely erudite. Poor Penicek, by contrast, did not seem so well prepared.

My assistant began to read from the book again:

"To make the writing reappear, take gall apples, crumble them into large pieces, leave them for an hour in *vincotto*, distil the resulting water, soak a cotton wad in it and dampen the writing."

"Right, we can start from there," proposed Penicek.

"Have you got any gall apples, idiot of a Pennal?" Simonis attacked him.

"I haven't but I know that Koloman Szupán is a real artist in these tricks."

"Really? He never told me," said Opalinski, who was his great friend, in surprise.

"Koloman is Hungarian: he has the blood of Attila, King of the Huns, who was more famous in his day for his skill in ciphering and deciphering messages, by means of invisible writing and such things, than for being the Scourge of God. He was a great diplomat," stated Penicek.

"Attila?" we all said in amazement.

"Attila."

Hungary got its name from the Huns, explained Penicek. Those fearsome barbarians occupied it in remote ages. It was part of ancient Pannonia, subjugated by Rome under the Empire of Augustus, and famous for its continual rebellions. In Pannonia, explained the Pennal, there was a certain nation close to the banks of the Maeotian Marshes. The people that lived and traded there were wild, misshapen brutes, unable to communicate articulately; they used a certain grunting sound that always seemed to finish with *hunhun*, from which they became known as the Huns, and then the Hungarians.

"By the way," my assistant asked Jan, "do you know where Koloman is?"

"No."

"No one's seen him," observed Penicek. "A pity. He's the one who knows Balamber's trick."

"What is that?" we all asked together.

The Huns – explained the Bohemian gazing upwards, as if searching in his own memory – had lived isolated from everything and everyone until the year of health 370. The Church of Christ was governed at that time by St Damasus, the Empire by Valens, and the Kingdom of the Scythians by Balamber. When hunting a deer, Balamber was drawn by it away from his lands, to the Maeotian marshes, which were frozen at the time. Without knowing it, he was the first foreigner to arrive in Hungary. After observing the view, Balamber forgot about the deer and began to consider the new lands before him and to explore them. When he got back home he talked about them and praised them so highly that the desire to take possession of those lands grew, and very soon the Hungarian lands were overwhelmed by a great invasion. Balamber crossed over the

Tanaïs, subjugated the Tauric Chersonese and the Goths who occupied it, and joining up with the Alans moved on towards the provinces of Moesia and Dacia.

"Nobody could resist him. He gave his messengers little pieces of
blank paper, from which only his allies could extract the messages of
the Scythian king."

On his way through these regions, however, Balamber died, and
was succeeded by Mundsuch, captain of the same nation. Mundsuch
finally conquered the lands of Hungary. His sons were Attila and
Bleda.

"Bleda did not last long: Attila, who had a nasty temper, very soon
killed him. Because of his cruelty he was known as the Scourge of
God, but he had inherited the secret of his grandfather Balamber,
and it was thanks to that – and not to his strength – that he was able
to descend into Italy undisturbed with a hundred thousand men and
put the peninsula to fire and the sword. But he also founded the
beautiful and most serene Venice, which – and it is no coincidence
– is the queen of espionage. It is said that the Doges secretly hand
down the secret of Balamber, left to them by Attila, from one to
another. And everyone knows the shady dealings that go on between
the Most Serene Republic and the Sublime Ottoman Porte."

Penicek was right, I remembered at that moment. Twenty-eight
years earlier Abbot Melani himself had told me that when the Pope
had called upon the whole of Europe to defend Vienna from the
Ottomans, only one other power, apart from France, had held back:
Venice.

"So this piece of paper could hold a secret message written using
Balamber's trick!" I exclaimed.

"Highly possible," confirmed the Pennal. "And in that case
Koloman is our last hope."

"First of all, let's read on," Opalinski proposed, returning to the
recipes of Doctor Abelius. "Perhaps we'll find less secret means."

"I agree," Simonis echoed him. "If we fail we'll look for Koloman."

To cancel something written, continued the little handbook,
some used lemon juice, *Spiritu vini* and *Sale armoniaco*, but if you then
added *Alumine piumoso* and distilled it in an alembic, the writing
would reappear. Of course, as my assistant's little room was hardly an
alchemical laboratory, we did not have any *Alumine piumoso* on hand,
nor even a simple alembic.

"There, maybe I've got it," exclaimed Simonis. "Here it says how to write something secret using normal words."

This happens, explained the book, when the words or letters that matter are counter-marked by little signs or hooks, or the words follow in a fixed number, or when the seventh or eighth word or letter matter, but in such a way that both meanings – the patent and the hidden one – work well in the context, so that the secret is not noticed by third parties and yet is understood by those who need to know it.

We pored over the paper but could find no trace of little marks, however miniscule. So then we tried the other method. But there were very few words and they were all short; one of them, "ad", consisted of only two letters.

"Sssapva, ooodoeu, solaone . . ." we all tried together, one of us taking the first letters, one the second, and one the first, second and third in succession, and then starting over again with the first . . .

Soon Simonis's room echoed with a confused mewling that lasted until we had exhausted all possibilities. In vain, alas.

The Greek leafed through his curious handbook again.

"Ah, there are writings that remain invisible until the paper is immersed in water or passed in front of the fire. This is much simpler."

"What?" said Cloridia, startled. "I have to take that piece of paper back to the palace just as it is!"

"Give it to me," I said to Simonis, taking the book from him and beginning to read: "Take vitriol or galanga, dissolve it in water, throw in powder of gall apples and stir it. After twenty-four hours filter with a clean cloth and use it to write; when it is dry you will not be able to see anything on the paper."

If you wanted to read what was written, concluded the recipe, you had to put the paper in clean water and after a few minutes white letters would appear.

But if the invisible writing had been done with the juice of onions or garlic, anyone who wanted to read it would have to hold the letter over the fire and at once reddish writing would appear.

The other systems indicated by Doctor Abelius were, unfortunately, even more complicated. If lemon juice had been used to write, in order to read it you had to grate a *Lithargyrium* nut, or silver foam, boil it in vinegar and then immerse the paper in it. This would reveal white script. But if the ink consisted of vitriol that had been crushed and dissolved in water, you would have to pulverise a dram of gall apples, pour a half measure of pure water over it, stir, sift with a cloth and wet the paper with this water; this would reveal black script.

Another way to make invisible writing and bring it to light, was to make an ink by dissolving vitriol in *vincotto*, filtering it with a linen cloth and leaving it to stand until it became clear. Then you took oat straw reduced to ashes and rubbed it with pure water on a coloured stone, until it became a convenient colour for writing. With this ink you then wrote – between the now dry invisible lines on the same piece of paper – a normal letter with nothing secret in it, so that no one would suspect there was anything hidden. Anyone who wanted to read the hidden lines would have to boil gall apples in wine, dip a sponge in it and wipe it delicately over the letter. The visible lines would disappear and the previously invisible ones would emerge in their place.

In short, the waters that should bring out the hypothetical writing on the Agha's piece of paper were complicated concoctions of ingredients that only an apothecary could supply. But the worst hypothesis of all was yet to come. If the writing had been done with a mixture of minced silver foam, strong vinegar and egg white, to read it we would have to burn the Agha's paper until it turned black: at that point white letters would appear.

"Have you gone mad?" my wife kept repeating as we read the book aloud, with her hands on her chest.

In the end she was persuaded to allow the least risky expedient: rapid immersion in water. But she did not want to witness the experiment, which made her extremely anxious, and took the opportunity to go back to our rooms to watch over Abbot Melani as he slept and to take care of our son.

Fortunately the Agha's paper was of the best and thickest, the kind used for messages to be sent by courier through rain and snow, over rivers, lakes and countless other obstacles. It was designed to stand up to all the discomforts of travel; I was sure it would resist. Almost as if it were a sacred ceremony, Simonis fetched a bowl of water, while Opalinski stretched out a white cloth on which we would lay the Agha's paper. With my heart pounding, I dipped it for an instant into the bowl, taking care not to wet the part with the Agha's phrase, for fear the ink would run.

Nothing happened, but fortunately the paper passed the test more or less unharmed. We waited for it to dry, placing a small brazier a little way off. Then we tried with the gentle flame of a candle stub to see if any hidden writing emerged. Nothing. For obvious reasons I discarded the carbonisation method, and resigned myself to trying the remaining methods. I told Simonis to make a list of what we needed: vitriol oil, alembics, *alumine piumoso, et cetera et cetera.* Then I gave it to Penicek.

"Here's some money," I said. "Go in your cart to the Red Crab apothecary, near the Old Market, and get everything."

"A pity good old Koloman Szupán isn't here with us," sighed the Pennal, screwing up his little eyes to stare at the list for the apothecary. "With all this stuff he would know how to get any secret out of the Agha's paper."

"I'd really like to know where he's got to," said Simonis.

"Perhaps Opalinski," the Pennal timidly ventured, "has some notion –"

"Not the faintest idea," the latter cut him short.

"A pity," repeated Penicek. "Perhaps Koloman is hiding because he's scared. After they killed Dragomir in that way . . ."

Opalinski lowered his eyes.

"If he's vanished because he's afraid," the Bohemian considered, limping towards the door, "it would soothe him to know that the dervish didn't really want to cut anyone's head off. It's a pity we can't tell him so."

"This evening I'll go and see if I can track him down in some tavern," promised Jan Janitzki.

"This evening will be late," insisted Penicek. "Signor Barber is right, this is the great chance to find out if the Agha's phrase conceals something or not. Signor Barber says truly: if we don't find anything on this paper, it means the Sublime Porte has nothing to do with this whole story. And so – as Signor Barber neatly puts it – we will finally have the proof that Dànilo, Hristo and Dragomir were not done away with for their enquiries into the Golden Apple."

"Bravo, Pennal! Incredible, there really is a glimmering of intelligence in that brute's head of yours!" exclaimed Simonis, pleased with the praise bestowed on him.

"All the same," I put in, "if Koloman is hiding, we could end up wandering all over the city . . ."

"He's at the House Goat."

❦

Opalinski knew where to find the Hungarian. Koloman had confided in his friend: he was hiding in the attic of an open-air inn, known as the House Goat, in the suburb of Ottakring.

Penicek had guessed correctly: after Populescu's death, Szupán was afraid. And so he had gone into hiding and had made Jan swear that he would not reveal his hiding place to a living soul.

But now the Pole had spoken. It was a question of tracking Koloman down to let him know the reassuring news about the dervish, and at the same time to seek his help in examining the Turkish Agha's paper. But Opalinski already seemed sorry he had let the secret out, and his face had turned dark.

"Come on, let's go," I exhorted him impatiently.

"If you don't mind, wouldn't it better if I went first to the apothecary to get the *remedia* before he shuts up shop?" the Bohemian proposed. "I'll come straight back, pick you up in the cart and we can all go to Koloman."

"If we all set out together we'll be quicker," I objected. "Once we get to Koloman, we can start the experiments with his help."

"With Signor Master's permission, if I may be so bold," Penicek timidly remarked, "doesn't Signor Master think it risky to let the Agha's paper leave the secure walls of this convent and to carry out delicate trials in a public place?"

"Good Lord, I hadn't thought of that," I said. "I must be really tired. You're right, we had better go and fetch Szupán and bring him here."

"On reflection," Opalinski put in, "despite the good news we'll be bringing him, it might take hours to persuade Koloman to lend us a hand in this matter. And, I repeat, even though we are friends, he has never talked to me about Balamber, Attila, ciphered codes or any of the rest. If he doesn't agree to help us, we could end up not having enough time to do the experiments by ourselves."

After further discussion we finally decided to try without Koloman. Opalinski's face brightened: should the experiments work, his Hungarian friend would never find out that he had blown the gaff on his hiding place. And so we sent the Pennal to the apothecary.

"And hurry!" roared the Greek, making the poor cripple jump.

The Bohemian student returned more than an hour later, panting and sweating from his hurried journey and from a long argument with the apothecary, who had been unwilling to sell him some of the preparations, which were potentially toxic. He had asked a thousand questions about what the devil all this stuff was for, and finally had kept him waiting a good while on account of the laborious Galenic preparation of a couple of *remedia*.

My assistant's little room was quickly turned into an alchemic kitchen, with the cauldron on the hearth full of smoking and foaming alembics, while the air was saturated with pungent smells.

"Nothing at all, damnation!" Simonis cursed impatiently.

The only effect achieved by all that busy activity was that the paper now had unsightly creases and singed margins.

"How can we put it back in Prince Eugene's diary in this state?" I fretted. "If Cloridia sees it, I'm done for!"

It was now two in the afternoon. We had been racking our brains for almost three hours over this little piece of paper, which refused to give up its secrets, if it had any. To the great dismay of Opalinski, our only resource now was Koloman Szupán.

১৯৪৩

On the way, Opalinski seemed in a state of mute anxiety. Perhaps he was wondering what Koloman would say when he saw us arriving.

I was in a grim mood too. If Koloman could not manage to extract anything from the Agha's paper, this would be good news in one way, since it would free us from the terror of the Turks. On the other hand, it would leave us in utter darkness: three students had died one after the other and the murderers (or the murderer) did not yet have a name.

I looked at Simonis: he was sitting opposite me, his dull eyes distractedly following the rows of vineyards running by our sides. Before setting out he had put a small bag around his neck, which he now stroked meditatively, probably sharing my serious thoughts.

"Why on earth did Koloman choose to hide in the House Goat?" I asked Janitzki.

"An Italian monk took him there. Koloman actually asked for shelter in a monastery, but they didn't want him there."

"Didn't your companion go to an Italian monk to get news of the Golden Apple?" I asked him at once.

"I remember that," confirmed Simonis, "an Augustinian who used to hear the confessions of the Turkish prisoners of war who wanted to convert."

"Yes, it's true, but I don't know whether it's the same one," answered Opalinski.

"What?" said Penicek in alarm. "Has Koloman gone mad?"

"Why?" we asked in unison.

"Didn't you hear that they arrested an Augustinian this morning? An Italian who has been accused of a string of murders and rapes."

A chill descended upon us.

Our lame cart driver, by contrast, seemed in a feverish state:

"So Koloman had to go and hand himself over to an Italian monk, of all people? I thought he was smarter than that!" he repeated, shaking his head, as he drove us outside the city walls, towards the suburb of Ottakring.

"Praguer brute!" Simonis reacted. "How dare you? Apologise and then shut up."

But either because of the praise he had received earlier from his Barber or from underlying fear, Penicek seemed to have no intention of shutting up. On the contrary, laying aside his humble and contrite air he persisted doggedly:

"Doesn't Koloman know that monks are the most treacherous and dangerous breed? And Italians to boot!"

"Why do you say that?" I asked, annoyed that this wretched lame Pennal, the servile laughing stock of his companions, should take such a knowing tone when talking about my fellow countrymen.

"Filthy Bohemian animal!" snarled Simonis, leaping to his feet and striking the driver on the back of his neck. "What's got into you? Apologise to Signor Master."

"Forget it," I said to my assistant. "But you," I said brusquely to the Pennal, being accustomed now to treat him as roughly as all the others did, "I asked you a question. What's wrong with Italian monks?"

Halfway through the sixteenth century, answered Penicek, made nervous by his Barber's reprimand, Martin Luther came along and lifted the stones off those whitened sepulchres and vipers' nests, the monasteries. All the things that had previously gone on in the dark were now exposed to the light. Many monks abandoned their orders, got married and joined the Lutherans. The number of Catholic monks went down alarmingly.

"Just what are you saying, Pennal?" Opalinski said indignantly. "Are you on the side of Luther's cankerous heresy?"

"What can you expect from a Praguer?" muttered Simonis.

"Go on, Penicek," I ordered him.

The ancient monastery of the Augustinian Hermits of Vienna, at the time situated next to the Caesarean palace, was on the point of closing down. The order was forced to seek the help of brothers from other countries. Reinforcements came from the religious houses of Italy, which had not been affected by the wind of the Reformation."

"A godless wind from the backside," added Opalinski.

But unfortunately the Italian fathers (especially those of a higher rank), being closer to and more familiar with Rome, felt somehow superior and worthier. They despised and mistreated their Viennese brothers and wove mysterious diplomatic intrigues with the foreign ambassadors in the Caesarean city.

"You mean the Italian brothers were spies?" I asked suspiciously.

"The imperial authorities were convinced of it."

As a consequence of certain visits or inspections in the monastery, suspicious characters of every type were found in the cloisters: bandits, plunderers and all sorts. The Italian monks were accused of exploiting the proximity of the royal palace and their links with the imperial court to spy on all those in the pay of France or other foreign powers, and in the end orders came to drive them out, forbidding them to return and decreeing that in future all fathers superior must be German-speaking.

The Germans were more honest, but they had other faults. They were a little cold in their faith, and, above all, incompetent. They lacked the human touch that, although often perverse, came naturally to their Italian brothers. They were great rogues, these brothers from the south, but they knew how to nurture souls and to win over people, and when necessary they were extremely wily and shrewd. Rome and the fathers general of the Augustinian order meanwhile insisted on having their own men on the spot, and in the end they won. The Italians were readmitted, then driven out again, taken back, thrown out yet again and so on, while the people looked on in amazement and wondered whether the problem was the dishonesty of those being expelled or the confused ideas of the expellers.

Meanwhile the Catholic Counter-Reformation got under way, the principal lines being dictated by Rome. The fathers superior sent some of their trusted compatriots to Vienna. The court could not refuse them, because in the meantime the Prior of the Augustinian monastery, who was not Italian, had fled to Prague just before an inspection, where he was finally arrested. He was guilty of serious financial malpractice, which had left the monastery up to its ears in debt, having broken the same imperial edicts that forbade the monks from selling off the property of the monastery, from turning themselves into wine traders, from trading in agricultural commodities, *et cetera et cetera*.

In short, within the holy walls peace was a chimera. When the Italians came back, quarrels and rows broke out continually. All privileged relations with the Emperor's court had broken down in an atmosphere of diffidence and mutual contempt. The monks continued to quarrel with the civil authorities; the fathers superior quarrelled with their subordinates, and also among themselves. If one of them bought a vineyard or a piece of land for the monastery, his successor would sell it, and then they would accuse one another of having squandered the order's money. The case would end up before the civil authorities, who would find faults on both sides, blaming all the monks, and so on, partly because the fathers superior were substituted too frequently, and this greatly multiplied the number of litigants.

Since no one was above reproach, the Italians had no difficulty in lording it over everyone. Acrimony, quarrels, backbiting, envy and calumny lit the fuse of hatred between the Teutonic monks and the Italians, and if the new prior tried to make peace, he would quickly be insulted by the Germans and get drawn into the intrigues of the Italians, who had a damnable gift for sowing discord and creating incomprehensible disputes out of nothing, so that everyone suffered, including the Italians.

"In the end the Jesuits got involved in the matter, obtaining a bull from Pope Urban VIII with permission to confront the Augustinian Hermits – Italians and non-Italians – and move them outside the walls, without any warning, into the suburb of Landstrasse, where they still remain. Their place was then taken by the Barefoot Augustinians, 'imported' from Prague, a far more virtuous order."

"The order of Pater Abraham from Sancta Clara," I said.

"The very one. And as far as I know there's not a single Italian among them," sniggered Penicek.

"Are you happy now, Pennal?" grumbled Simonis. "What have you proved with your tirade? That the monks from Prague are better?"

"Or that the Jesuits, as usual, are the cleverest?" added the Pole. "In any case the story of the expulsion of the Augustinians is as old as the hills."

"But the news of the Augustinian murderer . . ."

"Was he an Augustinian Hermit or a Barefoot Augustinian?" asked my assistant point blank.

"Mm . . . Hermit."

"Koloman's monk friend is a Barefoot Augustinian," snapped Simonis.

"So, nothing to worry about," I concluded with a sigh of relief, while the cart pulled up in front of the gate of a vineyard.

We had arrived at the House Goat. It was one of those delicious *Heuriger*, open-air inns kept by vine growers and their families, where you can go and taste *Heuriger*, the new wine produced in the vineyard at the back of the house. The House Goat was considered one of the best wine shops, but actually it was difficult to go wrong with the *Heuriger* inns: the white or red wine trodden in the family cellar is never less than decent, the turkey coated in breadcrumbs by the host's wife or mother is always crisp, the pork with caraway seeds as fragrant and juicy as the cheeks of the maiden with blond tresses who serves it to you piping hot.

Usually you pass through a gate and find a table under the trees, in an internal courtyard, where even the coarsest customer has the good manners to whisper (in such a place in Rome you would have to plug your ears against the noisy chattering, the guffawing and the clattering of plates, tables and chairs). If there is no room at the tables, you find a place in one of the niches carved into the centuries-old tree trunks, or you can eat at a makeshift counter, formed by rustic planks fixed roughly to a low wall or, if it rains, inside an old barrel quaintly kitted out with table, stools and lace cloths like a squirrel's den in a fairy-tale. At the entrance you are at once charmed by the graceful, gentle atmosphere, so that even if they served you vinegar instead of wine, and dry bread instead of turkey, you would eat and drink with relish all the same, revelling in the rustle of the branches, the twittering of the birds, the smile of the host's daughter and the peace that breathes forth from the blessed land where Vienna the Wise sweetly reposes. And as you rotate a glass of ruby-coloured new wine in your hands, and lose yourself in its vermilion depths, the clucking of the nearby hen house will sound like a chorus of Aegean virgins, the braying of the donkey on the nearby farm a verse from Sophocles; and you will not be surprised to find yourself recalling, as happened to me that day, the austere description of Austria by Enea Silvio Piccolomini which I had read before I came to Vienna, and in your memory it will almost turn into a poem:

> *The Archduchy of Austria above and below the Enns provides wine for Bavarians, Bohemians, Moravians and Silesians, hence the great wealth of the Austrians. They make the grape harvest last forty days, and two or three times a day three hundred carts loaded with wine enter Vienna from the suburbs, and every day one thousand two hundred horses, or perhaps more, are used in the work of the harvest. It does no harm to anyone's prestige to open a wine shop in their own house; many citizens keep a tavern, heat the place and do magnificent cooking...*

My wife and I dreamed of opening a wine shop one day, in the vineyard in the Josephine that Atto Melani had donated to us, I reflected, as I sat on a bench in the *Heuriger*, which was curiously deserted at that moment, while Penicek waited on the box seat and the other two went in search of Koloman. With my little boy I would keep up our profitable chimney-sweeping activity, in which my son would succeed me; Cloridia would find a steady job as a hostess in our *Heuriger*; our two daughters would join us, and they would help their mother in the kitchen and the wine shop, while we would find a couple of good strong boys from the neighbourhood to work in the vineyard, and, who knows, maybe they would ask our blessing to wed our daughters, and so the whole family, including (God willing) our grandchildren, would prosper in...

"Signor Master, Signor Master, quick!"

The voice came from afar, and from above. I looked around but could see nothing. I got up from the garden bench and walked a few steps. Simonis was calling to me from the attic of a service building, which looked onto the animal yard and was connected to the main house by a low building, perhaps the stables. He was at a dormer window, on the rear side of the building, and was waving to attract my attention, rousing me from the languor I had been lulled into by the idyllic setting and the first sips of red wine.

There was no need to climb the stairs and go all the way up there. Walking round in search of the entrance, I ran into a small crowd of people. They were clients of the *Heuriger* (so that was where they had all ended up) and with them were the host and his wife. They were gathered around the hen run. Then I saw.

At first I took it for a scarecrow, one of those figures made of old clothes and straw that are used to keep birds off the newly sown fields. But what was a scarecrow doing in a hen run? It was Koloman. It wasn't very different from the way we had found Populescu: Koloman too had been impaled, but by wooden pikes, not by candlesticks.

A fence of pointed poles, thrust deeply into the ground, protected the animals from raids by foxes, martens and wildcats, which could not reach their prey either by digging or by climbing. Impaled on the forest of sharp points, Koloman the great lover, Koloman the poor Hungarian waiter, Koloman the self-styled baron of Varasdin, was gazing eastwards, towards the great plain of his native Hungary. Chickens, hens and turkeys took no notice. They continued to scratch around calmly in the shady pen, disturbed more by our presence than by their scarecrow of flesh and blood.

"Murderers, beasts . . . They're just beasts," stammered Opalinski, stifling his sobs.

We were now in the little attic room from which Simonis had called out to me.

"Murderers? Who?"

It was my assistant who said this, without removing his eyes from the corpse.

"The ones who murdered Koloman," I answered, fearing that he was feeling the effect of this blow.

The Greek said nothing. He stood there, looking out of the dormer window. He looked up, to the roof, and then down, towards Koloman and the pikes. Then his eyes shifted again towards the stables that joined the building to the host's house. I followed the direction of his eyes, and at the window opposite ours I saw the shocked faces of two rosy-faced girls, probably the host's daughters. Beside them, on the wall of the house, a sundial showed that it was half past three. At that moment Simonis turned towards us:

"What if it were an accident?"

❧

Nothing was clear anymore. We had made a hasty departure from the House Goat and now we were wandering around the nearby high ground known as The Pulpit.

From the top of the steep hill, there was a view over the Caesarean city. It stretched out before our eyes, under the menacing shade of black rain clouds, while we were bathed in warm and inopportune sunlight.

Much had happened since we took our leave of poor Koloman, starting with the scuffle that had broken out involving Opalinski. Things had gone in this fashion.

In exchange for a hefty tip the host had agreed to wait another half-hour before calling the city guard.

The landlord stood gazing at us with an impatient air, waiting for us to go: he had not even asked our names. The only thing he was interested in was the money with which we had bought those few moments of peace for our final farewell to our friend; he thought we were friends or relatives of Koloman who had come to visit him. When the city guard eventually came he would simply show them the boy's body and say that he had fallen from the roof.

He had never seen or met him, he would say. Actually, he had met him most definitely the day before, when Koloman had been brought to him by the Italian monk to whom the student had turned for help. What had happened after that, the host neither knew nor cared to know. The money he had been given by the monk was enough, he said, though he was quite happy to take our offering as well.

We had just a few moments to ourselves before we slipped away. Koloman's death, the fourth, left only Simonis and Opalinski of the group of friends I had met at the Deposition just a few days earlier. It was all too obvious that their deaths were interconnected, and that I, in one way or another, was not unrelated to them. And yet we could find no evidence of a common motive or of a link between those deaths and myself. The enquiries into the Turks had led to a dead end. Ciezeber the dervish had nothing to hide, nor did the

Agha's phrase on the Golden Apple, and it was highly improbable that the paper on which it was written concealed anything either. And so Atto Melani's allusion to the fact that both Hristo and Dragomir were Ottoman subjects meant nothing. By contrast, each of the four victims had an excellent reason for passing into the next world. Dànilo's and Hristo's dangerous occupations had perhaps been fatal to them; the Armenian girl to Dragomir; and Koloman?

"He died at three, his regular hour for lying with a woman."

"Right," I said, remembering the hour marked by the sun dial, "and at the window opposite there were the host's two beautiful daughters. Do you think he fell trying to reach them?"

"Koloman, I've already told you, was a specialist in climbing over roofs and cornices for his romantic appointments. Perhaps this time he put a foot wrong. It's just that . . ."

"What?"

"It's just that it seems very unlikely to me that, terrified as he was, he would have felt like having a woman."

With Koloman Szupán, in short, it was very difficult to work out whether he had been killed or not. Although I myself had looked repeatedly at the place where it had happened, at the position of the body and the trajectory of the fall, although I had examined every detail in the little room in which Szupán had spent his last hours, I could but reach the same conclusion as Simonis: the only thing certain was that the Hungarian had fallen. God alone knew if he had been pushed.

Only Opalinski, overwhelmed with despair and remorse at having betrayed the name of Koloman's hiding place, seemed sure that his friend had been murdered. And he accused Penicek.

"Augustinian murderer, my foot! Filthy demon from Prague, I'll tear your eyes out!" he bellowed as we climbed aboard the Bohemian's cart, after leaving the House Goat.

We just managed to rescue the poor cripple before Opalinski, who was a great strapping fellow, choked him to death in his powerful grip. When he heard what had happened, Penicek repeated the story of the Italian monk, and that Koloman should not have trusted him, *et cetera et cetera*. But Janitzki attacked him without even letting him finish, so that Simonis and I had to grapple with him to prevent him from strangling the Bohemian.

"But you made a mistake, foul beast of the Evil One! You defenestrated Koloman! You just can't help yourselves, you Praguers!" yelled Jan, finally slackening his grip on the Pennal's throat.

At these enigmatic words from Opalinski, Simonis briefly explained that for centuries it had been a brutal custom in Prague to murder people by defenestration. The first such act had taken place on 30th July 1419, when a group of dissatisfied Bohemian nobles had broken into the town hall and thrown the mayor and his councillors out of the window, killing them. Since then the list of precipitations from windows had lengthened. A hundred years earlier a delegation of Protestants had defenestrated two Catholic counsellors of the Emperor, who had landed on a cart full of dung and thus been saved. A famous defenestration, finally, had been the trigger for the Thirty Years' War.

"When you left to go to the apothecary, you already knew where to find Koloman!" sobbed Opalinski now. "You did all you could to worm his hiding place out of me. And like an imbecile, I fell for it!"

The Pennal had come back after more than an hour. According to Jan Janitzki, he would have had plenty of time to go to the House Goat, defenestrate the Hungarian student and come back to us at Porta Coeli.

"That story about your discussion with the apothecary, you just made it up – confess!"

The Pole was raving. Penicek had saved my life, at the Prater, after Hristo's death. Janitzki's accusations made no sense. I told him so, looking for support for my words in Simonis's eyes.

"Jan, calm down. What you're saying is absurd. Tell him so, Simonis."

The Greek had been with me at the Prater; he knew that I owed my life to his Pennal. But my assistant, his face pale and shiny with cold sweat, was gazing into the air. It was impossible to tell if his eyes were impenetrable or simply vacant.

The Pole meanwhile had got out of the cart. Beside himself and shaking with sobs, he refused to stay another minute in the Pennal's company: he would go back to the city on foot.

"Go to the Red Crab and talk to the apothecary!" he shouted, as he set off. "We'll see if he backs up the lies of that demonic Bohemian!"

Penicek, purple in the face, sat there on the box seat, his terrified, bespectacled eyes wandering from me to his Barber, and then
to his Barber's hand, which was rummaging in his bag.

"To the Red Crab, Pennal!" ordered Simonis.

Penicek did not move.

"Turn round and get moving!" Simonis shouted, seizing him by
the neck.

The cripple took his eyes off us and, in obedience to his Barber,
turned and looked at the road; but he did not move the cart.

"I . . . I . . ." he stammered, "Janitzki is right, it's true, I wasn't at
the apothecary all that time."

I looked at him in astonishment, and Simonis did not let go of his
neck.

"I . . . I think I've solved the mystery of the Agha's phrase," he
said at last.

The poor cripple told us that, after leaving Porta Coeli to go to
the apothecary, he had driven in front of the little palace known as
Haidenschuss, or Shoot the Heathen.

"I look up and what do I see? On the front of the house there's a
little statue of a Turk on a horse, brandishing a scimitar."

"And so?" said Simonis. "That statue is famous, we all know it."

"Yes, I've seen it," I confirmed.

"Do . . . do you know the story of the statue?" asked the Pennal,
his mouth still quivering with terror.

"No," we said in unison.

Simonis ordered him to drive us up the nearby hill of The Pulpit,
so that passers-by would not get suspicious at our remaining
stationary, and Penicek began to talk. According to the tradition of
the Sublime Porte, the Ottoman's name was Dayi Çerkes, which is
to say Dayi the Circassian, and he had taken part in the first siege of
Vienna. As soon as Suleiman's mines had opened a breach in the
walls, he had rushed inside the city on his horse, scimitar in hand.
He knew that if the other Turks followed him, there would be no
escape for the capital city of the Holy Roman Empire. However, his
companions were not quite so courageous and did not follow him.
And so, left alone, Dayi Çerkes was attacked by the Christians and
killed. Emperor Ferdinand I honoured the courage of the dead hero:
he had him and his horse mummified and placed them under the
arch of the façade of a house, renaming the small square in front of

it Circassian Square. There you can still admire Dayi Çerkes sitting on his horse, fully armed. The Emperor ordered that the Giaour – which is to say the Christian – who had killed the Turk by shooting him in the back with an arquebus, should be bricked up alive in the wall of the house opposite, addressing these words to him: "Why did you shoot from behind at a soldier armed only with a scimitar? You should have confronted him directly with a mace and sword, not shoot from hiding." There the Giaour died amid a thousand torments. As the years went by the equestrian mummy deteriorated and was replaced by the statue.

"And so?" said Simonis.

"Dayi Çerkes entered the Golden Apple *all alone*. For his courage he is still venerated as a saint. If Vienna were to become Muslim, he would be its patron saint," concluded the Bohemian.

"Good Lord!" I exclaimed. "That's why the Agha said he had come all alone to the Golden Apple: he wanted to recall the Circassian's heroism . . . But why?"

"Well, I don't . . ." stammered Penicek. "Ah, perhaps it was a way to emphasise their own honourable behaviour as enemies, coming here just as Dayi Çerkes had done, in daylight, on a horse, armed only with his scimitar."

"So that's what Hadji-Tanjov had found out!" I remembered. "He said that the meaning of the Agha's phrase lay in *soli soli soli*. Now it's clear: he had discovered the story of the Circassian. That means the Agha's phrase holds no more mysteries – just like Kara Mustafa's head and the dervish's rituals," I exclaimed in disappointment.

"But someone did murder Dànilo, Hristo and Dragomir. And perhaps Koloman," objected Simonis.

"And Hristo on that note in his chessboard wrote 'The King is enclosed' . . . What does –?"

"We're here," Simonis interrupted me in a powerful voice, making Penicek jump.

We had reached the top of the hill. I was about to get out of the cart, but the Greek held me back.

"Now you'll drive around here," he ordered Penicek, keeping his grip on his neck, while his other hand was still thrust in his bag.

"What do you think?" I asked him.

"I just wonder: how could the Agha have been sure that Prince Eugene would understand the meaning of the phrase?"

"Right," I said, and I noticed that my incomprehensible assistant was for the moment in a happy phase of mental lucidity.

"Em, oh . . ." said the Pennal uncertainly, casting oblique sidelong glances at Simonis's bag with terrified eyes. Then his face lit up: "It's simple: the Shoot the Heathen palace belongs to the Most Serene Prince!"

"We could go there," I suggested. "Perhaps the residents will be able to tell us more about this story of the Circassian, something that will help us to understand more clearly."

"I fear not," answered the Prague student, still looking at the grassy meadow before him, which Simonis was forcing him to drive around in circles.

What he had recounted so far, Penicek clarified, was the Turkish explanation for the presence of the statue on the front of the house. The Viennese version was quite different. The tunnels dug by the Turks with their mines reached right under the walls. In order to keep track of this subterranean menace, the Viennese set up warning systems in their cellars, such as buckets full of water (when a mine exploded, even far off, the water would start to tremble), or drums with peas or dice on top of them, which would all leap up at an explosion, making a reverberating noise. Obviously a boy had to be set to watch over these systems, day and night. At the time of the first siege, in 1529, the house in question was lived in by a baker. It had two underground floors, used as a cellar. A boy who worked in the deepest cellar, a certain Josef Schulz from the city of Bolkenhain in Silesia, discovered the work on the Turkish mines and excavations thanks to the dice bouncing on a drum. He at once informed the commander of the city and so saved Vienna from ruin. Emperor Ferdinand consequently granted the corporation of bakers the privilege of holding an Easter procession every year in honour of that event, with flags flying and Turkish music. Later the cellar became a wine shop and was called the Cellar of the Turks. And the little statue is supposed to be the symbol of the Turks thwarted by the boy's alertness."

"Ah yes, I saw the procession of the bakers a week ago. So that's what it referred to," I said.

"If the residents of the palace don't know the Turkish version of the story, I imagine that you didn't learn it from them," said Simonis to Penicek. "So where did you hear it? And why did you take so long to get back to Porta Coeli?"

The Pennal gave a timid half-smile.

"I already knew the legend, but it was only today, when I lifted my eyes to that damned statue, that it became clear to me. And so I got out to question the inhabitants of the house, and that's why I took so long. But all they knew was the story I've just told. If only I had thought of it earlier! At this hour we would already have given up this absurd story of the Golden Apple!"

Penicek broke into sobs, giving free vent to his tension, torment and panic. He wept unrestrainedly, and he was still weeping when Simonis ordered him to drive the cart to Porta Coeli.

On the way back my assistant stared at him with the glassy eyes of a barn owl, behind which, as usual, I could discern nothing.

⋙∞⋘

17 of the clock, end of the working day: workshops and chancelleries close. Dinner hour for artisans, secretaries, language teachers, priests, servants of commerce, footmen and coach drivers (while in Rome people take but a light refection).

At the hour of our appointment with Ugonio at Porta Coeli I arrived exhausted and drained.

Our little boy was playing in the cloisters. I sent him to dine in the eating house with Simonis. I found Cloridia in Abbot Melani's rooms.

"Well?" My wife greeted me anxiously, when I knocked at Atto's door.

She wanted to know if we had succeeded in extracting anything from the paper with the Agha's words: she had to return the precious piece of paper to the wife of Prince Eugene's personal chamberlain.

I told her and the Abbot about Koloman's death, Opalinski's reaction and his accusations against the Pennal. My consort fell into a chair like a limp rag. Melani, barricaded as ever behind his dark glasses, stroked the pummel of his stick, immersed in impenetrable thought.

"And suppose it were an accident?"

"And suppose it were the monk?"

"And suppose . . .?"

Question after question piled up while I talked to Cloridia.

We both knew it: only the last of the three possibilities, the one that concealed within itself the name of Penicek, connected the deaths of all four students. This hypothesis left just one question open, and that was: why?

I explained, finally, how the Bohemian had solved the mystery, which was in fact no mystery, of the Agha's phrase: the Turks wanted to emphasise to Eugene that they had come to Vienna with the same integrity as Dayi Çerkes: all alone – that is, without any subterfuge. A metaphor that was perfectly clear to the Most Serene Prince, since the palace with the statue of the Circassian belonged to him.

"The Turks have nothing to do with it and that's good, I'm pleased. Koloman's death may well have been an accident. But someone killed the other three students one after the other. And I don't like that Penicek," she said, in a grim tone at last.

"But he saved my life," I objected.

"Don't exaggerate. Let's say he turned up at the right moment."

I didn't like Penicek either. I had never thought about it, but there was something dark and slimy about the twisted little rat, with his ferret-like eyes behind his glinting spectacles, which often made me look away from him. It was true that his arrival at the Prater had saved me from being stabbed, and now, with the story of the Circassian, he seemed to have made a definite contribution to the solution of the Agha's phrase. But even so I had never once thought of offering him even a *scudo*, instinctively profiting from his condition as Pennal. Alas, I had let myself be conditioned by the way he was mistreated by Simonis, or by the wisdom of his country, Greece, which first gave birth to the concept that what is beautiful is also good, while what is not beautiful conceals within itself evil. And Penicek was far from beautiful. In addition, he was lame, like the devil. But I was certainly not the person best suited to make such observations, as I was about to be superseded in height by my eight-year-old son.

"And what does Simonis think of this story?" my wife asked. "The Bohemian is under his command, it seems to me."

"Exactly. At first he put him on the spot. But then, after Penicek revealed the real meaning of the phrase . . . you know, Simonis is at times, how can I put it, hard to fathom."

"Yes, poor thing," agreed Cloridia, who had always had a soft spot for my bumbling assistant.

"It's convenient to play the idiot," Atto put in.

"What do you mean?" I asked.

"Nothing, for the moment. But Monna Cloridia put it well: the lame boy takes his orders from the Greek."

"And so? It's a student custom that . . ."

"I'm not interested in the form. I look at the facts," the Abbot cut me short. "In any case, Cloridia told me about the Agha's piece of paper. May I see it?"

"See it?" I said wonderingly.

"In short, I mean, can I hold it. I'm curious. If only my poor eyes could really see it!"

I pulled it from my pocket. It was a little worn by our deciphering experiments. I gave it to the Abbot. He opened it. He seemed to be trying to glean its contents by the light of the candle that stood on the table next to his armchair, but Cloridia, as soon as she saw the state to which our experiments, suggested by Doctor Abelius's handbook, had reduced the poor scrap of paper, snatched it from his hands.

"Oh my God! And now what? I certainly can't give the paper back in this condition!"

"Maybe, with a little trimming at the edges and some smoothing . . ." I stammered.

Thrusting the paper into her apron pocket, without another word Cloridia stormed out of Atto's room.

At that moment the pantry sister entered with dinner for Abbot Melani and Domenico, who was still ill. Atto did not want to move: we were waiting for Ugonio. But he was late.

On the pretext of going to eat something myself, and in order to let uncle and nephew dine in peace, I asked their permission to join Cloridia in our rooms. We were just a few yards away: if Atto needed us, he could call for us.

I found Cloridia busily fixing the Agha's sheet of paper. She was painstakingly trimming the singed edges. With the iron she would then smooth out the creases the water had produced.

Abbot Melani, Cloridia told me while she worked, had told her what had happened with Ugonio that morning – that the head craved by Ciezeber the dervish was the wizened one of Kara Mustafa, and not the one on His Caesarean Majesty's youthful neck. He had also told her about the ambiguous appointment that the *corpisantaro* had with Gaetano Orsini and how this was connected in some way with the two unidentified hanged men. Now that we were alone, I told her what had happened that morning after she had brought us the pamphlet with the news of the Grand Dauphin's suspected smallpox: Atto's confession and all the rest that I had learned from him, including Eugene's tremendous jealousy of His Caesarean Majesty. When I touched on the disconcerting revelations about the Most Serene Prince's intimate habits, my sweet spouse was less surprised than I had expected; indeed, she made a few salacious comments that cannot be repeated here.

"Bah," she remarked doubtfully at last, "however badly I might judge the Prince, do you know what I think? I'm sure he would not go so far as to wish for the Emperor to die. As for the rest, I already suspected he was a smart one," she concluded with a smile. "I bet it was he who had the Pálffy woman set up just here in Porta Coeli Street, almost opposite his palace."

"Gaetano Orsini said it was the Emperor in person, because of its closeness to the convent, where Camilla is."

"Perhaps both. In any case I wouldn't trust Orsini until Ugonio makes it clear just what his relationship is with him. And on that subject, what time is it? Wasn't he supposed to be here at five?"

It was almost six. The *corpisantaro* was late. Cloridia, however, could not be late: the time had come to give back the Agha's piece of paper. She urged me to keep an eye on Abbot Melani's requirements and left for Prince Eugene's palace.

A short while later, Simonis and my son came back from the eating house where they had dined. Cloridia's words on Orsini gave me an idea. I sent both of them to the Coppersmiths' Slope. They would knock at the door of Anton de' Rossi. Cardinal Collonitz's former chamberlain had asked Gaetano Orsini to arrange for his flue to be repaired. I was waiting for Ugonio and could not leave, but Simonis, with his vague air, could manage by himself to get information on the young castrato.

Having given my assistant and apprentice all the necessary instructions and sent them off, I was about to settle in my armchair when Doctor Abelius's handbook on the artifices of students slipped from my belt.

As I picked it up my eye ran over the titles of some of the mini chapters on the page where it had opened. It was not the part we had read and used for the Agha's paper. The pages were densely annotated in the margin; I recognised Simonis's unintelligible handwriting. Alas, it was written in Current, that German cursive which to the eyes of a Latin might just as well be Arabic. Growing curious, I glanced at the passages that seemed to have drawn my assistant's closest attention:

> *Do you wish to see if a wounded person will get better or die? Take rue juice and put it in his nose; if he sneezes he will get better, otherwise it means he is fatally wounded.*

It was just what Simonis had tried with Dànilo when we had found him dying on the ramparts. So my assistant had taken the trick from Doctor Abelius's handbook. After this there was a description of another technique to see if a wounded person was destined to die or not. Then there were remedies to make someone drunk without any harm, and other remedies to make a drunk person immediately sober, like drinking a lot of vinegar or putting a wet cloth on their pudenda. I had heard this from Simonis as well. Like his methods for not falling asleep: carrying a bat around with him, exactly as he had done the night of the Deposition and the night we had wandered round all the bowling alleys in Vienna in search of Populescu. When I came across the methods for testing the virginity of girls, I thought of poor Dragomir . . . I went on reading where the Greek seemed to have lingered with most attention:

> *To make someone sleep for three days in a row, take bile of a hare and make him drink it in wine: he will fall asleep at once. When you want to wake him pour vinegar into his mouth. Or take a sow's milk and place it where he sleeps. Or take bile of eel and mix it in a drink: he will sleep for three days. To wake him up, pour rosewater into his mouth.*
>
> *To make an animal stay with you, take a piece of bread and put it under your armpits. When it is soaked in sweat, give it to the animal to eat.*
>
> *To make an animal run with you wherever you want, give it a cat's heart to eat: it will follow you wherever you go.*

Doctor Abelius had written every student's gospel!

How to make sure that a dagger, sword or knife can cut an adversary's weapon: take the noble herb known as Verbena, crush it and mix it with mullein and urine, boil them together, leave the weapon in them for a while and you will soon note the difference!

To make a pair of pistols that look the same as others, but which with the same charge of powder and balls can fire further and more power-fully than others: have pistols made with a more resistant and heavier butt than usual. Apparently they will be the same as ordinary pistols. At the rear screw have a little tripod welded to insert into the barrel with a tube in the middle, through which the powder can fall on the ignition hole. Load the pistols as usual: they will fire further and more power-fully. The reason is this: the powder charge is lit at the centre and so more powder is burned.

The short chapters that followed had even more notes and comments penned by Simonis.

Camisole proof against shooting, clubbing or stabbing: take two pounds of the fish called ichthiocolla, shred it and leave it all night in vincotto, *then drain the* vincotto *and pour fresh spring water on it, cook until it becomes a thick muddy pulp, put in five ounces of fine leather rubber and leave it to dissolve in this hot pulp. Then put in four ounces of powdered smir, which has been prepared by heating it and cooling it many times in vinegar, and two ounces of old turpentine. Cook it all together again and spread this mixture on a thick linen cloth which has been stretched out on a smooth board and fixed with nails. Put another linen cloth on top and spread the mixture on this one too, and continue until you have placed ten or twelve linen cloths one on top of the other. Leave them to dry (in summer eight days are enough). Before they are completely dry, fold them and give them the shape you want. With this material you can make camisoles, helmets and such like. A camisole of this sort can be seen at Baron K's at Labach and also at N. in the Royal Kunstkammer.*

Swords, pistols, fighting clothes. What did my Greek assistant want with all this stuff?

Another material resistant to daggers, maces and guns: take ichthiocolla and fish glue, dissolve and squeeze until they become clear. Cook them ad consistentiam melleam, until they have the consistency of honey. Dip a linen cloth into this and when it has dried a little, spread the mixture on it with a brush and leave it to dry. Spread it again and leave it to dry as many times as necessary.

    Or, if you want to make a garment proof against a dirk, take a new heavy linen cloth and spread it with fish glue dissolved in water. Leave it to dry on a table. When dry, take yellow wax, resin and mastix, two ounces of each. Dissolve it all with an ounce of turpentine, mix it well and spread it on the linen until the cloth has sucked in the whole mixture.

And again:

    A collar proof against musket balls: take the skin of a racing or game ox that has just been killed, and on the cleaner side cut out a collar that is of your exact size and stitch it. Leave it to ferment for twenty-four hours in vinegar and dry it well in the open air.

All of this Simonis had meticulously underlined and commented on in the margin in his abstruse calligraphy.

    I thought back to Atto's sceptical remark on Simonis's ingenuousness. Clearly the Abbot suspected him. Absurd! In addition, Melani had refused to say another word. Maybe because he had too little to go on and not even he could be sure of anything now.

    And in any case, how could one help suspecting everyone? We were groping in the dark. Years ago, when I had followed false trails with Abbot Melani, sooner or later they would peter out, sending us back to the correct path towards the truth. But this time, having abandoned our initial false track, we now found ourselves in the dense tangle of a forest where everything shifted, slipped from our grasp, or turned into its opposite. I had suspected everyone: first Atto and Ciezeber, then Penicek and even Simonis; without counting Ugonio and Orsini, whose relationship was still unclear. All the others were dead: Dànilo Danilovitsch, Hristo Hadji-Tanjov, Dragomir Populescu, Koloman Szupán, the two mysterious hanged men of Ugonio's note. All of them apart from Opalinski. Should we suspect him as well? Whatever the truth was, the question remained the same: why had the students been murdered?

    In the shadow of the illness that threatened the Emperor (and the Grand Dauphin), there were too many deaths, too many culprits and no truth.

    The only ones not included among the suspects were Cloridia and myself: and now perhaps . . .

The paradox, however absurd it might be, took my breath away. The series of deaths had begun as soon as I had asked Simonis's companions to carry out research into the Golden Apple, but we had seen that this research had nothing to do with the murders.

Therefore the only connecting element was ourselves – or rather myself. I had already thought of this, but only now had begun to put two and two together: I was in fact the only real suspect. After meeting me, those poor students had started to die, just hours apart, like flies.

That was not all. They had been murdered just when they had an appointment with me and Simonis, or when we were looking for them. True, I had been with the Greek each time I had discovered a corpse, but he had known his university companions for a long time. It was he who had introduced them to me and who had even proposed that I should engage them. Why should he have wanted them to die just now?

Atto was right. If you are looking for a culprit, he had told me a few days earlier, look in the mirror: anyone who has an appointment with you dies.

Now Ugonio was supposed to come, but he was nowhere to be seen yet. Anyone who has an appointment with me dies . . .

20 of the clock: eating houses and alehouses close their doors.

Like a pack of panting hounds following an agile fox, it was only thanks to their great bravura that the orchestra managed to keep up with the serpentine glissades of the soprano. In the fiction of the oratorio, Alessio's mother sang her anguished rage against cruel destiny. On this rage the Chormaisterin had constructed a sprightly and superb edifice of vocal acrobatics, which, with its sinuous arches, depicted better than any painting, and explained better than any poem, the just anger of a mother grieving over her son's uncelebrated nuptials:

Un barbaro rigor
Fé il misero mio cor
Gioco ai tormenti
E il crudo fato vuol

Che un esempio di duol
L'alma diventi . . .[13]

While these indignant verses echoed in the Caesarean chapel, a
similar resentment filled my own heart, and the hearts of those who
were with me.

Ugonio had not turned up. We had waited for him for three
hours. It was clear that something must have happened to him. The
corpisantaro, who had begged for his keys back and had implored us
pitifully to treat them like gold until his return, would never have
missed the appointment of his own free will. Fearing the worst, I had
gone to the rehearsal of *Sant' Alessio*. What mysterious thread bound
Gaetano Orsini to Ugonio? What obscure threat had yet to be
revealed to us? After the tragic deaths of Dànilo, Hristo, Populescu
and Koloman Szupán, what new tragedy awaited us?

E il crudo fato vuol
Che un esempio di duol
L'alma diventi . . .

No, we would not wait passively. Camilla de' Rossi's furious and
sublime music fired my heart and spirit, exciting me to bold revenge.
I looked carefully this time at the Chormaisterin's Italian musicians
and wished I could put them all through the mill, and squeeze
from them, like a fistful of olives, the dishonourable truth of their
shady pursuits. I stared at the theorbist Francesco Conti and his
scrawny face: weren't they the features of one ready to sell his
honour for a handful of coins? I passed onto his round-cheeked
wife, the soprano Maria Landina, known to everyone as Landina, and
I said to myself: wasn't that florid face the image of a woman who has
grown fat on underhand dealings? And the tenor Carlo Costa, with
his pointed beard – didn't everything about him suggest a shameless,
double-dealing mind, wholly bent on evil? And Gaetano Orsini, with
his incessant prattle, wasn't he the epitome of the hypocritical huckster? Then I observed a second violinist with the crafty little eyes of
one who knew it all, a group of violone players with hooked noses
that betrayed greed, and flutists with the affected manners of
congenital liars. There came back to me, like an ill-digested meal

---

[13] *A barbarous rigour | Made my wretched heart | A toy for adversity | And cruel fate is*
fain | That an example of pain | The soul must now be.

regurgitated, Atto's tales of musician-spies like Dowland and Corbetta, and the conspiratorial and musical activities of Atto Melani himself, and I said to myself: you fool, do you really think you can shake hands with a musician and not find your palm greasy with a spy's guilty sweat? And I fell back on bitter reflections: on the cruel fate for Euterpe and Erato, sweet Muses of sounds, ever to find sly Mercury, lord of the wicked arts, at their heels. And I felt ashamed of having taken pride in the friendship of such people, who must have been laughing up their sleeves at my naivety.

But what weighed most heavily on me was the thought of the Chormaisterin. Was she, too, involved in this sordid practice of spying? A number of things about Camilla were still obscure to me. How, for example, had she guessed that Cloridia knew Turkish so well? Not even I knew that, and I was her husband! And yet the Chormaisterin had proposed her for the job in Prince Eugene's palace while the Agha was staying there, already quite certain of my consort's linguistic skills. And then there was her curiosity about Cloridia's past, her Turkish mother, and the fact that that she cooked with spelt, just as my wife did, and, finally, her acquaintance with Atto Melani. She had been introduced to him in Paris, she said, along with her husband Franz de' Rossi, nephew – so she said! – of Seigneur Luigi, Atto's old master. But what proof did I have of all this? If one questioned her on her past, Camilla would refuse to talk of her life before her marriage. She said she was Roman – Trasteverine, to boot – but she did not have the faintest trace of a Roman accent.

And then this Anton de' Rossi, Cardinal Collonitz's ex-chamberlain, must clearly have been a relative of Franz! Simonis, on his return from the Coppersmiths' Slope, had told me that he had not found the owner at home and had been unable to elicit much about Gaetano Orsini, except that their friendship was based on the fact that the young castrato, years ago, had taken lessons from Anton de' Rossi's deceased cousin, a court composer who had died prematurely, named Franz ... Why had Camilla wanted to deny this? Sitting next to Cloridia, I took the opportunity to tell her about it. She gazed at me open-mouthed: shades of suspicion fell on the person she now considered a dear friend. She furrowed her brows. I could guess what she was thinking. Some time ago the Chormaisterin had also denied being a relative of the Camilla de' Rossi whom Cloridia had known briefly in Trastevere: perhaps she had been lying then as well?

That evening *Sant' Alessio* was followed by a short rehearsal of another composition, also to be performed in the next few days.

It was now a sweet boy's voice that sang, and his innocence, I thought, was in sharp contrast with the murky hearts of the musicians all around. The composition was by Francesco Conti, the theorbist, and the Latin words sung by the boy seemed to have been written specifically to stir my desire for justice. First a heartfelt prayer to the Saviour:

> *Languet anima mea*
> *Amore tuo, o benignissime Jesu,*
> *Aestulat et spirat*
> *Et in amore deficit . . .*

"For your love, O sweet Jesus, my soul languishes, burns and sighs, and consumes itself with love"; oh yes, I said to myself sardonically, just the right words for this motley crew of crooked spies. Much more appropriate was the next stanza, which gave way to an *allegro moderato*:

> *O vulnera, vita coelestis,*
> *Amantis, trophea regnantis,*
> *Cor mihi aperite . . .*

"O wounds, celestial life, symbols of victory of the loving sovereign, open your heart to me!"

With all this tangled skein of suspicions I would have been very happy to open the heart of the beautiful and candid Chormaisterin. Oh yes, but I was even more eager to delve inside that of Gaetano Orsini – and very soon I would get the chance to do so, and to get all that I wanted from it.

"Four have already died. If Ugonio has ended up the same way you'll be the first to follow him."

"Four people dead? Ugonio? What are you talking about?"

At the end of the rehearsal Simonis, Penicek and Opalinski took Gaetano Orsini by surprise as he walked home.

I had told my assistant about Ugonio's disappearance and the need to put pressure on Orsini. Simonis had rushed round to

Opalinski's house and had persuaded him to make peace with Penicek. "We must remain united – if we start to accuse one another it'll be the end," he said. The Pole's anger, to tell the truth, had simmered down. He had begun to feel that he had accused the Pennal too precipitately, carried away by his despair at Koloman Szupán's death, which might have been accidental.

And so the three students moved in threateningly on Orsini. The young castrato was terrified, finding himself menaced by the muscles of the imposing Polish student, by the lanky Simonis and the shuffling, bespectacled Penicek, whose shifty, lopsided figure shuffling along in the dark had something decidedly fiendish about it.

I had simply pointed out the victim to them and then hidden round the corner. In the silence of the evening I could hear their questions and answers distinctly:

"It doesn't matter if you won't give us the other people's names – we already know them. It's too late for Koloman but if you don't spill where the *corpisantaro* is, you'll be spilling something else: your life's blood!" the Greek threatened him.

"The *corpisantaro*? I assure you there's been a mistake! You've got the wrong person, I have no idea what you're asking me, I swear," whimpered Orsini.

At a sign from Simonis, Opalinski punched him in the belly. Orsini bent double. The Pole gave him another backhander on his right cheek, while Penicek and my assistant gripped him from behind. The Pennal clutched his hair, pulling his head back, while Simonis twisted his arms behind his back. The poor singer, definitely not accustomed to such low-life techniques, moaned as Penicek covered his mouth.

"Take . . . take all the money I have on me . . . It's not much, but not so little either! Please don't kill me."

"So we haven't made ourselves clear," persisted Simonis. "We want to know about Ugonio, the *corpisantaro*. Was he supposed to come and see you? Or did you have an appointment somewhere? And what can you tell me about the two hanged men?"

"What are you talking about? I hate forests. I hardly ever leave the walls. I tell you," he said in a bewildered, imploring voice, "I don't even know who –"

Opalinski gave him two more punches in the stomach.

"We're fed up with your meaningless nonsense, do you understand?" whispered the Greek, while Jan went on: "Ugonio: the one dressed in a stinking greatcoat. The relic thief. Don't tell me you've already forgotten . . ."

Janitzki, just to be certain, smacked him robustly three or four times. Orsini stopped yelling. This earned him a hail of blows on the head and a piece of his own jacket thrust down his throat. The fight was ridiculously unequal.

"I've got a little money on me, take it all," Orsini offered again.

"Let's try again," repeated Simonis, paying no attention to the offer. "Ugonio, the one who talks a little weirdly . . . Make an effort."

"I'll take you to my house, if you like, I've got more money there . . ." answered the castrato, merely earning himself a series of six or seven raps on his head and face.

"At least ask him if he knows where he lives," suggested Opalinski.

"You're right. Did you hear my friend?"

Silence. Orsini was weeping. To make absolutely certain, Jan delivered a few more thumps, which had the opposite effect to the one desired: the castrato, clearly out of control, began to pray in a low voice. The reaction seemed too spontaneous not to be true.

"For this time we'll let you go. But if we find out you've been lying, and especially if you tell anyone about this conversation, well, you'll be in for a nasty surprise."

Orsini had now dropped to the ground. I felt a pang for the poor musician, whom I had seen yield to the fairly restrained violence of the three students like a piece of butter to a red-hot knife. Then I thought of the dead lads, of Ugonio, and my pity for Orsini diminished.

The three now came running in my direction. They ran on past me, giving me a quick nod as they went by. I followed them almost at once, running as lightly as possible on the pavement so as not to let Orsini know that a fourth man (and one well-known to him!) had observed the solemn thrashing.

"There are two possibilities: either he's a sly one, and tough to boot, or you've made a mistake," remarked Jan Janitzki Opalinski before setting off.

We also took our leave of Penicek. Then my assistant and I made our way back to Porta Coeli.

"Let's wait until tomorrow," I said before separating for the night. "If Ugonio hasn't got in touch by the afternoon, we'll go to the Cathedral of St Stephen. We'll look for the deacon he was going to talk to about the Archangel Michael's message. Ugonio told us he's a collector of relics – maybe that will help us trace him. But . . . what is it? Ah, yes, here you are: your book."

At that moment I had found Doctor Abelius's little handbook in my pocket. The Greek took it without saying a word. Then we took leave of one another.

Day the Seventh

WEDNESDAY, 15TH APRIL 1711

✠

5.30 of the clock: first mass. From now on the bells will ring in succession throughout the day, announcing masses, processions, devotions. Eating houses and alehouses open.

"Tomorrow night, do you understand? They're going to do it tomorrow night," said Cloridia, her voice eager and anxious.

"And so? What's the problem?"

Cloridia had once again been urgently summoned during the early hours of the day to the palace of the Prince of Savoy. The Agha would return that morning for a new audience, but not at midday as usual, but before dawn.

But just a short while later my dear wife returned from the palace. She had stolen a few minutes from her job to tell me the red-hot news she had heard.

As we already knew, the Most Serene Prince had been supposed to leave for the front the previous day, Tuesday. As His Caesarean Majesty's condition still seemed to be improving, the *condottiero* had finally resolved to leave the day after tomorrow, Thursday 16th April. He had written a letter to the Emperor officially announcing his intention to leave Vienna. This last piece of news could be traced back to one of Eugene's scribes, and so seemed more than certain. But this was not what was agitating Cloridia.

Before leaving, Eugene was to meet the Turkish Agha again. To talk about what (and at that hour, when the nobles were snoring), was a mystery, since they had seen each other just two days earlier. But nor was that the main reason for Cloridia's anxiety.

She had had a good deal to do that morning. First, to accompany two soldiers in the Agha's retinue to the kitchens to negotiate the unofficial purchase of liquors. Then to provide explanations for another pair of Turkish soldiers, who, beguiled by the sight of some couples behaving fairly freely during an *Andacht*, were asking for information about the habits of the local females (Cloridia had warned them against any harassment, which might provoke a diplomatic incident). Then she had had to obtain pen and paper for another Ottoman, a young man of a sad and contemplative temperament, who wanted to take home a sketch of Eugene's palace. After that she had had to resolve a row over prices between the two soldiers she had earlier taken to the kitchen to buy alcoholic beverages and one of the Most Serene Prince's cooks. Finally, Cloridia had been requested by the palace staff to remind some of the gentle guests (if the grim soldiery of the Orient could be so termed) at His Highness's residence that it was forbidden to make souvenirs of such items as ornaments, curtains, candelabra, the precious damask upholstery of the armchairs or the stucco from the walls. Cloridia had seen to all this while the Agha made his arrival at the palace and engaged in conversation with Eugene, this time in private audience, accompanied only by the official interpreters and the closest, most trusted counsellors.

At this point my sweet little wife had heard, as she passed in the corridor, a conversation between a small group of Turks (it was impossible to tell exactly how many, perhaps three or four, including the dervish) and another, German-speaking, person. One of those present acted as interpreter: why had they not engaged Cloridia? The matter under discussion seemed to be highly confidential. And indeed it was.

Prudently putting her ear to the door, she learned that the German-speaking person was none other than the Caesarean Proto-Medicus: Doctor Mathias von Hertod.

"The Caesarean Proto-Medicus!" I exclaimed. "And what was he doing with the Turks, in Eugene's palace, at such an antelucan hour?"

This was not the first parley between Ciezeber and the Proto-Medicus of Joseph I, Cloridia explained. The two of them, and the rest of the group, had referred to earlier conversations that they had had.

"Eavesdropping like that, of course, I couldn't understand everything they said, but I heard the most important news almost immediately – and very clearly. Tomorrow evening the dervish will tend to Joseph."

"Tend to him?"

"Yes, he'll give him a treatment – that's what I heard."

"So he is responsible for the improvement in his condition!" I said in amazement.

"Tomorrow will be just a repetition of the treatment, and it should be decisive. Von Hertod reported that Joseph's condition is improving continually, and so the treatment must be concluded tomorrow at all costs. If the people were to find out that the Infidels are collaborating on the Emperor's treatment, it could give rise to a great scandal."

As she had already said, the lion's share of the treatment was to be carried out by Ciezeber. In the conversation at Eugene's palace, they had talked about the dervish's instruments, his knowledge of such procedures and of the most suitable hour to do the operation.

"Do you think the Caesarean Proto-Medicus has realised that someone is plotting the Emperor's death?"

"I believe so, given the hour they met and the confidential nature of the meeting. The Proto-Medicus said that that at this point he could only trust Ciezeber."

"So that was what those rituals were for, the ones the dervish carried out in the woods near the Place with No Name," I said. "Ugonio told us they were for therapeutic purposes, but I would never have guessed *who* they were intended for! But," I objected, in a more doubtful tone, "when you think about it, it's an absurd story. We began by suspecting the Turks of wanting to poison the Emperor, and now we discover they're actually curing him . . ."

"It's simple," answered Cloridia, "if the Emperor died, his brother Charles would ascend the throne and the war would be over. It sounds paradoxical, but in fact the Sultan has every interest in Joseph remaining in good health. The conflict will continue, wearing out the Empire and the other Christian powers. Isn't it an excellent deal for the Ottomans?"

"But Abbot Melani told me that Charles has a weak character and Prince Eugene will persuade him to continue the war, and also that Joseph I is thinking of coming to terms with France, leaving them with Spain and keeping just Catalonia for his brother Charles. If that's really the case, it's more likely that the war will finish under Joseph than under Charles."

"Maybe the Turks don't know this."

"That seems unlikely, at least as far as the Emperor's peaceful intentions are concerned."

"Then perhaps they don't believe that Joseph's idea is likely to succeed. You know what the French are like: they want everything, or else it's war," said Cloridia, miming French intransigence with a wave of her hand.

"It's possible," I agreed. "But if that's the way things are, what happens to all Atto's theories about Prince Eugene conspiring against the Emperor to replace him with Charles, who is indecisive and would let him go on with the war? It would be very strange if the saviour of Joseph I were hiding in the Prince's palace."

"Quite. So Eugene might have nothing to do with it."

Cloridia was right. I was used to the notion that Atto's hypotheses and deductions were always correct, but this time he had clearly got hold of the wrong end of the stick! Besides, had not his conviction that the Turks were hired killers in the pay of Europe's warring factions been proved miserably wrong by the facts?

While Cloridia left me to go to back to the palace, urging me over and over again to look after the Abbot, Simonis came and knocked at my door as agreed. Now that I knew for certain that the Emperor was about to recover completely, I devoted myself with renewed zeal to the most important job that His Caesarean Majesty had entrusted me with: the Place with No Name awaited us.

❧

I went with my little boy and Simonis to the usual eating house for breakfast. Abbot Melani was with us. He was not used to waking up so early, and now he sprawled on his chair, listlessly nibbling at the abundant meal of sausages and mustard. In a coffee shop he would have found a breakfast more to his tastes. However, after what had happened to Dragomir Populescu and the things we had heard about the Armenians, the thought of setting foot in a coffee shop was a little unnerving.

I was about to tell the Abbot the devastating news reported by Cloridia but I held back. Atto had shown that he did not greatly trust Simonis. So I decided to say nothing. Instead I told him about the fruitless interrogation of Gaetano Orsini.

"Would you ask the host to bring me the latest gazette?" Atto asked my assistant as soon as I had finished my account.

"This is not a coffee shop, Signor Abbot: they don't have gazettes. But I happen to have the Diary of Vienna, hot off the press," answered Simonis, wondering at Melani's timing: on arriving in the eating house the Greek had set down on the table the newspaper he had just bought at the little palace of the Red Porcupine. "It's the issue covering the last three days."

What could the blind old Abbot want with a gazette in German, I asked myself, while I asked the host for some water for my son.

"Good. I imagine it is a newspaper that contains an obituary page for the city," said Melani.

"Certainly."

"Could you read it to me?"

The Greek looked at me questioningly. I signalled to him to proceed.

He opened the gazette and read:

"List of all deaths within and without the walls," he began in his slightly foolish voice, reading the title of the column. "On 11th April 1711 died the little daughter –"

"No, no, please, just the male adults."

"Let's see . . . here you are: Christof Lang and Matthias Koch, aged sixty-five and seventy-six, both at the poor people's home; Franz Zintel, aged thirty-two, brewer at the Spittelberg; Georg Schraub, aged forty-eight, cloth-cutter at the Windmill; Adam Kugler, aged forty, soldier of the Neubau guard; Michael Wißhoffer, aged forty, stone mason at the Liechtenthal."

"It's clear that these Viennese stuff themselves like pigs," broke in Atto, with a disgusted air. "Only those two at the old people's home died at an advanced age. The others all died very young, and I bet it was from indigestion."

"Shall I go on?" asked Simonis.

Atto nodded.

"On 12th April died Franz Johannes, aged seventy-four; Kaspar Wolff, aged forty; and Johann Graßberger, aged fifty-eight, both in hospital. On 13th April . . ."

While Simonis dutifully read the list of deaths, I gazed wonderingly at Atto, who was listening attentively, his neck taut like a bloodhound's.

". . . Carl Dement, aged thirty, student, at Landstrasse; Andre Treberitz, aged forty-five, soldier on leave at Wieden; Philipp Brixner, aged fifty-eight, fishmonger . . ."

"Are you looking for someone in particular?" I asked.

"Shhh! Just a moment," Atto hushed me.

"On 14th April," Simonis went on, "died Melchior Plaschky, aged fifty-four, on the Leopoldine Island; Rietter Blasi, aged thirty-eight, tailor on the Munich ramparts; Leopold Löffler, guard on the Carinthian ramparts; Lorentz Kienast, aged thirty-six, dyer on the Leopoldine Island . . ."

"Just as I thought. They're not there," commented Melani when Simonis had finished reading.

"Who?"

"Can't you guess? Your murdered friends. And it's not a mere oversight, or a decision not to include them: students are always dying like flies on account of their intemperate behaviour . . ."

"It's true," Simonis confirmed, looking at the gazette again, "for example, there's the death of this Carl Dement, a student."

"Populescu's body was disposed of by those colleagues of your cart driver, that what's his name . . . Penicek. All right. But Koloman and the first two?"

"It's true, damn it," I nodded, while my mouth gaped in amazement and Simonis furrowed his brows in thought. Koloman's body at the *Heuriger* had been handed over to the guards directly by the host; Dànilo Danilovitsch had been stabbed on the night of 11th April: a corpse on the ramparts certainly could not have escaped the soldiers' eyes. Hristo Hadji-Tanjov had died in the Prater on the 13th, two days earlier: the snow had certainly all melted by now and the guards must have found him.

"But how is it possible?" I asked.

"Simple. Someone made sure their deaths were not registered in the mortuary protocols."

"I don't see how: the guards will have called the city's medical officer and –"

"Exactly," he anticipated me, making me understand that he did not wish to talk in front of my assistant. "Now I must go back to my rooms a moment, I have forgotten something."

"Do you think that –" I persisted.

"I think what you think," he cut me off curtly. "So will you accompany me or do I have to go back by myself?"

Leaving my boy with Simonis to finish his breakfast, I noticed that my assistant was once again carrying the little bag that I had seen around his neck the previous day.

Atto and I set off towards Porta Coeli Street. He resumed the conversation:

"Whoever ordered this, shall we say, little cleansing operation is very powerful, and the person who carried it out is no mere pawn either. Do you know what this means?"

I shook my head.

"It means that behind those boys' deaths there is something big – very big."

"So why have you always laughed whenever I've tried to talk to you about these students' deaths and my fears?" I asked, barely restraining my acrimony.

"I told you this before and I've even repeated it, but apparently that isn't enough: I still do not believe they died because of their research into the Golden Apple, but I never said that their deaths were not linked to one another."

"Don't start shifting your position, Signor Atto. I remember clearly: you told me that Hristo was an Ottoman subject, as was Dragomir, and you let me believe that this was connected with their deaths."

"I spoke a little loosely, I admit. Actually, since the Sublime Porte invaded them, the Bulgarians have lived as refugees in their impregnable mountains and have practically no contact with their conquerors. And Romania is not entirely under the Ottoman Empire."

"What? And you've only just remembered this?"

"Shhh! Speak quietly, for goodness' sake," he hushed me, turning his head instinctively to left and right, as if his blind eyes could intercept any hidden spies. "I needed you to make contact with the Pálffy woman and I didn't want you to be distracted, racking your brains over the deaths of those good-for-nothings," answered the old castrato with brisk candour.

When we reached the convent, Atto struck the door of his room with the pummel of his stick.

The door was opened by Domenico, who was still weak from the fever of the last few days and the fluxion of the chest. He went straight back to cough in bed.

"I beg your pardon, boy," concluded Atto in a suddenly grim tone, seizing my arm. "I thought that, whatever the matter was, it only concerned the Empire, whereas I am here to serve France. And then

I was confident that if my letter reached Joseph I, all would turn out for the best. I would be ahead of anyone else. Instead . . ." And here he paused.

Oh yes, I reflected as he let me into his room, Abbot Melani would never believe that the interests of France and the Empire could be the same. In the theatre of war they seemed to be the two enemy captains. But the Emperor and the Grand Dauphin were at that moment on the same sacrificial altar, while the dagger raised over their hearts was in the grip of an unknown hand . . . Their hearts?

"By the way, Signor Atto," I said. "What were you doing the other evening in the alleyway behind the convent with that Armenian?"

Melani gave a start.

"What are you doing now, following me about?"

"I would never do such a thing. I overheard it by chance, on my way back from the eating house. The Armenian was talking about some people that had sold you, at a high price apparently, their master's heart."

"Did he say that? I don't think –" stammered Atto.

"Word for word, I remember perfectly. He gave you a little coffer and you gave him a little bag of money."

"Oh it was nothing important, just a –"

"No, Signor Atto. Let's put aside the usual nonsense, if you want me to trust you. Otherwise I'll turn around and leave you. And to the devil with you and the Grand Dauphin."

"Very well, you are right," he admitted after a few moments' silence.

His hands groped the knob of the drawer closest to him. He opened it and took out the little coffer he had received from the Armenian.

"Here it is. I'll give it to you, to show that your trust in me is not ill-founded," he said, handing me the little container.

I tried to open it, but in vain. It was locked.

"I'll give you the key before I leave. I swear it."

"I've already had experience of your oaths," I retorted in a sceptical tone.

"But you can open it whenever you want! You just have to force it. I only ask you not to do so now. I'll trust you," he added in a solemn tone, "if you'll trust me."

A great sophist, Abbot Melani, when it came down to trust. But I had to acknowledge that this time I had something concrete in my hands.

"All right," I said. "What do you want in exchange for the coffer?"

"That until you open it you ask me no more questions about the Armenian."

"When do you intend to leave again?" I asked after pocketing the coffer.

"As soon as I have understood who the shadow-man is."

"The shadow-man?"

"The man who acts as intermediary between the killers of His Caesarean Majesty and the Grand Dauphin and the instigators."

"A secret agent?"

"There is someone in Vienna who superintends and organises the moves of the perpetrators, whoever they are. It cannot be otherwise."

The shadow-man: Atto Melani was all too familiar with this role! Wasn't it the role I had always seen him play? Who, eleven years ago, had organised the conspiracy that had caused the war of succession to break out? Atto Melani was neither the instigator (France) nor the perpetrator (a simple scribe). But he had organised and guided the diabolical machine that had forged the will of a king, led three cardinals to betray the Pope in person and even obtained the election of one of the three traitors as the new pope.

Now for the first time I was seeing the Abbot wrong-footed by a new Atto Melani. Someone, who was of course much younger than him, and in the pay of other powers – Holland, England or who knows who – had taken the old castrato's place and was setting a fatal and ingenious trap for the Emperor.

"Maybe this shadow-man," I remarked, "is spying on our moves. He might be behind the murder of Dànilo, Hristo, Dragomir and, perhaps, Koloman."

"If so, it would be good to unmask him before we find him behind our backs."

☙❧

For once we allowed ourselves a little comfort. Abbot Melani would certainly not be able to reach Neugebäu on foot, or in our miserable chimney-sweep's cart. So Simonis engaged the Pennal, who transported us all much more commodiously and swiftly. Some obscure foreboding had induced me to leave our little boy at Porta Coeli, in the care of Camilla, who had generously agreed to look after him until either Cloridia or I returned.

As Penicek's cart made its jolting way towards our destination, I found myself picturing the corpses of those poor lads: Dànilo's agonised expression, Hristo's swollen blue face, Dragomir's mangled pudenda, and finally Koloman impaled on the pikes. I squeezed my eyelids tight and shook my head, trying to expel from my breast the wave of nausea and anguish surging within me. Death had reaped a rich harvest from the small group of students. Whose turn would it be next? Penicek? Or perhaps Simonis? Or Opalinski? I looked at my assistant sitting opposite me; his dull eyes were fixed inertly on the horizon, as if he had no worries. But it was just an act: I knew that, were he to be assailed by the most tremendous tempest, his gaze would remain the same. Penicek sat on the box seat. No one was questioning him and so he kept quiet, locked in his grim Pennal's cage, condemned to serve the Barber for one year, six months, six weeks, six days and six minutes. Finally I thought of Opalinski again: he too had trembled at the appalling sight of his Hungarian friend. And to think that until a short while ago Jan Janitzki had shown no fear. Inexplicable behaviour, in the light of subsequent events. I asked Simonis about it.

"Well, Signor Master, it's due to his occupation. Outside study hours, that is, of course."

"And what is it?"

"It's a little complicated, Signor Master. Do you know what the 'right of quarters' is here in Vienna?"

Since ancient times, Simonis explained, the Emperor had had the right to claim all rented property for himself and for the court. Ever since the ancient Caesars, travelling through their lands, had entrusted the Court Marshal with the task of requisitioning the lodgings needed for overnight stays. This custom, which takes the name of the right of quarters, had spread to Vienna as well, as the city became the seat of an increasingly large and important court, and of a growing number of functionaries, chancellors, musicians, copyists, dancers, soldiers, stewards, cantors, poets, servants, cooks, footmen, retainers, assistants, assistants' assistants, and parasites of all sorts.

"Many think that having an imperial functionary as tenant is both elegant and desirable. Quite the contrary!"

This was how things went. One fine day an imperial functionary would knock at the door and, with a decree in his hand, announce that from that moment on the apartment was at his disposal. In the space of a few days the owner and his family either had to accept cohabitation or move out. If the owner refused, they would forcefully requisition the whole of his house, or his shop, or even the entire palace, if it belonged to him. After this, without any bargaining, a derisory rent would be set by the imperial chamber. The imperial functionary, not content with this result, instead of using the confiscated apartment, would sublet it.

"And is that allowed?" asked Abbot Melani.

"Of course not. But in the shadow of the Caesarean court anything can be done," sneered Simonis.

The poor owner would thus find his apartment invaded by mysterious strangers who would carry off his furniture, rip out doors and windows, and often sublet in turn to the most disreputable types. The beautiful apartment would end up as a stinking den, a home to all sorts of shady business, including prostitution, sometimes even murders. There were even cases in which the occupiers, too slovenly to light the fire in the hearth, would make a big bonfire on the wooden floor, and the whole apartment would go up in flames. Meanwhile the imperial chamber, permanently in debt, would not even pay the rent. And if the owner protested the imperial functionary could actually follow the ancient custom of stoning him.

"This malpractice can become so bad," my assistant went on, "that at times it is the emperors themselves who evict the occupiers. Ferdinand I had an entire palace next to the royal palace emptied, because the functionaries who had settled there were always drunk and made so much noise that they disturbed the imperial sessions, and they were so incompetent in handling the stoves and fireplaces that they risked setting alight both their own building and the royal palace."

"And what does Opalinski have to do with all this?" I asked at the end of the explanation.

"It's simple: he acts as intermediary for the subletting agreements."

"Didn't you say they were illegal?"

"Certainly. In fact, they can present real risks: for example, when the owner of the apartment has friends at court and decides to get his own back on the functionary who expropriated him, or on the intermediary himself. Opalinski is used to risks, familiar with fear. It must be acknowledged: Jan is truly a courageous Pole. It's only now, after what happened to Koloman, that I've seen him get really nervous."

Meanwhile we had arrived in Neugebäu, greeted by the dazzle of its white marble. As a good son does with his tired father, I would have liked to show Atto, had his eyeballs not been deprived of light, Maximilian II's majestic building, its gardens, its generous fish ponds, its towers, the seraglio of the ferocious animals and the unconfined view that could be enjoyed from the northern terrace. Prior to entering the Place with No Name I had given him a brief description of its treasures and history, so that he did not arrive completely unprepared in this trove of memories, suspended between the tragic past of Maximilian and the present, no less sinisterly shaded, of the young Joseph. I had summarised Maximilian's struggles with the Turks, the birth of Neugebäu as a parody of the tent of Suleiman the Magnificent, the tragic death of the Emperor and the plots woven against him. I had of course said nothing of the only detail which he would never have believed: the Flying Ship and the supernatural wonders that Simonis and I had witnessed.

Atto had listened to my whole account of the dark history of the Place with No Name with extreme interest, nodding at those parts he already knew, prudently remaining silent during those that were new to him.

I could not, with my feeble oratorical powers, render the greatness of the place denied to him by his blind eyes, and I knew – or at least I felt – that he was afflicted by it to the depths of his soul, because this was the definitive proof of his decline: twenty-eight years earlier I had known him to be thirsty for all aspects of learning, every curiosity, every secret, and intent even on writing a guide to Rome in his spare time, so as to satisfy his creative bent and his appetite for knowledge. Now that his body betrayed him, his inner faculties were all slaves to circumstances; curiosity had to yield to resignation, haste to patience, intelligence to ignorance. Atto would never see Neugebäu.

Once we had reached our destination, after bidding farewell to the Pennal (he would come by to pick us up later), we went first of all to introduce our bizarre party to Frosch. The keeper of the Place with No Name, who had been surprised to see us arriving in Penicek's gig, cast a sceptical eye at Abbot Melani.

"**Is he a new apprentice, replacing the little boy?**" he laughed with coarse, bold humour, pointing at Atto.

Frosch asked us no questions about our previous day's work at Neugebäu. If he was not a skilful dissimulator (and drunkards generally are not), this meant he had not seen us take off in the Flying Ship, nor indeed land in it. I heaved a surreptitious sigh of relief: I certainly did not want to share with the drunken Cerberus the incredible secret of the flight that Simonis and I had undertaken.

We passed in front of the ball stadium and I cast a silent glance at the Flying Ship. It was where we had left it, lying limp on the ground. Its birdlike features, as awkward as they were bizarre, gave no intimation that it was capable of soaring lightly and nimbly among the clouds. I looked sidelong at Simonis: at the sight of the ship his doltish eyeballs seemed to grow wide and cloud over with emotion. Even Abbot Melani, unconscious of everything and locked in the darkness of his blind eyes, as he passed in front of the ball stadium, turned his head imperceptibly towards the Flying Ship, as if it had sent out an invisible, magnetic summons. "The power of blindness!" I thought. Those unable to see perceive what is invisible to the rest of us.

In the ball stadium only one detail had changed from our previous visits: at the far end of the great rectangular space were stacked the birdcages, full of their vociferous occupants. Atto heard the chattering noise and asked me about it. I turned and asked Frosch.

"**Martens. Last night they did away with half a dozen Indian pullets.**"

The keeper explained that he had put the cages in the ball stadium because the stable door had been broken, and the predators had immediately taken advantage of the accident. Tonight the birds of the Place with No Name would sleep safely: the stadium, whose doors were in good condition, presented no such risks. As soon as the stable door had been mended, the cages would go back there. For the moment, since the weather was now quite warm, the birds could even sleep in the open.

Atto was greatly struck when he heard the racket made by the lions, panthers and other fierce beasts: it was their meal time, and the hungry animals let out slavering howls. I briefly described the appearance and attitude of each carnivore, depicting how they gripped and tore at the red meats distributed to them by their keeper. He asked me if there was any risk of them escaping. I then told him of my encounter with Mustafa, on my first visit to the Place with No Name.

"Being blind, I wouldn't have a chance to escape from the lion. But then he'd find my bones getting stuck in his teeth, ha ha!" he joked.

During our first hour of work everything went smoothly. Abbot Melani remained at a prudent distance from us, sitting on a stool, taking great care not to get dusty: as soon as any dirty cloud reached his nose, amid sneezes and imprecations he would ask to be placed a little further off to spare his clothes, which were the usual green and black. It was surprising, I thought, how attentive the Abbot was to his outward appearance, even though he could not see himself in the mirror.

We took up our work at the point where we had left off the previous occasion. We entered the mansion by the main door and once again started with the large rooms on the ground floor. On the previous occasion we had finished the central entrance hall and the two side rooms. We went to the left, crossed the great terrace and reached the western keep, access to which was by a door. It was locked.

"We'll have to get the keys from Frosch," I remarked. "Meanwhile we'll try on the opposite side."

In the meantime I was trying to describe to Abbot Melani the wonders of the view that could be enjoyed from the terrace, the grandiose conception of the architect, the touching personal involvement of Maximilian, who must have followed the project from its outset to its realisation.

As we walked away, I thought I heard, from a direction that could not be identified, a noise – a long, shrill rumbling sound that I had heard before. But it was such a vague sensation that I did not dare to ask the others for confirmation, lest they should take me for a visionary or a coward. So we re-crossed the three entrance halls, and then came out into the open air again, onto the terrace in the opposite wing, finally reaching the eastern keep. Here the door was open.

Inside we found a broad space that resembled a large chapel.

"I think it was to be set aside for divine service," Simonis confirmed, "if only Maximilian had been able to finish it."

We set down to work. The job did not take long. As soon as it was over we went to the outside of the mansion and re-entered by the eastern keep. From here we visited the whole of the semi-basement floor. It was in the eastern keep, according to Frosch, that Rudolph the Mad had carried out his experiments in magic and alchemy.

However, we found no obvious signs of ovens, alembics or other such devilries. If that had once been the place where Rudolph celebrated his follies, time must have mercifully cancelled all traces. The ghosts that the Viennese (but also the chimney-sweeps, my fellow countrymen) fantasised about had left no marks of their presence.

Proceeding towards the central point of the house, we found the next room was a long gallery with round vaults, lit by broad, low windows that opened on the north side.

"This was where Maximilian wanted to set up his antiquarium, his collection of marvels. On the walls he wanted to display triumphal monuments, statues, tapestries and trophies," explained Simonis.

All we could see, however, was a bare stone corridor, made just a little more graceful by the fine curves of the ceiling. Every stone, I was saying to myself, seemed to express melancholy at its unfulfilled destiny, when Abbot Melani interrupted my thoughts.

"Did you catch that?"

"What?" said Simonis.

"Four times. It was repeated four times."

"A strange sound, right?" I said, thinking of the curious noise, halfway between an acute trumpet and a percussion instrument, which I had heard from the terrace.

"Not a sound: a vibration. Like the firing of a cannon, but muffled."

Simonis and I exchanged glances. It was no surprise that Atto should have heard a noise that was imperceptible to us: blind people are known for the acuteness of their tympani. But it could be something else: bizarre perceptions could also be attributed, alas, to the wandering mind of an old man.

Having completed our work of inspection and maintenance, we had come to the middle of the semi-basement. Just above our heads, on the ground-floor level, was the mansion's main entrance. From the point where we stood a couple of ramps descended underground, leading to a door that gave onto the rear of Neugebäu. From there we had a view that took in the gardens and the large fish pond to the north, and which widened out gloriously to the fields and woods beyond.

When we had finished our short reconnaissance, we went back towards the ramp and then towards the centre of the semi-basement.

We began to explore the west wing. We had just begun to examine the southern wall when the strange phenomenon re-occurred.

"Did you hear that?" asked Atto, perturbed again.

This time I had heard something too. A hollow and indistinct thud, as if above and around us a giant had gently set a Cyclopic bass drum vibrating. Simonis, however, had not noticed anything.

"We must finish the job," said my assistant, vaguely vexed that his hearing was not sharp enough.

"You're right," I agreed, hoping that I had been mistaken, or that work might magically wipe from my mind all memories of the arcane signal.

Rummaging in a bag of tools for a broom, and groping among a thousand irons of all kinds, my fingertips touched a quadrangular-shaped object. It was Hristo Hadji-Tanjov's chessboard, still wrapped in the little bag that its ill-fated owner had thrust it into.

In order not to risk losing it, I had put it among our tools, which I always put away securely. I pulled it out and dusted off the object that had saved my life three days earlier, but unfortunately not that of its owner. Simonis and I exchanged mournful glances.

"Poor friend," whispered Simonis.

"He realised long before Penicek that the meaning of the Agha's phrase all lay in *soli soli soli*," I said.

"What did you say?" Atto said with a start.

I explained how the chessboard had come into my hands, and I told him what Hristo had said to Simonis: our chess-playing friend believed that the secret of the Agha's phrase all lay in the repetition of those three mysterious words *soli soli soli*. When we had found Hristo's corpse, I added, the poor lad was clutching a white chess king in his fist. Finally, in his chessboard I had found a note that referred to checkmate.

"Yes, Hristo on the very day of his death had mentioned that he thought the words *soli soli soli* – that is, 'all alone' – were connected with checkmate," explained Simonis.

Abbot Melani quivered as if he had been stung by a wasp and stood up.

"Just a moment. Have I got this right? On the day of the audience the Agha said to Eugene that the Turks had arrived *soli soli soli*?"

"Certainly, what's new about that?"

"Wha-a-a-t? And you never told me?"

"Told you what?"

"That the Agha's phrase contained the words *soli soli soli*!"

Atto muttered a series of unrepeatable expletives to himself, as if to spare me a direct insult. Then he spoke aloud again:

"Just what were you thinking of? You realise what you've done?" he said vehemently.

I still did not understand. Simonis was listening in bewilderment too.

"To tell the truth, Signor Atto, I'm sure I did tell you. Didn't I explain that the Agha said 'We've come all alone to the Golden Apple'?"

"Just a moment: the phrase was in Latin, is that right?"

"Yes."

"Say it to me."

"*Soli soli soli ad pomum venimus aureum.*"

"And you, you ass, you ignorant beast, you translate *soli soli soli* as 'all alone'? The Agha's phrase means something quite different, curse it."

It had been a venial sin, but it had serious consequences all the same.

While we made our way back to the ball stadium for something to eat, now that the first part of the job was over, Atto began to explain.

Cloridia and I had believed that *soli soli soli* was just the repetition of a single term, which meant 'alone', and so we had given Atto the translation directly, 'all alone', or 'truly alone', not mentioning the original version.

Abbot Melani was raging. His legs trembled with anger, he muttered and mumbled swear words and curses, every so often addressing me with an accusing forefinger upraised.

"You young people . . . you're . . . all irresponsible, that's what you are! All you can do is get flustered and create disasters. Oh, if you only had a tenth of the brainpower and concentration needed for such things! And I brought you all the way here to Vienna so that you might help me!"

"Be careful, Signor Atto." I suddenly pulled him back by his arm.

While the old castrato was getting so worked up, before we started down the spiral staircase that led to the ball stadium and the animal cages, we noticed something truly bizarre. In the large eastern courtyard lay a huge stinking pile of dung.

"Good heavens, it must have been Mustafa," I said, holding my nose.

"I didn't think lions did such big ones," remarked Simonis with amusement.

Atto calmed down at last. We made him sit down on the stairs. With his hands quivering from the sudden surge of anger, he finally made up his mind to explain how things were.

"*Soli soli soli* is not just the stupid repetition of the word *soli*. On the contrary. It's a very famous Latin motto."

I listened in utter amazement.

"And if you had had the good manners to repeat to me literally the Agha's Latin phrase," Abbot Melani insisted, "instead of providing your own witless interpretation, we would have saved days and days of useless toil."

"So what does *soli soli soli* mean then?" I asked.

"The first *soli* is the dative singular of the adjective *solus*, 'alone', and so it means 'to the only one'. The second is the dative of the noun *sol*, 'sun'. The third is the genitive of *solum*, 'earth', and so it means 'of the earth'."

"And so *soli soli soli* means . . . 'To the only sun of the earth'."

"Exactly. Or 'to the only sun of the soil', if you prefer. In France it is a well-known saying, because His Majesty has had it engraved on his army's cannons. The Sun King likes to remind everyone of his power. But he did not invent the phrase – it was used, for example, by Nostradamus, in some of his woolly wafflings. And Nostradamus must have stolen it in turn from the ancient Romans."

"And why?"

"*Soli soli soli* is often found on sundials. It was probably an old Latin custom, which was handed down over the centuries. In any case its origin does not concern us. There are countless similar sayings, like *sol solus solo salo*, which means 'only the sun commands the earth and the sea', or '*sol solus non soli*, that is to say, 'the sun is just one for all', or again *sol solus soles solari*, 'only the sun consoles without a pause'."

As he spoke, Atto had got up again and started moving so we had now descended to the lower depths. We at once looked for Frosch to ask him if he had any water or wine to sell us, in particular because after his harangue Atto now felt thirsty, but the keeper was nowhere to be found. Near the entrance to the stable we found the tools and wooden planks with which he was mending the door. We heard a noise from far end of the ball stadium, where the birdcages were stacked. At once the birds became animated and the stadium was filled with their twittering.

"So the story of the Circassian has got nothing to do with it," I reflected aloud. "But why would the Agha have chosen this saying?" I asked, as we all three headed towards the ball stadium.

"Maybe it was a way of paying homage to Eugene," hazarded Simonis. "Perhaps the Agha just wanted to say, 'We have come to the only sun of the earth'."

"Unlikely," replied Atto. "Eugene is not the sun of anything. He is the commander-in-chief of the imperial armies, and that's all. *Soli soli soli* clearly refers to a sovereign."

"And so to the Emperor," I deduced. "But why use this saying in an audience with Eugene, instead of with the Emperor?"

Atto said nothing but looked thoughtful.

"Maybe the phrase has a double meaning," observed Simonis.

"And what would that be?"

"Let's see . . . instead of 'to the only sun of the earth', it could be translated as 'to the lonely sun of the earth'."

"And isn't that the same thing?"

"No. This second formulation would mean 'to the solitary sun of the earth', that is, to the Emperor," explained Simonis.

"And why would he be lonely?" I asked in surprise.

But I could get no answer. We had entered the ball stadium. The great arena, surrounded by high walls stretching upwards to the sky, was alive with the shrill squawking of the birds. Parrots and parakeets strained their uvulas to the utmost, filling the bowl of the stadium with strident screeches.

"Why on earth are the birds making all this row, boy?" Abbot Melani asked me, having to raise his voice to be heard.

We heard two or three heavy blows, like a mallet striking wooden boards. I explained to Atto that Frosch, concealed among the cages, was probably hammering nails into planks for the new stable door (even though it was not clear why he should be doing it among the birdcages).

The din, already deafening, was made almost unbearable by the reverberation of a new series of hammer blows.

"Curse it, these wretched birds are unbearable," said Atto again, trying to block his ears with his hands.

Protecting my own eardrums with my hands, I had almost reached the small birdcages when I noticed they were set right up against the wall, and so there could be no one behind them, certainly no Frosch, making those vexatious noises.

"Simonis!" I called my assistant, who had stayed behind with Atto.

"Look, Signor Master, look!" he echoed me, calling my attention in turn.

He was looking towards the opposite end of the great space, towards the doorway into the ball stadium, the one we had just entered by.

We were no longer alone. An enormous hairy biped, as tall and broad as two human beings, was baring its slavering canines and, even though I could not hear it on account of the racket made by the birds, was bestially snarling at us. Then it dropped on all fours and came bounding towards us, preparing to attack.

I knew nothing about ferocious animals, but instinct told me that it was enraged by hunger. Petrified, I observed the approaching beast, and with a last shred of awareness I heard the invisible black-smith rekindle chaos among the birds with new hammer blows, and then I heard a final screech – and only then did I realise that there was at least one other door giving onto the stadium, diametrically opposite the one that the bear had entered by.

While the parrots' squawking continued to assail my ears, I real-ised that the second door was hidden by the birdcages that Frosch had piled up on top of one another, and it was that door that some hidden carpenter was tormenting with his hammer blows.

Instinctively running away from the path of the bear, which was unmistakably heading for me, I had lost sight of Melani and Simonis, now hidden by the shape of the Flying Ship.

"Signor Master!" I heard Simonis call out one last time.

Then came the roar, and the tide vomited itself.

೨◦⊰

As in some crazed seer's dream, all creation erupted at monstrous speed from the door beyond the cages, almost as if behind it a capri-cious god had compressed all animal life from every age and place. A chaotic mass of flesh, blood, muscles, claws, manes, skins and fangs smashed their deafening way into the stadium, instantaneously pervading every inch of it like chalk dust thrown into clear water. The earth trembled at the passage of an enormous grey, be-trunked being, followed by the rumble of stamping bulls, of panthers which like black stars of ferocity seemed to absorb the ambient light into their dark fur, of tigers that spread out fanwise like the tentacles of a single feline octopus, of lynxes that almost seemed to fly with the savage energy of the living detonation that had hurled them into the ball stadium.

The birdcages were wiped out by the explosion like reeds in a tempest. The poor winged creatures that had not been instantaneously annihilated by the impact, or crushed by the beasts that burst into the stadium after the boom, rose into the air, filling the entire space above us with a crazy multicoloured cloud. The enormous bear that had rushed us moments before was now a mere trifle.

Where had it come from, the elephant that had knocked down the door, leading the great army of beasts? Why were these wild animals all free? How had they reached the back door of the stadium? None of these questions mattered: while the mad bellowing of the animals assailed my head and ears, I saw an entire army of brutes rushing towards me, and my legs ran as if self-propelled towards the only mad hope of escape.

"Simonis!" I yelled without hearing my own voice, drowned by the powerful trumpeting of the elephant, which had begun to run in a semicircle around the Flying Ship, while swarms of birds flew over it and the lions began a quarrel with the bears, making the walls of the stadium shake with their hate-filled roaring.

I will never know how I made it, since panic is the enemy of memory. I think I must have yelled unceasingly from the incursion of the elephant and its bestial convoy right up to the moment when, clambering with ape-like rapidity, I found myself breathless and voiceless aboard the Flying Ship. I was in such a state of unconscious terror that it was only when I saw Simonis dragging Abbot Melani aboard that I came partially to my senses.

Not far off a bear was tearing to pieces a sort of large pheasant; at once a pair of lions pounced upon it, driving off the bear and taking possession of the prey.

"Here I am!" I shouted, running towards my assistant.

In his attempt to scramble onto the ship, Atto had fallen awkwardly to the ground, and Simonis was almost lifting him bodily, in an attempt to get him on board. Of course, a lion could very easily board the craft as well, but at the moment it was as good a place to be as any.

Meanwhile the smell of the birds killed by the bears and lions must have gone to the heads of the other beasts. An amorphous forest of heads, fangs, claws and snorting nostrils was devouring the belly and genitals of a poor ox, kneeling on its hind legs, its eyes raised to heaven as it emitted a last gasp of agony.

While Simonis and I, both purple with effort, heaved Abbot Melani slowly onto the ship, I saw Atto's livid lips contract in a mute prayer. Just a few paces away a lioness, held at bay only by the crazy circling of the elephant, roared irately at him.

We had almost managed to drag ourselves and the Abbot aboard when I felt a sharp, cruel blow on my head, and a thousand stings tormenting the skin of my neck and my temples. A small flock of crazed birds had come swarming around us, and a young bird of prey was hammering at my skull. I had to let go of Atto to try and defend myself. Waving my arms around maniacally, my eyes half-closed for fear of being blinded, I thought I saw a kite, some parrots and other fowl of unknown breed.

The lioness meanwhile was getting closer, roaring threateningly and showing its fangs.

Suddenly the ship juddered, as if shaken by an invisible wave, and began to pitch. The elephant had stopped its mad circling and with its trunk had started to beat rhythmically on the opposite wing from the one we were on. By its side a panther, maybe the same one that had been making for me before I scrambled aboard the Flying Ship, was about to leap up, only halted by the continual oscillation of the vessel.

Finally the clamorous birds gave me some peace. I passed my hand over my head and then looked at my palm: it was bright red. Thousands of little wounds, caused by the birds' attack, were bleeding all over my head, trickling down my chin and my forehead. We finally got Abbot Melani on board, trembling and as pale as a sheet, and he only just managed to keep his balance and not fall straight back down. The ship had shaken so violently that we nearly tumbled as we climbed over the parapet of the cockpit.

"The elephant . . ." I gasped, pointing at the huge animal to explain to Simonis why the ship was shaking in that fashion.

But meanwhile the giant had been attacked in turn by the birds, and had let go of its prey and started to run wildly in a circle again, driving the birds away from its eyes with its swinging trunk and intimidating the lions, panthers and lynxes with its powerful trumpeting. The lioness that had seemed on the point of attacking us, confused by the pandemonium, had preferred to join the group of fellow creatures busily devouring the ox. But the ship now had a new occupier: the panther.

"God Almighty protect us," murmured Abbot Melani tremulously.

The beast had leaped onto the wing opposite the one we had climbed onto and was now moving towards us in slow measured paces.

There was no time to weigh pros and cons. Simonis snatched up the only tool we had: a chimney-sweep's broom.

"I left it here last time, Signor Master."

In the meantime the organised group of animals had finished massacring the ox, which lay on the ground in a pool of blood and guts. Not far off, two bulls had victoriously engaged in battle with a lion, opening its belly with a blow of their horns. The feline now lay with its bowels ripped open, roaring with despair and feebly swiping its paws in the direction of its assassin. All around was ferocity, blood and folly. A few animals had found the two doors out of the stadium; most seemed prisoners inside that crazed arena.

The smell of blood meanwhile had excited the panther that had climbed onto the wing of the ship, and it was staring at us with ravenous fury. We were all three clustered in the cockpit, pressed close to one another. As soon as the animal was below us, my assistant gave it a great blow on the head. The panther's amazement was obvious; clearly it had not expected any resistance. Meanwhile the ship swung a couple of times. All around, the mad festivity of the birds was dying down; the deafening screeches had ceased. Several birds had flown off, others were perched here and there, and yet others had ended up crushed or torn to pieces by the animals. It was now the deep bellowing of the larger beasts that prevailed. For want of other prey (the ox was now the preserve of the strongest and most domineering animals), they were now massing together around the ship. After the unleashed frenzy of their incursion, they had identified their next prey: us. Even the elephant, having finished his senseless circling, had come up to the ship and had started to threaten us with the buccin blast of his trunk. That was what it was, I thought – the silvery trumpet noise I had heard two days earlier at Neugebäu! And that was what had produced those thuds, like earthquake rumbles, that we had heard a few hours earlier in the mansion.

Meanwhile the panther, almost as if to get a foretaste of the assault, was amusing itself by attacking the wooden handle of the broom Simonis was stretching out to it, trying to bite it and seize it with its claws. My assistant managed to jerk it from its jaws and give it another resounding thwack on the head. The animal drew back angrily. Then it advanced again and Simonis, turning the broom around, shook its sharp bristles in its face. The panther jerked back, letting out a yelp of surprise, then it began to rub its right eye socket with its paw; one of the bristles must have got into the eye. It shook itself, throwing us a furious glance. We had played around too long; the animal was preparing to pounce. It would tear Simonis to pieces first, as he had irritated it, then me, as I stank of blood from the wounds on my head, and finally Atto.

The Flying Ship trembled. I turned round. A new and powerful weight now burdened the other wing: a large lion, far more fearsome than old Mustafa, was approaching with murderous intentions. We were caught between two fires: I prepared for the end.

The hull gave another judder. While the lion heaved itself onto the wing, on the opposite side the panther tensed its muscles, uncovered its canines, roared and leaped into the air. I did not even have time to utter a mute prayer to the Virgin, and with the animal almost upon us I yelled in fear and despair. Simonis held the broom, useless and ridiculous, out in front of himself.

☙❧

It was the same benign gods as before that decided our fate. The ship was shaken by yet another powerful judder, it rose and at the same time revolved.

The centripetal motion of the ship threw us all into the bottom of the craft, while out of the corner of my eye I saw the dark silhouette of the panther leap forward and smash its face into the keel. The animal let out a raucous and angry wail, but the time for its rage had run out: the Flying Ship quivered again, shaking off the panther. And the lion too, as I discovered moments later, had been rudely removed, as a lazy heifer sweeps away the tiresome flies with a care-less swish of its tail.

"What ... what's happened?" I heard Abbot Melani murmur, almost dead from terror, crouching with his head down on the planking of the ship, while below the ship we felt (because I was sure that I was not the only one to sense it) a terrifying and primeval force surge from the bowels of nature and drive us powerfully upwards, just as the spring breeze, amid the vines of Nussdorf, wafts the light dandelion spores.

And then there came that sound, the sweet, solemn tinkling of the amber gems dangling from the ropes above our heads, a kind of primitive hymn with which the Flying Ship celebrated our ascent to heaven. It pervaded the craft, transforming the miserable, poky space into a sublime garden of harmonies. Everything became possible: it was the same sound as the first time but also different, it was everywhere and nowhere, I could hear it and not hear it. It was as sweet as a flute and as sharp as a jangling of cymbals; if I had been a poet I would have called it a "Hymn to Flight", for it is a human weakness to impose colourful names on the ineffable, and to dip the fallacious brush of recollection into it, trying to create on canvas a landscape that never existed, like a dreamy drinker who raises an empty chalice to his lips, and savours in memory the ghost of wine that he never drank.

The celestial resonance of the amber stones found its counter-point, as on the previous flight, in a subdued lowing: it was the air flowing through the tubes that constituted the keel, the real belly of the vessel. At the stern the banner with the coat of arms of the Kingdom of Portugal began to flap gaily in the lashing wind.

"Simonis!" I shouted, as I finally rose from the planks at the bottom, where I had cowered to escape the panther's deadly pounce.

"Signor Master!" he answered, rising to his feet in turn, his face illuminated by a kind of delirious rapture.

"It's flying again, Simonis, it's flying again!" I exclaimed, embracing my assistant from relief at our escape, while beneath us we heard the beasts grunting, foiled by our flight.

I looked at the petrified figure of Atto: he no longer had his dark-lensed spectacles. He must have lost them amid the hubbub we had so miraculously escaped. He, too, had risen to his feet and was holding one hand to his left ear, as if to protect himself from that primeval sound, the Flying Ship's special hymn. With his other hand he clung to the vertical poles that held up the strings with the amber fragments.

Abbot Melani's face had a waxen and unreal pallor, except for a pair of livid rings round his eyes, from the glasses he had worn so long. It was as if a deranged painter had mocked him by coating his face with white lead, and had then spread ash around his eye sockets and hooked nose, turning him into a new version of Pulcinella. His goggling eyeballs were gazing outwards and downwards.

"But I . . . we . . . we're flying," he stammered in astonishment, and then fainted, collapsing like a withered grass snake on the floor of the ship.

And then I understood what I had, perhaps, suspected all along: Atto could see.

☙❧

My assistant – who was, after all, a medical student – felt Atto's pulse, examined his rolled up pupils, and finally, with a good few resounding slaps, brought him round.

Abbot Melani, his wig askew on his head, his four real hairs lashed by the impetuous wind, stared at me with goggling eyes and a tragic expression. He let out an "o-o-oh", low and monotonous, half way between a cry and a gasp. First he approached the parapet, still supported by Simonis, then stepped back, then leaned out again, going back and forth two or three times, dismayed by the great height we had reached.

Lions, tigers and bears roared with impotent fury at us; the elephant stretched its pliant trunk upwards by way of anathema; the birds, still savouring their freedom, flapped around us, intrigued by our craft, which soared lithely although the wings remained as still as statues. It may have been imagination (indeed, there was no doubt it was), but sharpening my gaze I saw the panther that Simonis had staved off with the broom and I thought I discerned a mute vow of hatred in its distant, almost invisible eyes.

"Yes, Signor Atto, we're flying," I confirmed. "And you can see perfectly well, it seems."

"My eyes see, yes," he confessed, letting his pupils roam the firmament, without even noticing what he was saying, overwhelmed by the power of the vision opening up around us.

Atto Melani's eyes and nose cleft the air, as fixed and immobile as the Flying Ship's wooden eagle's head, enigmatically outstretched towards infinity.

"But . . . couldn't we fly a little lower?" he implored.

Simonis and I looked at one another.

"Yes, Signor Atto, try and whisper into its ear!" I said with a sudden guffaw, venting the unbearable tension that was tearing me apart and gesturing towards the aquiline head at the ship's prow. "Maybe it will obey you."

Simonis joined in my liberating laughter, after which we confessed to Atto that this was not our first flight, and that two days earlier we had experienced the inexplicable power of the Flying Ship.

"You hid everything from me, boy . . ."

"And you pretended to be blind," I retorted.

"It's not what you think. I did it to defend myself," he corrected me laconically, and at last he looked out of the ship.

He gazed at the incredible landscape that stretched out before us: the Bald Mountain, the towers and spires of Vienna, the walls of the city and the clearing of the Glacis, the Danube with its tortuous curves, the plain on the other side of the river that stretched all the way to the kingdoms of Poland and the Czar; and then palaces, bridges, avenues, gardens, the hills with their vineyards, ploughed and cultivated fields, the roads radiating out of Vienna towards the countryside, lanes and streams, cliffs and gorges: everything was reduced to the size of an anthill, with us like haughty, all-powerful gods perched high above.

"Tell me: how do you manoeuvre this ship? How does it fly?"

"We don't know, Signor Atto," answered Simonis.

"What? It wasn't you two who lifted it into the air?" he exclaimed, and I saw the panic and terror on his face.

The poor Abbot had thought that Simonis and I were the artificers of its aerial elevation and thus fully in charge. And so I tried to explain to Melani that on the previous occasion also the Flying Ship had risen into the air not because it had been spurred in any way by us, but just because – so it seemed to us – it had sensed and granted our wish: the first time, our desire to fathom the mystery of the Golden Apple; this second time, our desperate wish to escape the fangs of the lions of Neugebäu.

"A wish? Wishing by itself is not enough to move a fork, let alone a ship into the air. Tell me I'm dreaming," retorted Melani.

At that very moment, with a slight shudder, the Flying Ship changed direction.

"What's happening?" asked Atto in alarm. "Who is controlling the ship at this moment?"

"It's hard to accept, Signor Atto, but it controls itself."

"It controls itself . . ." repeated Melani, bewildered, once again casting a dismayed glance downwards, and then staggering slightly.

Simonis darted forward to hold him up.

"My God," said Atto, shivering, as the Greek rubbed his arms and chest, "it's terribly cold, it's worse than being at the top of a mountain. And what about the descent? Won't we crash into the ground?"

"The other time the ship landed back in the ball stadium."

"But we can't go back into the stadium," spluttered Atto, turning pale again. "Not with all those . . . Help! My God! Holy Virgin!"

Suddenly, with a sharp creak, the ship had veered. With a gentle but definite swerve, the craft had turned left, and the centrifugal force almost projected Abbot Melani into the abyss. Luckily Simonis, who had remained by his side, grabbed him by a fold of his habit. I myself, to keep my balance, had had to snatch hold of one of the poles.

For a few minutes silence reigned between us, broken only by the whimpering of the octogenarian Abbot and the rustling of the amber stones, which filled the air with their ineffable harmony. Atto's eyes were now lost in the abyss. As if reciting the rosary, his lips murmured tremulous and incredulous orations to the Most High, to the Blessed Virgin and to all the saints.

Meanwhile the ship continued to adjust its route at regular intervals, carrying out an aerial survey of the city, segment by segment. With Simonis supporting him at each new juddering shift of direction, Atto, amid muttered invocations, commented on our voyage with dismay:

"A life, a whole life . . ." he mumbled, "a whole life has not been enough for me to understand the world. And now that I'm about to die this has to happen to me as well . . ."

The ship had completed a full circle above Vienna. It was then that I heard it. The harmonious rustling of the amber stones swelled and embellished itself with bizarre and ineffable variations; it became a counterpoint of whispers and tinklings in a constant crescendo. Finally the shining gems, almost like graceful orchestra players, regaled us with a golden-azure chiming, and a sense of inexorable sweetness wafted over the ship. Indefinable melodious delights, like the outlandish symphonies that one savours in the initial torpor of sleep, resounded throughout the Flying Ship, and I knew that Simonis and Atto were sharing them with me, and were as enraptured with them as I was, so that I did not even have to ask: "Do you hear it as well?" because all of this was with us and within us.

"*Soli soli soli . . . Vae soli,*" murmured Atto. "These amber stones. It's . . . a motif I know – a sonata for bass solo by Gregorio Strozzi. But how do they . . ."

He hesitated. Then to our surprise, he stood up, almost arching like a bow, and before falling back, he shouted:

"*Vae soli, quia cum ceciderit, non habet sublevantem se!*" he pronounced with a stentorian voice to the amber stones, which cast polyhedric arabesques of light onto his face.

"Oh my God, he's ill!" I shouted to my assistant, fearing the worst, while both of us ran to prevent him from collapsing on the floor of the ship.

"Ecclesiastes. He's quoting from Ecclesiastes!" answered Simonis, also beside himself, but it seemed to me shaken more by Atto's words than by his state of health.

We settled the Abbot on the planks. He had not fainted, but he seemed to have lost his senses. Before falling he had touched one of the amber stones with his wrinkled fingertips and the music had at once ceased, giving way to the original rustling noise. Simonis was now rubbing the old Abbot's temples, chest and feet.

"How is he?" I asked anxiously.

"Don't worry, Signor Master. He's very shaken, but he's getting over it."

I heaved a sigh of relief. I cursed the Agha and that weed Domenico, who was always ill. It had been a mad idea, now that I thought of it, to take the Abbot to work with us. Certainly, if I had had any idea what was waiting for us at the Place with No Name . . .

"We're on our way back," observed the Greek. "We're losing height."

The Flying Ship was descending. Staring into infinity with its empty wooden eyes, the aquiline head of the Flying Ship had finally pointed its beak towards the countryside of Ebersdorf and Simmering.

Would we land back in the ball stadium? In that case, would we survive? Atto meanwhile had come to his senses.

"We must change direction!" I yelled.

Our first attempts were wholly fruitless. We began to move carefully all three to one side of the ship, and then to the other, hoping to observe some change in the stability of the craft, but in vain.

"It's going straight down like a stone," remarked my assistant. "The only difference is that it's slow."

Massing together at the prow or stern seemed to have no effect on the progress of the vessel either. It was only then that the idea came to me. What had Penicek told us about the Jesuit Francesco Lana, and his experiments? To steer his ship he had conceived a system of guy ropes: even if unpredictable, it was worth trying.

I stretched up and pinched one of the ropes on which the pieces of amber hung. The yellowish fragments bounced around chaotically without ceasing to emit their indefinable and celestial humming, while the thread vibrated like a lute string. It was as if by disturbing the subdued and amorphous melody the natural course of events could be altered. In a flash of ineffable intuition it struck me that the Flying Ship and the music of the amber stones were the same thing, and it was as if it had always been so, and could not be otherwise. This dim perception, however bizarre, was no illusion: to my extreme astonishment, after a few instants the ship shifted to the left, then to the right and then to the left again.

"Jesus save us! What's happening?" exclaimed Abbot Melani, clutching Simonis's arm.

So it was true, I thought: the fragments of amber were in some way connected with the motion of the ship. In what fashion, it was not yet given to me to know (nor did I hope ever to find out), but for the moment I was happy to have found a way to influence the motion of the ship. I noticed that the sky, serene since the start of the day, had suddenly grown dark. In Vienna the sun and clouds alternate quite differently from the way they do in Rome: in the Papal City we have a kind of calm dialogue between two scholars; in Vienna it is like the squabbling of two suspicious lovers. Every three minutes the front lines are altered, it is impossible to say who or what is right or wrong.

"Hold tight," I warned my two travelling companions, and I repeated the experiment, this time tugging the rope with the pieces of amber more vigorously.

I had overdone it. The airship trembled violently, then the prow began to oscillate horizontally, as if the bird's head were seeking its direction: suddenly it became a challenge to stay upright.

"Aren't we overdoing things, Signor Master?" Simonis protested in a worried voice, while Abbot Melani clung to him with his bony hands.

Giving my companions in misfortune the time to hold on to something, I made some more cautious attempts, trying to limit the danger of our all being hurled into the abyss by the pitching of the ship.

In the meantime our altitude decreased, as did the distance between us and the Place with No Name, which now stood out clearly in the broad expanse of the plain of Simmering. The first drops of rain fell.

"Signor Master, I think the ship is returning to base," Simonis pointed out to me.

I looked: we were heading straight towards the ball stadium. I could not yet see if the animals were waiting for us within the great rectangle. It was highly probable that some of the animals would still be wandering around hungrily, if not in the stadium, then nearby. At least one of them was longing to see us again: the panther, whose eye Simonis had injured with the broom.

That was not the only development: at that moment great black drops began to pelt down. There was no time to lose, nor could I allow myself too many qualms.

"What on earth are you doing with those ropes now, boy?" Abbot Melani asked anxiously.

"Trying to stop us ending up in the jaws of some big cat."

Neither Simonis nor Atto tried to answer this: it was clear that we had to solve the problem of our safe return. We were not very high now. With my hands I tugged at three or four ropes and released them like hunting bows.

The ship gave a violent start, so that if I had not held on with all my might I would certainly have fallen. Atto and Simonis had crouched down on the floor. We were still heading for the ball stadium. What a crude and unworthy helmsman, I thought, the Flying Ship had found in me! The sublime Ark of Truth, the noble vessel come from the West to grant the Empire victory in war, the vehicle whose purpose was to crown the tallest spire of St Stephen with the Golden Apple, was now the victim of my clumsy attempt at sabotage. What a cruel twist of fate for the ship: it saved us and now we were betraying it by trying to divert the natural course of its flight and force it to the ground. Soaked by the rain, I got to my feet and gave another and harder jerk at the ropes.

This time the oscillation was so violent that I myself fell to the floor and was afraid we would be immediately thrown out. Atto and Simonis both swore. I did not have the courage to check the direction, fearing that some new, unforeseen lurch of the ship would knock me overboard. Getting up again, I gripped the ropes and pulled again, even harder. Finally it happened.

❧

The stones had stopped humming. I looked up: the fragments of yellowish matter were no longer vibrating spontaneously. It was as if they were dissipating some form of residual energy. The Flying Ship shook from top to bottom, like an enormous bird struck in a vital organ. It was a painful, convulsive shudder, a prelude to some catastrophe. If we had had gunpowder on board, I would have sworn that we were all about to be blown to pieces.

"Mamma mia, we're all dead," I heard Abbot Melani whisper, clinging to Simonis like a child.

I stood on tiptoes and, swaying as in the midst of an earthquake, I looked outside, towards the prow. At last we had changed direction. After momentarily regaining altitude, the Flying Ship had started descending again, now heading to the left. It was making for a corner of the plain of Simmering, a grassy expanse north-east of the Place with No Name. There, I thought, we would be thrown out.

As we braced ourselves for the impact, the simple rain became a violent storm. Perhaps it was better that way, if it meant no one would see our landing. A flash transformed our sail for an instant into a silver half moon, fallen from its niche in heaven and preparing to settle on the only strip of land willing to receive it. The rain came down in huge heavy drops.

"Hold tight!" I yelled as the belly of the Flying Ship grazed shrubs and tall plants, and I got ready for the crash. Then, as thunder burst nearby, I felt the first contact with the land and made the sign of the cross.

❧

"What are those pieces of amber for? How do they make that noise? Can one of you explain it to me?"

We had landed soaked through and exhausted but alive. Surprisingly, we had come down with little more than an awkward jolt. The Flying Ship had made contact with the ground without either breaking up or overturning, and we had only needed to hold tight to avoid being thrown out of the vehicle.

As soon as we had disembarked, the winged ship rose into the air again and headed for the Place with No Name.

"Maybe it's going back to the ball stadium," surmised Simonis.

As it sailed away, humbly exposed to the rain, I gave it one last look: would I ever see it again?

We were not far from the buttery of Porta Coeli, and we made our way towards it, trudging laboriously through the muddy fields. We did not know what had happened in the Place with No Name after our skyward escape; were the lions and tigers still roaming free?

Now we were drying our clothes in the little basement room, near the fireplace. Fortunately, we had met no one on our short walk: what would two chimney-sweeps be doing in the open country, in the company of a decrepit, bald old man (the Abbot had lost his wig), with a face of patchy white lead and carmine? His expression still showing consternation at the recent events, his clothes dark and filthy, his back bent and his gait awkward, Atto resembled a battered old elf who had fled from some strange fantasy land.

We now sat half-naked by the fireside, with our clothes laid out to dry, clasping warm cups of mulled wine, and we took stock of the situation. Abbot Melani regained confidence and fired a number of questions at us.

What was the function of the tubes that constituted the hull, with the noisy flow of air rushing through them? Did they provide the the power necessary for flight? And why did the ship fly a Portuguese flag?

This barrage of questions merely rebounded off the wall of our ignorance, despite the best efforts of our imagination. The tubes did seem to act as a propellant, even if we had no proof of that. The flag of the Kingdom of Portugal, however, was connected with the provenance of the ship. The gazette from two years earlier that Frosch had shown us reported that the aerial vessel had arrived from Portugal. That tallied with the information from Ugonio: the Flying

Ship had been sent to Vienna at the behest of the Queen of Portugal, sister of Emperor Joseph I. Its task was to place the Golden Apple, which had arrived in some mysterious fashion from the East, on the tallest spire of St Stephen's. Only in this way could the Empire triumph in the great war against France and its king, Louis XIV.

But the question that most concerned Atto was the first: how the devil had those amber stones performed the sonata for bass solo by Gregorio Strozzi?

"But why does that interest you so much?" asked Simonis.

"And why should you care?" snapped Melani rudely, who was beginning to find the constant presence of my assistant rather irritating.

The Greek was not intimidated.

"Why are you no longer blind?" he retorted, with his most foolish air.

"Listen, boy," said Atto to me, repressing his annoyance, "I advise you to send your workshop assistant to go and have a look, with due care, at that abandoned hovel – what's it called, Neugebäu? We need to know if the situation has calmed down."

The Abbot wanted to get rid of my assistant, whom he did not trust in the least, and especially to be spared his importunate questions.

"It's pouring down, Signor Atto," I objected. "And in any case I'd like to know myself how you miraculously recovered your sight on board the Flying Ship."

Atto lowered his eyes.

I persisted with my questions. Why on earth had he worn those dark glasses all this time? Was it to cross the border more easily and get into the Caesarean city? On the ship he had mentioned very vaguely that he had done it to defend himself.

"Well, what am I supposed to do with those bloodsuckers, my relatives?"

"Your relatives?" I said in amazement.

"My nephews and nieces, yes – those profiteers. Don't get the idea that my sight is good. Quite the opposite: I have advancing cataracts. That's why my Parisian doctor advised me always to wear green and black, two colours, he says, that are good for the eyes. And for the same reason I sleep barefoot in winter too: apparently it is very good for your sight. As for the rest, by the grace of God, I don't do badly."

Apart from the piles and gravel sickness, explained Atto, at his venerable age he was still sound of mind and body. The only problem was his nephews and nieces in Pistoia: they did nothing but ask him for money.

"Money, money, always money! They would like me to buy two smallholdings they have their eyes on, and so they want me to withdraw the savings I have in the Monte del Sale: yes, with the Germans at the gates I would get three per cent at best! And they want me to put iron hoops on the barrels on the Castel Nuovo estate. Oh, such luxury – do they think I find money under stones?"

Amazingly, Atto seemed to have already forgotten the feats of the Flying Ship and was now inveighing against his relatives. His nephews and nieces seemed to have no appreciation of what their old uncle did for the family; each of them was out for what he or she could get.

"They even had the nerve to ask me for money to buy an entire library! To which I answered that I would soon be needing *them* to send *me* money! Result: they all vanished into thin air. Such gratitude. And to think that I paid an intermediary for four years to find a wife for Luigi, Domenico's brother, one with the right dowry and lineage. Once I'd found the right girl, they got back in touch only to ask me, quite shamelessly, to send her a bridal gown from Paris – greedy skinflints! I answered that it wouldn't be ready in time for the wedding, and I suggested they should hire the same dressmaker as the Most Serene Princess of Tuscany and her ladies. Then I gave them permission to remove the diamonds from a portrait in my gallery to make two pendants for her ears and a small cross to hang round her neck on a black silk cord. But that wasn't enough, no!"

The Abbot was now in full spate. I had the impression that he actually had something else to tell me and was just waiting for Simonis to leave us.

"They insisted on the bridal gown," Atto continued, "heedless of the fact that the corallines of Oneglia and the armed boats of Finale had raided the galley that brought the courier of Lyons to Genoa and that sending a Parisian dress to the bride would be throwing money away, as happened to a lady who sent two dresses to the Pope's niece. I answered very brusquely, promising that if I could be sure of my income in the Kingdom of France, maybe they would see me in Pistoia before St John's day, in which case I myself would bring the bride her gown."

When the bride had resigned herself to getting married in a Tuscan gown and was pregnant, Atto went on, the nephews and nieces returned to the attack.

"The baby, according to the Connestabilessa who had seen him, was very beautiful. And so I rashly promised to send the mother strings of pearls and some other trinkets. I was waiting for a good opportunity to send them without any risk of theft, which never came; and I'm sorry that circumstances do not allow me to do all that I would like, but, as I have told you too, in Paris all we see are currency notes, and if you exchange them you lose half, and these notes have been and are the ruin of France."

All they were good for, his dear nephews and nieces, was demanding money, Atto said heatedly, every so often casting a side-long, impatient glance at Simonis. The violent memory of the beasts appeared to have faded in the thick smoke of his anger against his blood relations. But any good fortune, he said, and any riches that came to them, they took care to keep to themselves.

"They were very quiet, the cunning devils, when last year the Most Serene Grand Duke granted our family access to second-degree nobility, announcing that after five years genuine nobility would be granted. I only heard about it from other folk of the town."

Abbot Melani went on to explain that his relatives in Pistoia were always complaining: first they insisted on sending Domenico to Paris, to keep an eye on his wealth, then they even got jealous and suspicious of one another.

"Domenico is a lawyer, and the Most Serene Grand Duke of Tuscany gave him a post as secretary of the Council of Siena. I didn't want him to come to Paris, I don't need anyone. I said that it was not a good time to travel, with all the widespread poverty and the count-less murders, and the countryside rife with malign fevers and petechiae. There are so few of us left now that we have to be careful to look after ourselves, I wrote to the bloodsuckers, hoping they would leave me in peace. But it was no use: they turned to the Grand Duke, and His Royal Highness wrote to me that he considered it highly appropriate for Domenico, cadet of the family, to come to Paris: not being the eldest son he had no obligation to look after the interests of the house, and I need not worry about his position, they would keep it for him for as long as he needed to be away. Domenico was supposed to go back with me to Pistoia, or to set off by himself, but not before – just listen to this! – he had found out about all my interests! And I even had to reply to the Most Serene Grand Duke offering my humble thanks for the great kindness he had shown me *et cetera et cetera . . .*"

Simonis looked at me. I realised that he would rather go out and get soaked in the storm than stay and listen to this senile prattle. But it was still like the Great Flood outside. I indicated he should wait a little longer.

A year ago – Melani went on – Domenico had settled in with his uncle. In vain had Atto urged that his nephew should bring just a few things "because the suit he had on and half a dozen shirts would be enough"; he stayed for months and months, and his old uncle had to buy him a complete wardrobe. That was not all: Melani had had to send him money for the journey, and since thirty doubloons had seemed very little to his relatives, they had sent Domenico to Paris without even a servant.

"And I had been hoping he would bring a servant who knew how to cook, so that at last I could eat some Italian dishes. Selfish and miserly, that's all they are. And I know what I'm talking about, I know just how much money is coming into the family: when Domenico got his post as secretary of the Council of Siena the Grand Duke sent me a note listing all the emoluments and honours he enjoyed. One day or other I'll come out with it and write to those skinflints and tell them it's no good playing hide-and-seek with their old uncle, because the Grand Duke tells me everything."

As the months went by, however, the old Abbot had grown fond of his nephew, and even had him naturalised as a Frenchman.

"And the trouble that caused! The other relatives all got jealous, afraid that I was favouring him over them."

Simonis and I listened wearily to the endless harangue. Atto explained that the relatives should all have been grateful for this decision, because if he had died all his furniture and the income he received from his villa near Paris would have been given to anyone who asked for them.

"It is a right of the crown, which in France is called *aubaine*, and that is why most foreigners send for some relative of theirs and have him naturalised."

He was not in fact the first nephew that Abbot Melani had taken in to live with him.

"Three years ago I lost my dear nephew Leopoldo. He was blond and very good-looking. It was a great grief to me: he was only thirty-four. He went to the Lord after over twenty days of continual fever, with headaches and delirium. In His goodness God allowed him time to receive all the sacraments and he died a saint, which is the only consolation left to me. He had become a very good young man, of angelic behaviour, and was loved and esteemed by all who knew him for his fine qualities. I too fell ill at the same time that he did, and God in His mercy preserved me, so that the fruit of all my labours should not be lost."

Here Atto came to an emotional pause, but also listened carefully to see if it was still raining or not. It was. Casting a last disconsolate look at Simonis, who did not move a muscle, Melani started up again.

Thanks to family jealousies, he recounted, with the arrival of the first cold weather he had succeeded in sending Domenico back home. But then he returned, and so Atto took advantage of this to be accompanied to Vienna, instead of hiring a secretary whose wages he would have had to pay.

"I wanted to make up, at least in part, for what my vulture-relatives steal from me. But Domenico fell ill. When we leave Vienna, I'll send him straight back to Pistoia, together with the mortadellas."

"The mortadellas?" I said in surprise.

"Before embarking on the journey to Vienna, I asked my nephews and nieces to send me candied oranges and two of the best mortadellas that they make in Pistoia and to put them in the cases of wine that His Royal Highness the Grand Duke honours me with. I wanted to have these things for breakfast in the morning. After all, given that I couldn't make the journey except in a litter, I wanted to bring some flasks of wine along with me. Well, the skinflints sent me inedible mortadellas, hard and very peppery, and there wasn't a trace of a candied orange."

All they can do is beg, these relatives! thundered Melani, completely transformed from the trembling old man we had seen on the Flying Ship. Had it not been for him, he stated, at this hour they would still be the humble grandchildren of a bell-ringer, and not the descendants of a gentleman of the Veneto, he said, thus emphasising that he had been ennobled by the Most Serene Republic.

"It was I who carried out heraldic research and discovered that Machiavelli talks of a Castle of Melano in his *Istoria della Repubblica*, or *Istorie Fiorentine* or whatever it's called, and that its lord was a certain Biagio del Melano, from whom I am convinced we get the surname that these idlers are now so happy to boast of!"

Meanwhile the rain was letting up. Simonis felt his clothes and, although they were still damp, began to get dressed again, with Melani looking hopefully on.

"But you have to be able to carry out the offices of a lieutenant before doing those of a captain! I wrote to them in a letter. If only they would exert themselves as I had done, sweating for their daily bread," he declared sententiously, forgetting that his fortune had in fact begun with something one could hardly wish on others: emasculation.

But in the end, concluded the Abbot, it was almost impossible to elude all the requests of these money-grubbers.

"And so to save myself from being bled white, I had to pretend to be blind, and thus unable to serve His Majesty, and for this reason in straitened circumstances. I have to say that I gradually acquired a taste for it: blindness saves me a lot of trouble, also with the Grand Duke."

"With the Grand Duke?" I said wonderingly.

"Yes, in France he has some pupils with no talent either for soldiery or the court, and as unruly as they are foolish, and he wants me, as I'm on the spot, to advance their expenses. Yes, and who will guarantee that I'll ever get back the money that I lend them? With the war raging throughout Europe and raids by brigands and pirates – oh, very likely! And in any case what are the Grand Duke's pupils to me? The only possibility for such desperate cases is to become monks, so long as they never join the choir and remain either at table or in bed: which is to say, they go on with the same life they lead when they have no money to gamble with."

From Atto's words, it would seem that everyone wanted to take advantage of him.

"And finally, as you know, the expedient of my blindness enabled me to enter Vienna undisturbed."

But I objected that Domenico seemed to believe in his old uncle's blindness; or else he was a great actor, I thought to myself – like his aged relative, after all. And furthermore, the Abbot had confessed several things to me the previous day, even the fact that the letter in which Prince Eugene betrayed the imperial cause was a forgery that he himself had commissioned (but Atto did not allow me to say this in front of Simonis). So why had he not revealed to me that his blindness was all a sham?

"Domenico knows that I can see, but just a little, as is in fact the case, and since the others are now all so jealous of him, he has no interest in betraying me. As for your second question, I never reveal anything unless I am forced to."

Exactly. After the bad news of the Grand Dauphin's presumed smallpox, Atto had had no choice: he had been obliged to tell me that Eugene's letter was false, otherwise how could he have got my help? But if he had revealed his sham blindness at the same time, he would have lost all credibility with me irremediably.

Simonis was now ready. Having placed the little bag from which he was never parted round his neck again, he pulled on an oilcloth he had found in the room and slipped out of the door and headed for the Place with No Name.

"We must find out how the devil that ship flies!" Atto brusquely changed the subject, happy that the Greek had finally left us alone. "It's the greatest invention of all time! An army that possessed such a ship would win every war. You could drop bombs much more accurately than with a canon. You could spy on the layout of the enemy battalions, their consistency, the conditions of the land, everything, even know if a storm were arriving, if a river had dried up – everything you need to wage war."

All that Abbot Melani had appreciated of the wonderful Flying Ship and its qualities were its possible military uses. Ah yes, I said to myself, Atto was the same old intriguer as ever. Indeed, the more he felt his innermost being threatened by outward things, like the mysterious flying contraption that challenged our very conception of the world, the more he took refuge in the hard, certain and practical kernel of his own profession as a spy.

"If only I could tell the Most Christian King about it . . ." he sighed. "It would be my great return to favour! Everyone would say: Abbot Melani is advising His Majesty once again on military matters."

"I have no idea, Signor Atto, how that ship manages to fly . . ." I said, shaking my head.

"We'll talk about it later," the Abbot cut me short. "Now that your sham-fool of an assistant has gone, there's something more urgent I must tell you."

It was Gregorio Strozzi's melody, which Atto had thought he had heard being repeated by the amber stones of the Flying Ship.

Melani explained that in the margin of the manuscript copies of Strozzi's sonata which circulated at the time of its composition, about thirty years ago, a phrase from Ecclesiastes was jotted down: *Vae soli, quia cum ceciderit, non habet sublevantem se.* Which meant: "Woe to the Sun when it falleth, for it hath not another to help him up." It was this phrase that Atto had suddenly remembered on hearing the amber stones perform (if that was the right word) Strozzi's sonata.

"So Simonis was right," I said.

"What do you mean?" asked Atto, immediately suspicious.

"You didn't hear him because you had fainted, but he at once recognised that your words came from Ecclesiastes."

"Well, well," remarked Melani. "Erudition worthy of a biblical scholar! Isn't that a little singular for an assistant chimney-sweep?"

"Simonis is a *Bettelstudent*, a poor student, Signor Atto, and poor students are often highly educated," I protested.

"All right, all right," he cut me off, annoyed. "But explain to me how and why the amber stones played Gregorio Strozzi's sonata?"

"I haven't the faintest idea. I would say that the ship must have wanted to suggest to us the solution to *soli soli soli.*"

Atto was clearly exasperated. As I had seen him do in the past, he rejected the idea of having been a witness to arcane forces, and preferred to attribute inexplicable events to his own and to other people's ignorance of natural phenomena.

Without responding to my observation, Melani went on: as with the Agha's phrase, the quotation from Ecclesiastes could be translated, playing with Latin words that have the same sound, differently.

"Not 'Woe to the Sun', but 'Woe to him that is alone'. Woe to him that is alone, like Joseph, because when he falls, he has not another to help him up," concluded the Abbot.

"So the *soli soli soli* of the Agha's phrase could have a double meaning," I deduced. "Hristo was right!"

"Ah yes, the Bulgarian. Now explain carefully to me," said Melani. "What did he write in that note, before dying?"

"On the piece of paper hidden in the chessboard? He wrote: 'Shah matt, checkmate, the King is enclosed'. And when we found his corpse, he was clutching a white king in his hand."

"Right," he said with satisfaction; but his face immediately darkened: "Of course, if you had told me sooner . . ."

Then he fell silent. He had probably realised that the reason why I had not recounted the circumstances of Hristo's death was that at that time, before hearing that the Dauphin of France had also fallen ill and before his own confession, I had not trusted him. And, now that my suspicions had been allayed, I myself no longer had any desire to dredge up the matter. Meanwhile he began again:

"I told you the story of the two sieges that Joseph laid at Landau, you remember?"

"Certainly, Signor Atto."

"And I told you about the French commander Melac, who chivalrously offered not to shoot at Joseph."

"Yes, I remember."

"Good. Then you will also recall my explanation of his conduct: the good and ancient military rules resemble those of chess, where the enemy king can never be killed. 'Checkmate' in fact means 'the King is enclosed', 'the King has no way out', but not 'the King is dead'." Your Bulgarian friend must have been tormented by this thought, the thought of the King and his destiny, since you found a chess king in his hand after his death."

"And so?"

"And so the relationship between your Bulgarian friend's note and *soli soli soli* is that . . . they are the same thing."

"What does that mean?"

"*Soli soli soli* can be translated another way," continued Atto, "if the first and the third *soli* remain as they are in the phrase engraved on the French king's cannons, while the second is considered not as the dative singular of *sol*, 'Sun', but as identical to the first *sol* and is thus translated 'solitary', 'man alone'."

"And so that would mean . . . 'To the only man alone of the earth'."

"Exactly."

" 'To the only man alone of the earth' . . . It sounds a little strange," I remarked.

"But it works. If this explanation is correct, before he died your friend had understood the real sense of the Turks' message: 'We come to the Golden Apple, which is to say Vienna, to the only man alone of the earth'. A man alone, like the victim king of checkmate: the King is enclosed, the King is alone."

"And why would Joseph be the victim of checkmate?"

"That too you should be able to work out from what I have told you over the last few days," said Melani.

I was silent, gathering my thoughts.

"Yes, I understand what you mean," I said at last, breaking the silence that had fallen between us. "Joseph is alone, and he knows it. It is no accident that he is seeking peace with all his old enemies: to the west, France, to the east, the Ottomans and the Hungarian rebels, to the south, in Italy, the Pope, against whom the Emperor had even sent an army three years ago. His Caesarean Majesty's allies are the Dutch and English, who are actually his worst enemies: they are negotiating secretly with France and are afraid that Joseph, emerging victoriously from the war or making peace with the Sun King, might block their plans to replace the old European powers. And finally in Spain, his brother Charles is fighting the French, but he hates Joseph on account of the rivalry stirred up between the two of them by their father, the late Emperor Leopold. And Eugene, his military commander, has also hated him since the days of Landau, when Joseph overshadowed his glory. The Emperor is alone. Alone like no one else in the world."

"And now, I would add, in mortal danger," Atto completed.

"But why did the Turks choose to present themselves to Eugene with this sentence? What did they want to communicate?"

"It's the only question I can't answer. For the moment."

We stayed like this, in silence, gazing meditatively at the fire that flared up every so often, taking care that some lapillus should not singe the Abbot's clothes or mine, which were hanging there to dry. Soon Atto fell into a doze. The emotions of the last hour had been too much for the old man; it was only surprising that he had not lost his senses entirely the moment the animals burst into the ball stadium.

I thought back to his sham blindness and smiled. Abbot Melani in his old age had become the classic old skinflint from comedy, hounded by his relatives. Just a few days earlier I had been taken in myself and had believed Atto's complaints about his poverty. As I cogitated thus I felt drowsiness stealing over my tired limbs. In this semi-comatose state I went on to think about Hristo, about the Agha's phrase and the new meaning we had just discovered. And just as reason was yielding to dream, I had a flash of inspiration.

Now, at last, I knew why the Agha had said that phrase to Eugene.

It was just a question of putting two and two together, thinking of what Cloridia had heard that very morning from Ciezeber, who was looking after the Emperor.

The Ottoman embassy had arrived in great haste from Constantinople, bringing the dervish with them, in order to save the life of His Caesarean Majesty. They had come just in time, the very day Joseph I had been put to bed. Probably those who were on the Emperor's side had learned that someone was making an attempt on his life and had asked for help – why not? – from the Sultan of the powerful empire, the land that possessed medical skills undreamt of in Europe. And the Sultan, who (as Cloridia had understood) had all to gain from Joseph's good health, had sent Ciezeber.

Who had summoned the Turks? The answer was obvious: it could only have been Prince Eugene. It was certainly not a coincidence that it was in his palace that the embassy had been welcomed, and that it was there that the secret encounters took place between the dervish and the Caesarean Proto-Medicus.

Cloridia had hit the nail on the head here too: Eugene should not be counted among the Emperor's enemies, as Atto believed, but among his few friends, perhaps even the only one.

I had not yet had time to say so to Melani only because he had made it very clear that he did not trust my assistant. At that moment the sound of footsteps outside awoke Atto from his torpor. Simonis had returned from his reconnaissance.

"Judging by the elephant's trumpeting, I would say the situation has not improved at all," announced the Greek.

And so we confronted the event that had triggered off all our recent misadventures: the terrifying wild animals of the Place with No Name.

The incursion of the elephant and the other beasts into the ball stadium had come about because the animals had been channelled into a narrow space behind the stadium: a sort of blind alley, bordered by the external wall of the stadium, by the eastern keep of the manor house and by another wall. The animals had made their way there by a subterranean passage, which I guessed must lead to their ditches.

But where had the elephant come from? How was it possible to hide such a giant? We had seen no trace of it in the ditches along with the other beasts!

"There is an opening in the eastern keep as well, Signor Master," Simonis informed me.

I went over the events in my mind. On two occasions I had perceived the presence of the elephant: first on the great terrace on the upper floor of the manor house, when I had heard the trumpeting of its trunk, like that of a buccin. The second time was when we had been on the western side of the gallery on the building's semi-basement level. Evidently the great beast had its den in the western keep, at the westernmost end of the terrace, just above the gallery where we had heard its footsteps: we had not been able to enter the keep because Frosch had not given us the key. From here it had passed onto the terrace, then into the entrance halls and finally it had escaped from the manorhouse, turning left to pass under the archway of the *maior domus*. Once it had reached the eastern courtyard, that of the main entrance, it had deposited an organic evacuation: that was the source of the extraordinarily abundant faeces we had almost run into!

Finding no other way out, the elephant had entered the eastern keep, whose entrance into the courtyard, as I had verified myself, was always open. Inside the keep it had turned immediately right, entering the passage towards the narrow space behind the ball stadium, where it had met the animals that were emerging from the underground gateway of the ditches. Here the great mass of beasts of every possible breed, especially of the aggressive and ferocious, mauling kind, must have created a situation of uncontrollable fury. Tigers, lions and bears had found themselves face to face with the elephant, all crammed tightly together, in a suffocating mêlée. Panic had confused their feral minds, preventing them from finding the only possible solution: to enter the eastern keep, from which the elephant had emerged, one at a time, and from there to spill out into the main courtyard. The elephant had then resolved the situation by smashing down the door that led into the ball stadium: hence the sudden explosion of beasts into the arena where the Flying Ship lay. The elephant and the rest of the bestial horde had shattered not only the door but also the birdcages, unleashing general chaos.

So far, all was clear, but who had let the animals out of their ditches, and the elephant from its hiding place in the western keep? Where had Frosch been? Why had he previously said nothing about the elephant's existence? And how the devil had that colossus ended up in one of the keeps of Neugebäu?

৵৽৹

17 of the clock, end of the working day: workshops and chancelleries close. Dinner hour for artisans, secretaries, language teachers, priests, servants of commerce, footmen and coach drivers (while in Rome people take but a light refection).

Half an hour later we were inside the Pennal's cart, which we had intercepted on the road as it headed punctually towards the agreed meeting place: we wanted to avoid getting too close to the walls of the Place with No Name. A pleasant surprise awaited us: Penicek had stretched a robust tarpaulin over his cart to protect it from the rain. He appeared rather taken aback to meet us there, with the Abbot exhausted and wigless. After bidding us climb in, he set off again without asking too many questions; Simonis saw to that, mistreating him as usual, so he did not dare to open his mouth.

As the cart set off, I wondered what had happened to Frosch. He would certainly get into trouble if he could not justify his absence at the moment the animals were released from their cages.

"I will have to report to the imperial chamber what has happened here today," I said to Simonis. "As always in such cases, they'll come here for an inspection tomorrow and we'll have to be here too. They'll ask us a lot of questions, but as Master Chimney-sweep by court licence I can't keep quiet about this affair."

"I'll come too," Atto said swiftly.

I guessed why. The Abbot was not willing to leave Vienna without finding out more about the Flying Ship: if he could report something specific to the Most Christian King, his journey to the Caesarean city would be crowned by at least one success. I did not protest; it was useless to oppose the Abbot's obstinacy. And in any case no one would suspect a blind, decrepit old man. Dressing him in shabby clothes, with no make-up or wig, I would present him as a relative I was looking after.

"All right, Signor Atto," I replied simply.

While the Pennal's trap rumbled along slowly on account of the mud, with a new storm raging furiously, we picked up a peasant on the road.

As soon as he got in, gesticulating and yelling in a thick and almost incomprehensible dialect, the yokel explained that he had just seen a lion rampaging around and that was why he had asked for a ride. We feigned utter incredulity: unbelievable, a lion in this area? The man then explained that one of the wild beasts from Neugebäu, which were part of the castle's attractions for visitors, must have escaped from its keeper. We evinced further surprise at the news that Neugebäu contained not just one but numerous ferocious animals. The peasant, maybe to relieve the terror of his encounter with the lion, took pleasure in amazing us and said that, according to rumours in the countryside nearby, at Neugebäu there was even an elephant.

We opened our eyes wide in amazement and asked him to explain. He told us that Emperor Maximilian II, who had founded Neugebäu, had been presented with an elephant from Africa. Maximilian had arranged for it to travel overland from Spain to Vienna, thus giving the Germanic peoples their first opportunity to admire the breed of elephantine pachyderms. The beast had so impressed the Germans and Austrians that each of the numerous inns where it had halted had taken on the name of "Elephant Inn". With rustic ingenuousness the peasant told us that when it came to Vienna, the pachyderm had not only surprised the onlookers but also moved them: among the admirers was a young mother, who in her amazement dropped her newborn baby; amid the yells of the crowd the elephant picked up the little child with its trunk and returned it to its mother's arms. Maximilian had first placed the elephant in a purpose-built menagerie at Ebersdorf, near the Place with No Name. But then, in December 1553, the beast had died, and a chair, made from its left front leg, was all that remained of it. All? No, not quite all, the peasant corrected himself. Before dying the elephant had proved itself to be an elephantess, giving birth (a very rare event, apparently, among these pachydermic colossi) to a beautiful pair of "calves". Now, the keeper of the elephantess – the great-grandfather of the present keeper at Neugebäu – believing that the elephantess's death had been caused by the excessive strain of the Emperor's court ceremonial, felt sorry for the two exotic orphans. Fearing that sooner or later someone would come and take them away from their comfortable quarters at Ebersdorf, and put their lives at risk, he said not a word about the birth and moved the two little elephants into a stable in the countryside nearby, where he raised them, with the help of relatives, in great secrecy. After Maximilian's death the two little ones (in a manner of speaking) were transferred to the manor house of Neugebäu, which, after its creator's death, had fallen into neglect and decay. Their fate seemed to be sealed: victims and protagonists of a secret scheme, the two little elephants were destined to die alone and in secret in the gloom of the Place with No Name. But since Mother Nature is boundless in her mercy, among animals even incestuous love is permitted and can be fruitful: the two elephants were brother and sister, and their first youthful effusions resulted in a fine little male offspring, now kept at Neugebäu, healthy, lively and vigorous of character. Now, of course it was getting on in years, but it still possessed a notable temper.

"So we noticed," I was about to remark, thinking of the terrifying roar that had accompanied its incursion into the ball stadium, but I managed to keep my mouth shut.

"𝕬nd the two parents? 𝕯id they die?" asked Simonis.

"𝕿hey were stolen during the 𝕿hirty 𝖄ears' 𝖂ar. 𝕿o be eaten. 𝕿here was a famine," the peasant answered laconically.

Atto, Simonis and I all started in surprise. Pater Abraham from Sancta Clara was right: the Viennese appetite being what it was, no animal could feel safe in this city.

"𝕿alking about dead people," the peasant said, "today they found one in the woods, up north."

"𝕺h yes? 𝖂here?" I asked.

"𝕬t the 𝕿wo 𝕳anged 𝕸en."

I gasped with surprise. The peasant noticed.

"𝕯on't you know the place? 𝕴t's near 𝕾almannsdorf."

෴

Having left our passenger at a crossroads, we did not think twice. We had got him to explain, eventually, where and what the Two Hanged Men were: a clearing in the Viennese woods, to the north. It was called that, he explained, because they had once found the swinging corpses of two men executed on a gallows there, probably two brigands.

We arrived at our destination after a journey of almost two hours, first in a carriage and then on foot, in the neighbourhood of the charming village of Salmannsdorf. We reached our objective by following a steady stream of inquisitive onlookers through the woods. Our journey had been considerably lengthened by a detour: we had deposited Atto, too tired for any further activity, at the convent of Porta Coeli. On my return, free from Simonis's company, I would tell him what Cloridia had discovered at Eugene's palace.

Ugonio's body was lying on the rain-soaked grass. His appearance was not (and could not have been) much worse than usual. While the four or five greyish hairs on his head were covered by his hood, his face still presented the same wrinkled grey skin, and from his filthy overcoat peeked his black collar and his hooked, stained hands. Invincible and nauseating, the same cowshed stench still enveloped him. His half-closed eyes, yellow and gummy, still glittered dully with the bloodshot sclera of his rotten *corpisantaro* blood. Only a trickle of greenish slaver daubed his chin and testified to what had happened. If we had not known, we might have thought he was sleeping.

Suddenly there came a break in the clouds and a ray of sunlight, penetrating the foliage, touched the basket that Ugonio had brought with him and which still lay beside him. From the basket protruded various objects which had probably emerged at the moment the *corpisantaro* fell to the ground: two glass ampullae and a small pannier. The ray of sunlight transformed the two ampullae, making their respective liquids gleam: one golden, the other a fine ruby red.

Simonis and I pushed our way through the crowd of onlookers casually discussing the discovery of the body. In no way are Rome and Vienna more different than in their attitudes towards death. In Rome everyone thinks that talking of death brings bad luck; in Vienna the Great Liberator and all that accompanies it (the causes and circumstances of death, funerals, division of the inheritance, the subsequent rich banquet) are the subject of casual and spontaneous conversations. The Romans make fun of the Viennese: how the devil can they converse cheerfully about bereavements and corpses? They forget that in the city of the popes, death, especially violent death, is less widely discussed but more commonly perpetrated.

Ugonio, in a life spent between Rome and Vienna, had blended Italian and Austrian customs: he had died in the Viennese woods at the hands of an Italian. I could put a name to the murderer. It was all too obvious: Al. Ursinum, as was written in Ugonio's memorandum. Which is to say, *Alessium Ursinum*, the castrato Gaetano Orsini, who sang the role of Sant' Alessio. Farewell Ugonio, farewell for ever my friend, may God be with you. You have taken to the tomb the secret that bound you to Orsini. And farewell to the words of the Archangel Michael: now that Atto and I had finally understood the meaning of the Agha's phrase, it would not be much use to us. But I was still curious to know what message the Archangel had engraved with his sword at the top of the spire of St Stephen's, on the pedestal that had once held the sacrilegious globe of Suleiman the Magnificent and which, according to the prophecy, was still awaiting the real Golden Apple.

I stole a look at Simonis's face, wan with anguish. Another murder was rending our souls and further entangling the snarled thread of events. With my mind on the thousand homicides that steeped the Eternal City in blood every year, I looked at Ugonio's lifeless face and pondered again on his strange destiny. "After running every sort of risk in Rome," I repeated to myself, "you got yourself killed in Vienna."

"𝔓oor 𝔴retch!" a couple of old people commented at a short distance. "𝔥e got the 𝔴rong 𝔥erb."

"𝔗rue. 𝔗hese things happen . . ." echoed another.

Got the wrong herb? Defying the scandalised voices of the onlookers (mostly octogenarians with little to do but poke their noses into other people's business), I approached the corpse. I picked up the ampulla with the golden liquid and held it against the light.

"It looks like oil," said Simonis, who had joined me.

I pulled the cork out of the ampulla and spilled a drop onto my thumb and sucked it. He was right.

At once we checked the other ampulla, which, as one might have imagined, was vinegar. The pannier was full of herbs. A salad, that is to say, and freshly picked.

At this point our inspection was interrupted by three members of the city guard who had come to examine the corpse. They snatched the ampullae and salad from our hands. They examined them meticulously, shaking their heads as if deploring an accident that could have been avoided.

"Another one who's made the old mistake," said the tallest of the three, examining the leaves attentively. "Lily of the valley instead of ursine garlic."

"Ursine garlic?" I asked the gendarmes.

The three looked at each other and then burst out laughing, as if there were no corpse at their feet.

"*Italiano*, be careful! Or salad turns into poison,' one of the three answered mockingly.

Now everything was clear. After I had heard some explanations in dialect from the gendarmes (in Vienna the employees of the urban institutions almost always speak in the vernacular, unfortunately), it was Simonis who explained it all to me, as we made our way back to the cart.

Allium ursinum was the scientific Latin name of ursine, or wild, garlic: the long-leafed herb with its pungent taste which, in early spring every year, thickly carpets the soil of the Viennese woods with a brilliant shiny emerald green and spreads its spicy perfume everywhere. In Vienna it is normal to pick wild garlic to make salads with, or to cook with other dishes, a custom that has long died out in Rome. Ugonio evidently preferred it raw, and that was why he had brought a little oil and vinegar with him. That was what the annotation "Al. Ursinum" meant in Ugonio's note: not *Sant' Alessio* and Gaetano Orsini, but ursine garlic: an innocent harvest of fresh herbs. That therefore was the "urgentitious and appeteasing" affair that the *corpisantaro* had hinted at, not any plots with Orsini under the cover of the Chormaestrin's music! The subsequent words in Ugonio's note, the name of the Two Hanged Men, indicated the spot where the *corpisantaro* knew that he would find it in abundance. But instead, it was where he had found his death: wild garlic, as one of the gendarmes had explained to me, was almost identical to another plant, lily of the valley, whose leaves contain a swift and fatal poison. Even expert herb pickers had sometimes made mistakes and paid with their lives, just like Ugonio. Oh, how fragile a thing is a human being, if the life of a reckless relic hunter, hardened to all labours and all dangers, can be broken by a puny little wild plant!

That was why Gaetano Orsini, when Simonis and his companions had asked him, amid their pummelling, about the two hanged men, had said in bewilderment that he hardly ever left the city walls! He knew the name of the place and could not understand why they were talking to him about it.

It had all been pointless. The last tenuous thread that seemed to link us to a possible solution had frayed to nothing in our hands. If Ugonio had not been plotting with Gaetano Orsini, then our suspicions about Camilla de' Rossi's musicians remained no more than suspicions – or even fantasies, since they were based on nothing concrete. Ugonio's only business had been to provide Ciezeber with a false head of Kara Mustafa, as part of his customary trade as a hunter of fake relics.

The disappearance of the *corpisantaro* was another painful rupture for me. I had run into Ugonio twenty-eight years ago, in Rome, at the very same time that I, an inexperienced servant boy in a modest Roman inn, had first met Atto Melani, and through him the great capricious world outside the walls of my little inn, and the mad wheel of fortune that governs it.

Even then I had stared death in the face. Now the death of Ugonio closed the circle that had begun in those distant Roman days. The sense of completeness (not of perfection) that the events of Vienna brushed over my distant memories, like painters silently coating frescoes with a fresher glaze, took on a new tonality. A harsher, sadder and more ruthless one.

At least I had the consolation that Ugonio had not died at anyone else's hand: indeed, he had gone by gorging himself. I cast a last glance at his lifeless body. The shades and mephitic airs of the Roman sewers had bestowed on him the features of a burrowing mole. His passing now allowed him to be benignly caressed by the fresh Viennese breeze and by the April sunlight, which filtered tremulously through the foliage and rested maternally on his face, almost as if it wished to show me the divine breath that lies hidden in every man. More than a death, it was almost an elevation from the subhuman to the superhuman, this demise of the haggard old *corpisantaro*, I thought as I walked away. I made the sign of the cross and recited a short prayer for his twisted soul.

❧❧

On our way back I called in at the imperial chamber to report the escape of the wild animals from the Place with No Name. The clerk took note without batting an eyelid.

When we got back to Porta Coeli there was no point in trying to confer with Atto: he lay almost lifeless on his bed, too worn out by the day's adventures. Domenico, who had almost completely recovered at last, begged me not to insist: better to let him sleep through to the next day.

"𝕿𝖔𝖉𝖆𝖞 𝖜𝖊 𝖜𝖎𝖑𝖑 𝖙𝖆𝖈𝖐𝖑𝖊 𝖙𝖍𝖊 𝕱𝖔𝖚𝖗𝖙𝖍 𝕯𝖎𝖘𝖈𝖚𝖘𝖘𝖎𝖔𝖓: 𝕺𝖋 𝖇𝖚𝖞𝖎𝖓𝖌 𝖆𝖓𝖉 𝖘𝖊𝖑𝖑𝖎𝖓𝖌," Ollendorf greeted me, with the usual Teutonic smile that sends a shiver running down our Latin spines.

With my mind on quite other matters, I passively submitted to the German lesson. Our little boy and Cloridia, fortunately, proved much more attentive to the teachings of our good preceptor.

"𝖂𝖆𝖘 𝖋𝖚𝖗 𝖂𝖆𝖍𝖗𝖊𝖓 𝖜𝖔𝖑𝖑𝖊𝖓 𝖉𝖎𝖊 𝕳𝖊𝖗𝖗𝖊𝖓 𝖍𝖆𝖇𝖊𝖓? 𝕾𝖎𝖊 𝖌𝖊𝖍𝖊𝖓 𝖍𝖊𝖗𝖊𝖎𝖓 𝖎𝖓 𝖉𝖊𝖓 𝕷𝖆𝖉𝖊𝖓, 𝖚𝖓𝖉 𝖘𝖈𝖍𝖆𝖜𝖊𝖓, 𝖜𝖆𝖘 𝕴𝖍𝖓𝖊𝖓 𝖇𝖊𝖑𝖎𝖊𝖇𝖊𝖙," which is to say "What merchandise would your lordships like to have? Pray enter the shop, and see what attracts you," my little wife recited diligently.

A little later there came a knock at our door. It was Simonis. He had found a note from Opalinski in his room: he wanted to meet us the next day and fixed an appointment at seven a.m. in a palace near the southern ramparts.

I went back to the lesson with even less enthusiasm, and when Ollendorf had gone I was finally able to tell Cloridia all about the latest events, Ugonio's death *in primis*.

She was saddened, although less than me, naturally. For her the *corpisantaro* had only constituted a threat, not someone towards whom she could feel any attachment, however wavering. In any case, we did not talk much about it, so as not to distress our boy.

I settled down to read the newspaper: the *Corriere Ordinario*, of course. I had to admit that since these troubles had started, I had felt less and less inclined to take up the customs of my adopted city, and the impenetrable Germanic idiom was one of the first victims.

Cloridia had meanwhile foraged in the convent's kitchens for something to eat. I had not yet had any chance to eat and was starving.

"Mummy's little boy," she said to our son, with a tray in her hand. "Come and help me prepare Daddy's dinner."

"*Ich gehorsambe*", which is to say, "*I obey*," my little apprentice answered comically in German, and at once set out cutlery, a napkin and a glass in front of me.

The dinner was all based strictly on spelt. I knew who it came from, of course. How could I object? The Chormaisterin's fixation on the curative powers of spelt was shared wholeheartedly by Clorida, who had inherited it from her mother. In all her years in Rome, my wife had actually made very little use of her mother's recipes, but now, spurred by Camilla, she too had become a real fanatic. At first it had not bothered me, especially since the noble grain, a favourite food of the ancient Romans, had more than once cured our boy of his ailments, but as time went by I had tired of it. Chewing my way through this meal fit for ruminants, I settled down to read the *Corriere Ordinario*, which Cloridia had as usual obtained from van Ghelen's printing house.

The dispatches from Madrid, which had left there on 9th March, reported the preparations in Portugal (where the Queen was Joseph's sister) for the campaign against the Duke of Anjou. And so naturally I thought of the Golden Apple and the Flying Ship, which the Queen of Portugal had sent to Vienna. Then I read of the quarrels between the Duke of Vendôme and the Princess of the Orsini, "which are growing daily, the Duke saying loftily, that he cannot understand how the advice of a woman is followed in matters that should not even come to the ears of their Sex." I could well believe that the Duke of Vendôme might grow irritated with the gentle sex, I thought: had not Atto included him in the list of women-men? The name of Orsini, on the other hand, the famous intriguer known to everyone, reminded me of the homonymous and far from noble castrato, whom I had for a moment mistaken for the killer of poor Ugonio . . . How strange this evening's perusal of the *Corriere* was proving, I said to myself in vexation: instead of distracting me, every item reminded me of what I had just lived through. If such coincidences meant anything, what were they trying to tell me? I went on to the dispatches from Rome, which were also far from fresh, from 28th March, but here too the first name my eyes fell on was that of Connestabile Colonna: he had participated with His Holiness, the Supreme Pontiff Clement XI, at the feast of the Most Holy Annunciation. The Connestabile was Maria Mancini's son. In short, the gazette, wherever my eyes fell, was talking about me.

I threw it onto the ground impatiently and went on to read the pamphlet which accompanied the gazette. However, it only brought news from places that were distant and wholly unknown to me, like Mietavia, capital of a certain Duchy of Curlandia. Right at the end I found the latest news from Vienna:

The Most August Emperor having been ill with Smallpox since Wednesday, Prayers have been ordained and published since Sunday . . .

Things I already knew. I read on:

These days have seen the departure for the Low Countries by Postal Diligence of the Caesarean General Sergeant Count Gundacchero of Althan.

So Count Althan had already set off: which made it all the stranger that Prince Eugene was still lingering here. Perhaps the next day he really would leave, as he had announced.

That was the end of the Viennese news. I looked at the page again: there was something odd, like a false or missing note. Missing? Of course! The news of the Augustinian monk arrested for murder and rape! The Italian newspaper said nothing about it.

"Cloridia! The Diary of Vienna! Where's the Diary of Vienna?" I exclaimed, leaping from my chair.

"Here it is, here it is!" my consort said, pointing to the table by my side, where she always placed the paper that she bought at the Red Porcupine.

I could not find the news in the German-language gazette either.

Penicek had told me the previous day that it was on everyone's lips and he was surprised we knew nothing about it. But there was not a word about it in the gazettes. I went over to Cloridia, who had started brushing my work clothes and asked if she had heard anything about it, but she shook her head and looked surprised: at the palace of the Most Serene Prince they were usually the first to hear every little item of gossip – and if a monk had been arrested . . .! That was not the only thing. She had not heard a word about the serious crimes he was supposed to have committed either.

"Odd!" remarked my wife. "Who told you about it?"

"Penicek."

"Ah."

"Do you think he invented it, perhaps to . . .?"

At that moment, from the pocket of the trousers Cloridia was holding, fell a small object. It was the little box Atto had given to me.

"What is it?" asked Cloridia, retrieving it.

I told her that, according to Abbot Melani, it contained the explanation of his meeting with the Armenian. However, he had made me promise not to open it before he left Vienna.

"And suppose it were empty?" she objected.

I felt myself turn pale. I shook it slightly. An object of some sort rattled within. I heaved a sigh of relief.

"All right, the Abbot has put something inside," she admitted. "But are you really sure that it will explain his meeting with the Armenian? Maybe it's just a pebble."

I was on tenterhooks.

"I'm tempted to open it," I said.

"You'd be breaking your word."

"So what should I do?" I asked disconsolately.

"I'm almost sure your Abbot was sincere, this time. I've still got a few doubts, I'll admit, but the moment you suspect anything you can always force it open."

ॐ�

20 of the clock: eating houses and alehouses close their doors.

I was sitting in my usual place in the Caesarean chapel: it was time for the rehearsal of *Sant' Alessio*. This evening the orchestra was playing with more intensity of purpose than usual, the performance of the oratorio being imminent.

After Ugonio's tragicomic death – may he rest with God – the musicians had turned back into the innocent artists I had always really believed them to be. And yet I looked at Camilla de' Rossi's back as she waved her arm to coax a more intense vibrato from the violins, or a gentler muttering from the violas, and I asked myself some questions.

Why had she lied about Anton de' Rossi? Rossis are not necessarily all related to one another, she had said. But the ex-chamberlain of Cardinal Collonitz was indeed related to her deceased husband Franz. Cardinal Collonitz was the same man who years ago had baptised the Turkish girl who had been rejected by the nuns of Porta Coeli; it was Camilla herself who had told us about it. Franz and Anton de' Rossi, Franz and Camilla, Anton de' Rossi and Collonitz, but also Collonitz and Porta Coeli, and finally Porta Coeli and Camilla. What logic, if any, lay concealed amid all this tangle?

And why on earth, as I had been told by Gaetano Orsini (whom I only now knew to be harmless and therefore trustworthy), had the Chormaisterin never let herself be paid for the work she did for the Emperor? People who do not work for money, I argued, receive some other kind of recompense. What was hers? When Joseph had asked her to give up her job as a healer with spelt, she was no longer able to support herself and, rather than get paid for her musical compositions, she had asked His Caesarean Majesty to be allowed to stay at the convent of Porta Coeli, which was more like a punishment than a recompense.

Years earlier, Camilla and her husband Franz had arrived in the distant capital of the Kingdom of France to meet . . . Atto Melani. Was the journey undertaken for the purpose of meeting the pupil of Seigneur Luigi – or the spy of the Most Christian King? Could one really believe that Camilla had nothing to do with the shady dealings in which Atto had always been entangled? I noticed that Cloridia was looking at me gloomily: she knew my cogitations and shared them, but her heart wavered between them and her affection for the Chormaisterin.

From the mouth of the soprano, the plump Maria Landini whom I had believed just the previous day to be capable of the vilest crimes, Alessio's spouse mellifluously sang the wonders of love:

> *Basta sol che casto sia*
> *Che diletta sempre amor . . .*[14]

No, it was not possible. It was clear that behind Camilla's fabrications something lay hidden. I observed the Chormaisterin as she conducted, and I pondered.

> *. . .e fa' poi che eterna sia*
> *Fiamma ascosa entro del cor.*[15]

As I heard the soprano's words on the eternal flame of the passions, I told myself that doubt is just like love, a flame that torments and blazes incessantly. My perplexities about the Chormaisterin's musicians had vanished. But my burning doubts about this woman grew more painful by the hour. Porta Coeli and Camilla had been the starting point of my stay in Vienna. Now, after a thousand bloody

[14] *Let it be but chaste / Love always delights . . .*
[15] *And let it be an eternal flame / hidden within the heart.*

adventures, everything seemed to lead back to the convent and to the enigmatic composer.

With regard to the students' deaths, we no longer had any clue to follow. But with regard to the Emperor's mysterious illness there were still far too many questions left unanswered: what bound Camilla to Joseph the Victorious? What recompense did the Chormaisterin expect for the service she was rendering His Caesarean Majesty?

I could not say why, but I felt that the next day would bring a little light to my intellect, now befuddled by the bewildering labyrinth of events.

Day the Eighth

THURSDAY, 16TH APRIL 1711

✠

5.30 of the clock: first mass. From now on the bells will ring in succession throughout the day, announcing masses, processions, devotions. Eating houses and alehouses open.

The next day it was again impossible to shake Abbot Melani from his slumber. At dawn I returned to his rooms, and Domenico tried to prevent me from even entering, protesting that his uncle was in no fit condition. I did not give up, and after a short argument I managed to force my way in and approach his bed.

Unfortunately Atto's nephew was right: on account of the previous day's excessive exertions, and above all the emotions aroused, the Abbot was in an almost catatonic state. I managed to wake him and speak to him for a minute or two, but all I got was a dazed stare and a few muttered words. Even though I knew that Domenico would be listening to my words, I tried to communicate to Atto the gist of my most recent conversation with Cloridia: in all probability the Turks had arrived in Vienna with intents that were far from evil. Indeed, they wished to collaborate in healing the Emperor, and so his theorem was wrong, his suspicions about Eugene unfounded. But it was no use. After a while Atto closed his eyes again and turned away from me. Domenico, vexed and worried by my insistence, all but kicked me out.

Back in my rooms, I received the expected summons from the imperial chamber: that afternoon my assistant and I were to meet the authorities at the Place with No Name, where we would dictate a report on the events that had taken place there and sign it.

Meanwhile Cloridia had returned in great agitation after a brief excursion.

"The Most Serene Prince's carriage has left his palace. He has set off for the front again," she announced gravely.

The man who had plagued our thoughts for over a week was returning to his old job: the outer struggle against the French enemy, and the inner one between Dog Nose, Madame l'Ancienne and the Captain of Death.

But we had a job to do. It was almost seven o'clock: time for our appointment with Opalinski.

❧

It was a short journey, but it was at once interrupted by a wholly unexpected encounter.

"𝕰𝖍, 𝕴𝖙𝖆𝖑𝖎𝖆𝖓 𝖈𝖍𝖎𝖒𝖓𝖊𝖕-𝖘𝖜𝖊𝖊𝖕! 𝕾𝖙𝖔𝖕, 𝖜𝖆𝖎𝖙!" a familiar voice addressed me.

At first I did not recognise him. His head was bandaged, and he was leaning on a stick. As he came towards me I thought I was seeing a ghost.

"Frosch!" I exclaimed.

If he was not a ghost, the keeper of the Place with No Name had risked becoming one. Ceaselessly rubbing the bandages on his head, he told us what had happened when the animals went on the rampage and held us hostage in the ball stadium. While we were working in the mansion of Neugebäu, Frosch was in his usual place close to the animal cages. After which, as often happens in the case of sudden assaults, he could remember nothing. All he knew was that someone (it was impossible to say whether it was just one person or several) had taken him by surprise and bludgeoned him. He had remained unconscious for an indefinite period. He had only woken when Pup had licked his face with his trunk.

"Pup?"

"𝖄𝖊𝖘," answered Frosch, as if that pet name were the most obvious thing in the world for the elephant, probably hoping we would ask no questions about the secret he had kept all that time within the walls of the mansion.

When he re-awoke, the keeper went on, he had taken stock of the disaster, which could only have been caused deliberately. Weaving his way miraculously among the maddened animals in the drenching rain, his blood-soaked head throbbing painfully, the keeper had managed to bar all the exits from the Place with No Name, after which he had asked at the nearest farm for help.

Frosch recounted the whole story in great detail, speaking slowly and peppering his speech with frequent curses. He was still in pain and had clearly been drawing frequently on his bottle of Slibowitz schnaps. It was growing very late, but there was no way to get the befuddled keeper of the Place with No Name to be more succinct.

At first the peasants in the area, Frosch continued, had refused to help him, declaring that Rudolph's ghost had returned, that Neugebäu was haunted and what was more they had even seen a ship in the sky – at which point the keeper gazed at us inquisitively. However, since we had asked no questions about the elephant, he asked none about the Flying Ship.

Despite Frosch's efforts, some animals had escaped from the Place with No Name, and the hunt to round them up, which had spread into the neighbouring countryside, would go on for the next few days. I said that we had no idea who could have freed the animals, nor who had attacked him. We had escaped from Neugebäu, I declared, as soon as we saw some of the ferocious animals wandering around freely. Once back in Vienna, I told him, I had informed the authorities of what had happened and that very morning I had received a summons to draw up and sign a report *in situ*.

"𝕲𝖔𝖔𝖉; 𝖇𝖚𝖙 𝕴 𝖜𝖔𝖓'𝖙 𝖇𝖊 𝖆𝖇𝖑𝖊 𝖙𝖔 𝖒𝖔𝖛𝖊 𝖋𝖗𝖔𝖒 𝖍𝖊𝖗𝖊 𝖋𝖔𝖗 𝖆 𝖜𝖍𝖎𝖑𝖊," he said, massaging his bandaged head and pointing to the building he had just emerged from to take a short walk: the 𝕭ü𝖗𝖌𝖊𝖗𝖘𝖕𝖎𝖙𝖆𝖑, or City Hospital.

He went on to list all his wounds and the stitches that had been applied to them, and the number of tragic cases he had seen in the hospital, a place he hoped, once discharged, never to set foot in again, because he was sensitive by nature, and certain things he just could not bear, *et cetera et cetera*, and on and on he went until the Slibowitz sloshing around in his veins came pouring out in the form of tears. As often happens with alcoholics, Frosch ended his account by sobbing like a child. We endeavoured to cheer him up, and fearing he was about to faint we accompanied him back inside the Bürgerspital, where we entrusted him to the tender care of a young nun.

ॐ

The building was like a great many others near the southern ramparts. To find our meeting place we had to follow the instructions Opalinski had left us. Our encounter with Frosch meant that we arrived over an hour late.

As soon as we turned into the street, Simonis stopped me with his hand.

"Let's go back," he said.

"Why?"

"Let's try and arrive at the building by another entrance – you can never be too careful."

"But Opalinski wrote that we should follow his instructions."

"We'll find him just the same, Signor Master, trust me."

It was not difficult to arrive at the place stipulated. Houses in Vienna are often linked to one another. We slipped into the doorway of a small house situated in a side street, and passing from the corridor to the courtyard, we were soon at our destination.

"𝔗𝔥𝔢 empty apartment? 𝔍𝔱'𝔰 𝔱𝔥𝔢 one on 𝔱𝔥𝔢 top floor, 𝔱𝔥𝔢 𝔃𝔴𝔦𝔱𝔨𝔬𝔴𝔦𝔱𝔷 family 𝔩𝔦𝔳𝔢𝔰 there. 𝔒𝔯 rather, 𝔱𝔥𝔢𝔶 used to," said an old woman on the ground floor in a tone that was both sour and despondent, just before closing the door again. "𝔍𝔱'𝔰 𝔱𝔥𝔢 only one 𝔱𝔥𝔢𝔶'𝔳𝔢 already assigned to a functionary. 𝔗𝔥𝔢 other apartments are all closed, nobody knows till when. 𝔈𝔳𝔢𝔯𝔶𝔬𝔫𝔢 has been evicted. 𝔍'𝔳𝔢 just come to collect my last few things."

The old woman's voice was full of bitterness at the imperial functionaries, who had driven out all the inhabitants of the building. I was thus coming into direct contact with the effects of the right of quarters that Simonis had told me about: all the tenants had had to leave their homes at the behest of some court parasite. This latter, as usual, had illegally sublet the Zwitkowitz family's apartment, and Opalinski collected the rent of the new lessee.

We quickly climbed the stairs without meeting a living soul.

We immediately guessed which apartment it was, because the door was open. We entered. The place was half empty. Various items of furniture and paintings had been taken away recently; one could still see the marks on the floor and there were white patches on the wall where paintings, crucifixes and clocks had hung.

I was now well acquainted with Viennese homes, having seen dozens of them during my inspections of fireplaces. The objects on show in them and the architecture would make anyone's fortune in my home town; the possessions of a modest family in Vienna are the equivalent of five wealthy families in Rome. The walls are thick and solid, the windows large, the roof high, covered with tiles and crowned by impressive, well-built chimneys. The apartments generally have a hallway and well-supplied kitchen. The front door is broad, like the one we had just passed through.

"Jan, are you here?" said Simonis.

There was no answer.

"He'll have gone by now," I said.

From the first room one could turn left or right. We chose to turn right and so entered the kitchen. As usual in Vienna, there was a large oven and a great variety of utensils, such as would only be found in rich, well-furnished homes in Rome. In the Archduchy of Austria above and below the Enns the kitchenware is always of the best quality: the forks have three, and sometimes even four, prongs.

The Zwitkowitz family had carried away some furniture, but not their effects: on the floor were heaps or stacks of items of copper cutlery, metal jugs, brass pans, zinc bowls and glasses of every shape and form. Near a pile of plates, stacked in a corner waiting to be carried away, I spotted some red drops. I pointed them out to Simonis.

"Blood," he said evenly.

In the larders and storerooms of Vienna you will always find a great number of dishcloths, cloth napkins and serviettes, finely decorated with beautiful designs and patterns, because grease and oil flow like rivers in the kitchens of this city.

On a table I spotted a beautifully embroidered table cloth with its napkins, all neatly folded and stacked. Something struck me. I counted the napkins: there were just three. Not six or twelve, as was usually the case.

In Vienna the cooks use special spits, known as *Bratspieße*. They put three or four in the oven one above the other, so that the juice of the various meats that are speared on them, as they cook, can run down from the one at the top to the one at the bottom. Since no one likes to spend hours in front of the fire turning the spits, the Viennese have invented an ingenious automatic system – governed by weights, spheres and chains like a clock and powered by the force of the hot steam from the cooking – which allows the meat to turn regularly and so come to the table well cooked. Lying on the ground, I saw a rack with six *Bratspieße*. As usual they were extremely well made: the long tip, sharply pointed and equipped with little teeth that grip the meat and prevent it from slipping off, were detachable. However there were only four tips: two were missing.

"Opalinski, where the devil are you?" said Simonis again, but without much conviction this time.

From the kitchen we entered another room, very common in Austria, known as the *Stube*, which is a little like our dining room. It's where people spend most of their time because it contains a closed stove of a special kind, only found in northern countries. This produces a moderate and regular heat, and combats the harshness of the winter better than any fireplace. In the *Stube* the Viennese like to keep a great number of songbirds and they collect all sorts of strange ornamental objects (silk headrests, wall hangings, porcelain, pictures, chairs, mirrors, clocks, plates), which make it difficult to walk across the room without knocking over and shattering some nick-nack or other: concessions to luxury and vanity quite rightly disapproved of by Pater Abraham from Sancta Clara.

"There are more bloodstains," I added, looking at the floor and feigning calm.

"Yes. And they are more copious," observed Simonis distractedly, as if we were talking of a crack in the ceiling or a vase of flowers. Some of the stains were actually long stripes, as if someone had slipped in them.

Returning to the hallway, we noticed bloodstains there as well. We had not noticed them when we entered, because they were in the doorway to the left, while we had gone to the right. We passed through the left-hand doorway.

In Vienna, depending on the size of the family, every apartment contains at least one bedroom. The beds all have comfortable feather mattresses (ah, so much softer than Roman ones!), denounced, not unjustly, by Pater Abraham from Sancta Clara, since they inevitably lead to a softening of the spirit and body.

And so we entered the bedroom. The furniture was of the kind that had long been fashionable, the so-called rosebud style: a great mish-mash of amorphous and irregular decorations, not unpleasing in their way. The chairs had the classic leather backs and seats, fixed to the frame with nails. To the left, up against the wall, was a fine folding table. To the right there was a three-door wardrobe, with a niche and a little statue in the middle. Next to it stood a small cupboard carved in the form of a tabernacle, with a pair of statues on top and, in the middle, a clock. On the wall hung a small pendulum clock and a mirror.

In the centre of the room, finally, was a large double bed. A strange ferruginous smell hung in the air. In front of the bed there was an armchair facing away from us, with someone sitting in it. He turned round.

"You!" exclaimed Simonis.

Only then did I realise that the Greek had taken something from the bag he had been carrying around with him constantly over the last few days: a pistol. And he was aiming it straight at the the person who had greeted us: Penicek.

❧

"What's the matter? Don't shoot. I . . . I'm wounded," said the Pennal on seeing the weapon.

He got to his feet with an effort, his legs trembling. He was holding his right arm tightly with his other hand; between the fingers we could see the red of blood. From his left temple trickled another small crimson stream. Simonis and I stood there motionless, just three paces away.

"It was Opalinski," he went on, "he told me to meet him here."

"Us too," I said. "He sent us a note."

"When I arrived, he asked me if I had heard from you. He was waiting for you and he was very nervous. Seeing how late you were, he thought you were not going to come. Then I told him perhaps you were busy, because you had to go to Neugebäu today."

"And what do you know, Pennal, of what we are going to do or not going to do?" asked Simonis suspiciously, with his pistol still trained on him.

"You said so yourselves, when you got back, remember? But I wish I hadn't spoken! That was what ruined me. He pulled out a dagger."

He paused, supporting himself on the armchair.

"Jan had invited you and me to this appointment so that he could kill us all," Penicek went on, still shaken by his recent struggle, clutching his wounded arm. "Two henchmen were waiting in the street for you to arrive. As soon as they saw you enter the building, they were going to sneak upstairs, ready to come to their leader's aid, and kill you."

Now barely able to stand on his lame leg, he stared at us with frightened eyes, awaiting our reaction. We were frozen to the spot.

"At a certain point he attacked me, I defended myself, we fell to the floor and we fought. In the end. . ."

"In the end?" asked my assistant icily.

"He hit me on the head with something," he said, gesturing to the blood trickling down his face. "He thought I was dead and ran off."

"When did it happen?"

"I don't know, perhaps . . . a few minutes ago," he panted. Then he looked apprehensively towards the door. "If anyone heard us and comes in now, what . . . what shall we do, Signor Barber?" he asked in a broken voice.

"Let's get away at once," said Simonis.

"Where?" I asked.

"Somewhere quiet, to have a chat," he said, taking the Pennal by the collar and dragging him to the front door, paying no heed to his wounds or his lame leg.

❧

The spring had retroceded once again; the day was cold and unusually foggy, with very few people in the streets, except for a black carriage slowly trundling along in the same direction as us. We could not have chosen, in fact, a quieter and more secluded place than the one Simonis led us to: the small cemetery of the Bürgerspital, the city hospital near Carinthia Street, where Frosch had been treated. Inside the hospital grounds, which we slipped into without any trouble, there was a small graveyard set between the hospital church and the ramparts. A fine drizzle was falling, and there was not a living soul among the tombstones.

"Opalinski set a trap for us, and I fell right into it," Penicek began, pressing the wounds on his head with his hand. "That's if we really want to call him Opalinski."

He stopped for a moment. He continued to look downwards. His little wretched eyes were fixed on the graves all around us, his pupils darting feverishly from one stone to another.

"What do you mean?" I said at last.

"Opalinski doesn't exist, has never existed. His real name is . . . Glàwari."

❧

"Andreas Glàwari, to be precise," he said after a few moments' silence, "and he's Pontevedrine, not Polish. That's what he confessed to me, thinking that in a few minutes' time he was going to finish me off. He didn't imagine I would survive. So he amused himself by telling me all about it. And now, just as he told it to me, I'll pass it on to you. Everything."

Dànilo had been the easiest job. The first victim had imprudently revealed to Glàwari the time and place of the appointment, and so he just had to get there a little earlier to avoid any problems. The victim had ended up in the murderer's clutches without even recognising him. He had shown surprise only when the knife plunged into his liver like a hot blade into butter.

"When you found him dying, the only thing he managed to say was the name Eyyub and the forty thousand of Kasim, one of the thousand legends about the Golden Apple. Dànilo had learned it in his research. He thought he had been stabbed for this and, thinking it important, he spent his last breath in the attempt to tell you what he had learned. But in fact the Golden Apple had nothing to do with his murder."

With Hristo Hadji-Tanjov, the chess player, the procedure had been a little more complicated. The stubborn Bulgarian had guessed that it was not a good idea to talk in front of the whole group.

It was true, I thought, while the Pennal talked on: poor Hristo had fixed the appointment with me and Simonis in the distant Prater without anyone knowing.

"Glàwari, who always had all of us followed, already knew at the meeting at Populescu's house that Hristo was not going to come: his thugs had told him that he was heading for the Prater. And so he realised that the Bulgarian no longer trusted his friends."

"And he was right," I put in.

"But Glàwari had to come to the meeting with us, and so he ordered his two hired killers, two Hungarians to carry out the murder. He even told me their names: Bela and T rek; if those *are* their real names, of course. Anyway, they belong to his network of spies. In executing Hristo there was the risk of being overheard by the Prater's guards, or by any children who might have gone in to play. That was why the two Hungarians used a dagger. Luckily, he told me with a sneer, it all went well. It's true that his men could have caused a good deal of trouble, when they fired at us. They hadn't foreseen your arrival. Glàwari had given orders that they should eliminate any dangerous witnesses, but he didn't know that Hristo had an appointment with you, of all people. When the two killers saw how attentively you were examining the corpse they at once decided to do away with you. My arrival stopped them, luckily. And you know what, Glàwari even thanked me: he still needed you, he said. While he was telling me all this, every so often he would laugh," gasped Penicek, shaken by sobs, "and he explained that after thrusting the dagger into his neck they shoved Hristo's head into the snow until he stopped moving."

Then it was Dragomir Populescu's turn. In this case things reached the peak of refinement, Glàwari told Penicek, laughing all the while. Glàwari knew that the Romanian never hit it off with women, and he paid an Armenian girl to trick him. He fell for it easily: all he had to do was invite him to have coffee at the Blue Bottle, where she worked. The ingenuous Dragomir didn't suspect a thing.

"She was a brunette, a certain Mariza. On Glàwari's orders she arranged to meet him at the Andacht on Mount Calvary."

"So it was the waitress who served me and Atto just a few days earlier! How stupid of me, I took Atto right into the enemy's mouth!" I exclaimed, thinking how many secrets Melani had confided to me in that coffee house. Fortunately he had been prudent enough to tell me the most important things while we were out strolling.

"Everyone goes to the Blue Bottle, and people like Glàwari know it. There are always ears listening in there. It's easy with the Armenians: they'll spy for anyone who pays them well."

"So that same evening when they killed Dragomir, the old man at the Blue Bottle who frightened the Abbot by blathering about the Tekuphah, the cursed blood –"

"It was all set up for you. But the cruelty with which Populescu was murdered, including the discovery of the Armenian *tandur* with the mangled pudenda, followed a particular logic. You were supposed to suspect that it was revenge for Dragomir's excessive attentions to the young Armenian, whose family, like all those strange people, have cruel customs beyond all imagining. It was intended to put you on a false trail, or rather, on a trail that was not only false but also absurd, which would just make you go on with your investigations. And indeed you fell for it."

Breathing heavily on account of the pain in his arm, and shedding angry and desperate tears, the Pennal broke off briefly, and then resumed.

"The Armenian's traffickings, the Golden Apple, the Turks, the dangerous trade of each victim: all these possible explanations were used to keep you in continual uncertainty. And so you would go on investigating, until you finally made a false step which would allow Glàwari to identify the person whose orders you were following."

"Orders? What orders?" I said in surprise.

"In short, the person who set you poking into matters that didn't concern you."

"Opalinski, I mean Glàwari, thought we weren't acting alone?" I said in amazement.

"Exactly," repeated the Bohemian.

So Glàwari had really believed that our interest in the Agha's phrase had not arisen spontaneously, but had been inspired by someone else, someone much higher than us! But he had been wrong: Cloridia and I had grown suspicious all by ourselves, and it would have all ended there if Simonis had not offered to get his companions to look into things.

"So all those crimes were just a . . . little performance set up to keep you busy," Penicek summed up.

"A barbarous trick to see how we reacted," I repeated, aghast.

"Like a cat with a mouse," Penicek agreed, gasping more desperately. "And finally Koloman: it was a real stroke of luck . . ."

"Just a moment. Opalinski can't have killed Koloman: he was with us at Porta Coeli!" Simonis interrupted him, his face transfigured by suspicion, by perturbation, by repressed rage.

"Of course, of course," Penicek agreed at once, clearly scared of his Barber. "In fact Opalinski, or rather Glàwari, had killed Koloman before joining you at Porta Coeli. He had come to the convent with me with the deliberate intention of framing me. It was no accident that he threw him out of the window, in the Prague fashion. As I said, it was a real stroke of luck for him that you asked me to go to the apothecary. At that point he pretended to reveal unwillingly where Koloman was. Because from the moment I left Porta Coeli to buy the ingredients I no longer had an alibi, and would not be able to prove my innocence. We are all students of medicine, it's true, but Glàwari is better than me: he knew that I would have to wait for the Galenic preparations and, what's more, that at the apothecary of the Red Crab they were bound to get suspicious of that long list of things to buy. Ah, if only I had suspected something, I would have returned in the twinkling of an eye. I wouldn't have wasted any time arguing with the apothecary and I certainly wouldn't have racked my brains over the Agha's phrase in front of that stupid statue of the Circassian!"

"That means," I murmured, "that Opalinski's grief over Koloman's death . . ."

"It's always the truth that seems incredible, I know," sobbed Penicek. "It was all a cold-blooded performance on that devil's part! But one day divine punishment will strike him: a heart finds peace only if God wills it."

"That's why Jan, or Andreas, or whatever the devil his name is, at first didn't appear frightened by the murders!" I exclaimed, in stupefaction. "Polish courage, indeed!"

"Glàwari knew very well," added Penicek, wiping away his tears, "that at the fourth corpse your suspicions would inevitably fall on the survivors. It was me or him, therefore, and he had prepared everything. When by sheer chance you discovered the murder just before three p.m. and right opposite Koloman's window was the window with the host's daughters, Signor Barber surmised that Koloman had fallen out of the window by accident – an unforeseen hitch that caught Glàwari off guard and forced him to accuse me openly. But if you think carefully, he was the only one who had always known where Koloman was hiding."

"Why, God Almighty, why?" I repeated several times in confusion.

"I told you: he wanted to know who was behind you. He killed all the companions Signor Barber was fond of to induce you to reveal yourselves, to betray yourselves in one way or other, so that he could spy on your moves. He wanted to see if you were acting alone, or if you were under orders from someone higher up. Only Hristo had realised this, and that is also why he died. And there was another reason: he knew that it wasn't prudent to talk in front of the whole group!" the young Bohemian laughed hysterically, and then sighed: "Oh, Hristo! You have gone from our lives, but you will always live in our hearts."

Simonis and I stared at each other with a mixture of stupefaction, suspicion and anguish. Then the Pennal continued:

"The Turkish trail was a pure waste of time. There's nothing concealed behind the Golden Apple: it's just the Turkish name for Vienna. The enquiries into the Agha's phrase just served Glàwari to get you both alarmed. He wanted to unmask the bigwig who's above you."

Those words set me shivering, and at the same time they lit a lamp within me. So I had guessed right: there really was a link between me and the murders!

I ran my hand through my hair. By some tragic quirk of fate, the series of murders had begun with a mistaken assumption on Glàwari's part: he had not believed that the enquiries into the Golden Apple arose from any genuine interest on my part; he thought that I was carrying out an order. Penicek concluded:

"Finally there was me. Glàwari left me to the last because none of you loves me, you all despise me. I don't belong to your little band. You put up with me just because I'm a poor Pennal, and I act as your slave. I would be much more use as a culprit than as a victim. If he had killed me, you wouldn't have shed many tears. My death would not have spurred you to further investigations or action, which was what Glàwari wanted so that he could discover your secrets. You would all have been ready to believe in my guilt, as soon as Glàwari pointed his accusing finger at me."

These words stirred a sense of remorse which I had kept repressed for too long. How foolishly I had let myself be fooled by appearances! And how wrong I had been never to protest at the cruel treatment they inflicted on the poor Pennal!

"Up there, in the apartment, after massacring me," concluded Penicek, "time was ticking away and Glàwari felt things were getting too hot for him. You hadn't come, he was afraid you had smelt a rat and at last he decided to make off."

"Just a moment, I still don't understand," I stopped him. "Opalinski, or Glàwari, or whatever his name is, had known Simonis ever since their days together at the University of Bologna, like all the others, long before I arrived in Vienna. Is it a coincidence, or had he already got onto Simonis's trail? And if so, what was his motive?"

The Pennal did not reply at once. He seemed to have trouble in breathing. His wound gave him acute spasms. Then he spoke:

"He seems to be a man, but he lives in another world: one of solitude, lies and dirty games. Glàwari is a secret agent. One of the many whose task is to cover up a highly delicate operation. He told me no more than that. He had been chosen years ago to stay close on the heels of Simonis; that was why he was first sent to Bologna."

Simonis did not answer. His pistol was still trained on him, under a fold of his cloak.

"But Simonis and the others came to Vienna because of the famine two years ago!" I protested. "Two years ago now! I have only been here a few months. How is it possible . . ."

Here Penicek gazed at my assistant with eyes that gleamed anxiously:

"... that a *Bettelstudent* of medicine and an assistant chimney-sweep, ordinary simple Simonis, could be of such interest to a spy like Glàwari? Easy, if he too is not what he seems. If instead of being called Simonis Rimanopoulos, his name is Symon Rymanovic, a Pole with a Greek mother."

"You?" I exclaimed, turning towards Simonis.

"But don't think he's just a simple spy," Penicek interrupted. Then, breathing more shortly than ever, he addressed my assistant: "You, Signor Barber, apparently so absent-minded, are actually one of the best-trained, most courageous and faithful servants of the Holy Roman Empire. A loyal and generous defender of the cause of Christ, isn't that so?"

Simonis turned as white as a sheet, but did not answer. He slowly lowered his pistol. I looked at him again, astonished by what I had just learned. It was as if Penicek's words had wrapped the weapon and his face in an invisible shroud, which disarmed him and made him helpless: the shroud of truth.

"Now you'll excuse me, Signor Barber," gasped the Pennal at last, rising from the ground and heading towards the hospital. "This arm is too painful, I must get medication. My strength is at an end. Take me, Lord, into your hands."

He made off, still clutching his wound, limping and staggering towards one of the doors behind us which led into the hospital.

I turned to follow him with my eyes. At that moment I happened to glance at a gravestone:

> 𝔐𝔶 strength is at an end
> 𝔗ake me, 𝔏ord, into 𝔶our hands.
> 𝔄ndreas 𝔊làwari
> 1615–1687

And then the stone next to it:

> 𝔜ou have gone from our lives,
> 𝔅ut 𝔶ou will always live in our hearts
> 𝔅ela 𝔗 rek
> 1663–1707

And then another, even more mocking than the previous ones:

𝔄 heart finds peace
only if God wills it.
Farewell grandmother Mariza
1623–1701

It was too late. Simonis and I ran desperately in pursuit of Penicek. We were just in time to catch a glimpse of him as, with a nimble gait (where was the lame leg now?) he caught up with the black carriage that we had seen pull up at the Bürgerspital and calmly climbed into it. He bestowed a final glance of total indifference on us, closed the door and, tossing something out of the window, disappeared amidst the clattering of the hooves and wheels. We stopped running only when we reached the point from which the black vehicle had darted off into thin air. On the ground we saw what Penicek had just thrown away: his spectacles, which he had used to create the role of the timid, inexperienced Pennal. It was all too clear that we would never see him again.

❧

A few minutes later we were back in the same bedroom where we had found Penicek. Turning to the left this time, we found a door that gave onto the last room in the house, the only one we had not yet visited, probably a little study. The ferruginous smell I had noticed during our first visit had grown even thicker, more turbid and fleshy. Simonis went up to the door. It was locked but the keyhole was empty. With a few robust shoves he burst open the double doors, which sprang apart like a theatre curtain. Bouncing against the wall they closed behind us. Now there were three of us.

It was like a cross between a man and a beetle. It had two black antennae sticking out from its face, its head and torso were as red as warrior ants. Just before dying it had collapsed onto the armchair that was positioned there in front of us. The blood that soaked the torso had dripped onto the floor.

Hurled into his eyes with the swiftness of a skilled knife thrower, the tips of the two missing spits from the kitchen must have caught him by surprise. Then he had been eviscerated. The three embroidered napkins from the table had been thrust into his throat and fixed there by two twists of rope behind his neck, so that he had no way of crying for help. It was not clear whether he had bled to death (ten or twenty stab wounds are too many for anyone) or choked to death.

We both vomited.

"This time we're really in trouble," I began as soon as I could speak. "They saw us in the building. They'll come looking for us."

"Not necessarily. The false motive for the crime will help us," said Simonis with icy calm.

"What do you mean?"

"It'll look like a vendetta by Mr Zwitkowitz, or a quarrel among students."

"You don't stick a spit into someone's eyes for a quarrel."

"But for an eviction you might."

"Not in Vienna," I rebutted.

"In this city there are people from Half-Asia who would do it for much less."

"And Zwitkowitz sounds like a name from those parts."

"Exactly."

We walked out. The old woman we had seen earlier on the ground floor was no longer there. Out on the street I found my legs still shaking, while the icy air lashed our faces refreshingly. Everything – the street we were walking down, the buildings around us, the sky itself – seemed clear and distant at the same time. We walked all the way back to the convent without saying a word. I was expecting Simonis to say something, to explain, or at least to try. But he said nothing. Whoever he really was, he had been overwhelmed by the horror of Opalinski's murder no less than I had. I felt I had been catapulted into another universe. Everything was changing because of that wretched war, I thought, the War of the Spanish Succession.

The Age of Man was over, now the long agony of the world was beginning: the Last Days of Mankind.

᷐᠐᠙

"He was in the service of the great powers. Hidden men capable of overturning everything, of switching the moon with the sun. That's why the names of the dead students never appeared in the obituaries."

Dressed in fresh clothes, once again in a mood to act and argue, Atto Melani made these observations on Penicek's flight and the subsequent events, which I had briefly outlined after bursting into his room more dead than alive. Atto had sent Domenico out on some pretext. While the Abbot talked, I listened, my expression distant, overcome by all that had happened. We were alone, and free to talk of my assistant as well.

"It's no accident," he said, "that when the other students offered
to collect information on the Golden Apple, Simonis advised you not
to reveal to them that the dervish wanted someone's head. He didn't
want to dissuade them too soon – he needed them. On one point
Penicek did not lie: Simonis too was a spy. Idiot, indeed. I told you
so. He was eager to get his friends' help, at whatever cost. That's
how it is, when you live a life that is not your own, that belongs to a
secret master."

"Great heavens," I complained, "is there no one I can trust? Who
is Simonis Rimanopoulos, or rather Symon Rymanovic?"

"Who do you think he is?" the Abbot cut me short. "Maybe he
doesn't even know himself. Just ask yourself who he has been to you
up to this point. And do the same when you ask the same questions
about me. All that matters is who I am to you; the rest is vain and
fruitless speculation. Only God knows everything."

When there was talk of spies, Abbot Melani never lost a chance
to grind his own axe. How well it would have suited him if, all the
time I had known him, I had never asked myself who he really was!

"I'll speak to him. He owes me an explanation," I announced
after a while – without any great conviction, to tell the truth.

"Forget it. Things are complicated enough already. Why do you
need to know any more? In certain cases, like this one, where everything is cursedly confused and could turn lethal at any moment,
there's only one thing that is necessary: to understand for whom the
person beside you is working, whether for God or for Mammon. The
rest is just a hindrance. And you can trust Simonis."

Now, after the account I had given him, Atto had completely
reversed his opinion of the Greek. As certain animals do with the help
of their sense of smell, Melani the spy had recognised Simonis the spy,
and had finally established that he was not an adversary. Like the rest
of us, they had both been taken in by Penicek, and the great powers
that Atto talked of seemed to have attacked both of the kingdoms that
Atto and Simonis belonged to, and in the same way: the mysterious
smallpox of Joseph in Vienna, and that of the Grand Dauphin in Paris.

Atto and I proceeded to re-examine, step by step, the way things
now stood. On the eve of the Agha's arrival in Vienna, the dark forces
that were probably participating in the conspiracy against the
Emperor had decreed a state of alert. All those people like Simonis,
spies on the opposite side whose identities were known, were placed

under surveillance. Penicek was chosen to keep an eye on the Greek. That was why the Pennal had asked for him as his Barber! His leaders had probably designated him on account of his affinities in training with Simonis: he too was a student of medicine and had studied in Italy, in Padua. It was no accident that Penicek was the only one who did not belong to the little band of students who had come to Vienna from the University of Bologna.

At times he had not been able to learn or to foresee our moves because we did not always travel by cart. He had checked up on us day by day, taking us everywhere in that strange carriage of his, which was allowed to go everywhere and at any time of day. After sowing death among us, with a skilful reversal he had succeeded in attributing to Opalinski, whom he had just butchered, his own role: that of a bloodthirsty spy.

He was never caught off guard. We had found him in the apartment where he had just massacred poor Opalinski with atrocious cruelty, only because he did not know that his victim had an appointment with us.

Finally, his reconstruction of events. This was all true, so long as the two names Opalinski and Penicek were reversed. That was all. It was he, and not Opalinski, who had arranged everything. He had chosen that building requisitioned by the imperial authorities, so that we would believe that it had really been Jan who organised the ambush. But on account of our meeting with Frosch, we had arrived over an hour late. Thinking that we were not coming or, even worse, that we had smelt a rat, he had executed the poor Pole. As soon as he had completed his horrifying masterwork of violence, he must have heard our footsteps on the stairs. My assistant must have spotted or scented something: that was why he had suddenly made us turn back. Entering by the adjacent buildings, we were not seen by Penicek's hired killers.

The Bohemian, realising that his men were not going to be on hand to back him up, locked Janitzki's mangled corpse in the little study at the far end of the apartment, threw away the key and sat down to wait for us. He was in a trap; but with amazing coolness he pretended to be the victim, instead of the aggressor. We attributed the smell of blood that filled the room to the struggle between the two of them, as recounted to us by the Pennal (a term that now sounded painfully ridiculous for the murderous impostor). He undoubtedly had a hidden pistol on him, but first he tried the blood-less way: scaring us with the possible arrival of some passer-by alerted by the screams, he got us to leave the building as fast as possible without our discovering Opalinski's corpse. And so he avoided pulling out his weapon and confronting Simonis in a duel that could have been fatal to both of them. Seeing him leave in our company, the black carriage that was waiting for him in the street followed us, perhaps in obedience to a secret signal from Penicek.

The story he told us in the graveyard was actually a confession. He described all the murders he himself had committed, blaming them on Opalinski. He chose the best way to make things up: describe true events, and just change the characters' names. When he needed a false name, so as to provide corroborative details, or some heartfelt invocation to make it sound more convincing, he drew on the stones around him: Glàwari, Mariza, Bela T rek, and their respective epitaphs.

After the performance in the graveyard, he disappeared in the black carriage that had been lurking nearby at his orders. Outside the city he would have met up with other individuals of the same murky, bloody kind, other puppets manoeuvred by the invisible network that was polluting Europe.

The Bohemian (or Pontevedrine?) had fooled us all. Everything fitted in with his designs. When Simonis and I were on our way to our appointment with Hristo, Penicek, with the excuse of the processions, had tried to take us by long, tortuous routes and also to travel slowly and even to stop the vehicle, so as to delay our arrival at the Prater. He was afraid that his henchmen might kill us, as he himself had told us at the graveyard, attributing the notion to Opalinski. That was why my assailant, on seeing Penicek, had gone off without a fight! He had seen his master.

After the murder of Dragomir Populescu, Penicek had insisted on getting rid of the corpse; he had almost forced us. He knew that a third body could not just vanish into thin air, that sooner or later we would wonder why there was no sign of any investigation on the part of the authorities. And so he had come up with the idea of hiding the poor Romanian's body, charging two of his underlings with the task before our very eyes. Would we ever have suspected that they were not simple coach drivers?

With Koloman, the self-styled Prague student had deployed all his diabolic arts. The so-called trick of Balamber was an invention, as were Attila's cryptographic skills and Szupán's passion for secret codes. By voicing doubts with equal candour and skill and dropping the right remarks at the right moment, with little stories made up on the spot, he had led us to say and do just what he wanted. And yet when he was concocting these lies I had sometimes seen him waver and look into the air, as if in search of some good idea; just how had we all fallen for it? It had to be admitted that Penicek's powers of invention never failed him. Just think of the non-existent murderous Augustinian monk and the Circassian's palace, which, of course (there was no need even to verify it), did not really belong to Prince Eugene.

છ∙ક

I announced to Abbot Melani that there was other news. I had been trying to tell him about it since the previous evening, but he had been dead to the world in his bed. At Eugene's palace Cloridia had discovered that the Turks, principally the dervish, intended to collaborate in treating the Emperor, and they were going to act in concert with the Caesarean Proto-Medicus: the von Hertod Cloridia had seen going in person to meet Ciezeber. That very day they would administer the decisive treatment to Joseph, if they had not already done so.

"Wha-a-a-t? And you believed this madness?" he gasped, changing colour as soon as I had finished.

"But Signor Atto, it seemed likely to me that the Ottomans –"

"Likely my foot! How could you possibly think that an Indian dervish of the Ottoman faith could devote himself to the health of the Caesar of the True Faith? A less worm-eaten brain than yours would have dismissed such an idiotic idea immediately. But I'... amazed at Monna Cloridia. You and she have not understood a damned thing. This is the Emperor's death sentence!"

છ∙ક

There was no time for discussion. Half an hour later we were inside a hired carriage, like Penicek's, on our way to the Place with No Name. I could not be late: the police authorities were expecting me and my assistant to draw up our report on the events of the previous day. I could have gone to Neugebäu in our usual cart, but Atto, as he had announced the day before, insisted on coming along too. I had made him dress modestly and I had forbidden him his wig, false moles, white lead and carmine. I would introduce him as a blind old relative whom I was temporarily looking after. He made no objection.

And so there were three of us in the carriage: Abbot Melani, truly unrecognisable in this natural state, Simonis and myself. I had chosen not to bring our little boy with us but had left him at Porta Coeli, safely with Cloridia. My assistant fixed his gaze, no longer idiotic, on the horizon. I guessed he did not intend to talk; on the Abbot's advice, I did not press him. Atto himself sat scowling sullenly. The news of the secret operation that the Emperor was going to undergo had put him in an acerbic, touchy mood, almost as if he were in the service of His Caesarean Majesty rather than that of the Most Christian King of France.

Around our little group I could still smell the powerful, painful stench odour of blood. I pretended to myself that I could accept what I had seen. Deep down, however, I felt that I could not. The images and events of the last few hours were pounding at my senses and my memory. The Pennal's serpentine presence had gouged a deep trough of anxiety and alienation within me. He had been among us, but not of us. He appeared to be a man, but was of another breed: he was a helmsman of the new order, the Agony of Mankind. He had infiltrated our group by means of the Deposition, exploiting the university traditions, and had become Simonis's shadow.

How badly I had judged Penicek! I said to myself for the second time that day. Now I knew for sure: to evaluate a man you have to look him in the eyes. If they are wicked, as were those of the bespectacled ferret the Pennal, the soul that lies hidden behind them cannot offer anything good. Never let oneself be swayed by logic, that flawed human art, which leads us to judge our neighbour on the basis of his words and our fallacious reasoning: the eyes, mirror of the soul, never lie.

Simonis, I thought, did not have wicked eyes. He had never had them; not even for an instant had I ever caught that alienating sign in the pupils that makes one flinch inexplicably. In the Greek's glaucous gaze, both when he was feigning idiocy and when he was telling me about Maximilian II, I had always been able to swim as in the clear sea, even if only shorewards, since the spy that lay within him lurked in the sand of the submarine recesses. I had only ever perceived the blue horizon, without the murky sludge that clouds everything: the colour guaranteed the purity of the expanse that lay before me, but I was forbidden to dive beneath the surface.

But suddenly a surge of disgust overwhelmed me: a sham bespectacled cripple and a sham idiot, what a great combination! I had spent
all my efforts taking care not to get tricked again by Abbot Melani,
and I had never spotted these two behind my back. One lied for good
purposes and one for bad, but was I so sure that, if his mission
required it, Simonis would not sacrifice me and perhaps even my
little apprentice on the altar of the human aberration they call "just
cause"? I knew all too well what spies are like, I thought with a shiver.

"What sense is there in racking your brains with doubts and questions?" sighed Atto, whispering into my ear, as if guessing my cogitations from my long silence. "Everyone is responsible for his own
actions. Before God we will be alone on the day of the Last
Judgement. No one can hide his own crimes behind the pretext of
obedience, because he will be told: you could have disobeyed and lost
your life, but you would have gained it in the kingdom of heaven."

The Abbot was talking on his own account as well. I remembered
all too clearly when obedience to his King had led him to crime.

"But remember," he added raising his voice, "we are all working
for God, even those who do not wish to do so. God makes use of
everyone, as and when He wants; even that Penicek, however much
he may think to the contrary. Remember boy: not a single hair of ours
is lost without the Almighty wishing it. His loving designs are so
broad, that it is not given to us mortals to understand them."

I gazed grimly at Abbot Melani: he was preaching eloquently now
that he had come to the end of his life, but how many times over the
decades had he himself exploited me and exposed me to mortal
dangers for his own shady intrigues?

However, at that moment Simonis, surprised by Atto's words,
raised his eyes and they met the Abbot's. And then it was all clear
to me.

My heart saw all that the two spies, the young one and the old
one, communicated with their eyes in that eternal instant. For the
first and only time they talked to each other with no filters. I saw
between them an interchange of illusions, troubles, inward bereavements, resurrections, a determination to fight, cold-blooded reason-
ings and burning passions, and finally an awareness – innate in the
Greek student, gradually acquired by the castrato – of the divine
order of things. Their lives were mirrored in each other's eyeballs. It
lasted but a single mute moment, but it was enough to enlighten me.

Thirty years earlier they would certainly not have been on the same side, but would have fought one another – the spy of the Sun King and the faithful servant of the Holy Roman Empire – but now they both recoiled from the world's headlong precipitation into Godless darkness, and finally they met. That was why Melani had spoken thus in front of Simonis.

Like a putrid voiding of the bowels, the image of poor Opalinski skewered like a beetle rose up before my mind's eye.

"But why such atrocity?" I asked, shaking my head. "There was no need anymore. Penicek had come there to kill us. He no longer wanted to muddy the waters to drive us to go on investigating. The *tandur* with Dragomir's pudenda was needed to put us off the trail, but why ram spits into Janitzki's eyes and napkins down his throat, condemning him to that horrible death?"

"It was the only way for puny Penicek to overpower the size and strength of Opalinski," answered Simonis. "His men didn't come because they were downstairs waiting for us. And so he attacked Opalinski on his own. They fought and Penicek was wounded. He won by blinding him with the spits. The little devil must have been an expert knife thrower, and the eye sockets are among the few things we all have that are soft; pierce them and you get straight to the brain. The pain and suffering must have been unspeakable. He couldn't use his pistol because of the noise. He may have high-level protection but a shot would be heard by too many people, and the situation could have got out of hand. For the same reason he thrust the napkins into his victim's mouth, now that he could no longer see, to stop him screaming. The dagger did the rest."

My assistant's expertise and promptness in describing the dynamics of the murder depressed me more than ever. I had grown old, I thought, but once again I found myself the most ingenuous in the group; and this time I was faced with not just one but two spies!

"Sorry, boy," Atto cut in, addressing me. "What did you say? Penicek had come to kill you . . ."

"Yes, Signor Atto, as I had already told you . . ."

"Yes, yes, but it's just struck me that . . . My God! How had I failed to see it earlier?"

I did not manage to hear what Melani meant. At that moment we arrived at the Place with No Name, where we found a small squad of guards awaiting us.

As soon as we got out of the cart they made us enter the mansion. The atmosphere was vaguely unreal: there was not a single animal around now, and silence reigned. It was saddening to think that not even rough old Frosch was on hand with his habitual bottle and old Mustafa.

"What about the lions? Have you caught them all?" I asked, just to break the silence between us and our escorts.

"𝕷𝖊𝖙'𝖘 𝖌𝖔, 𝖑𝖊𝖙'𝖘 𝖌𝖔," said one of them, who seemed to be in charge, inviting Abbot Melani to follow us as well.

"Actually I had nothing to do with all the confusion yesterday. He's the one who has to make the report," protested Atto. "Couldn't I stay outside?"

The guards were adamant. We were led inside the mansion, down to the semi-basement. One of the men who was escorting us seemed familiar. We paused in the gallery to the west, where the day before we had heard the footsteps of "Pup", Neugebäu's secret elephant.

There now entered an individual dressed like a public functionary, whom I guessed to be a criminal notary. He began to read a document in German, of which I understood hardly a word. I turned questioningly to Simonis, while the notary went on reading.

"I don't understand anything either," Simonis whispered to me, looking very doubtful.

The notary stopped reading. It was then that things changed abruptly. The guard (if that was what he was) who had something familiar about him pulled out a set of irons, and from the tone with which the presumed notary shouted something at us, I gathered they were for our wrists. We were under arrest. But the operation was interrupted by a further surprise.

It was at that moment that something absurd happened. As in a drunken dream, Ciezeber came in and greeted us courteously in Italian.

❧

"The dervish!" I whispered to Simonis sotto voce, incredulously.

Ciezeber continued to smile cordially. For a moment in the semi-basement of the mansion there was an unreal silence.

"What's happening?" I asked.

"Perhaps you have already understood what the notary read to you. It's a decree by the imperial chamber. You are under arrest for conspiracy against the Empire, as well as for having made an attempt against the life of the Ambassador of the Sublime Ottoman Porte, Cefulah Agha Capichi Pasha."

"Conspiracy? There must be some mistake," protested Atto. "I'm from Italy and –"

"Silence, Abbot Melani," the dervish interrupted him. "We already know how you sneaked into Vienna. And don't pretend to be blind!"

Atto's cover was blown: the dervish and the strange band that surrounded us, whether they were guards or not, knew that Atto Melani was not the postal intendant, Milani. At that point I guessed it all.

It had all happened too quickly for us to save ourselves. Atto had had a flash of insight a moment earlier, but we had already arrived at Neugebäu, and it was too late.

There was one thing Penicek had omitted in his story at the graveyard: who our leader was, since he believed we had one. He wanted to kill us, a sign that he had learned what he wanted: who the bigwig was whose orders Simonis and I were supposedly obeying. And so he thought he had finally identified this person. And whom would he suspect if not Atto Melani? The sham cripple believed that Atto was the leader of a conspiracy, with me and Simonis under his command. He had met the Abbot as a passenger in his cart. It would have been child's play for him to look into his background and find out who he was. Of our group of four – Cloridia, myself, Atto and Simonis – two were spies. If anyone had told him that it had all begun with my own and my wife's simple suspicions, and that it had not been Melani who had suggested looking into the Agha's phrase (indeed, Atto's attention had been fully engaged in his forged letter and his pursuit of Madame Pálffy), he would never have believed it.

It was the typical mistake of petty spies: they think that their slippery way of reasoning must be applied to all mankind and they cannot conceive of initiatives, deliberations, and actions that arise from the free impulse of a spirit stirred by a pure sense of justice or a thirst for knowledge. They will not acknowledge in anyone else the true feelings they have banished from their own hearts. As the good Umbrian nun who had brought me up loved to repeat: "Treat your body ill, bad thoughts all minds will fill" – or, to interpret the vernacular anacoluthon, "He who treats his own body badly (and so lives dishonestly) thinks that everyone else reasons in the same wicked way." People of this sort are thus exposed to the whims of fate, which mocks them more often than they think.

But this time Penicek's mistake had been fatal to us. He had planned to kill us along with Opalinski, and then undoubtedly to kidnap Atto and torture his old limbs to get information from him. The plan had failed, of course, but how could we have believed that the sham cripple would leave things unfinished? During our last journey from the Place with No Name he had heard that Simonis, the Abbot and I would be returning to draw up the report for the complaint I intended to lodge. He knew where and when we could all be nabbed together. But now he could not eliminate us immediately: the functionaries of the imperial chamber were present and the thing had to have an appearance of normality. Of course, the accusation that these bullies were making against us was as false, hamfisted and brazen-faced as any cheap trickster's tale. Under the guise of an arrest was an organised ambush, I thought, as I recognised the guard who had something familiar about him: his eyes. They were the same deep dark eyes I had seen in the masked individual who would have killed me in the Prater had I not been saved first by Hristo's chessboard and then, irony of fate, by Penicek's arrival. All was lost.

"We have done nothing wrong, you can't arrest us," said my assistant in a calm voice, after studying the whole company intently: two functionaries, who actually looked tense and pale, the dervish and five guards, undoubtedly his own thugs.

At this point, having verified the arrest, the two imperial functionaries left. They asked no questions about the escaped animals, of course. Very different matters were at stake now.

"Be quiet, cur," answered Ciezeber with biting scorn, as if Simonis merited a special hatred. "None of the men with me understands the language you express yourself in, and I have no ears for the blathering of worms."

"And how does a dervish," said Atto, torn between fear and the desire for knowledge, "happen to know my language so well?"

Ciezeber, who was facing in the other direction, turned slowly with an amused and malicious smile. It was as if that were the first sensible thing any of us had said. Then he answered.

"I am one of those who know all languages, who are of all ages, who come from all countries in the world," he said, and then signalled to his men to chain us and disarm us.

The vanity of the dervish, who had wasted valuable moments on these remarks, provided us with the golden opportunity to save ourselves. A moment later and it would have been too late; it was worth attempting something desperate.

When Simonis leaped into action, none of our enemies was able to grasp what was happening. His flying kick smashed into the jaw of the closest armiger, but just before launching the attack, Simonis had pulled his pistol from his bag and thrown it to me, already loaded, I presumed. About a second later, one of the five fired at me, missing me by a hair's breadth. Nonetheless I felt an incandescent atom pierce my left thigh, and hoped it was nothing important.

In the three seconds that followed several things happened: Atto Melani fainted; the guard struck by Simonis now had a trapezoid-shaped face instead of a round one, which he clutched in both hands, apparently out of action; I fired into the face of a guard to my left, not knowing whether I had hit him or not; finally, after his successful kick, my assistant, fully erect and with no hint of a stoop, swivelled and plunged a knife into the closest armiger. This last man did not succeed in drawing his sword in time and, although managing not to take the knife in his belly as my assistant had intended, received a great slash on his neck, and it was quite likely that he would die from it fairly soon.

In the next two seconds, there were further interesting events: two of the armigers shielded the dervish, who withdrew in terror from a fight he had not considered possible; one of them fired at Simonis's chest and hit him at point-blank range. Meanwhile Abbot Melani disappeared without anyone realising. For a few seconds I faced one of the wounded armigers: it was the one who had been about to kill me in the Prater. Then I fled without being pursued.

As I ran I glanced back. Simonis, although struck full in the chest, was picking up the chains that had been intended for us, and then he swirled them round and twice struck one or two armigers, but these were just fleeting glimpses, as I was already running out of the half-basement into the courtyard of the *maior domus*. I thought I heard my assistant's footsteps behind me. There was no knowing how long he had left to live.

❧❧

Two of the (false) guards were probably out of action. That left three, plus the dervish.

When I got outside I caught a glimpse of Atto, limping to the left. Perhaps he had faked his faint, in order to make a break for it at the right moment, but he had not got very far and was already exhausted. From inside the half-basement we heard echoing shouts and then another shot. Someone had succeeded in reloading a pistol, I thought; they had killed Simonis, or he had killed one of the five, giving us valuable time. We panted our way into the main courtyard, from which we had entered, and saw the gate (usually open) locked and barred. Turning back and trying to escape from the opposite side of the mansion meant running into the dervish's clutches.

The next few moments occupy a dark, empty space in my memory. The fatigue, the certainty of imminent death and the small but smouldering crater of pain that I felt in my thigh probably prevented me from making any sense of events as I perceived them and from taking any decisions. I remember very little of Abbot Melani. I think I pushed and dragged him (there was no alternative, as his own strength were non-existent) down the spiral staircase that led to the animal cages, and then towards the Flying Ship, while expecting another pistol shot, sooner or later, to hit us in the back.

After which all I know is that we waited: Atto inside the ship, which I had heaved him into with difficulty, and I myself squatting among the broken planks of the birdcages, shattered the previous day by the incursion of the elephant and abandoned at the far end of the ball stadium.

Evening fell. I do not know how long we spent lurking in our two hiding places. Every so often we heard pistol shots, and we gathered that a two-way hunt was under way in the gardens of Neugebäu between Simonis and the surviving guards. On each side there must have been at least one functioning pistol, together with powder for reloading and sufficient desire (or need) to kill. It was a war of position: the objective was to hit, but without running any risks. Simonis could not get away; our enemies on the other hand apparently could not rely on any reinforcements. The close-range battle of the first few moments had given way to a shooting match in the dark, in which the winner would be whoever was best at hiding, reloading his weapon and exploiting the element of surprise. I wondered just how Simonis was holding out: just before I escaped from the semi-basement, he had been hit directly, and at close range.

At each new detonation we heard the lions make tired and tetchy complaints to the black sky over the moor of Simmering: the beasts of the Place with No Name, I thought, were back where they were supposed to be. The carcasses must have been removed earlier in the day. The shots did not worry me: each new exchange of fire told me that Simonis was still alive. Twice I heard the enraged yells of our enemies: it seemed likely that Simonis had hit someone, and that the others were giving vent to their pain or anger.

Every so often Atto and I would call out to one another, just for reassurance. We were stuck there with no weapons, and unable to engage in hand-to-hand combat (I was too small and the Abbot too old), in the darkness of the Place with No Name. With the darkness shrouding everything, there was no point in trying to get out of Neugebäu by climbing over the walls. I attempted a brief sortie into the main courtyard to check whether it was possible to open the gate. A couple of shots fired somewhere nearby persuaded me to return to my hiding place. Back in the ball stadium, passing by the Flying Ship, I heard Abbot Melani whispering a Hail Mary, pleading for his safety.

After a long time something changed. With a violent start I felt a couple of shots behind us: the action seemed to have shifted to the narrow corridor from which on the previous day the elephant Pup and the other animals had burst into the ball stadium. This, as I well knew, led straight towards the ditches with the wild animals.

Then for a while I heard nothing. I knew that Atto would stay inside the Flying Ship without moving a muscle. So I moved, and left the ball stadium. The moon was favourable; crawling along the ground I got close enough to catch a glimpse of the scene. I had some misgivings, and I found they were all too well-founded.

As pale as a tragic Pulcinella, gasping with fatigue, bent double with pain (in how many places had they hit him?), Simonis was in the middle between the two ditches of animals, balancing on the narrow wall that divided them. He looked like a circus acrobat who realised that the exercise he had chosen was too difficult and did not know how to make his excuses to the audience. Beneath his feet were two howling hordes of felines enraged by his audacious incursion. The faint moonlight may have deceived me, but I really thought I recognised, amid the roaring of the bloodthirsty beasts, the icily furious voice of the black panther that Simonis had struck with the broom just before our second flight in the Flying Ship.

To escape the shots of his adversaries, my heroic assistant had passed behind the ball stadium, as I had heard, and from there had slipped into the gallery that bordered the ditches of the animals, from where they could be observed. Here, however, the final act was about to be staged. Ciezeber's thugs had hemmed him in: there was one at each end of the corridor. To escape them, Simonis, like a tightrope walker, had begun to make his way along the wall that divided the lion cage from the cage containing other wild animals, hoping to reach the opposite side. But he had forgotten that the other end was blocked by an iron grating.

The darkness was only faintly relieved by the moonlight. I at once guessed what the matter was: they had run out of ammunition. It was now just a question of numbers, and Simonis was on his own. Probably he had hoped, by nimbly passing along the wall between the two ditches, to get beyond the abyss. Instead he had found himself up against a dead end: the wall terminated in a long series of iron bars, placed there to prevent anyone from accidentally falling into the ditches.

Approaching the scene of action had been imprudent on my part; if I were to try to steal away now, the dervish's henchmen might hear me. I noticed that Ciezeber had approached the beginning of the wall on which Simonis was dangerously poised, and was leaning forward as if he wished to address the fugitive. In the darkness I could barely discern Simonis, and I imagined that he could not see me at all. But suddenly I realised that he had spotted me. At that very moment the dervish spoke.

"Stop," he ordered Simonis in a dry, serious voice.

"I don't have much choice," answered my assistant in an ironic tone.

"You have no way out."

"I know, Ciezeber."

The dervish paused to take breath, then said:

"You know me as Ciezeber the Indian; others call me Palatine Caldeorum. Yet others, Ammon. But my name is of no consequence to me. I am one, no one, and a hundred thousand. But I need nothing, I look for no one, I do good to the poor and the imprisoned. I appear to be forty-five years old, but I have travelled for fifty-eight and I am ninety. I can become young again, change my facial features, smooth out my skin, make my fallen teeth return. My dominion is everywhere. I have trodden the roads of Turkey and Persia, I have been a guest of the Great Mogul in Siam, in Pegu, in Chandahar, in China. I have learned to suffer hunger in the desert of the Tartars, I have shivered with cold in Muscovia, I have been a pirate on the seas of the Indies. I have miraculously survived seven shipwrecks and have been locked in prison eight times, even in that of the Inquisition in Rome. Each time powerful protectors have got me out, but prison itself is nothing to me. On a pure whim, I once had all the other prisoners escape, and I remained in my cell."

Simonis said nothing. The dervish went on:

"I was thirty when I left my land. Then I was called Isaac Ammon. I was the firstborn son of Abraham Ammon, patriarch of the Nestorian Christians of Chaldea. For generations our family had proudly passed down the honour of the patriarchy, but it was of no value to me. I admired only one man: my mother's brother, who had retired to a mountain in Chaldea. He was like me, like us: more than a mere man. A great sage and astrologer, he lived as a hermit and treated all others as beasts. He raised me with the whip, teaching me the occult virtues of the herbs and the stars, their links with the stones, the animals of air and water, the quadrupeds, the reptiles. He revealed to me the periods and hours of the day to exploit these virtues, their temperament and the effects they have on men."

Simonis still said not a word. But Ciezeber did not seem disappointed by his adversary's silence.

"You'll say: why don't you shut up, dervish? Why are you telling me all this? Why don't you just kill me? But I'm not talking just to brag about myself. The loser must know he has lost, and suffer. We, the winners, feed on your pain: it's our lifeblood and our reason for living."

Then Ciezeber (or Palatine, as he said he was known) continued in a more relaxed tone, as if he had now said all that was important to say.

"It was a relative, my mother's brother, who enlightened me with real wisdom. This is nothing if you possess it, but everything if you do not know it. Thanks to it a healthy and whole man can live a thousand years, as in the days of Abraham and Noah: he just needs to keep away from women and excesses. My master, my uncle, was seven hundred years old."

I was listening to the words of a fanatic; and Simonis must have had the same idea:

"He must have a good many stories to tell," said my assistant sarcastically. "I imagine it was he who advised you which poison to put in the Emperor's dish."

The dervish took no notice of the irony.

"What do you know of poisons?" he answered, quite unruffled. "There are seventy-two different types, and the subtlest are not taken via the mouth. A pair of shoes, a shirt, a wig, a flower, a curtain, a door, a chisel, a letter: a thousand objects can be poisonous. But for each one there exists an antidote in nature. Some only work at certain hours, or on certain days, or weeks, or months – but they are all infallible. One just needs to know the condition and temperament of the person. In Joseph's case, you think it is poison and not illness. Well, the illness is poison, and the poison is illness. They are not alternatives, but the same thing: a disease induced by medical means. The smallpox was injected skilfully into the Emperor's limbs, as into those of the Grand Dauphin of France, obviously with the help of the traitors who can always be found among you Christians, and in both cases it will seem a natural death."

I held my breath: now we had the answer to our questions. The smallpox that had struck His Caesarean Majesty and the heir of Louis XIV was indeed an illness, but caused artificially, as if by poisoning!

Ugonio had told me that the instruments in Ciezeber's ritual were used to inoculate, but I had misunderstood the true meaning of "insanitary" and believed that their aim was therapeutic, not criminal.

"For you it's the ideal solution," remarked Simonis. "No one will suspect. It's not the first case of fatal smallpox in the House of Habsburg. Ferdinand IV, the elder brother of the previous Emperor Leopold, was carried off by smallpox fifty years ago. He was too clever, too cultured, too sharp, at the age of just twenty-one. Just like Joseph, no?" continued my assistant with bitter sarcasm. "Two annoying exceptions among the Habsburgs, who are emperors precisely on account of their mediocrity and malleability. As soon as one of them causes any trouble, away with him! Bring on the second-born. And all the better if he's a coward, like Leopold."

"Leopold, with his mildness, reigned for almost half a century," retorted Palatine inscrutably.

"But he himself was the source of one or two disappointments for you. It wasn't enough that he fled from Vienna when the Turks arrived in 1683: the Christian armies won all the same. Despite all your efforts, Palatine, your wishes are never quite fulfilled – it's your destiny."

"You think so? Everyone knows, and you yourself know it: the death of Ferdinand IV made this war possible," smiled the dervish.

"All of this – why?" asked Simonis in a cutting voice.

"That's the real question," answered the dervish. "But only those like you, like me, know it. *Why*. *How* and *who* are just distractions for the rabble. Maybe one day someone will suspect that Joseph the Victorious was assassinated and will wonder: who gained from it? Who had the power to cover it all up? Was it smallpox, or poison . . . Always *who* and *how*. We'll keep the people busy as in a game, preventing them from asking the most important thing, *why*."

"And yet it's not very hard to guess," said Simonis. "First of all the war: Joseph is thinking of dividing Spain with the French, and leaving Catalonia to his brother Charles."

I started. That tallied with what Atto had told me: the Emperor wanted to divide the Iberian peninsula, leaving his brother with just Barcelona and the surrounding area.

"That settles the Spanish question," continued Simonis, "and peace begins. But you want the war to go on, to reduce Europe to total ruin, and then impose an armistice on your conditions, so that you can do whatever you want."

Ciezeber kept silent, as if in agreement.

"Then there's trade," persisted my assistant. "War is bad for business – at least, for small-scale business. But your people are engaged in selling arms, building ships, designing fortresses: war is highly profitable for you. And it's big money. With peace, things dry up."

Ciezeber-Palatine answered with an amused whimper.

"Finally you want to get rid of dangerous rulers and replace them with more malleable ones. It's always been your strategy, but now you've perfected it. For centuries you have been busily laying waste to the world, conquering one city after another. By manipulating the Infidels you conquered Jerusalem. Then you moved northwards, taking Constantinople in 1453, then Budapest as well. It took centuries for you to obtain all this: enormous sums were squandered, armies were sent to wholesale slaughter, whole nations were annihilated. Only Vienna said no to you: despite the invention of Luther's schism with which you made Europe rot in the Thirty Years' War, your Ottomans lost the siege in 1529, and then the one in 1683. It was the last holy city before Rome, the final target. And so you had to reconsider your projects. Instead of attacking the Christian kingdoms directly, you concentrate on internal action: exterminating the kings directly. Then you take possession of the minds of their sons, the future sovereigns, by means of court tutors: tormenters of the spirit, whose only task is to crush the characters of the young princes and destroy all their good qualities. It's a technique you have known for centuries: here in the Empire, Rudolph, son of Maximilian II, was subjected to it. But from now on it will be your speciality."

And I remembered: had not my assistant told me that Rudolph the Mad, son of the creator of Neugebäu, had been bullied by his educators? Simonis and Ciezeber were referring to a subterranean conflict whose protagonists were such individuals as Ilsung, Ungnad and Hag, the conspirators who had plotted against Maximilian.

Simonis first looked up, towards the sky, then shot a meteoric and imperceptible glance at me, and finally down, towards the lions that were quivering and slavering, enraged by the prey that was so close but unattainable.

"Good. You know a great deal, and you suffer because you cannot do anything about it," replied the dervish. "So listen now: I tell you that Louis XIV, King of France, will die from poison. It will look like gangrene in the leg, but it will be an artificially induced illness. The doctors, who are the most ignorant of men, will be in the dark. Before the Sun King, it will be the turn of the Dauphin, the Duke and Duchess of Bourgogne, and their son the Duke of Berry: they will all end up the same way, with a skilfully induced false illness. The late King of Spain, Charles II, whose inheritance has set all the nations of Europe at each other's throats, even though he had just months to live, was poisoned in the same way. Now you know: the Emperor, Joseph the Victorious, is about to die. This evening the decisive inoculation will be administered."

I started again: Ciezeber was talking about the medical treatment that Cloridia had heard about that morning at Eugene's palace: but instead of curing, it would kill him. So Joseph had been betrayed by his own Proto-Medicus! And by countless others along with him. Abbot Melani was right.

"The Emperor will die – how can I put it? – poisoned by smallpox," continued the dervish. "It is a fitting end for one who thought himself so powerful that he could do without us: the only man alone on earth."

"Ah yes, *soli soli soli*," recited Simonis.

"Exactly. With that phrase the Agha announced to Prince Eugene how things are: either with us or against us. The Emperor thought he could do as he wished: finish the war in his own way, divide up Spain with the French, as if we did not exist. But the war will end on our terms, as and when we say. For Joseph thinks he governs the Empire, but actually he is a man all alone, who cannot even decide for himself: the Turks came *soli soli soli*, 'to the only man alone on earth'. Eugene of Savoy, who understands oblique phrasing, understood perfectly, and has chosen to abandon his sovereign and join us. There is your valiant general, your great hero: another traitor, like all the others."

I was listening in utter amazement. Thanks to Atto we had guessed the real meaning of *soli soli soli*; now we were learning why the phrase had been said by the Agha to Eugene of Savoy.

"You say 'we'. But who are you? Ottomans? The English? Dutch? Jesuits?"

"Are you so ingenuous? No, I don't believe it. You just want my confirmation, but you already know. We are everywhere and we are everyone."

I looked around: a pair of henchmen were standing stiffly by as their master talked away in a language incomprehensible to them.

"We are the real power," continued Palatine. "He, the Emperor, is as outcast and isolated as the most miserable beggar. The Turkish Agha said nothing but the truth to Eugene, which is there for all to see, but which no one does see. This is our power. We are every-where, omnipresent but invisible, we eat at your table, sleep in your beds, rifle through your purses, and you do not see us. We seem to be very few and isolated, but we are in fact legion. You think you are many, and yet you are all the same person – a man alone."

"You feel omnipotent: that's why you had the Agha pronounce his phrase in public."

"We never hide anything from you. It is you who have no eyes to see."

"No, Ciezeber, the people have eyes to see, but faced with your inhumanity no one believes what they see. And this is your real strength."

"Now be silent," the other man said. "The House of Habsburg will soon be extinct. Thanks to Joseph's death, Italy will have its own king, as will Germany."

"And that is why you had a poor child, just one year old, killed by your doctors – Leopold Joseph, the Emperor's little son."

"Italy has been broken up for centuries into a myriad of principalities," continued the dervish without replying, "and Germany into electorates for just as long. And yet both will become great nations, while the Habsburgs must come to an end once and for all, because we wish it, and history is in our hands."

"Yes, and after killing the kings and their sons and grandsons, you'll put the new heirs on the throne – all still children or mere youths – in the hands of tutors faithful to you, who will turn them into imbeciles, cruel and ridiculous," said Simonis, repeating what had just been said.

"Their subjects will rightly hate them, the crowned heads will fall under the axe of the people, which will therefore think it is controlling the revolution while all it is doing is implementing our designs," concluded the dervish. "A new order will replace the old world. For each new right we concede to the rabble, we will secretly abolish ten. Laws will get better, life will get worse. We will rewrite history: we will make fun of the ancients and convince mankind it is now living in the best of all possible worlds, so as to remove any desire to return to the past. We will spread artificial diseases to weaken the health of entire nations. Indeed, we are already doing so: you see how Joseph has ended up? The remedies we supply will be worse than the disease: the doctors and the propaganda are almost entirely in our hands. We will snatch babies from their mothers' breasts. The people will not even realise, and their weakness will be handed down to their children, and to their children's children. The tremendous wars which we will organise in the meantime will serve to destroy the documents of the past, to disperse its memory and to turn the world into a grey prison, to make man sad and reduce him to a state of resignation."

"Resignation? It's hard sometimes," said Simonis, jerking his head towards the beasts that roared angrily at him from the ditch.

The dervish did not grasp the irony, and went on as if nothing had happened, happy to humiliate Simonis with that grim and apparently inevitable vision of the future.

"Everyone will accept suffering as something normal, and those who are happy will be looked down upon. Oh, I ardently hope that envy will guide and illuminate the centuries to come! The imbecilic

masses will live in ignorance, but we will allow those like you, those
who have understood, to rebel just a little. We won't kill all of you:
quite simply, we will see to it that you are provided with false
prophets under our guidance, who will keep you under surveillance
and count you one by one, in case it is decided to eliminate you. But
take comfort: we actually need you. Your impotent suffering nour-
ishes us, and gives a joyful meaning to our task. What glory would
there be, otherwise, in triumphing over a herd of blind, deaf beasts?
There is no greatness in agreeing with the laws of nature. True
power consists in making water flow against the current, making the
mediocre triumph over the virtuous, rewarding injustice, praising
ugliness. We will separate man from nature. We will imprison
everyone in large windowless hives, people will end up ignorant of
how a hen's egg is laid, what a haystack is, or a common little dandelion plant. Our triumph will come when we can separate the people
from God as well, and we will take His place. This is what destiny
has in store, and we are destiny."

"You may be destiny, but without money, weapons and lies you
are nothing," answered Simonis in a strangely calm tone, as if the
dervish's endless lecture were all too familiar to him, and this last
objection was dictated more by duty than from any sense of real
utility, like a soldier who wearily fires his last shot against an overwhelming enemy.

"Money and weapons are useful," admitted Palatine-Ciezeber,
"but we are already very rich. Wealth bores us. Indeed, it no longer
exists: we are replacing gold with paper money, payment with promises. Wealth is an idea. And the most powerful weapon is the
dominion of ideas. Lies are part of the game, they make it more
amusing. Because we are –"

". . . you are all mad," Simonis interrupted him, packing into
these few syllables all the paternal sarcasm that the pranks of little
children, imbeciles and madmen merited. "No human being agrees
to sacrifice his own life just to inflict evil on his neighbour, and to
pass on his mission to his descendants. But you do. And if the world
succumbs to your vileness, it is simply thanks to the only real
weapon you have: madness."

Caught by surprise, Ciezeber remained motionless for an instant.
Then he nodded to the two henchmen. One of them headed towards
the tunnel that led out of the cages. In the meantime the other one,

after a good deal of fumbling, had succeeded in reloading his pistol, and he aimed it at Simonis's legs. It was clear what was about to happen: the first henchman would empty one of the two lion cages, the other one would shoot Simonis in a non-vital spot, maybe his foot. Then my assistant would have to fall into one of the cages, and obviously he would choose the empty one. There he would be at the mercy of the three enemies, who would drag him away by force. With torture they might be able to extort something interesting out of him.

"We will keep you just for a while," said the dervish, "then you will be free. Obviously you will go out and recount what happened to you here, but no one will believe you, not even your own people. We will slander you, and we will spread the word that we bribed you. Soon people will suspect that you can no longer be trusted. They will say: why was Simonis spared? You'll be alone, with no honour, no homeland. But alive."

"You're going too fast. You make it sound as if you've already succeeded. Because of you the world is getting worse and worse, it's true, but according to your plans it should have been ruined long ago. The truth is that you are desperate, because for centuries, for thousands of years, you have been struggling to eradicate Christ from the world, but the fruit of your efforts is always inferior to your hopes. Your problem is always the same: 'the stone that the builders rejected has become the cornerstone', as the Psalm says. The game is never really over, least of all yours. And so I ask you: are you really sure that it is you who direct the world? Have you never suspected that God leaves you alone – indeed, that He has even elected you for His own inscrutable ends?"

These were the very ideas that we had heard from Atto before we arrived at the Place with No Name. I smiled bitterly. The Abbot and Simonis were really on the same side: that of the humans, not of those who only appeared to be human.

"The world is the test bed of souls, Ciezeber," continued the Greek, "and you are no more than unwitting tools of this divine plan: we are all a part of God's plans, even damned souls like yours."

A shiver ran down the dervish's spine, making him shudder. Perhaps it was the cold. Or perhaps Simonis's words.

"And as for us," my assistant went on, "are you really sure that things will really go just as you said? Don't you think that at the last moment someone might spoil your party?"

At that exact instant Simonis's eyes sought out mine in the darkness, and he was certain that I was observing him. In the dark I could just make out a weak smile, perhaps a farewell. I realised that he was about to act, and that he expected the same from me.

"So who's going to prevent us?" Ciezeber said with a sneer. "Your two friends perhaps? Your little dwarf boss and that mummy Abbot Melani?"

The bow of possibilities had been stretched taut, the arrow of events was about to be launched. It was at that moment, enormous and deafening, that the noise began.

Day the Ninth
FRIDAY, 17TH APRIL 1711

✠

Midnight: three hours till the first cry of the night guard. The city sleeps.

An immense fracas, a grandiose and oppressive dirge, a primeval abyss of male voices exploded in the moor of Simmering. It came from all around and was directed everywhere. It set vibrating every clod, every plant, every stone, every one of the sharp-pointed stars that dotted the dark canopy of the sky. A piercing noise assaulted my ears, and I had to cover them with my hands to prevent them from being shattered by this scorching gale of screeches. It was if the throat of the whole of creation were growing agitated, as if the earth itself, the heavens and the waters had struck up a colossal counterpoint and were chanting in Turkish. Yes, this terrible and deafening litany was in Turkish, and as Ciezeber triumphed over Simonis, this faceless choir invoked the name of Allah, almost as if a new titanic Mahomet were shouting his own wild joy before sweeping away Vienna and its lands. And then I remembered what the students had learned during their investigations into the Golden Apple, and I understood; as Dragomir Populescu had told us, this was the chorus destined to repeat itself every Friday, and it recited "Woe to you, Allah, Allah!" as on that night when the forty thousand martyrs of Kasim had died. That harvest of blood was now being repeated, and the forty thousand were invoking vendetta. As the whole universe seemed to close in on itself above us, I learned that this was the night when the fate of the world would be sealed.

Then it was as if the horizon flared up, and the sound became so lacerating that it was not enough even to cover one's ears. Staggering with the pain tormenting my ears and head, I tried to stand up and I saw that at that very moment my assistant was dropping into the lions' cage.

Just so as not to deliver himself up to Ciezeber, he had surrendered his life. Simonis the humble chimney-sweep, Simonis the student with the foolish air, Simonis the Greek, had decided to end his life in heroic fashion. Better to be torn apart by lions than to confess his own secrets under torture. I gazed in terror at the darkness and with the eyes of imagination beheld the black panther, grimly mindful of the blows that had offended it the previous day, sink its jaws into my assistant's neck and chest, and inaugurate the orgiastic banquet in which he was torn to pieces and flayed, his human blood drunk, his veins sucked, his joints shattered, his muscles frayed, as if nature were seeking to indulge in the caprice of reversed butchery, and the blood of the forty thousand had to be avenged on Simonis alone. On his poor mangled body the wrath of two entire armies was being vented – one from the past, led by Kasim, and one from the present, led by the grim panther of the Place with No Name.

Meanwhile the dervish – he, too, covering his ears to defend himself from the deafening chorus, awkwardly jerking his elbows and pointlessly yelling – signalled to his men to come to his aid and protect him in his terror-struck flight from the Place with No Name.

My ears were still hurting, but it was time to act. While the dance between Ciezeber and his henchmen continued, I went back to the Flying Ship. Shocked as I was by Simonis's end, I had almost forgotten Abbot Melani. Although hampered by having to press my hands to my ears, I managed to pull myself aboard the aircraft just in time to feel its wooden frame vibrate and shake rhythmically. It was what I hoped: the only way to escape. Atto was also clamping his hands to his ears, but he removed his hands when he felt this phenomenon, almost a familiar one by now: we were rising.

But the ship, for the first time, was struggling. It lifted just enough to fly over the walls of the ball stadium and to take us out of the Place with No Name. However, its journey was not an easy one. It proceeded in jerks, tossed by powerful gusts, which swelled the sails and lifted it, and undertows, which dragged it downwards again. The amber stones, instead of chiming in their usual harmony, oscillated confusedly and buzzed in acrid concert, producing a metallic din, as in a battle from an earlier age. The light they emitted was grey and livid this time, like the face of someone confronted by horrific visions. Maybe it came down to that, I thought; too much horror had unfolded itself around the ship: Simonis's end, the wickedness of

Palatine and the new age ... Death weighed down its keel like ballast. It swayed awkwardly for a while and finally sank down, as if exhausted, in the dark countryside of Simmering. Atto and I stayed sitting in the ship, overwhelmed by the cries of the forty thousand.

But suddenly, just as it had started, the yelling of the martyrs of Kasim ceased. In those long minutes in which I had left him alone, Atto had realised what it was, and on his lean face I could see his amazement at this overpowering phenomenon. So what Dànilo Danilovitsch and Dragomir Populescu had recounted was not nonsense: the Turkish legend of the forty thousand was true – or at least it had become so that night, and so perhaps the legend of the Golden Apple was not wholly invented either. But Abbot Melani was constrained by the pride of one who has always thought he held the key that unlocks the labyrinth of existence.

Trying to gather my ideas and to recover lucidity, I told him what had happened to Simonis. I hoped that the excessive emotions the Abbot was once again exposed to would not endanger his life; I had not yet realised that it was my spirit that had been wounded most cruelly.

"It is not a coincidence that I arrived in Vienna just a day after the Turks arrived and after the Emperor fell ill," he suddenly said.

"What are you saying?" I said, turning pale.

Atto gave a faint smile.

"I knew nothing of it, have no fear. The truth is that we are at a crossroads in history, and at such moments the strangest things happen."

"Yes, it's a crucial turning point."

"I thought I was the one who could bring about this turning point, but I have been brushed away like a fly."

"The new forces . . ."

"New? They are ancient, they have just changed their strategy, and this pays better. Shall we name some names from the past? The Fuggers, for example, who financed the ascent to the throne of Charles V and then of Maximilian through their henchman Ilsung. But it is not important. What counts is their method. Their code of behaviour is not what we were accustomed to – the code of kings, their ministers, of diplomacy, of the old conventions – but another one, unknown to anyone but them. No general will do as Melac did during the siege of Landau and offer not to fire on the tent of the enemy's emperor. Those days are forever gone. Checkmate is abolished. From now on the enemy king will be killed as well – the dervish explained it clearly to your Simonis."

On hearing my assistant's name I saw his eyes again, gazing at me in his last instants of life. I felt myself shaking.

"He died torn to pieces by the wild beasts, like a Christian martyr," murmured Atto suddenly to himself.

"What?"

"Simonis. You're thinking of him, aren't you? So am I. His courageous end confirms it: he was part of the resistance against the new order that is about to emerge victorious from this war. Your assistant was, to use Penicek's words, on the side of Christ. And like an ancient Christian he was torn to pieces. But by now you too have understood that he was working as part of a network of which you knew and will always know nothing. Simonis, too, like the new faceless lords, is a sign of the approaching times. Do we know who he really was? No. Penicek? Again no. And Ciezeber-Palatine-Ammon? Even less. And yet they, and other equally anonymous beings, are playing dice with the world. The future is in the hands of shadowy networks of individuals with no names, no identities and no faces. Fortunately I am at the end of my career, boy: there is no room for people like me. I was the King's advisor, and His Majesty listened to me and then made his decisions, exposing himself to the judgement of his subjects, of the entire world and of history. The world was made of men. But soon it will be led by governments that function like this ship: if necessary, even without human beings on board. I didn't understand until now, do you realise? The shadow-man I was seeking everywhere does not exist. The new Abbot Melani does not exist. We were fighting against the void. There is just a group, up there, a collective intelligence, like an anthill. They are not individuals with independent mentalities. Taken singly they are puny beings, pipsqueaks. Only in a pack, like hyenas, are they to be feared."

"The Age of Man is over, the agony of the world has begun: the Last Days of Mankind," I said, repeating what I had thought when we found Opalinski's corpse.

"They have succeeded in setting fire to the world, these devils incarnate," Atto went on in a voice now quivering with rage. "And to think that I ingenuously came to Vienna on a peace mission. Peace, indeed! This war is just a lucrative affair of blood to quench the thirst of Beelzebub. And it will not end in the rebirth they have promised us, no, but in the greatest bankruptcy the world has ever seen."

His words dismayed me. I needed to hope, I desperately needed to hope. Otherwise I could not cope. It was all too much for me.

"But once there's peace –" I began.

"Then the war will begin," Atto interrupted me with a snarl of repressed fury.

"But all wars have ended with a peace!" I protested, clutching with all my strength at the banal optimism of my words.

"This one will not!" the Abbot snapped back with all the breath in his body. "This war did not take place on the surface of life. No! It raged *within* life itself: the world perishes and no one will know! Everything was yesterday, it will have been forgotten. Today will not be seen, and tomorrow will not be feared. It will be forgotten that the war has been lost, forgotten that it was begun, forgotten that it was fought. That is why this war WILL NE-VER END!"

"But once there is peace?"

"People will never have enough of war."

"But the people, through error –"

"They unlearn. Indeed: they UNLIVE!" the old castrato ended with a shrill cry, finally giving way to tears and sobs, hunched over in a corner of the ship, striking his breast like a soul in Purgatory.

Atto himself had made a decisive contribution to the outbreak of this war, this endless war, eleven years earlier. He, who had always believed he held the reins of the world in his hands, had been no more than a pawn in the hands of those like Ciezeber. He had only fully realised this now, and it had plunged him into despair.

The empty basin of the sky was illuminated only by a weak moon, almost entirely covered by clouds. The cold gnawed at us from head to toes. I curled up trembling at the bottom of the ship next to Atto. I should have taken the Abbot and left the ship where it had come to ground, but I felt broken inside, lost in a black night of the spirit that robbed me of all my strength.

I felt I had gone back to the days of our first adventure in Rome, where aboard a frail boat, in company with Ugonio, we had sailed the subterranean rivers beneath the Holy City, armed with just a paddle and our intuition. But this, as I had seen, was just one of many parallels between our present situation and the vicissitudes I had shared with Abbot Melani in the past. Now, just like twenty-eight years

earlier in the little inn where I had been working when I first met
Atto Melani, there was a case of a sick man who had perhaps been
poisoned – and on that occasion too there had been an attempted
murder by means of a deliberately produced contagion. Once again,
I was pervaded by the sense of a cycle coming to completion; as
similar events repeated themselves, I felt as if the real meaning of
what I had lived through was about to be revealed.

Abbot Melani, meanwhile, passed from weeping to a dark dreamless sleep, as I could tell from the expression on his face. I held him
in an embrace, so as to warm him with my body and prevent any risk
of death by exposure.

Lying like this on the hard planks of the ship, my eyes gazing at
the stars, I recalled Simonis's last words, and the daring action that
he had clearly signalled to me with them. The task I yearned for was
almost impossible, but I felt that I owed it to Simonis, poor Simonis,
mysterious Simonis, to make an attempt. I stared straight ahead,
trying to forget those instants in which I had seen him smile feebly
to me and then drop among the beasts, to his death. If we were to
tell the palace staff about the plot that was afoot to assassinate
Joseph, they would take us for dangerous madmen. We would have
to try some other method. Oh, if only the ship would take flight
again! I could put into action what I had haphazardly attempted
during the previous flight. I could fiddle with the ropes holding the
amber stones and so manoeuvre it. I dreamed of guiding the Flying
Ship towards the imperial palace, where I would carry out my
desperate plan. Using my skills as a chimney-sweep, I would drop
down into one of the great chimneys with the iron ladders typical of
the imperial residences and make my way to the apartments of His
Majesty Joseph the Victorious. There, on the sofa of some sitting
room, in plain view, I would leave an account of the plot hatched
against His Caesarean Majesty, imploring them not to subject him to
the inoculations prescribed by Ciezeber; or I would try to get one of
Joseph's butlers to listen to me, if I should meet one; or . . . well, I
didn't really know what, but something had to be done.

At that moment the ship, with a final effort (or so at least it
seemed to my confused spirit) took off again. I jumped to my
feet and with renewed vigour prepared to handle the ropes in
order to guide it towards the Caesarean Palace, but at once I felt
the ropes jangle weirdly beneath my fingers, and the ship judder

uncontrollably. A sudden unsettling jerk forced me to drop the reins (if they could be called such) of my winged steed, and so I left it free, as on the first flight, to guide itself. At once it appeared to me that the solidity and stability of the vehicle improved, and I felt relief. But it did not last long, alas. The Flying Ship was aiming – or so it seemed to me amid the purple nocturnal mist – for the spire of St Stephen's. And indeed it was. As the roofs and squares of the city glided beneath us, I saw the top of the cathedral tower getting closer and closer. I prayed that none of the city's fire-watchers, who always keep an eye on the cathedral, would spot the outline of our ship and raise the alarm.

"Not here, you wretched thing!" I shouted, beside myself. "You know where you have to go!"

As our craft got closer and closer to the spire, Simonis's death suddenly came rushing back to me. The roaring of the lions and the panther had been drowned out by the yelling of the forty thousand martyrs, and the beasts' jaws, hidden by the darkness of the night, had had seized hold not only of Simonis's helpless limbs but also of my spirit. The Last Days of Mankind, which had announced them-selves with Opalinski's death, had swallowed Simonis and were now breathing down my neck. For a moment I stood there full of anguish. It was then that I saw it.

At first I thought it was a hallucinatory effect of my sad lucubra-tions. Although it seemed alien in substance to the world of humans, the object was such that it was also visible to Abbot Melani, who had re-awoken and risen in the meantime, and who now stood gaping by my side.

It was a golden globe, suspended in the air, the size of an apple. No description could ever fully convey its appearance; a reminis-cence of it has stuck with me, albeit blurred and impenetrable. Certain dreams are difficult to remember, not because one's memory is weak, but because they can only live in the distorted state of mind of the oneiric world; like jellyfish dragged onto the shore, as soon they are transported to a state of wakened awareness they dissolve. In the same way, owing to my desperate and tormented state of mind at that time, I was granted an experience that I cannot now fully repeat and describe. All I can say is that the substance of the golden globe, suspended at a short distance from the prow of the Flying Ship, seemed midway between vapour and metal, as if the magic breath of an alchemist had transformed a sphere of gas into gold, and this latter once again into an aeriform substance.

It was then, enraptured by this arcane and fantastic vision, that I remembered: among the many prophecies about the Golden Apple that we had heard during the last few days, there was the one Ugonio had recounted. The War of the Spanish Succession, which was raging throughout Europe, would be won by the Empire only if the original Golden Apple of Justinian, which assures supremacy over the Christian West, were to be placed on the highest spire of the most sacred church in Vienna: the Cathedral of St Stephen, where one day the Archangel Michael had appeared, he who, according to tradition, holds the Imperial Orb in his hand as he drives out Lucifer with his sword in the form of the holy cross.

The ship gave a start. The wind had risen, and the swaying craft had knocked against the tip of the spire of St Stephen's. Out of the corner of my eye, even though enraptured by the vision of the golden globe, I glimpsed the coils and spirals that adorn the highest point of the glorious cathedral.

"What's happening? First that shout . . . now the Apple . . ." stammered Abbot Melani in a trembling voice, clinging onto my arm: he too had realised what the golden globe was.

But I was no longer listening. I now remembered that, according to Ugonio, on the pinnacle of St Stephen's were the seven mysterious words carved by the Archangel Michael.

It is from this point that my memories are overpowered by the shades of oblivion, and everything merges in a blurred magma: my attempt to lean out to try and see, despite the darkness, the inscription engraved by Archangel Michael's sword, the ship swaying with a new gust of wind, my body losing its balance, Abbot Melani tottering by my side and collapsing onto the floor of the ship, and I, with the help of my elbow, just managing not to fall out of the ship into the void. And then those long seconds half-hanging head downwards, with the unreal vision of the bell tower of St Stephen's, an immense humpback whale of stone, looming beneath the imposing roof of the cathedral. And again, the Golden Apple suddenly increasing in luminosity, and then, as I save myself from falling and manage to pull myself back into the ship, the Apple disappearing in a wispy trail of refulgent powder.

The epiphany was over and the Golden Apple had not returned to St Stephen's: Spain was destined to fall into French hands. The night in which the fate of the world was sealed had completed its parabola. The outcome of the war was already decided – that was what the Flying Ship wished to tell us – and with it the events of the years to come.

Then it was time to abandon ourselves to the pitching of the ship, and to its dumb and elusive will: to surrender, yield and turn away, while distant thunder announced a short morning downpour. Like an outburst of universal weeping, the rain would act as prelude to the new age: the Last Days of Mankind.

ॐ॰॰

Almost as if it wanted to give us a final helping hand, the Flying Ship once again landed amid the vineyards of Simmering, just a few yards from the convent's buttery. As soon as we had disembarked, the winged ship rose into the air again and departed, but not in the direction of the Place with No Name but to the west. I saw it sailing off ethereally and silently until it merged into the horizon and the clouds of the ashen dawn, towards the west, the Kingdom of Portugal, whence it had arrived two years earlier.

With my remaining strength, I dragged the Abbot to the nearby buttery of the convent. I do not know how my poor, short homunculus's limbs managed to support the weight of the old castrato. I leaned against the door in exhaustion and realised it was ajar. At that moment it was thrown open.

"My love!" I heard a cry.

I just managed to see Cloridia, and Camilla de' Rossi who was with her. While the Chormaisterin offered ready support to Atto, Cloridia smiled at me and held me tight, her face streaked with tears. What was my wife doing there? Why was Camilla de' Rossi there too? Were they looking for us? And how did they know that we would arrive at that very spot? These thoughts whirled round my head like bothersome flies. After Penicek and Palatine, I certainly did not have the strength to face the ambiguities and mysteries of the Chormaisterin! I frowned, but Cloridia held my hands gently and shook her head:

"I know what you're thinking, but don't worry. Camilla has cleared everything up."

I had no time to hear any more. Overwhelmed by it all, I fainted in my wife's arms.

꘏

"But ... these are portraits of our girls!" were the first words I managed to utter.

I had come to myself just a few moments earlier on a couch next to the fireplace. When I opened my eyes I was at once seized with an attack of vertigo: cruel, stabbing pains tormented my whole body. Cloridia had taken something from a little box and put it into my hand. I looked. It was a chain, from which hung a pendant in gold filigree, in the shape of a heart. It opened up. Inside there were the miniatures of two charming girls' faces: my daughters when small! What were these portraits I had never seen before? Was this another of my dreams?

"No, love. They're not the girls. Not exactly," smiled my wife.

Then, as my thoughts ordered themselves with difficulty and my whole being was convulsed with inward turmoil, Cloridia told me the whole story.

When it was all clear, I turned my head in search of Abbot Melani. Sitting by the fire, he was wrapped from head to toe in a woollen blanket, and was talking wearily but intensely with Camilla. Our eyes met. It should have been a happy moment, that was how he had imagined it; but we could not enjoy it, not now.

꘏

The horse pulling the buggy raced swiftly through the night on the way home, back to Vienna. Abbot Melani groaned at each jolt of the wheels. We had to be quick, very quick. We had to stop the hand that was raised against the Emperor. But how? In the first place, how would we enter the Hofburg?

I could not think, except with immense effort. Of all that I had lived through in the previous hours, only one thing had remained with me: a sound. It was the reverberation of the yelling of the forty thousand of Kasim. It was no longer present, but its roar still lived within me, like a foot that has left its print, and the vibration in my guts became deafening at times. I found it hard to discern sounds, even my own voice. I was not deaf, but deafened.

Nonetheless, once we reached Porta Coeli, even before getting out we heard a resounding rumble of carriage wheels. A two-horse carriage had pulled up abruptly in front of us. It bore the imperial coat of arms. Two footmen got out bearing torches.

"Open up, quickly!" they shouted, knocking insistently at the door of the convent.

"Are you looking for me?" asked Camilla, who had already grasped the situation, approaching the door. "I'm the Chormaisterin."

"Is it you? Then hurry up," one of them answered, thrusting an envelope with the Caesarean seal at her, which she opened at once.

"It's His Majesty," Camilla informed us with, an anxious quiver in her voice, after reading the note. "He's summoning me. At once."

This was the answer to our prayers: I would enter the Hofburg in Camilla's wake; with her I would get right to the Emperor. We left Cloridia and Atto at the convent.

The Caesarean palace stood out against the gloom, still immersed in the darkness of the night that had decided the fate of the world. We knocked at a side door. Despite the hour, it was opened at once. I guessed that Camilla must have made frequent and confidential use of that entrance, since the servant who opened up did not protest or ask who we were. They made us wait in a small room, and a few minutes later a footman with a sleepy face arrived. At once he and Camilla embraced and kissed fraternally.

"How is he?" asked the Chormaisterin.

He answered with a serious gaze, saying not a word.

"Let me introduce Vinzenz Rossi, a cousin of my late husband," Camilla said then. "He'll get us what we need."

Vinzenz came back a moment later with a page's costume: it was just my size. I changed into it and we set off along the corridors, guided by the footman and the dim light of his candle.

In addition to the darkness that filled the rooms of the Hofburg, and which also enveloped my tired limbs and exhausted spirit, I recall only an endless series of corridors, staircases and then more corridors. Finally a large antechamber, and then another one. A silent and velvety bustle of more footmen, doctors and priests. Nervousness, lowered eyes, a sensation of impotent expectancy. I saw a woman, shaken by suppressed sobs, half covered by a veil, walking away accompanied by two maidens and supported by someone whom I heard addressed as "Lord Count of Paar". Was this the Empress? I did not dare ask. We were allowed to proceed quickly, with discretion but no subterfuge: all the service staff seemed to recognise Camilla.

Finally the last great door opened and we entered.

The Chormaisterin talked in a subdued and even voice. Outlined by the light of a candle holder set behind him, I could just glimpse the haggard profile of the invalid breathing to the rhythm of agony.

When Camilla had approached the bed, no one had dared to go up to her and urge caution. Only Joseph had turned to the new arrival, but without the strength to make any sign of greeting.

The entourage of doctors was made to withdraw to the far side of the room, as did the father-confessor, clutching to his chest the chalice of the Holy Sacrament from which His Caesarean Majesty had just taken communion. They went to join the Apostolic Proto-Notary, who was still holding the oil of extreme unction, which had just been administered in the presence of the Apostolic Nuncio. It was for the Nuncio that Camilla had been working on her *Sant' Alessio*; instead, he now found himself bestowing the Pope's last benediction on the dying Caesar.

Now Camilla was whispering into the Emperor's ear; he was simply listening. All around, it was as if the whole room were holding its breath. Camilla could have been infected by the fatal sickness, and yet she knelt at the bedside as if at a child's cradle. Then she rose, and it seemed to me (I cannot swear it on account of the gloom) that she dared to caress the head of Joseph the Victorious.

I guessed that I would never know what she had said to him. I was right.

10.15 of the clock

> Then Roland feels that death is now upon him
> As from his ears his brain comes oozing forth.
>
> Then Roland feels that he has lost his sight,
> He struggles to his feet with all his force;
> The colour now has vanished from his face.
>
> Then Roland feels that death is clutching at him,
> It passes from his head down to his heart.
>
> Then Roland feels his time is fully over,
> With one hand he has struck upon his chest.

He offers up his right-hand glove to God:
The Archangel has seized it from his hand.
Above his arm he keeps his head low-bowed,
With hands close-joined he's come now to the end.

It was over. His Caesarean Majesty, successor of Charlemagne on the throne of the Holy Roman Empire, had handed his glove to the Archangel and given up his soul to the Most High. His suffering was finally over. Fever had consumed him like a burning flame, pain had prostrated him until he fainted, vomiting fits had scraped his bowels. Then the disease had flayed, devoured, and mangled him from within.

Joseph the Victorious died like the Paladin Roland, defeated by the Infidels in the retreat from Roncesvalles.

He had remained lucid to the last. Shortly before ten he had had the strength to ask his chaplain to approach with the blessed lamp and had placed his hands on it in the Christian fashion. The chaplain, kneeling by the bed, held the lamp up and also the young palms of Joseph the Victorious, which had no strength left in them. And so, gazing eagerly at that light, His Majesty had listened to the oration for the dying murmured by the father-confessor, who had tottered from the torment of it all and had had to be supported.

In his last moments His Majesty had been shaken by a violent convulsion: black blood had spilled from his eyes and ears; mucus and bits of brain had come dripping from his nose; derma, tissues, vessels, capillaries and lymphatic ducts had burst under the action of a thousand mines bursting silently. It did not seem to be – it was not – a simple illness: Evil itself, with its wicked arts, had torn the body of Joseph the Victorious asunder, and had taken pleasure in so doing.

When the Queen Mother, present throughout, approached and knelt to kiss her son's now upturned hands, we all knew that it was truly over.

I hid no longer. Still dressed as a page, amid the crowd of courtiers attending the imperial death in the antechamber, I made my departure unobserved.

I went down the stairs clutching an extinguished candlestick, just to give my hands something to do. And so I strode on, while my heartbeats, which had paused the instant my king had yielded up his last breath, began throbbing once again, beat after beat, and a few minutes later, they were hammering wildly, piercing my chest like a sharp burning dart. The gasping pendulum of flesh and lymph that vibrated in my chest dug and dug into my bowels and then surged back up, to my very eyes. My swollen eyelids pulsated painfully, and I imagined them full of the same ferruginous humours which I had seen, to my horror, pouring from my young Emperor's half-closed and contorted eyelids, while his pupils had rolled backwards and the heavens had dissolved in universal weeping.

I could barely make out where my legs were taking me. I was staggering, and I thought I would not be able to go very far. I dragged myself painfully until I came in sight of the ramparts. It was then that a new impulse took possession of me. I stopped struggling, my thighs became hard and strong, my heart beat regularly: I began to run. I ran with no restraint or aim, and I yelled with all the breath in my body. I hurled the extinguished candle from me, tearing off my wig, tailcoat, cravat and shirt, yelling and shrieking bare-chested, and my jaws throbbed and I wanted to explode in a thousand proclamations of horror. But no one could hear me: I was shouting all alone and running all alone, convinced that blood, instead of tears, was coursing down my cheeks, and I did not bother to dry it, not caring that it might leave a red trail on the pavement. I saw my fresh red blood being joined by the black blood that spurted from the mangled bowels of the Pontevedrin Dànilo Danilovitsch, and my yell merged into that of the forty thousand martyrs of Kasim; I saw the cold, coagulated blood of the Bulgarian Hristo Hadji-Tanjov, and my yell became a whistling blizzard; and then again the black blood of the Tekuphah invoked upon us by the old man in the Armenian coffee house, which had gushed down Atto's face from the pudenda of the Romanian Dragomir Populescu, severed like the sex of Uranus from which Venus was born; and the sharp poles soaked in the blood of the Hungarian Koloman Szupán from Varasdin, and again the blood that the iron spits had sent spurting from the beetle eyes of the proud Pole Jan Janitzki Opalinski; and finally, the Greek blood of Simonis, Simonis, my friend, my son, blood of my blood, which had quenched the thirst of the panther of the Place with No Name, whose fatal roar had shaken my chest, drowning out the cries from my own innards and merging with the yelling of the forty thousand martyrs.

The red trail of blood that I imagined marking my progress was now a long trail of death. Thanks to it, I repeated to myself, Cloridia would find me again. My veins were bursting at the thought of all the innocent blood that had been shed, but they also quivered at the notion of other blood, the blood of Judas, cursed *in saecula saeculorum*, which had flowed in trickles during the ritual in the woods from the wounds of the dervish Ciezeber *alias* Palatine, the Chaldean or Armenian or Indian traitor, or all these things together. And above all, the unshed blood of Penicek, the foul spawn of Lucifer. On all that blood the sun rose each day, itself tinged with blood *soli soli soli*, "to the only sun of the earth", a blood-stained sun, just as my young Emperor had been suffocated in blood, "the only man alone on earth."

Then I raised my fists to heaven and proclaimed: let the sky darken, the moon and vermilion sun cease their course, women cover their faces, banquets be suspended, every mouth be rendered dumb, all doors be bolted. It is over! The Emperor is no more. Death and injustice have had their dark triumph.

The echo of my bloody folly and no other sound came to me from the wreckage of creation: a sad fanfare with which my dead – but also the millions and millions of soldiers who are dead, dying or about to die from this war, the war without end – accuse me of still living. What have you died for? Ah, if only you had known, at the moment of sacrifice, of the profits of war, which increase despite – nay, *with* – your sacrifice, and grow fat on it! All of you, victors and defeated, have lost the war: it has been won by your murderers, the usurers of meat, of sugar, of alcohol, of flour, of rubber, of wool, of iron, of ink and of arms, who have been compensated a hundred times over for the devaluation of other people's blood. That is why you have rotted and will rot for centuries and centuries, generations on generations, in mud and water. You will stay alive until they have stolen enough, lied enough, fleeced mankind enough. Then, away with you! Bring on the next one, under the executioner's axe. They will go on dancing until Ash Wednesday and Lent in this great tragic carnival, in which men have died under the cold eyes of those like Palatine, and the butchers have become philosophers *honoris causa*.

And you, the sacrificed, you have not risen up and will not rise up against this plan. You, down there, murdered and cheated! You have supported and will support the freedom and welfare of the strategists, parasites and buffoons, just as you did your own misfortune, your own coercion. They have sold and will sell your skin at the market, but also ours. You that are dead! Why do you not rise again from your ditches? To call this breed to reply, with the contorted faces you had in death, with the mask that your youth was condemned to wear by their diabolically demented scheming. Rise up then, and go out and face them, wake them from sleep with the scream of your agony: they were capable of embracing their women in the night following the day they flayed you. Save us from them, from a peace that is contaminated by their presence.

Help, slaughtered ones! Help me! So that I shall not have to live among men who ordered hearts to stop beating, mothers to grow old on the tombs of their children. As God is my witness, nothing but a miracle can redress this atrocious affair. Awaken from this rigidity, come forth! May future times listen to you!

But if it were true, as Atto says, that the ages will no longer listen, would a being above them listen? My Jesus! The tragedy composed of scenes of mankind decomposing – carve this tragedy into my flesh as You did into Your own, so that the Holy Spirit who has pity on victims may heed it, even if it has renounced forever all contact with a human ear. May it receive the fundamental note of this age. The echo of my cruel folly, which makes me equally responsible for these sounds, may it count as Redemption.

Redemption, redemption. I repeated this and nothing else over and over. I was now half naked, and I no longer had anything to pluck from my chest. So I began to plunge my nails into my arms, my shoulders, my neck, my cheeks hollowed by that cry, my belly and my navel, which had once bound me to the mother I had never known. I ran bare-chested all day, tearing shreds of flesh from myself, from my ears that I might hear no more, from my tongue that I might speak no more, from my eyelids that I might see no more, from my nose that I might breathe no more, and biting my very fingers, that I might touch no more. I ran through fields and craggy gorges, and my single long cry ran through every clod of earth with me. My eyes were open, but I was running blindly. I saw and did not see, I heard and did not hear. At last a distant melody reached me, enveloped me, confused the soles of my feet, and my feet recognised it and wavered in their mad flight and at last danced to its subtle song. Without arresting their march, my soles swivelled freely and my arms followed docilely and also drew broad figures in the air to the sound that (now

I recognised it) was a violin, *that* violin. And then I saw . . . I was at Neugebäu. The cry from my chest gradually died down into the modulation of that old musical motif, which I now called by its name: a Portuguese melody known as *folia*, or Folly.

My bare feet now trod the gardens of the Place with No Name, but they were no longer uncultivated and abandoned; graceful blue and gold mosaics decorated them, pure fresh water leaped in a jet from the lovely fountain of alabaster in the middle and blessed everything around it with its freshness. It fell on my shoulders as well, washing my wounds of their coagulated blood.

It was only then, for the first time, that I truly saw the Place with No Name. As if my wounds had opened up the Kingdom of the Just to me, my eyes became new and superhuman, and in an explosion of retrospective truth they showed me the true and living face of Maximilian's creation, the glorious life it had been conceived for, and never attained: the roofs glittering with gold; the garden towers rising capriciously in the Turkish fashion; flower beds and luxuriant bushes teeming with buds; rare plants; trees bearing oranges, lemons and exotic fruits; precious floral creations; generous leaping fountains, whose silvery waters cascaded down onto beds of gleaming inlaid marble; the façade of the mansion decorated with a thousand lintels, sculptures, capitals, all adorned with delicate artefacts in embossed gold; the walls standing proudly with their robust battlements; a great bustle of carriages, servants, labourers, secretaries and footmen, all in the velvet clothes of two hundred years earlier; and finally, in the background, the wild but subdued sound of the animals, while the immense masterpiece of the imagination that was Neugebäu was so consciously harmonious that its bellicose symbols (the towers, battlements and lions) seemed to announce a message of peace, just as its creator, Maximilian the Mysterious, had been a man of peace.

I sobbed at the thought that this timeless vision was being granted to me only this once. I thought back to Rome, to the Villa of the Vessel, which had lived so long and retained so much of its past life; its walls still full of mottoes, it narrated the splendour of an age that would never return and, almost like a Medusa in reverse, imparted its wisdom to anyone whose eyes should fall on those mottoes even for an instant. But Neugebäu, the Infant with No Name cut down along with the womb that had given birth to it, had never lived its moment. Its day had never come; hatred had aborted it before its time. Only the gardens had been allowed a single brief glimpse of life, but those parts of the Place with No Name that were intended not for nature but for human spirits had awaited life in vain. All that the castle of Neugebäu could tell the visitor or the curious passer-by was: "My kingdom is not of this world." So what had all my existence been until that moment? What was the meaning of those lives that had been cut down before their prime, the lives of Joseph I and Maximilian II, and – eleven years earlier in the Villa of the Vessel – the unrealised destinies of the Most Christian King and his beloved Maria, and – even earlier, thirty years ago, again in Rome, in the Inn of the Donzello – the martyrdom of Superintendent Fouquet and the hatred that despoiled his mansion at Vaux-le-Vicomte, that great swaggering statement in stone that had lived just one night, that of 17th August 1661? What were they all but Beings and Places with No Name, with no history because they had been deprived of the history that was their right, all of them therefore preludes to Neugebäu? Of what had they spoken to me? Why had they approached me, why had they sought out my poor, obscure life and painfully dazzled it with their mournful effulgence?

৵৽

I do not know how it was that Cloridia found me and took me back to the convent. I lay on the bed, inert. I saw and heard my wife and my little boy bending over me. Next to them, in the armchair of green brocade by my bed, and reduced to a dejected shadow of his former self, sat Abbot Melani and his nephew. My eyes wandered over their faces, lingered on their mouths. They were all saying something to me. Domenico wanted to shake me; Atto, whimpering, blamed himself for everything and proposed calling a doctor; Cloridia, devastated by the disaster that had befallen me, in which she insisted on finding a touch of heroism, begged for a sign of understanding for her and our child, if not from my lips, at least from my expression.

And once more I went back in my mind to eleven years earlier in Rome, to the luxurious Villa of the Vessel built in the shape of a craft like the Flying Ship, and abandoned like the Place with No Name. And yet again I thought back to Giovanni Henrico Albicastro, the strange Dutch violinist dressed in black, who had seemed to fly over the battlements of the villa and, playing a Portuguese melody called *folia*, or folly, and declaiming verses of a poem entitled "The Ship of Fools", had taught me about life. I would never find out if he and the unknown helmsman of the Flying Ship were the same person, but that mattered little now: it was time to put Albicastro's warnings to good use.

In my chest I had started to yell again and had never ceased, but my lips, obedient to those ancient exhortations, had fallen silent. I had become dumb. My wife wept and I wanted to say to her: how can I speak to you with this din in my ears? Can't you hear it too? Only occasionally did the yelling change to the song of the *folia*, and then I would moan. I wanted to tell Cloridia that I loved her, but at once my interior yell started up again.

And so, lying as an invalid on that undesired bed, I once more fell prey to my Furies. I suffered from that silence, which was like a place anyone could enter and be sure of a welcome. I ardently wished that my silence would close around me, as in a burial chamber at the centre of which lay mankind, my tragic hero.

Ah, if it were possible to let posterity hear the voice of this age! I tormented myself in my sweat-soaked blankets. Then external truth would give the lie to internal truth, and our descendants' ears would recognise neither one: that is how time makes essence unrecognisable and prepares people to condone the greatest crime ever committed under the sun and under the stars.

Only in the archive of God is essence safe. No, it is not for your death, all my friends, fallen in war and in peace, those who died yesterday, today and tomorrow, but for what you have lived through, that God will wreak his vengeance on those who inflicted it on you. God will turn them into shadows, the shadows they are within, shadows that have mendaciously clothed themselves with the guise of real men. He will strip them of their flesh, in which they conceal their own empty souls. He will provide bodies only for the thoughts produced from their stupidity, for the feelings of their wickedness, for the tremendous rhythm of their nullity, and he will make them move, like marionettes, on the Day of Judgement, so that the righteous may see what perished under His Hand.

I had embarked on the long road of silence in anticipation of the day when, as Albicastro had taught me, "the bow will be drawn". But the Dutch violinist, eleven years earlier, had also warned me: it is not in this world that the bow will be drawn. And Christ Himself has admonished us: "My kingdom is not of this world."

While waiting for the Kingdom of God, where should I take shelter? Albicastro, the Vessel, the Place with No Name: it was as if my adventures alongside Atto were coming together to form a single great design, the key to which would be found during these very days. Life, which had amazed me and taught me much, and before which I had always regarded myself as an empty vessel, receiving and giving nothing back except greater fullness; that life of mine now seemed to fold in on itself, to return to old themes, teachings I had already heard, almost as if it did not intend to teach me any new things. Why?

Day the Tenth

SATURDAY, 18TH APRIL 1711

✠

I was in bed, immersed in my new silent world. I had just heard various items of news from Cloridia: at dawn the previous day the sun had risen more scarlet than ever, almost as if it were announcing that Joseph's last drop of blood was about to be shed. The Viennese had been right to consider this phenomenon an ill omen. Special emissaries had been sent to the Diet of Regensburg to announce the Emperor's death to all the prince-electors. The inevitable pamphlets with obituaries had appeared in abundance, especially in Italian:

> *Nel Fior degli Anni, ed in April fiorito*
> *Il Maggior de' tuoi Figli, AUGUSTA, muore:*
> *Saggio fù nella Reggia, in Campo ardito,*
> *Fù de' Guerrieri, e de' Monarchi il Fiore.*
> *Lagrima Austria, e nel Dominio Avito . . .*[16]

Reading these was unbearable for me. I had quite other things to think of: the Grand Dauphin, son of His Majesty the Most Christian King of France, had died. The news had reached Vienna the previous day. Today my wife had brought me the pamphlets, which were full of details.

The Dauphin had died without communion or confession, and the Archbishop of Paris had even forgotten to have the church bells tolled. But what was even more surprising was that one of the doctors, Monsieur de Fagon, had assured the King that the Dauphin was in no danger. The very night he died, Monsieur de Boudin, his first doctor, had been to see the King during dinner to tell him that his son's illness was taking its normal course and that he was getting better by the day. But just half an hour later he had come back to tell

---

[16] In the flower of his years and in flowery April, / The eldest of your sons, AUGUST LAND, dies: / Wise he was in the Palace, on the Field bold, / Of Warriors and of Monarchs he was the Flower. / Weep Austria, and in the ancestral Dominion . . .

him that the fever had returned with extraordinary violence, and there were fears for his life. The King had at once risen from the table and run to the Dauphin's chamber, to find him already dying and unconscious. He had not had time to make his confession, having only just had extreme unction. However, as he had confessed and taken communion on Easter Saturday, the King confined himself to censuring the doctors for their ignorance, in not recognising and foreseeing the vicissitudes that this illness was subject to.

The doctors said in their defence that the Dauphin had died after suffocating during an apopleptic fit. His body was so ravaged that the court surgeons did not wish to open it for fear of dying from the operation, since the innards and the heart were supposed to be taken to Val de Grâce. And the smell was so terrible in the room where he had died that the body had to be taken to St Denis two days later with no funeral ceremony, in a lead sarcophagus carried by a simple carriage. Two Capuchin monks were supposed to travel with it but they were unable to bear the great stench from the body, even though the sarcophagus was closed and fully lined with lead.

The Grand Dauphin was greatly loved by the good and peace-loving French people, so that the streets of Paris were filled with people weeping, from the humblest to the gravest. They knew that with his death France had lost a great opportunity to live in peace at last.

ॐॐ

Now that it was all over, I clearly saw not only my own failure, but that of Atto as well. His plan (to force the Empire to put an end to the war) had been totally swept away by events.

He had succeeded in just one mission: to get Cloridia to meet Camilla, her sister.

Two days earlier, in the buttery, Cloridia had explained everything to me, and each piece of the mosaic had finally slipped into place. My wife had begun by telling me about her mother, the Turkish mother she had always been so reluctant to talk of until then. She had been the daughter of a janissary doctor, she said, and had grown up in Constantinople. From her father Cloridia's mother had learned the rudiments of an ancient oriental medical art which treated people with spelt. During a voyage, however, when barely adolescent, the girl had been captured by pirates and sold as a slave.

There then followed a part of the tale that I had heard. As I already knew, Cloridia's mother had been bought by the Odescalchi family, the moneylenders for whom my late father-in-law had worked, and the sixteen-year-old Turkish girl had given birth to my wife. When Cloridia was twelve, her mother had been sold again and Cloridia herself kidnapped and taken to Holland.

Here began the part of the story I did not yet know. Now that I was lying in bed and was surrounded by so much death, I asked my wife in gestures to repeat the story to me, the only one with a happy ending, and so provide my cogitations with some temporary comfort far removed from the fury of tragic events.

Cloridia held my hand, her beautiful face dissolved in tears, and while waiting for yet another doctor she agreed to tell it over again. Three doctors had already been, and had declared that I was in perfect health. My voice would probably (but not "certainly") come back, they said confidently.

The Odescalchis, Cloridia lovingly recounted all over again, stroking my head, had sold her mother to Collonitz, the cardinal who had been one of the heroes of the siege of Vienna.

From him she had had another daughter in 1682. Collonitz had had her raised discreetly by his Spanish lieutenant, Gerolamo Giudici, also ceding the mother to him. Giudici had kept both of them in service in his house, where the mother had transmitted to the daughter her medical skills and her perfect knowledge of Turkish as well as Italian. When the girl was thirteen years old, in 1695, she already had a respectable education, especially in music. She played, even composed, but above all sang: the young, hot-blooded King of the Romans saw her performing and became infatuated with her. She seemed to return his love. So Collonitz, wishing to guarantee her safety, baptised her personally in the church of St Ursula on the Johannesgasse, and through Giudici had her sent to the convent of Porta Coeli.

It was, in short, the story of the young Turkish girl rejected by the nuns of the convent, which Camilla herself had told us a few days earlier.

The sisters had protested against the arrival of the Ottoman girl: they were all schoolgirls of noble birth, while the new arrival was a slave. Afraid of being locked away (another convent might always accept her), the girl had fled. No one knew where she had gone or with whom.

"She had fled with her music-teacher, Franz de' Rossi," my wife explained to me.

Joseph's musician, who was also Luigi Rossi's nephew, gave her the name of Camilla, like her Roman cousin in Trastevere, whom Cloridia also remembered.

"Our mother had called her Maria," said Cloridia, smiling and wiping the silent tears that wet my pillow.

I was not moved by this story, whose stirring vividness was almost outrageous when seen against the unnatural death of the Emperor, of the Grand Dauphin, of Simonis and his friends. I was crying for the opposite reason: the refuge that I sought in Cloridia's story, I was unable to find. Her consolation at having finally found a grave where she could mourn her mother did not soothe my despair; her joy at having discovered the blood of her blood in Camilla did not console me for the blood that had been shed.

I thought with sombre dejection that in almost thirty years of marriage Cloridia had never been wrong in her assessments: every time I was lost in doubt, she saw everything clearly and gave me the correct advice. But now she had actually believed that the dervish wished to contribute to the recovery of the Emperor, thus dragging herself and me into a fatal mistake. She, like Atto, had been vanquished by the new times. And I realised now that nothing, not even my sweet and wise wife, could offer me any relief from the sensation of hopeless slaughter that had overwhelmed my spirit.

While I observed her thus through my tears, Cloridia proceeded all unawares with her story. Franz and Camilla had got married, and from this point we had already heard the whole story from the Chormaisterin. When the War of the Spanish Succession broke out, they had returned to Vienna, where unfortunately they found that Camilla's mother (and Cloridia's) had died. Franz went back into Joseph's service, and with him his wife. However, the young King of the Romans did not recognise the Turkish slave he had once been infatuated with. A year later Franz died.

Joseph, even without recognising her, felt newly attracted to Camilla, so much so that he bestowed on her (as we already knew from Gaetano Orsini) his friendship and confidence. In response to Joseph's feelings, the young woman composed an oratorio for him once a year for four years in a row, but refused all payment, a mystery that had aroused my suspicions.

Camilla had now explained this: she had been afraid that if her name ended up in the hands of those in charge of making payments from Joseph's private coffers or from the funds of the court employees, they would ask her questions about her identity. With the Viennese mania for bureaucratic precision, sooner or later they would find out who she really was.

And so she preferred to support herself by travelling around the villages of Austria and working as a healer with the spelt-based medicine she had learned from her mother, which fortunately derived from the same ancient tradition that had inspired the holy abbess Hildegard of Bingen centuries earlier. This allowed Camilla to proclaim herself a disciple of Hildegard, concealing her Eastern origins. She could not practise in Vienna, since the **Examiniert und Approbiert**, or university licence, was required. In addition, Cardinal Collonitz remained alive until 1707, so it was better not to show herself too much in the Caesarean city.

At the end of the previous year, 1710, Joseph had asked her to settle in the capital permanently because he needed her advice. Instead of agreeing to be paid she told him that she no longer felt able to compose and asked permission to enter a convent. His Majesty placed her in Porta Coeli, opposite the young Countess Pálffy. Eugene of Savoy had managed to set the Countess up in Strassoldo House, close to his own palace, so that he could make use of her to keep tabs on Joseph.

When the Emperor asked her to arrange an oratorio in honour of the Papal Nuncio, she chose, as I already knew, the last one she had composed, *Sant' Alessio*. What I did not know as yet was that this oratorio had a special meaning. Camilla had portrayed herself in it: like Alessio, she had returned without anyone recognising her. Who could say whether Camilla – just like Alessio, who is recognised by his parents and his betrothed only on the point of death – had revealed herself to Joseph in their last encounter? Cloridia told me that her sister had preferred not to say anything to her; she prayed night and day to overcome her despair.

The young girls portrayed in the heart-shaped pendant were therefore not my daughters, but Cloridia and Camilla as children. The necklace had belonged to their mother – it was one way for her to fill the void, both daughters having been prematurely snatched from her – and, after her death, it had remained in the home of Girolamo Giudici, Collonitz's lieutenant.

The previous day, when Atto, Simonis and I had still not returned from the Place with No Name, Cloridia, in her alarm, had turned to the Chormaisterin. Together they had at once set out from the convent towards Neugebäu by cart, and then, having realised from afar that something strange was going on, Camilla had suggested taking shelter in the buttery that the nuns of Porta Coeli owned nearby. On the journey, fearing some intrigue of Abbot Melani's, Cloridia had finally made up her mind to force open the little chest that he had entrusted me with, on condition that I should not open it before his departure, and which had remained in her hands. And there she had found what she would never have expected: her own portrait as a child, alongside another child that Camilla instantly recognised as herself. At that point the Chormaisterin had confessed everything. She already knew the whole story: thanks to Atto, of course.

Here my wife's tale ended. After asking her to repeat it to me four times, I let her go. The silence I fell back into dried my tears and left room for clearer meditation. Everything slipped gradually into place. The background to Atto's and Camilla's acquaintance, for example.

In Paris, in September 1700, Camilla had told Abbot Melani her own story and that of her mother. Knowing about my wife's past, Atto had realised that the future Chormaisterin and Cloridia could not but be daughters of the same mother. He had revealed his intuition to Camilla, but had pretended to have no idea where to find Cloridia . . . whereas he had in fact just returned from Rome, where for ten days he had met my consort almost daily.

As usual, Melani was looking out for his own interests. He did not want Franz de' Rossi and Camilla to go to Rome, as they would certainly have done if they had heard that Camilla's sister was there. After the intrigues in which he had deceived and exploited me, he certainly did not want Cloridia telling her sister all his misdeeds. Atto would much rather that Franz and Camilla went back to Vienna, where they could be very useful to him, since the war for the Spanish succession was about to break out. It had not been difficult to find the arguments to persuade them to remain in the Empire: as Camilla had reported, he had told them that Vienna was the real centre of Italian music, the papacy being in decline, France impoverished by the crazy expenses of battles and ballets, and the golden age of Cardinal Mazarin long over.

He had backed up his arguments with a white lie: he had said that he was indebted to me and Cloridia (true), and that for this reason he was trying to trace us (false, he knew perfectly well where to find us: he had just abandoned us at Villa Spada). Finally he had promised Camilla that he would inform her of any progress in his search. In this way he had found a pretext to remain in contact with Camilla and Franz, in case he should need some favour in Vienna.

And this was yet another of the various reasons that had driven Atto finally to settle his debt, making the bequest to me through a notary in Vienna: he wanted to put an end to the separation between the two sisters once and for all, and make Camilla meet Cloridia. However, he had interposed another difficulty: he did not want the Chormaisterin to reveal herself to my wife before Atto himself had left Vienna. "I don't want to be thanked," he had said to Camilla with false modesty. The reason was very different: he feared my wife's rage, once she discovered that for eleven years Atto had kept them apart.

The old Abbot had hoped to depart from Vienna before the revelation. But events had prevented him from secretly setting off and abandoning us, as he had done in Rome eleven years ago, and twenty-eight years earlier, when I had first met him. At any other moment I would have assailed him with a barrage of accusations, questions and reprimands; but not now. Even if I wished to, without the gift of speech I could not. It was better this way: Cloridia, touched by the old castrato's flimsy subterfuges, had readily forgiven him.

Cloridia's account also dispelled the last cloud that hung over Atto. We now knew the meaning of the phrase I had heard the Armenian say to Melani, that the house servants had "sold their master's heart": it simply meant that, via the Armenian, Atto had commissioned the theft of the heart-shaped pendant at great expense! It had nothing to do with the Emperor, or with the Agha's Armenians.

I laughed wryly to myself at the tangled web that had had me going round in round in circles, amid deliberately created red herrings and misleading clues, while behind my back the whole world was about to be turned upside down: earth would become water, water earth and the sky fire.

❧

Finally the sound that deadened all thoughts for me faded away and I heard no more than a distant echo. I dozed off.

When I re-awoke I found Atto sitting in an armchair by my bed. Our destinies were now more closely linked than ever. As Vienna had nothing more to offer us, Atto would take us back with him to Paris. Just a few years earlier he would never have made so generous an offer, but now he had come to the end of his life and intended to die in God's grace and so was happy to do so. He had persuaded Cloridia to accept the offer: he would pay us handsomely to enter his service, and he would see to it that our son received a suitable education.

"I'm sure that I'll soon manage to persuade the Most Christian King to let me go back to Pistoia; then you and your family will come with me," he had announced.

I had not seen Camilla again. Where had she ended up? I looked at Cloridia and I caressed her damp cheeks, unable to console her. She had found a sister again, flesh of her flesh. But she had lost the husband she knew. She now had another one; less satisfying, less cheerful, less able to show his love for her, but highly determined. I already felt within me a growing desire to take up a sword, a very special sword. Soon the time would come.

❦

While the thoughts and reconstructions of the recent past filled my brain, Vienna plunged into sadness. If Joseph had still been alive, that Saturday it would have been the turn for us artisans and traders, with our respective apprentices, to recite the prayer of the Forty Hours. A very different ceremony awaited us: instead of this oration, we would queue up to go and honour his dead body. We had heard it from the sisters of Porta Coeli: the poor mangled body of His Caesarean Majesty, embalmed by the court chirurgeons, lay ready for the funeral wake on a bier in that part of the royal palace called Ritterstube, or Loggia of the Cavaliers. That evening the wake would be inaugurated, but only for the members of the high nobility, who every hour throughout the night and the next few days would follow one another two by two in paying their last respects to their dead Ceasar. From the next day the body would be displayed to the people as well, who would swarm into the Loggia of the Cavaliers and would be able to keep watch over the bier from the four altars erected for the occasion until the evening of 20th April, when the exequies would be held.

And at last I learned where Camilla had ended up. Every day between the hours of ten and eleven and eighteen and nineteen the court musicians would sing Psalm 50 in Latin before the imperial corpse. By express order of Joseph, who in full possession of his faculties had arranged everything before the end, the exequies would be conducted by the Chormaisterin.

At Atto's request, Camilla had agreed to take him with her and she had just come back to pick him up. While the Abbot prepared to take his leave of me I made my resistance clear: how could I fail to attend this last appointment with the Emperor I had seen die? I got out of bed, shaking off Cloridia's amorous embrace, put on my best clothes and, rejecting my wife's warnings with dumb obstinacy, I joined the Chormaisterin and Abbot Melani.

While we were waiting for Camilla to come back with the carriage (he did not want to walk even a few paces), Atto forestalled the question I would have liked to ask him, and which he had seen in my eyes:

"No, there is no risk in my showing myself. The plan of those damned souls has succeeded, the Emperor is dead. And after a state murder, the conspirators – killers and hirers – always disappear. The system withdraws into itself; some go away, like Eugene, others remain in hiding to monitor the situation, but the general rule is: for two to four days do not act in any way, do nothing at all. They will see that we go and watch over the body, but they will not intervene. They know that we can no longer do anything."

In the Loggia of the Cavaliers, which was decked out for mourning and illuminated by countless candles, archers and trabants mounted guard over the funeral bier. It was placed on three steps and ornamented with stuccos in burnished gold. Above it hung a baldachin in black velvet with silk fringes.

His Caesarean Majesty was perfect. He lay just where he had so often received visits and honours, and presided over numerous events and ceremonies during his brief life. His clothing and cloak were in black silk and lacework of the same colour. On his head was a tawny wig and a black hat, by his side a dagger and around his neck a small emblem of the Golden Fleece. The sarcophagus was spangled with crimson velvet and also ornamented with stuccos in burnished gold. His head lay on a double cushion. The embalmer had worked well. I was struck by the absence of smallpox pimples on his face: the result of his skill or a sign of foul play?

In front of the Emperor a large silver crucifix bestowed its blessed protection. To the side was a holy water sprinkler. On the right were the Caesarean insignia: the crown, the Imperial Orb, the sceptre and the Golden Fleece on a golden cushion; on the left the crowns of the kingdoms of Hungary and Bohemia. Not far off, covered with black taffeta, were an urn and a silver shrine: in accordance with the customs of the House of Habsburg, one contained the heart and tongue of Joseph, the other his brain, eyes and internal organs. On two chaises longues draped in black sat the court chaplain and four barefoot Augustinian friars, who murmured the litanies for the dead.

Then, from afar, I saw them again. They were all there: the castrato Gaetano Orsini (still with some marks of bruising), Landina, the soprano wife of the theorbist Francesco Conti, and the others. I did not let myself be seen: how could I greet them, voiceless as I was? I observed them, their wan faces and lost expressions. They had had to bid farewell to the *Sant' Alessio*; the planned performance of the oratorio in honour of the Nuncio had obviously been cancelled. What would become of them, now that their beloved Joseph was dead, now that their young benefactor, who had so greatly expanded the musical staff of the Caesarean chapel, was no more? Would his brother Charles, when he returned from Barcelona to sit on the long-desired imperial throne, keep them where they were or sack the lot of them?

Vinzenz Rossi came up to us. He exchanged signs of fraternal consolation with Camilla, and while the Chormaisterin prepared to direct the chorus of musicians, he invited us to sit in a corner, where we would be able to stay until the end of the choral performance. I knew Psalm 50 and, while the musicians sang in Latin, I repeated the words mentally in my own language:

> *Purge me with hyssop, and I shall be clean:*
> *Wash me, and I shall be whiter than snow.*
> *Make me to hear joy and gladness;*
> *that the bones which thou hast broken may rejoice.*

So it was that the chorus of universal mourning was all one with the void that possessed me. The grief of every imperial subject entered me, passing through my body drop by drop, and my body was a vague spark of sadness, borne on the wind of that song of imploring despair. Nonetheless, my thoughts did not soften. While all around me subdued weeping, sniffling noses and sobs shook the air, I remained cold and impenetrable like a grey chip of slate. The impassive lens of my suffering focused on every event, and like a skilful surgeon I subjected it to anatomical inspection, dissecting it with the scalpel of reason.

Sitting next to Atto on an uncomfortable velvet seat, I continued to reflect, measuring the present with the yardstick of the past.

At the time of our first meeting, in September 1683, Abbot Melani had come to Rome to carry out the secret mission that the King of France had entrusted him with. It was not till later that he had had to carry out his own investigation, because he discovered that no one had explained to him either the real nature of, or the reasons for, his mission.

When we met again in 1700, Atto had been mysteriously stabbed in the arm on his arrival in Rome, and for this reason he had had to undertake a series of enquiries to find out who was threatening him. But actually, on that occasion too, he had a secret mission to carry out for the Sun King, and from the beginning he knew perfectly well what steps to take: to forge a will, with the help of his conspiratorial friend Maria Mancini; to stage a fake quarrel with Cardinal Albani, the future Pope, and so on, with the diabolic skills he was accustomed to employing.

This time, in Vienna in April 1711, things had gone very differently. The Abbot had come to the Caesarean city to urge Eugene of Savoy to conclude the war. He knew from the very beginning what he had to do (hand over the forged letter to the Emperor), but on account of Joseph's illness his attempts had soon proved futile, and in the end they had been swept away by the obscure manoeuvres of someone much more powerful than Atto, but without a face. Now we knew that it was a question of an entire system, and not a single person.

This was the descending parabola of Abbot Melani, as he himself had fully understood. After reaching the heights of his diplomatic career in that warm Roman summer eleven years earlier, he was now in steep decline. It was a new age. Atto was just a little old man, a memory of the past.

These were not the only comparisons I made between past and present. Joseph the Victorious was dead, but his wake pointed back to another sad day: the death of Maximilian the Mysterious. There were so many things, and great things at that, the two unfortunate emperors had in common!

They had both gone into battle leading their armies in person, and had been tolerant towards the followers of Luther. They were forever bound to the Place with No Name: Maximilian for having created it, Joseph for having desired its restoration, rendered impossible, alas, by his death. Schönbrunn, too, had been founded by Maximilian, and extended mostly by Joseph. They were both polyglots, and intellectually more gifted than most of their predecessors and successors.

And yet all this glory had ended in nothing: Maximilian had soon been forgotten, and the same thing (I am prepared to bet) will happen to Joseph, if the dark forces that lead Ciezeber-Palatine are not halted.

They both died prematurely of illness, and were both subjected to medical treatments that were suspicious, to say the very least. Both, finally, were succeeded by their brother, and not by their son. Oh, how easy for even the most innocent spirit, to see in these twin destinies the stamp of a single murderous will!

It was not the first time that I had observed the murder of a distinguished person at close quarters. Twenty-eight years earlier I had witnessed the death of Nicholas Fouquet – the Most Christian King's Superintendent of Finances – the inevitable conclusion of a life fully exposed to calumny and hatred. Once he had been removed, his envied castle at Vaux-le-Vicomte was plundered and stripped, and thus abandoned, like the Place with No Name.

The Loggia of Cavaliers now resounded with the sombre chorus of musicians, and I made their invocation my own:

> *Create in me a clean heart, O God;*
> *and renew a right spirit within me.*

Oh, Joseph the Victorious! Your death itself already reveals and lays bare the culprit. The assassination of the hero of Landau could never have been the work of one of your peers. If the Sun King, even when it would have been easy for him, refused to have you kidnapped or killed in battle, how could he have assassinated you so furtively? It is low people that murdered you: people low in spirit. Your death is the end of an era: the era of the great kings, of great personages, when sovereigns did not dare to knock off another king's head, as Abbot Melani taught me when I met him in Rome. We are in another century. Dark forces are on the rise, plots are stirred up by people with no faces or names, and above all no rules.

The choir conducted by Camilla, rendered sublime by the heavenly voices of Orsini and Landina, exhorted us to trust in the infinite wisdom of God:

> *Then will I teach transgressors Thy ways;*
> *And sinners shall be converted unto thee.*

I watched Atto pray humbly, every so often casting a glance at the body of the young Caesar, stretching his wrinkled neck to do so. He had been the first to understand the new times. The people who may have been behind Joseph's death, who at first had seemed to rule themselves out one by one, are all part of this play-acting. The new masters are undoubtedly in charge, the lords of the Last Days of Mankind. But all the others, like the lions I had seen sinking their teeth into the carcase of the dying ox at Neugebäu, have found their profit in this death as well. Nothing is missing. England and Holland, the instigators, have prevented the Empire from becoming too powerful, upsetting the equilibrium between the European powers. Then there are the accomplices: the Jesuits have taken their vengeance on the only Emperor they have not educated and who had them banished; his brother Charles, who will now be emperor, has crowned his hatred for his elder brother; the ministers of the old guard, whom Joseph had driven out or reduced to obedience, are sneering with satisfaction; and finally Eugene of Savoy, or Madame l'Ancienne, whatever one wants to call him, has been avenged for the humiliation of Landau, when that little boy Joseph dared to steal the limelight from the greatest invert-general of all ages. Finally, the hired killers: Islam, as ever, has been manipulated to do the dirty work of some faction of the West.

So who was responsible? All of them. They all armed a crazy dervish with a hundred names: Palatine, or Ammon, or Ciezeber, who is perhaps seven hundred years old. Or perhaps it's the opposite: it is the dervish, and those who like him have many names but no surname, who have manoeuvred England, Holland, the Jesuits, the ministers and even Eugene and Charles, to get the infamous deed carried out.

It was stifling in the mortuary chapel; beads of sweat trickled from people's wigs and all around people gasped with the heat.

Perhaps Joseph the Victorious had wanted to restore the Place with No Name, I thought, because he felt he was strong enough not to have to care about the forces still living that had devoured Neugebäu and Maximilian. And instead . . .

I looked at Atto again. He looked back at me and, for an instant, it was as if his eyeballs spoke to me sadly. It was undoubtedly a mere dream, brought about by the sepulchral atmosphere of the place and time:

"Impress Joseph's wan face into your memory, boy. You will not see any more sovereigns like that. Kings in future will be just limp puppets in the hands of networks of people with no leaders, of headless monsters that will listen to nobody who is not already one of them. But anyone who enters their circles is a prisoner. There will come a day when the people will go down into the streets from who knows where, as they did during the Fronde on the day of the mysterious barricades, when nothingness vomited forth hosts of hotheads from all sides, ready to destroy everything, all authority, every sacred symbol, every human boundary. As in Prague, during the funeral of Maximilian II. But it will not last for just one day, or three days. No, there will come a time when terror will wander the streets naked, armed with axes and scythes, for years and years, and it will cut the tongue of truth and the heads of the just. They will call it Liberty, Equality and Fraternity: however, it will be nothing but organised slaughter and disguised tyranny."

I took my eyes off Atto's. A group of nuns had entered the mortuary chamber, and they were reciting a rosary. Then Atto and I looked at each other again.

"You will hear no more teachings from me. Now that you know, you will not need anything else to understand the events of the world to come. All the rest – the future political alliances, the future wars, the future financial crises – all of it counterfeit. Everything will have been decided beforehand by the children, grandchildren and great-grandchildren of Joseph's assassins."

And then I thought back almost thirty years to when my late father-in-law had inveighed against the marriages between relatives among the monarchs of all lands, the eternal incest among the ruling houses. With a sudden flash in his eyes, Atto told me that matters were very different now:

"From now on the matrimonial alliances, relationships and consan-guinity will be kept secret – indeed, top secret. Nothing will be done in the light of day anymore, to prevent anyone from pointing out where truth is, to have them branded as madmen should they do so."

I thought back to Albicastro, the strange violinist I had met eleven years earlier during my second adventure with Atto. He too had expounded a similar prophecy to me, and now I understood its full significance: it contained the instructions needed to face this new world.

The Flying Ship, the vessel abandoned by all but still able to fly – with its first mysterious helmsman, who had arrived from Portugal, like the tune that Albicastro was always playing, the *folia*, and who had been secretly executed – was the heavenly sign that forces contrary to those teachings had been unleashed.

I kept silent. But was it right?

Paris

EVENTS FROM 1711 TO 1713

✠

The journey to Paris was very long, painful and punctuated by innumerable halts. Although assisted by Domenico, Cloridia and myself (now recovered except for the voice), Atto had to travel constantly in a litter.

We had sold my profitable chimney-sweeping business very quickly to a family of Italians. Camilla, with the influence of Porta Coeli to back her, had handled the negotiations brilliantly: nuns, as is well known, are always highly skilled negotiators. I had sent the proceeds from the sale to our two girls in Rome: it was the longed-for dowry.

I would have liked to sell the vineyard with the house in the Josephina as well: I was terrified at the idea of abandoning the property like that, until who knew when. But Cloridia did not agree and had asked her sister for help. So Camilla reassured us that she would keep an eye on it personally. Abbot Melani approved: "What the merchants want to do is strip us of our lands, giving us waste paper in return, which, at their own whim, may turn out to be worth nothing at all from one day to the next. Land has no price, my boy: it feeds us and so makes us free."

In Paris Atto lived in the Street of the Old Augustinians, in a rented apartment belonging to a certain Monsieur de Montholon. Curious, I thought; we had left the convent of the Augustinians of Porta Coeli to come and live in a street named after the same religious order.

At first I had thought I would be a servant of Atto's, a footman or something similar. But when I arrived I realised I was not needed at all: the old castrato had a great swarm of house servants. And even though the old housekeeper had retired, and Cloridia had therefore quickly found a place for herself in the Abbot's house, while our little boy filled his days with study, I could not really see what there was for me to do, without even the gift of speech.

I did not yet know that Atto had some very particular projects in mind – and he had been planning them for some time now.

It was not the first time that he had asked me to go and live with him. He had offered me the chance twenty-eight years earlier, in 1683, but I had refused, outraged by the Abbot's thousand intrigues and lies.

Now he could finally make his wish come true. In order that I should not feel superfluous he put me in charge of numerous things and gave me a salary worthy of a cardinal's secretary. I spent most of the time, to tell the truth, just listening to him. He began one day, almost by chance, to tell me about his origins, his infancy and his childhood dreams, more and more confidentially, omitting nothing, not even the terrible day when the barber turned up at his father's house with the blades that were to castrate him, confining his dreams to one inevitable path.

Very soon Atto was in full spate. He held forth to me day and night: during meals, with his mouth full, after leaving everyone else outside the door, until late at night, when he found it hard to fall asleep and tore me from my conjugal bed to keep him company. Cloridia understood the old castrato's whims and was patient: she had grown very fond of the now almost totally harmless old man.

Abbot Melani told me everything, absolutely everything: what I did not yet know of him, intrigues and secrets that shocked me, unforgivable sins which he would soon have to account for before the Most High. As he relived that past, sometimes he was overcome by dejection. At other times he seemed resigned to the fact that he must pay the price of the penitent sinner. And so, during the three years I remained with him, the numerous decades of his long life went sweeping before my eyes, until he began to recall the years of his maturity, and then he told me what I already knew, or rather what I thought I knew, stories I had lived through with him and where I thought I had uncovered everything, understood everything, and instead . . .

❧❦

In other respects, our lives together with the old castrato ran smoothly. We received regular letters from our daughters, who had finally got engaged to good young men, of modest circumstances (in

Rome, capital of usury, it could hardly be otherwise), but full of goodwill.

From the very beginning, our stay in Paris was plagued by the continual squabbles between Atto and his relatives. Domenico, as Abbot Melani had told me in advance, was soon sent back to Tuscany. A certain Champigny assiduously visited the house now and acted as secretary: Atto dictated to him all the missives that he sent to his relatives in Italy, so that his nephews and nieces would continue to think that he was irremediably blind. Domenico would not betray him: he knew that a substantial bequest awaited him by way of reward.

It was a continual tug of war, not unlike a squabble among children. In June the Abbot vainly rebuked his relatives for not having sent him the candied oranges, as if Paris were not full of Italian patisserie shops! Then he went on to complain about the little wood he owned in Tuscany, which was going to rack and ruin from neglect. In August the Abbot finally wrote to his relatives that he knew perfectly well how much money entered the Melani household, because when Domenico had obtained the post of secretary of the Council of Siena, he had been sent a note from Florence of all the emoluments and honours the household enjoyed. After this blow, his nephews and nieces, in an attempt to appease him, promised to send him a fellow villager with a sausage and mortadella of excellent quality, not like the hard, peppery one that they had sent him before he set out for Vienna.

But it was not only sorrows that came from Tuscany. His lands, indeed his country house itself, were being visited at that time by the Connestabilessa Maria Mancina, his old and adored friend, the one whom I myself had seen intriguing with Atto eleven years earlier in Rome, and who had changed the destiny of Europe.

When letters came from the Connestabilessa, all clouds would vanish from Atto's face. He would at once make plans to travel to Versailles for an audience with His Majesty, to ask permission to join Maria in his Pistoia.

Every year it was the same story: when the warm weather came, Maria would arrive at Atto's Tuscan villa. The old castrato would have the carriage prepared and would drive off to ask the King for permission to return to Italy. After which, at every refusal, he would chafe miserably. But between one attempt and another, the Abbot, despite the heat, would travel back and forth from Versailles to Paris unstintingly, almost like a young man, such was the force that drove his limbs when he thought of his Connestabilessa, the only woman the old castrato had ever loved in his life. And to say that they had not seen one another for fifty years.

The Grand Duke also continued to torment him with requests to assist his favourites. In autumn that year Atto had a fall in his bedroom, from which he hardly ever emerged for the whole winter, despite feeling in good health. The candied oranges, the high-quality mortadella and sausage, to which he had added a request for *manteca* cheese and orange-flower sweets, had still not arrived. Meanwhile he sent emissaries to Pistoia to report on the condition of his house and the appearance of his little nephew. Their task was also to get the longed-for delicacies (the Abbot would not give up) and to announce to his nephews and nieces that if the war ended in spring they would see him arrive in Pistoia, where he would stay for a whole year.

But a year later, in March 1712, peace had not come yet, and I was surprised to hear from the Abbot's own mouth words of bitter repentance at having engineered, twelve years earlier, the election of Pope Albani. He now missed his late friend, Cardinal Buonvisi, so much so that he had copies made of some of his letters which he had already sent to Pistoia so that they might be preserved for posterity.

"If he had been pope," he whined, "Tuscany would not have been oppressed by the *Alemanni*, and peace would have been made years ago. But since God wished to castigate the Christian world, he called that great man to himself two months before the election of the reigning pontiff, because if he had been alive and healthy, he would have become pope and not Albani, and I might have ended my days in Rome and not in France!"

As announced by Palatine, the war continued to rage and the people to get poorer, and so it would go on until Europe, totally destroyed, would be at the mercy of the peace that had been decided and settled by the merchants. The Abbot also ended up at their mercy: the payment of his pensions was suspended, both those of the King and those of the Hôtel de Ville, and in order to pay the thousand francs of monthly rent Atto had to start drawing on his savings.

But this was not possible for everyone. Poverty was so widespread that even people recommended by the Connestabilessa ended up behaving like common cheats. A certain Monsieur Jamal, for example, suddenly set off from Paris and changed his name so as not to pay the Abbot back the two hundred francs he had borrowed. Fortunately Madame Colonna intervened at once to settle the debt.

Amidst these tribulations, the longed-for candied oranges, finally sent by his nephews and nieces, got stolen on the journey.

Atto's only consolation was to learn from the letters of the Most Serene Grand Duke that his new-born great-nephew, for whom the Grand Duke had acted as godfather, had greatly pleased the Connestabilessa, reminding her of one of the little stucco putti that they make in Lucca. And as soon as he read news of Maria Mancini, Atto was off at the first light of dawn to beg the King yet again to let him return to Pistoia.

In 1713 Atto had two great-nephews, but his health would now not allow him to walk two paces in his room without support and he could no longer even go to mass. Furthermore, Atto was now truly blind. In a moment of inattention he had written to his nephews and nieces that "my final misfortune is I cannot read or write anymore," which amazed and infuriated his relatives, and the Grand Duke as well, who had believed him blind for years. His friend Monsieur de la Haye, who had recovered his sight at the age of eighty, had given him hope, but no such miracle came about in Atto's case.

Sensing that the Abbot would not live long, the Grand Duke sent Domenico to him in the summer. Atto was very weak, but still hoped for a miracle that would allow him to return to Pistoia.

In that same year, 1713, France hit rock-bottom: the economy was in such a state that according to Abbot Melani a hundred years of peace would not suffice to pay the King's debts. All the kingdom's revenue was tied up, and for this reason it was feared that the accounts of the Hôtel de Ville's revenue were being falsified. For two whole years pensions had not been paid, even though half the kingdom survived on that income. Atto had now gone though all his cash savings, and did not know how to pay the rent, and the return to Pistoia now took on the meaning of a flight *in extremis*: fortunately he was still very rich in real estate.

In November 1713 he learned that Maria was still in his house in Pistoia, and hoped that the King would finally set him free. Peace was almost made: Prince Eugene and the Marshal of Villars had met up in Rastatt and it was thought that before Christmas the armistice would be signed. Europe was in ruins. Atto planned to return to Versailles as soon as winter was over, in April, to beg the Most Christian King to let him go back home. Gondi, the Medicis' secretary, was looking for a house for him in Florence, in Borgo Santo Spirito: as soon as he found a suitable residence he would let him know. Atto, in fact, had no intention of retiring from political life and, heedless of his age, planned to travel between Florence and Pistoia.

He trusted that with the coming of peace the King would finally agree to let him go, and so he wrote to everyone in Pistoia. He could not know that this was to be his last letter to his nephews and nieces.

In that harsh winter, while Atto lived his last few months of life, I went into a bookshop that I often visited, owned by a Pontevedrine. Another customer, who was following me, overtook me on his long legs and got served before me. His face was wrapped in a thick woollen scarf. He asked the bookseller if he had a book of stories: *From Half-Asia* was the title. The bookseller said in surprise that he had never heard of it. As he turned to walk out the customer grumbled in vexation:

"Pontevedrines, bah. Half-Asia!"

I raised my eyes as in a dream and saw the glaucous eyes of a slightly stooping spindleshanks whom I well knew winking at me slyly from behind his woollen scarf . . .

He thrust something into my hand and then disappeared rapidly down the road. I would have liked to chase him, but he was much younger and faster; I would have liked to shout, but I was dumb; I would have liked to cry but it would have been useless. I laughed, more and more heartily, and feeling as light as a feather I lowered my eyes to see what he had thrust into my hand. It was a slim volume:

Doctoris Henrici Casparis Abelii

Studenten-Künste

There was a small bookmark. I opened it. It indicated – as I had anticipated – the page concerning the artifices to make clothes resistant to weapons, to put someone to sleep for three days and finally to get dogs to obey one. In a flash I could see it: the panther and the other animals drugged or tamed, my assistant escaping down the tunnel that emerged onto the plain of Simmering. And of course, Frosch had even told us about it. I had forgotten; Simonis had not. In the margin was a scrawled message from Simonis, or Symon, or whatever his real name was: "Thank you." And I was happy.

$\partial \infty$

One night I dreamed of a mysterious being, concealed in a pure white, perfumed cloak, turning up in the Flying Ship and lifting me up to the bell tower of St Stephen's. There I saw the pedestal that long, long ago had held the Golden Apple. In its place stood the Imperial Orb, symbol of the Archangel Michael, defender of God's people. The being pointed out some words written there. They were the seven words of the Archangel Michael:

> *Imprimatur*
> *Secretum*
> *Veritas*
> *Mysterium*

And then, a little below these: *Unicum* . . . And the last two words inscribed by the Archangel? The Flying Ship, as if at the mercy of a storm, lurched away from the spire. I floundered, desperately seeking a handhold so that I could finish reading the message, but in vain. "*Imprimatur et secretum, veritas mysteriumst!*" the ineffable entity pronounced in a stentorian voice, adopting the concise practice of ancient epigraphs, which omits verbs and adverbs. "Let the secret be uncovered, the truth remains a mystery!" he translated.

Then he continued: "*Unicum* . . ." "There remains only . . ." What remains? Here the entity revealed itself to me. It removed its hood and revealed a smiling face: it was Ugonio. I woke with a start and so now I do not know how the sentence ends. But perhaps it is best not to investigate too closely: it might just be another of the *corpisantaro*'s harebrained messages, like the *allium ursinum* or the *Gran Legator* and the *Albanum* of the events of Villa Spada, which many years ago had thrown me and Atto off the trail in our investigations . . .

Paris
6ᵀᴴ JANUARY 1714

✠

Someone accidentally jostles me and jerks me back to the present. The few bystanders are moving: Abbot Melani's funeral is now at an end. The silver angels that have compassionately supported his mortal remains during the ceremony now return the bier to his old servants, and they make towards the side chapel near the high altar, opposite the door to the sacristy, for the entombment. The place is ready, open and empty, awaiting the coffin. The funerary monument by the Florentine Rastrelli will soon ornament the chapel with a noble bust of the Abbot, for any French subjects who pass this way to remember him by.

It took the epidemic of catarrhal influenza, recorded in the medical annals and well described by Doctor Viti in his treatise, to break the old Abbot's resistance. The first symptoms began in December: fever; coughing; some slight inflammation of the throat; low, weak pulse; copious spitting of thin blood. Atto joked: "Here's the Tekuphah," laughing to overcome his fear at having really reached the end. We treated him with massages and barley water, which made him sweat and brought about great improvements. But the spitting was still copious, though now it was white. The doctors declared: "spurious lymphatic pleuritis": cryptic words that sounded like Ugonio talking. They administered myrrh mixed with camphor, laxatives, emollients and even whale sperm, a remedy that was so expensive that the Abbot lost all the benefit when the moment came to pay.

When the worst was over, Atto once again had all his wits about him and had recovered his usual spirits. However, I often saw him by the window, absorbed, with his half-closed eyes ranging over the grey slate rooftops, while he hummed for the umpteenth time an aria written for him by Luigi Rossi, and – I was sure of it – thought with a smile of the boy king listening to him in the castle of Saint Germain, sixty years earlier. And perhaps he thought of the capricious intertwining of fortune and bad luck, of jealous fits, friendships, betrayals, impossible loves; of acts of violence endured; of one in particular, and of the destiny it had implacably determined. Observing him unseen, I liked to imagine that he was using the delicate scales of memory to weigh up faults and merits, knowing that he had served music and the Most Christian King with equal loyalty; and that soon it would be time to serve a greater master.

Domenico, Champigny and I still feared the excessive catarrh he had in his chest and the slight tertian fever that disturbed him during the day. We prayed he would get through the winter, but he appeared resigned to the will of God. He was fully prepared and ready for the great step, and discussed his death with firmness and constancy, instructing Domenico on a number of things that he wanted carried out afterwards, and personally making sure that all his writings and books were packed up and delivered to Count Bardi, the envoy of the Medici in Paris, who could then send them on to Pistoia. There were too many secrets hidden in Abbot Melani's letters and memoirs to run the risk of leaving them in the house after his death!

Just over a week ago, on St Stephen's Day, 26th December, I heard him complain: "The season could not be more contrary to my convalescence," immediately adding with a touch of vanity: "But even the most robust are feeling it." What an optimist Abbot Melani was! He talked of his death, but he did not really believe in it. What he stubbornly called convalescence was actually agony.

After four days, on 30th December, he insisted on getting out of bed, saying that he felt suffocated, so that we had to humour him by putting him on a chair. Even that was not enough: he wanted to walk a few paces across the room, supported by me and Domenico. But as soon as he tried to move, he exclaimed, "Alas, I can't make it", and we had to make him sit down at once. He had fainted and we put him straight back to bed. Cloridia rushed to our summons, and bathed him with the water of the Queen of Hungary, sent to him most considerately every year by Gondi, the Grand Duke's secretary, and it soon brought him round. But just a quarter of an hour later the illness seized hold of him again.

"Don't abandon me," he said, and then lost consciousness and remained like that, without speaking or moving, for almost four days, to the amazement of the doctors, who had never seen such a resilient heart in a man of eighty-eight. The day before yesterday, Wednesday 4th January, two hours after midnight, he opened his eyes and looked at me. I was seated by his bed. I had never abandoned him, as he had done with me three years earlier; I took his cold bony hands in mine. He murmured: "Stay with me." Then, with a long sigh of weariness, he went.

∂∾⊚

As I cross the church of the Barefoot Augustinians, I feel as if Atto is still by my side: like that other time, that freezing 20th April three years ago, in another church, also – by a twist of fate – of the Barefoot Augustinians. The occasion was the exequies of His Caesarean Majesty Joseph the Victorious. Nothing in the world could have stopped me being there: the only other funeral I have ever attended. I cannot follow Abbot Melani's bier without feeling lashed by the icy north wind of memories.

In the Loggia of the Cavaliers the Emperor, having received the benediction of the Bishop of Vienna, had been transferred to a new sarcophagus, draped in black and gold velvet, and sealed forever with golden nails. The coffin was adorned with gold all over: the locks, the keys, the handles and the initials I.I., Joseph I, engraved in the middle. The Barefoot Carmelite Sisters of St Joseph had covered the bier with the cloth they always preserve for the burials of the Caesars. At the foot they had placed the crowns of Bohemia and Hungary; at the head the Caesarian insignia with the Golden Fleece; and in the middle the dagger and short sword with their imperial eagle hilts. The urn with the heart and tongue of the deceased had been trans-ported, in the absolute silence imposed by the ceremony, to the Loretan Chapel of the church of the Barefoot Augustinians, and placed there among the other eight urns containing the hearts of his predecessors, starting with the young Ferdinand IV who had begun the tradition out of devotion to the Madonna of Loreto. Immediately afterwards, the shrine containing the brain, eyes and bowels had been taken in a six-horse carriage escorted by a procession of candles to the Cathedral of St Stephen and placed there in the archducal crypt: twenty-two other collections of grey matter and internal organs, those of the previous Habsburgs of Austria, would silently receive it.

During the ceremony, black night had stolen in, and with it had come the much-feared farewell. We returned to the Loggia de'

Cavalieri, where the Queen Mother and the other members of the imperial family had arrived in the meantime – all except the widow Queen, whose great grief had detained her in the palace with her youngest daughter. Followed by the whole court and the Papal Nuncio, the bier was then transported along the low corridor of the palace to the church of the Barefoot Augustinians and placed there on a black litter, around which, in the hour between 20 and 21, every funeral rite had been solemnly celebrated. The Augustinians then handed things over to the Capuchins for the interment.

And now it was the moment of the people. The faithful subjects had come from all around into the church of the Capuchins, and at 21 hours, announced by the powerful tolling of the bells of all the churches in the Archduchy of Austria and illuminated by thousands and thousands of torches protected by glass lanterns and fixed to every bell tower to vanquish the mournful darkness, the Emperor's lifeless body made its entrance between two dozen white torches, their flames flickering in the furious wind, carried by the scions of the nobility. It was awaited by the city guard, with their banners held upside down, while from the dark belly of the drums the rhythmic rumble of death reverberated all around.

Atto and I were also awaiting the deceased, almost suffocated amid the immense crowd. I could barely make out the procession; right behind the bier walked the Queen Mother, impassive and impenetrable, surrounded by three gentlemen of the chamber and illuminated by the torches of seven noble scions: Her Majesty Eleanor Magdalen Theresa had just been named Regent. Abbot Melani, as I would learn later, with the help of Camilla and of Vinzenz Rossi, had succeeded in getting the forged letter of Prince Eugene into her hands, to put a stop somehow to the Prince's desire for war and prevent him from becoming equally powerful under the future emperor Charles. Atto knew very well that Eugene would continue the war against France even without his allies England and Holland. There was no knowing whether that letter would finally be of any use or not.

Behind the Queen Mother came Joseph's sisters and elder daughter, also escorted by a cluster of torches, buffeted mercilessly by the raging wind.

The court musicians intoned the *Libera me Domine* and Joseph was at last escorted to his final resting place: the crypt of the Capuchins.

In that very year the Emperor had prophetically enlarged it, doubling its capacity. Now it would receive him in the large central sarcophagus, the golden key to which would be preserved forever in the imperial treasure chamber along with all the other tomb keys of the Habsburgs of Austria. And so ended the barely thirty-three years of the earthly adventure of His Caesarean Majesty Joseph the Victorious, first of his name.

Vienna

DECEMBER 1720

✠

After Abbot Melani's death I left Paris, as did Domenico.

The War of the Spanish Succession is over. It has left behind it thirteen years of famine, devastation and death. In 1713 the Treaty of Utrecht was signed, in 1714 the Peace of Rastatt and that of Baden.

Everything has gone as Atto foretold: the English merchants have grabbed the most appetising booty. England has snatched Gibraltar and the monopoly of slaves from Spain, and the North American colonies from France.

But it is not only the instigators but also the accomplices of these new times who have been rewarded.

Emperor Charles VI, brother and successor of Joseph, has been awarded the Spanish Netherlands, Milan, Mantua, Naples and Sardinia. In Spain, on 11th September 1714, the Franco-Spanish troops of Philip of Anjou, now King Philip V of Bourbon, entered Barcelona and put a bloody end to the independence of the city Charles had abandoned in his haste to ascend the longed-for imperial throne.

The Savoys have been raised from the rank of double-dealing dukes, as Atto described them, to that of kings, and have been awarded Sicily: all thanks to Eugene. And so the Italian peninsula is caught in the Savoyard vice: to the north Piedmont, to the south Sicily. The perfect prelude for the other project of the dervish's friends: that one day Italy will have a king.

In 1713 Landau was besieged once again, but this time by the French, as it had remained under the Empire since 1704, when Joseph reconquered it for the second time. Yet again the garrison commander, Prince Karl Alexander von Wüttemberg, had to coin money using his own gold and silver dining service. A repetition, though in reverse: this time the French won. It was Prince Eugene's fault: if he had not gone on with the war to the bitter end, the Empire would have kept Landau.

Atto's prophecy about Eugene has come true: Charles VI made him (and makes him) do what he wants. Delivering the forged letter to the Queen Mother has proven totally useless.

But on the horizon, clouds are gathering for the Caesarean dynasty: as the dervish foretold, the House of Habsburg will soon peter out and Germany will have its own king. Charles VI has no male children, just two girls. And the heir to the imperial throne can only be male. To tell the truth, Charles's firstborn was a son, born four years ago, in 1716, but he died just a few months later: exactly what happened to Joseph's little son. What a coincidence.

Charles VI's heirs should be Joseph's daughters. But obviously he does not relish the idea. This was made clear in 1713 when, even though he still had no progeny after five years of marriage, he issued the Pragmatic Sanction: on his death his own children, if any – not Joseph's – would ascend the throne. Therefore it will be his elder daughter, Maria-Theresa, born three years ago, who will inherit. An arbitrary act, in every sense. The other countries in Europe refuse to accept it, and so for years Charles has been pleading with them, one by one, imploring them to recognise the Pragmatic Sanction. In exchange he makes endless promises, even the surrender of territory. Anything to prevent a daughter of his hated brother from sitting on the throne.

But Charles's hatred is weakening the Empire. The German princes are chafing: the moment is coming when Germany will secede (as Palatine predicted) and will have its own sovereign, no longer in Catholic Vienna.

In short, as Atto feared, this war has marked the end of the world, but has not replaced it with a new one; no, the agony of humanity has simply begun. Now it is an oligarchy that coldly decides the destinies of lands thousands of miles away: the colonies of the New World and the Italian territories were reorganized from Utrecht. Political alliances are no longer the fulcrum of international diplomacy, but just token operations: they are decided by the financial backers of the crowns. And those, like the Most Christian King or Joseph the Victorious, who will not let themselves be manipulated, are rendered impotent, along with their descendants. Dynastic rights or military conquests no longer count for anything; only just money, or rather finance matters. Wasn't it during the war of succession that coins began to be replaced by paper?

౽ఞ

From the friends we still have in Paris, I have heard that life has got harder there; even harder than in Rome, and that is saying something.

Five years ago, in 1715, the Sun King died: of gangrene, exactly as Palatine had foretold. And he died almost without heirs. Between 1711 and 1712 *all* his legitimate children and grandchildren died (this, too, was predicted by the dervish), except a child aged two, Louis, saved by his nurses, who locked themselves up with him in a wing of the palace, preventing the doctors not only from touching him, but even from seeing him. They were convinced that the other members of the royal family had not died from their sicknesses but from their treatments . . .

Atto Melani had been right: "With a king like the Grand Dauphin, France would finally emerge from its downward spiral of arrogance and destruction; England and Holland want the opposite to happen. The country must continue to degenerate, the court must be hated by the people. It annoys them that the Most Christian King has adult sons and grandsons; the ideal would be if there were no heir, or if he were a baby, which amounts to the same thing."

The days when the Most Christian King, aged just four, ascended the throne are over. In those days, to defend the country from the interference of other powers there were the Queen Mother, Anne of Austria, and the Prime Minister, Cardinal Mazarin. Now there is no longer a queen, nor a prime minister.

"Louis XIV has taken everything into his own hands," said Atto. "After his death a regency would leave the country at the mercy of the first scheming meddler, who might just happen to be sent by England or Holland to set off a mine under France's backside."

Exactly. The death of the Most Christian King is exactly what Palatine's friends were waiting for: just a few months later their man dropped in from Holland. It was the Englishman John Law, with his theory of finance, which led France to an economic collapse unprecedented in centuries and centuries of history.

This year the swindler's treatise was published: *Money and Trade Considered*. There was a French translation, but I never managed to find it. I do not know English but my son does; Atto knew that England would be the real winner of the war and, although reluctantly, he arranged for him to be taught the merchants' language, alongside Italian, Latin, Greek, German and French.

And so, finally, thanks to my little boy's reading (actually he is now a handsome lad) I can see in plain black and white the heresy with which Law delivered the death blow to France: according to him the best incentive for the country's productive growth is ... loans and property in banknotes! Not the good old coins of old, which were worth their weight in gold. In short, he was a friend of the usurers.

With this cheap huckster's fib he managed to persuade the Regent Philip II of Orléans to let him found the General Bank in 1716. The war of succession has brought France so low that the Regent hoped to have found the solution to his debts in this man Law. From 1718, under the new name of the Royal Bank, the insti-tute issued gigantic quantities of notes, which it distributed to the French with promises fit for nincompoops, demanding in exchange all the gold, silver and lands they owned. If their goods were worth a hundred, Law would give them a note with the words: "This is worth five hundred", with the promise they could have their property back whenever they wanted it. The subjects of the Kingdom of France all rushed to entrust their property to him, in exchange for scraps of paper stained with ink.

It is incredible how ingenuous these French are: they feel supe-rior to everyone else and are always ready to glorify themselves, but then they go flocking after the first charlatan that comes along.

In January this year, the Regent even granted Law the post of General Controller of Finances, the job held by Superintendent Fouquet and then by Minister Colbert!

It did not last long. In March Palatine's friends delivered the final blow: they circulated doubts about Law's credibility, and all of a sudden the French went rushing to the Royal Bank to ask for the gold, silver and lands that they had pawned for his banknotes. The Regent first halved the value of the banknotes, then stopped all payments. "We no longer have anything," the bank candidly responded to the French subjects. The bank was closed, John Law fled to Venice and the French were left stony broke.

Atto had foreseen it, the dervish had predicted: the typhoon of financial ruin and popular outcry struck France, and then passed on to the rest of Europe, already prostrated by the war of succession.

Money, for centuries and centuries has always had the same value, but now that there is just paper and no more gold or silver, it is worth less every day. I am among the privileged few who can sleep easily: I still have the vineyard in the Josephina.

⌘

And so I went back to Vienna. But the city is no longer what it was. On the bell tower of St Stephen's is the magnificent bell that Joseph had had cast from the Turkish cannons, which the people soon nicknamed Pummerin. It did not ring for the Emperor's thirty-three years, as had been planned: death came first. And so they hung Pummerin in October, and inaugurated it in January 1712 to celebrate the arrival of the new Emperor, Charles VI. A few months later, in December, divine wrath fell upon the usurper: the plague broke out, and raged for the whole of 1713, carrying off eight thousand innocent victims. And here was another echo from the past, another circle closing in on itself: the *secretum pestis* that thirty years earlier had saved Vienna from the contagion deliberately procured by the besieging Turks could do nothing against the scourge of God this time.

I have heard of the bad end of Countess Marianna Pálffy, Joseph's young lover, whom Abbot Melani had vainly tried to approach. As soon as Joseph had died, the Queen Mother, the ministers and the whole court lashed out at her, even forcing her to give back the presents received from her deceased lover. Fallen into disgrace, banned from the court, she was forced into a lowly marriage, to the despair of her father, the poor Count Johann Pálffy ab Erdöd, one of the most faithful and valiant commanders of the Caesarean house.

From the day of Joseph's death the sun no longer rose blood-red: it was truly an omen, famous throughout the city, and was still being talked of today. The almanac of the English fortune-teller, after correctly prophesying Joseph's death, now sells widely throughout Vienna. It truly is a golden age for the English.

The Italians, on the other hand, so well-loved by the Habsburgs up to the time of Joseph, are no longer popular. The French are arriving, summoned by the man who was their bitterest enemy in

Spain: Charles VI. Italian itself, cultivated by Joseph, is being gradually supplanted by French as the court language. As soon as he arrived
in Vienna, Charles sacked all the palace staff who had served his
deceased brother. The first to fall were the court musicians favoured
by Joseph. He replaced them with others, including very few
Italians. Obviously Camilla's services were no longer required, nor
have her oratorios been performed since.

Overwhelmed by her memories, Cloridia's sister asked and was
allowed to change convent. She is now at St Lawrence, seeking
peace. The good musicians often go to visit her, but she does not
wish to see anyone, except my wife.

Despite everything, Vienna, the capital and Caesarean residence,
is still the best place to live in these times. In no other city can one
live so well if one wishes to be secluded from the world.

I am finally living in the house with the vineyard in the Josephina
that the Abbot one day gave me, which fostered so many dreams and
hopes in my and in my family's hearts.

The girls are now in Vienna as well; 𝕰𝖝𝖆𝖒𝖎𝖓𝖎𝖊𝖗𝖙 𝖚𝖓𝖉 𝕬𝖕𝖕𝖗𝖔𝖇𝖎𝖊𝖗𝖙, they
have obtained their midwives' licences and are both mothers.
Cloridia has a wine shop selling *Heuriger* or new wine, with the help
of our son and our two sons-in-law, bright young Romans very happy
to leave the capital of usury in search of a life worthy of the name.
Hands are needed to cultivate the vineyard, and, of course, hoeing in
the sun – for my boy too – is healthier than breathing soot. And in
winter we can stay inside in the warmth instead of freezing on the
rooftops. Even though chimney-sweeps are well paid in Vienna, one
cannot put a price on one's health. And in any case, they no longer
need anyone to clean the chimneys at Neugebäu: the new emperor
does not want to restore it.

Of course, with the education that my son received at Abbot
Melani's home, he could aspire to something greater. He could
continue to study, acquire learning and knowledge: but to know is to
suffer. And anyway, as Abbot Melani said, land feeds you and so
makes you free. The best choice is still the one Cincinnatus made.

❧❦

I have finally found the answer to my query. Now, only now, can I
hear their voices distinctly. I have not heard the yelling again, nor the
song of the *folia*. I remain in religious silence. But I now hear all

those spectres that appeared to me at the Place with No Name whispering among themselves. They have formed a circle around me. I see landscapes and faces that are not unknown to me: the French castle of Vaux-le-Vicomte fades into the Roman Villa of the Vessel and the Place with No Name; and Superintendent Fouquet into Maximilian II and Joseph I. And two dates that I have encountered many – too many – times, come back to me: the 5th and 11th September.

The 5th September was the Most Christian King's birthday, but also the day when he had Superintendent Fouquet arrested. It was also the day Suleiman died and the day Maximilian, ten years later, succumbed to agony. On that same day, over a century later, Vienna under siege came close, thanks to an Armenian traitor, to falling prey to the Infidels. My wife Cloridia, who sometimes likes to amuse herself with the occult science of numbers, which was her specialty when young, has informed me that the sum of Louis XIV's birthday is 5, and also Suleiman's day of death, while that of the arrest of Fouquet is 10, which is to say twice 5.

On 11th September 1683 the Christian troops arrived to free Vienna with the battle that would be fought at first light on the following day. And again it was 11th September when I first met Abbot Atto Melani. The same day in 1697 Prince Eugene defeated the Turks in the famous Battle of Zenta, and in 1709 the French at Malplaquet. On 11th September 1702 Joseph conquered Landau for the first time. The same day in 1714 Barcelona and Catalonia, abandoned by Charles, finally fell into the hands of Philip V with a bloodbath.

Only now do I finally understand: I have returned to where I started from. You have received, you will not receive anymore, I hear them whisper to me. Now you must give. You have learned, now you must teach. You have lived, now you must give life.

From the day of my arrival in Vienna, in 1711, everything gradually began to talk to me of the past: first just in hints, like the resurfacing of Cloridia's mother on Camilla's lips. From the time I finally visited the Place with No Name, the events of the past and those of the present interwove their frantic double gallop: from the Flying Ship to the death of Ugonio, whom I had met twenty-eight years earlier, up to the news in the *Corriere Ordinario* and the *Wiennerisches Diarium*, which in one way or another spoke to me of the past.

Life, in imparting its teachings to me, had chosen to repeat old tunes from the past: it indicated that it was time to give back what I had received. It was time to transform myself, from the spectator that I was, into an actor for other spectators; to turn from schoolboy into teacher, for new schoolchildren; to change from a vessel into a source of living water, to be poured into other vessels. As in the parable of the talents, I was called not to bury the money that the Lord had entrusted to me but to risk it, investing it in order to multiply it. In what form? I had already been given the answer: with the past. With the experience accumulated and with the tales that Abbot Melani had told me in the three years spent with him in Paris. Atto's life would become my life, his memories my memories. Art would be my shelter and my workshop.

And so, that which thirty years ago had been just a pastime for a young inn servant, and seventeen years ago had become a task *una tantum* given me by Atto, has now become a life choice.

I write of the last century, of time now lost, the last century of mankind. In my books I transfuse what I have experienced with the Abbot, and what I have experienced through his tales. My ear has discovered the sound of actions, my eye the gesture of speeches, and my voice, where it limited itself to repeating, dictates to the pen so that the fundamental note shall be fixed for all time.

It is a lengthy task to pour so much of the past onto paper! At times I ask: "Will I have enough time? Am in a fit condition to do it?" Cradling in my hand the coin of Landau that Cloridia never returned to Prince Eugene's chest, I fear that I will not have the strength to keep a close hold on this past, which already seems so far away. For the most part I work when everything around me is asleep. I will need many nights, perhaps a hundred, perhaps a thousand or more, to transfer to paper the imprint of time.

Our senses make many mistakes and hence falsify the real appearance of life, if such a thing exists. In my transcription, which I try to make as accurate as possible, I do not alter sounds or colours, I never separate them from their cause, which is where intelligence locates them after hearing and seeing them. I describe the hundred masks that every face possesses; in some personages I represent every gesture, however slight, that was the cause of mortal upheavals and led to variations in the light of our moral heaven, unsettling the serenity of our certainties. In transcribing a universe that is to be entirely redesigned, I do not fail to represent the reader, but with the measurements not of his body but of his years – years that he unconsciously drags about with him wherever he goes in life, a task that is increasingly arduous and which finally overwhelms him.

We all occupy a place, not only in space, but also and above all in time. So, this concept of incorporated time, of the years spent that are not separate from us: this is the truth, the truth suspected by everyone, and which I have to try to elucidate. And on the day that, having "drawn the bow" and separated the wheat from the chaff, the master of my fate will ask me to account for myself, I will pour into His Hands the fruit of my labour.

かめか

A quill pen and a piece of paper: I have no other way of communicating with men. I have not regained my voice, I have remained dumb forever. In some part of these notes appear these words: "I suffered from that silence, which was like a place anyone could enter and be sure of a welcome. I ardently wished that my silence would close around me." Well, now it has. I could not present myself more fittingly as servant of the black thread in a white field – an image that reminds me strongly of Hristo's chess-board, which saved my life.

The pen is my voice, and, apart from occasionally helping my two sons-in-law to hoe the vineyard, writing is the only job that a dumb man can do. A printer in Amsterdam kindly prints and sells my books. I send my manuscripts up there, into free Holland: "Under the sign of the Busy Bee" is the address, and I like to think that it is a metaphor for my humble but unflagging work.

Sometimes the old discouragement seizes me. I, who had eyes to see the world in this way, with a fixed stare that affected it and made it become what I had prophetically seen it to be – if Heavenly Justice was behind this, it was unjust that I had not been not annihilated beforehand; I repeat this to myself from the depths of my soul.

Have I deserved that my mortal anguish should be appeased in this way? What is it that proliferates in my nights? Why was I not given the power to strike down the world's sin with a single axe-blow? Do my books touch any consciences? Why am I not given the intellectual strength to force violated mankind to start shouting? Why is my shouted response, which I entrust to pen and paper, not louder than the shrill command that dominates the souls of a terrestrial globe?

I preserve documents for an age that will not understand them, or which will live so far from what happens today that it will say I was a forger. But no, the time to say this will not come, because that time will not be. In my books I write of a single immense tragedy, the defeated hero of which is mankind, whose tragic conflict, being that between world and nature, finishes with death. Alas, since it has no other hero than mankind, this drama does not even have any other audience. But what does my tragic hero perish of? He is a hero who perishes as a consequence of a situation that intoxicated him, even as it constrained him.

Ah . . . if mankind one day, by the grace of God, should emerge safely from this adventure – however afflicted, impoverished and aged – and the magic of a supreme law of retaliation should give it the power to call them to answer one by one – them, the ringleaders of universal crime, who always survive: Palatine, Penicek, and all the other serfs, the henchmen and satraps, Beelzebub's little slaves. Ah, if we could lock them up in their temples and then draw by lot a death sentence for one in ten, but not kill them; no: slap them! And say to them: what, you didn't know? You didn't imagine that following upon a declaration of war, among the countless possibilities of horror and shame there was the chance that children might go without their mother's milk? What, you didn't measure the tribulation of a single hour of anguish in an imprisonment that lasts for years? You didn't measure the tribulation of a sigh of nostalgia, of love soiled, violated, murdered? And you did not realize how tragedy could turn into farce – or rather, given the coexistence of the present monstrous situation, and the old formalist delirium – into comic opera? Into one of those revolting comic operas so popular today, whose texts are an insult to the intelligence and whose music is a torture.

Under the shelter of this new demon from England called finance, hysteria overcomes nature. Its armed henchman is paper. The gazettes have experienced a real boom in these years, one that shows no sign of letting up. And as a young man I wanted to be a gazetteer! Fortunately Abbot Melani, in that distant, so distant 1683, did what was needed to put me off the idea.

They are nothing but machines, these newspapers, which feed upon the life of men. The life that these machines devour is naturally no more than it can be in such an age, an age of machines; production that is stupid on the one hand, and mad on the other, inevitably, and both bearing the stamp of vulgarity.

Paper rules the military and has crippled us even before there were any victims of the cannons. Had not all the realms of fantasy already been stripped bare when that sheet of paper imprinted by the press declared war on the inhabited land? It is not that the press set in motion the machines of death, but it drained our hearts, so that we can no longer imagine how things would be without newspapers and without war. It is to blame for that. And all the people have drunk of the wine of its lust, and the kings of the earth have fornicated with it, and we fell because of the Whore of Babylon, which – having been printed and propagated in all the languages of the world – persuaded us that we were enemies and that there must be war.

🙐🙑

There, it is done. As far as writing goes, I have written. I have done my duty, to the very end. Have I been fed to life? Well then, I feed my life to pen and paper. My books combat the gazettes. It is good. No one can deny that I have attained my perfection. "The stone the builders rejected has now become the cornerstone," recites the Psalm, as Simonis said to the dervish that night at the Place with No Name.

Like the chariot of the sun careering at a dazzling gallop, other words from Simonis pierce my thoughts: the game is never really over, the world is a test bed that the Almighty has prepared for souls and so we are all a part of his plans, even His enemies. I forgot those words too quickly, even though they sent a shiver down the dervish's spine. I'm sorry, Simonis, my despair – unbridled Cassandra of the Last Days of Mankind – prevents me from letting them germinate within me, at least for now.

Meanwhile I find my salvation, all alone, in my silence, with my silence, which has made me so – as the age wishes – perfect.

Only Cloridia has gradually understood; she smiles serenely and our embraces have the warmth of earlier days. My two good sons-in-law, however, do not wish to understand, and every day they come to try and shake me out of this silence of mine, now absolute. They would like me to cry, so that at least with my eyes I should appear afflicted or enraged, so that I too should believe that life is out there, in the superfluity of the world. I do not bat an eyelid. I replace my quill in the inkwell and gaze at them, rigid and motionless, and I make them run off again, infuriated. On my account my daughters study these new treatises of nervous pathology, so fashionable among young doctors, who only know how to hold a scalpel to dissect corpses, but can no longer compose a small poem. As if science could exist without letters ... My daughters propose injections and balsams, they hover around me to persuade me to get my vocal cords examined by some renowned doctor.

No, thank you. Thank you, everyone. Enough now. I want to stay as I am. This is our age; this is life; and in the meaning I give to my work, I want to continue like this – dumb and impassive – to be a writer.

Is the stage ready?

Raise the curtain!

Pistoia
1644

✠

The carriage groans, the horses foam at the mouth while the dust that enters our compartment envelops us like a cloud of misapplied rouge. We will eat a good deal of this stuff on our way to Rome. We have only been travelling for a quarter of an hour, and my poor limbs are already creaking like the axle of our coach.

I lean out of the window, gaze back and in the morning mist I see the roofs of Pistoia gradually become veiled. Soon they will vanish. Then I look ahead, towards the invisible, distant zenith where the embrace of the Holy City awaits us.

My young lord, the eighteen-year-old Atto Melani, stays in his seat. His eyes are closed. He opens them every so often, looks around himself and then closes them again. It almost seems that the great journey is of no interest to him, but I know that it is not so.

Atto's baptismal godfather, Messer Sozzifanti, before entrusting him to me, had given me profuse advice: "His nature is impulsive. You will have to keep an eye on him, advise him, temper him. Such refined talents must be made use of: he will have to obey the master we found for him, the great Luigi Rossi, in all things, and win his sympathy. Let him avoid bad company, behave righteously, and never give scandal if he wishes to acquire honour. Rome is a nest of vipers, where hotheads always fall into error."

I nodded and thanked him, before bowing, without asking any questions. I already knew what I had not been told: the essence.

I have in my care the most talented castrato that has ever been seen in the Grand Duchy of Tuscany. In Rome the greatest teachers will transform him into the greatest soprano of our age. He will become rich and celebrated.

It is easy to guess that it will not be simple to make him behave sensibly. He comes from a poor family (his father is the humble bell ringer of the Cathedral of Pistoia) but the Grand Duke's brother, the powerful Mattias de' Medici, already holds him in the palm of his hand. I just glance at him, the young Atto, I see the cleft in the middle of his chin tremble a little and I understand everything. While he keeps his eyes closed, and pretends to be asleep, I can almost hear his chest swelling with pride at the protection he is being afforded by the powerful, and his eyes flickering under his eyelids, trying to grasp the dreams of glory that are dancing before him like crazy butterflies. Instead of thinking of petticoats, like young men of his age, his head is filled with dreams of glory, honour and social ascent. No, it will not be easy to bridle him.

And anyway: why should a young castrato be wise, and behave prudently, given that he has been set on the road to Rome by a mad and atrocious night in his childhood, when he was placed in a bathtub and had his virtues snipped by a pair of scissors, and, as the water turned crimson and his shrieks filled the room, what stepped from the bathtub was no longer a male but an atrocious freak of nature?

No, it will not be easy to keep a check on the young Atto Melani. In Rome interesting days await me, I am certain.

Veritas is written on the cover of this book [. . .]

In this comforting belief I close my book, which is at the service of truth. I have had to report so much darkness and despair. Lies and prejudice are as thick as fog over my homeland, but we wish to remain restless and not lose courage . . . *Vincit Veritas!*

(Karl Emil Franzos, From Half-Asia)

Letter

✠

Vatican City, 14th February 2042
To Don Alessio Tanari
Centrul Salesian
Costantia – ROMANIA

Dear Alessio,
This comes to bring you news of myself. On opening the parcel, you will have realised: I have sent you a copy of the new work I have received from my two friends, Rita and Francesco. Renewing a now well-established tradition between them and me, they have sent me their third work even before publication.

I am sure that you will enjoy reading it too, just as you were able to put your reading of the two previous books to good use. By the way, did you notice? After *Imprimatur*, their second book was published under the title *Secretum*. And to think that it was I who sent it to you, just a year ago. At the time I was in Romania – in Costantia, or the ancient Tomi, where Emperor Augustus had exiled the Latin poet Ovid and where you now are.

Who would have guessed that things would have altered in such a short space of time? With the death of the old pope and the election of this German pope everything has changed. His Holiness has had the benevolence to appoint me cardinal and assign me to the Holy Office. When I happen to pass in front of a mirror and see my reflected image unworthily adorned with all that purple, I find myself smiling as I recall that just a year ago, an exile in Romania, I thought I was destined to quite other purple: that of martyrdom.

And you, how do you find your new position as missionary in Romania? How does one feel after laying aside the robes of monsignor and donning those of a simple priest again? It may have struck you as a demotion, but is it not wholesome for the spirit to consider things as they appear? Don't you agree?

The Holy Father (who no sooner emerged from the conclave than he took the decision to transfer you and, with equal swiftness, summon me back) told me the other day that he remembers you very clearly, when you were my pupil at the seminary. A mission to Costantia for an undefined period is, in His opinion, what is required by the powerful ambitions you already nurtured as a young man. I mean spiritual ambitions, of course.

But let me return to the work I enclose here, and to my two old friends Rita and Francesco. His Holiness has already read it and, as he is originally from the Teutonic lands where the events narrated take place, he greatly enjoyed the narrative waltz between history and literature, which interweaves quotations from archival sources with allusions to Shakespeare, Proust and Karl Kraus, finally winking at the reader with burlesque anachronisms transposed from the most famous Viennese operettas, such as Franz Lehár's *Merry Widow* (from which the imaginary little state of Pontevedro and much else are taken), Johann Strauss Jr's *Die Fledermaus* (where Frosch is the jailer), *Countess Mariza* by Emmerich Kalmann and, of course, the *Bettelstudent* by Karl Millöcker.

In the parcel I am also sending you a recording of a chorus: the medieval motif of *Quem queritis*. I was listening to it in the very days when I was reading my friends' third book. Before explaining the reason for this dispatch, I must make some preliminary remarks.

Imprimatur Secretum Veritas Mysterium: this, according to my friends' work, is the message carved by Archangel Michael on the spire of St Stephen's. Or is it just a harebrained invention of the *corpisantaro* Ugonio? As soon as I read it, I suspected that it came from some *Flos sententiarum*, those collections of famous Latin mottoes, like *in vino veritas* or *est modus in rebus*.

As the "narrating I" justly observes, the inscription followed the epigraphic custom of omitting verbs and adverbs, and the entire sentence was *Imprimatur et secretum, veritas mysteriumst*, where *mysteriumst* obviously stands for *mysterium est*.

The use of the conjunction *et* in the sense of "even", and the verb *est*, "is", understood in the second part of the saying, were in keeping with the tradition. But the whole thing did not lead towards Seneca or Martial, nor to Cicero or Pliny. The use of the term *imprimatur*, "let it be printed", which among other things designates the *nulla osta* given by the ecclesiastic authorities for the publication of a book, provided a clear reference to the printing of a text, and therefore indicated a date well outside the classical period. They were not the words of a Roman writer, nor even of one from the late or Christian empire, but of one from modern times.

I looked it up in various anthologies of Latin sayings, including the dated but excellent one by De Mauri published by Hoepli. I found nothing, not even a vague resemblance.

But I repeated that motto over and over again, in private, like a secret, heretical rosary, or those words of mysterious power that Tibetan monks are said to mutter monotonously for an entire life in the silence of their monasteries.

And then that *Unicum* ..., that truncated conclusion which alludes to something that is left: what remains in the wilderness of uncertainties to which we are condemned by the unknowableness of truth? The answer, as I had not realised, was already dancing in the air. The song of the nuns, the music that came constantly from the stereo not far from my desk: the *Quem queritis*, from the medieval liturgical repertoire with Russian performers, a memory of my exile in Tomi – *Mitbringsel*, as the Holy Father would say.

The title, *Quem queristi*, is not an affirmation. It is a question. The Latin text, a dialogue, goes:

– *Quem queritis in sepulchro, christicole?*
– *JESVM Nazarenum crucifixum, o celicole.*
– *Non est hic, resurrexit sicut predixerat, ite nunciate quia surrexit de sepulchro.*

Quem queritis? JESVM. Jesum, Jesus, that sweet name whispered something to me. Something I already knew, but that was not clear to me. But what? After hours of vain concentration, on impulse, I tried writing it down: JESVM, in the Latin form, with V instead of U.

The next step suggested itself. Underneath, I transcribed the words of the mysterious message:

> Imprimatur
> Et
> Secretum
> Veritas
> Mysterium

It was an acrostic. And this acrostic revealed the name of Jesus, IESVM. In the accusative: it was the answer to my questions. *IESVM unicum.* "Only Jesus"; Jesus is the only certainty.

That was what the *Quem queritis* wanted to tell me. It is one of the final scenes in the Gospels, which in the Middle Ages was simplified for the people to sing and recite. The images are very simple, almost primitive. Mary Magdalen and Mary go to the sepulchre of Jesus. An angel, of dazzling appearance and in snow-white robes, announces himself with a tremendous commotion and the guards of the sepulchre fall down as if dead. Then the angel (or the angels, depending on the version) reveals to the women that they will not find Jesus there, because He has risen again as he had predicted, and he invites the women to spread the word among His disciples.

In medieval musical performances the Gospel passage (Matthew 28: 1–6; Mark 16: 1–8; Luke 24: 1–7; John 20: 1–18) is reduced to a few basic lines:

– *Whom are you seeking?*
– *Jesus of Nazareth crucified, O angels.*
– *He is not here, he has risen again as he foretold, go and announce that he has left the sepulchre.*

IESVM is accusative, because it is the object of something, it answers the question: whom are you seeking? We are seeking Jesus. It therefore answers *the* question, the only real question for those who have faith. Whom are we really seeking, whom must we seek, if not Jesus? Who remains if not He?

Quem queritis? The answer is *Jesum*, which in certain paleo-Christian epigraphs on tombs (recalling the episode of the angel announcing Christ's resurrection) was written *ISVM*, with V to indicate U, and omitting "e" or in certain cases writing it as IᵉSVM, with the "e" in superscript. Alongside it, on the same tomb, one would find the symbol ATTΩ, which means that the alpha and omega of life, its beginning and end, are under the temple of God, represented by the double "T". But it can also be read "Atto".

We are all Atto, or rather, ATTΩ: whether we like it or not, we are all under the great roof of the Lord.

I know that two words are missing of the seven that form the message: let us hope the whole thing is not simply the fruit of Ugonio's frightful imagination . . .

Go in peace
Card. Lorenzo dell'Agio

NOTES

✠

Emperor Joseph the First's smallpox – The Flying Ship and its inventor – Ciezeber-Palatine – The Place with No Name and its enemies – Eugene of Savoy – Joseph the Victorious – The censored biography and the secrets of Charles – Atto Melani – Camilla de' Rossi – Ottoman customs, embassies and legends – Ilsung, Hag, Ungnad, Marsili – Bettelstudenten and chimney-sweeps – Free time, taverns, feasts and other details – The Viennese and their history

Emperor Joseph the First's Smallpox

Emperor Joseph I died at 10.15 on Friday 17th April 1711. He was not yet thirty-three years old. The official diagnosis was smallpox.

A preliminary observation: smallpox, a horrific disease which has now (almost completely) disappeared, has never been overcome by any treatment. In short, there is no cure for smallpox.

If you consult the famous *Harrison's Manual* (Dennis L. Kasper, *Harrison's Manual of Medicine*, 16th edition, New York 2005), a basic study text for every medical student, you will read that smallpox is, along with anthrax, one of the ten class-A (the most dangerous), "special surveillance" viruses in the struggle against bio-terrorism.

In 1996, delegates from 190 nations passed a resolution: on 30th June 1999 all smallpox samples still existing in the world would be destroyed. This did not happen. At the CDC in Atlanta, USA (Center for Disease Control and Prevention), they still exist.

When Joseph fell ill on 7th April 1711, no one at court was sick with smallpox. Later studies (see, e.g., C. Ingrao, *Joseph I. der "vergessene Kaiser"*, Graz-Vienna-Cologne, 1982) report that at that time a smallpox epidemic was raging throughout Vienna. This is not true.

The historian Hermann Joseph Fenger, in his report on all the epidemics that affected Vienna from 1224 (*Historiam Pestilentiarum Vindobonensis*, Vienna 1817), makes no mention of a smallpox epidemic in 1711. Neither does Erich Zöllner (*Geschichte Österreichs*, pp. 275–278).

But we wished to check this for ourselves. At the Vienna City Archives we consulted the *Totenbeschauprotokolle*, the reports compiled by the city's medical authorities for every death. We examined the reports for the months of March, April and May 1711 thoroughly: there was no smallpox epidemic. What is more, the number of deaths remained average for the period.

Until ten days before he died, Joseph I was a young man at the height of his powers and in a state of perfect health, an active sportsman and a great hunter.

The medical report describes the corpse's face as covered by copious pustules. However, no mention is made of them in the printed gazette of the day, which described the Emperor's death and his body as put on display (*Umständliche Beschreibung von Weyland Ihrer Mayestät / JOSEPH / Dieses Namens des Ersten / Römischen Kayser / Auch zu Ungarn und Böheim Könih / u. Erz-Herzogen zu Oesterreich / u. u. Glorwürdigsten Angedenckens Ausgestandener Kranckheit / Höchstseeligstem Ableiben / Und dann erfolgter Prächtigsten Leich-Begängnuß / zusammengetragen / und verlegt durch Johann Baptist Schönwetter*, Vienna 1711). Besides, a face disfigured by blisters would certainly not have been shown to his subjects. Could this have been the work of the embalmers?

According to the medical diary kept in Latin by Doctor Franz Holler von Doblhof (Vienna State Archive, Haus- Hof- und Staatsarchiv, Familienakten, Karton 67), with the onset of the earliest symptoms the Emperor was vomiting mucus and blood. As soon as he died, the diary reads, "from both nostrils and from the mouth blood dripped for a long while." The neck was swollen and "*atro livore soffuso*": dark blue from an internal haemorrhage. At the autopsy, carried out by the same doctor, the liver and lungs are described as "blue and gangrenous, lacking natural colour" ("*amisso colore naturali, lividum et gangrenosum*"): another haemorrhage, it would seem. On account of the unbearable smell, the autopsy was concluded without opening the skull.

This medical description is catalogued today as "haemorrhagic smallpox", a particularly virulent and deadly variant. The strange thing, however, is that this type of smallpox has not always existed.

Before Joseph's death, no medical treatise refers to smallpox having a haemorrhagic tendency.

The first to talk of smallpox was Galen, followed by the doctors of the tenth century, the Persian Rhazes, Alì Ben el Abbas and Avicenna, and then, in the eleventh century, Costantine the African, secretary to Robert Guiscard. All of them engage in lengthy and detailed descriptions of smallpox and the possible complications and progressions, but none of them mentions the possibility of a haemorrhage. Quite the reverse: the progress of smallpox is described as usually benign; only in a few cases where the patients are already weak does it lead to death. This remains true right up to the sixteenth and seventeenth century. Ambroise Paré, Niccolò Massa, Girolamo Fracastoro, l'Alpinus, Ochi Rizetti, Scipione Mercuri and Sydenham, to mention just some of the best-known names, all devote long chapters of their works to smallpox, but there is no trace of haemorrhagic smallpox. They, too, describe the illness as very common and benign: it was fatal only in the huge pandemics unleashed by wars and famines. Smallpox is usually described in the chapters dealing with infant diseases, and is often lumped together with chickenpox and measles. Rhazes, in his *Treatise on Smallpox and Measles*, makes a very detailed distinction between the two illnesses: "restlessness, nausea and anxiety are more frequent in measles than in smallpox; pain in the back is more characteristic of smallpox." Ambroise Paré (*Oeuvres*, Lyon 1664, livre XX, chap. 1–2) devotes no more than a chapter to smallpox along with measles, expostulating on the details in order to distinguish between the two illnesses. Such clarifications seem totally incomprehensible to modern readers: today smallpox is, unfortunately, completely different from the almost always harmless measles. The horrible pustules of smallpox and the terrible syndrome as a whole are totally unrelated to the little red spots of measles and the accompanying discomforts. Sydenham, too, drew a differential diagnosis between smallpox and measles: a sign that from the tenth to the sixteenth century smallpox remained the same, a contagious disease that could be confused with measles. Joseph's own daughter, Maria Josepha, had contracted it in January 1711, three months before her father, and recovered from it: on this occasion, too, there was no sign of any haemorrhages.

The first testimony that we have of haemorrhagic smallpox is, in fact, the medical report on Joseph I.

Two years later, in 1713, the Greek doctor (some say he was from Bologna), Emanuele Timoni, in his treatise entitled *Historia Variolarum quae per insitionem excitantur*, refers for the first time to a new practice adopted in Constantinople: subcutaneous inoculation.

A preliminary remark: inoculation is simply the term to indicate the ancient means of immunising, before the English doctor, Edward Jenner, at the end of the eighteenth century, established the method of vaccination that is still in use today. Inoculation consisted in taking a serum from smallpox pustules where the course of the illness was milder and more benign, and by means of a cutaneous incision injecting it into a healthy patient, with the aim of provoking a form of smallpox that would also be mild. The patient treated in this manner should fall slightly ill for a short time, thus protecting himself or herself permanently from the risk of contracting smallpox in a serious form. It was universally known that smallpox never struck the same individual twice.

Obviously subcutaneous inoculation can also be carried out with intentions that are not preventive but criminal – using a more lethal form of the virus.

Timoni reports the presence in Constantinople of two old female fortune-tellers of Greek origin, known as the Thessalian and the

Philippoupolis, who had been carrying out inoculations in the Ottoman capital on the "Frankish" – which is to say, non-Muslim – population since the end of the seventeenth century. The Muslims refused to be inoculated. In 1701 and 1709, a few years after this practice had begun to spread in the city, Constantinople suffered the first mass outbreaks of death from smallpox. However, the two fortune-tellers were not lynched but acclaimed. Certain well-known doctors had arrived declaring that without the intervention of the two Greek women the epidemic would have been even worse. And very soon this notion was endorsed by the local clergy, which opened the way for inoculation *en masse*.

The year after the events reported by Timoni, in 1714, the Venetian ambassador in Constantinople reported the practice of inoculation in his work *Nova et tuta variolas excitandi per transplantationem methodus nuper inventa et in usum tracta*.

Subcutaneous inoculation spread throughout Europe two years later, between 1716 and 1718, when the wife of the English ambassador in Constantinople, Lady Mary Wortley Montagu, officially imported it from Turkey into England. On her travels she promoted inoculation in all the European courts with great enthusiasm, even having her own children inoculated. In 1716 she passed through Vienna, where, as her diary informs us, she met Joseph's widow and daughters. In 1720 in England she persuaded the King to have some prisoners inoculated. From 1723 inoculation became widespread.

However, in those same years, smallpox, rather than getting weaker, ceased to be a "benign illness" and became mortal in almost all cases. It was no longer considered an infant disease. The symptoms were much more serious than those described in the preceding centuries and above all were unmistakeably hideous: there was no longer any likelihood of confusing the horrible smallpox pustules with those of chickenpox or, even less likely, with the little red spots of measles.

Marco Cesare Nannini's essay, *La storia del vaiolo* (Modena 1963), provides some terrifying statistics. In the twenty-five years following upon the introduction of inoculation, 10 per cent of the world's population died. There were numerous cases of haemorrhagic smallpox. Inoculation soon proved to be an excellent instrument of colonial conquest: the Indians of America were decimated in this fashion, from the Redskins to the Indios. E. Bertarelli (*Jenner e la scoperta della vaccinazione*, Milan 1932) reports that in Santo Domingo alone, for example, 60 per cent of the population died in the space of a few months. In Haiti, smallpox, imported in 1767, rapidly killed two-thirds of the inhabitants; in Greenland it exterminated three-quarters of the population in 1733.

In Europe, between the introduction of subcutaneous inoculation and the end of the eighteenth century, sixty million people died of smallpox (H.J. Parish, *A History of Immunization*, London 1965, p. 21). At the end of the eighteenth century very similar estimates were formulated (D. Faust, *Communication au congrès de Rastadt sur l'extirpation de la petite vérole*, 1798, *Archives Nationaux de France*, F8 124). In 1716 smallpox caused 14,000 deaths in Paris, and another 20,000 in 1723; in 1756 mass deaths occurred in Russia, as they had done in 1730 in England, where in little more than four decades 80,505 deaths were recorded from smallpox; in Naples, in 1768, in a few weeks, there were 6,000 deaths; in Rome, in 1762, another 6,000; in Modena, in 1778, following upon a single instance of subcutaneous inoculation, an epidemic was unleashed that decimated the city in the space of eight months; in Amsterdam, in 1784, there were 2,000 deaths; in Germany in 1798, 42,379; in Berlin alone, in 1766, 1,077 deaths; in London, in 1763, 3,528. England did great business with inoculation: Daniel Sutton had founded a flourishing inoculation business, with branches that spread to the remote western territories of New England and Jamaica during the second half of the century.

How many people died from smallpox before inoculation? A few examples from London: 38 deaths in 1666, 60 in 1684, 82 in 1636. In short, hardly any.

At the court of Vienna, before Joseph's case, smallpox had struck only Ferdinand IV. But after Joseph the disease exploded, and by the end of the eighteenth century it had killed nine more Habsburgs. There were countless cases of haemorrhagic smallpox in those years, and *all* ended with the death of the patient.

Here are two descriptions of the illness for the sake of comparison. The first is by Scipione Mercuri, the famous Roman doctor who lived from 1540 to 1615 (*La commare*, Venezia 1676, libro terzo, cap. XXIV, p. 276, *Delle Varole e cura loro*), and therefore prior to the introduction of inoculation. It will be noted that Mercuri, too, considers smallpox and measles as similar (he deals with them extensively also in *De morbis puerorum*, lib. I, *De variolis et de morbillis*, Venetiis, 1588).

The second description of smallpox is by Doctor Faust, taken from the essay already cited of 1798, and therefore at the height of the vaccinatory euphoria.

Here is Mercuri:

> *I will now deal with the universal external illnesses; and first of all the commonest, which is the* 'roviglione' *known in this country as* 'varole'. *Between* 'varole' *and measles there are some differences: nonetheless because both of them receive the same treatment, I will deal with them together.* 'Roviglioni' *or* 'varole' *are little pustules, or blisters, which break out all over*

the body, particularly spontaneously with pain, itching and fever, and when they break they become sores … The signs that pre-announce their arrival are stomach ache, hoarseness, redness in the face, headache, copious sneezing. The signs that reveal them as having already arrived are delirium, little pustules or blisters over the whole body, now white, now red, now larger, now smaller, depending on the different bodies of the patients. 'Varole' for the most part do not kill, except occasionally when, either because of the air or due to other mistakes committed by the doctors, as many people die as in a plague.

And here is Faust's description in 1798:

With countless pustules, smallpox presses in from head to foot. It is as if the body is immersed in boiling oil, the pain is atrocious. With suppuration, the face becomes monstrously swollen and disfigured; the eyes are closed, the throat enflamed, blocked and unable to swallow water which the rale demands incessantly. The invalid is therefore deprived at the same time of light, air and water; his eyes emit pus and tears; the lungs exhale a fetid smell; the dribble turns acrid and involuntary; the excrement corrupt and purulent, and the urine is equally thick. The body is all pus and pustules and cannot move or be touched; it moans and lies motionless, while the part on which it lies is often gangrenous.

There is an equally horrific verse description that Abbot Jean-Joseph Roman wrote in 1773 in his poem *L'inoculation* about a sufferer from smallpox:

> *A pain not felt before attacks him now,*
> *His eyes are filled with seething scorching liquid;*
> *And dribble, running from his foaming mouth,*
> *Does naught to quench the thirst that burns his palate:*
> *He has no longer use of his chained senses,*
> *Amid dark clouds he only sees grim shades,*
> *His voice is toneless, and his mangled body*
> *Is but the prison of a downcast spirit.*

❧

The description of the haemorrhage found in Joseph I appears very similar to the "smallpox purpura" described by Dr Gerhard Buchwald, a German doctor almost ninety years old now, in his book *Vaccination. A Business Based on Fear*, 2003 (original German title: *Impfen: Das Geschäft mit der Angst*, Munich 2000). Dr Buchwald is one of the rare doctors still alive to have personally observed and studied smallpox cases. In 2004 we sent him the documentation concerning Joseph's illness. We then had a long conversation on the telephone. Based on his own experience Buchwald claims that damage to the blood vessels is only and exclusively found in cases of smallpox induced by viruses injected into the vessels. The same conclusion can be read in his book (p. 50 of the German edition), which states that the haemorrhagic course of the disease is to be attributed to the recent injection of the virus and always ends in death.

In short, for Buchwald there is no such thing as naturally occurring haemorrhagic smallpox; it is caused by the introduction of the practice of inoculation/vaccination.

ॐ

There are numerous studies on smallpox that make the claim that subcutaneous inoculation had been known in China and India for millennia. The same propaganda was spread in the eighteenth century to inspire confidence in the practice. It is false.

As far as China is concerned, the Jesuit father D'Entrecolles, a missionary in Peking, is often cited as a source. But he wrote in May 1726, no earlier than that, and does nothing but quote a passage from a Chinese book which describes the practice of immunisation from smallpox, but by inhalation and not inoculation. There is no connection with inoculation, therefore; indeed, the Jesuit specifies that according to Chinese doctors it would be lethal for smallpox to enter the body by means that were not natural (like the nose), but through an incision in the skin. The famous treatise of the history of Chinese medicine by Chimin Wong and Wu Lien-Teh (*History of Chinese Medicine*, Shangai 1936) makes the same claim and adds that some medical historians point to India as the place where inoculation began.

The famous Indian doctor, a professor at the University of Calcutta, Girindranath Mukhopadhyaya, in his *History of Indian Medicine* (Delhi 1922–29, vol. I, pp. 113–33), examines all the claims about the practice of inoculation in India having its roots in the distant past. Mukhopadhyaya reaches the same conclusion as us: there is no evidence of this. There are doctors – nearly all English – who have written studies in which they claim to have heard stories from ancient times that refer to this practice. One of them, a certain Doctor Gillman, has even unearthed a Sanskrit treatise of medicine that mentions inoculation. Mukhopadhyaya had the text examined by two Sanskrit scholars, who recognised it as an "interpolation": a blatant forgery, in short. In the ancient Indian treatises of medicine by Caraka, Suśruta, Vāgbhata, Mādhava, Vrnda Mādhava, Cakradatta, Bhāva Miśra and others, Mukhopadhyaya could not find the slightest allusion to the practice of smallpox inoculation. Furthermore, in the hymns to the Goddess Śitalā, taken from the Kāikhanda by Skanda Purāna, it is explicitly stated that there is no remedy for smallpox except prayers to the goddess. And yet Mukhopadhyaya says emphatically, "no one has yet questioned the notion that inoculation was frequently practised in India."

Mukhopadhyaya suspects, as we do, a conspiracy to provide a pedigree first for inoculation and subsequently for vaccination, so that the masses would be induced to trust these practices and to let them be carried out on themselves and on their children.

(In addition to forgeries, the history of smallpox contains numerous embarrassing silences. The inventor of vaccination – which was what inoculation subsequently developed into – the famous English doctor, Edward Jenner, vaccinated his own ten-month-old son with material extracted from the pustules of a smallpox victim, and the child was left mentally handicapped and died at the age of twenty-one. Later on, in 1798, Jenner vaccinated a child aged five, who died almost immediately, and an eight-month pregnant woman, who just a month later miscarried a baby covered in pustules similar to smallpox. Despite these experiences, Jenner sent samples of the material used for these experiments to the ruling houses of Europe, which made widespread use of them on orphan children to develop new diseases in order to be able to extract new samples of infected material. Every manual of medical history carefully avoids reporting these facts.)

༖

Let us return to the eighteenth century. Soon several voices were raised against inoculation. The tragic case of Madame de Sévigné was pointed to; she, too, fell ill of smallpox and died in 1711. However, it was not the illness that killed her but, amid atrocious suffering, the doctors' treatment of it (cf. J. Chambon, *Traité des métaux et des minéraux*, Paris 1714, p. 408 ff.). In the mid-eighteenth century Luigi Gatti, an Italian doctor in Paris, treated Madame Helvétius's smallpox, performing all sorts of somersaults and pirouettes in front of the invalid, firmly convinced that cheerfulness was the only possible remedy, and that it was only medical treatment that made smallpox fatal. For mysterious reasons, Gatti was to change his opinion drastically, suddenly becoming a highly active (and extremely wealthy) inoculator.

Van Swieten, in the nineteenth century, reported that noble and wealthy patients almost all died, while the common people, who did not undergo any treatment, survived (cf. *Rapport de l'Académie de Médecine sur les vaccinations pour l'année 1856*, p. 35).

That was not all: rumours began to circulate that inoculation, when it did not kill, was entirely useless. There were cases of people who, despite having undergone inoculation and having suffered the smallpox caused by it, nonetheless fell ill of the disease, even years later. The *Mercure de France* of January 1765 (vol. II, p. 148), for example, reports the case of the Duchess of Boufflers.

But the worst fear was yet to come: did inoculation unleash smallpox even in people who had already had it? It was well known, as Avicenna himself said, that "smallpox only strikes once in a lifetime", granting perpetual immunity. According to numerous doctors opposed to inoculation, artificially induced smallpox subverts this law of nature. The proof? A very famous case: Louis XV of France, who had had smallpox at the age of eighteen, died in 1774 aged sixty-four. Of smallpox. In circumstances almost identical to those of Joseph I.

There was something special about Louis XV: as a child he was the only one who survived the incredible outbreak of fatal diseases that struck the children and grandchildren of his grandfather the Sun King, decimating the Bourbon House of France between 1711 and 1712. Count De Mérode-Westerloo (*Mémoires*, Brussels 1840) reports that Palatine had prophesied these deaths to him in 1706, describing them as murders. Little Louis in 1712 was just two years old, the second-born of the Duke and Duchess of Bourgogne. His parents and elder brother had died of smallpox, but Louis had been saved: his nurses, at the first signs of the child's illness, had literally barricaded themselves in the bedroom with him, preventing the doctors from even seeing him. They were convinced that it was the doctors themselves who had killed the other members of the royal family. And so Louis was spared Palatine's prophecy, and when he attained his majority he ascended the throne of France as successor to his grandfather Louis XIV. France, in the meantime, had been afflicted by years and years of Regency rule, during which the malign John Law, the inventor of banknotes, had been given free rein, leading the kingdom to an unprecedented financial disaster, as recounted by the chimney-sweep.

But certain "prophecies", sooner or later, always come true . . . At the age of sixty-four, Louis XV no longer had any brave wet nurses to protect him.

His death closely recalls that of Joseph I. Both were enemies of the Jesuits (Louis XV actually suppressed the Society of Jesus) and Louis XV, like Joseph, had to endure the menacing announcement of his own death, unfortunately accurate, from a preacher. It was 1st April 1774, a Thursday in Lent, and the Bishop of Senez pointed at the King from the pulpit and exclaimed: "Another forty days and Niniveh will be destroyed!" Exactly forty days later, on 10th May, Louis XV breathed his last (Pierre Darmon, *La variole, les nobles et les princes*, Brussels 1989, pp. 93–4).

Up to a week earlier, examining his boils, he had continued to murmur in amazement: "If I had not already had it, I would swear that this was smallpox." Finally on 3rd May, realisation struck him: "It is smallpox! . . . It is smallpox." With the mute assent of those around him, he turned his face away and said, "This is truly incredible."

A bitterly ironic death in many ways, not least for the fact that Louis XV had always been a tenacious opponent of the practice of inoculation.

ॐ

Having concluded our historical research into smallpox and having received Dr Buchwald's opinion on Joseph's death, we passed on to the final stage: the search for a pathologist who would support our request to exhume the Emperor's body and who would be prepared to analyse it.

. We at once rejected the medical exhumers who are so fashionable today: they exhume the bodies of historical figures from the past essentially to develop new vaccines, and are usually sponsored by the colossi of the pharmaceutical industry.

We turned to various Italian and Austrian university professors, but nobody was interested in the matter; indeed in many cases they actually seemed annoyed.

There was something familiar in all this: in 2003, when we needed to find graphological experts to examine the last will and testament of the King of Spain Charles II of Habsburg, most of the experts had run a mile for fear of annoying the present Spanish king, Juan Carlos of Bourbon. So when it came to a matter of smallpox . . .

Meanwhile we sent an application by registered mail to the Denkmalamt of Vienna (the office in charge of preserving historical monuments) to start the paperwork for the exhumation of the body of Joseph I. We knew that the procedure would be a long one and did not wish to lose any time.

In the hope of finding someone a little more courageous, we proceeded through mutual acquaintances. And so we hit upon the name of Professor Andrea Amorosi, a pathologist from the same city as one of us. Amorosi works at the Department of Experimental Medicine and the clinic of the "Magna Grecia" University of Catanzaro, in southern Italy. Initially we had a very good relationship. Professor Amorosi was attentive and helpful. After studying all the documentation that we sent him, he was excited by the idea of exhuming Joseph's body; it was he who informed us that smallpox is on the class A "special surveillance" list in the struggle against bio-terrorism. Our initiative, therefore, could cause a stir in the scientific community.

We asked if it would be possible, after all this time, to prove whether Joseph had been poisoned, killed by an artificial smallpox, or had instead died from natural smallpox. In the case of a poison, he answered, it should not be too difficult, since at the time they mainly used metals, which can be traced by modern equipment. The poisons used today, he declared, leave no traces.

In the case of death by inoculation, the professor went on to explain, the question was more complicated, but not impossible. It would be necessary to exhume several bodies, not just Joseph's. The ideal situation would be to have bodies that had died from smallpox long before Joseph, when smallpox

was not so lethal, in which case it would therefore be reasonable to assume
that death was due to natural smallpox – and bodies that had died from
smallpox later in the eighteenth century, in the age of inoculation. Then
DNA sequences would have to be taken from these bodies and compared
with those of Joseph I. Professor Amorosi kept us on the phone as he
continued to explain all the possible ways to detect a possible artifical cause
in the young emperor's death, using an abundance of scientific terms.
Lacking his professional expertise, we are unable to report Professor
Amorosi's ideas and intentions with the appropriate terminology.

We arranged with Amorosi that first of all he would send us the pages
from Harrison's manual on internal medicine concerning bio-terrorism, and
in the meantime he would talk with some of his colleagues, whom he did not
identify as yet, with the aim of forming a team to carry out the exhumation
and analysis of the bodies.

We never heard from him again.

We never received the photocopies from the Harrison manual (we got
hold of them by ourselves), nor did we succeed in talking to Professor
Amorosi again. He never replied to our emails. Our numerous phone calls,
over a period of months, all ran up against the insuperable barrier of his
secretary, nurse or assistant, who regularly asked us for our names, put us on
hold and then told us that Professor Amorosi was not there. Then one day
we shifted tactics, calling and refusing to accept yet another vague and off-
putting response. We insisted, we called back five times the same day, then
the next day, and so on for a week. Each time we explained the whole matter
from scratch, even though we could sense that the person at the other end
of the line did not wish to listen to us. We began to recognise their voices,
and the voices recognised us. Our interlocutors contradicted themselves,
and one of them after the briefest of greetings put the phone down on us.
The people on the other end of the line were armed with a good deal of
patience; they could have treated us worse. In June 2006, when for the
umpteenth time we pronounced the words "exhumation", "smallpox",
"inoculation", finally a weary voice whispered to us: "Just how old are you?
Do you realise what you're doing? Let it go. And leave the professor alone."

We did not call again. For the first time since we had started our investigations into the past, we felt really frightened. The voice was not threatening.
Quite the reverse: it seemed sincere. It was clear: Professor Amorosi had been
intimidated by someone, to the point that he refused any contact with us,
even to the extent of simply inventing a pretext and wriggling out of the
business. Perhaps we really were playing with fire. We opened the chapter on
bio-terrorism in Harrison's manual on internal medicine. We read and re-read
the same passage, as if it was only now that its significance had struck us:
despite the continual urgings of the World Health Organisation to destroy

every test tube sample of smallpox, at the CDC in Atlanta in the USA they still preserve these and carry out experiments of all kinds. The manual emphasised how the recombinant (or artificial) smallpox is much more devastating and dangerous than the natural one.

We went back to Professor Buchwald's book. The book reports every sort of malpractice committed until just a few decades ago to hide the number of deaths due to the anti-smallpox vaccine, and to pass them off as natural smallpox: substitutions of clinical records, suppression of reports and other things. The horrifying photos (pp. 49 and 50) of Waltraud B., a child horribly covered with pustules and scabs from smallpox provoked by anti-smallpox vaccine, and of the blood issuing from the eyes and open mouth of the corpse of a young nurse who died at Wiesbaden in the sixties from haemorrhagic smallpox, also caused by vaccination, caused our pens to drop. And not only metaphorically.

As this book goes to press, the registered letter containing the application for the exhumation of the body of Joseph I, and a subsequent reminder, have received no answer from the Denkmalamt of Vienna.

The Flying Ship and its Inventor

The gazette of 24th June 1709 kept by Frosch reporting news of the arrival of the Flying Ship in Vienna is authentic. An example can be seen at the Vienna City and State Library. It is not the only eye-witness account of the Flying Ship: other gazettes reported the flight of the extraordinary device. The Diary of Vienna gazette of 1st June 1709 actually contains an engraving showing the Flying Ship (*Wiennerisches Diarium* Nr. 609, 1–4 June 1709, pp. 1–2) and the item read by the chimney-sweep is taken word for word from the newspaper.

Modern historians know perfectly well who the inventor and helmsman of the Flying Ship was: not the mysterious violinist Albicastro, as the chimney-sweep supposes, but a Brazilian priest, as reported in the *Wiennerisches Diarium*, Bartolomeo Lorenzo de Gusmão (1685–1724). He was an extraordinary figure: a Jesuit, scientist, adventurer, inventor, possibly a charlatan, undoubtedly a genius, who has gone down in history as having perhaps flown not only the first airship but also the first aerostatic balloon, decades before the Montgolfier brothers.

The flight of his wooden ship (if it really happened) was reported all over Europe; in addition to the Viennese gazette, printed news sheets were issued in London and in Portugal.

Did the ship projected by Gusmão really take off? Opinons differ. The expert on the history of flying, Bernd Lukasch, does not rule out the idea at all. But according to the historian Fernando Reis, the Passarola (this is the name Gusmão gave it) was just a fable invented by Gusmão to draw the attention of detractors and inquisitive souls away from his real experiments, centred on hot-air balloons. And the gazettes? According to contemporaries, they were the work of Gusmão and a close friend, the Count of Penaguilão, who had set up the gigantic prank with the assistance of other friends. But this is not certain either. Gusmão's life was shrouded in mystery up to the very end.

Between 1713 and 1716 the eccentric Brazilian travelled around Europe and made a name for himself with inventions of all kinds: a system of lenses for cooking meat by sunlight; a mill that ground much faster than any already existing; a machine for the exploration of peat bogs, and other unusual ideas. He settled in Paris where he earned a living first as a herbalist, and then, with the help of his brother, as secretary to the Portuguese ambassador to the Sun King. After returning to Portugal, thanks to his brilliant gifts as a scientist and orator he first became a member of the Royal Academy of History, and then acceded to the post of court chaplain. But then his troubles began: he was accused by the Inquisition of sympathising with the crypto-Jews. Furthermore, as Saramago records in his *Memorial do Convento* (*Baltasar and Blimunda*), he was involved in a scandalous trial, where the suspects included the King of Portugal, a brother of the Sovereign, their lovers, witches and prostitutes. Some suspect that behind the ecclesiastic authorities' fury against Gusmão there lay hostility towards his aeronautical research. One of his brothers, perhaps to save him from the clutches of the Inquisition, declared that Gusmão was mad. To escape a possible conviction, the Jesuit secretly left Portugal and fled to Spain, trying to reach Paris. But in Toledo he was seized by a malignant fever and taken to hospital, where he died a month later, aged just thirty-nine. Even in these last moments he was not idle: just before dying he converted to Judaism. The truth about the Flying Ship is buried forever in Gusmão's grave.

To conclude, one should not be surprised to discover, as reported in the gazette Frosch showed the chimney-sweep, that the pilot who came to Vienna on board his Flying Ship in 1709 was arrested and imprisoned, rather than borne in triumph as the first aviator in history. The Austrian soul loves tradition and distrusts anything new. Even at the beginning of the twentieth century, Emperor Franz Joseph was hostile to the introduction of electricity and lifts.

The experiments and theories of Francesco Lana, Ovidio Montalbani and Geminiano Montanari are taken from the texts they themselves published starting from the second half of the seventeenth century (see the bibliography).

Ciezeber-Palatine

From the recesses of history there emerges several times the mysterious figure of a dervish, as the chimney-sweep describes him. In a "flying sheet" (a sort of short gazette handed out in the streets) containing a report of the Turkish audience with Eugene (*Beschreibung Der Audientz des von tuerckischen Gross-Sultan nach Wien gesandten und alda ankommenden Cefulah Aga Capichi Pascia*, Vienna, 9th April 1711) mention is made of an Indian dervish named Ciezeber in the ambassador's retinue. In the account given by the chimney-sweep he will finally reveal himself under the name of Isaac Ammon, known as Palatine. Here again we are talking of a figure that really existed. And his political predictions on the future of Europe, formulated decades, even centuries ahead, have proved incredibly accurate. As already mentioned, reference is made to this extraordinary sorcerer figure, and his plots and prophecies, in the *Mémoires du feld-maréchal comte de Mérode-Westerloo* (Brussels 1840, vol.2, pp. 150–85 and 293). The author of these memoirs, which remained in manuscript form until the nineteenth century when they were published by a descendant, was a Belgian man-of-arms and diplomat, in the service of the Empire but often at odds with Eugene of Savoy. He gives a very unflattering portrait of Eugene, thus earning himself the displeasure of modern historians (see, for example, H. Oehler, *Prinz Eugen im Urteil Europas*, Munich 1944, pp. 369–75). Palatine (his name was in fact Isaac Ammon, as the chimney-sweep records), despite being the eldest son of an important family of Nestorian patriarchs, was close to the circle of dervishes in Babylon (*Mémoires*, p. 159–160). An expert healer and connoisseur of poisons, he successfully cured de Mérode himself of a serious illness. De Mérode remained close to him for eight years, and recorded his prognostication of the secret poisonings of numerous personalities: Louis XIV, the Dauphin, the Duke and Duchess of Bourgogne and their son, and also the Duke of Berry, the King of Spain Charles II and above all Joseph I. With regard to this last named, Palatine speaks of an "Emperor", but there is no doubt that it was Joseph because De Mérode-Westerloo dates his acquaintance and conversations with Palatine (p. 150 and 160–61) around 1708, when Joseph I was Emperor. Palatine was also in touch with Eugene of Savoy: De Mérode-Westerloo recounts (p. 293) that he heard with some concern, in 1722, several years after losing touch with him, that the strange character held talks with Eugene and gathered information about him.

Palatine's uncannily accurate predictions of death include the following: that of the Sun King (who in 1714, three years after Palatine's pronouncement, would indeed die of gangrene in the leg, as forecast by the dervish in the chimney-sweep's tale and in De Mérode-Westerloo's memoirs); that of the Duke of Berry, who died in May 1714 (grandson of Louis XIV and third son of the Grand Dauphin, the Duke died of an illness, as predicted by the dervish); that of the Grand Dauphin himself, who expired on 14th April 1711, just three days before Joseph; and finally those of the Duke and Duchess of Bourgogne in 1712: an incredible series of deaths that historians have termed "the hecatomb".

The Place with no Name and its Enemies

All the information and descriptions provided by the chimney-sweep on the "Place with No Name known as Neugebäu" (as it appears in the archive documents), are confirmed by the historians as well as by the numerous studies published and listed in the bibliography. Today the manor is known as Neugebäude. That Maximilian II in his final years was obsessed by the thought of completing Neugebäude, as Simonis recounts, is confirmed by the Venetian ambassador Giacomo Soranzo: cf. Joseph Fiedler (ed.), *Relationen venetianischer Botschafter über Deutschland und Österreich im 16. Jahrhundert*, Vienna 1870, p. 217.

The ferocious black panther itself really existed. It is reported in the *Wiennerisches Diarium* (today *Wiener Zeitung*) n.483 of 17–20th March 1708: on the afternoon of Sunday 18th March, Joseph, with his consort, and a retinue of knights and ladies, accompanied his sister-in-law, Princess Elizabeth Christine of Brunswick-Wolfenbüttel, to Neugebäude. Since his brother Charles was in Barcelona claiming the Spanish throne, Joseph had represented him at the wedding by proxy celebrated between Charles and the German princess in Vienna. Before she set off for Spain to join her husband, Joseph wished to pay her the homage of showing her the wild beasts kept at Neugebäude, especially the two lions and the panther, which had only recently arrived.

After the death of Joseph I the manor continued to decay relentlessly. Not only did the restoration work come to a halt: Maximilian II's creation became the victim of an incredible series of omissions, indecisions, errors and general exampes of ill will, which almost seem to have been orchestrated by malign forces.

When Charles ascended the throne after his brother's death, he abandoned his predecessor's restoration projects and left the castle to fall to pieces. The gardens lapsed into decay, and the last traces of the wonderful flower beds, pot plants and hedges disappeared. With the ascent to the throne of Charles's daughter, the famous Maria Theresa, things got even worse. At the request of the imperial artillery, the empress authorised the use of Neugebäude as a powder magazine. At her express order the precious columns supporting the grandiose panoramic terrace to the north were carried away. The perimeter towers underwent modifications so that powder could be stored, the four main ones were destroyed and the boundary wall heavily altered. The ball game stadium (from which the chimney-sweep tells us the Flying Ship took off) was covered with a roof, then divided into several storeys by means of a wooden structure, which in the end was destroyed by fire, along with the roof.

In addition to the columns, Maria Theresa's soldiers dismantled fountains, stucco work, ornaments and possibly pieces of walls and bricks, and took them away to Schönbrunn. Some of the marvellous Tuscan columns of Maximilian's palace were thus reutilised in the central part of the colonnade of Schönbrunn, on the side that looks out onto the famous gardens. Deprived of its columns, the great terrace of Neugebäude to the north was subsequently walled up, turning the castle into a kind of large, obtuse box.

Other columns plundered from Neugebäude went to form the framework of the Gloriette, the elegant triumphal arch, complete with two long terraced wings, that rises on the green hill behind Schönbrunn, and which figures in thousands of postcards and tourist brochures of Vienna. Various other items, useful for building massive walls, were probably set in the walls of the palace's side wings, work on which began after Joseph's death. The Viennese archives say nothing about this immense operation of stripping and recycling; no one will ever know in what point of the walls of the Schönbrunn these fragments are silently lurking, witnesses to an unfulfilled dream. Other materials for which no specific use could be found went to form the so-called "Roman ruins" of Schönbrunn: a clumsy and melancholy composition of capitals, cornices, decorative statues and lintels in the Renaissance or pseudo-antique style, after the fashion of a Piranesi view, set in a corner of the great park of Schönbrunn, in the guise of a ruined Roman temple.

And so every year, when thousands of tourists go to Schönbrunn and admire the impressive façade on the garden side, or the Gloriette, or the false Roman ruins, without knowing it they are also gazing at Neugebäude. Why, instead of honoring and saving the masterpiece of Simmering, did Maria Theresa choose to strip it and secretly bury its remains in another creation? People have pointed to her proverbial parsimony: the valuable sixteenth-century columns of the Place with No Name could not be left to rot in the wind and rain. Fair enough: but then why did the cautious Maria Theresa spend the absurd sum of a million gulden (the tourist guides point out to visitors that at that time a successful doctor or lawyer would earn 500 gulden a year) on the oriental-style sitting room on the first floor of Schönbrunn? If she really intended to curb expenses, the glorious sovereign need not have commissioned the great imperial bed covered in gold and silver brocade, a single piece of incalculable value, which, freshly restored, is once again on view in the great Viennese palace.

The secret debt of Schönbrunn to Neugebäude does not end here. As has been observed (Leopold Urban, *Die Orangerie von Schönbrunn*, typewritten degree dissertation, Vienna 1992), the Simmering complex is indeed "the mother of Schönbrunn". In various ways a comparative study of the two masterpieces "reveals surprising similarities" (*ibid.*, p. 62): for example, the layout of niches, arches and walls in the palace's orangery and in the parts of the castle devoted to animals; similarities that can also be found in the underground gallery from the western stretch of Neugebäude (where, at the end of the chimney-sweep's story, the illegal arrest is carried out by the dervish and his henchmen). Even the ornamental masks of Schönbrunn seem openly inspired by those of the fountains of Neugebäude. It could be added that the motif of the rows of columns supporting a long panoramic vault, interrupted by a central body, is common to the Gloriette and to the manor of Simmering; and that the essential elements (pond/fountains at the rear, large courtyard/garden enclosed by walls) are found both at Neugebäude and at Schönbrunn. Were Neugebäude to be restored, it is quite possible that the modern tourist would greatly prefer it to Schönbrunn. Despite all this, no one has done anything to save the Place with No Name; quite the contrary.

After the havoc wrought by Maria Theresa, her successors also seemed to be possessed by a mysterious destructive impulse. The centuries that followed were marked by spoliations, neglect, fires, and even the disastrous stationing of military troops during the clashes between the imperial army and the Napoleonic army. In 1922 the city of Vienna decided to build the city's crematorium within the walls of the upper garden of Neugebäude, which irremediably damaged the physiognomy of the entire complex. Where rows of flowers and fruit had once been laid out charmingly, where ivory Turkish-style towers had soared gracefully, and where avenues and groves had led harmoniously into one another, crematorium ovens and gravestones now stood grimly. A curious detail: many of the green areas occupied by the crematorium are not used at all. Was it really necessary to locate it here, of all places?

In 1952, in order to make way for vehicles, a Renaissance fountain, an admirable work by the sculptor Alexandre Colin which Maria Theresa had had moved from Neugebäude to Schönbrunn and which had been placed in the courtyard of the orangery (Urban, p. 71 ff.), was dismantled and left in pieces on the ground, in the open air. As time went by, various parts disappeared, probably ending up in some private garden. In 1962 a serious fire in the east wing of Neugebäude irreparably damaged the chapel, which was being used as a store for cinema reels. Proposals for restoration work were constantly being put forward, but invisible forces seemed to block them at every step. No one, except the common Viennese citizens in love with their city, seemed to care a jot for the only Renaissance villa still standing north of the Alps. In 1974 a great plan of restoration was announced, but never carried out. In 1982 a proposal was made to use the castle for the city's historic armoury collection. Two years later there was fresh talk of restoration. In 1986 the newspapers emphatically announced that some archaeological excavations had been carried out, which threw light on certain important details of the construction and the history of the complex. But in 1993 another major fire brought down a large portion of the roof. Rumours began to circulate in the city that the underground station of Stubentor had been created using bricks taken from Neugebäude (instead of materials found on the site, as a plaque inside the stations claims). Just a few years ago an incredible proposal for the demolition of the castle circulated. After all, wasn't that more or less what had been going on for years now? Fortunately Neugebäude found a bold champion: Othmar Brix, president of the 11th district of Vienna, within whose jurisdiction the castle of Maximilian II lies, generously set in motion a number of initiatives and petitions for the restoration of the castle. However, almost as if persecuted by the same mysterious enemies as his protegé, Brix suddenly died in 2003 aged just fifty-nine, without having seen any of his projects carried out. The road that leads to the venerable manor now bears his name. It is only in recent days that restoration work has begun on the Place with No Name, although no final use has been decided for the complex (cultural centre, museum or other institution). The flow of finances is always governed by the contorted logic of politics, and the spectre of demolition is forever lurking round the corner. For this reason an association of citizens imbued with a noble spirit of voluntary work has for some years now been defending the ancient walls, organising guided tours and a summer festival of cinema and music inside the main courtyard. Only in this way, perhaps, will it be possible to keep at bay the mysterious forces that for centuries have apparently been trying to consign Maximilian's dream to oblivion, together with its glorious historic associations.

The mythology that surrounds the Place with No Name, it should be noted, was not invented by the authors. Accounts of the ghosts at Neugebäude and Rudolph II's alchemic experiments as narrated by Simonis regularly emerge in the Viennese newspapers: see the *Neues Wiener Tagblatt* of 4th April 1940, p. 6 ("Ein Besuch in Wiens Gespensterschloß", which is to say, "A visit to Vienna's castle of ghosts"); and the *Volkszeitung* of 28th January 1940, p. 7 as well as the *Neue Freie Presse* of 7th September 1937, p. 6. Cases of ghosts that terrorised the *Nachtwärter* (night sentinels), soldiers guarding Neugebäude when the castle was a military store were reported until at least the nineteenth century. Up to the 1930s the inhabitants of the plain around Simmering avoided Neugebäude for fear of unpleasant encounters.

And the elephant? It is well known that Maximilian II did have an elephant brought to Vienna from the Iberian peninsula, and that a famous inn on the Graben (one of the celebrated streets that form the ancient centre of the city) took its name from i. The inn survived for almost three centuries and was then unfortunately demolished. There is nothing to prevent one from imagining, therefore, that the pachyderm found a home, as the chimney-sweep reports, in the place that Maximilian had chosen for his precious seraglio.

Eugene of Savoy

First of all, the Agha's little slip of paper. In the documents of Eugene's military campaigns is a copy of a report to Charles (*Feldzüge des Prinzen Eugen von Savoyen. Nach den Feld-Acten u. anderen authentischen Quellen hrsg. von der Abtheilung für Kriegsgeschichte des k.k. Kriegs-Archives*, Vienna 1876–1892, vol. XIII, Suppl. p. 14, chap. 7, Vienna 11th April 1711):

> *Finally on 7th afternoon the Turkish Agha arrived, to whom I granted audience on 9th. I attach for Your Majesty a copy of the written message that he delivered to me.*

What about the original of the message? There is no trace of it in the documents, as the reader who has read the historical appendices to *Imprimatur* and *Secretum* will perhaps have already guessed: certain operations are always carried out in the same way, whether it concerns covering up a pope's misdeeds, forging a king's will, or endeavouring to conceal a plot to harm an emperor.

What is this message from the Agha and why on earth should Eugene have sent it to Charles? It was to Joseph I that he should have been reporting, unless it was a question that Joseph must not hear of but which Charles already knew about.

The machinations of Atto Melani. Abbot Melani had very cleverly devised the trap of the forged letter from Eugene of Savoy, and he came close to achieving his aim. It was true, as Atto himself recounted, that an apocryphal letter, which attributed to Eugene the project of betraying the Empire, was delivered to Philip V of Spain, who then sent it on to the Sun King and to Torcy, who finally prevented it from going any further, as Atto complained to the chimney-sweep. It was not until May 1711 (about a month after the events described by the chimney-sweep) that Eugene, having arrived in Tournai, in Flanders, was informed of the existence of the letter, but he succeeded in proving his innocence. The whole affair can be read about in Eugene's correspondence held in the State Archive of Vienna or reproduced in the documents of Eugene's military campaigns: in particular, the letter in which Count Bergeyck wrote to Eugene that he had received a mandate from Philip I to ask him if the letter was authentic and, if so, to negotiate with him (State Archive of Vienna, Kriegsakten 262, 22.3.1711; Kriegsakten 263, 3.5.1711); Eugene's indignant reply (State Archive of Vienna, Grosse Korrespondenz 93 a, 18.5.1711), and the letters to the Queen Mother and Regent Eleonore Magdalene Therese and to Charles (*Feldzüge des Prinzen Eugens* XIII, Suppl., pp. 32–3, 13 and 17.5.1711) and to Sinzendorf (State Archive of Vienna, Grosse Korrespondenz 73 a, 18.5.1711), in which Eugene sent a copy of Bergeyck's letter and expressed all his dismay; and finally the answers from the Regent, from Charles and from Sinzendorf, who recognise that he is not in any way implicated (State Archive of Vienna, Grosse Korrespondenz 90 b, 3.6.1711; 31.7.1711; Grosse Korrespondenz 145, 21.5.1711).

Atto's analysis of the relations between Eugene, Joseph and Charles reflects the historic reality with surprising accuracy. For example, it is true, as Atto claims, that Eugene managed to have more influence at Charles's court than at that of the unfortunate Joseph. Eugene would, in fact, manage to persuade Charles to continue the War of the Spanish Succession all alone, when the allies had already made peace with France. Then, not content with this, he would proceed to the war on the Turkish front.

But above all, the jealousy Eugene felt towards Joseph as recounted by Atto Melani is far from unfounded. It is historically authenticated that Eugene was excluded from the Battle of Landau of 1702 so that the stage would be left free for Joseph, as Onno Klop reports (*Der Fall des Hauses Stuart*, vol.11, Vienna 1885, p. 196). Furthermore, it is true that Joseph did not allow Eugene to go and fight the French in Spain, where Eugene had hopes of achieving great things, as Onno Klopp recounts (*Der Fall op. cit.*, t. XXIV p. 12 ff.).

Atto Melani's reflections on the personality of Eugene of Savoy are also perfectly in keeping with the reality of the historical documents. It is not surprising that official historiography devotes little attention to the murkier side of the great *condottiere*. In all the thousands of books and articles (over 1,800 have been counted) that have been published over the last three centuries celebrating Eugene, hardly any reference is to be found to his private life. The reason is very simple. Eugene left no personal papers: only letters of war, diplomacy and politics. Nor can any private correspondence worthy of the name be found in the archives of the numerous personalities who corresponded with him. There does not seem to have been any personal or intimate side to his existence: all we see is his granite-like exterior as a soldier, diplomat and statesman. An almost inhuman heroic figure, who has no room for feelings, weaknesses or doubts.

As for women, none seem to have left any mark on this bellicose monolith. Eugene, one of the richest and most celebrated (and hence one of the most eligible) men of the age, never married. A few women have been associated with his name, above all Countess Eleonore Batthyany, his "official lover" from 1715 onwards. But even in what remains of his correspondence with her, no trace can be found of an intimate relationship in the real sense of the word. Perhaps the female sex was more useful than congenial to Eugene: it seems to be historically proven that the *condottiere*, as the chimney-sweep writes in December 1720, set up Countess Pálffy, Joseph's very young lover, in Porta Coeli Street (and so close to his own palace) so that he could watch over her and exploit her more easily (Max Braubach, *Prinz Eugen von Savoyen*, Vienna 1964, vol.3 pp. 21–2). The Viennese postman Johann Jordan, in his *Schatz /Schutz / und Schantz Deß Ertz-Herzogthumbs Oesterreich*, a carefully compiled street guide printed in 1701, reports on page 107 that a certain Agnes Sidonia Countess Pálffy, an old relative of Joseph's lover, lived in the Strassoldo House in Himmelpfortgasse, the building owned by von Strassoldo, the directress of the convent's novitiate (cf. Alfons Žák, *Das Frauenkloster Himmelpforte in Wien*, Vienna, 1906). A few years before Marianna arrived, therefore, the Strassoldo House had already been occupied by another woman from the Pálffy family.

There is no doubt that Eugene's early years in France were unruly, unconducive to education and even dissolute. As the English historian Nicholas Henderson writes: "There can be no doubt of the existence of shadows in Eugen's early boyhood. He belonged to a small, effeminate set that included such unabashed perverts as the young Abbé de Choisy, who was invariably dressed as a girl, except when he wore the lavish ear-rings and make-up of a mature woman." (N. Henderson, *Prince Eugen of Savoy*, London 1964, p. 21). It was in those days, according to some letters of Louis XIV's sister-in-law, Elizabeth of the Palatinate Countess of Orléans, that the homosexual adventures referred to by Atto Melani took place. Elizabeth had known Eugene personally from the days when he was still living in Paris. She recounts to her aunt, Princess Sophia of Hanover, that Eugene's nickname was Madame Simone, as Abbot Melani recounts, or Madame l'Ancienne; that in his relations with his contemporaries the young Savoy "played the part of the woman"; that in his sexual revels he coupled with the Prince of Turenne; that the two were considered "two vulgar whores"; that Eugene would not have put himself out for a woman, preferring "a couple of fine page-boys"; that the ecclesiastic benefice he had sought was refused because of his "depravity"; that it was only in Germany that he may have forgotten "the art" he had learned in Paris.

Eugene's most important biographer, Max Braubach, in his monumental five-volume account of the life and works of the great soldier, did not give much space to Elizabeth's letters and their implications. Another historian, Helmut Oehler, reports her pungent remarks, but attributes them solely to

Elizabeth's personal resentment against Eugene: at the time they were written (1708–10), the Italian military commander was opposing the peace between the European powers and France, a peace that Elizabeth – given the dramatic situation in which Louis XIV found himself – hoped for ardently. In fact, this is not exactly true: Elizabeth wrote openly about Eugene's homosexuality even years after the war had ended.

However, it is impossible to avoid the suspicion that it is Oehler who allows himself to get carried away; when he has to talk of another critic of Eugene, the Dutch Count Mérode-Westerloo, who left some vitriolic jottings on the *condottiere*, he changes register very markedly, defining Mérode-Westerloo a "know-all", "charlatan", "salon gossip", "parasite", and a "reprehensible individual" who "led a useless life", and whose memoirs are little more than an instance of "senile dementia". Finally Oehler explains that he deliberately ignored some passages by the Dutch diplomat because passing on Mérode-Westerloo's "idiotic prattlings" is a "disgusting" task.

In the end it was only to be expected that the partisan historiography should have triumphed in Eugene's case: a military hero can have no stain, least of all that of sexual inversion. The artificially created figure of the upright, irreproachable soldier triumphed – it is hardly a surprising – during the years of the Nazi regime; see, for example, the biography of Eugene by Viktor Bibl: *Prinz Eugen. Ein Heldenleben*, Vienna-Leipzig 1941, complete with a dedication to the army of the Third Reich.

The first of Elizabeth's letters to accuse Eugene of homosexuality is reported in Wilhelm Ludwig Holland (ed.), *Briefe der Herzogin Elisabeth Charlotte von Orléans*, Stuttgart 1867, in *Bibliothek des Litterarischen* [sic] *Vereins in Stuttgart*, Band CXLIV, p. 316:

To Madame Louise, Countess of the Palatinate – Frankfurt

> *St Clou, 30 October 1720*
> *[. . .] I would not have recognised Prince Eugene in the portrait to be found here: he has a short wide nose, but in the engraving it is long and pointed. His nose is so turned up that his mouth was always open, and you could see his two upper central teeth entirely. I know him well, I often tormented him when he was a child. At the time they said that he would soon take vows, and he was dressed as an abbé. I assured him that he would not remain so, which turned out to be the case. When he abandoned the habit, the young people called him "Madame Simone" or "Madame l'Ancienne", and it was said he played the part of the lady with them. So you see, dear Louise, that I know Prince Eugene well; I knew all his family, his father, his mother, brothers, sisters, uncles and aunts, he is not at all unknown to me, in short: it is impossible that he has a long pointed nose.*

Another passage (letter from Elizabeth to her aunt on 9th June 1708) in Helmut Oehler, *Prinz Eugen im Urteil Europas*, Munich 1944, p. 108:

Prince Eugene is too sensible not to admire Your Highness. But since Your Highness wishes to know the real reason why Prince Eugene was called Madame Simone and Madame l'Ancienne, just as Prince Turenne was, it is because the two of them were called, if I may be allowed the term, two vulgar whores and it is said that they were so accustomed, and at every moment gave themselves à tout venant beau *and played the role of the ladies; Prince Eugene may have unlearned this art in Germany.*

From another letter in 1710 (Oehler, *Prinz Eugen op. cit.*, p. 109):

Eugene does not put himself out for women, a couple of fine pageboys would suit him better.

From another letter in 1712 (Oehler, *ibid.*):

[. . .] If value and judgement make a hero, Prince Eugene is certainly one; however, other virtues are also required, whether one has them or not. When he was Madame Simone and Madame l'Ancienne, everyone looked on him as a petite salope, he also ardently desired a benefice of 2,000 talleri, which was refused because of his débauche. For this reason he went to the imperial court, where he made his fortune.

The other accounts that Atto gives of homosexuality at the court of France are all authentic too, as can be verified in Didier Godard, *Le goût de Monsieur – L'homosexualité masculine au XVIIe siècle* (Paris 2002), and in Claude Pasteur, *Le beau vice, ou les homosexuels à la cour de France* (Paris 1999).

The description of Eugene's palace in Porta Coeli Street (today's Himmelpfortgasse, where the Prince's former residence now hosts the Austrian finance ministry) is also entirely accurate, including the position of the future library on the first floor: it was in those rooms that the Prince's rich collection of books was started, which later became part of the imperial library and subsequently the National Library of Vienna.

Joseph the Victorious

The descriptions of the sieges of Landau led by Joseph and all the details relating to it, including the story of the coins that the French commander Melac ordered to be made from his silverware, are confirmed by G. Heuser, *Die Belagerungen von Landau*, Landau (2 vols.) 1894–96.

The procession that forced Penicek's cart to slow down on the afternoon of the fourth day really happened. A leaflet on the death of Joseph I (*Umständliche Beschreibung von Weyland Ihrer Mayestät / JOSEPH / Dieses Namens des Ersten / Römischen Kayser / Auch zu Ungarn und Böheim Könih / u. Erz-Herzogen zu Oesterreich / u. u. Glorwürdigsten Angedenckens Ausgestandener Kranckheit /*

Höchst-seeligstem Ableiben | Und dann erfolgter Prächtigsten Leich-Begängnuß |
zusammengetragen | und verlegt durch Johann Baptist Schönwetter, Vienna 1711,
p. 6) provides the list of orders and confraternities that took part in the
Forty Hours prayer. On 12th April, at that hour, shortly after five p.m.,
the Oratorian brothers were swarming towards St Stephen's, along with the
confraternity of the Immaculate Conception and the corporation of knife-
makers; their turn for prayers was from six to seven p.m.

The name of the Caesarean Proto-Medicus Von Hertod is confirmed in
the above-cited *Umständliche Beschreibung*, which faithfully reports every
detail on the death of Joseph and on the long funeral ceremony.

For the funeral apparatus described at the beginning, everything is
taken from *Apparatus Funebris quem JOSEPHI I. Gloriosissim. Memoriae . . .*,
Vienna 1711.

The enemies of Joseph I did indeed include the Jesuits, as Atto Melani
claims. The account of the expulsion of the Jesuit Wiedemann by the young
emperor, as given by the chimney-sweep on the third day while looking
through his collection of writings on Joseph, is authentic (cf. Eduard Winter,
Frühaufklärung, East Berlin 1966, p. 177). None of the panegyrics and the
gazettes mentioned by the chimney-sweep are invented: every reader
familiar with the history of the periodical press will have recognised the
famous *Englischer Wahrsager* ("The English Fortune-Teller"), the calendar
whose fatal prophecy for 1711 is reported by the chimney-sweep.

The story of the sun rising with a bloody tinge is not an invention either:
it is reported by Count Sigmund Friedrich Khevenhüller-Metsch, reproduced in the diary of Prince Johann Josef Khevenhüller-Metsch: *Aus der Zeit
Maria Theresias. Tagebuch 1742–1776*, Vienna-Leipzig 1907, p. 71):

> *This grievous death was not only foreseen by the English Fortune-Teller in his*
> *calendar, but was also pre-announced by the Sun itself, which for some days*
> *began to rise with a blood-red colour.*

This strange phenomenon is very similar to something that happened in
Russia in 1936, a circumstance recalled at the beginning of the 1994 film
Burned by the Sun, by the Russian director Nikita Mikhalkov, about one of the
Stalinist purges.

As the chimney-sweep recounts, after foretelling the death of Joseph,
the *Englischer Wahrsager* seems to have sold in great quantities: judging by
the copies still preserved today, up until the end of the eighteenth century
it enjoyed a far wider circulation than the other almanacs of the time.

The story Atto Melani narrates of the proposed kidnapping of Joseph is
also true. The traitor Raueskoet made the suggestion to Louis XIV, who
rejected it (cf. Charles W. Ingrao, *Josef I., der "vergessene Kaiser"*, Graz-Vienna-
Cologne, 1982, p. 243 n.98, and Philipp Röder von Diersburg, *Freiherr*,

Kriegs und Staatsschriften des Markgrafen Ludwig Wilhelm von Baden über den spanischen Erbfolgekrieg aus den Archiven von Karlsruhe, Wien und Paris, Karlsruhe 1850, vol. 3 p. 97).

The Censored Biography and the Secrets of Charles

Eugene's envy, Charles's rivalry: why has no historian ever investigated the hostility that surrounded Joseph the Victorious? Did the glory he gained in Landau cost him dear, as Atto Melani suggests to his friend the chimney-sweep?

According to Susanne and Theophil Antonicek (*Drei Dokumente zu Musik und Theater unter Kaiser Joseph I* in "Festschrift Othmar Wessely zum 60. Geburtstag", Tutzing 1966, p. 11–12), when Joseph was alive a sort of underground war over music developed between the young emperor and his brother (and consequently also among their counsellors): Charles accused his brother, quite openly, of wastefulness. After Joseph's death, the superindendent of music Scipione Publicola di Santa Croce was ordered to present the accounts of his directorship, and many of the deceased emperor's favourites (including Santa Croce himself) were dismissed, but once the purge had been effected Charles's regime of austerity softened rapidly, and the golden period of court music that Joseph had inaugurated continued as before.

There had always been jealousy and quarrels between the two brothers. Joseph was probaby surrounded by other hostile and secretly malevolent individuals. There should have been a historian to recount his great victories at Landau, illuminating the prestige that the young emperor achieved there, and the secret malice that it had unleashed among those present. A work of this sort would perhaps have prevented Joseph from being condemned to oblivion.

Well, in fact such a work was written, and it is of monumental proportions, consisting of twelve large manuscript volumes. Fate – or rather Emperor Charles VI, Joseph's brother – decreed that it should remain in manuscript form buried deep in an archive, unknown to everyone. Re-examining the affair, as we have done, helps to reveal how the threads of history, fastened in remote ages, can remain taut and tense until the present day.

The time and place were Vienna in the spring of 1738. Twenty-seven years had elapsed since Joseph's death, and two since the death of Eugene of Savoy. On the imperial throne sat Charles, Joseph's brother. A learned man of letters, Gottfried Philipp Spannagel, wrote a series of pressing letters to a noblewoman, the Countess of Clenck (National Library of

Vienna, Handschriftensammlung, manuscript Codex 8434). Spannagel was
one of the superintendents of the imperial library, a post that he had
obtained thanks to his great erudition in matters of law, genealogy and
history. He had spent several years in Italy and wrote fluently not only in
Latin, German and French, but also in Italian. Eleven years earlier, in 1727,
he had obtained the post of court historian, and then that of custodian of
the imperial library. In addition, Spannagel had also held a very sensitive
appointment: for two years he had given history lessons to Archduchess
Maria Theresa, Charles's daughter. It was she who, thanks to the Pragmatic
Sanction mentioned by the chimney-sweep, was to succeed to her father's
throne, trampling over the natural rights of Joseph's daughters. Gifted with
greater virtues than her father, Maria Theresa was to become known to
history as the great reformer of the Austrian monarchy. Spannagel, the
learned scholar and preceptor of the imperial family, wrote to the Countess
of Clenck to arrange a meeting with Charles: the Countess apparently had
excellent relations both with the Emperor and his consort. Spannagel was
concluding an impressive historical work in twelve books, which he wished
to bring to the Emperor's attention. The work was written in Italian, the
language his protagonist had been so fond of. The title was *Della vita e del
regno di Josefo il vittorioso, Re et Imperadore dei Romani, Re di Ungheria e di Boemia
e Arciduca d'Austria* (*Of the Life and Reign of Joseph the Victorious, King and
Emperor of the Romans, King of Hungary and of Bohemia and Archduke of Austria*;
National Library of Vienna, Handschriften Sammlung Codex 8431–8435 e
7713–7722). It was the first biography of Joseph in which full light was
thrown on his heroic deeds, within the great historic framework of the years
ranging from his boyhood to his death. In order to publish it Spannagel
needed not only permission but also material support from the imperial
crown. He therefore repeatedly asked the Countess of Clenck to arrange a
meeting with Charles, or at least a recommendation to his consort. But after
a whole year, in spring 1739, the librarian was still waiting for some sign of
agreement from on high, indispensable for the publication of his lengthy
work. We have just a short note from the Countess in which, in addition to
vague reassurances, the lady fixed an appointment with Spannagel to inform
him of the answer he had so long been waiting for. What this answer was, we
learn from subsequent events.

Della vita e del regno di Josefo il vittorioso is the moving testimony of a
sincere admirer of Joseph I, who, in the correspondence attached to the
work (Codex 8434, paper 272 ff.), several times calls Joseph "my hero".
Without falling into mere apologia, Spannagel's biography offers a lively and
full-blooded portrait of its subject, and highlights his intellectual, moral and
military virtues. Three episodes are studied with particular attention: the
victories in the two sieges of Landau of 1702 and 1704, and the failed

participation in the 1703 campaign, in which the Bavarian fortress was reconquered by the French, exactly as recounted by Atto Melani.

Spannagel asks himself: why was Joseph not able to participate in the military campaign of 1703? The answer is highly significant. Within the court there were those who wanted to keep him at home, and not for good reasons. The motives adduced for this opposition (Codex 7713, p. 105, c. 239r and ff.) were, of course, "the lack of necessary things" and the "insufficiency of the revenue", as well as the "considerable number of enemies" together with the "abundance of all things they had to make war well". But this did not explain everything, says Spannagel. One must also consider whether the men who were in charge of political and military affairs on the imperial side were really giving of their best. "Such an examination and comparison would be a bold, odious and arduous enterprise," because it would also be necessary to "scrutinise the will, spirit and heart, which have hundreds and hundreds of inscrutable expedients". So inscrutable that Joseph's true friends had some doubt whether "the enemies were served with much greater fidelity than were the Emperor and the King of the Romans; and that without this defect there would never have been so many difficulties and so many disasters."

In short, someone was playing the traitor. Or at least, was consciously avoiding doing his duty. For what reason? In the end, it came down to the lack of "good harmony" between Joseph and his father's ministers, as well as "some kind of jealousy", on account of which the ministers closest to Leopold were "on their guard against ministers of the rising sun" – that is to say, Joseph's ministers. But according to these latter, the only way to "preserve the House of Austria from final ruin" was for "the King of the Romans to be able to put into effect great things, worthy of his noble talents". If anything was to change, and if there was to be a real shift of direction at the head of government, Joseph's star needed to shine brightly at last: exactly what had begun to happen at the capture of Landau in 1702.

Spannagel, whose date of birth is not known, but who probably died in 1749 (Ig. Fr. V. Mosler, *Geschichte der k.k. Hofbibliothek zu Wien*, Vienna 1835, p. 148) was a contemporary of Joseph I, and had been present at many of the events he reports. He could have spoken by hearsay, or he could have cited oral testimony, but from extreme scrupulousness he cites (Codex 7713, pp. 124–26; Appendix to Book V – Letter Z) documentary sources provided by the Chancellor himself: letters from Prince Salm, Joseph's old educator, to the Count of Sinzendorf during the early months of 1703. Here there are open references to the "bad designs of this government", and to the "extreme necessity" of a change in the ministers and the urgency to replace them with "capable people, upright and accredited, who can alter things and stop abuses". Writing to Sinzendorf, Salm adds bluntly that "given the hostility of the present government towards the King of the Romans, until this is changed, I say frankly that I cannot advise the King to join the military campaign."

Therefore it is true, as the preceptor of Charles's family says, that Joseph was the victim of "bad designs" – or, to put it more bluntly, of envy. For this reason he was prevented from going to war in 1703, and hence from making his star blaze anew.

Charles did not like the biography of *Josefo il vittorioso, Re et Imperadore dei Romani, Re di Ungheria e di Boemia e Arciduca d'A. ....* Negotiations were soon held. Through the Chancellor, Charles suggested some cuts to Spannagel (Codex 8434, papers 280–86), above all, the part explaining why Joseph was prevented from going to war himself in the 1703 campaign: an affair that Spannagel had reconstructed also thanks to documents provided by the Chancellor, reproduced in the appendix to the work. Despite his sovereign's insistence, Spannagel courageously refused to make any cuts, because that would have jeopardised the integrity of the work. He might eventually take the advice given, but only after completing the work.

But something else disturbed the Emperor. The historian must apologise (Codex 8434 papers 297r–298v e 292r) for having "made a mistake" in describing Charles's education: it is not true that he defined it as "modest". In any case, the passage would be immediately corrected, and Spannagel recorded that he was still awaiting documents that he had requested in order to describe the youthful years of the current emperor more accurately.

Spannagel was perhaps too courageous, too keen to tackle delicate subjects, and perhaps he unwittingly committed the crime of *lèse majesté*. The seed of envy is always fresh: in the end the historian was never received by the Emperor, and his biography was never to be published.

Perhaps in an attempt to ingratiate himself with the Emperor, Spannagel began to write a history of the reign of Charles himself, in Latin. But the work was never completed, and the pages of the work actually devoted to Joseph's brother (cf. Susanne Pum, *Die Biographie Karls VI. Von Gottfried Philipp Spannagel. Ihr Wert als Geschichtsquelle*, unpublished dissertation, Vienna 1980) are ridiculously few. The historian who had loved Joseph must have found it hard to appreciate Charles.

The censoriousness of the successor of Joseph the Victorious did not end here. In 1715, four years after Joseph's death, Charles had already carried out a singular operation: he assigned two functionaries to go through all the correspondence preserved in the desks and in other furniture belonging to his father Leopold and his deceased brother. This meticulous examination lasted almost four months (from 28th January to 20th April, and from 26th August to 19th September).

In the end, having received the list of documents, Charles ordered that a large portion of them be burned, personally noting, page by page, which papers must not be passed down to his descendants: primarily, anything of personal or family interest. The State Archive of Vienna still holds the careful record of this examination with Charles's annotations (Haus-, Hof- und Staatsarchiv, Familienakten, Karton 105 n.239). What is striking, among the private papers of Joseph listed by the functionaries, is the great number of letters and memoirs concerning Landau: a simple glance is enough to show just how important the double triumph in Bavaria was for the young *condottiere*. Among the papers sent to the bonfire were dozens and dozens of letters between Joseph and Charles, between the brothers and their father and their wives, plus many more whose contents are not clear. When it is a matter of personal correspondence, the following words are written in the margin: "burn so it does not reach the public."

Why had such a great mass of documents been abandoned for four years? (This is even odder when one considers that not only papers but also jewels are listed among the items examined.) What mysterious force drove Charles to destroy so many valuable family memories? Was the truth of the relations between the two brothers concealed there? Or was there something revealing about Joseph's death? The bonfire Charles ordered means that we will never know the answer to these questions.

Atto Melani

The news of the arrival of a certain Milani in Vienna at the beginning of April, which the chimney-sweep tells us that he read with amazement in the newspaper, is not invented. According to the *Wiennerisches Diarium* of 8–10 April 1711, page 4, on 8th April a certain Signor Milan, an official of the imperial post from Milan, entered the city by the so-called Scottish Gate, and he settled at the post station. (*Schottenthor . . . Herr Milan / kayserl. Postmeister / komt auß Italien / gehet ins Posthauß*). Anyone in Vienna can check this item at the National Library, or in the city library of the Rathaus, as with all other quotations from newspapers of the day.

By a strange coincidence, both Atto Melani and Joseph I had their funerals in a church of the Barefoot Augustinians: in Vienna the Augustinerkirche, in Paris the church of the Barefoot Augustinians of Nôtre Dame des Victoires. Atto's funeral monument (a work by the Florentine Rastrelli, as the chimney-sweep correctly notes), can no longer be seen; it was probably destroyed during the 1789 revolution. His remains are thus forever lost, thrown into the Seine during the revolutionary frenzy, as happened with the royal family of France, including the corpses of Mazarin and Richelieu. However, a copy of the monument can be seen in Pistoia, in the Melani chapel inside the church of San Domenico. The Pistoia cenotaph gives us the only surviving portrait, among the many that existed, of Atto Melani: a bust representing him in his abbot's robes, with a proud stare, and a capricious cleft in his chin. The authors published it for the first time in the volume they edited, *I segreti dei conclavi*, Amsterdam 2005.

All the details of the relations between Atto and his relatives (including the sending of candied oranges and mortadellas), the aches and pains of old age, his passion for expatiating on his haemorrhoids, the circumstances of his death, his contacts with the Connestabilessa, the account of the great famine in France in 1709, the financial crisis of 1713, his last words before dying, his burial and a thousand other details, are confirmed in his letters kept in Florence in the State Archive (fondo Mediceo del Principato 4812, *lettere al Granduca di Toscana e al suo segretario, l'abate Gondi*) and in the Biblioteca Marucelliana (Manoscritti Melani vol.9, *lettere ai parenti in Toscana*). As regards the relations between Atto Melani and Connestabilessa Maria Mancini Colonna, see the historical notes in the appendix to Monaldi & Sorti, *Secretum*, Edinburgh 2009, where many passages from Melani's letters are published for the first time.

In Atto's correspondence one also learns that in 1711 he was indeed one of those who collaborated with Torcy, the powerful prime minister of the Sun King, as he proudly recounts on the third day. But the letters sent from France to Tuscany during those years reveal that at the French court his opinions were no longer heeded, which is not surprising, given his advanced age. In a letter from Paris to Gondi on 23rd February 1711, for example, Atto reveals that he travelled to Versailles but that Torcy did not receive him.

Atto's desire, despite his extreme old age, to end his days in Tuscany is also expressed (cf. also the notes in the appendix to *Secretum, op. cit.*). On 17th December 1713, eighteen days before his death, he wrote:

> *I have already resolved to go to Versailles to beseech the King to grant me permission to spend two years in Tuscany, to see if my native air will restore my strength and, what is most pressing, my sight; because not being able to write by hand myself, I am no longer of any use to His Majesty and His Ministers; in particular because the older ones, whose confidence I had, like M.r di Lione, Tellier and Pompone, have passed away; they acted as protectors with the King, whereas now, if I do not go and speak to him myself, it comes into no one's mind to do so. I could hope that Signor Marchese de Torcy would favour me, but he is so circumspect that I have never been able to get him to present M. de Maretz with a memorandum for the payment of my pension.*

In Florence Atto was not held in any great esteem either. On 30th of the preceding March, Gondi wrote to the Grand Duke of Tuscany:

[Abbot Melani] takes the trouble to give me his opinion . . . thinking that I wish to be so enlightened.

However, Gondi let him have his way just to appease Atto's relatives in Tuscany.

From the family's correspondence one learns that on 12th April 1711 Atto did indeed have the colic, as described by the chimney-sweep. The false blindness, which he adopts mainly to reject his relatives' requests for financial support, is confirmed by the letters that he sent in those years from Paris to Tuscany. On 23rd March 1711 he wrote to Gondi: "My health is always vacillating on account of the variety of weathers that we have here, but even more because of my great age, considering that although I can no longer read or write with my own hand, God grants me the grace of retaining my mental faculties at the age of eighty-five, which I will attain on 30th of this month."

His blindness, which in 1711 already seemed to be well advanced, only started in actuality two years later: on 6th February 1713, when he had truly lost his sight, Atto wrote to Luigi Melani, Domenico's brother: "And then as a last stroke of ill luck, I can no longer read or write. And yet Monsieur de la Haye, my friend, regained his sight at eighty!" Afflicted by faltering memory, like so many old men, Abbot Melani had forgotten that he had been claiming to be blind for quite some time now.

Camilla de' Rossi

The spelling today is Camilla *de* Rossi, without the apostrophe.

A certain Camilla de Rossi was born and lived in the Trastevere quarter of Rome. She was a shopkeeper, from whom Franz de Rossi borrowed his bride's new name. Her will is still in existence (Archivio Capitolino of Rome, 6th December 1708, deeds of notary Francesco Madesciro).

As the Chormaisterin herself recounts, Franz de Rossi was a musician at the court of Vienna and died of *Lünglsucht* (phthisis) at the age of forty, on 7th November 1703, in an apartment block in the centre of the city, the Niffisches Haus. The Vienna City Archive holds the deed (*Totenbeschauprotokoll*) certifying the death of Franz de Rossy, using the spelling often found in public administration documents for foreign names:

Der Herr Frantz de Rossy königlich Musicus im Nüffischen Haus, in der Wollzeile, ist an Lünglsucht beschaut. Alt 40 Jahre.

Franz de Rossi is referred to as "königlicher Musicus", a musician of the King and not of the Emperor; he was therefore in the service of Joseph I, who in 1703 was still King of the Romans, and not of his father, Emperor Leopold I.

The death is also reported in the *Wiennerisches Diarium*, 1703, n. 28, 7–10 November 1703:

Den 7. November 1703 starb Herr Frantz Rosij / Königlicher Musicus im Nivischen Haus in der Wohlzeil / alt 40. Jahr.

However, almost no trace remains of the Chormaisterin, apart from the scores and libretti of her oratorios. What Gaetano Orsini tells the chimney-sweep is true: the composer never received any payment for her musical services. The lack of any mention in the books of the imperial administration makes the figure of Camilla almost invisible. Fortunately the *Wiennerisches Diarium*, as the authors have discovered, reports the performances of oratorios on Good Friday in the same years that Camilla de' Rossi's oratorios are dated (1707–1710), and it is no accident that Joseph I attended them, as he appears to have commissioned Camilla's four oratorios. Apart from this indirect confirmation of the activity and presence of the composer in Vienna, all of the authors' searches in the archives have proved fruitless: Vienna State Archive – Hofarchiv, OMaA (Obristhofmarschallamtabhandlungen) Bd. 643 (Index 1611–1749); Bd.180 (Inventaria 1611–1749); Bd.181 (the valet Vinzenz Rossi, probably the cousin of Franz mentioned also by the chimney-sweep, appears there); OMeA (Obristhofmarschallamt), Protokolle 6 e 7; Karton 654, Abhandlungen 1702–1704; Hofkammerarchiv, NÖHA (Niederösterreichische Herrschaftsakten), W-61/A, 32/B, 1635–1749, Fol. 455–929: list of various writings by musicians employed by Hofkapelle, Kammermusik and Hofoper (some years are missing, with a large gap from 1691 to 1771); Gedenksbücher, 1700–1712. No trace of Camilla in the birth, marriage and death certificates (*Geburts- Trauung- und Sterbematriken*), which start from the second half of the eighteenth century; the same is true of the *Conscriptionsbögen* (a sort of census of homes and occupiers), which do not start until 1805; above all, there is no trace of any payment to Camilla in the private coffer (*Privatkassa*) of Joseph I, from which payments were made to various musicians. Susanne and Theophil Antonicek (*Drei Dokumente, op. cit.*) have published the list of musicians paid by Marquis Scipione Publicola di Santa Croce in the years 1709–1711 as "music superintendent" of Joseph I. No mention is made in these documents (pp. 11–29) of Camilla de Rossi.

The information on other Italian musicians in Vienna is taken not only from the Viennese archives but also from L. Ritter von Köchel, *Die Kaiserliche Hof-Musikkapelle in Wien 1543–1867*, Vienna 1869, and B. Garvey Jackson, "Oratorios by Command of the Emperor: The Music of Camilla de Rossi", in *Current Musicology*, 42 (1986), p. 7. Gaetano Orsini really did sing for Camilla de' Rossi's oratorios, and was among the musicians who received payments from Joseph's secret coffers (cf. Vienna State Archive,

Hofkammerarchiv, Geheime Kammerzahlamtrechnungen 1705–1713, *varii loci*, ad es. c.10v).

The convent of Porta Coeli really did exist. Unfortunately it was demolished by order of Emperor Joseph II in 1785, along with many other convents in the city. The archive of Porta Coeli, which survived the demolition, is kept at the Vienna City Archive.

The story narrated on the fourth day by Camilla of the Turkish slave girl assigned to the novitiate at Porta Coeli and rejected by the other nuns is also authentic. Cf. P. Alfons Žák, "Das Frauenkloster Himmelpforte in Wien", in *Jahrbuch für Landeskunde von Niederösterreich*, new series, VI, (1907), Vienna 1908, p. 164: "In the year 1695 a Turkish slave girl of Gerolamo Giudici, the Spanish lieutenant of Cardinal Leopold Count Collonitz, was baptised at Saint Ursula, and she was to be educated at the convent of Himmelpforte. The nuns protested against the arrival of the girl, since they were all noble novices, while she was a slave. Even the Kaiser agreed with them, on 3rd September 1695, and after the lieutenant applied to the Viennese consistory on 12th September, requesting them to oblige the convent to take the slave into the novitiate, on 16th September, the request was turned down."

Nor should the sudden appearance of Camilla de' Rossi in the buttery near Neugebäude occasion any surprise: the convent of Porta Coeli did in fact possess some properties near the Place with No Name, as is attested by the documents concerning the convent held at the Vienna City Archive.

It is quite plausible that Camilla de' Rossi should have retired to the convent of St Lawrence. This is not only because it is impossible to find any trace of the musician after 1711, either in Vienna or in her native Rome, but also due to a surprising account given by Lady Montagu, the famous English writer and traveller, who, visiting the capital of the Empire in 1716, writes:

I was surprized to see here the only beautiful young woman I have seen at Vienna, and not only beautiful, but genteel, witty and agreeable, of a great family, and who had been the admiration of the town. I could not forbear shewing my surprize at seeing a nun like her. She made me a thousand obliging compliments, and desired me to come often. It would be an infinite pleasure to me, said she sighing, but I avoid, with the greatest care, seeing any of my former acquaintance; and, whenever they come to our convent, I lock myself in my cell. I observed tears come into her eyes, which touched me extremely, and I began to talk to her in that strain of tender pity she inspired me with; but she would not own to me that she is not perfectly happy. I have since endeavoured to learn the real cause of her retirement, without being able to get any other account, but that every body was surprized at it, and no body guessed the reason. I have been several times to see her; but it gives me too much melancholy to see so agreeable a young creature buried alive.

(*Letters of Lady Mary Wortley Montague: Written During Her Travels in Europe, Asia, and Africa, to which are Added Poems by the Same Author.* Paris 1822, pp. 37–38).

The therapies used by Camilla de' Rossi, based on the medicine of St Hildehard of Bingen, are all authentic. There is nothing surprising in the fact that the Chormaisterin learned these skills from her Turkish mother: as Karl Heinz Reger (*Hildegard Medizin*, Monaco 1989, p. 11) reports, some scholars see clear influences of Islamic culture on Hildegard's writings.

Ottoman Customs, Embassies and Legends

All the descriptions that Cloridia gives of Ottoman customs, such as the particular concept of hospitality (the guest as *muzafir*), Populescu's account of the harem, the dervish's ritual, the Armenian use of the *tandur*, Atto Melani's descriptions of the derebeys and the rebels of Giaur-Daghda, including his reflections on "men without a conscience", faithfully reflect the accounts given by contemporary travellers visiting the Ottoman Empire and their scandalised reactions to customs and ways of thinking that were so different from those in the West. See, for example, Maccari, *Diario del mio viaggio di Costantinopoli presentato alla Maestà dell'Imperatore Leopoldo I*, Ms., 67 cc. This is a stupendous manuscript in Italian, kept in the manuscript collection of the National Library of Vienna, which the authors will publish in the near future.

Accounts of the Ottoman Empire remained practically unchanged from the sixteenth to the nineteenth century. See, for example, Ferriol, *Wahreste und neueste Abbildung des Türckischen Hofes . . . 1708, 1709 . . .*, Nuremberg, 1719; and the Piedmontese princess Cristina di Belgioioso, "La vie intime et la vie nomade en Orient", *Revue des Deux Mondes*, 1855. Belgioioso, among other things, describes how she herself witnessed the magic dancing ritual of dervishes, who made cuts all over their bodies which then inexplicably healed within a few seconds, just as described by the chimney-sweep.

During our research in Istanbul we had the good (and ill) fortune to track down, at an antiquarian's in the Grand Bazaar, the *disjecta membra* of a Venetian diary on Constantinople from the end of the sixteenth century; unfortunately the antiquarian had already stripped it of its cover and frontispiece, and had cut out all the individual pages in order to sell the engravings for 150 euros each. This kind of malpractice is, alas, common among antiquarians throughout the world; to our way of thinking, it should be severely punished by the law. Yielding to our heartfelt supplications, the antiquarian courteously allowed us a rapid examination of the fragmentary writings on the back of the engravings.

The Turkish legends that the students investigate (principally, that of the golden apple and the forty thousand of Kasim) are all genuine; they are reported, for example, by Richard F. Kreutel (ed.), *Im Reiche des Goldenen Apfels. Des türkischen Weltenbummlers Evliyâ Çelebi denkwürdige Reise in das Giaurenland und in die Stadt und Festung Wien anno 1665*, Graz-Vienna-Cologne, 1957.

The myth of Dayı Çerkes, or Dayı Circasso, recounted by Penicek, corresponds to the version provided by Kerstin Tomenendal, *Das türkische Gesicht Wiens*, Vienna-Cologne-Weimar 1999, p. 187 ff. The Turkish version of the legend is narrated in the excited travel account of the Turk Evliyâ Çelebi, who visited Vienna in 1665. The statue can still be admired on the façade of the palace. The address is: Heidenschuss 3.

Equally true is the inhuman practice of the kidnapping of Christian children by the Ottomans that Atto Melani describes. Robert Mantran discusses it in *La vita quotidiana a Costantinopoli ai tempi di Solimano il Magnifico*, Milan 1985 (original edition: Paris 1965), pp. 104–105:

> *After the second half of the fourteenth century, which is to say, after the conquest of a part of Balkan Europe, the Ottomans, in order to ensure the regular recruiting of an army that was expanding in strength and size, used a system that profoundly disturbed Christian consciences but which for a long period of time proved of great service to the Turks: we allude to the dev irme, the "harvest". This system consisted of the annual or biannual culling, in a certain number of Christian families of the Balkans, of male children under the age of five. Separated completely from their parents, these children were sent to Anatolia, to Muslim families where they were brought up in the Muslim fashion, taught Turkish and initiated into Turkish and Islamic habits and traditions. At the age of ten or eleven they entered the educational institutions of the palaces of Hadrianopolis and Gallipoli and, after the conquest, Istanbul, and from this moment on they were termed* acemi o lan. *Depending on their aptitude they were sent to the army or to the palace, where they became pages and were termed* iç o lan. *There then followed a procedure that saw them rise from rank to rank, and if they succeeded in attracting the attention of the sultan or of a sultana or of some favourite, there was nothing to stop them from gaining access to the highest offices, even that of Grand Vizier. Having practically forgotten their origins and owing their own position solely to the favour of the sultan they showed him the utmost devotion and had no other ambition than to devote themselves to his service.*

As regards the provenance of the upper classes of the "harvest", see Giorgio Vercellin, *Solimano il Magnifico*, Florence 1997, pp. 11–12:

It is impossible to overestimate how much the presence of the Ottomans in Europe during the years around the Reformation influenced the course of history on our continent, starting with the history of the countries between the Rhine and the Danube. The Protestants were the principal beneficiaries of the conflict of Charles V and Ferdinand I with the "Infidels", so much so that the greatest expert in relations between the Ottoman world and the Christian world, Kenneth Setton, has gone so far as to state ("Lutheranism and the Turkish Peril", in Balkan Studies, *III, 1962) that without the Turks the Reformation could easily have suffered the same fate as the Albigensian Revolt. The Empire's strength was based on the crucial function of the janissaries, a highly specialised infantry corps created by Sultan Murad I (1362–1398) almost a century before the formation of the first regular army in France. Issuing from the singular institution that was the* dev irme *[. . .] and distinguished by their white headgear, the janissaries were about a thousand in number in the fourteenth century, 5,000 in the following century and 12,000 in the age of Suleiman."*

The description of the Turkish procession in Himmelpfortgasse is closely based on accounts of the visit, which were printed and distributed at the time: *Beschreibung der Audientz . . . op. cit.*, Vienna, 9th April 1711.

The two subsequent audiences of the Agha at Eugene's palace, respectively on 13th and 15th April 1711, are confirmed in A. Arneth, *Prinz Eugen von Savoyen*, Vienna 1864, vol. 2, p. 159. Arneth, however, makes a mistake: he says that the Agha left again on 19th April. This is not true. The farewell ceremony with Eugene's substitute, the Vice-president of War, Count von Herberstein, took place on 16th May and is described in the printed report entitled *Die an dem Tuerckischen Abgesandten Cefulah Aga, Capihi Pascia, ertheilte Abschieds-Audienz, mit Beschreibung aller Ceremonien so darbey ergangen,* zu Wien, den 16. May 1711.

In addition the supplement of the *Corriere Ordinario* of 3rd June 1711, *Foglio Aggiunto*, (p. 91 of the year 1711) reports that the Agha did not leave until 2nd June, "making for Constantinople with five boats assigned to him, and he took with him various things, which he bought here, including some Casks with Pocket-Knives, Scythes, and Sickles, and similar Utensils."

Further details on the various Turkish embassies to Vienna in those years come from R. Perger and E. D. Petritsch, "Der Gasthof 'Zum Goldenen Lamm' in der Leopoldstadt und seine türkischen Gäste", in: *Jahrbuch des Vereines für die Geschichte der Stadt Wien*, 55 (1999), p. 147 ff.

During the Turkish siege of Vienna there really was a betrayal by the Armenian Schahin and his servant, as Koloman recounts to the chimney-sweep on the fifth day; see K. Teply, *Die Einführung des Kaffees in Wien*, Vienna 1980, p. 35 ff.

The story of Kara Mustafa's lost head is also wholly authentic. Cf. Richard F. Kreutel, "Der Schädel des Kara Mustafa Pascha", in *Jahrbuch des*

Vereins für Geschichte der Stadt Wien, 32/33 (1976–1977), pp. 63–77. There was actually a second head of a Turk in the city Zeughaus of Vienna, at the address no. 10, Am Hof. It belonged to Abaza Kör Hüseyin Pascha, who fell near Vienna on 24th August 1683 at the Battle of Bisamberg (cf. Kerstin Tomenendal, *Das türkische Gesicht Wiens. Auf den Spuren der Türken in Wien*, Vienna-Cologne-Weimar 2000, p. 186). The head of this forgotten war hero was kept as a companion to that of the more celebrated Kara Mustafa, and was listed in the catalogues only until 1790. It had probably disappeared from the warehouses before that date, maybe long before, which is to say when it was stolen by Ugonio . . .

Ilsung, Hag, Ungnad, Marsili

The essential information on Ilsung is all confirmed by Stephan Dworzak, *Georg Ilsung von Tratzberg*, typewritten degree dissertation, Vienna 1954.

As Simonis recounts, in 1564 David Hag was appointed on the advice of Georg Ilsung to the post of court paymaster (*Hofpfennigmeister*): cf. Vienna State Archive, Haus-, Hof- und Staatsarchiv, Familienakten, Karton 99, recommendation of Ilsung to Maximilian II of 3rd October 1563.

It really was Ilsung who advised engaging the mysterious healer Magdalena Streicher to treat (or to kill?) the dying Maximilian. This is reported in a letter from the doctor Crato von Crafftheim to Joannes Sambucus published by M.A. Becker, *Die letzten Tage und der Tod Maximilians II*, Vienna 1877, p. 41. On David Ungnad see Hilda Lietzmann, *Das Negebäude in Wien. Sultan Süleymans Zelt – Kaiser Maximilians II. Lustschloss*, Munich-Berlin 1987.

It was indeed Luigi Marsili (all the details concerning him are historically accurate) who taught the Viennese to prepare coffee, as the chimney-sweep says. In his leaflet *Bevanda asiatica, brindata all'Enimentissimo Bonvisi, Nunzio apostolico appresso la Maestà del'Imperatore etc.*, Vienna 1685, the Italian commander explains for the first time how to toast the beans, grind them and mix them with boiling water. The other information on Marsili contained in Atto Melani's account is confirmed by the numerous other works cited in the bibliography appended to this book.

Bettelstudenten and Chimney-Sweeps

In issue 280 of the *Wiennerisches Diarium*, which reports the news from 7th to 9th April 1706, and which is held in Vienna's city library, we discovered a very rare account of the Viennese *Bettelstudenten* of the age, never unearthed by any historian:

Wednesday 7th April. For some time now it is to be noted that, despite the frequent Edicts published, many wandering students – and others who join them, but who are not truly such – are still to be seen begging night and day in the streets and in front of the churches and houses, even during the school term; these, feigning to study, devote themselves to idleness, to theft and robbery, like the tumult of 17th and 18th January last which broke out inside and outside the city, also at Nussdorf (for which detailed inquiries are still being carried out to identify the culprits and punish them severely) and they tarnish the good name of the other students. This lamentable mendicancy – which is the word for lounging about and succumbing to vice under the pretext of study – must be seriously uprooted: to this end it is necessary to complete the task laid down by the former Resolutions of his Caesarean Majesty; to this aim the Rector, the Caesarean Superintendents and the Consistory of this most ancient University were exhorted to issue a special Edict and to give a final warning to the Bettelstudenten *who were roaming around and not studying: within 14 days they must depart from here and go to their homes or anywhere else. Failing to do so they will be seized by the guards and taken ad Carceres Academicos, where suitable punishment will be meted out. Those impoverished students, on the other hand, who daily and continuously apply themselves to their studies, must seek a study grant in the Alumnates or some other means of subsistence; only those who are unable, because of the numbers, to obtain such assistance, or those who have no choice but to seek alms outside lesson times, will be allowed to continue in this fashion until the arrival of new orders. But they must always bear their identity badge, get it renewed every month and show it if requested. Otherwise they will not be recognised as real students, but as vagabond students and will be immediately punished.*

It is possible to verify that the chimney-sweep never invents anything by studying the numerous sources that describe student life at the beginning of the eighteenth century: for example, Rudolf Kink, *Geschichte der kaiserlichen Universität zu Wien*, Vienna 1854, or Peter Krause, *"O alte Burschenherrlichkeit". Die Studenten und ihr Brauchtum*, Vienna 1987, or Uta Tschernut, *Die Kärntner Studenten an der Wiener Universität 1365–1900*, typewritten degree dissertation, Vienna 1984. The bizarre student ceremony known as the Deposition, during which Penicek is appointed Simonis's Pennal, follows an ancient and genuine tradition, as is explained by Wolffgang Karl Rost, *Kurtze Nachricht von der Academischen Deposition*, Jena (no publication date).

The tricks, expedients, superstitions and devices used by Simonis and by his student friends are taken from the highly entertaining Henricus Caspar Abelius, *Leib-Medicus der Studenten und Studenten-Künste*, Leipzig 1707.

Even the tiniest detail concerning the wretched life of chimney-sweeps in Italy is authentic; see, for example, Benito Mazzi, "Fam, füm, frecc, il grande romanzo degli spazzacamini", in *Quaderni di cultura alpina*, 2000.

Equally authentic is the description of the happier life led by Italian chimney-sweeps in Vienna and the many imperial privileges granted to their corporation: cf. Else Reketzki, *Das Rauchfangkehrergewerbe in Wien. Seine Entwicklung vom Ende des 16. Jh. Bis ins 19. Jh., unter Berücksichtigung der übrigen österreichischen Länder*, dissertation, Vienna, 1952. All the details of the Gewerbe IV, the business number four, donated by Atto Melani to his chimney-sweep friend, can be checked in the deeds of the chimney-sweeps' corporation held in the Vienna City Archive (Wiener Stadt- und Landesarchiv), including the vineyard and the house "close to the church of St Michael" in the Josephina suburb, which has now become the beautiful district of Josefstadt.

Free Time, Taverns, Feasts and Other Details

All the details concerning the incredible number of feast days, of processions, the continual absences from work for all kinds of religious observances, the general level of comfort even in the lowliest strata of society, and also the antelucan hours of the start of day, including the call of the night guard ("Now rise O Servant, praise God this morn, the light now gleams of a new day's dawn"), inns, games, taxes, spies, free time and all other descriptions of life in Vienna, are authentic in every detail, starting with the Hetzhaus and the animal fights.

As Gerhard Tanzer records in his admirable degree dissertation on amusements in Vienna in the eighteenth century (*"In Wienn zu seyn ist schon Unterhaltung genug!" Zum Wandel der Freizeit im 18. Jh.*, Dissertation zur Erlangung des Doktorgrades der Philosophie, Vienna 1988) and in the essay that derived from it (*Spectacle müssen seyn. Die Freizeit dr Wiener im 18. Jh.*, Vienna-Cologne-Weimar 1992), between 1707 and 1717 there was great resistance on the part of innkeepers to the taxing of bowling alleys, exactly as Simonis tells the chimney-sweep when they go looking for Populescu. Those, like the Romanian student, who denounced rule breakers, were as common as mud. The payments handed out to them exceeded the revenues from tax, but people soon resigned themselves to looking on the bright side: the sums won at gambling all added to the money in circulation; the important thing was that money should not be sent abroad! And so in later years, as with dancing, gambling proliferated wildly. People danced and gambled everywhere, grumbled the conservatives, even when the Holy Sacrament was passing in procession outside the tavern.

The number of taverns in Austria at the time, and the list of dishes devoured at wedding dinners is taken from Franciscus Guarinonius, *Die Greuel der Verwüstung menschlichen Geschlechts*, Vienna 1610.

Despite what the reader may think, the scene in which diners indulge in all sorts of wild behaviour, witnessed by Atto, the chimney-sweep and Domenico on the fourth day, is not in any way an exaggeration on the authors' part; the actions reported (blowing on hot food and spattering oil into other diners' eyes, pouring wine down people's shirt fronts, using napkins to blow one's nose, pulling the tablecloth to bring the roast meat closer etc.) are all amply described – in order to castigate them! – by the famous court preacher, the barefoot Augustinian Abraham from Sancta Clara (cf. also E.M. Spielmann, *Die Frau und ihr Lebenskreis bei Abraham a Sancta Clara*, typewritten degree dissertation, Vienna 1944, pp. 125–126).

The incredible secret exchanges of bread and wine between Turks and Viennese during the 1683 siege are historically substantiated too: see K. Teply, *Die Einführung... op. cit.*, p. 30. But as Teply points out (p. 35), when the historian Onno Klopp (*Das Jahr 1683 und der folgende grosse Türkenkrieg bis zum frieden von Carlowitz von 1699*, Graz 1882) dared to question the conduct of the civilians who had defended the besieged city two hundred years earlier, he was immediately silenced by a hostile chorus of journalists, politicians and academics, with questions even being raised in the city council.

Nothing is invented in Koloman's account of the incredible variety and quantity of fish that once reached Vienna. It was not until the 1780s that things changed: Emperor Joseph II closed many monasteries – which had previously been the main suppliers of good fish – and did away with many religious feasts with obligatory fasting. The fish recipes created to circumvent this obligation fell out of favour. Very soon the Viennese adopted a saying from the Elizabethan age, with which the Protestants indirectly made fun of the Catholics: "He's a good person, he doesn't eat fish."

The alehouse known as The Yellow Eagle (*Zum Gelben Adler*), also known as the "Greek tavern" (*Griechenbeisl*), situated in the meat market (today's Fleischmarkt), where Simonis takes Atto and chimney-sweep at the beginning of the sixth day, is still active. It is the famous inn where, according to legend, during the plague of 1679, the storyteller Augustin composed his famous Lied: *O du, lieber Augustin, alles ist hin . . .*

The Blue Bottle Café (*Zur Blauen Flasche*) really existed and was the first place authorised to sell coffee.

The inn known as the House Goat (*Zum Haimböck* in German) still exists today. The tavern, which has splendid food and is much loved by the Viennese, is now called 10er Marie (*Zehner Marie*). It took on the new name in the mid-eighteenth century, combining the street number with the name of the host's beautiful daughter. Unfortunately it is no longer surrounded by the beautiful vineyards of former days, but by ugly apartment blocks: to rediscover the unspoilt countryside described by the chimney-sweep one has to climb up to The Pulpit (*Am Predigtstuhl* in German), on the hill now known as Wilhelminenberg, where the chimney-sweep goes on the sixth day.

A small clarification on the Buschenschank, the hostelries similar to the Roman *fraschette*: today they are commonly known as *Heuriger*, taking their name from the new wine that is served there.

The poor quality of the wines of Liesing and of Stockerau, referred to by Cloridia, is noted in an almanac for the year 1711, *Crackauer Schreib-Calender auff das Jahr nach Christi Geburt M.CC.XI durch M. Johannem Gostumiowsky, in der Hochlöbl. Crackauerischen Academia Phil. Doct. Ordinarium Astrologiae Professorem, und Königlichen Mathematicum*, Krakow 1710.

The Viennese have always had a particularly sensitive palate when it comes to wine. It is well known that in 1453 Emperor Frederick III, enraged by a particularly unsuccessful grape harvest, decreed that the wine should be used instead of water to mix the cement needed to build the Cathedral of St Stephen.

The theory that the Habsburgs might descend from the Roman Pierleoni family, as Atto declares to the chimney-sweep, corresponds precisely to the ancient heraldic treatises in vogue in Vienna in the eighteenth century, including the dishonourable deeds of the Roman family (cf., for example, Eucharius Gottlieb Rynck, *Leopolds des grossen Römischen Kaysers wunderwürdiges Leben und Thaten aus geheimen Nachrichten eröffnet und in vier Theile getheilet*, Leipzig 1709, I, 9 ff.)

The Turkish cannonballs stuck in the walls of Vienna, which Ugonio would have liked to steal and then sell, are still visible in the places in the city listed by the *corpisantaro*.

The *Neuer Crackauer Schreib-Calender, durch Matthias Gentilli, Conte Rodari, von Trient*, Krakow 1710, the almanac for 1711, in which the chimney-sweep reads the tally of the days since the birth of Jesus Christ, is kept in the City Library of Vienna (Wiener Stadt- und Landesbibliothek).

The legend of the Tekuphah is authentic: to read it in its entirety see W. Hirsch, *Entdeckung derer Tekuphot, oder Das schädliche Blut*, Berlin 1717.

The system of quartering rights as described by Simonis is entirely accurate: see Joseph Kallbrunner (ed.), *Wohnungssorgen im alten Wien. Dokumente zur Wiener Wohnungsfrage im 17. und 18. Jahrhundert*, Vienna-Leipzig 1926.

The list of the dead that Atto reads in the *Wiennerisches Diarium* is taken directly from issue no. 803 of the newspaper, 11–14th April 1711. The statistics on the dead in 1710, reported by the chimney-sweep, are confirmed in a supplement of the *Corriere Ordinario* of Vienna, 7 January 1711. The same is true of the dead recorded in Rome the same year (see Francesco Valesio, *Diario di Roma*, t.IV, anno 1710, p. 368 ff.).

In Vienna news of the sickness of the Dauphin of France arrived on 14th April 1711, the same day on which Cloridia gives Atto and the chimney-sweep the gazette bearing the news.

There is no element of fantasy in Penicek's description of Hungary: his account faithfully corresponds to the sources between the seventeenth and eighteenth century. Cf. Casimir Freschot, *Idea generale del regno d'Ungheria, sua descrittione, costumi, regni, e guerra*, Venice 1684.

The information on the widespread use of Italian in Vienna is confirmed by Stefano Barnabè's manual (*Teutsche und Italianische Discurs*, Vienna, 1660 and *Unterweisung Der Italienischen Sprach*, Vienna, 1675) and above all by Michael Ritter's excellent text, *Man sieht der Sternen König glantzen*, Vienna 1999, p. 9. Ritter confirms that in Vienna Italian was not only the official court language, as the chimney-sweep tells us, but the dominant idiom *tout court*.

Cardinal Kollonitsch ("Collonitz" is the old spelling) really was one of the pillars of Viennese resistance against the Turks, as Gaetano Orsini recounts, and was indeed in close touch with the family of Pope Innocent XI Odescalchi, who financed the Christian armies that triumphed in the battle of 12th September 1683 (cf. the historical notes in the appendix to Monaldi & Sorti, *Imprimatur*, Edinburgh 2008).

The description of the tavern where Hristo Hadji-Tanjov played chess is confirmed in Michael Ehn and Ernst Strouhal, *Luftmenschen. Die Schachspieler von Wien 1700–1938*, Vienna 1998.

The *Wiennerisches Diarium* was indeed sold, as the young chimney-sweep recounts, in the palace known as the Red Porcupine (Rothes Igel). According to the *Historisches Lexikon Wien* by Felix Czeike (Vienna 2004, III, 300) it was not until 1721 that Rothes Igel hosted the editorial office of the *Wiennerisches Diarium*. However, in the *Wiennerisches Diarium* of 1711 one already finds the words "Zu finden im Rothen Igel", which is to say "it can be found at the Red Porcupine".

The Viennese and Their History

The Viennese – historians, scholars, professors, but also the common people and those residing in the surrounding area – are all highly sensitive to anything concerning the Habsburgs: woe to anyone who casts the slightest doubt on the noble imperial lineage! Joseph and Charles were universally loved, Prince Eugene should have been canonised, and the resistance of the besieged citizens in 1683 was nothing but heroic. While Onno Klopp, as has been seen, takes a rather different approach and is a great historian, Arneth is often unreliable. For example, he takes his information on the death of Joseph I from the biography of Wagner (a Jesuit!), gets the date of the Agha's departure from Vienna wrong (see above) and constantly tries to convince the reader that Joseph I was surrounded by nothing but harmony and love. Arneth then describes in impassioned language Charles's presumed grief on hearing of his brother's death, claims that Joseph bade farewell to his "beloved consort", but says nothing about the cruel treatment meted out to his young lover, Countess Marianna Pálffy.

Even today, anyone who dares to contradict the rose-coloured vulgate version is brusquely silenced, almost as if one were dealing with current politics (in a non-democratic regime), and not with history from the remote past. This is a minor defect of the Viennese, but it is also their most valuable quality: in their country everything is always fine, and woe to anyone who makes so bold as to claim the contrary, especially if a foreigner. The good side of this – and by far the most important – is that by dint of believing in and propagating the notion that everything is fine, they have succeeded to some degree in defending their world from the destructive forces of our squalid age, so that in no other capital city in the world can one live so well as in Vienna. It is a factor that writers who criticise Austria harshly, like Elfriede Jelinek, should bear in mind. And these are the words of two authors who have been forced into exile from their beloved homeland, Italy. Thank you, citizens of Vienna.

BIBLIOGRAPHY

✠

Archive sources:

Hofkammerarchiv, Vienna.
Haus- Hof- und Staatsarchiv, Vienna.
Handschriftensammlung der Österreichischen Nationalbibliothek, Vienna.
Wiener Stadt- und Landesarchiv, Vienna.
Wiener Stadt- und Landesbibliothek, Handschriftensammlung, Vienna.
Archivio Paulucci de' Calboli, Forlì.
Archivio Storico Capitolino, Rome.
Archivio di Stato di Firenze, Archivio Mediceo del Principato, Florence.
Archives du Ministère des Affaires Etrangères, Paris.
Biblioteca Marucelliana, Fondo Melani, Florence.
Biblioteca Nazionale Centrale di Firenze, Fondo Manoscritti, Florence.
Biblioteca Forteguerriana, Carte Melani, Carte Sozzifanti, Pistoia.

⁂

Various authors, *Smallpox and its Eradication*, World Health Organization, Switzerland 1988.
Various authors, *Memorie intorno a Luigi Ferdinando Marsili*, Bologna 1930.
Abelii, Henrici Casparis, *Leib-Medicus der Studenten und Studenten-Künste*, Leipzig 1707.
Abraham a Sancta Clara, pater, *Huy! Und Pfuy! Der Welt Huy Oder Aufrischung Zu allen schönen Tugenden: Pfuy Oder Abschreckung.von allen schändlichen Lastern (etc.)*, Würtzburg 1707.
Abraham a Sancta Clara, pater, *Mercks Wienn / Das ist deß wütenden Todts ein vmbständige Beschreibung ... zusammen getragen ... Von ——*, Vienna 1680.
Abraham a Sancta Clara, pater, *Etwas für Alle, das ist: Eine kurtze Beschreibung allerley Stand- Ambts- und Gewerbs-Persohnen (etc.)*, Würtzburg 1699.
Abraham a Sancta Clara, pater, *Etwas für Alle*, Dresden 1905.
Idem 1960.
Abraham a Sancta Clara, *Gack/Gack/Gack/Gack, a Ga einer wunderseltzamen Hennen in dem Hertzogthumb Bayern. Beschreibung der berühmbten Wallfahrt Maria-Stern in Taxa etc.*, Vienna 1687.
Ackerl, Isabella, *Die Chronik Wiens*, Vienna 1988.

Aichholzer, Doris, "Klosterleid, Fehlgeburten und Türkengefahr. Das Themenspektrum in Briefen adeliger Frauen vom 16. zum 18. Jh.", in *Wiener Geschichtsblätter*, 54, 1999, 117–133.

Alpinus, Prosperus, *De Medicina Aegytiorum Libri IV*, Venice 1591.

Altfahrt, Margit, "Den professionisten ist wider ihrer Störer alle Assistenz zu leisten. Unbefugte Schneider in Wien des späten 18. Jh.", *Studien zur Wiener Geschichte, Jahrbuch des Vereins für Geschichte der Stadt Wien* 52/53 (1996/1997), 9ss.

Ancioni, Gian Battista, *Panegirico a Gioseppe I re di Germania e imperatore romano, trionfatore augusto*, Vienna, van Ghelen, 1708.

Andrée, Hilda, *Geschichte rund um ein Büro. Über die Rauhenstein-, Ball-, und Himmelpfortgasse, ihre Häuser u. prominente Bewohner*, Vienna 1943.

Antonicek, Susanne u. Theophil, "Drei Dokumente zu Musik und Theater unter Kaiser Josef I.", in *Festschrift Othmar Wessely zum 60. Geburtstag*, Vienna 1982.

Apparatus Funebris quem JOSEPHI I. Gloriosissim. Memoriae . . ., Viennae, van Ghelen 1711.

Aretin, Karl Otmar, Freiherr von, "Kaiser Joseph I. zwischen Keisertradition und österreichischer Grossmachtpolitik", *Historische Zetischrift*, 215. Band, 529–606.

Arneth, Alfred, Ritter von, *Maria Theresia's erste Regierungsjahre*, Vienna 1863.

Arneth, Alfred, Ritter von, *Prinz Eugen von Savoyen aus den handschriftlichen Quellen der kaiserlichen Archive*, Bd. II, 1708–1718, Vienna 1864.

Arneth, Alfred, Ritter von, *Die Relationen der Botschafter Venedigs über Österreich im achtzehnten Jahrhundert*, Vienna 1863.

Ar-Razi (Razes), *Über die Pocken und die Masern (ca. 900 n. Chr.)*, Leipzig 1911.

Außzug und Vormerkung deren Kaÿs Leopoldinisch- und Josephinischen Briefschaften und Schriften Verfasst 1715, 28. Jänn. – 20. Sept., mss.

Baechtold, Jacob, *Des Minoriten Georg König von Solothurn Wiener-Reise. Wienerische Reiss-beschreibung*, Ms. Nro. 32, 326 carte, in quarto.

Baltzarek, Franz, "Die Wiener Stadtbibliotek 1690–1780", in *Wiener Geschichtsblätter*, 25–27, 1970–72, 69–71.

Baltzarek, Franz, "Das Steueramt der Stadt Wien und die Entwicklung der städtischen Rechnungskontrolle bis zur Mitte des 18. Jh.", in *Wiener Geschichtsblätter*, 21–24, 1966–69, 163–169.

Bankl, Hans, *Die kranken Habsburger*, Munich-Zurich 2001.

Barnabè, Stephanum, *Unterweisung Der Italienischen Sprach*, Vienna 1675.

Barnabè, Stephanum, *Teutsche und Italianische Discurs*, Vienna 1660.

Bastl, Beatrix, "Feuerwerk und Schlittenfahrt", in *Wiener Geschichtsblätter*, 51, 1996, 197–228.

Bastl, Beatrix; Heiss, Gernot, "Tafeln bei Hof: die Hochzeitsbankete Leopolds I.", in *Wiener Geschichtsblätter*, 50, 1995, 181–206.

Baudrillart, Alfred, *Philippe V et la Cour de France d'après des documents inédits tirés des archives espagnoles et des archives du ministère des affaires étrangères à Paris*, Paris 1890.

Bauer, Wilhelm, *Josef I.*, Mitteilungen des Oberösterreichischen Landesarchivs, 4 (1955), 261–175.

Becker, M.A., *Die letzten Tage und der Tod Maximilians II.*, Vienna 1877.

Belgioioso, Cristina, di, "La vie intime et la vie nomade en Orient", *Revue des Deux Mondes*, 1855.

Benedik, Christian, "Zeremonielle Abläufe in habsburgischen residenzen um 1700. Die Wiener Hofburg und die Favorita auf der Wieden", in *Wiener Geschichtsblätter*, 46, 1991, 171–178.

Benedik, Christian, "Die herrschaftlichen Appartements. Funktion und Lage während der Regierungen von Kaiser Leopold I. bis Kaiser Josef I.", in *Österreichische Zeitschrift für Kunst und Denkmalpflege*, 51, 1997, Heft 3–4, 552–569.

Benedik, Christian, *Die Wiener Hofburg unter Kaiser Karl VI. – Probleme herrschaftlichen Bauens im Barock*, dissertation, Vienna 1989.

Benedikt, Heinrich, "Der erste Kafeeschank Wiens und der Mann, der die Wiener Kaffee kochen lehrte", in *Bustan*, 5, 1964, 20–22.

Berg, Heinrich; Fischer, Karl, "Vom Burgerspital zum Stadtbräu. Zur Geschichte des Bieres in Wien", *Wiener Geschichtsblätter*, Beiheft 3/1992.

Berney, Arnold, "Die Hochzeit Josephs. I.", in *Mitteilungen des Instituts für österreichische Geschichtsforschung*, 42 (1927), 65–83.

Berney, Arnold, "Die Hochzeit Josefs I", *Mitteilungen des Instituts für Österreichische Geschichtsforschung*, XLII, 1867.

Bersohn, Mathias, *Studenci Polacy (Die polnischen Studenten auf der Bologneser Universität im 16.u.17.Jh.)*, Krakow, Czas 1890.

Bertarelli, E., *Jenner e la scoperta della vaccinazione*, Milan 1932.

Beschreibung Der Audientz / Deß von dem Türckischen Groß-Sultan Aus Constantinopel nach Wien gesandten und alda ankommenden Cefulah Aga / Capichi Pascia / Wien den 9. April 1711.

Bibl, Viktor, *Maximilian II., der rätselhafte Kaiser*, Leipzig 1929.

Bibl, Viktor, *Prinz Eugen. Ein Heldenleben*, Vienna-Leipzig 1941.

Bibliotheca Eugeniana. Die Sammlungen des Prinzen Eugen von Savoyen, Ausstellung der Österreichischen Nationalbibliothek und der Graphischen Sammlung Albertina, Vienna 1986.

Bili ski, Bronisław, *Le glorie di Giovanni III Sobieski vincitore di Vienna 1683 nella poesia italiana*, Warsaw-Krakow 1990.

Böhm, Bruno, *Die, Sammlung der hinterlassenen politischen Schriften des Prinzen Eugens von Savoyen'. Eine Fälschung des 19. Jh.*, Freiburg im Breisgau 1900.

Botto Micca, A., *Razes e Avicenna: i due primi descrittori del vaiolo e del morbillo*, "Il Dermosifilopatico", fasc. 8, 1930.

Braubach, Max, *Prinz Eugen von Savoyen*, Vienna 1964.

Braubach, Max, *Geschichte und Abenteuer. Gestalten um den Prinzen Eugen*, Munich 1950.

Braubach, Max, *Die Geheimdiplomatie des Prinzen Eugen von Savoyen*, Cologne and Opladen 1962.

Bräuer, Helmut, *". . . und hat seithero gebetlet". Bettler und Bettlerwesen in Wien und Niederösterreich während der Zeit Kaiser Leopolds I.*, Vienna 1996.

Briefe der Lady Marie Worthley Montague während ihrer Reisen in Europa, Asia und Afrika, Leipzig 1724, 19–55.

Broucek, Peter; Hillbrand, Erich; Vesely, Fritz, *Historischer Atlas zur zweiten Türkenbelagerung*, Vienna 1683, Vienna 1983.

Brown, Edward, *An Account of Several Travels through a Great Part of Germany: in Four Journeys. III. From Vienna to Hamburg*, London 1677.

Buchberger, Reinhard, "Lebl Höschl von Wien und Ofen: Kauffmann, Hofjude und Spion des Kaisers", in various authors, *Hofjuden und Landjuden. Jüdisches Leben in der Frühen Neuzeit*, 217–395.

Buchwald, Gerhard, *Impfen. Das Geschäft mit der Angst*, Munich 2000.

Buchwald, Gerhard, *Vaccinazioni. Il business della paura*, Milan 2003.

Celoni, Toti, *Le grandi famiglie d'Europa: gli Asburgo (I)*, Milan 1972.

Chambon, J., *Traité des métaux et des minéraux*, Paris 1714.

Chandler, David, ed., *Robert Parker and Comte de Mérode-Westerloo, The Marlborough Wars*, North Haven 1968.

Chimin Wong, K.; Lien-The, Wu, *History of Chinese Medicine*, Shanghai 1936.

Codex Austriacus, Vienna 1777.

Copia, Röm. Käyserl. Majestät allergnädigster Verordnung / Den neu aufgerichten Banco in Wienn betreffend.

Coreth, Anna, *Österreichische Geschitschreibung in der Barockzeit (1620–1740)*, Vienna 1950.

Corriere Ordinario, 1700–1720.

Crackauer Schreib-Calender, auff das Jahr . . . 1711 . . . durch M. Joannem Gostumiowsky, Vienna 1710.

Czeike, Felix, "Die Apotheke 'Zum Roten Krebs' ", in *Wiener Geschichtsblätter*, 43, 1988, 15–18.

Czeike, Felix, *Historisches Lexikon Wien*, Vienna 2004.

Darmon, Pierre, *La variole, les nobles et les princes. La petite vérole mortelle de Louis XV*, Brussels 1989.

De Bin, Umberto, *Leopoldo I e la sua corte nella letteratura italiana*, Trieste 1910.

De Freitas, Divaldo Gaspar, *A vida e as obras de Bartolomeu Lourenço de Gusmão*, San Paolo 1967.

Della Bianca, Luca, *Manuale di caffeomanzia*, Rome 2003.

De Mérode-Westerloo, conte, *Mémoires*, Brussels 1840.

Der Baum des Erkäntnüsses Guten und Bösens / Bepflantzet gey der Grufft des Aller Durchlauchtigsten / Großmächtigsten Fürsten und Herrn / Herrn JOSEPHI Erweihten . . . Breslau 1711.

Der Schmertzliche Erfolg des unverhofften Absterbens Ihro Röm. Käyserl. Majestät JOSEPHI, wie solches den 17. dieses Monats April 1711 mit allgemeiner Bestürtzung vorgefallen / und darauf die solenne Beerdigung geschehen ist, Vienna 1711.

Des Grossen Feld-Herrns Eugenii Herzogs von Savoyen, Kayserl. Und des Reichs general-Lieutenants Felden-Thaten, Nuremberg 1739.

Diario della villeggiatura fatta dalla Santità di N.ro S.re PP. Clemente XI in Castel Gandolfo l'anno 1710, ms.

Die an dem Türckischen Abgesandten Cefulah Aga, Capihi Pascia, erteilte Abschieds-Audientz, Mit Beschreibung aller Ceremonien so darbey ergangen, Zu Wien den 16. May 1711

Die Presse, 12 February 1982, 5.

Dini, Giuseppe, *Diario pieno e distinto del viaggio fatto a Vienna dal Sommo Pontefice Pio Papa Sesto*, Rome 1782.

Dolch, Oskar, *Geschichte des deutschen Studententums*, Graz 1968.

Donin, Richard Kurt, "Das Neugebäude in Wien und die venezianische villa suburban", in *Mitteilungen der Gesellschaft für vergleichende Kunstforschung in Wien*, 11. Jg., Dez. 1958, Nr. 2, 61–69.

Dubost, Jean-François, *La France Italienne XVIe–XVIe siècle*, Paris 1997.

Duindam, Jeroen, *Vienna and Versailles. The Courts of Europe's Dynastic Rivals, 1550–1780*, Cambridge 2003.

Dworzak, Stephan, *Georg Ilsung von Tratzberg*, Dissertation, Vienna 1954.

Ecker, Ludwig Viktor, "1683–1933: 250 Jahre Wiener Kaffeehaus: Festschrift des Gremiums der Kaffeehausbesitzer", in *Österreichische Kaffeesieder-Zeitung*, 1933.

Ehalt, Hubert Christian, *Ausdrucksformen absolutistischen Herrschaft, dargestellt vor allem am Beispiel des Wiener Hofes unter Leopold I., Josef I. und Karl VI.*, Dissertation, Vienna 1978.

Ehn, Michael; Strouhal, Ernst, *Luftmenschen. Die Schachspieler von Wien. Materialien und Topographien zu einer städtischen Randfigur 1700–1938*, Vienna 1998.

Eilenstein Arno, ed., *Abt Maximilian Pagl von Lambach und sein Tagebuch (1705–1725)*, Salzburg 1920.

"Einige genealogische Auszüge aus zwischen 1566 und 1783 bei der niederösterreichischen Regierung publizierten, derzeit im Archive des k. k. Landesgerichtes Wien befindlichen Testamenten adeliger oder für adelig gehaltener Personen", in *Monatsblatt der Kais. Kön. Heraldischen Gesellschaft, Adler*, nr. 274, Vienna, October 1903, V. Bd., Nr. 34.

Eisler, Max, ed., *Historischer Atlas des Wiener Stadtbildes*, Vienna 1919.

Eisler, Max, *Historischer Atlas der Wiener Ansichten, Das barocke Wien*, Vienna and Leipzig 1925.

Erasmo Da Rotterdam, *Il lamento della pace*, Milan 2005.

Ernstberger, Anton, *Europas Widerstand gegen Hollands erste gesandschaft bei der Pforte (1612)*, Munich 1956.

Faber, Elfriede M., *300 Jahre Kunst, Kultur & Architektur in der Josefstadt*, Vienna 2000.

Fadda, Bianca, *L'innesto del vaiolo: un dibattito scientifico e culturale nell'Italia del Settecento*, Milan 1983.

Fantuzzi, Giovanni, *Memoria della vita del conte Marsigli*, Bologna 1770.

Faust, D., *Communication au congrès de Rastadt sur l'extirpation de la petite vérole*, 1798, *Archives Nationaux de France*, F8 124.

Feldzüge des Prinzen Eugen von Savoyen. Nach den Feld-Acten u. anderen authentischen Quellen hrsg. von der Abtheilung für Kriegsgeschichte des k.k. Kriegs-Archives, Vienna 1876–1892.

Fenger, Hermanus Josephus, *Historiam Pestilentiarum Vindobonensis*, Vienna 1817.

Ferriol, *Wahreste und neueste Abbildung des Türckischen Hofes . . . 1708, 1709 . . .*, Nuremberg 1719.

Feuchtmüller, Rupert, *Das Neugebäude*, Vienna-Hamburg 1976.

Fiedler, Joseph (ed.), *Relationen venetianischer Botschafter über Deutschland und Österreich im 16. Jahrhundert*, Vienna 1870.

Fischer, Karl, *Der Wienerwald*, 44, 1989, Heft 1.

Fischer, Karl, "Brände im Bereich der Wiener Hofburg", in *Wiener Geschichtsblätter*, 48, 1993, 45–52.

Fondra, Lorenzo, *Del maneggio alla Corte Cesarea*, ms.

Fracastoro, Girolamo, *De sympathia et antipathia rerum liber unum, De contagione et contagiosis morbis et curatione libri III*, Venice 1546.

Franzos, Karl Emil, *Aus Halb-Asien. Culturbilder aus Galizien, der Bucowina, Südrussland und Rumänien*, Leipzig 1876.

Freschot, Casimiro, *Idea generale del Regno d'Ungheria*, Bologna 1684.

Freschot, Casimiro, *Mémoires de la Cour de Vienne*, Cologne, 1706.

Gründliche Wiederlegung des ietzo regierenden Türckischen Käysers Mahomet des Vierdten . . . Nativität, Vienna 1694.

Fritsch, Susanne, "Essen im Augustinerkloster in Wien", in *Fundort Wien*, 6, 2003, 188–197.

Fuhrmann, Mathia, pater, Alt- und Neues Wien, Vienna 1739.

Furlani, Silvio; Wandruszka, Adam, *Österreich und Italien. Ein bilaterales Geschichtsbuch*, Vienna 2002.

Garvey Jackson, Barbara, "Oratorios by Command of the Emperor: The Music of Camilla de Rossi", *Current Musicology*, 42, 1986, 7–19.

Gherardi, Raffaella, *Potere e costituzione a Vienna fra Sei e Settecento. Il "buon ordine" di Luigi Ferdinando Marsili*, Bologna 1980.

Giese, Ursula, *Wiener Menagerien. Ebersdorf / Neugebäude / Belvedere / Schönbrunn*, Vienna 1962.

Gladt, Karl, *Almanache und Taschenbücher aus Wien*, Vienna-Munich 1971.

Godard, Didier, *Le Goût de Monsieur. L'homosexualité masculine au XVIIe siècle*, Béziers 2002.

Goldmann, Artur, *Die Wiener Universität 1519–1740*, Vienna 1917.

Görlich, Ernst Josef, "Graubündner in Wien", in *Wiener Geschichtsblätter*, 26, 1971, 211ss.

Greuel, Veronika, *Oratorien am Wiener Hof. Die Komponistin Camilla de Rossi*, in: various authors, *Frauen in der Aufklärung*, Frankfurt 1995, 426–447.

Gschliesser, Oswald, "Die Bekämpfung der Fremdenwörter durch den Reichsvizekanzler Grafen Schönborn im 18. Jahrhundert". Innsbruck. *Beiträge zur Kultur und Wissenschaft*, III, 1955.

Guarinonius, *Die Greuel der Verwüstung menschlichen Geschlechts*, 1610.

Gugitz, *Aus den Totenbeschauprotokollen*, M-Z, XVIII Jh., typewritten degree dissertation, p. 619.

Gugitz, *Aus den Totenbeschauprotokollen*, 1648–1699, typewritten degree dissertation, 120 e 437.

Gutierrez, David, *Storia dell'ordine di Sant' Agostino, vol.II, Gli Agostiniani dal protestantesimo alla riforma cattolica (1518–1648)*, Rome 1972.

Hadamowsky, Franz, *Magdalena. Wiener Marionettenspiel*, in JbGStW, Bd. 32–33 (1976–1977), 17–31.

Haintz, Otto, *König Karl II. von Schweden*, Berlin 1958.

Harl, Ortolf, *Die Ausgrabungen im ehemaligen Himmelpfortkloster*, in JbGStW, Bd. 34 (1978), 9–23.

Harrer, Paul, *Wien. Seine Häuser, Menschen und Kultur*, Vienna, typewritten degree dissertation.

Harrisons Innere Medizin, XVI ed., Berlino 2005 (original edition: Dennis L. Kasper, ed., *Harrison's Manual of Medicine*, XVI ed., New York 2005).

Henderson Nicholas, *Prince Eugen of Savoy*, London 1964.

Herchenhahn, Johann Christian, *Geschichte der Regierung Kaiser Josefs I.* 2 Bde. Leipzig 1786–1789.

Heuser, G., *Die Belagerungen von Landau*, Landau (2 vols) 1894–1896.

Hilscher, Elisabeth Theresia, *Mit Leier und Schwert. Die Habsburger und die Musik*, Vienna 2000.

Hirsch, W., pater, *Entdeckung derer Tekuphot, oder Das schädliche Blut*, Berlin 1717.

Histoire anecdote de la Cour de Rome. La part qu'elle a eu dans l'affaire de la Succession d'Espagne. La situation des autres Cours d'Italie et beaucoup de particularités de la dernière et de la présente Guere de ce Pais-là, Cologne, chez Jacques Le Jeune, 1704.

Historisch-Politische Gedancken über den durch das unvermuthete und höchstschmertzlichste Absterben Sr. Ömischen Käyserliche Majestät Josephi Veränderten Zustand in Europa, Frankfurt 1711.

Historisches Museum der Stadt Wien, *Das Barocke Wien. Stadtbild und Straßenleben*, 20. Sonderausstellung, June–September 1966.

Hofmann von Wellenhof, Viktor, *Der Winterpalast des Prinzen Eugen von Savoyen*, Vienna 1905.

Holland, Wilhelm Ludwig, ed., *Briefe der Herzogin Elisabeth Charlotte von Orléans*, Stuttgart 1867.

Horn, Sonia, *Wiener Hebammen 1643–1753*, "Studien zur Wiener Geschichte, Jahrbuch des Vereins für Geschichte der Stadt Wien" 59 (2003), 35–102.

Horn, Sonia, *Examiniert und Approbiert. Die Wiener medizinische Fakultät und nicht-akademische Heilkundige in Spätmittelalter und früher Neuzeit*, Dissertation, Vienna 2001.

Huard, Pierre; Wong, Ming, *La médecine chinoise au cours des siècles*, Paris 1959.

Hummelberger, Walter; Peball, Kurt, "Die Befestigungen Wiens", *Wiener Geschichtsbücher*, Bd. 14.

Ingrao, Charles W., *Josef I., der "vergessene Kaiser"*, Graz-Vienna-Cologne 1982.

Jedlicska Pál, *Gróf Pállfy-Család*, Budapest 1910.

Jelusich, Mirko, *Prinz Eugen. Der Feldherr Europas. Der Traum von Kaiser und Reich*, Graz-Stuttgart 1941.

Jordan, Johann, *Schatz / Schutz und Schantz deß Ertz-Herzogthumbs Oesterreich / Das ist Ein sehr genaue / und ordentliche Beschreibung aller Gassen /Plätz / Palläst / Häuser und Kirchen der berühmten Haubt- und Kayserl. Residentz- Statt Wienn*, Vienna 1701.

Josepho Primo Augusto Rom. Et Hungariae Regi, In expeditione ad Rhenum Landavia recepta triumphatori, in urbem reduci Applausus Emblematicus, Wien, bey J.B. Schönwetter Universitätischen Buchhändler im Rothen Igel, 1702.

Kallbrunner, Josef, ed., *Wohnungssorgen im alten Wien. Dokumente zur Wiener Wohnungsfrage im 17. und 18. Jh*, Vienna 1926

Khevenhüller-Metsch, Johann Josef, Fürst, *Tagebuch 1742–1775*, Vienna 1907–1925.

Kink, Rudolf, *Geschichte der kaiserlichen Üniversität zu Wien*, Vienna 1854.

Kinz, Maria, *Zauberhafte Josefstadt*, Vienna 1990.

Klausgraber, Andrea, *Afrikaner in Wien im 18. Jh.*, Diplomarbeit, Vienna 1998.

Klopp, Onno, *Der Fall des Hauses Stuart und die Succession des hauses hannover in Groß-Britannien und Irland im Zusammenhange der europäischen Angelegenheiten von 1660–1714*, Vienna 1875–1888.

Klopp, Onno, *Das Jahr 1683 und der folgende große Türkenkrieg bis zum Frieden con Carlowitz 1699*, Graz 1882.

Kluge, Heidelore, *Hildegard von Bingen – Frauenheilkunde*, Rastatt 1999.

Klusacek, Christine; STIMMER, Kurt, *Josefstadt*, Vienna 1991.

Knöbl, Herbert, *Das Neugebäude und sein baulicher Zusammenhang mit Schloss Schönbrunn*, Vienna 1988.

Koch, Herbert, "Wohnhaft in Wien. Geschichte und Bedeutung des Meldewesens", *Wiener Geschichtsblätter*, Beiheft 3/1986.

Köchel, Ludwig, Ritter von, *Die Kaiserliche Hof-Musikkapelle in Wien von 1543 bis 1867*, Vienna 1869.

Kölbl, Anita, *Die Ursulinen in Wien 1660–1820*, Vienna 1997.

Kramer, Hans, *Habsburg und Rom in den Jahren 1708–1709*, Innsbruck 1936.

Krause, Peter, *"O alte Burschenherrlichkeit". Die Studenten und ihr Brauchtum*, Vienna, 5. Auflage, 1987.

Kretschmer, Helmut; Tschulk, Herbert, "Brände und Natur: Katastrophen in Wien", *Wiener Geschichtsblätter*, Beiheft 1/1995.

Kretschmer, Sigrid, *Wiener Handwerkerfrauen*, Vienna 2000.

Kreutel, Richard F. *Der Schädel des Kara Mustafa Pascha*, "Studien zur Wiener Geschichte, Jahrbuch des Vereins für Geschichte der Stadt Wien" 32–33 (1976–1977), 63–77.

Kreutel, Richard F.; Spies, Otto, ed., *Leben und Abenteuer des Dolmetschers Osman Aga*, Bonn 1954.

Kreutel, Richard F., ed., *Im Reiche des Goldenen Apfels. Des türkischen Weltenbummlers Evliyâ Çelebi denkwürdige Reise in das Giaurenland und in die Stadt und Festung Wien anno 1665*, Graz-Vienna-Cologne 1957.

Kreutel, Richard F., ed., *Kara Mustafa vor Wien: Das türkische Tagebuch der Belagerung Wien 1683 vom Zeremonienmeister der Hohen Pforte*, Vienna 1955.

Kübler, P. *Geschichte der Pocken und der Impfung*, Berlin 1901.

L'Acceso Gelato (pseudonym), *Applausi della Fama e del Danubio al Giorno del Glorioso Nome dell'Augustissimo Imperadore Giuseppe. Poesia per musica* etc., Vienna, Anna Francesca Voitin 1706.

Lana Terzi, Francesco, S.J., *Prodromo ouero saggio di alcune inuentioni nuoue premesso all'arte maestra opera che prepara il p. Francesco Lana . . . Per mostrare li piu reconditi principij della naturale filosofia*, in Brescia per li Rizzardi, 1670.

Lana Terzi, Francesco, S.J., *Magisterium Naturae et Artis* Brescia 1684.

Landau, Marcus, *Geschichte Kaiser Karls VI. als König von Spanien*, Stuttgart 1889.

La schiavitù del generale Marsigli sotto i tartari e i turchi da lui stesso narrata, ed. Emilio Lovarini, Bologna 1931.

Law, John, *Money and Trade Considered with a Proposal for Supplying the Nation with Money*, Paris 1720.

Lettre de SS. le Pape Clement XI. A S.M.I. l'Imperatrice Regente du 3. May 1711, avec les reflexions, qu'une personne de qualité a faites pour un de ses amis, s.l., s.d.

Levinson, Arthur, "Nunziaturberichte vom Kaiserhofe Leopolds I. 1670–1679", in *Archiv für österreichische Geschichte*, 106, 1918.

Lietzmann, Hilda, *Das Neugebäude in Wien, Sultan Süleymans Zelt – Kaiser Maximilians II. Lustschloß*, Munich-Berlin 1987.

Lorenzi, Ernst, Kaiser *Leopold I. Seine Familie und seine Zeit*, Diplomarbeit, Vienna 1986.

L'origine del Danubio, Venice 1684.

Ma, Klaralinda; PSARAKIS, Brigitta, "Akkreditiert in Wien. Zum Gesandschaftswesen in unserer Stadt", *Wiener Geschichtsblätter*, Beiheft 1/1996.

Ma, Klaralinda; PSARAKIS, Brigitta, "'. . . ein ungeheurer herrlicher Garten . . .'. Wien aus der Sicht ausländischer Besucher vom 15 bis zum 19. Jh.", *Wiener Geschichtsblätter*, Beiheft 3/1988.

Maccari, *Diario del mio viaggio di Costantinopoli presentato alla Maestà dell'Imperatore Leopoldo I*, Ms., 67 cc.

Maier-Bruck, Franz, *Klassische Österreichische Küche*, Vienna 2003.

Major, Ralph H., *A History of Medicine*, Illinois 1954.

Mancusi Sorrentino, Lejla, *Manuale del perfetto amatore di caffè*, Naples 2003.

Mantran, Robert, *La vie quotidienne à Costantinople au temps de Soliman le Magnifique et de ses successeurs (XVIe et XVIIe siècle)*, Paris 1965.

Manzi, Leonello, *Vaiolo, vaiolizzazione, vaccinazione a Bologna dai primi del Settecento ai primi dell'Ottocento. Con documenti inediti*, Bologna 1968.

Marsigli, Luigi Ferdinando, conte, *Bevanda Asiatica*, Vienna, van Ghelen 1685.

Marsigli, Luigi Ferdinando, conte, *Dissertazione epistolare del Fosforo minerale ò sia della pietra illuminabile bolognese*, Leipzig 1698.

Marsigli, Luigi Ferdinando, conte, Relation deßen, das ihm bey Anlaß der Übergab Breysachs begegnet, 1703.

Marsigli, Luigi Ferdinando, *Autobiografia*, Bologna 1930.

Massa, Niccolò, *Liber de febre Pestilentiali, ac de Pesticijs, Morbillis, Variolis* etc. Venice 1556.

Masson, Frédéric, ed., *Journal inédit de Jean Baptiste Colbert marquis de Torcy, ministre et secrétaire d'État des affaires Étrangères pendant les années 1709, 1710 et 1711*, publiés d'après les manuscrits autographes, Paris 1884.

Mattioli, Nicola, padre agostiniano, *Fra Giovanni da Salerno*, Rome 1901.

Mattl-Wurm, Sylvia, *Wien vom Barock zur Aufklärung*, Vienna 1999.

Mausoleum Josephi I. des Heiligen Römischen reichs Kayser . . ., welchen die frühzeitige Todt . . . am 17. April 1711 . . . in die Ewigkeit versetzt hat, Vienna, Lercher 1711.

Mazzi, Benito, "Fam, füm, frecc, il grande romanzo degli spazzacamini", *Quaderni di cultura alpina*, 2000.

McKay, Derek, *Prince Eugene of Savoy*, London 1977.

Memorie della vita del generale conte Luigi Ferdinando Marsigli, Bologna 1770.

Mercure de France, Paris 1765.

Mercuriale, Girolamo (pseud. of Scipione Mercuri), *La commare*, Venice 1676.

Mercuriale, Girolamo (pseud. of Scipione Mercuri), *De morbis puerorum*, Lib. I, *De variolis et de morbillis*, Venice 1588.

Merlo, Valerio, *La foresta come chiostro*, Milan 1997.

Millöcker, Karl, *Der Bettelstudent*, Stuttgart 1958.

Montalbani, Ovidio, *Nubilogia. Discorso meteorologico delle nuvole* di O.M. il Rugiadoso Accademico della Notte, fra gl'Indomiti lo Stellato, Bologna 1642.

Montanari, Geminiano, *Le forze d'Eolo, dialogo fisico-matematico sopra gli effetti del Vortice, ò sia Turbine, detto negli Stati Veneti la Bisciabuova, che il giorno 29 luglio 1686 hà scorso e flagellato molte Ville, e Luoghi de' Territori di Mantova, &c. opera postuma del Sig. Dottore Geminiano Montanari Modenese, astronomo e meteorista dello studio di Padova*, Parma 1694.

Mosler, Ignaz Freiherr von, *Geschichte der k.k. Hofbibliothek zu Wien*, Vienna 1835.

Mukhopadhyaya, Girindranath, *History of Indian Medicine*, Delhi 1922–1929.

Müller, Klaus, *Das kaiserliche Gesandtschaftswesen im Jahrhundert nach dem Westfälischen Frieden (1648–1740)*, Bonn 1976.

Musikgeschichte und Gegenwart (MGG), Kassel-Basel-London 1963.

Nachricht von dem Fliegenden Schiffe / So aus Portugal / Den 24. Junii in Wien mit seinem Erfinder / Glücklich ankommen. Von neuen nach dem allbereit gedruckten Exemplar in die Naumberger Meß gesandt. Anno 1709.

Nannini, Marco Cesare, *La storia del vaiolo*, Modena 1963.

Natter, Martina, *Die vier Oratorien con Camilla de Rossi Romana*, Diplomarbeit, Innsbruck 2003.

Neuer Crackauer Schreib-Calender ... auff das Jahr ... 1711 ... Durch Matthias Gentilli, conte Rodari, von Trient, Vienna 1710.

Neuer und sehr bequemer Wand- und Sack- Calender / Auff M.DCC.XIII ... von dem Warschauer Authorn, Vienna 1712.

Neues Wiener Tagblatt, Donnerstag 4. April 1940, 6.

Neufeld, Hans, *Studien zum Tode Maximilians II.*, Dissertation, Vienna 1931.

Neu Wiennerisches Studenten-Calenderl, Vienna 1715.

Niderst, Alain, *Les français vus par eux-memes: Le siècle de Louis XIV. Anthologie des mémorialistes du siècle de Louis XIV*, Paris 1997.

Oberhummer, Eugen, "Ein Jagdatlas Kaiser Karl VI.", in *Unsere Heimat*, new series, VI, 1933, nr. 5, 152–158.

Ochi Rizetti, Heronimus, *De Pestilentibus, ac venenosis morbis* etc. Brescia 1650.

Oehler, Helmut, *Prinz Eugen im Urteil Europas. Ein Mythus und sein Niederschlag in Dichtung und Geschichtsschreibung*, Munich 1944.

Opll, Ferdinand, "Italiener in Wien", *Wiener Geschichtsblätter*, Beiheft 3/1987.

Opll, Ferdinand, "Markt im alten Wien", *Wiener Geschichtsblätter*, 34, 1979, 49ss.

Opll, Ferdinand, "Innensicht und Außensicht. Überlegungen zum Selbst- und Fremdverständnis Wiens im 16. Jh.", in *Wiener Geschichtsblätter*, 59, 2004, 188–208.

Opll, Ferdinand, *Wien im Bild historischer Karten*, Vienna-Cologne-Graz 1983.

Österreichische Kunsttopographie, Band XIV, Baugeschichte der k.k. Hofburg in Wien bis zum XIX. Jh., Vienna 1914.

Otruba, Gustav, "Wiens Gewerbe, Zünfte und Manufakturen an der Wende vom 17. zum 18. Jh.", in *Wiener Geschichtsblätter*, 42, 1987, 113–148.

Otruba, Gustav, "Die Wiener Rotschilds. Aufstieg und Untergang einer Familie", in *Wiener Geschichtsblätter*, 42, 1987, 148–168.

Paré, Ambroise, *Les Oeuvres*, Lyons 1664.

Parish, H.-J., *A History of Immunization*, London 1965.

Pasteur, Claude, *Le beau vice, ou les homosexuelles à la Cour de France*, Paris 1999.

Paulucci De' Calboli, Fabrizio, *Cenni biografici dei Cardinali della fam. P.d.C.*, Forlì 1925.

Perger, Richard; Petrisch, Ernst Dieter, *Der Gasthof "Zum Goldenen Lamm" in der Leopoldstadt und seine türkischen Gäste*, "Studien zur Wiener Geschichte, Jahrbuch des Vereins für Geschichte der Stadt Wien" 55 (1999), 147–172.

Perger, Richard, "Die ungarische Herrschaft über Wien 1485–1490 und ihre Vorgeschichte. Zum 500. Todestag des ungarischen Königs Matthias Corvinus (gestorben 6. April 1490 in der Burg zu Wien)", in *Wiener Geschichtsblätter*, 45, 1990, 53–102.

Perger, Richard, "Die Haus- und Grundstückskäufe des Prinzen Eugen in Wien", in *Wiener Geschichtsblätter*, 41, 1986, 41–84.

Peter des Großen, Czar, *Tagebuch vom Jahre 1698 bis zum Schlusse des Neustädte Friedens*, Berlin-Leipzig 1773.

Piccolomini, Enea Silvio, *Historia Friderici III Imperatoris*, Cap. I, *De Urbe Vienna*, 1426–1429, Italian translation *Vienna nel '400*, ed. Baccio Ziliotto, Trieste 1958.

Pils, Susanne Claudine, "'daz er mih nit halb so lieb hadt alß wie ich ihm . . .'. Liebe und Sexualität im ehelischen Nicht-Alltag von Johanna Theresia und Ferdinand Bonaventura Harrach", *Studien zur Wiener Geschichte, Jahrbuch des Vereins für Geschichte der Stadt Wien* 52/53 (1996/1997), 397–414.

Pils, Susanne Claudine, "Bestimmte Männlichkeit. Überlegungen zur Erziehung adeliger Knaben im 17. und 18. Jh.", *Studien zur Wiener Geschichte, Jahrbuch des Vereins für Geschichte der Stadt Wien* 60 (2004), 275–285.

Pils, Susanne Claudine, "Hof/Tratsch. Alltag bei Hof im ausgehenden 17. Jh.", *Wiener Geschichtsblätter*, 42, 1987, 77–99.

Pipers, *Enzyklopädie des Musiktheaters*, Munich 1997.

Pomposer Einzug Ihro Königl. Majest. Josephi I. Römisc: und Hungarischen Königs / u. Mit Ihro Majestätt Wilhelmina Amalia Röm. Königin / Königl. Gespons. / u. So Den 24. februarii 1699 zwischen 4. und 5, Uhr . . .

Praesagium Josephi propriae mortis, Leipzig 1711.

Pum, Susanne, *Die Biographie Karls VI. von Gottfried Philipp Spannagel. Ihr Wert als Geschichtsquelle*, Hausaufgabe, Vienna 1980.

Quincy, Louis-Dominique, "Mémoires sur la vie du Comte de Marsigli", 2 Bände, Zurich 1741.

Ramazzinus, Bernardinus, *Rede von der Ansteckenden Seuche des Rindviehes im 1711 Jahre*, Hanover and Lüneburg 1746.

Rapport de l'Académie de Médecine sur les vaccinations pour l'année 1856, Paris 1857.

Raschauer, Oskar, *Schönbrunn, der Schlossbau Kaiser Josephs I.*, Vienna 1960.

Rauscher, Peter, "Zwischen Ständen und Gläubigern. Die kaiserlichen Finanzen unter Ferdinand I. und Maximilian II. (1556–1576)", *Veröffentlichungen des Instituts für Österreichische Geschichtsforschung*, Band 41, Munich 2004.

Razzell, Peter, *The Conquest of Smallpox: the Impact of Inoculation on Smallpox Mortality in Eighteenth-Century Britain*, Sussex 1977.

Reger, Karl Heinz, *Hildegard Medizin*, Munich 1989.

Regola di S.to Agostino con l'espositione di Ugone da S. Vittore et consitutioni della religione del divoto Giovanni di Dio, Rome 1617.

Reketzki, Else, *Das Rauchfangkehrergewerbe in Wien. Seine Entwicklung vom Ende des 16. Jh. Bis ins 19. Jh., unter Berücksichtigung der übrigen österreichischen Länder*, dissertation, Vienna 1952.

Rennhofer, Friedrich, *Die Augustiner-Eremiten In Wien*, Würzburg 1956.

Ricaldone, Luisa, *Italienisches Wien*, Vienna 1986.

Riedling, Gabriele, *Kaiser Karl Vi.*, Diplomarbeit, Vienna 1986.

Riemann, *Musik Lexikon*, Mainz 1961.

Rigele, Brigitte, "Sardellendragoner und Fliegenschutz. Von Pferde im Alltag Wiens", *Wiener Geschichtsblätter*, 50, 1995, Heft 45.

Rigele, Brigitte, "Mit der Stadt aufs Land. Die Anfänge der Sommerfrische in den Wiener Vororten", *Wiener Geschichtsblätter*, Beiheft 2/1994.

Rinck, Eucharius Gottlieb, *Joseph des Sieghafften Röm. Käysers Leben und Thaten*, Cölln 1712.

Rinck, Eucharius Gottlieb, *Leopolds des Grossen / Röm. Käysers / wunderwürdiges Leben und Thaten aus geheimen Nachrichten eröffnet und in vier Theile getheilet*, Leipzig 1709.

Ripellino, Angelo Maria, *Praga magica*, Turin 1973.

Ritter, Michael, *"Man sieht der Sternen König glantzen". Der Kaiserhof im barocken Wien als Zentrum deutsch-italienischer Literaturbestrebungen (1653 bis 1718)*, Vienna 1999.

Röder von Diersburg, Philipp, *Freiherr, Kriegs- und Staatsschriften des Markgrafen Ludwig Wilhelm von Baden über den spanischen Erbfolgekrieg aus den Archiven von Karlsruhe*, Vienna-Paris-Karlsruhe 1850.

Roman, Jean-Joseph, *L'inoculation*, Paris 1773.

Roselka, Rosemarie, "Die Begräbnisfeierlichkeiten für Kaiser Maximilian II. 1576/77", *Mitteilungen des Instituts für Österreichische Geschichtsforschung*, 84 (1976), 105–136.

Rost, Wolffgang Karl, *Kurtze Nachricht von der Academischen Deposition*, Jena, s.d.

Rota, Ettore, *Il problema politico d'Italia durante la guerra di successione spagnuola*, "Nuova Rivista Storica", anno XVIII., gennaio-febbraio 1934, fasc. I, 1–167.

Rotter, Hans, *Die Josefstadt*, Vienna 1918.

Rummel, Friedrich, von, *Franz Ferdinand von Rummel, Lehrer Kaiser Josephs I. und Fürstbischof von Wien (1644–1716)*, Vienna 1980.

Sant' Agostino, *La Regola*, Rome 1986.

von Sartori, Josef, *Sammlung der hinterlassenen politischen Schriften des Prinzen Eugens von Savoyen*, Tübingen 1811.

Schlöss, Erich, "Über die Begegnungen des Zaren Pete I. mit Kaiser Leopold I.", in *Wiener Geschichtsblätter*, 49, 1994, 149–162.

Schmidt, Irmgard, "Josef I. und Wien (zum 250. Todestag des Kaisers)", in *Wiener Geschichtsblätter*, 13–16, 1958–1961, 311–316.

Schöpfer, Gerald, "Die 'Erste Hilfe' im 18. Jh.", in *Wiener Geschichtsblätter*, 30, 1975, 143–144.

Schulte, Aloys, "Die Jugend Prinz Eugens", in *Mitteilungen des Instituts für Österreichische Geschichtsforschung*, 13 (1892), 470–521.

Schwabe von Waisenfreund, Carl, *Versuch einer Geschicte des österreichischen Staats- Credits- und Schuldewesens*, Vienna 1860.

Schwerdfeger, Josef, *Eine Beschreibung Wiens aus der Zeit Kaiser Karls VI.*, Vienna 1906.

Scritti inediti di Luigi Ferdinando Marsili, raccolti e pubblicati nel II centenario della morte, a cura del Comitato Marsiliano, Bologna 1930.

Slanec, Hans-Christian, *Wien und die Wiener in Reiseberichten und Beschreibungen deutscher Reisender des 16.–18. Jh.*, Diplomarbeit, Vienna 1994.

Söltl, J., "Von dem Römischen Papst. Ein Vortrag für den römischen König Josef I". *Historische Zeitschrift*, VI, 1861.

Sommer-Mathis A., *Theatrum und Cerimoniale. Rang- und Sitzordnungen bei theatralischen Veranstaltungen am Wiener Kaiserhof im 17. und 18. Jahrhundert*, in *Zeremoniell als Höfische Ästhetik in Spätmittelalter und Früher Neuzeit*, ed. J.J. Berns & Th. Rahn Tubingen 1995, pp. 511–33.

Spannagel, Gottfried Philipp, *Della vita e del Regno di Josefo il Vittorioso Re ed Imperadore de' Romani, Re di Ungheria e di Boemia nonché Arciduca d'Austria*, mss. in 12 vols.

Spielman, Elisabeth Marie, *Die Frau und ihre Lebenskreis bei Abraham a Sancta Clara*, dissertation, Vienna 1944.

Spielman, John P., *The City and the Crown. Vienna and the Imperial Court 1600–1740*, West Lafayette 1993.

Spielman, John P., *Leopold I of Austria*, New Brunswick, New Jersey 1977.

Spuler, Bertold, "Die europäische Diplomatie in Konstantinopel bis zum Frieden von Belgrad (1739)", in *Jahrbücher für Kultur und Geschichte der Slaven*, neue Folge, XI, Heft III/IV, 1935.

Srbik, Heinrich, Ritter von, *Der staatliche Exporthandel Österreichs von Leopold I. bis Maria Theresia*, Vienna and Leipzig 1907.

Steidl, Annemarie, "Auf nach Wien! Die Mobilität des mitteleuropäischen Handwerks im 18. und 19. Jahrhundert am Beispiel der Haupt- und Residenzstadt", *Sozial- und Wirtschaftshistorische Studien*, Bd. 30, Institut für Wirtschafts- und Sozialgeschichte, Universität Wien, Vienna 2003.

Straub, E., *Representatio Maiestatis oder Churbayerische Freudenfeste. Die höfischen Feste in der Münchner Residenz vom 16. bis zum Ende des 18. Jahrhunderts*, Miscellanea Mavarica Monacensia 14, Munich 1969, pp. 117–46.

Strehlow, Wighard, *Hildegard-Medizin*, Freiburg im Breisgau 1997.

Strehlow, Wighard, *Hildegard-Heikunde von A-Z*, Munich 2000.

Suttner, Gustav, Freiherr von, *Die Garelli*, Vienna 1888.

"Tanzveranstaltungen und Tanzformen am Hofe", in *Innsbrucker Historische Studien*, 14/15 (1994), 65–76.

Tanzer, Gerhard, *"In Wienn zu seyn ist schon Unterhaltung genug!" Zum Wandel der Freizeit im 18. Jh.*, dissertation, Vienna 1988.

Tanzer, Gerhard, *Spectacle müssen seyn. Die Freizeit dr Wiener im 18. Jh.*, Vienna-Cologne-Weimar 1992.

Teply, Karl, "Karl Eugen Leopoldstätter alias Mehmed Efendi – ein hofbefreiter Kaffesieder im Wien Kaiser Karls VI.", in *Wiener Geschichtsblätter*, 25–27, 1970–72, 374–384.

Teply, Karl, "Die erste armenische Kolonie in Wien", in *Wiener Geschichtsblätter*, 28, 1973, 105–118.

Teply, Karl, "Türkische Gesandtschaften nach Wien (1488–1792)", in *Österreich in Geschichte und Gegenwart*, 20, 1976, 14–32.

Teply, Karl, *Die Einführung des Kafees in Wien: Georg Franz Kolschitzky, Johannes Diodato, Isaak de Luca*, Vienna 1980.

Teply, Karl, *Türkische Sagen und Legenden um die Kaiserstadt Wien*, Graz 1980.

Thiriet, Jean-Michel, *Über die Herkunft der Italiener in Wien vom Ende des 16. Jh. Bis zur Mitte des 18. Jh.*, "Studien zur Wiener Geschichte, Jahrbuch des Vereins für Geschichte der Stadt Wien" 52/53 (1996/1997), 156–165.

Thiriet, Jean-Michel, "Mourir à Vienne aux XVII°.XVIII° Siècles. Le cas des Welsches", in *Studien zur Wiener Geschichte, Jahrbuch des Vereins für Geschichte der Stadt Wien* 52/53 (1996/1997), 205–217.

Till, Rudolf, "Woher und wie die Kipfel nach Wien kamen", in *Wiener Geschichtsblätter*, 25–27, 1970–72, 66–69.

Timoni, Emanuele, *Historia Variolarum quae per insitionem excitantur*, Venice 1713.

Tomenendal, Kerstin, *Das türkische Gesicht Wiens*, Vienna-Cologne-Weimar 2000.

Topka, Rosina, *Der Hofstaat Kaiser Karls VI.*, Dissertation, Vienna 1954.

Trawnicek, Peter, "Wien 1716. Die Stadt im Spiegel ihrer Totebeschauprotokolle", in *Wiener Geschichtsblätter*, 58, 2003, 104–129.

Treiber, Johannes Philippus, *De excussione fenestrarum*, Halae Salicae, Hilliger 1737.

Tschernuth, Uta, *Die kärntner Studenten an der Wiener Universität 1365–1900*, dissertation, Vienna 1984.

Tschol, Helmut, "Gottfried Philipp Spannagel und der Geschichtsunterricht Maria Theresias", *Zeitschrift für katholische Theologie*, 83, 1961, Heft 2, Sonderabdruck, 208–221.

Turba, Gustav, ed., *Die pragmatische Sanktion*, Vienna 1913.

Umständliche Beschreibung von Weyland Ihrer Mayestät / JOSEPH / Dieses Namens des Ersten / Römischen Kayser / Auch zu Ungarn und Böheim Könih / u. Erz-Herzogen zu Oesterreich / u. u. Glorwürdigsten Angedenckens Ausgestandener Kranckheit / Höchst-seeligstem Ableiben / Und dann erfolgter Prächtigsten Leich-Begängnuß / zusammengetragen / und verlegt durch Johann Baptist Schönwetter, Vienna 1711.

Urban, Leopold, *Die Orangerie von Schönbrunn*, Diplomarbeit, Vienna 1992.

Urban, Leopold, *Die Orangerie von Schönbrunn*, Vienna 1999.

Valesio, Francesco, *Diario di Roma 1700–1742*, Milan 1978.

Vandano, Vittoria, *Le grandi famiglie d'Europa: gli Asburgo (II)*, Milan 1972.

Vercellin, Giorgio, *Solimano il Magnifico*, Florence 1997.

Vienna Gloriosa, id est Peraccurata & Ordinata Decriptio Toto Orbe Celeberrimae Cesareae nec non Archiducalis Residentiae Viennae, Vienna 1703.

Viti, Ludovico, *Chi cerca, truova. Dialoghi d'un Romano, e d'un Bolognese Professori Celebri di Medicina sopra la Cura de' Vaiuoli occorsi in perugia L'Anno 1712. . . . aggiugnendo in fine un breve Discorso dell'Influenza Catarrale del 1713*, Perugia, Pe'l Costantini Stamp. Camer. 1713.

Volkszeitung, 212, 3 August 1937, 3.

Volkszeitung, 13, 14 January 1940, 7.

Voltaire, *Le siècle de Louis XIV*, Paris 1751.

Wagner, Franciscus, S.J., *Historia Josephi Caesaris*, Vienna 1745.

Wagner, Michael, "Zwischen zwei Staatsbankrotten. Der Wiener Finanzmarkt im 18. Jh.", in *Wiener Geschichtsblätter*, 32, 1977, 113–143.

Wandruszka, Adam, *Österreich und Italien im 18. Jh.*, Vienna 1963.

Weaver, Robert Lamar, *Materiali per una biografia dei fratelli Melani*, "Rivista italiana di musicologia" 12 (1977), 252–95.

Wehdorn, Manfred, "Das Neugebäude. Ein Renaissance-Schloss in Wien", *Perspektiven*, 2004, 2.

Werner, Christian Ludwig, *Allerschmertzlichste Trauer-Gedancken, bei des Röm. Kaysers JOSEPHI I. allzufrühzeitigen Todes-Fall . . . bezeugt und dargelegt*, Vienna, Lercher 1711.

Wessely, Othmar, *Josef I.*, in MGG (1958), Sp. 181–185.

Wiener Stadt- und Landesarchiv Wien, *Historischer Atlas von Wien*, 1980–2005.

Wiennerisches Diarium, 1700–1720.

William Haanemanns Verwunderlich- Englischer Wahrsager oder ausführliches Prognosticon, Augsburg 1710.

Winter, Eduard, *Frühaufklärung*, East Berlin 1966.

Wyklicky, Helmut, "Die Beschreibung und Beurteilung einer Blatternerkrankung im Jahre 1711", in *Wiener Klinische Wochenschrift*, Heft 27, 5 July 1957, 69 Jg., 971–973.

Žák, Alfons, *Das Frauenkloster Himmelpforte in Wien*, Vienna 1906.

Zambrini Francesco, *Volgarizzamento del Trattato della cura degli occhi di Pietro Spano, codice Laurenziano citato dagli accademici della Crusca, ora per la prima volta stampato*, Bologna 1873.

Zöllner, Erich, *Geschichte Österreichs*, Munich 1990.

Zöllner, Erich; Gutkas, Karl, "Österreich und die Osmanen, Prinz Eugen und seine Zeit", *Schriften des Institutes für Österreichkunde*, Vienna 1988.

Zschackwitz, Johann Ehrenfried, *Leben und Thaten Josephi I. Römischen Käysers, sambt der unter Sr.Majestät glorwürdigsten Regierung vorgefallenen Reichs-Historie. Alles mit behörigen Documenten bekräfftiget (etc.)*, Leipzig 1712.

Pieces of Music Performed in *Veritas*

✠

1. "Crucifixus et sepultus est" (p. 00)
    Gioacchino Rossini, *Petite messe solemnelle*. The gentle reader will
    forgive the anachronism (Rossini lived in the first half of the
    nineteenth century), but this piece was performed in 1902 by
    Alessandro Moreschi, the last castrato of the Sistine Chapel,
    the only emasculated singer whose voice was ever recorded. The
    original is kept at the Discoteca Nazionale in Rome.

2. Arrival in Vienna (p. 00)
    Johann Joseph Fux, *Serenada en Ut majeur* K352: *Fanfare ex C – Marche*.

3. "Credi, oh bella, ch'io t'adoro" (p. 00)
    Camilla de Rossi, *Oratorio di Sant' Alessio*.

4. Procession of the Turks (p. 00)
    Giovan Battista Lulli, "La ceremonie des Turcs", from:
    Molière, *Le bourgeois gentilhomme*.

5. "Resurrexit" (p. 00)
    Joseph I, *Regina coeli*

6. "Cielo, pietoso Cielo" (p. 00)
    Camilla de Rossi, *Oratorio di Sant' Alessio*.

7. "Duol sofferto per amore" (p. 00)
    Camilla de Rossi, *Oratorio di Sant' Alessio*.

8. "Sonori concenti" (p. 00)
    Camilla de Rossi, *Oratorio di Sant' Alessio*.

9. "Un barbaro rigor" (p. 00)
    Camilla de Rossi, *Oratorio di Sant' Alessio*.

10. "Languet anima mea" and "O vulnera, vita coelestis"
    (pp. 00–00)
    Francesco Conti, Cantata *Languet anima mea*.

11. "Vae Soli" (p. 00)
    Gregorio Strozzi, *Sonata di basso solo*.

12. The Day of Wrath (p. 00)
    Josef Johan Fux, *Kaiserrequiem*, K 51–53: "Dies Irae".

13. The Wake (pp. 00–00): Josef Johan Fux, *Media vita in morte sumus*.

14. The Farewell (pp. 00–00): Josef Johann Fux, *Kaiserrequiem*:
    Kyrie Eleison.